About the author

Annette Young holds a BA (Honours) degree in History from the University of Sydney, and a Doctorate in English Literature from the University of New South Wales. She currently divides her time between research, piano and violin, raising four gentlemen, and writing Volume Two, *Outside Heaven's Sway.*

Join Annette's mailing list at annetteyoung.net

goodreads.com/annetteyoung

Pre-release praise for *By Violence Unavenged*

'Extremely well researched, historically, musically and linguistically.
Every chapter is full to the brim with action. A spectacular read.'
Christine McCarthy

'Tremendous depth…akin to Tolstoy … the author has the story, the
people, the world, entirely in hand.'
Warwick Adeney, Concertmaster, Queensland Symphony Orchestra

'A truly fine story and an enthralling read. Very much recommended!'
Regina Doman

'Descriptive panache, engaging pace and memorable characters …
clearly written by a musician, a kind of polyphonic saga, with the
interweaving themes of war, history, suffering and the search for truth.'
Wanda Skowronska

'The reader is impressed by the depth and breadth of her knowledge
not only of Austria, but of the entire European (and Turkish)
background to the Great War and its aftermath… a beautifully written
novel of great inventiveness and originality. It is a pleasure to read
Annette Young's prose and to enjoy her wide learning.'
David Daintree AM, President 2008-2012, Campion College Sydney

'this novel is so beautifully crafted'
Susan Reibel Moore, author of *What Should My Child Read?*

BY VIOLENCE UNAVENGED

In the Hearts of Kings
Volume One

Annette Young

This book is a work of fiction set in a world of real places and historical events. It is peopled with characters representing diverse views of the political and social currents of the period. Where actual historical characters appear, including public figures from the political and artistic world, their dialogue, opinions, and actions within this tale are entirely of the author's own invention, inspired by accounts of their lives and writings, and are contrived to serve dramatic purposes and to give readers a believable context for the story. They are to be enjoyed but not to be believed.

Cover Images

Gustav Klimt (1862-1918): Jurisprudence 1903 (detail), University of Vienna faculty ceiling paintings, oil on canvas 430 cm x 300 cm. Lederer collection. From a photograph. Original destroyed by fire set by retreating German forces in 1945 at Schloss Immendorf, Austria. (CC-PD, Wikimedia Commons.)

"Adolf Hitler on his triumphal journey in the Mercedes through Vienna after the Anschluss of Austria". Copyright: bpk, Berlin, licensed image 00005798.

Montage by Francis Young, from a concept by the author.

Illustrations

(Page 12) Peter Brandt, Map of 1937 Vienna, commissioned for *By Violence Unavenged*, 2018. All rights reserved by the illustrator.

(Page 378) Ein Volk, Ein Reich, Ein Führer, Nazi propaganda 1938. (CC-PD, Wikimedia Commons.)

ISBN-13: 9780987435132 paperback
ISBN-13: 9780987435149 hardback
ISBN-13: 9780987435156 ebook

Typeset in Bookman Old 9.5 pt

24 May 2019
Distant Prospect Publishing
8 Roy St Lorn NSW 2320 Australia

NATIONAL LIBRARY OF AUSTRALIA

A catalogue record for this book is available from the National Library of Australia

BY VIOLENCE
UNAVENGED

Dedication

To Charles,
a truly blessed friend,
without whom
this book never would have been written.

Acknowledgements

To Lev Raphael, for his patient assistance with Yiddish. To Don Bible for his advice regarding Gestapo ranks and ID. To Professor Dr Otto Biba, Director, Archiv, Bibliothek und Sammlungen der Gesellschaft der Musikfreunde for kindly supplying details on the Musikverein. To Ralf Siebenbürger for his help in fine-tuning all things Austrian, from German grammar, modes of address, and historical details, to the more trivial, but no less essential, points concerning coffee, cake, and wine.

To my beta readers: Martin Cooke, Jacinta Woodnutt, Laura Pearl, Toni Stevens, Regina Doman, Mark Morey, Warwick Adeney, Mishka Góra, and Dr Susan Moore, I cannot tell you how grateful I am for your feedback, suggestions, and encouragement.

To my husband, Francis, for all his help with the cover and layout, and for his forbearance and encouragement. To my four 'boundary riders' – John-Paul, Patrick, Max, and Ben – who never cease to inspire.

'O duca mio, la vïolenta morte
che non li è vendicata ancor', diss' io,
'per alcun che de l'onta sia consorte,

fece lui disdegnoso; ond' el sen gio
sanza parlarmi, sì com' ïo estimo:
e in ciò m'ha el fatto a sé più pio'.

Dante,
La Divina Commedia,
Inferno, XXIX, 31-36.

'My guide, it was his death by violence,
for which he still is not avenged,' I said,
'by anyone who shares his shame, that made

him so disdainful now; and—I suppose—
for this he left without a word to me,
and this has made me pity him the more.'

Dante,
Divine Comedy,
Inferno, XXIX, 31-36,
Trans., Mandelbaum.

Contents

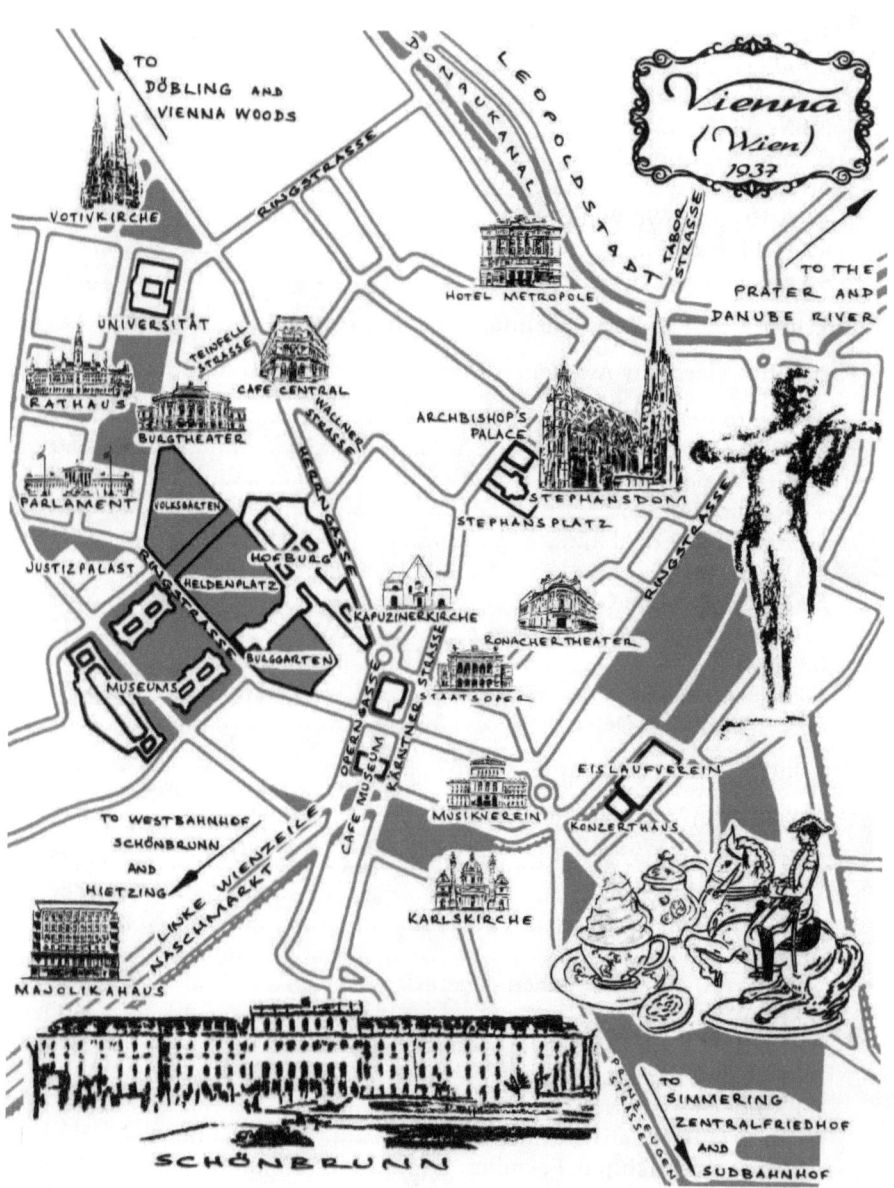

Prelude

.

To Master Roderick Edward Raye

Dear Roddy,

Forgive me my earlier refusal to tell you what you so ardently wished to know. That you are brimful with questions is understandable, and you have every right to be informed; but I have good reason to dislike interrogation, even from my half-brother, and require the freedom and privacy of paper and pen to order my thoughts. Furthermore, and despite your protests to the contrary, I doubt you have the patience to listen to your middle-aged sister. Instead, I have written my story.

Most likely, your history books told you that following the Armistice which ended the Great War for Civilisation, the victorious Allied nations (Britain, France, the United States, and Italy) demanded a pound of flesh from the Central Powers, namely Imperial Germany and Imperial Austria. Since Austria, with Germany, was responsible for the hostilities, Austria and Germany should pay.

The Big Four, as the Allies were called, forbade any subsequent Austro-German union or alliance. They punished Germany under the Treaty of Versailles by dismantling her burgeoning empire, stripping her of European territory, limiting her armed forces, and demanding millions in reparation. Imperial Austria they dismembered into either democratic republics or smaller kingdoms, based on language or ethnicity, under the Treaty of Saint-Germain, thereby satisfying nationalist and socialist revolutionaries from those parts.

But they overlooked one remote and deeply loyal southern outpost in Sydney, Australia: a suburban Liechtenstein in Gordon Crescent, Stanmore, which was ruled by one Mr Roderick John Raye - our father.

To a young man in turned-up jeans my historical references must seem extraneous, when in fact they form the canvas of a tale rivalling the Bayeux Tapestry for length. The Empire along with the War and its aftermath, comprise the warp. Traversing the weft, as twisted as crepe, are the concerns of the heart.

Hopefully, Roddy, my tableau will help you make sense of the brave new world that has emerged during these past decades, and of your place in it. So, permit me to embroider my account; and I will leave you to ponder the details.

Phoebe Raye Krizman

Phoebe Raye Krizman,
Vienna, Austria,
Christmas, 1956.

Part One

•

Fiat iustitia,
et pereat mundus

•

1921-1936

Let justice be done, though the world perish
Motto of Ferdinand I, House of Habsburg
Holy Roman Emperor 1558-1564

1

Of Foreign Lands and People

I FIRST BECAME AWARE of Imperial Austria and Dad's curious association with it one pleasant summer afternoon in February 1921, when I was seven. To my fanciful young mind our home in Stanmore was indeed a palace. Italianate in style with its smooth stucco façade and large bay windows, it presided over a lawn court where bordering roses, pansies, and petunias presented a lavish but respectful gathering of botanical lords and ladies in waiting. A central tower and handsome Roman arch guarded the front entrance, and balconies with wrought iron tracery crowned the mezzanine. Inside, the spacious rooms were elegantly appointed with cedar fretwork, gold fittings, and fireplaces whose patterned tiles paid tasteful homage to the paper on the walls. The wallpaper, in turn, deferred to the paintings and pretty china, which abundant ornament enhanced our home's regal but restful charm.

As you know, Roddy, Dad returned from the War without his legs, and crippled in his right arm. He was quite chipper about his injuries (at least, with me he was); but it was his nature to be chipper. He said he was lucky his legs came off below the knee, for he still had use of that joint, and so could walk quite well with wooden limbs. Dad fancied he resembled Felix the Cat when he wore his legs. 'Reckon I'm a bit like old Felix eh, Possum?' he'd smile at me as he stomped about, imitating that favourite feline character, 'Better ask that orthopaedic chap to make me a tail, too.'

Truly, there was something cat-like about him, which impression was not lost on me when I entered his downstairs suite that February afternoon. Sleekly built and smartly groomed, he was perusing a map on the polished oak table. His sharp nose led the way, and seemed aided in its quest by invisible whiskers, for it twitched astutely. Meanwhile, the fingers of his left hand stalked across the printed territories, as if hunting prey. He paused when I entered, welcomed me as he always did, and tossed me his tobacco pouch.

'Neat and tight, Poss,' he instructed. He needn't have, for I knew how he liked his smokes. I took a small handful of tobacco, savoured its rose and clove aroma, and sprinkled a column across the paper which I then rolled and sealed, twisting the ends like lolly wrappers. The finished product I placed in his silver cigarette case. For the two years since his return, I had been Dad's *aide-de-camp*. We learned many things together, like fastening buttons and tying shoelaces; although, since I was much smarter than he (so he said), I usually ended up doing his buttons and laces for him. He reciprocated by teaching me to read; and we spent hours at the parlour table writing letters on slates and comparing our efforts.

Dad explained that the map featured many new countries. In the north, on the edge of the Baltic sea, was Poland and the Free City of Danzig. Below Poland was Czechoslovakia, which I struggled to sound out.

'You pronounce C-Z as "ch", Poss,' advised Dad.

'Like in Czerny?' I asked, referring to one of my favourite pianoforte books.

'That's right. In fact, Mr Czerny was from that part of the world. And see that country to the east? That's Hungary.'

'They've misspelt it, Daddy. It should be H-U-N-G-R-Y.'

'Crikey. They better fix that. Now, this tiny country is German Austria, a very beautiful place indeed. I'll take you there someday. Once upon a time, all these lands were ruled by the oldest family in Europe, a family of emperors and kings: The Habsburgs, they're called. These days, Kaiser Karl's in exile.'

'Here's a kingdom, Daddy.'

'Hmmm, The Kingdom of Serbs, Croats, and Slovenes. That's Bitzerland.'

'Bitzerland? Why Bitzerland?'

'"Cause it comprises bits o' this, and bits o' that, *meine Prinzessin*. And here's the Crown Jewels!' he nodded in the direction of the doorway. His dark, oriental eyes gleamed, while a smile spread from under his immaculate, pencil thin moustache, which caused the scar on his cheek to smile in consort. Maman, dressed in her loose, creamy linen day-dress, her wavy, honey-blonde hair scalloped into a chignon, had returned from giving piano lessons. I ran to her, wrapped my little arms around her cosy figure, and told how I could read 'Czechoslovakia'.

'Roddy, must Phoebe roll the cigarettes?' she kissed Dad hello and brushed aside the black curl which had fallen onto his forehead.

'You can roll the next lot, Jules,' he kissed her.

'We can afford rolled cigarettes. There's no need to scrimp,' she scolded meekly, her soft, doe-like eyes incapable of anger. The word 'scrimp' afforded her some trouble, for she lisped, and she pronounced her R's in the French way. 'Time for tea, ma petite.'

Such was our Peace after years of wartime separation and carnage: a loving family, a beautiful home, a joyous life.

Two days later, Maman did not come to wake me up. I woke by myself. Rubbing my eyes in dozy puzzlement, I wandered out of my room and trotted down the hall.

'Miss Phoebe!' Dad's nurse ran up the stairs, took my hand, and led me away from Maman's door.

'Is Maman asleep?'

'Yes, miss. She's fast asleep. Let's go to your father.'

2

Nothing Else but Mad

MAMAN WAS DEAD. Like the baby magpie that fell out of our tree. Like a fly shrivelled on the windowsill. Like the worm I found squashed on the pavement.

Dead.

Grappling with the horror of never hugging Maman again, I was in no condition to make sense of the policemen milling around that mid-February morning. I clung to Dad and refused to be parted from him. Since the many discussions I heard that day exceeded the limits of my experience, the details here recorded derive from information I acquired years later through sources far more reliable than my seven-year-old self.

The detective in charge pronounced the death a suicide. On her dressing table, Maman had left a note to Dad stating that she found the burden of looking after him too much to bear. An empty bottle of Veronal at her bedside revealed her chosen means. The detective looked at Dad, forlorn and crippled, and deemed his conclusion logical. Dad was adamant that Maman was not depressed. Only that night she had told him she was expecting another baby, and her news had filled them with joy. How could he be certain the child was his? questioned the detective, dubiously arching an eyebrow at Dad's walking stick and limp right hand. Could it be that Maman, overwhelmed by the guilt of having conceived another man's child, had decided to take her own life?

Furious and upset, Dad insisted the note was a forgery. True, the handwriting was identical; but given the previous night's merriment, the letter made no sense. If Maman was happy, as indeed she was, why would she have killed herself? She may have taken something to help her sleep (she often did); but perhaps her medication had been tampered with? There was morphine in the house. That would have killed her. Dad knew Maman was sensitive to opiates: she once fell dangerously ill from the pain killers administered to her following an appendectomy at the age of fourteen. Then she would have known exactly what to do, countered the detective. Yes, and no, Dad argued. Maman did not have access to the morphine. It terrified her. Where was the morphine? It was in the charge of the nurse, (Dad took morphine to alleviate the pains he suffered due to his injuries). The nurse was questioned, and the morphine examined. Finding the doses intact, the police dismissed the idea as the flighty notion of a distressed man who could not accept that his wife had taken her own life and that he was the cause of it. Instead, they upheld the barbiturates theory. How else could one explain the empty bottle of Veronal?

Dad persisted. Maman's death was out of character. If she had decided to take her own life, she would have left a trail of evidence. He could always tell how she had spent her day, and often amused himself by strolling through the house to work it out. It made for good tea-time conversation. If Maman had been gardening, she would forget to clean her trowel. If she had been sewing, a spool was sure to have rolled unnoticed under a table. If she had been playing the piano, Dad would know what piece it was because the music would still be on the stand. If she had been reading, she would leave her book, page down, next to her chair. So, if Maman had written a suicide note, her bureau would still be open, her pen unwiped, her ink bottle devoid of its lid, and her waste paper basket overflowing with failed attempts. And if Maman had taken a sleeping potion, a single dose would not have killed her unless it had been substituted.

'By whom?' queried the detective. Who would want to kill Maman?

The person who entered our house that fateful night.

Dad explained that he had slept peacefully but had been roused by the sound of footsteps on the attic stairs, which were above his room. (Due to his ailments, he slept downstairs, apart from Maman, which fact only served to underscore the police assessment of their marriage). Concerned, he rang for the nurse and requested she investigate. No one was there. Dad, meanwhile, was certain he had heard a door. Perhaps he had, for his hearing was sharp despite his years in the trenches. He instructed the nurse to lock the attic and bring him the key, and insisted she check the back door before retiring. The police also checked the back door but found no evidence of anyone entering or leaving. The nurse confirmed Dad's story but attributed his wakefulness and obsession to a nightmare.

The police searched the attic. Certainly, items had been moved; but Maman had been there recently, and, true to form, had left it in a mess. There were no other fingerprints, apart from mine; but I did not factor in the investigation. Since our attic contained all the usual unwanted or past-loved paraphernalia, there appeared to be nothing out of the ordinary. Instead, the police concluded that the noises Dad heard were induced by shell shock. It was typical: they received hundreds of reports against Fritz and Abdul by diggers who claimed that Kaiser Bill or Johnny Turk had tunnelled their way to Sydney. But Dad did not suffer from shell shock. Admittedly, he had his share of bad dreams; while his attempts to come off the morphine had brought about some strange behaviour. He was sensitive to sudden noises, too. Only the previous Sunday, the ringing of the bell at Mass prompted him to shout in alarm and fling himself, Maman, and me under a pew. Such episodes, however, were rare. The detective thought him hyperactive; but Dad maintained that he had always been excitable. Nevertheless, the police suspected that Dad was nothing else but mad, that there was no intruder, and that Maman took her own life.

The doctor agreed, even though he thought Maman's death odd for she had been in remarkably good spirits – better than he'd ever known her. But Maman had a history of melancholia which, coupled with the evidence to hand, led him to rule that her unfortunate and tragic death was probably self-inflicted.

Inconsolable, Dad refused to accept the official conclusion and clung to his theory that Maman was murdered. He badgered the police, the doctor, and even the priest until he was issued a restraining order. He questioned the neighbours to such an extent that they, too, made formal complaint. And the more they protested, the more he persisted. The more he persisted, the more they attributed his behaviour to shell shock. The more they attributed his behaviour to shell shock, the more paranoid and obsessive he became. The more paranoid and obsessive he became, the more reason they had to declare him socially unfit. The nurse administered morphine to keep him under control.

Then one day I came face to face with a grim old woman who said she was my Aunt Sara. Aunt Sara arranged to have Dad admitted into a home. On parting, Dad passed me a key.

'Keep it safe, Poss,' he whispered, hugging me tight.

I clutched the key in my tiny hands as I stood on the front steps and watched two men escort him to a motor car.

Aunt Sara packed my things, locked our home, and took me to live with her.

3

Into Hemlock

WITH HER GREY HAIR, meagre frame, sombre high-necked blouses, and black skirts that swished as she walked, Aunt Sara Raye McDonald should have been Dad's aunt, not mine. She was, in fact, sixteen years his senior; but to my child's eyes, she seemed thrice that.

Aunt Sara lived far across the harbour on Sydney's North Shore, which to me explained why I had never met her. She had a son, Ian Raye McDonald, who was 'abroad on military service'. Upon studying his photograph which held pride of place on the mantelpiece in the front parlour, I thought him a very kind, adventurous-spirited chap who would have made a fine older playmate. So, I waited with curiosity and impatience for him to come home. Aunt Sara said she expected him any day, and in anticipation made sure his room was dusted and aired. As for Uncle James McDonald, he had passed away before the War. Uncle McDonald had been a successful businessman, a fact attested by the grand house and its many servants.

The house featured a long hallway. Half-way down stood a grandfather clock whose steady tick-tock would stop before the hour and grind into a discordant chime. Convinced that inside its cabinet was imprisoned a genie, I took to tip-toeing down the hall, fearful that the genie might leap out and capture me. Sometimes the clock would strike as I passed, and I would run for my life, and instead be caught by Aunt Sara, who would scold me for running, and for believing in fantastical beings.

There was also an organ which I discovered during a solo expedition to the drawing room. Fascinated by the stops and pedals, I climbed onto the stool and began to play. To my delight, the instrument produced remarkable thunderstorms. For this profanity Aunt Sara sent me to bed without supper and thereafter kept the room locked.

And she forbade me from playing with the toys in Cousin Ian's room. Why not? I asked. They were Ian's toys, not mine, said my aunt.

'But Cousin Ian looks too old to play with them.'

'They are not to be played with by a child like you,' she answered, insinuating that I was inferior to her son, who had always been 'a good boy' like the child who preferred the verse of a Psalm to a gingerbread-nut.

To prove my biblical knowledge, and thereby my worthiness to play with Cousin Ian's toys, I decided one evening to tell Aunt Sara all I knew of the lithographs in her sitting room. The lithographs depicted the ten plagues of Egypt; and the tempests, frogs and pestilence so graphically portrayed, I feared as much as the genie in the clock. Nonetheless, I told Aunt Sara of Pharaoh's repeated refusal to free the Israelites, and of the divine retribution he and his people incurred. Similar punishment, she replied, would befall me because I, too, was sinful.

'Why am I sinful?'

'You are the fruit of adultery,' which explanation held no meaning for me whatsoever.

'Is that why you don't love me?' I asked; but Aunt Sara refused to elaborate.

I chanced to learn more about my origins from Aunt Sara's maid whom I overheard in conversation with the cook after church the following Sunday:

'She's a pretty little thing,' remarked the cook, referring to me. 'But how can you be so sure?'

'It happened in the family home,' the maid watched cook take the lamb from the oven. 'The missus saw with her own eyes Mr Roderick sneaking out of the hussy's room at dawn in nothing more than his dressing-gown. They married within months— you can guess why. And in the Church of Rome to boot. I met him once— handsome devil,' she added, having respected cook's hush. 'A ladies' man if ever there was. Miss Phoebe was born the following January, nine months to the day.'

'It's a wonder she took the little bastard in,' replied cook, whose derogatory tone confused me. The only time I had heard the word bastard was when Dad spoke of friends who had survived the War, on which occasion it was qualified with 'lucky'.

Lucky, I was not. From that day forward, the servants treated me like an unwanted house pet – an animal to be fed and sheltered by request of its owner; but because it served little useful purpose, was barely tolerated by those charged with tending it. The kitchen cat fared better, for she kept the mice at bay and was rewarded with bowls of milk and a cosy place on cook's lap. Whenever I came for a drink or a biscuit, the servants shooed me away. Yet neither was I a lap dog, doted upon by its mistress and fed titbits from her plate. My pedigree was insufficient. Indeed, I was a lesser creature: a child. I was to be seen and not heard; adequately kept; and disciplined according to my circumstance and station, which latter policy implied that I was much in need of reform. Aunt Sara implemented a regime of nutritious meals, regular exercise, early bedtimes, sermons, and Sunday School, none of which I liked. Not that I was unused to good food, fresh air, rest, and even catechesis for that matter. Simply, the routine and so forth with which I was familiar, Dad (and Maman to a lesser degree) adorned with songs and stories, games and rhymes. Aunt Sara monitored my activities with sterile formality.

My domestic remediation she complemented with an equivalent academic one. She removed me from my parish school in Stanmore and sent me to a nearby private establishment where I was instructed not to aspirate the letter 'H'. I liked the school about as much as I liked Aunt Sara, and frequently absconded. Naturally, my wanderlust only underscored her opinion that I was a law unto myself and in need of stricter surveillance. So, she placed me in the charge of a governess; but the change failed to curb my behaviour.

Little wonder, she concluded. I had Dad's profligate nature, which first I assumed was something good but forbidden, like most things associated with him, such as putting three teaspoons of sugar in tea when one should suffice, making the Sign of the Cross before praying, singing loudly, or reading stories about witches and goblins. The dictionary, however, corrected my understanding, defining profligate as wasteful or extravagant; and I suppose putting three teaspoons of sugar in one's tea was wasteful (Aunt Sara certainly thought so); but when later I questioned her, Aunt Sara said Dad was a profligate because he was reckless and immoral. So was my attempt to catch a ferry across the harbour, penniless and unaccompanied, and committed to avoid a reading lesson. It mattered little that I already knew how to read, and that the literature provided did not interest me. As for my questions, they deemed me impudent.

I stared at Aunt Sara in her black blouse, its high collar fastened by a mourning cameo. She tightened her lips and swallowed. Her eyes, like Dad's, were dark and a little slanted; but they did not twinkle as his did. They were hard and beady, like a snake's. And the venomous righteousness she spurted numbed my every capacity.

Fortunately, memory supplied an antidote. I thought of Dad in his ivory summer suit with its paisley necktie, matching handkerchief, and jaunty boater, leaning on his walking stick, his withered right hand concealed in his trouser pocket as he waited for me to come out of school, eager to hear my news; of his cheery greeting and our leisurely walk home, punctuated by frequent stops to admire a garden or greet a passer-by; of the many bedtime stories he told me about Gregory Allegri, a magical horse which featured in every historical event imaginable, from Hannibal to Napoleon. How could he be reckless and immoral when he was only ever kind, and when that kindness crowned a determined struggle to overcome enormous injury? For I had also seen him weep, cradled like a child in Maman's arms.

'My father is a very brave man. Maman said he was very brave because he came back from the War,' I retorted, recalling a conversation in which Maman tried to explain his missing legs and crippled arm. Dad's 'coming back' was of the deepest importance to her. 'I will tell you more someday, ma petite,' she used to add.

'There are plenty of brave men who did not come back,' Aunt Sara replied while my eyes welled with tears. Never would I hear what more Maman would say. 'Furthermore, your mother was a trollop whose suicide demonstrated her weak and immoral character. And your father's injuries are just recompense for his godless conduct.'

'Then, if God punishes people for the bad things they do, why has He not punished you? You are evil and cruel. I hate you and I hope you die!'

I wondered at the power of my words. Pallid and quaking, Aunt Sara put her hand to her breast and bade me leave the room. Thereafter, brief greetings at morning and night marked the limit of our contact. For that, I was grateful.

Meanwhile, Dad languished in Graythwaite, a home for severely disabled war veterans. Aunt Sara allowed me to visit him once a week. When I first saw him, he held me close and cried. Aunt Sara attempted conversation, but Dad had words and ears only for me his pride and joy. With every subsequent visit, however, it seemed he had drifted to another time and place. Soon he was unreachable. In fact, he no longer spoke English. Nor did he recognise me. Aunt Sara resorted to her usual verbiage on divine retribution, to which Dad responded by shouting at her and hurling a crucifix which struck me hard on the brow. There was much blood and the blow nearly cost me the sight in my right eye.

An uncanny whimper, animal in nature, broke my sobs. Then followed a wail, the cry of a man more dead than alive: an imploration from the abyss voiced in a language only Heaven understands.

Dad's lament was the last I was to hear of him. My aunt banned me from visiting, and no amount of running away would alter the situation. Aunt Sara then made other arrangements for my welfare.

She put me in an orphanage.

4

A Better World

HAVE YOU READ *Jane Eyre*, Roddy? If so, perchance you might think Aunt Sara like Aunt Reed, which was the conclusion I reached when I read Brontë's novel at age fourteen.

In hindsight, however, Aunt Sara was not a vain and indulgent woman. She was righteous, certainly, but she was not hypocritical. She disciplined herself as harshly as she did me. Falsehood was abhorrent to her, and therein lay the catch: she was convinced of the truth of her observations. Speaking with authority, and using phrases I did not understand, she attributed qualities to my parents which conflicted with my experience of their kindness. And because I knew she did not lie, I worried that she might be right. Baffled, I grew resentful; and I embraced Jane Eyre's rebellious and hostile sentiments. Glad to be rid of my aunt, I entered the orphanage as a boat to a harbour.

Nor was the orphanage a Lowood School. True, the institution provided a rudimentary education and trained girls for domestic service; but it was run by Josephite nuns who took a far more benign approach to salvation than the oppressive and sanctimonious Mr Brocklehurst. There were some unpleasant personalities, but overall the Brown Joeys (as they were known) were amiable, no-nonsense characters who fed and clothed us as best they could, and saw that we were pious, literate, and house-trained. Such duties left them little time for deviant or clandestine activity. Besides, their resources were scant. There were no luxuries for anyone.

Compassionate, the nuns sullied not Maman's name and troubled to inquire after Dad who was 'very ill' and 'could not be seen'. Instead, they encouraged me to pray – they themselves prayed rosaries and had Masses offered for his recovery. But what did a Mass, however devoutly offered, mean to me? Mumbled in Latin, with its careful ritual of bows, genuflections, crossing of hands and long silences, it only reminded me of all I had lost.

As for the other girls, many of their situations were far worse than mine, for the War and the Influenza epidemic had wreaked havoc on families. The nuns endeavoured to find homes for all of us. Meanwhile, we sought solidarity in our misfortune, and in our determination 'to leave the past behind and make the most of what God's given you' as our wimpled mentors liked to say.

Aunt Sara had prepared me well for the orphanage. Her cold-hearted and judgmental treatment taught me not to expect affection. Indeed, to desire love would have been my undoing. But I cannot credit myself for my endurance. I would not have lasted very long at all if it had not been for someone you know very well indeed.

I first met Mrs Epstein shortly after I arrived, in the winter of 1921. It was an encounter I will never forget, one reason being that in all my seven short years (and subsequently for that matter) I had never met a plainer person.

That winter's afternoon she gave a concert at the orphanage. The nuns welcomed the event as a much-needed treat, since everyone was convalescing from illness. There had even been a couple of cases of polio. Mrs Epstein played the violin for us, accompanied on the piano by Mr Epstein.

Cross-legged, I sat spell-bound, in the front row, watching and listening, and, above all, yearning. I had never heard a violin before, despite there being one in our home. I remembered discovering it during a visit to the attic with Maman:

'Qu'est-ce que c'est?' I asked as I pulled it out.

'C'est un petit violon,' Maman paused from rummaging through a trunk of clothes. 'No, no, no, ma petite!'

Her urgent whisper demanded I cease plucking the strings and immediately put the instrument down. 'Pas maintenant! Peut-être un autre fois.'

But that other time never came. For the music stopped when Maman died, and Aunt Sara locked the organ in the parlour.

Mrs Eptsein then played a tune that Dad used to sing with Maman accompanying him on the Bosendorfer. It was an odd song, I thought, for it was about the sickness of poor Dauphin Duncan of Lieberville, which I assumed was in France; and of Bessy, his lady, who soothed him. Dad sang it with great reverence; which I thought appropriate given his injuries, when on bad days Maman would take him in her arms and comfort him by singing to him. So preoccupied was I with my memories that I must have begun singing myself.

'Do you know this tune?' she stopped playing

'It's called "Handy Music",' I replied once I realised she was looking at me, for her thick glasses distorted her gaze. And I suppose the music was handy because, like all music, once you knew it by heart, you could take it anywhere and it made you feel better.

'Would you like to sing it?'

I stood with my legs astride, like Dad, and placed one hand on the side of the piano. My other hand I put in my pinafore pocket, as Dad would his hand in the pocket of his plush plum-coloured smoking jacket. I glanced fondly at the pianist, the way Dad did Maman, and nodded for him to begin, whereupon I awaited my entrance. Then I sang with all my might:

> In olden times 'midst evil groans I stand and
> Vomit in Lieberville with cries and screams
> A steaming horse, was formerly in something:
> A stomach in my best velvet coat,
> In my best velvet coat.

'I don't like being sick,' I told Dad when in commiseration I recounted to him my experience with Influenza when I was five. 'Do you like being sick?'

'I'd rather not be.'

'Then why are you so happy?'

'I reckon happiness is more to do with being loved than being healthy.'

'I love you, Daddy,' I threw my arms around him.

'I love you too, Poss.'

Mr Epstein at the piano prompted me by singing, 'Oft hat'. Pleased that he also knew the song, I commenced the second verse even louder than the first, and hoped that in doing so Dad might hear it and be happy again:

> Of that I suffer dinner half unfinished,
> Then suffer Hell on Earth accordingly.
> An hymn will Bessie sigh and sing so softly,
> And hold and kiss her drunk and dear dauphin,
> And hold and kiss her Duncan dear.

Upon finishing, I curtseyed. I knew how, because Maman had taught me when I performed a piano solo as part of a concert for returned soldiers. Mrs Epstein asked me my name, and how I came to know the song so well. I recounted my parents' musical evenings, and, my memory enlivened, told with much enthusiasm how an Irishman with a mighty bass voice used to come to our house to give Dad singing lessons, after which he would stay to tea, and, if Dad was well enough, more music making.

'And did your father teach you that song?'

'Oh no,' I declared, 'I learnt it all by myself.'

'Do you like music?'

'Very much. But I don't like being sick.'

The following day Mrs Epstein returned with a small violin especially for me. Consumed by the sound and the means involved in achieving it, I devoted myself to the instrument, while Mrs Epstein devoted herself to teaching me. She taught other girls, too, but I sensed that I was special because I made rapid progress. Mrs Epstein responded by teaching me twice a week.

The best lesson took place at her home on Friday afternoons. Over the years that amounted to many, many houses. The Epsteins tended to move every three months or so in response to complaints about their practice from neighbours who could not stand the noise; although what was so unpleasant about it, I don't know. It seemed, also, that landlords objected to the capsicums they cultivated in the gardens of their various rented premises. The underlying reason, though, was that the Epsteins were 'German', and wartime antipathies had by no means faded. But, as you know, although she spoke the language, Mrs Epstein was not German, she was Australian. And Mr Epstein was not German, either. He was Austrian. But most people were oblivious to such distinctions.

On Fridays I had a piano lesson with Mr Epstein. At that time, he resembled Franz Schubert, for he had sideburns and wore small, ovular glasses like the composer's; which resemblance made me feel privileged to study with him.

But best of all was that Mr Epstein baked Challah. He always let me help him with the final kneading and braiding, and while the bread was rising, he would give me my lesson. After the lesson, we put the bread in the oven and Mrs Epstein would teach me violin. It was difficult to concentrate in that lesson because the house would fill with the wonderful sweet smell of the baking bread; and my lesson invariably finished early, so insistent was I upon being present when the golden loaves came out.

At sunset we celebrated Sabbath. Mrs Epstein would place two candles on the table and light them. Then she would wave her hands over the candles before closing her eyes to say the blessing. Mr Epstein let me sip wine. We washed our hands, again with a blessing, and enjoyed our meal, the highlight being (for me, at least) the Challah which fortunately we ate first. The remaining evening, we spent playing games and telling stories. With a bedtime blessing from Mr Epstein, I retired to a room all my own. Saturday, we spent in a very relaxed manner, with a goulash and strudel for the main meal. Finally, on Sunday morning, the Epsteins took me back to the orphanage in time for Mass.

I implored them to adopt me. After all, they had no children of their own, why should they not? Other girls were adopted. But it was out of the question; and Mrs Epstein told me as much in such a way (gently but with indisputable firmness) that I never dared ask again.

And what did the nuns think of all these lessons and Sabbath rituals? Believe it or not, they encouraged them. Well, they encouraged the lessons. They never knew about any Jewish observances, for I didn't say anything about them, nor did Mrs Epstein. Regarding music, given my proficiency it promised to be a viable livelihood, not to mention a far more desirable form of employment than domestic service. Practice was vital in the deepest sense of the word. On a higher level, musical prowess constituted just use of God-given talents, the nuns instructed. Provided I do my chores, complete my lessons, and fulfil my religious obligations (weekly confession, rosary, and daily Mass), I could practise as much as I pleased.

Like a Byzantine tomb, I presented a plain, unadorned and altogether uninteresting exterior. My peers thought me pretty, but my physical endowments were the result of Nature's benevolence. There was nothing artful in my presentation. I dressed neatly and modestly in whatever well-made clothes came my way. My grooming likewise befitted my age and station: my tresses were braided; my sole ornament a Miraculous Medal. My imagination, however, glittered with tesserae: glorious mosaics of gypsies and fairies, of knights and princesses, dragons and monsters, all expressions of my music, and rippling with colour and adventure, but, unlike the Ravenna mausoleums, devoid of theological symbolism.

I should have had more faith, but nothing came of my petitions to make Dad well again. My outward piety instead served as brickwork to protect me from nuns and teachers. Deeming me a well-behaved child and a model of industry, they let me be; as did the other girls who had their own survival to consider. Thus respected, I kept my musical world intact which, for me, was tantamount since it provided a lifeline to a happier but increasingly remote past and blocked the memory of Dad's cries.

All in all, the orphanage was secure, safe, and sufficient in everything save homeliness. There I stayed until my fourteenth year when the nuns required that I make my own way. Once again, I begged Mr and Mrs Epstein to take me in.

They declined.

A better arrangement had been made:

An aunt was coming from Paris to look after me.

5

Firebird

ASIDE FROM AUNT SARA, from whom I never heard, I did not know of any other family; and as I awaited my aunt's arrival, I dreaded facing another Puritan.

Upon introduction, I learned that Miss Ailine Devereaux was my mother's sister. Unfortunately, Miss Devereaux did not resemble Maman at all. True, she had the same compact, cuddly figure I vaguely recalled hugging; otherwise, she was darker in complexion. But there was a familiarity about her eyes that put me at ease. Not that they were like Maman's large brown orbs; they were a lively green. I wondered, too, at her soft calf shoes with their heels and straps; and her stockings, silky and sheer – a fascinating contrast to Sister Mary Paul, whose legs were concealed by her long brown habit, and whose rosary dangled from her ample girth. And when Miss Devereaux turned to leave, I gasped at the sight of the firebird embroidered in a sunset of colour on the back of her emerald velvet coat.

While we travelled to Stanmore, Miss Devereaux told me that she had lived most of her life in Paris, the city of her birth, and had traversed Europe in her youth. She had even sojourned in Morocco (to escape the Influenza after the War). Although her English was fluent, she often lapsed into French, and only corrected herself when she realised I did not understand.

'Bien,' she concluded as our cab pulled outside my childhood home. 'But Aunt is a little too formal a mode of address, n'est-ce pas? I do not like to think of myself as your aunt; it is so old-maidish and passé. And under no circumstance will I be called Aunt, Tante, Tatie, Tata, or Aunty. Besides, you are too grown-up— more than I expected. How old are you?'

'Thirteen.'

'Then we will be friends instead; and you may call me Ailine.'

Weeds filled the garden and the lawn was unmown; but I was consoled by the sight of my swing hanging from the tree at the front. The house itself was a vault. Much of the furniture remained, like bones undecomposed; but the knick-knacks, plants, paintings, and books were gone. Dad's downstairs suite – the rooms converted for his express use after he returned from the War – was empty. I ventured up the wide wooden staircase and paused outside Maman's door. Shaking, I opened it and breathed a sigh when I found her body not lying on the bed. Nothing remained of Maman: her bed was stripped, her dressing table devoid of trinkets, her wardrobe empty. Fortunately, my room had retained its child's bed and nursery prints. Even the doll's house was intact.

'Your mother used to play with it when she was a girl,' remarked Ailine, who had followed me much of the way. 'Her father, your grandfather, made it especially for her.' I knew nothing of my grandfather and said so. Ailine explained he was of Hungarian descent. He had been born on the Victorian goldfields and had worked in Sydney before travelling abroad.

'It's beautiful,' I whispered as I studied the miniatures inside. Ailine said they were all Maman's work. 'Can we make the house like this again, Ailine?'

'Provided you don't expect it to happen all at once,' she replied as she left.

Beside my bed I placed my one photograph which had been taken the Christmas before Maman died. Maman had tied my hair with a pink satin bow to match the sash I wore round my waist. The photographer, a kindly gentleman with ginger hair, had organised us in the front parlour: Dad sitting proud and erect in his Sunday best, Maman behind him, and me at his right side trying my utmost to keep still despite the heat, thinking of the cake and ices to follow. To think that two months later we would be parted forever! I remembered Dad wandering about on the stumps of his legs, his trousers trailing; unshaven; his shirt collarless; a cufflink on his right sleeve, his left cuff undone and draping over his hand; questioning all and sundry; the neighbours' hostility, Aunt Sara's intervention, and our final separation. And I threw myself on my bed and wept.

'You are still here? I have made tea and you do not come! But what is the matter?' Ailine sat beside me and I poured out my sorrow.

'It is a tragedy, yes? A tragedy. Poor Juliette! Poor Roderick! Poor, poor Phoebe! Come now, we must start afresh. From Death comes Life. You must be like the Phoenix and rise from the dust of your past. Come with me. I have something especially for you.'

She led me down the back wing of the house to a large room which she said was hers when she was my age. Since it had been my grandfather's wish to be laid to rest in Australia, the family had come here for the last years of his life.

'Where is he now, Ailine?'

'I assume he is buried with your grandmother.'

'Bobeshi!' I hugged her, excited at the recollection of happier times. Bobeshi was my grandmother, who gave me my first piano lessons. How magnificently she played! But how sad that she died of Influenza before Dad came home. 'Oh Ailine, I used to lie under the Bosendorfer spellbound by Liszt's Rhapsodies; or I'd fall asleep near the pedals, soothed by Chopin's Berceuse. And when she performed Mussorsgky's Gnome, I used to scream. Oh, and Baba Yaga, what a frenzy! I would hide in the curtains and pretend I was Vasilisa! Can you play the piano like Bobeshi?'

Smiling, Ailine denied that she could. 'Can you?'

'I can now! Anyway, Ailine, you have green eyes, just like Bobeshi! You really are family, aren't you?'

'Yes, I am family. And I have a present from Paris, especially for you. I hope it fits. I did not expect you to be so well-grown.'

She presented me with a red dress made from the softest velvet, with a wide, white lace collar and an enormous sash. Loosely styled, it seemed more suited to a younger child. Nonetheless, having lived only in hand-me-downs, it was very special. I imagined myself as Rose Red and said so.

'Perhaps, then, you will marry a Prince!' laughed Ailine, who congratulated herself on choosing so well, although the dress barely fitted.

'I will wear it to Sunday Mass,' I told her as I smoothed the front.

'You don't expect me to take you to Mass, do you?'

'Don't you go?'

'I was only dunked because of the Dreyfus Affair— a loathsome court case about a Jewish officer accused of leaking information to the Boche. Went on for decades.'

'Oh, so you're Jewish?' I concluded after Ailine enlightened me as to the identity of the 'Boche' and the rift between Catholics and Jews which the case had provoked. Well, if my aunt's being Jewish meant we would eat Challah in my own home, I was glad. But I must have gabbled a bit too much about my Sabbaths with the Epsteins, for Ailine reminded me that tea was ready. And no, she wasn't Jewish, either.

A few days later, my photograph disappeared.

'I am so very sorry, ma chèrie,' Ailine replied when I asked her about it. 'I was dusting your room. The vase tipped and soaked it. Why did you place them so close together? I tried to dry it out, but it was beyond salvation. I'm afraid I had to burn it. There was nothing more I could do.'

'You might have told me,' I stammered, trying to hold back my tears.

'But I did. Just now. It was an accident.'

I ran to the backyard where indeed a pyre had been lit. I grabbed a stick and raked through ashes. Nothing was left of my photograph. But I did find the remains of another. What else had she destroyed? Were there other photographs? Other pictures? My puzzlement increased with the passing weeks. It became quite plain that Ailine never dusted my room. She never dusted anything.

Ailine made up for my loss by inviting me to play with her cosmetics, an impressive array of curved bottles, atomisers, crystal jars, and trinkets enough to make a film star envious. Like my peers at the orphanage, I was fascinated by the silver screen. By appointment we would steal away from the nuns and gather behind the gardening shed where we would meet those who had obtained situations. We spent the time smoking, leafing through magazines and studying the smouldering eyes and painted lips of Clara Bow and Mary Pickford. Such gatherings constituted a pact forged years ago. I, in turn, upheld the tradition, purchasing a dozen Luckies with my earnings as a picture show pianist, which job earned me considerable kudos.

I watched Ailine smooth her complexion with ivory powder. Using deft but delicate brushstrokes, she shaped her lips into a cupid's bow. She plucked her brows, then pencilled them into elegant slopes. Her green eyes she outlined with kohl and shadowed with blends of grey and turquoise. She combed and darkened her lashes; her cheeks she softly rouged. That she should let me try for myself was an honour. Only I was not to use the powder. 'You will look like a phantom,' she said. My own efforts were disastrous; but thanks to Ailine's skill, I could have passed for twenty-one.

'Would you like to brush my hair, Phoebe?' she handed me a silver brush with soft bristles.

Previously, hair for me had been hidden under wimples or restrained in braids and buns. Ailine, however, had beautiful hair and plenty of it. My last experience of flowing hair was Maman's golden tresses. Ailine's locks were a glossy, deep brown, and I marvelled how they danced over her shoulders. In gratitude she let me watch her sculpt them, twisting and piling them on top of her head, framing her face with stray curls, and letting soft ringlets fall. The finished work of art (for Ailine's hair was indeed a work of art) she enhanced with a silk scarf tied round her head, its ends falling down her back in a waterfall of colour.

'Now, may *I* brush your hair, Phoebe?'

Sighing in disapproval, Ailine undid my braids, liberated my curls and applied long, sumptuous strokes.

'Quelle jolie petite fille! Comment comme son père! Et sa

maman! You have your mother's face and your father's complexion. What dark eyes he had, and what beautiful olive skin – light and flawless – not a bit swarthy. Un Nijinksy. And he had rosy cheeks when he was young, like you.'

'Did you know Dad?'

'Intimately. You have his black curls, too. Your eyes may be dark, like his, but they are your mother's: comme un épagneul. If you were blonde, you might pass for her. Your lips and cheeks are her very own. Why Phoebe, you don't need a photograph! Just look in the mirror! Mais—Qu'est-ce-que? Cette cicatrice? What is this here?' She indicated the scar on my brow.

With deep regret I told her of the incident in the veteran's home, when Dad hit me.

'I noticed it when I made up your eyes but didn't like to ask. Oh dear, I shouldn't have mentioned it. You'll ruin your mascara. There, there. Try not to cry. He has gone quite mad, yes?'

'Have you seen him?'

'I tried, but—' She shook her head. 'They told me he will never, ever recover. But this,' she added, indicating my scar, 'This we can fix.' And she arranged my hair on top of my head so that it enhanced my curls and concealed my defect. What a transformation! I looked like a princess. Ailine twisted my locks round her fingers and cooed compliments.

Mrs Epstein deemed my coiffure too sophisticated. She had other concerns, too, the most pressing being my need for a full-size violin that would do justice to my ability and to the more advanced repertoire I was studying.

'What do you expect me to do about it?' Ailine shrugged when Mrs Epstein visited one Sunday.

I marvelled at the contrast between my two guardians. Ailine wore silk pyjamas, and her feet were bare, for it was hot. The weather seemed not to affect Mrs Epstein who wore her customary tweed suit and sensible brogues. How was it they should converse with such familiarity?

'I am sure funds can be arranged,' replied the straight-forward Mrs Epstein.

'Merde! She won't find anything here in this backwater. You cannot lend her one?'

'I have already done so. At least take her to Smith's, Lina. They're bound to have something.'

Ailine conceded with much ennui, and Mrs Epstein departed.

'Can we go tomorrow, Ailine?' I asked.

'Why bother?' Ailine dismissed me with a wave of her hand, and I regretted my imposition. 'There's probably something in the attic.'

Hitherto, I had avoided the attic because of its association with Maman's death. Then I remembered the circumstances of our last visit. I dashed up the stairs to the top of the house.

The attic was locked. But the key Dad had given me, which I had kept safe the past seven years, opened the door – a tricky manoeuvre requiring two hands and much jiggling of the lock. The violin was exactly where I had left it near the open trunk, when I showed Maman what I had found: a half-sized violin in a tiny case. Of course, it would have been perfect for a small child. Now, it was a toy. I laughed at the trick my memory had played, when amidst the clutter I glimpsed another violin case, and a very battered one at that. Inside was a beautiful instrument with a rich amber varnish, and a curious mark on its neck. Unfortunately, its strings were broken, and it lacked a chin rest. The bow was also in disrepair, its hair a tattered mess of bug-eaten strands.

'What have you found?' whispered a voice.

'Oh, Ailine!' I gasped as much from surprise as delight, 'A Guarneri del Gesù! Isn't it beautiful?'

'Lucky you!'

'I'll have it repaired at once!'

Mr Hunt at the local music shop was most impressed when I showed him, although he doubted the instrument was a Guarneri, as did Mrs Epstein. The bow he wouldn't touch. Being a fine Louis Bazin, it deserved a first-class rehair at Smith's. The violin he fitted with a new chin rest and the best strings. With its full curves, fine purfling, and beautiful wood and varnish, it showed much promise.

But it was not easy to play. Indeed, the instrument was quite cryptic. The lower strings sounded dark and poignant, while the upper registers were brilliant; yet they, too, possessed a mysterious timbre. To transition from low to high required considerable skill with the bow. 'That bow is better than you,' remarked Mrs Epstein who thought it superlative. Playing well required much patience on my part. It was like listening to a gifted storyteller who spoke with a foreign accent. Either you swept aside your inner prejudices and preferences and paid attention, or you missed out on a captivating, colourful tale. To my chagrin, my tone seemed harsh; and I caught only the occasional glimmer of beauty, a magical feather of sound falling into my possession. But a glimmer was all I needed to pursue my quest.

Meanwhile Ailine, delighted at having suggested I look in the attic, encouraged me to give my imagination its fullest expression, not only in sound, but in every aspect of my person. Nor did she complain of the hours I spent practising, be it violin or piano. She was equally consumed by her own pursuits, most of which were confined to our capacious front parlour which she had converted into a studio.

After the War, Maman, at pains to keep Dad busy, encouraged him to take up painting. Once he learned to control the colour and co-ordinate his brush with his left hand, it became a means to express his nightmares as well as engage in the beauty all about him. Brow furrowed in thought, he would pause before his masterpiece, which in hindsight by no means deserved that description, although I was impressed at the time.

'Reckon I'm still to find my feet, Possum,' he lamented, hugging me.

'You haven't got any feet.'

'What? Where've they gone to now? Ah! It's you! You took them!'

Ailine, however, could paint or draw anything, as I discovered when a box of her paintings finally arrived from Paris. I helped her hang them and was intrigued to find that some were very modern, while others were skilled copies of old masters. The latter I most admired and said so.

'C'est le pain', she shrugged, and explained that the sale of such works provided income. 'C'est bourgeois. That's real art,' and she pointed to what I thought was a still life, but which turned out to be a portrait of a man comprised of parts of a violin and torn pieces of music.

'It looks like my violin.' I noted the similarity between the ochre paint and my instrument's golden varnish.

'Whether it resembles *your* violin is incidental. It's not about *your* violin, it's about form.'

'Oh.' But I was unsure whether I ought to be thankful for the edification, or stupid, given that Ailine had to communicate an apparently fundamental principle. 'It still looks like my violin. Why did you make it a man?'

'It is not a man. It is Art. Now, I need to ask you a favour.'

Thinking that she might feature me as a Raphael Madonna, I was excited and flattered when she requested I pose for her. Ailine bid me undress. 'You may wear my robe while I finish setting up. It's Japanese silk. You'll look so pretty in it. And have a sip of tea. I brewed some specially.' When I crept out from behind the screen, she smiled and guided me to the velvet chaise lounge she had prepared. 'Now take off the robe and lie here. It's very comfortable.'

Trembling, I loosened the gown only slightly.

'You'll have to remove it some time.'

'But I don't want to.'

'I felt the same at your age. There's no need to be ashamed. We all have a body, and yours is quite beautiful. The world's not a convent, darling.'

'But I don't want to,' was all I could say. I wanted to run away, but could not, for I felt quite confused. Nor was my body able to fulfil my mind's instruction.

'Perhaps you could pose as a Sultana, like in the *Arabian Nights*? It's much easier when you pretend to be someone else,' I heard Ailine say. 'That way you'll understand that the painting is not about you. Deception is the essence of Art. We create, that others might believe.'

Clashing colours and bold lines formed the ligature whereby she strangled my innocence. Bare-breasted, wearing billowy trousers, and savouring grapes whilst draped across a sofa, I was an Odalisque, a concubine in her possession. Ailine dashed her signature, Devereaux, across the bottom of the work.

'Why did you paint me like that?' I cried.

'Comment-elle regarde son nombril! How many times must I say it? It's not about you! Who do you think you are?'

Ailine made a point of showing the painting to her numerous friends, so much so that whenever anyone looked at me, I was convinced they could still see my breasts. I begged her to get rid it; and to my relief, she obliged.

But the Odalisque proved that I was not quite ready to live with her and she arranged to send me to boarding-school. St Dominic's, the school she selected (for a brief time it was her own *alma mater*), turned out to be only a few suburbs away.

'But why must you send me away, Ailine?'

'How can I possibly paint with the freedom I need if I don't?'

'I am fourteen and have employment. I don't have to go to school.'

'And if you stay, you do so on my terms, for I am your guardian.'

'You're not my guardian! You do nothing to look after me! Besides, it's my house!'

'Your house? It's as much mine as it is yours. We're family. But I'm in charge. So, either you go to school or you walk the streets. You cannot live here.'

6

Harpies

IKE BIRDS OF PARADISE flying into a chicken coop, we landed at St Dominic's. Well-heeled parents cocked their heads at Ailine's vibrant robes and stared at the delicate gold chain round her right ankle. A nun in a white habit glided swanlike towards us. She knew Ailine, for her warm greeting and subsequent enquiries were affectionate and well-informed (I soon learned that they had shared the same dormitory). Ailine, however, considered her a foreign species, predatory by nature, which should have become extinct aeons ago, and took flight.

My peers thought me more akin to Aesop's jackdaw. Since my red dress no longer fitted me, being too short, too childish, and too tight across my breast, I indeed looked a bird in borrowed feathers. They demanded I explain myself. In the orphanage I had been in the same predicament as my fellows. Each of us had been consigned to that institution because of domestic trouble connected with the War, and we felt much solidarity because of it. But I had just witnessed mothers and fathers bid daughters good-bye and was now surrounded by girls chatting about their family holidays. To admit Maman was dead cost me much; and all I could say of Dad was that he had been 'in the War', which explanation usually sufficed. Not so now. Was it because of Ailine? Was it my darker complexion? Was it my garment that rendered me pretentious?

'You're a War Baby,' sneered one. That I had been born in January 1914, before the War's outbreak, made no difference. Since bullies tend to overlook such details and drawing their attention to finer points only exacerbates their teasing, the girl deemed my denial and justification prevaricatory, insinuating thereby that she was better informed.

Her position was later verified by the prettiest and most popular girl in the class who rumoured that my mother was already pregnant when she married, and that my father abandoned her for the War. She had it on good authority, for our mothers had gone to school together. 'Not true! He may have gone to War, but he came back! He came back!' was all I could say; for that was all I knew. Only at night in the dormitory when I lay in my bed, cuddling my little soft horse and listening to their snores, did they give me respite. Then, during those midnight hours, Aunt Sara's canker rotted my memories. Her aspersions, along with her maids' conversation, reinforced my peers' allegations. But while my child's innocence had protected me those years ago, the knowledge I subsequently acquired rendered me far more vulnerable.

My parents had committed fornication. By the age of fourteen, I knew exactly what that meant, and had the nuns to credit for it. With my class, I was due for Confirmation, and underwent rigorous instruction in the Creed and the Ten Commandments. Sister Bernard's lesson on the Sixth Commandment might have emphasised modest dress and conduct, the duties of the married state, and the virtue of chastity; but it was supplemented in the playground, common room, and dormitory with a less expurgated version courtesy of my peers. Certain more precocious class members then challenged Sister for details and were firmly reminded that fornication was a mortal sin.

So was suicide. But on this occasion, I assumed the role of Grand Inquisitor. I questioned Sister Bernard, referencing the matter in generalities rather than singling out poor Maman who, Sister implied, was eternally damned because Sister upheld that contempt for one's God-given life justified divine contempt. But what of repentance? If Maman had taken her own life, would there have been time between commission and expiry to ask for pardon? Or was her soul hurled hellward ere she could beg for mercy? What if she intended to ask pardon? But Sister Bernard would not tolerate more involved discussion.

The more compassionate Sister Mary Magdalene agreed that one never could be sure and concluded that it was imperative to pray for the dead. Nonetheless, she regarded it indisputable that suicide, committed with full knowledge and understanding, merited the Inferno. For me, therefore, it became critical that Maman was murdered. Had she received death at another's hands, the likelihood of her eternal punishment would be less severe, the flames of Hell instead reserved for her murderer should they die with their sin unshriven.

Immediately after class, I hurried to the cemetery. I discovered my grandparents' graves in the Catholic section. Bobeshi, or, as her headstone inscribed, Fleurdelys Devereaux Volcot, departed this life 1919, was buried next to my grandfather Digby Devereaux, called to God 1908. Maman's grave was nowhere to be seen. Further desperate inquiry brought me to a separate plot. Poor Maman lay in the unhallowed grounds reserved for those who took their own lives.

Then and there I rejected all I had been taught. For years I had hewn stones from the quarry of Hope to build a stronghold for my soul. Although I knew of miracles in which mystics were sustained exclusively by the Christ's Body and Blood, I, poor creature of passion and feeling, quite lacked that grace; and the rations I permitted in the form of prayer and sacraments were as monotonous and unpalatable as bread and water, dished up as they were on the battered tin plates of sanctimony, severity, sentimentality and, at times, outright hypocrisy. Now, with the discovery that Maman's possible repentance, let alone God's mercy, had not even been considered, my fortress crumbled. The callous ostracism of my mother by those invested with the power of the keys induced me to shun the idea of a divinity – particularly a loving, paternal, creator being – and of a church entrusted with the care of souls. I ceased hearing Mass and abandoned prayer. Prayer would not save Maman, as it had done nothing to help Dad.

If I was to have anything to do with religion, I decided I would be Jewish and sought refuge with the Epsteins. I demanded they let me live with them; but they refused to take me. Not even repeated running away would convince them of my need. I also refused to attend school. When she learned of my truancy, Mrs Epstein approached Ailine who refused to take me back since she did not plan to stay. Only after Mrs Epstein threatened to report her irresponsibility to the police did she comply 'for the time being'.

7

Le Cadavre Exquis

MY HOME HAD MUCH CHANGED when I returned. The house was filthy; the garden overgrown; my swing dangled broken from the tree like a body gibbeted. Neighbours rumoured that a wild party had been held; and I soon experienced one for myself: a three-day orgy of drinking and dancing, with couples availing themselves of my bedroom for erotic acts.

All but one of Ailine's guests departed, Daphne Wood. About twenty years old, slight and adenoidal, she wore tailored jackets, men's shirts, waistcoats, cufflinks, and neckties. These she matched with a skirt as a concession to her boss, a local businessman for whom she worked as a stenographer. On evenings and week-ends, she pulled on trousers. She enjoyed experimenting with her appearance, receiving (and welcoming) much advice from Ailine who recommended she visit the barber for a page-boy cut and exchange her hated spectacles for a monocle which, according to my aunt, had become a trend among certain French *intellectuelles*. Use of the monocle required practice, and her effort to hold the item in place at first caused her already enlarged nostrils to flare and her mouth to scrunch. But Daphne was determined to master the art, since she wished to be a writer and live in Paris.

Ailine doted on her, greeting her with a kiss on either cheek, and calling her 'Mon Cher Daphnis'. The Paris trip promised to be an exciting venture for the pair of them, for my aunt intended to accompany her young friend. In between planning their trip, they took to rearranging furniture whereby they made a nest for themselves in the back wing of the house. Such displays of fondness might have irked me, but their isolating effect meant I could practise without interruption; and if I took my meals alone, I managed to avoid them altogether.

Daphne particularly wished to improve her French and sought Ailine's help. Ailine proved a willing, if rather unorthodox teacher who eschewed the grammar books in favour of a more idiomatic approach involving conversation and games. One such amusement was 'Le Cadavre Exquis' which she said was played in every artists' circle on the Left Bank.

'Le Cadavre Exquis' was a simple exercise involving pencil and paper. Players took turns to write a single word following a designated syntactic pattern, for instance: article, adjective, noun, verb, article, adjective, noun. They concealed the word by folding the paper concertina fashion before passing it to the next participant. Curious sentences resulted, vis: 'Le Cadvre exquis boira le nouveau vin' (the sentence which apparently gave the game its name); and, 'The quickening twilight clings to hopeless burdens'. Ailine suggested Daphne also use the game as inspiration for her fiction.

Harry followed Daphne. Scruffy, unkempt, in need of a space to work and a cheap food source, he arrived with a truckload of sculptures which he deposited on the front verandah. Ailine took him in and, along with lodgings, supplied him with live models (herself mostly) and began wearing long, flowing garments which she discarded whenever required. On the occasions she was unable to pose, she made me substitute; but after a couple of sittings, Harry complained I was 'immature', 'frigid', and 'sullen', and rudely dismissed me.

'Odious man!' Daphne stormed into the music room where I was practising piano one evening. She lit a cigarette and offered me one. It was the first time someone had offered me a cigarette in months. We sat outside together, smoking in silent commiseration.

'I thought she cared for me,' she sighed.

'She cares for none but herself,' I replied.

After that, we enjoyed private picnics of an evening: simple affairs of bread, fruit, and cheese. I played piano for her while she read me her stories, most of which featured women driving ambulances across Flemish battlefields, flying planes, or combatting abusive husbands. She told me of her dreams for a new life in Paris and listened to my woes in turn. 'Don't let anyone stop you,' she advised as she offered me chocolate (on pay days, we would always end our picnics with a bar of her favourite, Small's Gentleman's Club). 'You can do anything you want. You can, you know. Find a way.'

'You shouldn't associate with her,' Ailine cautioned during a rare moment of personal interest. 'She's a bad influence.'

'I can do as I please,' I retorted, buoyed by Daphne's resolve.

'We'll see about that.' And she began re-ingratiating herself with my new friend. Furious, Daphne took the next boat to Marseilles. Had I the means, I would have followed her save that it meant relinquishing my home to my aunt. So, I held my ground, even if it meant enduring Ailine and abiding by her terms.

Meanwhile, artists and intellectuals came and went. Ailine had a knack of making a hearty cassoulet last a week through whimsical additions courtesy of the grocer and butcher, on the occasions she bothered to shop. Accompanied by bread and wine, this rustic cuisine enjoyed a high level of bohemian appeal, being a significant departure from the meat and three to which most of her guests were accustomed. Aside from Harry, there was Arthur, who was in the theatre, and who spent the day wandering about in a silk dressing gown doing vocal exercises. Ailine thought he had a 'marvellous torso' which she liked to paint. In tandem with Arthur was Cedric, who wrote poetry when he was not working in menswear. Others called in at whim. A strange smell of stale blooms permeated Ailine's studio, the by-product of the opium she smoked with her friends (which sessions offered me further relief from their other diversions). There was little point in questioning it. It was not my place to ask questions. My role was to endorse everything my aunt said, heed everything she did, and service her every request. And if I did not wish to do so, then I lived as a shadow. Ailine referred to me as 'The Child of my Dead Sister', which she soon shortened to 'The Child'. This deathly legacy assumed physical form when, as my figure filled out, I was obliged to wear clothes Maman had worn at the same age, for Ailine would buy me none. My attendance at school became a form of respite. As for my music, I relied on it as an addict would cocaine.

Months later, a book of poems chanced to come into my possession. Items belonging to my parents had a way of turning up in second hand stores; and in this case, it was a copy of Byron's poetical works. The book disturbed me much. It was inscribed 'Ex Libris Roderick Raye' in a tidy but florid copperplate which must have been Dad's style before he lost the use of his hand, and therefore had belonged to him before the War. Equally disconcerting was that a photograph of Ailine marked one of the pages. When I demanded she explain, Ailine decided it was time I learnt 'The Truth'. She once had to learn 'The Truth' at my age: that the man whom she thought to be her father was not, and that her own father had abandoned her mother before she was born.

'The Truth is not pleasant, dear,' she continued without pausing from her painting: a hideous, contorted portrait of a child, a product of her imagination for she made use neither of sitter nor photograph. 'And I am sorry to say that the only reason your father married your mother was because she was expecting you. When it came to men, your mother was a whore. But the Truth is that your father loved me. That is why that picture is in that book. Speaking of Byron, your father rivalled Don Juan for affairs. Aside from you, who knows how many other children he fathered? Still, when all is said and done, I was his first and only true love. He told me so. That was why he enlisted: to run away with me. We planned it all. During the War he stayed with me in Paris. He would have remained with me forever, save that he was wounded. But that did not prevent us corresponding afterwards. Your mother found out and was so upset that she ended her life. I would have cared for your father had he not become so deranged. And that is why he wishes to have nothing to do with you. He never wanted you in the first place. That I look after you shows that I bear no grudge. And what gratitude do you show?'

None, of course, dirty tainted creature that I was.

Had my parents' devotion been a sham? But I had witnessed Maman muster every ounce of physical and moral strength to care for Dad. And I had watched Dad exercising his wit and humour to the utmost as he struggled to master his wooden legs and to manage without the use of his right arm. Despite their hardship, they were happy in each other's company. Had it all been a charade? Was there no love at all?

Sadly, I was not an angelic being endowed with intuitive knowledge; I was not an ethereal composite of moonbeams and sunshine as my name implied. I was dependent upon my senses. And when memory finds no confirmation in sights and sounds it loses authority. Ailine's account amplified the playground rumours and Aunt Sara's assertions. Flames engulfed Maman. Dad's wooden legs became hooves, his thighs those of a goat, his withered hand a claw. His scarred face with its dark, pointed features and glowering eyes menaced my dreams; and had it not been for The House of Cards I would have followed Maman to an outlying grave.

8

House of Cards

I F MRS EPSTEIN HAD HER WAY, she would make everyone learn a stringed instrument and play in a quartet. There would be fewer wars, she opined, if more people played chamber music. For the string quartet encapsulated how society should be: a republic of four equal yet distinctive parts; the quality of the music played being dependent on the contribution of each member, and on the benevolence, trust, and respect between them. With this explanation she tried to quell the bickering of the four disparate schoolgirls, among whom I was one unfortunate, she had gathered to form a string quartet.

Not that I paid much attention at the time. To me, the analogy evoked Ailine's dinner conversations. 'Society is but a random gathering of individuals competing for self-expression,' my aunt philosophised, cigarette in hand and a bottle of red nearby. Apparently, self-expression involved the release of the individual from every form of control. Birth was the first, being the moment when the newborn is liberated from the constraints of the womb. 'Throughout its formative years the child must free itself from the mother, then the family to fully realise its individuality.' Which, I suppose, was the theory underlying her treatment of me. Self-emancipation was a continuous process, for Ailine considered social institutions to be vehicles of individual repression.

Marx and Freud enriched her discussion. My aunt appreciated the dialectics of class struggle, but she disliked the subordination of the individual to the class system. 'If you ask me, *that* is the true struggle,' she maintained, heedless of the fact that I did not ask her; although I shared her views regarding the subordination of the individual to a repressive system. The subconscious was the realm of the free Self; opium the key that unlocked dreams and desires, suppressed memory and submerged experience which could then be expressed in Art – creations which followed their own laws, rather than observe ancient strictures concerning tone, perspective, and composition. Whoever could most successfully attain freedom of expression, and hence most fully realise their individuality, was the true Superman. The artist, according to my aunt, was supreme.

While I mused on the supremacy of the artist, Mrs Epstein produced a deck of cards and built a tower; and as she balanced card against card, she explained how the give and take of friendship was the foundation for music making. The tower fascinated me. Many a time I had tried to construct a house of cards and had failed to complete even a single unit. Mrs Epstein, however, succeeded in building four storeys before she removed a card from the base and let the tower crash, as I thought it ought long ago. For what did music making have to do with friendship? Certainly, I enjoyed playing with others, but for Music's sake, nothing more.

Nor did I wish to play second violin, which was the part Mrs Epstein had assigned me. I wanted to be first violin. Instead, Della Sotheby took first violin. She was a petite, gentle, rather delicate girl who spoke with a proper British accent, and, according to Mrs Epstein, had age and maturity to her advantage, for she was two years older than me. Admittedly, Della seemed kind enough; but Mrs Epstein had asked Pim Connolly to be the viola player. Pim was Head Prefect of St Dominic's, had a temper to match her fiery red hair, and was accustomed to wielding her considerable weight (she was built like an Amazon). I had already fallen foul of her in the school boarding house.

Had it not been for the cellist, I would sooner have played all four instruments myself. Tall, gangly, short-sighted Lucy Straughan was a capable player. Crippled by polio, introverted, and fastidious, she too shared my reluctance to play in a group. She did not, however, share my reluctance for friendship. Motherless herself, she understood my troubles. With her Irish wit and warmth, her peculiar talent for gaucheness, and occasional flash of temper, I came to love her as a sister.

So, whatever our views might have been regarding republics, we formed an ensemble; and despite our misgivings and differences, the four of us did eventually become friends, to the point that our quartet became a mutually supportive house of cards. We named it accordingly: The House of Cards Quartet.

But Mrs Epstein had other motives for bringing us together. She entered us in a competition at the Conservatorium and encouraged us to prepare by giving private performances. Little did I expect her to arrange a concert at Graythwaite, the veteran's home where Dad lived.

Although none of us liked the idea, Della, Pim, and Lucy could rationalise the benefits of such a performance; while I could only envisage a half-crazed, legless man who shouted in foreign tongues, who in his youth had indulged in numerous affairs, and who had escaped a failed marriage from which I was the unwanted issue.

Pim, Della, and Lucy tried to appease me with advice about not bearing grudges; about giving second chances; about prayers being answered; about the need to be loved; how music heals the soul; how people who suffer need the most care of all. They muddled me with their wisdom; and, while I valued their affection and genuine attempts to comfort, I wished they would leave me be; for crowning my friends' concern, was my teacher's betrayal.

Mrs Epstein knew Dad. She had known him for years.

'So, do you mean that in the seven years you have been teaching me you have been visiting my father, who is not mad, while I have been barred? Why has he seen you and not me?' I later demanded of her. 'And why have you never told me?'

'Phoebe, I cannot explain everything now. All I can tell you is that after your mother suicided, your father suffered a nervous breakdown. Mr Epstein and I were among the few people who could communicate with him.'

'But why you?'

'It's a long story. Anyway, he's better now, and he wants to see you.'

How I hated my youth, my innocence, my helplessness! True, there was the reassurance that Dad was not insane as Ailine had said. But why had he not seen me? And why had Ailine lied? Had he really regained his health? What would he be like? Would he be the father I treasured from my early childhood? Or would he be one of those surly figures, silent veterans who only talked if they had a pint, and then unpleasantly? Could it be true that he wanted to see me again?

He wanted to see me! He wanted to see me!

But did I want to see him?

Mr Epstein was playing the piano when I interrupted him that evening, for I was staying with the Epsteins at the time. If he was involved in the conspiracy, he would have good reason; and if he had any explanation, I knew it would be an honest one.

'Do you know my father?'

'Ja, I know him.'

'How long have you known him?'

'Many, many years. Do you recognise this?' he indicated the music he had paused from playing.

'It's Schubert. I can tell without looking.'

'When you were seven you called it, "Handy Music".'

'Did I?'

'I remember that afternoon in the orphanage when you sang this very song. I knew you could be none other than Roderick

Raye's daughter.'

'You knew even then? Why did you not say?'

'Because we were uncertain he would recover, and we did not wish to upset you. So, we decided to look after you and bring you back to him should his health improve. That was why we never adopted you. You weren't ours to adopt; and we did not wish to compromise your affections, nor raise your hopes.'

'I see,' I murmured. 'But I don't recall the lyrics to be anything like those. Is that German?'

'Yes,' he laughed. 'I will sing for you?'

> *Du holde Kunst, in wieviel grauen Stunden,*
> *Wo mich des Lebens wilder Kreis umstrickt,*
> *Hast du mein Herz zu warmer Lieb' entzunden,*
> *Hast mich in eine beßre Welt entrückt,*
> *In eine beßre Welt entrückt!*
>
> *Oft hat ein Seufzer, deiner Harf' entflossen,*
> *Ein süßer, heiliger Akkord von dir,*
> *Den Himmel beßrer Zeiten mir erschlossen,*
> *Du holde Kunst, ich danke dir dafür,*
> *Du holde Kunst, ich danke dir!*

'Now I remember! Only I thought it was about being sick. I didn't realise it was in German.'

'I myself heard your father sing it many times. How he will love to hear you perform! Be brave, Phoebe. Go and play for him.'

9

Truth

I N THE RECREATION ROOM at Graythwaite, amidst the worst of the War – the limbless, sightless, disfigured, dimwitted men – there was no sign of Dad. During our performance, I fumbled passages and frequently lost my place before a crooked scrape of my bow jolted my attention away from that strange audience. Finally, I glimpsed him: a thin, frail man being wheeled into the room by Mrs Epstein, his missing legs covered by a blanket.

Upon introduction, Dad ignored me and instead jested with Lucy, Pim, and Della, none of whom knew what to make of his biting wit, let alone his picking on minute aspects of our performance, his every remark designed to tease. I floundered about what to do or say, when I caught from behind his menacing gleam a twinkle I recalled from long ago. Amidst his sport, however, he kept glancing at my violin, and the fingers of his left hand twitched.

'Do you play?' Lucy, in her very straight-forward manner, voiced what I suddenly desired to know.

Dad attacked her with rhetorical questions, raising his voice to an embarrassing height before demanding I pass him my instrument. He grabbed it and strummed the strings. Then he dashed a passage down the fingerboard and spun the violin around, whereupon he froze.

'Where did you get this?' he demanded, interrogating me about the instrument's whereabouts until in desperation I pleaded I was telling the truth.

Tenderly he kissed it. 'Juliette,' he murmured, 'My beautiful, darling doe, how you could sing!'

'What's the matter, Roddy?' asked Mrs Epstein; for Dad, mesmerised by the instrument, had lapsed into a strange silence.

'It's mine.'

Almost incoherently, he began to ramble about how the violin came into his possession before requesting us to leave. And when we hesitated, out sprang the demon who hit me when I was seven.

'Get out!' he thumped his fist on the arm of his chair. Then he added in a sadder, softer tone, 'I'm sorry. Please go.'

That Dad was a violinist was all I could think of on the ferry trip to Mrs Epstein's that afternoon; and while Mrs Epstein explained how she had met him when they were students in Vienna, and what she understood had happened between him and Maman prior to the War, I rummaged through the trash pile of gossip piled high in my memory in a desperate search for the childhood experiences I knew to be true.

Perhaps my reunion with Dad at Graythwaite prompted recollection of my very first visit to the soldier's hospital where we were introduced. I was five at the time. Prior to that, I had only ever heard Maman mention Dad with affection; and although he was a stranger to me, and a peculiar stranger at that, I had sensed he was kind. Now I had to trust my child's perspicacity. Despite his cutting wit and tempestuous conduct, the kindness still glimmered.

And how tenderly he had kissed that violin! He said he acquired it during the War and had named it Juliette, Maman's name. So, if there had been a rift between Maman and Dad, and that Dad and Ailine had been intimate as Ailine maintained (which view Mrs Epstein shared albeit with reservation), that rift had been repaired. I pictured Dad's troubled face, the sudden sadness in his dark eyes, and the equally sudden fury: a man confronting deep loss. That violin was precious to him. Maman was precious to him. Since it was impossible that he should lie when so unexpectedly troubled, I was convinced that Ailine was the liar.

Home I ran as fast as I could. I thrashed through the garden wilderness and pushed past the broken swing. It fell, its rope rotten and frayed.

An odd calm filled the house. Ailine's studio was unusually tidy. Paintings were piled, and there were no paints or brushes anywhere. Nor was there a whiff of opium. Down the hall I dashed and up the stairs, calling furiously.

Ailine appeared on the landing.

'I know the truth! I know the truth about my father, and the truth about Maman! And the truth about you! You lied to me! Why did you lie?'

'The Child's a lunatic!' she called, and I turned to find Mr and Mrs Epstein at the bottom of the stairs. 'Get her out of here!'

'I told you not to go anywhere near your aunt!' Mrs Epstein pulled me away.

'But how else am I to learn if I don't confront her?' I tried to wriggle free, but my teacher and her husband held me firm.

'Talk to your father!'

10

Mercy

D AD WAS READING when I summoned the courage to visit him on my own a few days later. He had a private room in a cottage on Graythwaite's grounds. Neat and trim in dark trousers and a red velvet waistcoat, he was wearing his wooden legs and sat in a leather grandfather chair.

'No one told me you played violin,' I began.

'Can't play half as well as you,' he smiled, tears overwhelming his dark eyes as we embraced. 'I thought I'd never see you again.'

'Mrs Epstein told me that you suffered a nervous breakdown.' After Maman's death, Dad had retreated into his student days in Vienna. He spoke only German and recognised only the people connected with those years. 'Are you better?'

'Much better, thank you.' The scar on his cheek had faded; his eyes were attractively lined; his curls slicked back, and his pencil thin moustache was as elegant as ever. 'But what your teacher didn't tell me was how beautiful you are. Comme ta chère maman. Tu ne te rappelles pas comment tu as parlais français avec ta mère?' Seeing my bewilderment, he paused. 'I said: You don't remember how you spoke French with your mother?'

'Not at all.'

'Do you remember Maman?'

'Tell me about her, Dad.'

'Well,' he drawled, putting aside *Les Miserables*, 'She was like a mountain flower— a rare bloom – orchid or monkshood – one you climb long and hard to find: Your beautiful Maman was not for the faint-hearted. Just as well I like mountain climbing. I like flowers, too.'

They met in Vienna through her mother's (Bobeshi's) salon, to which he was invited to perform. Dad was nineteen at the time and was studying at the Academy. He frequently dined and performed with Madame Devereaux, her two daughters, and her celebrated guests. Only when Bobeshi, whose hands were troubled by arthritis one winter, could not accompany him as she was wont on such occasions, did he have much to do with Maman, her youngest, who shyly offered to play. Together they learned Beethoven's Kreutzer Sonata, their practice interrupted by skating, long walks, and ardent conversation. 'That sonata was our musical Matterhorn; and if your mother could conquer the Kreutzer, I reckoned she could handle anything. Played it yet?' I confessed I had not. 'Well, you're in for a treat.'

Dad proposed, and Maman accepted; Bobeshi, however, refused permission, insisting that Maman was too young (she was eighteen at the time), and, being a talented singer and pianist, ought to pursue personal success before 'settling down'. Dad, two years older, with a promising international career ahead of him, she deemed equally unready. Marriage could be postponed until Maman turned twenty-one. Soon after, the Devereaux family left Vienna for Paris, and later returned to Australia. Dad arrived in Australia for Maman's twenty-first birthday, when he again proposed. Again, Bobeshi declined permission.

'In the end we decided the only way we could marry was to have a baby.'

'So, I was conceived out of wedlock?'

Sadly, he acknowledged the fact. 'But it wasn't a fling, Poss. Planned to take your mother back to Vienna after the wedding. People are less rigid over there, and the circumstances soon would have been forgotten. After all, we married, which was what we intended all along. Unfortunately, Maman was too sick to travel, so I had to return alone. Had concerts I couldn't cancel. Worst decision I ever made,' he sighed. 'Didn't see you until you were five months old. And what a change had come over your mother! Blamed me for all her troubles and shut me out. Tried in every way to make it up to her. Lina recommended taking her back to Vienna. When Maman was fifteen, you see, her father's death upset her deeply and the only remedy was a grand tour. That's why they came to Vienna in the first place.'

'Ailine recommended you take Maman to Vienna? But she told me you were going to run away with her.'

'Did she now?'

'Mrs Epstein thought so, too. Did you love Ailine?'

'Can't deny I was keen on her at first. What a peach! Damn good cellist.'

I winced at his words and recalled the photograph Mrs Epstein had shown me: a photograph of the quartet she and Mr Esptein had formed in Vienna with Dad on first violin and Ailine, of all people, on cello. The Klimt Quartet they called themselves.

'We were friends, Phoebe, nothing more.'

'But Ailine said—'

'I was going to take your mother to Vienna,' he declared as if testifying in court. 'She needed a change of scene and a more forgiving society. Bloody War put a stop to everything.'

'Mrs Epstein mentioned you had a hard time of it.'

'If you didn't enlist, or at least attempt to enlist, no one wanted to know you.'

'Not even your family?'

He grimaced. 'Musical establishment even demanded I perform the Mackenzie concerto instead of the Beethoven as arranged. I refused. They then accused me of having German sympathies. Didn't help that I was a court musician.'

'A what?'

'I was employed as a musician by Emperor Franz Josef of Austria. I played in the Habsburg court. British authorities suspected me of espionage and threatened imprisonment if I didn't sign up. Joined the Light Horse. No ordinary foot soldier for me,' he swaggered in self-mockery.

'And you left Maman and me?'

'Yes, I abandoned you and your mother. I was going to desert and cross the line somehow, back to Wien. Didn't work out too well. Got bloody sent to the Dardanelles. Then I found that fiddle.'

A shrapnel wound to the cheek followed by a serious bout of gastric put Dad out of action for much of the Gallipoli campaign; and by the time he recovered, he learned he was heading for France. He purchased the violin for a song in Cairo, having convinced the seller it was good only for tapers. Nothing could have been further from the truth. All it needed was a few adjustments. Oddly, the instrument reminded him of Maman, for it was a little wide at the hip; and it sang the way she did, with a full, rich tone. A beautiful spinto soprano was how he described it.

To his mates, though, he showed off, boasting how the instrument was shaped like a girl he knew back home. And when they prodded him for details, he strung them along until he jokingly admitted it was his wife. All but one laughed. 'Pulled me aside and said if he had a wife with a corker of a figure like that, he wouldn't make light of it. Well, Poss, that was as good as a kick in the pants— especially after the poor bastard got his head blown off. Anyway, got that fiddle to Paris and had it repaired. It's an early Vuillaume and it's modelled on the violin Paganini used to own. How about that?'

'And Maman?'

'Ah, yes. Well, that winter, it was cold: freezing cold; so cold your clothes froze, your hair froze, your grub froze, your pony froze, and they stayed froze. Even the rats froze. Well, Maman sent me a parcel – first time in two years (we weren't writing, Poss) – and inside were several pairs of socks knitted especially.' He chuckled at the memory, for the socks were so poorly knitted that none matched. 'About the same time, another letter arrived from a nurse explaining that your mother had been sick. She was already anxious and sad when she was expecting you, but it became worse after you were born. Couldn't nurse you. There's a name for it: post-partum depression—'

'Was it because of me?'

'She had worries of her own. Anyway, poor Maman was right to blame me. I followed my own selfish ambitions when I should have stayed at her side. Should have tried to understand. Instead, I left her a second time.

'The way I saw it, alone on that muddy battlefield in France, was that regardless of her actions towards me, I, the stronger party, had failed to look after her in sickness and in health. I had broken my wedding vows. Problem was I couldn't hop on the next convoy back home. Wrote of course, many times. She wrote, too. Letters are on that shelf over there. Meanwhile, I had to live with what I'd done. And when I could no longer bear it, I took myself to the padre and made the first serious confession I ever made in my life. Went to Confession once or twice in the past, but it was a bit like tossing off sins the way I'd take off my gloves and toss them into my top hat. I'd hand the hat and gloves to the footman, dance every waltz and polka, and put them back on without a thought. Well, after that confession, I was determined to get back and beg her forgiveness. And I did. Came back on my knees.'

'Maman used to say you were brave because you came back. Is that what she meant?'

He nodded. 'I knelt and asked her forgiveness; and she gave it to me. And now I'm going to ask the same of you.' He knelt before me. 'I've let you down, Poss, and I'm sorry. I've been a rotten father.'

I knelt, too.

'You got sick, Dad.'

'Will you forgive me?'

'Of course. But it's not all your fault.'

'As our Jewish friends like to say, *Der Mensch tracht und Gott lacht*: Man proposes, and God laughs. I'm afraid life hasn't quite gone as planned.'

'There's still time to make it better, Dad.'

'You're right there.'

'Then what happened?'

'Let me see... It was the last months of the War. Spent most of my time in France escorting troops and running messages; and being fluent in French and German, I was often called upon to translate— My Canadian's not bad, either,' he winked. 'Didn't see much action. Come September 'eighteen, though, I was called up for front line work. Had some leave due, so I returned to Paris to visit Lina. Hadn't seen her the entire War.'

'Did you have an affair?'

'We visited the places your mother knew when she was growing up. But listen,' he cautioned, for, thinking he was evading my question, I started to interrupt. 'I've been tempted, Phoebe, in many ways; but believe me when I tell you, I've always been faithful. And your aunt needed some happy memories, not to mention consolation. They were dreadful years. Anyway, I left the fiddle with her, and, if I survived, planned to fetch it and explain that she had mistaken my feelings. Any affection I had for her was merely that of a brother-in-law for a sister-in-law, while your mother I loved more than any other, despite my mistakes. It had ever been thus, and so it would remain. Didn't expect this,' and he grimaced at his legs and shrivelled hand. His arm was crippled by nerve damage from the shoulder injury he suffered when he was thrown from his horse amidst the thick of battle; while subsequent infection had resulted in the loss of his lower limbs. 'In the end, I wrote. Took me years before my hand was good enough. Not the sort of letter you can dictate.'

'And Maman found out?'

'Didn't find out. I told her. Told her everything. She was relieved. She'd tried writing to Lina but never received a reply. All we could do was hope my letter would reach her. Well, seems it did. I know that now.'

'How?'

His lips twisted, as if he was unsure whether to smile or frown, while tears again began to well.

'Did Maman suicide, Dad?'

'No, Possum, Maman was murdered. And your violin told me all I needed to know.'

11

Vindication

HOW DID DAD KNOW? Someone had put the violin in the attic of our Stanmore home, and must have done so after I visited with Maman and found the smaller instrument, and before the attic was locked the night Maman died. The key to the attic was unique and had remained in my possession since Dad entrusted it to me the day we parted. Thus, the only person we knew who could have left the violin there was Ailine, given that Dad had left it with her. In his letter, written in 1920, in which he explained the extent of his injuries and why he had never returned, he had requested she sell the instrument and keep the proceeds. Evidently, she did no such thing, even though when she visited Dad at Graythwaite in 1927, she told him it had gone 'to a good home'.

'Catch was, Possum, she wavered. For a split second, she fished for an answer. Unusual for someone who always has answers. She lied. What's more, she knew that *I* knew that she lied.'

'I saw that look, too, Dad, when I told her I knew the truth. I didn't know what I know now, but she knew something. So, that was it!'

'Which means she must have come to Sydney back in February 'twenty-one, when Maman died. Then there's the note they thought your poor mother left—'

'Could Ailine have written it?'

'Reckon so. She's clever like that. By the way, I've still got it. It never felt right. See what you can make of it.' Judging from its well-worn creases, Dad must have spent hours mulling over it, comparing it with Maman's letters. The handwriting appeared identical: a loopy upright *écriture à l'école primaire*; but the unfortunate note lacked the clumsiness, the crossings out and the ardent emotion that characterised Maman's correspondence.

'Don't tell me he's conned you into that!' Mrs Epstein was convinced Dad was paranoid – the consequence of shell shock from which she thought he would never recover. Dad would wrangle anyone into raising Maman's case with a police inspector, she said. Furthermore, thinking Maman to be excessively melancholic, she had never questioned her death. Maman suicided; and the sooner Dad accepted it, the better.

To convince anyone of the murder, we needed more substantial proof, a tall order considering the lapse of years. But we found Maman's diary tucked away in the secret drawer of a china cabinet in the living room in Stanmore. Written the night she died, its final entry told of her quiet triumph in having surprised Dad with the news that she was expecting. Filled with hope, she wrote of her plans to economise on meals and clothes; and of Dad's decision to teach foreign languages: hardly the words of a woman about to take her own life. Given also that she tended not to write when depressed, as later research established, the police instead ruled her death as suspicious and reopened the case.

Finally, Dad was believed. When next I visited, I saw a man, who, for all his frailness, was full of sprightly charm, gifted with dancing wit and energy, and ready to face the world. True, he was also faced with a police investigation, and even had to endure questioning; but since these were steps towards vindication, he remained calm and became all the stronger. So great was his improvement that his doctors soon pronounced him well enough to return home. Of course, he needed assistance with his legs and with the fundamentals of dressing and grooming; but such requirements were easily met by a valet.

To find the murderer posed a different problem. One could suspect Ailine; but to pin the crime on her was not so straightforward. The violin in the attic and the forged note indicated the possibility of her being involved but did not explicitly identify her as Maman's killer unless she confessed; and to obtain a confession, she needed to be found. Ailine, however, had disappeared.

'If she's caught, Dad, will she hang?'

'Law's an ass, Possum. Needs a stick to prod it, and a carrot to entice it. Even then it can barely manage a trot. Let's not get too far ahead of ourselves.'

'But will she hang?'

'That'll depend on the court. Leave Lina to the police. Meanwhile, we need to give Maman a proper burial.'

Mrs Epstein was the most sorely affected. How could one of her closest friends commit such a heinous crime, and against her own sister, no less? She was dismayed at her perceived role in the affair; for she had maintained correspondence with Ailine since the end of the War, had informed her of Maman's death and Dad's breakdown, and had provided her with updates concerning Dad's health. Acting on assumptions regarding Ailine's friendship with Dad, she repeatedly encouraged her to come out to Australia with a view to look after Dad and me, and nearly gave up on the idea when Ailine suddenly agreed. She then blamed herself for what I had suffered.

'I cannot believe I was so naïve! To think I had been feeding her information— playing right into her hand!' She drew the worst conclusions, becoming convinced that Ailine attempted to ruin both Dad and me. Dad warned her that she was losing perspective. Mr Epstein agreed.

Being matter-of-fact personalities, Pim and Lucy were disinclined to speculate.

''Twill work out one way or another, Phoebe,' Lucy remarked one day, 'And you're needing to trust it will work out for the best.'

'How can you be sure of that?'

'Did I say I was sure now? All I said was you're needing to trust.'

'You know perfectly well things don't simply work out for the best, Lucy. You have to do something.'

'You've got a point,' added Pim, for once in my favour, 'Just don't get obsessed about it.'

'I'm not obsessed about it.'

'You always get obsessed about things.'

'I do not!'

'Anyway, I'm warning you: I don't think it's wise to get obsessed with murder. Find something else to be obsessed with.'

Only Della shared my interest in the hows and whys and wherefores:

'Can you imagine what your aunt thought when she received that letter from your father?' She leant forward from her pillow, her eyes wide with feverish excitement, for she was ill and confined to bed. 'Do you think it made her angry?'

'I suppose so.'

'Do you think she planned the murder before she left Paris?'

'She must have. After all, my mother was poisoned, and poisoning is quite calculated, isn't it? And then to disguise her death as a suicide by forging a note—'

'Well, that's very deliberate. Can you imagine writing something like that?'

'Dad says Ailine is very clever.'

'Mrs Epstein thinks your father was the real target. She believes Ailine was so jealous of your mother and father that she thought she could do more harm by killing your mother. I mean, given your father's injuries, if she elected to kill him she may have been doing him a favour by putting him out of his misery.'

'But he wasn't miserable— not like that.'

'Still, it was very, very cruel. What does your father think?'

'Dad hardly talks about it. It's as if he doesn't want to know why. I suppose he's relieved he's finally been proven right. He seems sad rather than angry— sad in a sort of horrified way, if that makes any sense.'

'I get shivers down my spine. Imagine! Your aunt stole into your house, switched the medicine, and hid in the attic. And nobody knew she was there! It must have been stifling! I mean, it was the height of summer, wasn't it?'

'Yes. Then she crept out in the early hours of the morning, tip-toed to my mother's room, and planted the suicide note—'

'Although first she would have had to check whether your mother was dead.'

'How?'

'By putting a mirror to her mouth to see if it would fog up. She probably used a hand mirror. Did she wear gloves?'

'I don't know.'

'Did the police search for finger prints?'

'I don't think so.'

'Then, while your aunt was in your mother's room, your father woke the nurse and made her check the attic—'

'And while the nurse was checking the attic, Ailine crept out of the house.'

'Perhaps she was nearly discovered! I mean, maybe she intended to go back to the attic, or maybe she intended to kill your father, too, but she saw the nurse and hid. Or she opened the door of your mother's room and spotted the nurse walking past, so she thought it safer to leave while she could. Your poor mother! Do you think she knew she was dying?'

'I have no idea. She went to bed happily that night. She probably took some medicine to help her sleep, not realising it had been substituted. How long do you think it would have taken?'

'Strychnine kills very, very quickly. It sends you into convulsions until you can't breathe any more. They used strychnine in *The Mysterious Affair at Styles*. Have you read it?'

'No. Anyway, it wasn't strychnine. Dad suspects it was morphine. How do you die from morphine?'

'I don't know about morphine. Did she say her prayers?'

'She always said prayers before bed.'

'Did she go to Confession?'

'Sometimes.'

'Do you think she's in Heaven?'

'I don't believe in heaven. And I don't believe in hell, either. Nor do I believe in God. I stopped believing in all that a long time ago.'

'Don't you pray for your mother?'

'I used to, but I gave up. Nothing ever came of it.'

'But Phoebe, don't you think that finding out your mother was murdered was an answer to prayer?'

'It was learning the truth. And it doesn't change the fact that she died. All it does is change peoples' attitudes towards it. You have no idea how much that sickens me. They used to be judgmental; now they're sympathetic; and suddenly Maman is taken from the bowels of Hell and counted among the Blessed in Heaven as if it were the work of their own hands.'

'Well, I pray for your mother. And I pray for you, too. I pray a lot these days— can't do much else lying here apart from read. I say, did the police find Ailine?'

'She's disappeared.'

'Perhaps she threw herself over The Gap.'

'How I wish! But they haven't found a body.'

'Have they been looking?'

'Yes. They have to—'

'Otherwise, I suppose the case is a bit like our quartet. It's a house of cards. I mean, if the police have insufficient proof and Ailine can't be apprehended, the case collapses.'

'That will never happen. I swear, while I breathe, that will never happen.'

'But if they can't find her, what will you do?'

12

Reparation

DELLA DIED PEACEFULLY on New Year's Day 1929. Weakened by the stifling effects of tuberculosis, her heart gave out; and she slipped to her heavenly home, having been given final absolution and the Last Rites.

Her death revived what little faith I had. Deprived of consolation after Maman's sudden passing, I had floundered as one tossed from a ship on high seas, my faith a raft too flimsy to withstand the waves of doubt and disbelief, deception and cruelty which had often engulfed me. Now, I had friends with whom I could share my sorrow. We grieved together, remembered together, prayed together. Lucy and Pim, both inclined to devotion, were ever thoughtful and kind; so, I never felt isolated or neglected, as I had when Maman died.

What's more, I had Dad. The horrors of war, the loss of mates in battle and through war-associated illness and injury, not to mention his own physical sufferings and the terrible loss of Maman put Dad on close terms with the Reaper. Most significantly, his sorrows had not embittered him; and of his faith I will say more in time. He respected my need to mourn and my desire to be alone; he listened when I wanted to talk; and he hugged me and let me cry. Even though he had known her only a short while, he was very fond of Della. Being both violinists and sharing a common fondness for literature, not to mention their natural affability, they had quickly become friends; and the rapport they enjoyed endeared Dad much to her family. He lit a candle for her at church after Sunday Mass – an act which I welcomed rather than shunned; for it reminded me of when I did the same with Maman while he was at war.

The empathy, support, and devotion of my father and friends stirred in me the desire at least to imitate their serenity and piety. I returned to the sacraments which I had abandoned since leaving the orphanage. Furthermore, the sense that Della was truly at peace encouraged me to consider Divine Justice more favourably, and to conclude that maybe dear Maman was also in heaven; and it pleased me much that a place in Hell was reserved for Ailine.

❖ ❖ ❖

During our many conversations, I probed Dad about his early years, and was astonished to learn that aside from Aunt Sara, he had family still living.

'You have grandparents; another aunt, Rachel; and an uncle, Alec,' he explained.

'Then why did they not take me in? Why? Is it because—' I couldn't bear to say, and Dad didn't enlighten me. 'Where do they live?'

'The Rat.'

'You mean Ballarat? Mrs Epstein said you were from Ballarat. Can I write them?'

From my grandmother I was delighted to receive not only a reply, but an invitation. But when Dad heard my garbled plans involving several changes of train, he refused to let me travel on my own.

'Then, why don't you come?'

Had the idea never occurred to him? Apparently not, considering how his eyes widened at my question. A thoughtful silence curtailed his surprise.

'We'll overnight it in Albury,' he resolved.

Having greeted the wheezy gentleman who joined our compartment and helped us with our luggage, Dad did the unthinkable: he extinguished his cigarette, the near-permanent appendage that dangled from the corner of his mouth. He had not been on a train since the War; and as the locomotive hastened southward, I wondered what memories rattled through his mind. At times a tear formed, which he blinked back. Then his mouth twitched in a suppressed half-smile. His hand tensed, and he muttered a little before attempting again to read. But he could not concentrate. Why doesn't he smoke? That was his usual means of keeping the demons at bay. I offered him a cigarette of my own. He declined; and I feared his restlessness would worsen. Then what would happen? The wheezy gentleman offered peppermints. Dad's hand shook as he tried to fish one out of the packet; but sucking a humbug soon calmed him. The moment the gentleman left our compartment at Goulburn, however, he reached for his Luckies.

'Gas,' he remarked as he lit up, nodding after our departed companion, 'Can always tell.'

'I'm a bit worried they might all be like Aunt Sara,' I voiced my own apprehensions concerning his family.

'Could be worse,' he puffed. 'They might all be like me.'

Little by little he spoke of his upbringing, portions of which I already knew from Mrs Epstein. Given the length of our journey, Dad told stories enough to fill a book; but a paragraph or two must suffice for now. His father, John Alexander Raye, at the tender age of sixteen had set out from his native Scotland to the Victorian goldfields, where he made a fortune from the find of some nuggets, abstention from intoxicating liquor, and the sale of copious amounts of tea. The latter enterprise he carried out in partnership with a Chinaman, one Lee Yeung Peng, or Billy Penn as he was popularly known. John Alexander later married Mr Penn's daughter, Irene; and therein lay the explanation for Dad's intriguing dark eyes: he was part Chinese.

There were four surviving children. Aunt Sara was the oldest, Dad the youngest, and Uncle Alec and Aunt Rachel were in the middle. Dad credited his Chinese grandfather with encouraging his musical talents, smuggling him into the local convent for piano lessons with a resident Bavarian countess, and arranging violin lessons with one Mr Szabo, an Hungarian with gypsy blood and prodigious skill. Within years Dad was performing in theatres and halls across the district, much to his family's consternation. But it seemed that he also shared his father's enterprising and adventurous spirit; for when he, too, was sixteen, he sought his fortune across the sea; not to dig for gold and trade in tea, but to study music in Vienna, thanks to his grandfather's bequest.

Long his account may have been; nonetheless, I still had to fill in the gaps: that his father had opposed his musical endeavours and agreed to his Viennese adventure on the proviso that after three years Dad return to work in the family business. Three years passed, and Dad refused to come home. In response, his father cut his allowance. 'Made my career,' was all Dad said when I probed him. He returned to Australia to claim what remained of his inheritance, which was his legal right when he came of age, and to marry Maman. Being a staunch Presbyterian with an ingrained suspicion of papal authority, Dad's father objected. Not only was Maman foreign, she was a Catholic. Even worse, she was a Jewess who had converted to the 'wrong' faith for the 'wrong' reasons. And he was furious when he found out that Dad, too, had converted.

'Did you convert only to marry?' I asked.

'Bit of a career move. Catholicism's *de rigueur* in Wien, so I crossed the fence. Proved both reasonable and advantageous. Besides, I could handle a Mass with a bit of Mozart. Made for quite a pleasant Sunday morning.'

Dad's father refused to attend the wedding; and when he learned that Maman was already expecting when she walked up the aisle, he deemed the marriage improper. Then, after War was declared, he threatened to disown his son if he did not enlist.

'What about Uncle Alec? Did he join up?'

'Had to manage the business.'

And Dad had never seen his family since. His mother and Aunt

Rachel tried to visit when he returned, but he refused to see them. 'They got the glory, and I got the guts,' he added ruefully, referring to the Military Medal he had earned after dashing across the battlefield to deliver a timely message, which action saved a battalion and resulted in his injuries. The medal he sent to his parents.

'We don't have to go, Dad.'

'Yes, we do. I promised your mother I would when I was ready. "You might have come back half a man, Roderick Raye," she told me once, "But you'll be twice the man you ever were when you can embrace your parents." As for you, Poss, who am I to deny you a family?'

'Grandmother said she would kill the fattened calf.'

Dad shrugged. 'I'm no prodigal.'

'I think they'll be glad to see you, anyway.'

Grandmother Raye welcomed us with open arms and brought us inside a very grand Victorian residence which boasted a wide staircase, stained-glass windows, and generously proportioned rooms, each with a fireplace. On one mantlepiece, I was surprised to find a photograph of Dad in his Light Horse uniform, with that flamboyant spray of 'kangaroo plumes'[1] in its slouch hat, glaring as if to say, 'Take that and be damned the lot of you'. His bedroom was filled with memorabilia: concert notices, photographs, prizes, and even a gramophone recording.

But nothing would change Grandfather Raye's view that his youngest son was a dilettante and a deviant, and a Papist to boot. Now nearly ninety, and gruff and stern with his white spade beard, Scottish burr, and fierce blue eyes, Grandfather complained of everything from Dad's choice of necktie to his frequenting the local pub. Dad, however, remained his wily, witty self, and ignored the jibes which years ago had provoked endless quarrels. 'Seen enough pointless fighting to last the rest of my life,' was all he said when privately I protested his treatment. Nevertheless, Grandfather ensured Dad's every need was met; and at the end of our stay made a point of showing him the tree which he had planted in his memory. Upon seeing the tree, one of the hundreds lining Ballarat's main boulevard commemorating those who had served in the War, Dad cried a decade of tears.

For me the reunion was a joyous affair. I had a family. I relished looking from one to the other: all of them fine-boned, slight, energetic, and dark-eyed save for Grandfather. Charming, peaceable, and submissive, Grandmother Raye knew her place to be in the home, and she kept it perfectly. Uncle Alec presided over the family business (an extensive network of tea rooms, among

---

[1] *Kangaroo plumes*: emu feathers

other things), and had a knack for profit. He had married late, after the War, and had fathered six children in five years. Aunt Rachel was a spinster devoted to the care of her ageing parents. Conscientious she might have been in this regard, but there was a spark of wit in her otherwise placid demeanour that pleased me much. Furthermore, being a maiden aunt, she had time and energy to spare, and was delighted to meet her baby brother's only daughter, upon whom she knew she could lavish attention without any risk of reproach. Through tea parties and shopping sprees, we became firm friends.

Dad was the toast of the town, catching up with what remained of his boyhood chums at the barber's and the pub, and even seeing Mr Szabo, who was now very old indeed. He dreaded Sunday, however. Mass being celebrated at an earlier time, he had to make his own way to St Patrick's, for Grandfather denied him the use of the carriage; and if he wished for a ride home, he had to wait outside St Andrew's Presbyterian where the rest of the family worshipped, and which occupied a rival position on the opposite side of the road. I accompanied him for solidarity. Unusual for the Rayes was the silence that dominated the return journey, and which prevailed until the serving of Sunday dinner.

'Good sermon, Rachel?' Dad inquired.

'Since when have you shown an interest in sermons, Roddy?' Aunt Rachel laughed. 'He could hardly sit still when a boy.'

'And thrashed he was for it,' Grandfather vigorously whet the carving knife. He was still strict about hands in pockets and sitting straight.

Dad winced.

'It was a good sermon, thank you, Roddy,' remarked Grandmother.

'And yours?' ventured Aunt Rachel.

'Whore of Babylon, arrayed in purple and scarlet colour,' mumbled Grandfather.

'The Whore was in fine form today,' Dad replied, 'Rendering unto Caesar, that which is Caesar's—'

'And be it known that not a penny of mine will ever line the coffers of Rome,' Grandfather growled.

'Priest didn't mention money. More about justice and authority. Talked of the responsibility of those in power to govern wisely and uphold truth; and about the deference we ought to show to those who have authority over us. Like parents. Isn't that right, Poss?'

'Papists,' Grandfather humphed. 'Money, power, and wicked abomination, every man his censer in his hand.'

'Not too many bells and smells this morning. Low Mass.'

'Mint sauce, Roddy?' asked Grandmother.

'Sounds great, Mum. Now, what about a toast?' Dad raised his glass, which had nothing but water. 'To family, eh?'

He made up for the alcoholic deprivation later that afternoon. While Grandfather was snoozing on the verandah, Dad announced that he was heading down to the rubbidy-dub for a tiddly wink.

'We'll keep that one quiet,' Aunt Rachel whispered to me.

Aunt Rachel reciprocated our visit, coming to Sydney for Maman's interment, and braving a Catholic requiem and burial. On the anniversary of Maman's death, a requiem Mass was offered for the repose of her soul, and her remains were transferred to a plot Dad had purchased in Waverley Cemetery. Some months later he had a monument erected: a broken pillar flanked by two angels, one playing a violin, the other in joyous song, at the base of which was carved:

> *Sacred to the memory of*
> *Juliette Marie Raye,*
> *Beloved wife of Roderick,*
> *Loving mother to Phoebe,*
> *Departed this life*
> *16th February 1921*
> *Aged 28 years*
> *'Be ye therefore merciful'*

We also visited Aunt Sara, who was buried alongside her husband across the harbour at Gore Hill. Much to my relief, I had learned in Ballarat that Aunt Sara had passed away a few years before.

'I don't know why Roddy bought tea roses,' Aunt Rachel mused as we walked together, 'I told him Sara preferred yellow roses, but he wouldn't have it any other way. Chalk and cheese, those two,' she sighed. 'All things considered, it was very noble of Sara to care for you, Phoebe dear. She never understood Roderick, who would let his heart rule his head,' which latter observation was Aunt Rachel's take on the immoral circumstances of my conception.

'She was a cruel and horrible old woman.'

'Hush, Phoebe! She meant well, love. She tried to do what she thought was right, especially after what happened to poor Ian.'

And she explained how my cousin Ian Raye MacDonald disregarded his mother's protests and volunteered the moment he turned eighteen. He went missing in action at Passchendaele and was not presumed dead until after the War ended.

'Sara never recovered from the shock of it. She always hoped he might come home. Sadly, he never did, whereas your father—'

'She told me he deserved his injuries.'

'It was the only way the poor dear could justify the situation. Sara blamed herself for what happened to Roddy. I'm afraid she was the one who had been the most insistent about his joining up.'

'Do you mean to say she made my father enlist yet she wouldn't even allow her own son—?'

'It was my own stupid doing,' Dad interrupted from his post at the graveside.

'She tried her best to make amends,' apologised Aunt Rachel. 'Taking you into her care was part of that. But, as she said to me many a time, it was very hard to love you. You didn't want to be loved.'

'No, I didn't. Not like that.'

'In the end, she was too sick to even try,' Aunt Rachel sighed. 'She had cancer, dear.'

'That's no excuse.'

'She bore it with great courage.' Believing Dad to be occupied once more with his own thoughts but not wanting to take a chance, she whispered, 'She had a breast removed. It was very humiliating for her. And there was nothing anyone could do to cheer her. Poor Sara couldn't understand why she had been made to suffer like that. She fought right to the bitter end. It's very sad to see someone depart this world in such anger.'

'She made life hell for herself and everyone else.' I decided that Aunt Rachel's apology was her way of saying that she herself had had a hard time of Aunt Sara.

'For which she is only to be pitied. Well, she's at peace now, I hope, with her loved ones. For she was loved, Phoebe. She was loved very much.'

It turned out that to assuage her guilt, Aunt Sara had appointed Dad heir to the bulk of her considerable estate. Dad had little real need of it, for he was comfortably off in his own right. Maman's inheritance, coupled with his own private income, sufficed to last a lifetime provided he was careful. Aunt Sara's bequest made him as rich as Phil the Jew. In this matter Dad proved himself every inch a Raye: frugal, enterprising, and financially astute.

'Well, if I've been lucky with anything this side of the grave, it's money,' he sighed, his dark eyes tinged with sorrow. Silver and gold would never replace his legs, would never restore the use of his arm, would never bring back Maman; but it enabled him to divert his attention from his own loss by using his considerable fortune for others' sake. When Mr and Mrs Epstein were evicted yet again, he invited them to live with us and set aside part of the house for that purpose. Some months later he saw them settled in a home of their own a few streets away which he helped them purchase. It was the least he could do for them, he said, given all they had done for us.

When the stock market crashed late in 1929, Dad's business

acumen stood him in good stead. While our Stanmore residence maintained its grandeur, I watched five families gradually move into the neighbouring villa, which formerly was the habitation of a single elderly couple. Our other neighbours abandoned their large gabled home, which afterwards could neither be let or sold, as was also the predicament of some newer dark brick bungalows further down the street. Of the properties still inhabited, gardens lost all sense of decoration, having been turned to agricultural purpose, while the family inside struggled on a meagre income. The neighbourhood grew melancholy. People lived from one day to the next. Small, struggling bands of men not yet on the susso wandered out to work (which was true for some, but for most 'going to work' meant a trip to the park or pub). Dwindling numbers of Newington boys in suits and boaters walked to school. Ladies in last year's clothes made trips with pennies saved for weeks, probably months. And all the passers-by began to eye our home with envy, admiration, or suspicion.

What did Mr Raye do?

Well, prior to the Crash, Dad had sold Aunt Sara's mansion and invested in numerous smaller properties. These he refurbished and sold at a profit, or else put up for rent. As the economic depression took hold, casting thousands out of work and rendering families homeless and impoverished, Dad put his real estate empire to ingenious purpose.

'The poverty of the rich man is characterised by two things, Possum: generosity and moderation,' he instructed me during one of his more serious moments. He made a point of renting houses at a reduced rate to tradesmen. In return, they carried out the necessary maintenance, and availed themselves for work on other properties as required. Mr Jones the plumber, for instance, kept a house in Paddington, and repaired the pipes in the Redfern house of Mr Smith the painter, who in turn decorated Mr Jones' Paddington home, while Mr Scrubb in Surry Hills fixed roof tiles, and Mr Finch of Enmore provided joinery. Rather than rely on income from low rents, Dad gave French and German conversation lessons at Fort Street and Newington College, sang in wireless commercials, taught violin, conducted occasionally, and adjudicated competitions and exams.

Throughout those difficult years he sheltered some twenty families who might otherwise have raised their children in 'Happy Valley', one of several coastal shanty towns and tent settlements constructed from old sacks and corrugated iron. Indeed, he acquired a reputation for assisting anyone out of work. Many a time an itinerant would knock on our front door requesting help. Dad would always find him something to do, pay him for it, give him a meal and a bed for the night if needed, and send him off with a reference (or keep him on if he could). By these means the fountain was installed at the back of our Stanmore home, the parterre constructed, and flowerbeds kept brimful with annuals.

Landscaping projects of this kind were part of Dad's extensive beautification of our home, which he was determined to restore in memory of Maman. Items such as Bobeshi's set of Limoges porcelain (which, we discovered, Aunt Sara had stowed away for herself) were returned to their rightful place in our parlour. Harry's statues, which the latter had abandoned on the verandah, found leafy homes in our garden. Meanwhile, Dad, who had an eye for novelties and bargains, snaffled curios at auctions.

Prominent in the decoration was the Graythwaite Gay and Hearties, a collection of some two dozen portraits which Dad had painted during his years in the veterans' home. On subsequent visits to Graythwaite, I had the good fortune to meet a few of his sitters and was intrigued to see how Dad had captured some quirky traits. Each was painted in a naïve style: the faces highly individualised, but simplified like icons, and set against plain backgrounds. Dad quartered the Hearties in Ailine's former studio. The paintings covered every inch of wall with the effect that the room, which became his own studio, assumed the richness and intensity of an Orthodox shrine.

In gazing at the faces I felt as if I had indeed entered into a communion with the living and the dead, made all the more real by Dad's stories: of Jim who time and again protected my father and ultimately gave his life for him, because Dad was married and he was not; of Artie who was illiterate, yet who could read the land as a book; of Jack who had a degree in mathematics, although if you met him, you would never have believed it, for he was like a child of three. One, however, was headless; and Dad had painted the poor fellow's head, grinning like Poor Yorrick, upside down next to his body, just as he had seen it on the battlefield. There was also Kurt, a Bavarian prisoner of war and a friend from Dad's time in Vienna, who looked as if he had stage fright. Not that the tableau was a glorification of the War – headless Harry especially precluded such interpretation – nor did it pay homage to the lofty notion of the 'supreme sacrifice'. It was Dad's tribute to his mates, a means of laying some of the 'poor blighters' to rest in a manner denied them during the hostilities; and a way for him to come to terms with their loss and with the horrific nightmares he had suffered.

Towards himself, Dad was frugal. Certainly, he enjoyed small luxuries – wine with his meals (which were simple overall), and an after-dinner liqueur – and he smoked a packet a day. But during those years he never bought himself a new suit, a hat, or even a shirt, choosing instead to wear his old clothes, most of which dated from before the War, and were tailored in the finest Viennese style.

Towards me, he made up for years of separation. Given that I had abandoned school, Dad set about teaching me himself, reviving those treasured days after he returned from the Front when he taught me my first lessons. We plunged into literature and history, our discussions fuelled by tea and cigarettes, and, in the evenings, a liqueur or two. Dad also taught me French and German, whereupon I realised I shared his gift for languages, for I rapidly acquired fluency in both tongues. 'Don't you remember, Possum?' he asked me, 'Your mother and grandmother only spoke to you in French; so, you prattled in French before you did in English. German, too.'

'You spoke to me in German?'

'And sang to you.'

'I don't remember any of it. How could I forget?'

'You didn't forget. You blocked it out. And now it's all coming back.'

My education also had a practical side, for Dad insisted I accompany him on his rounds. Every Wednesday we took a tram through Sydney, a pleasurable excursion involving lunch and what we nicknamed the Eternity Quest. 'He's at it again!' Dad tapped his stick on the word Eternity chalked in copperplate on a Pitt St pavement. 'They missed that one,' he indicated the inscription on the stairs at Stanmore railway station, relishing that the mystery graffitist had outwitted the authorities so bent on cleaning up after him. In the afternoon, we called on tenants. Over cups of tea and inordinate small talk, Dad kept an eye on the families in his charge, supplying books, clothes, food, or medicine as required; and passing treats, hidden in his sling, to the barefoot children who dogged him down the dusty streets. Many a youngster liked to imitate him (Dad was slightly bow-legged and used to kick his wooden legs out from the knee when he walked); and when from the corner of his eye he spied a rascal in the act, he would give his cane a twirl, wriggle his haunches and waddle along like Charlie Chaplin. Come nightfall, however, I saw what the trip had cost him. He was exhausted, the stumps of his legs tender from his exertions.

Our weekly trips comprised part of an ordered routine: Dad rose early and breakfasted in his room. Immaculately groomed, he emerged to take his morning walk, via the church, to the barber for his daily shave and a manicure or trim. He returned to join me for coffee, during which we discussed the daily papers in English, German, and French. And there was much to discuss, particularly after Adolf Hitler became Chancellor in Germany in January 1933.

❖ ❖ ❖

'So, it's Mussolini in Italy, Mr Jardine and the Marylebone Cricket Club, and now Herr Hitler in Germany. Who is this Hitler fellow?' Dad asked over one such morning coffee.

'Don't you remember, Roddy?' prompted Mr Epstein (who often popped in for elevenses). 'From Wien? Gustl's friend, Adolf?'

'Gustl?' Dad raised an eyebrow. 'Gustl Kubizek? Schwammi, nein!' Playing on Mr Epstein's physical resemblance to Schubert, Dad always called him 'Schwammi', a variation of the composer's own nickname.

'Who's Gustl Kubizek?' I interrupted their Viennese banter which within seconds had turned the clock back to 1907, when as students, crammed in the gods at the Hofoper, they saw Mahler's production of *Die Walküre*.

'Studied conducting at the Conservatory,' Dad tossed me the answer in German. 'Reckon I sent Rachel one of Adolf's picture postcards. Wonder if she kept it... Adolf,' he chuckled to himself, 'Adolf... *der Maler...*' And off he went to attend to his correspondence, as was his custom after coffee, amusing himself en route with puns on Maler and Mahler.

Some months later I caught him reading what he said was 'Adolf Maler's' autobiography, which had been sent him specially from Germany.

'Funny that Adolf wanted to be a Maler,' he remarked. 'I'd imagine he wouldn't want much to do with any Mahlers now.'

'What are you going on about, Dad?'

'Adolf's got a bone or two to pick with the Jews, I can tell you that much, Possum. Mahler was Jewish,' he added, seeing that his observation made little sense to me. 'Seems he has something in store for Austria, too. Wants what those scoundrels at Versailles called German-Austria to return to what he calls the German Motherland.'

'Well, if Austria is German speaking, why should it not be?'

'I'm a Viennese citizen and I speak fluent German; but somehow I doubt that in being part Chinese, I'd qualify as a German according to Herr Hitler. This isn't about language; it's about blood.'

'But the Austrians were ruled by German princes.'

'German princes? Habsburgs were more than "German". You can't get more European than a Habsburg. And Germany – especially Bismarck's Germany – was never Austria's "Motherland". Coming home to the Reich? Balderdash! Austrians have been resisting the Piefke for centuries.'

'What's a Piefke, Dad?'

'What a Viennese calls a Prussian. They're none too fond of Prussians in Wien.'

13

Two's Company

MEANWHILE, THE POLICE conducted a two-pronged search of shipping records: to ascertain whether Ailine had left the country and to detain her if possible; and to establish her being in the country at the time of the crime. Passenger lists for 1928 produced no evidence of an 'Ailine Devereaux'; which meant that if she had departed, she had done so under an assumed name. They probed us to think of alternatives, particularly ones associated with family, such as Walkowicz, from which Bobeshi's surname Volcot derived. Another possibility was Walker. Being a common surname, it led to an extensive investigation which unfortunately yielded nothing. Earlier records uncovered a Mrs A. D'Evereaux who had arrived from Marseilles late in January 1921. Mrs Albert D'Evereaux, however, remained in Sydney, where she died in 1925.

'I know Lina was in the country in 'twenty-one,' said Dad. 'You saw her, Poss. We were picnicking in the garden. You took yourself on an expedition and ended up nattering with someone at the front gate. Maman called you back and you told us you were talking to a lady who was just like Bobeshi. Maman walked down to see; but the woman had left. She couldn't make her out, but later said to me she could have sworn it was Lina. Didn't think much of it at the time; but it's odd how some happenings lurk in your memory.'

'I don't remember that at all; although Ailine does look rather like Bobeshi.'

Dad agreed. 'Doesn't prove anything, though.'

Would they never find her? Surely it could not be so difficult? Dad reminded me that the police had plenty to do besides chasing a crime committed a decade ago.

'Do you think Ailine was jealous?' I asked. 'Mrs Epstein reckons she killed Maman because she was jealous that you loved Maman and not her.'

'Well, that'd be pretty pointless, because I'd still love your mother.'

'Mrs Epstein said Ailine wanted to destroy you by destroying the people you loved.'

Dad disagreed.

'How can you be so sure?'

'Because she loved me.'

'And she didn't love her sister?'

'Half-sister.'

'Anyway, it's ridiculous saying she loved you. She only loves herself.'

'Perhaps it has nothing to do with love— that is, not in the way you think. Best leave the matter be, Poss. Let the ducks and geese do what they're trained to do; and you better do the same. How's that Haydn?'

'Haydn! Why can't we play something else for once?'

After Della died, we reconfigured the quartet and named it the Hirondelle Quartet in her honour. Lucy remained on cello; Mrs Epstein took my place as second violin, which support role she preferred; and Mr Epstein replaced Pim on the viola, Pim having moved to Moss Vale to help an aunt. To my immense satisfaction, I realised my ambition of playing first violin, which role I found more daunting than expected, since I was responsible for much of the interpretation, and felt awkward having my own teacher look to me for cues. Fortunately, I had Dad's very capable assistance (he knew the quartets of Haydn, Mozart, and Beethoven by heart).

'I suppose she told you a string quartet was a four-voiced republic,' he once observed, referring to Mrs Epstein.

'Yes.'

'Always let them think that. They play better when they do,' he winked. 'Truth is, it's an autocracy. A benevolent autocracy, but an autocracy, nonetheless. You're in charge, and don't forget it.'

But I could not exercise the same authority. While I might have inherited Dad's skill, I could not shape the music the way he did; nor could I explain my ideas in a calm and ordered manner. I did not have his knack of winning hearts, of commanding respect, of joyful entertainment, as was borne out when he joined us one evening, requested the use of my violin, and advised Mr and Mrs Epstein and Lucy, who were skilled at improvisation, on their accompaniment to 'L'Amour' from *Carmen*. Then, he took up my violin, plucked out the tune with a formidable left hand pizzicato, and sang the counter-melody falsetto. The pizzicato tango, as they called it, became an act at parties, student concerts, and soirees, and in Dad's winsome performance I saw the brilliance and charisma that had captivated audiences in the pre-War years.

I also saw my own inadequacy. If Dad was a monarch of the stage, gifted by Divine Privilege, I was a serf committed to a life of toil. I practised long and hard; but the hours I devoted to my craft, and the paltry results, made me feel incapable and inadequate, particularly regarding any piece with which Dad was familiar. And when we performed quartets, I became overwhelmed by what I sensed was the others' expectation for me to fill his shoes. The situation was not helped by the fact that I detested playing Haydn, whose music my cohorts preferred. Time and again I was over-ruled or marginalised by the hoi polloi of second violin, viola and cello, all of whom liked resolving matters democratically to such an extent that I resorted to tyranny. Finally, I abdicated, and left the Hirondelle Quartet to its fate.

Lucy then suggested we form a piano trio. It was obvious why: she wanted to spend more time with Della's brother, Wally. I suppose I should have been wise to it when I saw him kiss her at Della's wake. For he did kiss her, on the cheek; and she smiled and returned his affection.

Girls thought Wally handsome, mainly because he was tall, tanned, and athletic. In truth, he was all bone and sinew, with a prominent Adam's apple, and a mop of sandy blonde hair that was forever falling into his sky-blue eyes. His other features were so irregular that his face seemed a make-do assemblage of unwanted parts. His mouth was too large, his lips too thin, his gapped teeth too small; his cheekbones were low and prominent; and his nose was angled like a dog's leg, thanks to a collision with a cricket ball.

Wally and Lucy began hiring skiffs and sculling down the river. A bicycle followed the boat; for Wally, who was studying Medicine, thought that Lucy's polio-stricken legs could be strengthened by exercise. Soon, the tall, gangly Lucy required only half-leg braces, and took to wearing plus-fours when she pedalled at the back of the tandem. Her cheeks grew rosy, her milk-white skin glowed, and her sleepy, short-sighted green eyes shone behind their thick glasses. Lucy herself even managed to look quite feminine, despite her boyish figure and cropped black hair.

But the other side-effects were far worse. My best friend added cricket to her interests, cheered Wally when he played club matches, and nursed him when he broke his nose. The two of them followed the tests on the wireless, and, when the Bodyline controversy arose, talked of nothing but bowling. Then Wally converted to Catholicism and accompanied Lucy to Sunday Mass. He also began accompanying her on the piano and resumed lessons to build his skills. They performed the Beethoven A Major Cello Sonata together first at a soiree, and later at a Conservatorium concert.

'Why didn't you ask me?' I demanded of my friend. 'I've always played the Beethoven with you.'

''Tis relaxing for the lad, with all his studies; and he feels close to Delleen when he plays,' she replied. 'He plays well, does he not?'

'For an amateur. But what about me?'

'And that's why I'm asking you now, will you not consider a piano trio? Or is it that you don't like him?' she probed.

'It's not that— It's— Whenever I have anything to do with him, I feel as if he's studying every inch of my anatomy!' I blurted and blushed. Nothing escaped Wally, whose probing gaze was but the cold, hard tip of the iceberg of his thought, the latter a dangerous mass of psychological and physiological analysis which his medical training only encouraged.

'He's doing nothing of the sort,' Lucy soothed. 'It's yourself's the trouble. Would it not please you to play the Mendelssohn? The D Minor Trio?'

'You would have to suggest the Mendelssohn, wouldn't you?'

''Tis a favourite, is it not?'

'Why can't we play something just two of us?'

'We can still do things together, but 'twill not be the same.'

'What do you mean?'

'I mean, Wally and myself are engaged to be married.'

'What about piano quartet?' suggested Mr Epstein when he heard my plight.

'That won't work! Pim's married and living in the country and has two children already! She's too busy with nappies to even bother with her viola nowadays. Why does everyone have to get married?'

'I do not think you will end up old maid.'

'I have no intention of marrying. I have no interest in men whatsoever. What are you doing?'

'Checking the colour of your stockings,' replied Dad, who had ducked his head under the table. 'Ha! As I thought!' he emerged, his eyes gleaming, 'Blue.'

'They're nothing of the sort!'

'You don't want to be an old maid, dear,' added Aunt Rachel who was holidaying with us.

'You never married.'

'That's because my fiancé died at Amiens. So, you're going to spend your life caring for your father?'

'That is the idea.' My vocation, I had decided, was to look after Dad and play violin, and one day make the concert platform as a soloist.

'There's no need for that.'

'But I want to.'

'You leave your father to me. Enjoy your life, Phoebe, and give it everything you've got.'

'I can't give it anything at present. All the cinemas are getting wired for sound, so there's hardly any work, and I won't play piano trios. If three were ever a crowd, it's playing Mendelssohn with Lucy and Wally.'

'Then I think I might be able to help. One of my best students has returned from Germany,' Mr Epstein resumed. 'If you like, I could talk to him. I am certain he would be most happy to form ensemble.'

Upon introduction, Mr Eric Rudd looked promising. Unlike Lucy and Wally, he was closer to me in height and build, that is, perfectly average and pleasingly slender. His hair, lush and slick with Brilliantine, was dark brown, his skin a healthy bronze, his eyes midnight blue. Open and cheery in manner and expression, he had an attractive smile. 'Chrome and bakelite,' remarked Dad, who considered him an elegant take on Mr Cagney. 'Nonsense,' I countered, 'He's just like Clark Gable.' Wally thought him 'flashy', for he wore a black and white pin-striped suit, a scarlet tie, and two-tone shoes. From his surname, Lucy wondered whether he was Irish like herself.

'Irish? I'm of German descent,' he laughed. 'Turns out Rudd's a corruption of Ruttenberg.'

A few more questions on Dad's part revealed that his German was very good. He had spent the past three years working in the Bechstein factory in Berlin, his father having sent him to study the fine points of 'goanna manufacture' as he termed the piano industry. Now back in Australia, he had the dilemma of finding permanent employment, a near impossible task given the economic situation. Meanwhile, he was making ends meet through the odd gig, a few violin students, and tuning the occasional piano. Dad also suspected bootlegging, but that notion was unsubstantiated.

And what did Mr Rudd think of Herr Hitler? 'I met him,' he declared. 'Visited the showroom with the boss's brother and his wife. I found him charming, affable, committed – Everyman's champion, if not Everyman himself. Good bloke. Nation's right behind him. I mean, before he came to power, a loaf of bread was a luxury— You think it's tough here, but it's been like that in Germany since the War. Anyway, the country's being transformed! Employment's on the rise and relief work's put food on every table. You should see the highway they're constructing! Thanks to Chancellor Hitler, my cousins enjoyed their first summer holiday in over twenty years. National Socialism's the solution to the financial crisis. We could do with similar initiatives here. Mr Lang was on the right path with that Bridge. If you ask me, an

Australian national identity is what we need to bring this country together.'

'But what of the Jews, Eric?' Mr Epstein queried, while Dad murmured, 'We've Buckley's of that'.

'Don't worry, Mr Ep. Not that many German Jews. Only seems like more because every second doctor or lawyer you meet happens to be one. The Ostjuden are different. They're Russian immigrants. Poles didn't want them. Nor did the Soviets despite their supporting the Revolution. More orthodox ones stick out like a sore thumb; but they tend to be Zionist. Germany's a half-way house. It'll get sorted somehow or other.' Indeed, the only downside of Germany's new situation was the forced closure of his favourite clubs and cabarets; and he was peeved by his father's urgent mandate to return home.

He proved himself an excellent violist: dependable, easy-going, and familiar with the repertoire (particularly Schumann and Brahms which were far more to my taste). Full of initiative, he even recommended we change the name of the group, since Hirondelle Quartet sounded too Latin-French for his taste. It might have honoured Della's memory, but a native Australian name would be more in keeping with the Zeitgeist and would probably secure us more work. My suggestion of the Kookaburra Quartet was debunked by Wally who argued that we'd end up being called the Laughing Jackasses. 'Could call it the Goanna Quartet,' Eric joked before assuming a more serious vein and proposing 'Katandra' as an alternative, Katandra being an aboriginal word for bird song. Lucy and Wally (the more reluctant parties) approved only because the name maintained an indirect link with Della who had loved all things avian; while I was eager to cut ties with the past if it meant putting us on a more equal footing.

Besides, Eric needed support. One crisp Autumn afternoon, he showed me his former home. An imposing Victorian residence, across the railway line from my own place, it was now divided into flats, its wide verandah enclosed with iron offcuts and scavenged timber panels. Eric explained that his father, a piano salesman, once owned several showrooms in Sydney. After the Crash, no one could afford a piano, and those who had them couldn't afford to tune them. The family business collapsed; and by the time Eric arrived from Berlin, his parents had moved to Glebe where they managed a tiny corner store and lived in the three rooms above.

'You can see why I need work,' he grinned when I called by one day and found him wearing an apron, sleeves rolled, stacking tins and looking daggers at the grubby urchin lurking near the jar of oatmeal biscuits on the counter.

'Something will turn up, Eric. Don't worry.'

'Suppose we're luckier than most. Family next door did the moonlight flit last night; and the Ginger Meggs who just nicked off lives in a stable down the road. Anyway, we can whirl away our cares on the dance floor, can't we? What about it, Phoebe? I've been saving for weeks to ask you out.'

My only previous experience of dancing – lessons undertaken at Dad's insistence – had involved blundering youths unsure of their right and left, fearful of error, and incapable of distinguishing between duple and triple time. Eric possessed full command of every move. He was not at all awkward about where to put his hands or feet, had a fine sense of rhythm, and guided me with ease. How thrilling it was! We spent evenings mastering steps and routines, especially the tango which he had learned in Berlin. 'I played with an Argentinian band. The only way to play the tango is to dance it first,' he smiled, and swung me into position.

And when Lucy and Wally married in October 1933, the word was that the bridesmaid and her beau outshone the bride and groom for style.

14

Mother and Child

M Y COMINGS AND GOINGS with Eric, Dad viewed as a cat would a fieldmouse in long grass. He also began mentioning someone called Cilla. Given his habit of casual reference to persons and subjects familiar to himself yet foreign to others, it fell to me to make the necessary connections.

Cilla soon featured too often for comfort, which compelled me one morning to blurt, 'Dad, who is Cilla?'

'Cilla?' he echoed in his absent-minded 'I thought you knew' tone of voice. 'Oh, she's Jack's sister.'

Brain-damaged at Passchendaele, Jack was Graythwaite's 'professor' of Mathematics. As for 'Cilla', her full name was Mrs Priscilla Driscoll. Further prompting revealed that she was widowed when her husband died at Gallipoli and had lost her only daughter to diphtheria soon after. She then supported her ageing mother who, in turn, looked after the unfortunate Jack who was first admitted to Graythwaite for respite care.

Whilst visiting Jack, she met Dad. A teacher of Modern Languages, she had a good command of French and German, which skills enabled her to communicate with him. Apparently, 'Cilla' was partly responsible for his 'coming to'. In speaking German, she could converse in the language of his world, and yet was not of that world, which fact she was required to explain, for he was much agitated that he could not place her anywhere in Vienna. During subsequent visits, she passed Dad volumes of Goethe and Schiller; and after some months, Dad asked in English, 'Who are you? I don't believe we've been properly introduced,' which were the first words he had spoken in that language since his breakdown. Following their mother's death, Jack became a permanent resident at Graythwaite, which meant 'Cilla' saw Dad on a weekly basis. Such was the case when Dad and I were reunited in 1928.

'Then why haven't I met her?'

'Would you like to?'

And meet her I did at Jack's funeral late in 1933.

I thought her an orderly, sensible, intelligent person who perhaps was quite pretty in her youth, given her petite stature, regular features, grey eyes, and wavy light-brown hair (which, I suspected, she coloured). Her practical, forthright manner and keen sense of humour suggested that she had faced life with courage and resolve. Certainly, she was well-positioned to handle anything Dad threw at her. In fact, she had a way of managing him (and everyone else) in that annoying manner of teachers who think they must apply the instructorial rigour and organisational demands of their profession to every person and situation regardless of whether they are in the classroom or not. What I found even more peculiar was that Dad was amenable to it.

Mrs Driscoll, for me, remained of little consequence until Eric escorted me home after a ball the following New Year's Eve. Being a balmy summer's night, the windows were wide open. Laughter floated from the front parlour— not simple delight in wit, but warm, affectionate chuckles. I bid Eric good-night and entered the house.

It pleased me to think that Dad, like Lucy's dear father Mr Straughan, the gentlest, kindest soul I have ever known, led the quasi-monastic life of the widower: a life that was chaste and frugal, like my own, spent in loving sacrifice for my sake, as I did for him; a life devoted to my care and well-being, and to Maman's memory. The idea that he could be in any way involved with another woman had never occurred to me.

Dad and Mrs Driscoll were lounging on the couch. Apparently, get-togethers of this sort were a regular event and had been so for years. Whenever I was out working or, more recently, dancing, they went to the pictures, enjoyed a meal, and journeyed homeward for a drink or two. Dad then arranged a cab for his lady friend, and, by the time I arrived, was sitting in his favourite chair, reading or snoozing, as if nothing untoward had taken place.

After my discovery, Mrs Driscoll accompanied Dad to concerts and was his partner at dinners and entertainments. She proved accomplished enough to play the piano for him while he sang; and had the gall to offer to accompany me, which I declined. She joined us for Mass, and afterwards for Sunday dinner, and began receiving instruction in the Faith.

Given the nature and constancy of her presence, and sensing the necessity for diplomacy, she broke through the professorial barrier and invited me to call her Cilla instead of Mrs Driscoll, which I did.

I called her Scylla.

'And I suppose that makes you Charybdis,' Dad remarked.

'And are you Odysseus?'

'Well, if I am, and if memory serves me well, Circe advised Odysseus to sail closer to Scylla, for Charybdis would drown his entire ship. Should I sail closer to Scylla?'

'How would I know? I'm Charybdis, not Circe. Anyway, you wouldn't dare.'

But he did dare.

He proposed.

And Scylla accepted.

'I hope you're not going to be like your aunt over this,' cautioned Mrs Epstein when we met at Dad's wedding that April. 'With your silent manner and curled lip, you look uncannily like Lina. Don't you dare begrudge your father his happiness.'

'As if I would be so spiteful. Would I murder someone? I think not.'

The wedding was small, confined to close friends and family (although only Aunt Rachel came up from the Rat). I had to admit that Scylla had quite good taste. Her pert pillbox hat was neither silly nor pretentious; her sky-blue ensemble simply and attractively styled. No doubt it would serve her well in the years to come. Dad had splashed out on a new suit. He carried on with his usual sparkle; but in quieter moments I noticed him watching the company with an elated expression I had never seen. Even more disconcerting was that Scylla was equally joyous. From the church steps she threw her bouquet which, to my embarrassment and misfortune, fell my way. And as much as it was my instinct to catch it, so it was my instinct to let it go.

'Trust Phoebe to drop the bundle!' laughed Pim, who was expecting number three.

'She'll be dropping a few more if she ever ties the knot!' called someone else.

Eric picked up the bouquet, bowed most chivalrously, and handed it to me, salvaging my self-respect by inviting me to play the damsel.

'For my Best Girl,' he kissed my hand.

The happy couple returned from their honeymoon in time to hear me perform the Brahms Double with Lucy. Our performance had been years coming. While Lucy and I had learned the concerto at school, we had been unable to present it in any capacity because of the Crash. Finally, thanks to Eric who compiled an ensemble from various contacts, and Dad who provided the funds, we arranged a concert at the Conservatorium.

We made our curtsies. Lucy, who usually dreaded that first

entrance, beamed; and when she nodded at the audience, she lingered a little on the centre row and sent Wally a winsome smile. Dad was nearby with Scylla beside him. He put his hand on hers, and I was certain he squeezed it. Then Scylla looked at him and smiled. He wriggled gleefully in his seat. She nestled beside him.

The event was reported in the morning paper thus:

Last Friday night, we were treated to a performance of Brahms' Double Concerto by two accomplished young ladies. Pretty Miss Phoebe Raye, the violinist, possessed the grace and poise of a wood nymph, and her flashing eyes bewitched us from the first. Mrs R. Walsingham (Lucy) Sotheby, the tall and striking 'cellist, was awkward by comparison, until she took her seat.

In her dark, dramatic opening, the young 'cellist transported us to the northern forests, her instrument's sonority creating a rich autumnal tapestry of storms and swirling leaves; her second movement evoked the warmth of the fireside; her finale, an impish and virtuosic Germanic fantasy, was performed with astounding athleticism and maturity.

Miss Raye, by contrast, was a mere sapling. While her scintillating technique reminded me of her father, a celebrated violinist whom I had the pleasure of hearing before the War, she is yet to acquire his memorable warmth and vitality. True, her tone was pure and delicate, like blossoms on a tree in early spring. Her brittle phrasing, however, betrayed the green wood of her youth; and her interpretation, while passionate, lacked the nourishment of experience. Enter a rustic tavern, and we would find our 'cellist by the hearth, beckoning us to join her for a stoup of ale and an exciting tale of robbers and stolen treasure. Our violinist we would encounter on a Paris Pavement drowning her sorrows in absinthe. Although she is not without promise...

'Did you ever receive a bad review, Dad?' I asked, laying the paper aside and facing a host of anxious, adult faces. Along with Dad and Scylla, Mr and Mrs Epstein were keen to hear news.

'June 1913. Bruch Number 1. Same critic, I might add: Lord Byron.'

'It's Mr George Gordon.'

'We called him Lord Byron,' Mrs Epstein smiled.

'What did he say, Roddy?' asked Scylla.

Dad cleared his throat and feigned a pompous British accent as he quoted verbatim: 'Our Ballarat virtuoso seems to have frittered away his time in Vienna carousing with rogues in the manner of Prince Hal instead of devoting himself to the rigours of conservatorium study. His technique is all too reminiscent of the Jew and the Gypsy; his manner too relaxed; his interpretation too bohemian. In short, his performance lacked the restraint that is the hallmark of English accomplishment.'

'And he was right, yes?' Mr Epstein chuckled.

'Although I don't recall you being quite so amused at the time, Roddy,' Mrs Epstein remarked.

'You're right there, Annie,' chortled Dad.

'You should have seen him, Phoebe,' Mr Epstein nudged me and nodded at Scylla, 'It was fireworks display: Pa-pa-pa-pa-pa, boom! "English restraint? It's Bruch for Pete's sake!" although he used much worse expression. "What does he want me to play in? A straight jacket?"'

'I don't know how you all can make light of it!' And I ran to my room.

'What's the trouble?' Dad requested permission to sit on my bed, my decision to unlock the door being much delayed. 'Now, are you upset because your best friend received a better review than you? Come on, Possum, don't let a critic blight your friendship. Admit it: Lucy Long's extraordinary (Lucy Long was Dad's nickname for Lucy). Gave a ripping performance the other night. She's achieved what every musician dreams: she's found her voice.'

'And I haven't?'

'I think you're yet to find it. It's only an opinion, Phoebe, and not a low one, not by any means.'

'He called me a sapling!'

'Could have been nasty and called you a weed. Do you think it was unfair?'

'Am I a sapling?'

'A very healthy one. You played well: beautiful tone, top notch technique. Just need to get your roots down. Lord Byron's right: You need experience, and that takes time.'

'What time have I got?'

'What—? Don't use me as a benchmark. Listen, I was lucky to achieve what I did early on.'

'Luck? Hard work, more like. And talent. I've worked so hard, Dad!'

'There, there. It's already begun to pay off. You continue to do the best you can with the time you have. And don't give in. Don't go drowning your sorrows in absinthe, either. Speaking of sorrows...' he drawled into one of his penetrating silences.

'Dad, why did you have to marry her?'

'Come with me.'

'Where are we going?'

'Up to the attic.'

In the attic was a hideous painting of a mother and child which had caused much controversy, being one of the works Ailine had left behind. Mrs Epstein at first took a liking to it and hung it in her studio; but as her antipathy towards Ailine increased, she began to hate it, and left it behind when she moved. Dad then hung it above his desk. I hid it. Dad found it and hung it back. I insisted the painting be destroyed. Dad insisted upon the painting staying, and compromised by hanging it out of my sight, in his dressing room. When Scylla, too, voiced her dislike, he removed it for good.

'One word from *her* and up to the attic it goes!' I complained.

'It was a painful reminder of her own daughter.'

'And you think it's not a painful reminder for me?'

'Clearly, it is. Now, back to Cilla. In you, she has a chance to have another daughter. If you play your cards right, you'll have a mother and a friend. And that doesn't mean she'll take Maman's place. She'll never replace Maman. She knows that. Nor do I want to tie you down looking after me. You need to see the world and get some of that experience you sorely need.'

'I wish you didn't love her.'

'When you love someone, you'll never wish that. Your best friend, for instance. Have you gone all green-eyed because she's married?'

'Why would I be green-eyed over that?'

'Wouldn't want you to resent her happiness. Things won't be easy for Lucy, Poss. I mean, children and all. And if I were you, I'd celebrate her every success. Life's precious. You know who that is, don't you?' he nodded at the painting.

'Ailine painted it, I know that much.'

'It's Lina herself and her daughter.'

'What?'

'She had a child of her own.'

'Was she married?'

'No.'

'Then, who's the father?'

'I'm not at liberty to say.'

I feared the worst. 'Don't tell me it's you.'

'Me? No. Happened while I was courting Maman. Little girl's name was Sabine.'

'The child looks sick, and the mother, too. I think that's why I hate the painting so much.'

'Sabine had Cerebral Palsy. While I knew about her birth, I didn't know about her handicaps until later, when your mother was expecting you. Maman worried herself sick that you might be the same and that she wouldn't be able to look after you. Tried to reassure her. Told her the best doctors were in Vienna, and that if there was something wrong we would do everything in our power to look after you and keep you with us. You see, Poss, Lina was forced to put Sabine in an orphanage.'

'Might have guessed.'

'She couldn't bear it, Phoebe; which was why she returned to Paris before the War. I met Sabine in 'eighteen. Poor little girl couldn't do a thing for herself. Broke Lina's heart when she died a few months later. She was only seven.'

'I didn't know Ailine had a heart to break.'

'Some hearts break so hard it's almost impossible to piece them together.'

'It would seem so, given that she was heartless enough to murder Maman. I hope the police find her soon. Why is it taking so long?'

'I'm afraid it might take even longer, Possum. They've closed the case.'

15

Sleuthing

GIVEN THE CURRENT economic clime, the police had insufficient resources, financial or otherwise, to throw at a murder inquiry more than a decade old. 'Plenty of babbling brooks keeping the ducks and geese swimming happily for the moment,' was how Dad put it. 'Haven't closed the case for good. Reckon if something definitive turns up, they'll reopen it. As for you, Poss,' he added gravely as he plodded down the attic stairs, 'how you handle this will affect your relationship with every-*one* and every-*thing*. Be careful.'

'Crikey, that's dreadful,' Eric remarked when I poured out my troubles at Lucy and Wally's the following afternoon. We had finished rehearsing early, for I had a terrible headache and could not concentrate. Lucy and Wally thought an aspirin and fresh air the best remedy, and Eric offered to walk me home. 'But something tells me you're not going to take this lying down.'

After some roundabout questioning (no easy matter where Dad was concerned), I learned the name of the nurse who had helped Maman look after him when he came back from the War. Weeks passed before I finally tracked her.

Miss Beryl Hicks lived with her sister Joan in a terrace near Lewisham Hospital where she had worked since leaving my parents' employ. I remembered her as an enormous and very formidable person, solid and practical – quite capable of lifting a slight man like Dad. She had not changed. When she opened her door, I thought I had come face to face with a bull, for her head was set on a thick, short neck which in turn was wedged between sturdy, square shoulders and a powerful chest. Upon greeting me, she flared her nostrils and pressed her lips taut; and when she lowered her head, I thought she would charge.

'Miss Phoebe Raye! Am I glad to see you,' she bellowed low and heartily as she herded me inside. But if Nurse Hicks was a bull, she was more like Ferdinand, for her home was a meadow of chintz, while she herself was clad in a sensible floral. We sat at a table spread with a cloth embroidered in lazy-daisy and took tea in pretty cups, accompanied by cake fresh from the oven, buttered, and sprinkled with sugar and cinnamon.

'I was thinking about your mother only the other day when I received your letter,' she continued. 'We had a lass brought in. Barbiturate overdose. Couldn't do anything for her. It reminded me of your mother, for she was of similar age and build, with a history of depression to boot. But that was where the similarity ended.'

'How do you mean?'

'What I mean is this, Miss Raye: when I found your mother that awful morning she was dead as a doornail.'

'But if she had overdosed you would expect that, wouldn't you?'

'Yes, and no. Milk or lemon?' Handling the silver tongs with surgical precision, she placed a circle of lemon in my tea. 'I suppose they told you your mother overdosed on Veronal. Well, the problem with that is that she was dead when I found her.'

'But—?'

'You see, Miss Raye, barbiturates work slowly. It would have taken a day at least for your mother to die. She would have been comatose by morning, not dead, for she retired after midnight that night. Furthermore, there was foam about her mouth which indicated that she died soon after taking the medicine.'

'Did you tell the police?'

'Not at first. I assumed it was the Veronal. Only thought it odd in hindsight. When I did raise the subject, the police ruled it out. Classic case of suicide, the inspector said. Well, if it was, I thought, it wasn't the barbiturates that killed her. Mind you, she and Mr Raye had had a bit to drink that night. Perhaps it was the alcohol— but they never drank to excess. They *enjoyed* their liquor. Maybe being pregnant made her more sensitive, and the tragedy was an unfortunate accident; but that didn't explain the note, did it?'

'Do you think it might have been morphine?'

'If it was, she didn't get it from the house supplies. I checked those. And it doesn't explain the empty bottle of Veronal.'

'Was there a glass?'

'There was; but the police didn't examine the contents.'

'Besides, my mother was happy, wasn't she? I mean, there was no reason for her to suicide.'

'That's right. It didn't make sense. She was devoted to your father, and he to her. Whatever had happened between them before the War – and there was gossip, I'm afraid, Miss, nasty gossip – they had put behind them. And as far as I was concerned, if it was a bad situation made good, their devotion was only to be admired. I was proud to work for your parents. So, it was murder after all?'

'Yes, but they've called off the case.'

'Shame. Whoever killed that kind, gentle, quiet, dear girl was a nasty piece of work, make no mistake. I hope they swing, for her sake and yours. Wait till Joan hears about this.'

'So, your old man was right about the opiates?' Eric led me onto the dance floor and eased me into a tango promenade. Eager to improve our routine, we had begun taking classes.

'It seems that way,' I smiled. His aftershave hinted of sandalwood.

'You're getting good.'

'It's fun.' I had become attuned to his subtle language of feet, hips, and hands, his gentle shifts and lunges, and relished my skill at following his indications. We fashioned a sinuous pattern of cross steps and pivots, our synchrony the source of mutual delight. With Eric to guide me, my every move felt graceful and supple, his support so secure that anything seemed possible.

'If it wasn't Veronal, then what was it?'

'Ailine uses opium. I suppose she brought some with her and substituted Maman's sleeping medication with it. Otherwise, she could have purchased it. It's not difficult to obtain. Do you think it's worth a check?'

'Popped in to a few apothecaries while you were taking tea. Don't know how useful it's going to be. Look, if the nurse's convinced your mother's symptoms were more in keeping with an opiate overdose, and not Veronal, isn't that enough? I reckon we'll have more luck if we investigated hotels. See if anyone remembers your aunt. After all, she must have stayed somewhere.'

Our search of hotels and guesthouses was exacerbated by the fact that many establishments were no longer operational or were not in operation at the time. Beginning first in the Stanmore vicinity, we extended our inquiry to neighbouring suburbs. Public house after public house yielded no clue, until we arrived at The Royal Hotel in Leichhardt. The proprietor vaguely remembered Ailine because of her foreign accent. He summoned a chambermaid who took one look at the photograph I showed her and exclaimed,

'Why, she's the lady with the violin! And the reason why I remember, Miss, is because she *didn't* play it. My Poppa played, you see, and I used to like hearing him fiddle away, but I never had an opportunity to learn. When I met her, I asked if she would play us all a tune. But, you know what? She seemed annoyed by it. As if it were beneath her to play. She didn't like me asking questions, so I buttoned up. Still, I couldn't resist a peek while she was out one day. It wasn't well looked after— broken strings, and the bow was a mess. Now wasn't that a shame?'

'Was this the instrument?' I opened my case and showed her Dad's violin.

'Oh, I couldn't say, Miss.'

'Do you remember her name?' Eric asked.

'Let me see, let me see...' She rummaged through every available space of memory as if she were searching for a precious item misplaced by a patron, and that her livelihood depended upon its recovery. 'Stern!' she announced in delight. 'Eileen Stern. Odd that she should have an English name, considering she was foreign. I suppose she'd married a soldier. Do you play, Miss?'

'I do. And for your pains, I will play you anything you wish!'

At last, thirteen years after the crime, we had a name! Sure enough, the hotel register revealed that Eileen Stern stayed for two weeks in February 1921 and checked out on the eve of Maman's death. Now we could search the shipping records, where there was bound to be an Eileen Stern who disembarked in early 1921, and who returned to the Continent shortly afterwards. From there we could track her, perhaps even discover who else might remember her. We could determine whether the date of her departure fitted with the date of her receiving Dad's unfortunate letter. Wally recommended we have the maid sign an affidavit; but by the time we arranged the matter, she had perished in a house fire.

'Don't worry, Poss, at least we have a name,' Eric soothed, 'even if we don't have a testimony. We can still search the shipping records.'

'But how on earth are we going to do that?'

'Leave that with me.'

'Sleuthing! Why doesn't he get a proper job?' Dad complained when I told him. 'He's a decent enough musician. Could form his own band given his dance hall expertise. And tangos! What the deuce was he doing in Berlin?'

But for all his carping, Dad was conducting investigations of his own. His lively foreign correspondence had increased in recent months, and hardly a day passed when he did not receive a letter or packet from the Continent. Most recently, he had taken to reading an Austrian newspaper, *Der Christliche Ständestaat*, which he was sent on a regular basis, for he had begun to follow the political situation intently.

'Austrian Chancellor Dollfuss's been assassinated,' he announced in a paroxysm of alarm the following morning. 'Left to bleed to death with neither doctor nor priest to attend him. Could mean war.'

'You're not serious, Roddy?' Scylla sipped her tea.

'Said that back in 'fourteen, and continued sipping tea, Cill.' Dad frowned from over the top of the *Herald*. 'Seems Hitler's mob's responsible – Nazis or whatever they call these National Socialists. Austrian troops have been mobilised and Italian forces are on the march. Closed the Austro-German border and Wien's under martial law. Forty rebels executed on the spot. Happened on Wednesday.'

For days afterwards, he combed the papers. His beloved Austria was fighting for her independence! 'They've suppressed the Nazis in Styria,' he reported. 'Still fighting in Carinthia.' 'Mussolini's cancelled military leave.' 'Imposed martial law in Salzburg.'

'Europe's gotta unite against Hitler!' he declared.

'Hitler had nothing to do with it,' groaned Eric. 'It was the Austrian Nazis.'

'Caught one of the scoundrels trying to get back to Germany with plans for a Putsch in the soles of his shoes, or don't you read the papers? Even the Swiss are complaining about being used as a traffic route for explosives. Whole dinkum plot was hatched in Berlin.'

Apparently, order was soon restored; but Dad was deprived of his regular supply of information. Letters and parcels from Vienna ceased, much to his frustration and concern. Little wonder he seized the opportunity for first-hand news when one Mr Egon Kisch was purportedly arriving down under.

Now it was Eric's turn to panic, which sentiment he shared with officialdom. 'He's a Communist!' he complained. 'He burned down the Reichstag! They can't let him in!'

Indeed, Mr Kisch, a Czech journalist and writer, had been involved in the Communist uprisings in Austria at the end of the War, in addition to his later exploits in Germany where he was arrested for his involvement in the Reichstag fire, imprisoned, and subsequently expelled. He was a prominent member of the Comintern, and his visit to the Antipodes was organised by likeminded Australians who also happened to share Dad's interest in matters abroad, and who were similarly concerned about the prospect of war. Dad, with Scylla in tow, began trotting off to discussions at Pakies and dining at certain quayside restaurants where these individuals were known to gather.

Meanwhile, the Australian authorities caught wind of Mr Kisch's presence on the *Strathaird*, barred him from entering the country, and confiscated his passport when the ship docked at Perth. Upon arrival in Melbourne, he was detained on board before he decided, literally, to plunge into Australian waters as the *Strathaird* left port. Suffering a broken leg, he was then required by Sydney's immigration authorities to take the dictation test before he could legally enter the country.

'Scottish Gaelic!' laughed Dad, who had gone to the harbour to meet the visitor who now had achieved larrikin status, 'They had to resort to Scottish Gaelic to keep him out!'. A court case ensued; and Dad relished the decision that since Scottish Gaelic did not count as a European language, Mr Kisch could visit.

'Surely we have every right to bar him?' insisted Eric. 'He's a Communist for crying out loud! They wreaked havoc all over Berlin.'

'But if Mr Kisch respects our laws, should he not be given freedom to speak?' queried Dad.

'He's anti-national.'

'That's a good thing, isn't it?' Which reply led Eric to surmise that Dad's real estate enterprise was a devious form of collectivism set in opposition to the State; which notion Dad encouraged. 'I met him once,' he mused.

'Who? Kisch?'

'Probably crossed paths at some point. No, Mr Trotsky. Played chess with him in Wien. Fascinating grasp of history. Had this knack of seeing every event as a form of class struggle, I believe he called it. Extraordinary. I was very taken with it. I mean, there was some grim poverty back then. Justifies socialism, don't you think?'

'You're too right there. The rabid individualism of capitalism encourages exploitation, whereas communal collaboration benefits everyone.'

'Indeed, Mr Rudd. So then, upon what do you base your community? Herr Hitler's blood and soil?'

'I suppose so. Lucky for us, we Australians don't have the problems that exist overseas.'

'Well then, if it's blood and soil you favour, you might as well leave the country to the abos.'

'Come on!'

'I'll tell you something more,' Dad chuckled, 'Not long after I met Mr Trotsky, I had an audience with Emperor Franz Josef. You could make appointments like that before the War. Didn't matter if you were a prince or a dustman. Well, I met with the Emperor to ask for citizenship. I wanted to marry, purchase property, and build my life in Vienna. He heard me out, asked me about my fiddle and about Jules; and when he heard that I intended to convert and marry in the Church, he even recommended a priest. Talk about Jesuitical, I thought when I met with the padre, for the Emperor wasted no time passing details. Bloody conspiracy. Anyway, it got me my citizenship.

'At the time, I congratulated myself on my achievement; but in hindsight I reckon it had more to do with the Emperor than with me. He had taken the trouble to tend to me – body and soul. So much for being a monarch – he was as much a servant as his footman. You see, in his eyes I was a person and I mattered – not as an anonymous component in one of Mr Trotsky's class struggles – but as an individual who had something to give, and, because no man is an island entire of itself, needed somewhere to belong, both here and for eternity.

'Now, had blood and soil been the basis for citizenship, what interest would the Emperor have had in a mongrel like me? But there was a largesse about the Habsburgs who can be credited with encouraging some of the greatest achievements known to mankind; whose empire was bound by something far greater than race, or class, or language; and it had been like that for seven hundred years. Now, Mr Rudd, I don't find quite the same principles at work in our brave little Austrian Republic. Nor do I find it in Herr Hitler's Reich. Seems to be missing from Stalin's Russia, too, come to think of it. So, I think it's rather important we hear what our Czech comrade has to say about the situation, whether we agree with him or not. You coming?'

We made a day of it, taking a picnic and joining the crowds who had gathered at Sydney's Domain to listen. Troubled by his broken limb, not to mention that the gentleman who introduced him died of a heart attack while on the podium, Mr Kisch delivered a brief message urging a united front against Nazi Germany. But Dad, with Scylla, Eric and me in tow, managed to corner him afterwards. Amidst fond reminiscence, he raised the subject of the Berlin fire.

'The fire?' echoed Mr Kisch. 'The Nazis enjoy theatricals. Do not believe the German press, Herr Raye. It was a false flag.'

'Giving gammon, eh?'

'Poppycock,' scowled Eric whom Dad henceforth called 'The Red'.

16

A Hundred Suspicions

'I WISH YOU WOULDN'T keep calling him that, Dad. Eric's not a communist,' I complained some months later.

'Every Fascist's a communist in fancy dress,' Dad shrugged.

'Just because he holds different ideas to you doesn't mean you should tease him. You'll end up like grandfather, especially if you start sniping at him about religion.'

'You bringing up religion? This is getting serious. Fancy him, do you?'

'I think he's rather sweet,' I blushed.

'An Alpha Plus, eh?'

'A what? He's a Unitarian, if you want to know— Not that it matters.'

'Unitarian? Hmmm... And what does he do with his time? Tangos and stacking tin cans?'

'Stop putting him down! The past few years haven't been easy for him. Imagine exchanging a mansion for a few tiny rooms above a shop; having the best private school education and no career; having to give up studying overseas and return to ruin. It's not his fault his parents went under.'

'You met them?'

'They're nice.' Mr and Mrs Rudd managed their tiny corner store as a version of their former showrooms: the shop was spick and span; customers were treated as royalty; Mr Rudd père wore his one remaining double-breasted suit; Mrs Rudd coiffed her hair herself. 'And as you well know, they weren't the only ones to suffer from the banker's conspiracy.'

'The what?'

'That's what Eric reckons the Crash was about: International Jewish banking firms manipulating the economy to bring about societal collapse – a sort of revolution from the top down.'

'Told you he was a Communist. He's too much time on his hands.'

'At least he's looking for work.'

'How long've you known him? Eighteen months? And he still hasn't a proper job. And your compassion doesn't help. He's a layabout. Had a pretty good time of it in Berlin, it seems, from what I gather...'

'Have you been checking up on him?'

'A not very eligible young man shows untoward interest in my only daughter, and she asks whether I've been checking up on him? Too right I have. Where's he taking you tonight?'

'*The Mystery of Edwin Drood*, followed by *I'll Love You Always* at the Capitol.'

'Crime and romance, eh? You don't want to miss that. Bring him in for coffee when you come home.'

'I hate to think what he wants to talk to you about,' I warned Eric that evening as we walked home arm in arm. 'He grilled me about you before I left.'

'Well, do I have news for him. Got me a job as a clerk with P&O.'

'Eric! You're not serious! Really?'

'Start on Monday. Means I'll have access to their passenger archives. Never know, perhaps Eileen Stern sailed on the *Orsova*, or the *Ballarat*, or—'

'Oh, Eric! You champion!'

Dad and Scylla were playing Bridge with Mr and Mrs Epstein when we announced our good news.

'Shipping clerk?' Dad continued to peruse his cards, 'What sort of a job is that? Four spades, by the way.'

'Four spades! Four spades! Dad, you criticise him for not having a proper job. Now he finally has a proper job, and you denigrate him. Don't you see how important this is? Eric will be able to look through records. If he finds anything, we can notify the police and they can resume the investigation!'

'What's your response, Cill?'

'Six spades. Roddy, listen to Phoebe.'

'Yes, Dad, listen. We have a witness— well, we had a witness, and we have evidence. If we have—'

'We might have a hundred suspicions, Possum, but they don't make a crime. Without a confession, any evidence you dish up is circumstantial. The violin in the attic? We only have your word for it, which counts for little because of your age at the time. The medicine? It was never tested. We might assume Nurse Hicks is correct, but it has nothing to do with Lina. The note is a forgery, and of that Lina is capable; yet only she can testify as to whether she wrote it. The contradiction between the note's contents and your mother's diary entry is the only indication of murder; but nothing will explicitly connect Lina save her own free admission. Same applies for any shipping records.'

'Why must you always play devil's advocate?'

'Because our case has to be foolproof if we are to succeed. And the only way we can succeed is with a confession—'

'Which we can obtain if—'

'If. *If* we find her. You're right. Find Lina and we have a chance. Shipping records won't tell us where she is.'

'But they'll indicate at least where she went. And then—'

'All right, all right, settle pettle. So then, if we knew where she was, what would you do?' Dad scrutinised me from over the top of his pince-nez.

'I would seek her out immediately and make her confess.'

'You'd scour Europe for her, would you? And then?'

'I would bring her to a court of law and see her hang!'

'And *that's* what I'm afraid of!' He slammed his cards on the table, and his dark eyes flashed. My head was too full of the gallows to articulate any further argument. Besides, why should I have to argue my case? Ailine was guilty, therefore she should hang. Surely, he could not oppose that?

'It's only fair,' Eric began.

'Fair?' Dad pounced on him.

'Well— I mean, she murdered— She ought to hang.'

'You've given the matter thought, haven't you? And tell me, Mr Rudd, why are you so interested?'

'Roddy, Eric's right. And Phoebe needs to see justice done,' Mrs Epstein urged.

'A noose around anyone's neck is not justice, Annie.'

'Lina murdered her own sister – your wife and Phoebe's mother – and you're prepared to let her get away with it? Do you care more for her than for your nearest and dearest?'

'I care for them all. Pause a minute, Annie. Do you think that because a dear friend has betrayed your trust, and has harmed those you love, you have a right to see her hang? Lina's punishment will come in due course: if not in this life, it will come in the next.'

'Don't you think that a trial might precipitate the outcome for which you hope?'

'And what might that be? Annie, you can't guarantee how the case would proceed in court. Without a confession, the evidence is insufficient to convict her. And who's to say Lina will confess? I can't testify on grounds of health— too easy for the defence to prove I was of unsound mind; nor will I put my daughter in a position whereby her testimony is critical to the outcome she desires. If Lina's convicted, Phoebe'll gloat over the gallows; if acquitted, she'll drown in guilt.'

'You cannot protect her, Roddy.'

'I can; and I will. She's my daughter.'

'You cannot protect her from herself. I hate to think what

Phoebe will do if the case fails to proceed. And having you turn your back on it exacerbates the problem.'

'I am not turning my back!'

'Perhaps we could write to friends abroad,' suggested Mr Epstein. 'Those who survived the War.'

'Not many of those left, Schwammi.'

'But someone might know of Lina's whereabouts. It might take time, but it would be worthwhile, yes?'

'Perhaps. But Lina had a different circle of friends. Meanwhile, all we can do is look to ourselves. Regardless of the resolution, in whatever form it takes, be it now or hereafter, forgiveness is paramount.'

'Forgiveness, Dad? She murdered my mother!'

'She murdered my wife!'

'You don't care about Maman!'

'Now just a—'

'Then why did you marry *her*?' I pointed to Scylla and relished the outcry I had longed to hear. 'Phoebe!' Mrs Epstein protested, while Eric let out a soft whistle. 'How could you? Now you're going to abandon poor Maman forever! And me! You don't care about me, either! You only care about yourself: your comfort, your pleasure, your amusement, how you can wittily outsmart—'

'*That* is untrue!' he seethed.

'Roddy, sh,' Scylla reached across the card table and patted his hand, 'Let her alone. She's upset.'

'Phoebe has neither your patience, nor your forbearance, Roddy,' Mrs Epstein added, 'Nor did you possess those qualities at her age. And look what happened!'

'With the result that she knows the price of folly and the consequence of passion.'

'I wouldn't bank on it.'

'You cannot make me forgive, Dad!'

'No, I can't. But I can show you how. Possum, over the years I've been stripped of everything: my legs, my livelihood, my integrity. But come what may, no one can take away my right to choose. And I will choose what I know to be right. Years ago, I broke my marriage vows and left your mother in her darkest moment. I drove my dear wife to attempt suicide. And she forgave me, wretch that I am. Do you have any idea what it is to be forgiven like that?'

'But you were sorry, Dad. I doubt Ailine is.'

'And that is why her sincere and free confession is vital—'

'Sincere and free confession?' scoffed Mrs Epstein. 'Lina is not some noble tragic in a Russian novel. She will lie and scheme, and manipulate—'

'Like some villain in a Russian novel, eh?'

'Which is why she must be punished!'

'Punished, yes. Hanged, no. Forgiven, always.'

'But she's not sorry, Dad!'

'How do you know? Whether or not she is makes no difference to me. Regardless of the wrong, regardless of Lina's disposition, regardless of the outcome, I will honour your mother's memory by extending her mercy. I will forgive. I do forgive.'

'And I do not!'

17

A Proposal

ITHOUT THE DIRE possibility of the gallows, Dad might have exercised more determination regarding Ailine's arrest and prosecution; but he could not bear the idea of a hanging. Should a verdict of guilty be delivered, there would be little ground for appeal. The deliberate substitution of drugs, along with the forged note, testified to cold-blooded murder. Life imprisonment, therefore, was unlikely. Once convicted, Ailine would hang by the neck until she was dead.

Nor could he be certain that fear of such punishment would guarantee repentance on Ailine's part; and with that assessment, I agreed. Whatever remorse Ailine might have for her crime more likely would stem from having been found out rather than from any consideration of its gravity, both essentially and consequentially, in this world and the next. Ailine was a law unto herself. She had no belief in God, and was contemptuous of any doctrine concerning Death, Judgment, Heaven, Hell, and Purgatory. If those were her beliefs so be it, I reasoned. Dad, however, was staunchly Catholic; and the duty of Charity, coupled with his eschatological convictions, demanded he consider Ailine's final destiny. He did not wish her to endure the flames of Hell for all eternity.

Nothing I could say would convince him to leave Ailine to her fate in the name of justice and right. 'It's not justice, and it's not right,' he retorted.

'But murder is a vile and wicked act. Ailine knew she would hang if she were caught. That's why she must be condemned.'

'You're quite right, Possum,' he agreed for once. 'Murder is vile and wicked. I cannot fathom the degree of hate, the utter lack of regard for life, the extent of pride that could drive someone to think they have a right to determine another's end. But tell me this: is execution any different?'

'The despicable nature of the crime justifies despicable punishment.'

'An eye for an eye?'

'Ailine murdered Maman. Ailine deserves to die.'

'I see. So, hate and vengeance, masquerading as justice, constitute the twofold ply of your hangman's noose? Seems as much a prideful determination of your aunt's end as murder. Lina shouldn't be given a chance to right the wrong?'

'How can she? Since Maman didn't get a second chance at life, Ailine should be flung into the bloody mire of Hell's Fifth Circle.'

'Your Faith's tied with pink tape, eh?'

'The possibility of an afterlife is one of the few notions that justify my belief in God.'

'And the marvel of Divine Mercy is what justifies mine. I've lived long enough to learn that there's a certain economy about life. I don't know how this will all pan out, Possum, but I am convinced that nothing happens that is not intended for our salvation. And that applies to Lina as much as it does you and me. Lina might murder,' he concluded, 'but I am a better man than that.'

'And a stubborn one.'

'He's like the cat that walks alone,' Scylla sighed when out of sheer frustration I complained to her, 'Cannot be tamed, cannot be lured, cannot be bribed; will only respond to the highest ideals; and even then, he'll do it on his own terms. You won't change him, Phoebe.'

'But it's not right!'

'Phoebe, I'm not going to argue about it, but I will say this: Your father's a fine man. Given all that he has endured, he could have been angry and bitter, but he isn't. Instead, he has the strength of character to do good in the face of evil. I love him for it; and, for better or for worse, I will stand by him. What about you?'

I refused to talk to him and found any excuse not to be home. When we were not playing quartets at Lucy and Wally's home in Lewisham, Eric and I danced the night away. I made a point of rising late, took my meals apart, and practised much of the day. Since I was sufficiently independent, I considered moving out altogether.

'And would that be wise, Phoebeen?' Lucy asked one afternoon, 'He'd miss you terribly, I'm thinking.'

'I wouldn't ostracise your father however much you disagree with him,' Wally cautioned, 'And you've got to admit he has a point: whatever the outcome, you have yourself to deal with.'

'Which doesn't justify inaction,' I replied.

'You can be sure the bad deed will catch up with the evil doer,' Lucy moralised.

'No, you can't. I bet Ailine's laughing somewhere in a Paris alley, thinking how clever she is.

'She could be dead, for all we know,' shrugged Wally.

'How I wish!'

'And if she is, you've worried yourself silly for nothing.'

'We can always count on you to be positive, can't we, Wally.'

'The sooner we find her, the sooner we'll know,' concluded Eric.

'Haven't you found anything in the shipping records?'

'Haven't been idle, Phoebe. Promise.'

Upon arriving home, I tip-toed down the hall to avoid Dad who was in his study.

'That you, Poss?' he called.

I glanced at his partially written letter. What tricks was he up to now? All I could translate from the German was *may it please your Eminence*, written in his post-War left-handed italic.

'You know where these came from?' Dad fondled the Rosary next to his inkwell. 'They were a gift from Archduke Karl von Österreich as he was at the time.'

Here we go again, I sighed. Another lecture on the Austrian royalty. I knew it well: Archduke Karl succeeded Emperor Franz Josef to the throne in 'sixteen, at the height of the War. Immediately, he set about providing relief to his people who were cold and starving; and attempted to negotiate an end to the conflict, only to be driven out of Austria following the revolutions two years later. 'Didn't abdicate like the German Kaiser,' Dad explained one former occasion, 'so technically he still holds office— Well, his son does, Crown Prince Otto. Emperor Karl died in 1922, aged only thirty-five, while exiled in Madeira, having made an unsuccessful attempt to reclaim the throne of Hungary'. The restoration of the Habsburgs was the solution to the European crisis, he maintained. Dad followed the monarchical situation obsessively, mainly via correspondence, and was delighted to learn of the recent relaxation of laws which had prohibited select members of the royal family from entering their former domains.

'European crisis? It's all in his head,' Eric once scoffed when I told him.

'If he had his way, Dad would revive the Holy Roman Empire,' I replied.

'Which was neither Holy—' he nudged.

'Nor Roman—'

'Nor an Empire!' we both laughed.

'You remember Archduke Karl?' Dad prompted.

'How could I forget?' I murmured as I examined my fingernails. My polish had chipped.

'Happened after a concert – Mendelssohn Concerto – the night you were born. Announced your arrival to the audience before my encore. Archduke Karl came backstage to offer his congratulations. He had recently become a father again himself – we were roughly the same age, you see. Sensing I was lonely without Maman, he invited me to lunch. Turned out a very pleasant afternoon. Talked of federation, would you believe. Given the situation of the Australian colonies, he wanted to know my experience.

'Well, did I regret not paying attention at school! Sensed the issue was vital to him. Anyway, did my best. He in turn was impressed how a nation had been formed without bloodshed and had preserved its links with the Mother Country. After that, our conversation drifted to music, history, art, family, travel, and eventually faith. I told him I'd recently converted, how I was having doubts – for at that stage I did have doubts, and family opposition didn't help. He listened thoughtfully, and upon our parting reached into his pocket. Gave me these,' he nodded at the beads.

'"I will pray for you," he said, "And you, please, pray for me. You see, Herr Raye, we must help each other get to heaven. After all, that is what it is all about, yes?"

'Took the beads, of course – you don't refuse an archduke – although I found his innocence embarrassing. But, as is often the case, those awkward moments are the ones that make you think. Mind you, it took all the mud in Flanders to bring that one home. Packed those beads when I left for the trenches. Needed them then. Prayed that Rosary ever since: prayed for him, prayed for Jules and Cilla, prayed for you, and prayed for Lina— Yes, I pray for her. Kaiser Karl was right: we must help each other get to heaven, else what is it all about?'

'I've got to go, Dad. Eric and I are dining out.'

'Hold your horses, young lady. You see, Possum, I'm writing to Cardinal Innitzer of Vienna. There's been a call for testimonies regarding the holiness of Emperor Karl. They want to open his cause for canonisation – make him a saint. 'Bout time I wrote.

'Anyway, while compiling my thoughts, I realised how lucky I am to have had such opportunities— Sadly, through no fault of your own, you've not had the same good fortune. So, cut to the chase, I've decided it's high time we travelled to Wien.'

'What?'

'Wouldn't mind showing you the sights and taking you to some splendid concerts— Why, we could attend a concert every night, and two on Sunday! Not to mention theatres and coffee houses, and woods and mountains and gardens, and churches, palaces, and galleries. And that's but the beginning! Haven't mentioned the people you'd meet. You could even have a few lessons from old Rosé. Be nearly eighty by now. Be good to see him again. What about it?'

'Are you serious? When?'

'We'd go tomorrow if we could.'

'What about Scylla? I suppose you've already told her.'

'She's all for it. She can come, can't she? Listen: We'll spend a few months in Wien, for you to get a taste – make new friends, try a different way of life, learn more about where you fit in this big, wide, wonderful world. Then Cilla and I'll travel home, and you can decide whether you want to stay on. I've still the apartment there, so you needn't worry about where to live.'

'What about Eric?'

'Reckon he'll be here when you return, backside on his clerk's stool, scratching away in that shipping office.'

'When are you leaving?' Eric asked as we shared fish and chips at the quay, snuggled against the winter chill and watching the lamplight play on the water's inky ripples.

'Next year sometime.'

'Well, hopefully I'll have uncovered some clues by then.'

'I do hope so, Eric. You see, if we find anything— if Ailine returned to Paris, for instance— I could track her down.'

'Paris is a train ride from Vienna. Easy peasy. Wish I could come. Will you smuggle me?'

'If I did, Dad would toss you overboard. I'm going to miss you.'

'I'd stowaway for another kiss like that.'

'You don't have to come to Vienna for a kiss, silly.'

'Goody,' he hugged me and played with my curls. 'Kiss me again?'

'If you like.'

'You bet. And more. Phoebe, I've been meaning to ask you, and now's as good a time as any. I love you, and I think you're the most beautiful girl in the world,' he brushed the salt and oil from his hands, and knelt before me. 'I've got a job. It's not much, but it's a start. And if nothing better comes along, I can work my way up.'

'Whatever you do, I'll support you all the way. You know that, don't you?'

'I know.' And he brandished a diamond ring. 'It's only paste; but will you marry me? I'll buy you a proper rock as soon as I can.'

'I'm giving my consent only because if I don't there'll be more trouble!' Dad declared after Eric requested his permission. 'You're twenty-one, so I can't prevent you. But there'll be no wedding until after we return from Wien. Give your bloke time to sort himself out. A shipping clerk for a son-in-law! Hardly know his parents.'

'Perhaps you ought to do something about that.'

A reasonably pleasant dinner ensued. Dad and Scylla were hospitable and charming, Mr and Mrs Rudd well-mannered and cordial; although I sensed that everyone was making best of the situation. The Talk followed, with Dad putting a few hard words on Eric regarding his marital obligations. If he wished to marry me, he would have to convert.

'And while Mr Rudd is preparing himself, I'll prepare you by taking you abroad.'

'You don't want me to marry him, do you, Dad?'

'Well, I'm not going to marry him.'

'I'm sorry, Eric, I didn't expect him to be so churchy!' I sighed.

'You're his only daughter. He wants the best for you.'

'But to make you talk with the priest— All those classes! I can't believe he thinks you've not been properly baptised. He's such a fusspot!'

'It doesn't matter. Honestly it doesn't. I'm marrying you, and that's what's important.'

'You're awfully good about it.'

'I'd go to the moon for you.'

'You don't have to do that. The moon is already here in your arms.'

'And what a beautiful moon she is! And when we marry, she'll soon be a full moon.'

A few weeks later, and much to Dad's delight, a letter arrived from Vienna: the first overseas reply to his announcement of our trip.

'Is it from Professor Rosé?' I asked.

Dad shook his head. 'From young Hubert. Baron Franz-Hubert Maria Schütze von Rechtschaffen. Hubie for short. He's my godson,' he added with considerable relish.

'Your godson?' I could not help my testy emphasis of that last word. As always, the most surprising information he delivered in the most candid fashion.

'What's more, his father's your godfather.'

'I didn't know I had any godparents, let alone your having a godson.'

'You? Godparents? Of course! Herr Professor Kurt Schütze, and his wife Baroness Klara von Rechtschaffen. Had it all arranged before you were born, only the kerfuffle in Europe made it impossible for them to attend your Baptism, which would otherwise have been in Vienna. Annie and Reuben stood in their stead.'

'So, are you telling me now that the German soldier in that

painting in the studio is my Godfather?'

'That's right.'

Kurt Schütze, or 'Schützie' as in warming to his subject Dad preferred to call him, was originally from Bavaria, and had studied oboe and bassoon at the Vienna Academy, which was where he met Dad. Religious to the point of excess, he had been victim of a constant barrage of taunts, questions, and arguments on Dad's part, which was hardly a recipe for friendship; but somehow the man managed to survive. He even won a few rounds. Indeed, Dad attributed his conversion in part to his friend's long-suffering and thoughtful counter-argument.

Meanwhile, they attended concerts, played in orchestras and ensembles, holidayed and hiked together, and made the rounds of balls and parties. Dad was Best Man at Schützie's wedding and became godfather to his second son, which latter gesture he reciprocated when I was born. But that was life before the War.

Then, in 1918, amidst the carnage and confusion of the Western Front, they chanced to reunite when Kurt Schütze, serving under Crown Prince Rupprecht, was taken prisoner. Dad escorted him to camp. An auspicious coincidence, it enriched not only Dad's supply of cigarettes (for health reasons, Schützie did not smoke), but also his understanding of matters pertaining to the Sixtus affair, the Austrian attempts to negotiate an early peace, the revolution in Russia, and the desperate situation in Vienna. After the War, Kurt Schütze became a Professor of Music at the Vienna Academy and Principal Oboe in the Vienna Philharmonic. He was also patriarch of quite a large family.

'Reckon there's about six little Schützies. Haven't seen Hubie since he was a babe in arms. We've enjoyed a regular correspondence over the years. Been a while since I heard from him. Odd that... Interesting young man...'

'How?'

'Why do you want to know? I thought you were getting married.'

'That is the idea. Although you've done nothing about it. You could at least set a date.'

'Crikey!' he muttered, stubbing his cigarette. The news perturbed him so much that he hurriedly excused himself and spent the remainder of the morning in his study. He re-emerged with an envelope in hand and set off in his determined way to the post office.

18

Pack Up Your Troubles

D AD DECIDED WE WOULD LEAVE the following March, which meant we would arrive in Vienna by Easter. The very thought of an Austrian spring had him singing 'Wien, Wien nur du allein' as he pottered about. Then, a foretaste of what was to come arose when the Vienna Boys' Choir arrived in Sydney. The organisers were much in need of a translator, and at a loss how to entertain a bunch of energetic Austrian youngsters. Someone remembered Dad having connections and requested his services. At concerts and parties, I witnessed much bowing, smooth-talking, and nonsensical pleasantry – *Gemütlicheit*, Dad called it.

Scylla suggested we host an afternoon tea for the choristers. Mr Epstein, whose family owned a bakery in Vienna, assisted her in preparing treats our guests were bound to enjoy. It was a happy occasion, with boys running through our house and playing games on the lawn with Eric; the garden drenched in late-winter sunshine; Dad in the best of humour; Scylla radiant, capably supplying conversation and cake as required. Weaving in and out of cheerful groups, all chatting in German, offering biscuits, cake and lemonade, I wondered how my family might have been had Maman lived, and I had been raised in Vienna.

But what was the world coming to that we required passports? 'Bureaucratic rigmarole!' Dad declared. 'Could travel anywhere before the War, no questions asked!' Still, he had no qualms about playing his Viennese citizenship to his advantage, dining with the Austrian consul, and penning lines to persons in high places to secure tickets to operas, concerts, and plays. Come Christmas, he was exhausted, and for the first time in eight years he declined to sing in the *Messiah*. Scylla recommended we cancel our annual trip to the Rat, but Dad was adamant about seeing his family. He was much revived by the festivities, bursting into the drawing room for afternoon tea singing 'Drink, Drink let the toast start!' at the top of his voice, while arching an eyebrow at Grandfather; and teasing his nephews and nieces by not reacting when they stamped hard on his wooden feet, then feigning paroxysms of agony at the gentlest touch. Indeed, that Christmas was a truly Dickensian celebration with carols, charades, and musical chairs; a family feast of jokes, stories, and recollections. How happy we all were!

Two weeks later, Grandfather died at the ripe old age of ninety-eight.

The second trip took its toll. Wearied by the mid-summer heat, Dad found walking unbearable; nor was a two-day journey in a cramped railway carriage a recipe for comfort or consolation. It was hot as Hell. A respectful funeral was held, despite it being a hundred degrees in the shade. Following the wake, the immediate family gathered for the will, after which Dad withdrew in silence and plodded upstairs to his room.

'Not now, Poss,' was his only response to my query.

From outside his locked door, I heard him sob.

'Dad!' I called.

But only Scylla he permitted to enter.

'What happened?' I asked Aunt Rachel.

'Grandfather disinherited him.'

In keeping with family circumstances, Grandfather had altered his will several times over the years; but from 1913, all that pertained to Dad remained intact. Grandfather did not jest when he declared that not a cent of his would line the coffers of Rome; and while his youngest son remained a Roman Catholic he would never enjoy his father's hard-earned wealth. 'Of course, it's not the money he cares about,' Scylla later explained, 'It's the resentment behind it. Your father's shattered. He thought he had made his peace with your grandfather years ago. Not so, it seems. Talk about ruling from the grave.'

'Can he contest the will?'

'It's tighter than a hangman's knot. Now, Phoebe,' she held up a warning finger, 'It's not the family's fault. There is little point in taking out your anger on them.'

'I don't ever want to come here again!'

'How do you think they feel? For now, it's up to us to stand in your father's place and carry on. He's too distressed to face anyone at present; but, I tell you, there is not a bitter bone in his body. Are you with me?'

The family hushed as we entered the dining room. Scylla brought the full measure of her classroom experience to bear on the situation. Quickly, but calmly, like a teacher returning to class after a playground fight, having comforted the victim and sent the bully to the principal's office, she glanced at the maid and smiled at the family gathered around the damask spread table laden with silverware, crystal, and gilt-edged china.

'He's resting,' was all she said, which comment assuaged Grandmother and Aunt Rachel, who clearly were worried as to how much guilt they would be made to carry.

'Would you like some water?' offered Aunt Rachel.

'Thank you,' Scylla replied, and proceeded to talk of our forthcoming trip as though she were presenting a lesson, answering the various polite inquiries intelligently and comprehensively. Perhaps her informed manner and jolly hockey sticks enthusiasm suggested that, like me, she was keen to get away; but she made no mention of the fact.

Her concerns she reserved for Dad who did not appear until breakfast. Although subdued, he could not resist a joke; and somehow the top of his boiled egg landed in Aunt Rachel's tea.

Aunt Rachel loved him for it.

'Better pack those kit bags,' Dad resolved.

The moment we arrived home, he set about further trip preparations. Scylla and I were each to have a new ensemble, and he happily helped us select fabrics and styles (particularly if we let him have the final say). Any extra purchases we could make in Wien where there would be plenty to delight us. I, in turn, refrained from pestering him about my wedding.

'I suppose everything really does happen in good time,' I mused as I curled up with my book in the window seat of our front parlour. Having visited Maman's grave that morning, we were enjoying a lazy February afternoon at home. Whatever grudge Grandfather bore, Dad did not return it. 'Would you have felt differently if we were not so comfortably off, Dad?' I ventured to ask one day. 'Wealth and poverty are each binding in their way, Possum; but nothing is as soul-stifling as resentment.'

'He's right. No matter what happens, we can choose how things affect us. Perhaps time will also tell what happens regarding Ailine. How I wish Eric would find those records! Or maybe Fate will guide Justice down a different path. If Ailine is not caught, tried, and punished for murdering Maman, she might be convicted for some other crime. Frank and Cora got away with murdering Nick the Greek, but who knows what will happen next?' I thought as I avidly turned the page.

The doorbell rang. It was the postman. 'Funny that the postman should call when I am reading a novel which has nothing to do with a postman, despite having postman in the title. Modern fiction,' I smiled as I laid my book aside and answered.

'Letter for Mr Roderick Raye, Esquire, M.M.,' he began. He was not our usual man, and his announcement dwindled into a query, for he became distracted by the plaque on the front of the house. 'Schönbrunn?' he stared at the gold Gothic letters on their jet-black ground, 'That's German, i'n' it?'

'Austrian,' I replied. 'It's named after a palace in Vienna.'

'Mean anything?'

'It means beautiful spring.'

'Don't see any spring,' he observed, perusing the garden.

'It's out the back.' It would be taking irony too far, Dad had once remarked, to call the house Schönbrunn and not have a spring of some sort.

'Oh,' grunted the postman.

'Phoebe, mit wem sprichst du?' Dad called, and I heard the soft rubber 'puck' of his stick as he clomped down the hall.

'Er ist nur der Postbote, Vati,' We had been conversing in German since our return from the Rat.

'Grüß Gott,' Dad bowed. 'Du hast für mich schon unterschrieben, Phoebe?' He hooked his stick over his crippled arm, fixed his pince-nez, and perused the envelopes in question. 'Ah, gut! Der österreichische Konsul in letzter Sekunde! Danke schön, mein guter Herr,' he let his glasses dangle from the ribbon fastened to his waistcoat, nodded at the postman, and took up his stick. 'Grüß Gott,' he bowed and puck-clop-clopped back inside.

'Bloody Gerry,' the postman mumbled.

Given our high rate of correspondence, it was little wonder the postman called again next morning. Dad made a point of answering. I peeked out the drawing room window and braced myself for the exchange.

'Mornin',' he drawled with his usual 'heat 'n flies' economy.

'Military Medal?' The postman needed to reconcile the 'M.M.' behind 'Roderick Raye, Esquire' with the suspicious, Gothic inscription on the façade, as well as with the man who now greeted him with such a broad accent, whereas yesterday he spoke perfect Deutsch.

'Bellicourt,' Dad explained.

'Gallipoli,' responded the postman. 'Third Infantry.'

'Thirteenth Light Horse.'

'Devil's Own?'

'That's the one. You collect stamps?'

'My son does.'

'Arf-a-mo.'

Dad returned with an envelope. The previous postman had been an avid philatelist, and Dad had always saved his stamps for him.

'Seems Herr Hitler's a bit of a Wagnerphile,' Dad mused as the postman examined its contents. 'Can't say I share his enthusiasm. That's Parsifal. You like Wagner?'

'What's this say?'

'Wise man,' I thought. Had the postman offered an opinion on Wagner, he would never have completed his rounds.

'Hmmm, "Die Saar kehrt heim!"' Dad read. '"The Saarland comes home!" Chickens more like, I reckon. Now, I wonder, could I ask a favour? I've a letter here needs posting. Would you be so kind?'

The postman took the letter, thanked him for the stamps, and bid him good day. Dad glanced at the front window and winked at me. To return to Frank and Cora would be futile. Within seconds he would enter to share his little joke and report on the news to hand. But there was an odd silence; and before I could enquire, I heard his stick clatter.

'Dad?'

Amidst scattered letters he stooped, unable to speak, his good hand clutching his heart.

19

Shipping News

THE BLUE NUNS at the Lewisham Hospital said Dad had suffered a heart attack; and while they attended him, I attended to his admission forms. What did they expect me to say? Admittedly, few words were required. Yet such concise responses produced a most inaccurate picture of his person and character, which would render the medics' impression of him totally false and their treatment of him inappropriate. Oh dear! How could Dad be reduced to a form?

'Phoebe!'

Wally, in his white doctor's coat, jogged to my side. His preliminary inquiry as to my reason for being at the hospital he immediately substituted with a concerned, 'Is everything all right? And what about Cilla? Does Cilla know?'

'Not yet. I haven't had a moment, and I've no money for the telephone. She's at Mark Foys' and is meeting a friend there for afternoon tea.'

'I'll send a boy with a note. Would you like to telephone Eric? Here's a couple of pennies. Shall I tell Lu? You know we're only a stone's throw away. Pop in for a cup of tea or a meal or—'

I cut him short with a thank you.

'Chin up, Phoebe. Your father's in the best of care.'

'He's not going to die, is he?' I demanded of the nun who arrived at my side.

'He has requested a priest, Miss Raye. That is all.'

Father Moran passed me, greeted me briefly as was his custom, and continued along the hospital corridor, his purposeful stride concealed by his cassock, his vials and viaticum in his leather bag. A regular visitor to our home, he usually joined us for a meal, a liqueur, and some healthy intellectual discussion. Now he was to perform the Last Rites. Was it more important that Dad see him and not me?

Another vast white habit and sky-blue veil sailed toward me, her face a fixed and solemn figurehead.

'Is he— Has he—?'

'He's resting,' soothed the nun. 'You may see him, but he needs to stay calm. Come.'

That Dad was the sole patient in a small ward relieved me much. He needed privacy. Without his legs he looked like a child in bed.

'He's been through a lot,' the nun whispered as she glanced at the wooden legs propped in the corner.

'Felix Culpa, he calls them,' I welcomed her inquiry. 'Dad used to say it was a Happy Fault he came home from the War. The left leg's Felix because it's his good leg, and the right leg's Culpa because it used to jam on him when he first got it. Don't know what sort of Happy Fault he's going to see in this, though.'

'They're a hardy lot, those boys from the bush,' the nun smiled, 'Although, from what I've seen, that War added twenty years to their lives. I'll leave you with him. Quiet now, remember.'

'Tell God your plans, eh?' Dad murmured.

'God may be laughing, Dad, but I most certainly am not. Are you comfortable?'

'Listen, Poss,' he struggled to speak, 'if things don't work out, promise you'll go to Wien for my sake, won't you?'

'Of course, I'll go, Dad. I promise. You'll come too if you rest.'

He drifted back to sleep, much weakened by his efforts. I stroked his hand and found it softly shaped around his rosary. Unable to pray myself, I, too, folded my hands around it and hoped that if he was praying in silence, he was praying for us both, and that he would not die in the process.

A serene expression floated across his face. 'Ah Jules,' he sighed, drifting once more to consciousness. 'She was beautiful, you know... Your mother... Beautiful... Not all adazzle like some women... Beautiful deep inside... Beautiful... Come what may, Poss, always forgive... Better that way...'

❖❖❖

'I don't know what you were thinking when you filled out those forms, but they look like the front page of the *Times*!' Scylla hurried into the room.

'Shh! What could I write? They'll never look after him properly if they don't know all about him!'

'They'll find out soon enough. There, there, Phoebe. Poor girl! Does his family know?'

'I haven't spoken to anyone yet.'

'We ought to send a telegram.'

'I'll do it.'

'Are you up to it?'

'I suppose so. I need to call Eric, too. What should I say?'

'Keep it simple if you can. Don't alarm them unnecessarily. Something like Roddy ill. Hospital. Serious but stable. How does that sound?'

'Don't alarm them?' I thought, 'They ought to be alarmed! Grandfather's bitter prejudice nearly killed Dad, and his family never came to his defence. Never have they stuck up for him! Cowards! Shame on them! And still he laughs and jokes and carries on, never burdening them with his troubles, while they are happy that he smiles. Now look what's happened! I hope they're sorry when they find out! And why is there never a working public telephone when you need one?'

'You just caught me,' Eric answered. 'What's up, Poss?' The line grew quiet as I garbled my unfortunate news, so quiet that I thought it had gone dead.

'Hello?' I called, 'Eric! Are you there?'

'Crikey! He's— he's not—?'

'He's in a serious but stable condition.'

'I'll come toot sweet.'

He waved as he swung off the crowded tram, his momentum propelling him to my side, and he spun me in his arms and kissed me.

'Any more news?' he asked.

'No. Scylla's with him, but she'll be leaving soon. Dad will be all alone, and there's nothing I can do. They won't let me stay. Oh Eric, I feel so useless!'

'There, there, Poss. You look ragged. Have you eaten?'

'No. Wally mentioned something about a cup of tea—'

'That's the ticket. Come on, we'll call on Lu. And while we're walking I'll tell you something that ought to cheer you up: I found her! Eileen Stern sailed from Marseilles to Sydney in December 1920, and departed on February—'

'Which coincides with the dates given by the hotel proprietor!'

'What's more— and this is the clincher: I checked the lists for 1927. Another Eileen Stern arrived in Sydney in October that year, again from Marseilles.'

'Which is when Ailine came out.'

'And she left the following September.'

'So, she went back to Paris after all,' I sighed.

'Aren't you pleased?'

'Of course!'

'You might have shown a little more gratitude. I've been

searching for months.'

'I know you have. And I am thankful. Only Dad's so ill. We'll have to call off the trip.'

'That's unfortunate— well, for you it is. Can't deny I'm a bit glad. Perhaps we can marry first and honeymoon overseas?'

'I can't make any plans. Not now. Oh bother!'

'Don't worry. It was foolish of me to suggest it. It's just that— Well, I hate having to wait, that's all.'

'Will you let yourselves in for I'm up to me elbows in salmon!' Lucy called from the kitchen. 'God between us and all harm, Phoebeen, what sad news about your da,' she wiped her hands on her apron, limped forwards with open arms and embraced me. 'I'll wet the tea and we'll sit and chat. Mary and the saints it's hot! You'd think the summer will never end, and when winter sets in summer cannot come soon enough. Wally said you might drop by so I'm making extra. You don't mind fish cakes, Eric, it being Lent and all? Now tell me all about it.'

My account of Dad's misfortune I ended with Eric's latest news, while Eric explained the considerable measures he took to access the information, and Lucy bumbled about with sugar and milk.

'He's been searching for months, Lucy, and now he's found the details that prove she was here when Maman died!'

'And may the cat eat the two of you!'

'I don't know why you're so annoyed.' When Lucy was angry she always invoked the cat.

'And I hope the devil eats the cat! Listen to you gabbling about the shipping and your poor dear da lying sick. And don't you go troubling him with your shenanigans. Can you not hire a detective? A— Who is it you been reading about?'

'Hercule Poirot?'

'Aye, one of them fellows. Any more news, Wally lad?'

'I checked how he was doing on my way out,' Wally made his greetings, kissing Lucy and welcoming Eric with a handshake. 'Fast asleep. He's all right, Phoebe. What's this?' he took the letter Lucy passed him from her apron pocket.

'It came this afternoon, and 'twas all I could do to refrain from opening it myself.'

Wally raised an eyebrow as he dubiously fingered the envelope.

'Wally-lad, you been waiting how many months, and when at last the letter comes you cannot bring yourself to lift a finger? 'Tis as good a time as any is it not?'

'What's it about?' I asked, but Lucy looked over her husband's shoulder and smiled while he read.

'I guess it's official, Lu,' Wally hugged her and laughed. 'We're going to Oxford!'

20

Bon Voyage

AND LUCY COMPLAINED of my shenanigans? Eric and I had been quite open about our investigation; whereas she and Wally had been scheming for over a year, making secret applications to universities abroad. Wally wished to continue his research into disease and had so impressed some Oxford institution with his findings on tuberculosis that he was offered a place.

'Reckon last season's haul of wickets played a part?' Dad asked when Wally told him his news during his rounds of the wards.

'If it did, then at least it's been good for something, Mr Raye. Speaking of hauls...' he glanced at Dad's bedside table where jars of lemon curd and potted meat propped up handmade get-well-soon cards featuring children's drawings of flowers, pirates, and horses.

'Could open a shop.'

'Don't know there's a demand for aspic.'

'Any more of that calf's foot jelly, Possum?'

'No, Dad. Mrs Stubbs sent some rose hip jam,' I produced another jar from my basket.

'Must be getting better. Tell Cill to bring scones when she comes.'

'Well, I'm pleased to say your blood pressure's down,' Wally undid the strap from Dad's arm, 'Bit more bed rest and you'll be right as rain.'

'When do you set sail, Doctor?'

'May. Give us a few months to settle in before term starts.'

'Got a job for you, Poss,' Dad whispered with a shifty look the moment Wally departed, 'Fish in my trouser pocket and you'll find a key. Now, that key opens a box at Stanmore Post Office. Will you check it once a week while I'm tied up here and bring me anything you find?'

Curious myself as to its prospective contents, I took to going daily, just in case. I found the post box empty, which fact seemed to please Dad more than if a letter were deposited.

'What's it about, Dad?' I asked.

'A personal matter,' he replied. 'And whatever you do, don't tell Cilla.'

Five weeks later, having celebrated his forty-sixth birthday with a dram of smuggled kirsch, and having charmed every member of the medical staff, Dad came home. Frail, a little greyer, relying more heavily on his cane, he lingered in the front garden, surveying with mellow pleasure the mass of pansies and petunias which he never expected to see again, and complimented the gardener for his work. His moustache having grown too thick for his liking, he rectified the next morning with a trip to the barber, which earned him a school-ma'amish scolding from Scylla who was wary of him over-exerting himself.

That he should take an overseas holiday the doctors heartily endorsed. A long sea voyage would be restorative, provided he didn't handle the trip details. Scylla rebooked our passage for July, while Dad envisaged a glorious autumn filled with concerts and operas and walks in the woods, followed by a white Christmas. Naturally, we would remain in Vienna for Carnivale, and he insisted upon having ball gowns made and purchasing fur coats (we were going to need them). Come Spring, we would resume our tour, bringing it to a fitting conclusion by spending the following May with Lucy and Wally in Oxford.

'What about our wedding?' Eric asked as we lay on the beach, soaking up the dregs of the summer.

'Dad won't discuss it until after we return, which means we won't be married before October. It's awfully long to wait, I know. And I've no idea when I'll look for Ailine. He's planned everything with such detail that I'll be lucky if I have a day in Paris. I'll have to fit in a side trip of my own while he and Scylla are busy elsewhere. Anyway, at least it gives you a chance to improve your credibility.'

'How do you mean?'

'Dad's being a frightful snob about me marrying a shipping clerk.'

'It's getting boring without the sleuthing. And I'll hate it if all that work comes to nothing.'

'I've been thinking, Eric. The Trocadero's opening soon. They're bound to be on the lookout for something novel. Why don't you form a tango band?'

'With you as my leading lady?'

'How did you guess? We could play a few duets and dance into the bargain.'

'What about the money?'

'I have some savings— quite a lot, actually. I could give you some money before I go. That way you could make a start with auditions, arrangements, and rehearsals. Then, when I return, we can work on our routines.'

'Sounds like a plan. You really are a sensation!'

'I would do anything for you.'

'Race you to the water!'

In early May, Mr and Mrs Sotheby held a party for Wally and Lucy. Typical of the Sothebys, it was a grand event with dinner, a dance band, and numerous guests.

'I wish my cousin had written sooner,' I heard Mr Rudd remark to Mr Epstein. 'Back in 'thirty-three I could have helped. No chance now. And your family? Are they concerned?'

Dad was holding a council of war with Mr Sotheby, manoeuvring salt cellars and cutlery, wine glasses and napkins to illustrate how the newly independent nations of Mittel Europa had little hope of withstanding a German invasion.

Mr Sotheby countered that such an invasion was unlikely, given that France and the Soviet Union had signed a pact. Germany wouldn't wage a war on two fronts again.

'Hmmm,' Dad perused his topography, 'Is that why Hitler's remilitarising the Rhineland?'

Not wishing to discuss bacteria with Lucy, Wally, and their medical chums; and having neither the patience nor the inclination to join Scylla and Mrs Rudd, who were listening to Mrs Sotheby's analyses of the latest fashions, I wandered onto the back verandah where Eric was smoking a cigarette. He offered me a light, and I joined his contemplation of the clear night sky.

'Been thinking of your little brainwave, Poss,' he interrupted my starry thoughts. 'Reckon that band's a goer. I'll advertise auditions in the paper and book a venue.'

'I know you can do it, Eric. And if we get a head start before I leave, I'll be able to help.'

'You're already helping enough. You are such an inspiration! Generous, too.'

'It's nothing. We'll work together. I'm looking forward to it. How much will you need?'

'About twenty pounds. Can you manage that?'

'Of course. I've two hundred saved. How soon do you need it?'

'What about Monday?'

Our lips just touched when someone coughed.

'Might I have a word, Mr Rudd?' Dad invited Eric inside. Following part of the way, I watched them enter a sitting room. I crept to the door and leant against it. Glasses clinked, and I thought I heard Dad say, 'Prosit'. Perhaps they were fixing a wedding date at last.

'I'll be looking forward to when you come next May,' Lucy appeared at my side. Beyond the word 'plans', there was no chance of my hearing more. 'Wally wants to visit Ireland before he starts,' she added after a pause.

'How do you feel about that?'

''Twill be good to see family again, but much has changed.'

'On both sides, I imagine.' Eric seemed to be talking about our proposed band.

'Aye. Would you mind if we sit?' Lucy brought me to a corner of the living room, far away from Dad and Eric's discussion. 'Listen, before I leave, Phoebe, I been meaning to tell you something me dad told me when me mam died,' she peered at me through her thick spectacles. 'There was an inquest, you know, and her death was pronounced an accident of war. The soldier, a captain in the British army, who authorised the shooting was also present. After the decision was handed down, he came to me da and apologised. Then he extended his hand and asked if there was any way he could help. Dad hesitated. The officer seemed genuine enough, and dad had to accept the situation as an accident. But the handshake could be misread by others who hated the British. Not that me da was that fond of them himself. Still, he decided to shake even though he might be shot for seeming a traitor. He slept well that night, knowing he had made peace. Fortunately, the officer was true to his word and helped us with our passage here. I suppose what I'm saying, Phoebeen, is that should you cross paths with your aunt, and should she extend her hand, I hope you'll do what is right. And may God grant you a sound sleep.'

'There you are!' Eric swaggered towards us. 'Been looking everywhere for you, Poss. Pardon me, Lu, but this little lady and I have something to celebrate. Strike me lucky, Phoebles, lookie here! One hundred pounds!'

He brandished a cheque, and tottered from the effort required to pull it from his suit pocket. 'A hundred pounds!' he called and waved the paper like a handkerchief. 'He gave me a hundred bloody pounds! And here I was thinking your old man a skinflint!'

'Eric, sh! Put it away!' I saw Lucy look aghast as I reached for Eric's arm. Eric stepped back, causing me to fall on him as if I were drunk. Sniggering, he whirled me onto the dancefloor and thrust his hips close.

The band was playing a foxtrot, but Eric persisted in dancing a tango. Every step became more serpentine, our curves and dips exaggerated and out of time. The room was more confined than the spacious halls to which we were accustomed, and as we smoothed our way round we collided with Mr and Mrs Sotheby.

'Eric, please,' I whispered, for I sensed a hush, not from

fascinated dance hall crowds as was often the case, but from family and friends. He grinned and plunged me so far backwards I could see Wally draw apart from his colleagues. Mr and Mrs Epstein had left the floor and were standing with Scylla. Thankfully, there was no sign of Dad. The band ceased. Eric remained suspended over me, his hold firm, reeking of whiskey. I turned my head and saw a walking stick.

'That'll be all for the moment, thank you, Mr Rudd,' Dad gave Eric a prod, handed him his stick and watched him blunder away. 'Miss Raye, may I have the pleasure?' he bowed.

'Can you manage, Dad?'

'Easy does it. Haven't danced a foxtrot since the War.' He nodded at the band master.

'I've never seen him drunk,' I whispered.

'Always a first time, and you're not to blame.'

By allowing me free rein, he masked his inability. I, in my turn, did my best not to render him a fool. I need not have worried; Dad knew what he was capable of. What a wonderful partner he must have been! Gifted with natural poise and grace; imbued with the rhythm and sense of the music; every faculty attuned. How handsome, and oh, how kind!

As I lay in bed that night, I remembered how Maman taught me to play some of Schubert's Llandler on the piano. We treated Dad to a concert. 'Brava!' he cheered, 'Encore!' And he invited Maman to dance. While I played, I heard their gentle laughs as they fumbled steps they thought were lost to them. Maman apologised that she was so clumsy. Dad chuckled at his errors.

'May I try, Daddy?'

'Of course! Permit me the honour, meine kleine Prinzessin,' he bowed.

Maman sat at the piano. Dad held out his hands: both hands. He became young again, and whole, dressed in white tie and tails, his chin cleanshaven, his dark curls falling rakishly over his forehead. I felt his right hand softly touch my back shoulder. No longer was I a little girl, but a woman in a black and gold gown. My own right hand I rested upon his left and we glided into a waltz, gently at first, for Maman played the Kaiser Walzer, sweeping and noble. Through a palace sun-filled and golden we danced, our feet borne by clouds, a full orchestra playing. But where was Maman? Where was she? Maman was crying. The orchestra lost first its soft bass pulse. The brass fell out of time with the percussion. Violins and cellos tangled their tunes. The flute played flat. Drums rumbled, shaking me hard...

Scylla, wrapped in her dressing gown, her hair in rollers, loomed over me. Her eyes were wet and bloodshot.

'Phoebe, I'm sorry to wake you. It's your father.'

Interlude

.

Vienna, Christmas 1956

'Buddy Holly gone to bed yet?' Peter yawned as he entered the kitchen.

'His light's on,' I sighed. 'I hope I haven't upset him again; but I had to tell it the way I saw it.'

'Let him work it out. Well, I'm calling it a night. Merry Christmas, Sonček.'[2]

Back in the living room, I curled up on the sofa, resumed my cross stitch and enjoyed the midnight calm, the happy slumber of husband and children. Hints of liqueur and cloves, the remnants of our celebration, mingled with the fresh pine and honey scents from the tree aglow with candles. On the sideboard opposite, a lamp illumined our nativity figures. Another lamp enabled me to stitch amidst restful darkness. I threaded my needle and continued to worry over the crack of light under the door at the far end of our apartment.

Young Roderick was still awake.

He arrived in November, the day the Soviets invaded Hungary; a short, slight young man, nineteen years old: a shy, scholarly version of the rockabilly, with dark curly hair and black horn-rimmed glasses, wearing an overcoat and tartan scarf undoubtedly picked by his mother. His violin identified him, and the apprehensive raising and lowering of the shoulders as he stood on the platform of Vienna's Westbahnhof railway station, trying to get his bearings in a foreign land, his passage complicated by the

---

[2] *Sonček*: (Slovenian) Sunshine.

Suez crisis.

Little Klem and Mellie could not hide their excitement at meeting their uncle from Australia; and their childish grammar and nonchalant blend of German and English put him at ease far more than my welcome.

But the moment we arrived home, Roddy launched his attack. Question upon question he fired about Dad and me, Maman and Ailine.

'Roddy, stop! Just stop!' I cried.

'I have a right to know!' he shouted.

To my initial relief he retreated into scales and German grammar, emerging only to silently partake of family meals. He had an audition to prepare. As the weeks passed, however, I concluded that solitude was both his preference and defence, and that sullenness came naturally to him.

I knew eventually I would have to tell my story for the children's sake. Without understanding the past, how else would they make sense of the present? How would they shape the future? But they were too young to know: Klem was eight; Mellie, six. Besides, we all needed this blessed time to wallow in childhood. Roddy, however, rolled in like a tank with revolving turrets ready to gun anything within the range of his inquiry. Viewing me through a periscope of Innocence, he fired in earnest, unaware of his capacity for destruction.

It was wrong of me to think him an enemy. He was my half-brother, after all. And how he resembled Dad! More disturbing, though, was that he had been mothered. It was the ease with which he leant against the kitchen table that I hated. Then I envisioned a whip in his hand. That was when I cried and shielded myself from him and hated myself for hating in the face of another opportunity to love. I never expected to have a brother to love; but I feared my story would enhance the disparity of our respective experiences and drive us apart.

His angry retort and subsequent aloofness compounded my dilemma. I had disturbed him as much as he had me. Why was he so morose? And he had a point: to a degree he was entitled to know. But did he have the capacity to understand?

'You will have to tell it sometime,' urged my conscience. So, I began to write, tentatively at first, fearing the permanence of my inscriptions. Odd words, random thoughts and memories I jotted on scraps of paper. Soon I was writing furiously while the children were at school, scribbling pages at dawn and in the dead of night.

It was an unusual Christmas present: a thick notebook accompanied by a curt letter of explanation – a far cry from his other package, the cable knit cardigan sent by air mail, Cilla's handmade gift. Still, he was politely receptive (he said nothing about the cardigan) and retired to his room like Eeyore with his balloon and empty pot.

'I didn't think anyone was up.'

Roddy stood in the shadows, slippers on his feet, his cosy checked dressing gown wrapped around striped flannel pyjamas, the top button of which was fastened against the cold.

'Would you like some mulled wine?'

'That'd be beaut. Thanks.'

'I suppose I can fill you in a bit,' he watched me warm the spicy brew. 'I was born here. In Vienna, I mean. Mum said she had to honour Dad's wishes and go. Why didn't you come?'

'I couldn't, Roddy.'

'Did you marry Eric— Mr Rudd, I mean?'

This time he had sense enough to stop probing.

'Apparently, Mum attributed her illness to grief, then sea sickness,' he continued, having respected my silence. 'Given her age, a baby was the last thing she expected.'

'I hope you didn't mind me calling her Scylla.'

'She often called you Charybdis. By the way, we used to call her Olive Oyl— Mrs Ep, I mean.'

'Mrs Epstein? Olive Oyl? I would have thought Pop-eye more appropriate— her glasses and all.'

'Nah, it was 'cause she's a perfect fifty-seven— nineteen-nineteen-nineteen. Bean-pole. I was christened Roderick Edward— Edward after the king, although that was a bit of a blue duck,' he muttered, looking down in self-deprecation.

'I thought Edward was in honour of your maternal grandfather.' And I watched him smile as he swirled his wine.

'I'm really sorry about Dad,' he resumed.

'He suffered a massive heart attack. I understand he didn't suffer.'

'I mean, you must have missed him terribly. Mum always said I was a blessing— mixed one, I reckon. But you— You must have been angry— That unfinished business with your mother.'

'It's all right, Roddy.'

'It's not all right! Growing up in that house was like living with ghosts: your mother, Dad, and you; but Mum couldn't bring herself to move. So, what happened? When did you come to Vienna?'

'The following year. Mind you, I didn't intend to stay.'

'Why?'

'Unfinished business.'

Part Two

•

Honi soit qui mal y pense

•

April 1937

Shame on him who thinks evil of it
Or
Evil be to him who thinks evil

Edward III, King of England, 1327-77
Motto of the Order of the Garter

21

Unfinished Business

'IT'S BEEN OVER A YEAR NOW and she's still in mourning,' I overheard Aunt Rachel in the front parlour.

'Lucy says she's written letter after letter, and no reply. She's very worried,' replied Mrs Sotheby.

'Same with that other friend of hers— Refused her offer of a month in the country— Wouldn't even see her when she came to visit, which was very inconsiderate. I said as much; and all Phoebe said in reply was that it was inconsiderate of Pim to presume her company was any comfort for the loss of her father. She's hardly worked the last year. When she does, she practises day and night for weeks on end until she exhausts herself. Afterwards, you'd think she'd never played in her life. I worry she'll have a breakdown— Or worse. I've hidden the medications. She should have gone with Cilla. Any news from Lucy?'

'One would think that after three years of marriage she'd be in the family way. But no. Although she does have news of Eric. He arrived in Oxford just before Christmas. It seemed that some calamity had befallen him in Berlin. Something about his family not meeting citizenship requirements, whatever that means.'

'Serves him right,' I thought as I gazed at the naked fingers of my left hand.

'I'm sorry, Poss,' Eric's words echoed across void and meaningless months, and I shivered at the memory. The night had been a cold one – unusual for October. Since Dad's funeral, I had hardly seen him. He was respecting my need to mourn, he said, his voice chill.

'But why should that stop you from visiting, Eric? I miss you!'

'There's no easy way to say this, but I should be honest. I can't marry you, Phoebe. There's someone else.'

'There's never been anyone else! What do you mean?'

'After I came back to Australia, I thought I'd never see her again. But an opportunity's come up. I've got a job with a cruise band. I'm going to start over in Berlin.'

'What? On Dad's generosity?'

'Like you, he wanted me to succeed. That's why he gave me the money. Surely, you don't want me to remain a clerk? Anyway, it would be caddish of me if I didn't admit my true feelings.'

'You don't love me?'

'I don't think you're the right girl. I didn't expect you to be so emotional—'

'My father's dead!'

'Anyway, I told you. There's someone else.'

'What's her name?'

'Frida.'

'It was callous of him, waiting until the poor girl was alone before breaking off the engagement,' continued Aunt Rachel, 'To make matters worse, he's back! Phoebe came home in hysterics after playing for a ball last Saturday night. Eric was there, in the company of another young lady.'

'No!'

'Roddy suspected he was a gold-digger. The moment Phoebe and Eric became engaged, he changed his will and tied up the money in a trust. Cilla said that the night Roddy passed away he gave Eric a cheque and told him to clear out and make something of himself. Well! So much for honouring a dead man's wishes. The scoundrel was right by Phoebe's side for the funeral, comforting her and treating her almost as an invalid; but, the moment he learned he couldn't lay a finger on her inheritance, he dumped her. Phoebe's fortune is hers alone, regardless of whom she marries. Now I wonder if she'll marry at all. She hasn't left the house since she last saw him.'

'Well, that's why we've come. Lucy says here that—'

I entered the front parlour to find not only Mrs Sotheby, but also Mr Sotheby taking tea with my aunt.

'Phoebe, love, you remember the Sothebys, don't you?' Aunt Rachel's banal welcome carried the assumption that either I was mentally deficient, or a child needing assistance with common courtesy. 'Come and have some tea, dear.'

'We're planning to spend a few months abroad and were wondering whether you'd like to accompany us,' Mr Sotheby began.

'Lucy's invited you,' added Mrs Sotheby.

'What a splendid idea!' accorded Aunt Rachel. 'A voyage! New sights, and old friends.'

'But I don't want to go to Oxford.'

'Think of the opportunity, dear.'

'I want to go to Vienna.'

'But—'

'How plainly must I speak?'

'I suppose that could be arranged,' considered Mr Sotheby.

'A few days in Vienna would be rather nice, Desmond.'

'Days? I want to live there!'

'I don't think that's very wise, dear,' advised Aunt Rachel.

'Why not? If Scylla can spend over six months in Vienna with her cousin and his wife, I'm quite capable of doing the same. I'm twenty-three, I'm independent, and I am fluent in German. I have people to visit, so I wouldn't be alone. Besides, it's what Dad wanted. I promised him. You can't—'

'Then what say you to this?' interrupted Mr Sotheby. 'Instead of sailing to Southampton, why don't we cruise to Const— Ah! Is-tan-bul they call it now. Then we could take the Orient Express via Vienna. Letty and I could spend a few days there to get you settled, continue to Paris, and thence to Oxford. You could join us later. How about a Parisian shopping spree as well as a Viennese one, Letty?'

We booked our passage for June.

The *Oronsay* sailed into a perennial Summer, every northward mile more temperate than the last. Upon embarking, I thought the great white liner a titan; but after a day's journey, it was a mere speck on a vast ocean expanse. Leaning over the deck, I shuddered to think of the strange creatures and ancient wrecks below: bodies tossed overboard, circling the globe, and dumped on foreign shores, their hopes and dreams dissolved in relentless tides. Once resonant with purpose, their insignificance was terrifying when measured against Time. Were there no Eternity, they would count for naught.

I passed through the cortex of passages to my cabin in the first-class lobe of the ship. Compact, it was conducive to privacy and thought; and its polished walnut cabinets with their chrome trims were like Dad's coffin. Locked in my cabin, with no one to love, I felt as good as dead.

But I had to live. I had unfinished business. Life, it turned out, had been Dad's parting gift to Scylla: a son – yourself, of course, Roddy. All he had given me was a post box key which I had returned, and Kaiser Karl's rosary. Of course, there was my substantial inheritance and all he had taught me over the years. But there was also a murder he had failed to resolve.

Mr and Mrs Sotheby, who possessed in equal measure that wholesomeness and decadence that seems to define English eccentricity, revelled in the weeks of wining and dining, games and sports, amusements and entertainments, and encouraged me to share their pleasure by inviting scores of young men to their table.

They all wanted something – I could sense it in the way they danced: the soft, slow pressure of their slimy hands; the energy coiled inside their physique; their eyes on quests they knew were barred to their bodies; their conversation frivolous or mundane. Did they think me a pipe? But if I told them I wished to avenge a murder, I would attract the worst of them. Else they would mock me. That a pretty woman, a wealthy woman, should toy with crime, was silly.

I preferred to feign sea sickness than friendship. However, as the humidity increased, I had genuine reason to take to my cabin. The ship crossed the Equator, and I left my fellows to their absurd rite of passage: a visit from 'King Neptune' (a crew member draped in seaweed, wearing a crown and holding a trident). Lying on my bed, I leafed through my scrapbook of notes and photographs which documented all I knew of Ailine. What did Dad ever see in her? I wondered as I studied her photograph. True, she was very pretty; but Dad had a knack of seeing into souls. Did he ever realise how fickle and self-centred she was? How decadent and deceitful?

And she once had a child of her own: Sabine, who died aged seven. Fancy abandoning her in an orphanage! And what did she get up to in Paris during the War? She claimed she had had an affair with Dad, which was a lie. But I suspected other affairs. After the War she sojourned in Morocco. Sometime in 1920, she returned to Paris where she received the letter Dad had written explaining his injuries. Then she came out to Australia under the name Eileen Stern. Why did she choose that name? Eileen was obvious. But Stern? She killed Maman and returned to Paris, a murderess. What was her purpose? And she had the gall to come back to abuse, manipulate, and destroy me. Why was I her target? Had she always been so evil? We are all born with Original Sin, or so we are taught. But how is it that goodness radiates from some people, and not from others? What prompts a person to cross that threshold from virtue to vice? Or vice to virtue?

In Ceylon, dark skinned native boys dived for pennies. Grinning with delight, their white teeth shining, they seemed happy in their jungle paradise. Covetousness, however, led to theft, and they squabbled over paltry treasures. Were they noble savages corrupted by Western evils, or did all societies have their ills?

From Colombo, we sailed to Aden, then Suez and Port Said. Mr Sotheby, an adventurous sort despite being almost seventy, had booked a train to Alexandria so we could experience Egypt before sailing to Istanbul. As Aunt Rachel said, a trip like this was an opportunity not to be missed. I had agreed with the Sothebys to meet in Oxford for Christmas. That gave me until December in

Vienna. En route to Oxford, I decided I would stop in Paris and find Ailine. I had her address, thanks to Mrs Epstein. 'I cannot guarantee anything, Phoebe,' she remarked as she handed it to me, 'I wrote years ago and received no reply.' At least I could start in Paris. Someone there would know. A gallery maybe. Or Daphne, if she was still there. I would visit Ailine, confront her about Maman, show her my evidence, and secure her confession, after which—

Should I kill her, or should I force her to take her own life?

That Ailine should suffer the same ignominy as poor Maman seemed fitting. I could acquire the opiate in Vienna. What dose would I need? It wouldn't do to make a mistake. Perhaps cyanide would be more effective. How could I make her take it without recourse to a court of honour?

Perhaps I should poison her secretly after all, the way she did Maman.

But I wanted her confession!

So, if I executed, what weapon should I use? Something easy to handle that would kill swiftly and decisively. After all, Ailine was not an old woman, nor was I a young man. A blow to which part of the head would cause sudden death? Where would I purchase such a weapon? How would I hide it? But what woman travels with an axe in her trunk?

I lay on my deckchair and studied anatomy; and took to visiting the pool. Men in swimsuits, flaunting their diving skills, provided opportunity aplenty to ascertain the position of the heart in relation to the ribs.

Women, however, are more complex.

The mirror became my teacher. I lifted and separated my breasts and pressed my sternum. My heart lay behind. How do you plunge a knife into the heart? If I used a letter opener, would the blade suffice in length and temper? How would I angle the stroke? From above or below? And how many times?

Was I capable of such a frenzy?

It is more difficult to stab a woman. And more difficult for a woman to stab.

Besides, what happened to the blood?

It wouldn't do to have her blood on my hands...

Perhaps poison was the best method after all.

I would buy the poison in Alexandria where no one would notice or care.

22

Diversion

SINCE MR AND MRS SOTHEBY'S enthusiasm for the exotic aligned with my secret need for a toxin, we exchanged the boulevards and officialdom of Alexandria's colonial precincts for stuccoed alleys cluttered with stalls. My chaperones examined trinkets and haggled in English and French, while I studied bowlfuls of spices pungent in the heat. Splayed carcasses made me shudder, as did the bleating lambs awaiting slaughter nearby. Dark-skinned men in robes and tarbooshes squatted around silver hookahs and eyed with suspicion my tee-straps and Spanish heels. Undaunted, I watched cobras of steam rise and twist from their curious apparatus, and inhaled draft upon draft of lemon and crushed herbs.

'Hardly a poison,' I concluded, when I was shoved into a pile of baskets. Relieved to find my handbag not stolen, I recovered my balance and promptly collided with a man in urgent pursuit. But if he called for help, it was not for my sake. Others darted from stalls and side streets. Shutters burst open and bearded onlookers thrust their heads. Arabic cries engulfed my own, while the madding crowd jostled me into a small square where a woman huddled against a wall wailing, pleading. To no avail. Rocks struck, hurled by the men gathered around her. Blood trickled from her temple. A second volley battered her skull. Angry shouts drowned her weakened pleas. Walls caved. Robes blurred. My knees crumbled. I stumbled, was scooped up and borne away.

For how long and how far I was carried I knew not, only that I came to my senses with the help of salts. 'Hush,' soothed a man, 'Je vous promets que vous êtes en sécurité.' From a rosy haze emerged an ivory silk-linen suit with modest lapels, even top-stitching, and hand-crafted buttonholes. The man himself was clean-shaven and olive-skinned; his countenance, with its aquiline nose and high cheekbones, refined; and what remained of his dark hair was closely trimmed and on the verge of silvering. He placed the salts on a low table and signalled in the direction of the open door before leaning into his chair and crossing his legs: a picture of ease and calm with one hand lounging in his jacket pocket.

Embarrassed and drowsy, I fingered the fringe of the embroidered shawl which covered me. An enormous gilt-edged dressing mirror revealed that I lay propped on a lacquered chaise lounge scattered with pink satin cushions, in an alcove lined with billowing gossamer curtains in soft shell tones, some tied with gold tassels. The walls were a rich terracotta, and the room hinted of fresh coffee and jasmine.

A woman entered, her fulsome figure lavishly swathed. From a silver tray she served me a gold-etched glass of warmed milk. Honey sweet and laced with cinnamon it proved a comforting restorative, as did its companion rose-scented almond cake.

'Where am I? What happened?' I asked, unable to rouse my French to consciousness.

'You fainted,' the man replied in a foreign version of my native tongue, 'And I happened to be behind you when you collapsed.'

'So much blood,' I murmured, 'Why—?'

'The woman had committed adultery, the traditional punishment for which is stoning.'

'But how did they know?'

'She was carrying another man's child.'

'I had no idea such practices still existed.'

'Unfortunately, they do. Even though Islamic law is no longer upheld in Egyptian courts, many cleave to the old customs.'

'Did she die?'

'I hope not. Fortunately, the police intervened. Might I suggest, Mademoiselle, that it is far too hot to wear black in this clime.'

'I am mourning my father.'

'Peace be on you, and the mercy of Allah and His blessings. In this part of the world, however, sobriety suffices for mourning. A simple white dress, for example, would render you more comfortable. You are alone?' he added, much concerned.

'I am in the company of parents of friends of mine. Well, I was. We're due to embark for Istanbul this afternoon. Oh dear! I must find them! Where am I?'

'Hush, you are quite safe; although you are not, shall we say, in the most savoury part of town. But on my honour, you have my most sincere assurance that you have come to no harm. On which ship are you sailing?'

'The *Izmir*.'

'Then we will be travelling companions,' he smiled. 'Would you permit me to escort you to the port? I know the streets well and will guide you along the most discreet route.'

He assisted me to my feet and introduced himself with a bow, sweeping his left hand from his heart to his lips and finally to his forehead, which graceful gesture he finished with his palm and fingers suspended upwards, as if to include heaven in the greeting.

Mr Kerem Solak was his name, and he was a Turk from Istanbul itself.

'Thank heavens we've found you!' Mrs Sotheby dashed into view only minutes before we were to board. 'We thought you'd been kidnapped for the white slave trade! What a to-do! But Phoebe, who is this?'

I introduced the gallant Mr Solak and explained the circumstances of our meeting while Mr Solak acknowledged their thanks with a tip of his panama. Might he join us for dinner? I requested of Mr Sotheby, who overcame his initial disconcertment by issuing a formal invitation.

Upon joining us at table that evening, Mr Solak whispered to the waiter; and from the tenor of their exchange, I detected an opportunity to repay his kindness.

'I will take care of your food,' I whispered.

He raised an eyebrow in surprise, his eyes betraying gratitude before they blinked, revealing a more cautious expression.

'I don't mind. I'm quite used to it. I had to do the same for my late father.'

'Was it the War?' inquired Mrs Sotheby as I cut Mr Solak's lamb.

'It was my misfortune, Madame, to be mauled by a cur when I was sixteen.' But while his face remained calm, his affected arm, which had never left his jacket pocket, twitched. 'I lost my right hand.'

'Mr Solak, how terrible!' Mrs Sotheby, like me, must have imagined a rabid dog in frenzied attack.

'Do not be too concerned, Madame. It was many years ago, and, luckily for me, I am naturally left-handed.'

'May I inquire what is your line of work, sir?' asked Mr Sotheby.

Our guest was a merchant who traded in gemstones and estate jewellery, having fallen into that occupation through escorting White Russians to safety after the deposition of the Czar. 'They paid me well, in Fabergé and Cartier,' he added with a smile, while his emerald dress ring implied that his jest contained some twenty-two carats of truth. Since his business took him across the Mediterranean, and even as far as South Africa and China, he had much in common with Mr Sotheby who also had travelled extensively. Meanwhile, like Desdemona, I feasted upon their stories as if they had been served me on a platter.

When the band commenced, Mr Solak had the sensibility, not only to discern his hosts' preferences, but also their concerns regarding himself, and indicated his readiness to take the floor by inviting me to join him.

'Considering your kind assistance with my meal, I thought you might make allowances for foxtrots,' he jested as he helped me with my chair. 'I am sorry I have no hand to guide you.'

Of which I am glad, I thought. You have no hand to manipulate me, to press and push me where I do not wish to go, to make me act in a manner at odds with my person.

'My wrist stump will not bother you? Some women would loathe to look at it, let alone touch it.'

'I think we will manage very well.'

For the first time that evening, he freed his right arm with its empty cuff and offered it.

'Do you like dancing, Mr Solak?'

At least he knew how to navigate without embarrassment and had enough sense to step in time; and he improved with every dance. 'This is a pleasure of which I am most unworthy,' he whispered.

What beautiful green eyes he had: jade, with smoky rims and copper sunbursts! Closer I nestled, trusting his gentle embrace and consoled by the simplicity of his every move. Here was no risk of entanglement, no artful seduction.

Istanbul glowed across the shimmering sea. Kerem leant over the deck rail and indicated with his panama the Blue Mosque which bubbled from the shoreline, its minarets like giant spears, its golden cupolas gleaming. Rosy Hagia Sophia crouched nearby; and the domes and spires of the Topkapi Palace were clustered along the leafy promontory. Swift, stately gulets swept about the harbour; more modest single-masted fishing vessels with scarlet sails darted in competition; and broad ferries laden with goods and passengers chugged across the Bosphorus. Rowboats cluttered the coast. Springing from the water's edge, boxlike buildings punctuated here and there by minarets progressed steadily up mosque-crowned hills. A long, low bridge lined with boats and busy with trams and pedestrians linked the two massive headlands: Thracia, the end of Europe; and Anatolia, the beginning of Asia.

'Where do you live, Kerem?' I lolled my head against his shoulder.

'Close your eyes, my houri, and listen to the lapping waves. How free they are! Then listen to my heart and feel it pulse in time. That is where I live.'

'Of all the men you meet these past weeks, you set your heart on one twice your age and a cripple to boot!' Mrs Sotheby complained as we checked in at the Pera Palas.

'I'm not in love with him. And what does it matter if he's missing a hand?'

'I know another woman who, at a similar age, fell for a man old enough to be her father,' teased Mr Sotheby.

'Desmond!' Mrs Sotheby laughed. 'At least you were all of a piece. He's not married, is he, Phoebe?'

'He's a bachelor.'

'Thank heavens! Even if he were married, he would think nothing of having six wives, I'm sure. Goodness! You've spent every waking moment with him.'

'It has been a very pleasant diversion.'

'Three days at sea! What could you possibly have to say to one another?'

'Everything and nothing at all. And aside from talking, we danced, and strolled, and played chess.'

'Well, at least there's nothing romantic about chess,' Mrs Sotheby fanned herself and sighed. 'And he's coming at what time?'

'Seven o'clock tomorrow morning. Kerem recommended we sightsee before it grows too hot.'

'Capital advice!' enjoined Mr Sotheby, while his wife murmured over my use of Mr Solak's first name, 'And what a lucky stroke to have a local for a guide, eh?'

The next morning, a knock interrupted my formulations about how I could implement Kerem's suggestion and purchase a costume in a lighter colour. Mrs Sotheby, no doubt, who would seize upon a shopping venture to avoid him. Instead, a bell boy handed me a bunch of bright and cheery tulips courtesy of the gentleman himself. Two boxes accompanied the flowers. I removed the lids, carefully loosened the tissue, and lifted out a white organdy dress and matching wide-brimmed hat. With its princess seams and delicate flounce, the dress neither belittled my years nor my youth and seemed too flattering on that account. As I fastened the row of covered buttons and adjusted my new chapeau, I wished that I, and not my reflection, epitomised such purity.

'Still, it's consoling he thinks no evil of me, yet disconcerting given my plans. But why should I not permit myself a joyful interlude, a brief pleasure? A little tourism is as much a reality as avenging a murder most foul— perhaps more so, since it pertains to present circumstance; whereas the notions plaguing my thoughts, although rooted in truth, are quite improbable. They will send me mad if I am not careful. I will enjoy my innocence – or the illusion of it – while I can.'

'How could such beauty inspire severity?' I wondered as I stared at the domed expanse of the Blue Mosque; for the shouts, the clattering stones, and the desperate, bleeding woman back in

Alexandria disturbed the peace I might have felt in that sacred place. Yet, if ethereal space and intricate tesserae epitomised Divine harmony and splendour, then sin was truly a blight on the cosmos. Perhaps, therein lay the justification for the brutality.

Even so, why should God be so mindful? Here I was, dwarfed by geometry: Numerical Perfection. Still. Simple. Silent. Thus diminished, was I of any worth? And what of my actions? The busy cogs of my thoughts? The ebb and flow of my feelings? The mosque was centuries old. How many generations had trod, trod, trod before me? Given such human insignificance amidst God's grandeur, what did our actions matter?

And yet it is said that moving a mere grain of sand affects every part of the immeasurable whole; that even the hairs on our heads are counted. I studied the massive columns and followed their heavy fluting to a band of lapis lazuli upon which was inscribed an Ottoman message in gold.

'Did you know, Phoebe,' Kerem began, 'that somewhere lies a tile inverted or misplaced: an ancient custom whereby we humbly glorify Allah by not emulating His perfection.'

'The fault is well-concealed.' I scoured the mosaic, but the glorious contest of leafy motifs baffled my efforts. 'You would think the artist might have wished to make his mistake more visible. Or is that what you mean by humble glorification?'

'Our flaws are an intricate part of our nature; also, it is our habit to conceal rather than expose them. My missing hand, for instance.'

'But that is merely a physical limitation, and not of your own doing. Regarding our moral weakness, we engage in all manner of deceit.'

'I doubt you have such flaws to disguise.'

'As likewise I doubt you.'

'Then maybe we are both bedazzled.'

'I cannot find the tile. The decoration is too far away. Can you?'

'I have long since abandoned my search. Whatever defects you might have so beautifully hidden, I believe you are incapable of wrong-doing.'

'I don't know that I have any capacity for crime, if that's what you mean. But I have entertained vile temptations.'

'We are all capable of atrocity, which few of us would commit even if we had opportunity. But such thoughts belong to another realm – one we should avoid. Is it not better to consider virtue, that multi-faceted jewel which requires a setting to enhance its beauty, and a skilled craftsman to cut and polish it to perfection?'

Mrs Sotheby, meanwhile, feared that opportunity had arisen for any number of atrocities and introduced me to Reverand and Mrs Winterbotham. Accompanying them was their son Richard, a young chap up from Cambridge. Very decent. Very respectable. Very neatly combed hair. And very aware that his parents expected him to converse with me. The Sothebys had accepted the Winterbothams' invitation to join them for a guided tour of the Topkapi Palace.

'You must respect your chaperones, Phoebe,' Kerem curtailed my protest with a fond look.

'After all, Mr Solak must have seen the palace a hundred times,' added Mrs Sotheby.

'In truth, Madame, I have never set foot inside. I have little desire to revisit that era. I am relieved that Turkey is now a secular, democratic nation.'

'My father was wary of the republics created after the War.'

'One look at the rest of Europe, Phoebe, and I suppose he had reason. But I think the democracy experiment has been more a question of leadership and vision. It has been our good fortune to have Mustafa Kemal, the Father of the Turks, as our president. He has overseen our children's education, the mechanisation of our industry, and the reform of our language. We have dignity and rights; our women, freedom and opportunity; our primitive customs and barbaric laws have been quashed. So, I will leave the palace to you and attend to business of my own,' he tipped his hat. 'Perhaps I can show you the bazaar after your tour? You will require refreshment, and no doubt will wish to purchase souvenirs. Some knowledge of Turkish might help.'

Thanks to Kerem, the Sothebys and their new friends did quite well at the bazaar. Thoroughly exhausted, they conceded to his escorting me to the Pera Palas on foot, which involved a leisurely excursion across the Galata Bridge; and my safe deliverance secured their consent to my spending our final evening in his company.

Kerem suggested a favourite meyhane, the Turkish equivalent of a tavern, where conversation was cherished, in Istanbul's 'Little Paris', reasonably close to the station.

'Well, I can honestly say that I am not fond of guided tours,' I informed him. 'Being told what to look at, what I ought to know, to move on when I would prefer to linger, makes me feel a prisoner. Anyway, the palace was like a citadel where the Sultan and his court could live for months at a time. I saw Mohammed's Sword; and the Tower of Justice afforded the most magnificent view of the city and harbour. I liked the Harem most of all, although I would not have liked to live in it. Still, Kerem, I had no idea I would enjoy Istanbul so much!'

'You have certainly taken a liking to our coffee,' he smiled, lifting the candle on the table for me to light my cigarette.

'Not only the coffee,' I inhaled.

'The baklava?'

'Oh yes!'

'And the balik ekmek we shared near the bridge?'

'I never thought a fish sandwich would taste so good.'

'A fresh catch prepared by the fisherman himself. And what of the raki?' He laughed as I winced at the memory of the aperatif's potent anise flavours.

'Kerem, how I will miss you!'

'But it is necessary that you go, Phoebe,' he prompted.

'I must get to know my father's world. And I have a family matter of some importance which requires my attention in Paris. Do you ever visit Vienna?'

'Occasionally. Ordinarily, I would not expect to travel there for some time to come; but I think I will alter my plans. Next week I sail to the Far East. When I return, perhaps we might enjoy an opera together, or a concert, or even a dance?'

'I would like that very much.'

'Meanwhile, we have our memories spread upon the table of our hearts like the platters here before us. This silver dish, for instance, gleams like your beautiful eyes in the candlelight. And here, in these mussels with their lingering flavours, are the joys we shared as we walked across the Bridge. When I bring my cup to my lips, I will remember the caress of your beautiful hands, so gentle and yet so strong. What will you remember, Phoebe?'

'These dolmades are the tulips you sent me which, when I placed them in a vase, grew a meadow in my heart. Whenever I wear this yazma, I will remember when you picked it out from that stall in the bazaar. I couldn't work out how to wear it at first, and you tried to help—'

'I wasn't much use, was I?'

'We managed together. And the colours are so pretty! Cobalt and turquoise, and amethyst, and gold! They are as rich and varied as our conversation. And the sweet sherbet I sip, well, that is the story you told me as we sat on the deck of the *Izmir* and contemplated the stars: the story of Hüsrev and Shirin. Tell it me again, Kerem.'

'I will tell you the fragment I remember best, when Hüsrev sees his beautiful princess for the first time: Softly he moved through the garden, when of a sudden he gleamed Shirin, bright as a moonbeam, bathing in a pool, her long dark curls spread across the water. Filled with Love, King Hüsrev became as a fiery sun. And yet tears rolled from his eyes, so taken was he with her beauty. Unaware of his presence amidst the jasmine, Shirin continued to bathe, the water lapping her fair frame. Then she fell asleep on a bed of hyacinths; and upon waking the following day, she beheld him. Ah, Phoebe, when next you behold me, as you did that day in Alexandria, what will have passed?'

'Who can tell?'

'And how will I contact you?'

I scribbled my Vienna address. He kissed the paper and tucked it inside his top waistcoat pocket. Then he placed before me a tiny velvet box. Inside was a pair of earrings: sapphire pendants set in platinum filigree.

'Kerem! Thank you! How beautiful they are!'

'*You* are beautiful. Put them on, Phoebe, and feast me with another memory.'

On board the Orient Express, I sought to spend the hour before bed curled up with a cigarette and a book when I discovered my cigarette case was missing. I assumed it was in my handbag and blurted as much to the Sothebys. And no, I had not smoked since leaving the meyhane in Istanbul. Kerem's company, his final kiss soft as a cushion; his hand stroking my cheek; his beautiful green eyes with their mysterious dark rims; the prospect of a letter; these delights had filled my every minute. And I remembered my tears when he took a red rose from its vase and presented it to me as we left, knowing it would be months before I would see him again; and how, like Lot's wife, I took one last, longing look at our table still scattered with bowls and napery; save that what I was leaving was no Sodom, but a place of loving friendship.

'Perhaps I left it in the meyhane,' I murmured.

'Was it valuable, Phoebe?' asked Mrs Sotheby.

'It was sterling silver! Furthermore, it belonged to Dad! It was engraved with his initials, R.J.R.; although they could have been mine, for their curlicues intertwined so that the first R could be mistaken for a P.'

'I have a feeling, my dear,' remarked Mr Sotheby to his wife, 'that our charge has entertained the company of a very charming and very accomplished thief.'

'Kerem would never do such a thing! Besides, I always put my cigarettes in my handbag, and hours have passed since we dined. What with organising our tickets and luggage, making the train, and saying good-bye, I have been thoroughly distracted!'

'Is there any way we can find out, Desmond?'

'I doubt it. If he took it, by the time we notify police and they track him down, he would have disposed of it. A sly old fox if ever I met one.'

'Shame on you for thinking evil of him!'

'You are too compassionate, Phoebe,' observed Mrs Sotheby. 'Heavens! A theft! I suppose the next thing will be a murder!'

'Don't be ridiculous!'

❖ ❖ ❖

He lied to you, he lied to you, he lied to you, he lied to you... the train clacked through the night.

I don't believe that for a moment!

You lied to him, you lied to him, you lied to him, you lied to him...

You let him think you were better than you are. Never did you tell him your sinister plans.

'A family matter? Is that what you call it?' Dad raised an eyebrow.

'You're very coy, dear,' observed Aunt Rachel.

'How did he describe you? A houri, eh?' questioned Dad. 'Peri more like. Wouldn't see the likes of you this side of Paradise.'

'I have committed no crime.'

'You've considered it.'

'It's your fault! You wouldn't take any action!'

'Imagine if there was a murder!' exclaimed Mrs Sotheby.

Only in fiction could one conceive an elaborate conspiracy against a murderer acquitted by a corrupt court. I wouldn't have stabbed Cassetti while he slept. I would have confronted him, and then stabbed him, if I could stab at all. A letter opener would suffice. Plunge it hard. Under the ribs and into the heart.

'They caught him!' Mr Sotheby tapped his egg with a silver spoon.

Furious men in robes and turbans hurried down the street with Kerem in tow.

'What are you going to do?' asked Della in her broderie night-gown, propped with pillows on her sickbed.

What are you going to do? What are you going to do?

'Take up that axe and chop off his hand!' called a man from a balcony high in the square.

'Don't make me do it! He doesn't deserve it! It was only a silver case! I cannot do it! I love him! I love him!'

'I love him!' I cried.

'He must be punished!'

'But I forgive him! Let it be someone else! Anyone but him!'

'Pick up the axe!'

I raised the axe and brought it down hard. Blood gushed. Ailine's head rolled to the ground, and Maman began to sing:

> *Sleep then my princess, oh sleep*
> *Slowly the grey shadows creep*
> *Forest and meadow are still*
> *Peace falls on valley and hill*
> *Luna appears in the sky*
> *Holding her lantern on high*
> *Stars now their night watches keep*
> *Sleep then my princess, oh sleep*
> *Goodnight, goodnight*

23

City without Walls

U PON ARRIVING AT VIENNA'S Westbahnhof, Mr Sotheby proposed an open carriage ride through the city and organised for our trunks to be sent ahead. Leisurely we clopped toward the Ringstrasse which, as you know by now, Roddy, is Vienna's main boulevarde. According to Dad's 1905 Baedecker, it replaced the old fortifications which had withheld marauders for centuries, most notably the Ottoman Turks in the famous siege of 1683. 'Only their coffee got in,' remarked the coachman, a solid, puffy cheeked, affable character; his drawl a lazy melody that syncopated with his horse's hoofs.

The Hofburg Palace (the former Imperial Winter Palace) extended its vast wings in open embrace, as if to welcome us into the Ring. Before the palace lay a vast and verdant square – the Heldenplatz – in which stood two rampant equestrian statues: Prince Eugene of Savoy, who liberated Hungary from the Infidel Turks; and Archduke Charles of Austria who had boldly resisted Napoleon and the spread of the French Enlightenment. I turned to the left, only to wonder at another magnificent square – the Maria-Theresien-Platz – which served as a gracious conduit to a set of buildings which matched the Hofburg's grandeur. Knowledge rather than fortitude and authority was their purpose, for the edifices turned out to be the Museum of Natural History and the Art Gallery. Lush, leafy, and brimful with roses, the Kaisergarten (now known as the Burggarten) greeted my right gaze.

Opposite, a smaller park partially obscured the Justizpalast (Palace of Justice) before we passed the sweeping Palladian façade of the Parliament, and that other testament to Counsel, the steep-roofed, Flemish styled Rathaus or town hall. And, because all work and no play make Jack (or Hans) a dull boy, the Burgtheater wisely provided a venue for amusement. Wisdom herself was represented by the University, built like a Baroque palace; while the Votivkirche served as the house of Piety.

Certainly, cleanliness was next to godliness in Wien. Our horse paused outside the church, and no sooner did it finish its business than a boy ran up and shovelled the droppings off the cobbles. Otherwise, all proceeded with the utmost calm. A bright red tram dinged politely as it drifted along its rails. If anyone was in a hurry, be it in motor or on foot, they did not let on. Even the sun seemed to take its time reaching the horizon, preferring instead to bathe the city in a lingering, gentle golden light. The sky remained a glorious Wedgwood blue, a perfect backdrop for those great white buildings. The one peculiarity was that the Ringstrasse's opulent edifices seemed rather pretentious given that Austria, once destined to rule the world, now claimed sovereignty over a mere six million 'German Austrians'.

And instead of rule by emperors on horseback, as was the case in Dad's day, the government of this Lilliput republic, ostensibly devoted to 'Faith and Fatherland', had fallen into the hands of a bespectacled gentleman of goodly disposition for whom vigorous outdoor activity or aggressive confrontation held little appeal. Even his scowl was a half-baked attempt at severity by one who seemed more inclined to meekness. That is, if the occasional poster was any indication.

'That is Herr Bundeskanzler Schuschnigg,' the coachman observed my interest.

'And the square cross underneath?'

'Is the symbol of the present government, the Fatherland Front,' he spat into the gutter.

'But what about those crosses? The black ones on Herr Bundeskanzler's eyes?'

'They're swastikas, Phoebe,' added Mr Sotheby.

'That'll be Hitler's gangs at work,' the coachman sighed, 'But don't you worry about that Piefke nonsense, Fräulein. Vienna has better to offer; and the Metropole is one of her finest hotels.' He halted in front of a palatial building, its entrance flanked by imposing Corinthian columns. 'Enjoy your holiday.'

'I hope our accommodation meets your expectations, my dear,' Mr Sotheby teased his wife as we entered.

'Will we see the Duke of Windsor?' she asked, swaying in time to the Strauss being played by a distant string ensemble.

'Quite likely. And let me tell you, I wouldn't have dreamed of booking a room here before the War. How times have changed! And I believe we're in time for tea.'

The dining hall was brimful with tourists, specimens the world over, enclosed in an opulent menagerie with a stained-glass ceiling and fed choice morsels by attendants in dinner jackets. They were on display, to stare and be stared at, oblivious of the urban wilderness beyond.

'Verzeihen Sie mir, gnädiges Fräulein.' A waiter presented me with a letter on a silver tray; and I hesitated before using the accompanying knife to lift the seal. The letter, which welcomed me to Vienna, was from Frau Klara Schütze-Rechtschaffen, the wife of Dad's old friend.

'What does it say, Phoebe?' asked Mrs Sotheby.

'Professor and Frau Schütze-Rechtschaffen are currently in Salzburg for the Festival; but will be making a special trip to Vienna to meet us.'

'How very kind. When, dear, when?'

'August 17. When is that? With all the travelling, my days and times are quite mixed up.'

'Why, that's today!'

Minutes later, the waiter reappeared with a calling card signifying the arrival of the persons in question.

Attired in a Chanel suit, Frau Professor Klara Schütze resembled a delectable creation of a master pâtissier: a plump piece of choux filled with fresh cream. Her face glowed as if lightly glazed; filaments of spun toffee formed her hair, which was rolled in the French style; and her eyes were soft and warm, like caramel. And Professor Schütze? Well, the man seemed in the same state of alarm as when Dad encountered him on the Front some twenty years ago, and which he had captured so brilliantly on canvas, the only difference being that the professor had lost most of his hair. What remained was grey and cropped. Beady and pale, his blue eyes surveyed me like eagles perched either side of the rugged narrow promontory of his nose; while his mouth was tense, ready to snap at his prey.

But if I was astonished, Professor Schütze was more so. When I held out my hand (quite high, for he was a tall man) he took it, bowed, and finished his courtesy with an incredulous gaze. Was it something of Dad's expression he had seen in me? Or was it Maman? His wife, while more composed, perused my mourning in a worried, maternal fashion.

'Welcome, Miss Raye,' she began in precise and careful English. 'How good to meet you! Your dear, late father taught you German, yes?'

Delivered in German, my affirmation prompted her to continue in her native tongue. Again, she welcomed me, enquired after my trip, expressed her sorrow for my loss with an effusive 'Mein Beileid', and recounted with joy her time spent helping Scylla, adding excitedly that she herself was soon to become a grandmother.

'Karl-Alois, our eldest son, married his childhood sweetheart last year, and our first grandchild will be born in October.'

I introduced the Sothebys. Finding a language in which we could all converse with ease took some working out. While my German was good, Mr Sotheby was not proficient, and Mrs Sotheby had no knowledge of the language whatsoever. Professor

Schütze understood English but was embarrassed by his lack of skill. Of this, his wife was aware and deferred accordingly, despite her competence. It turned out that French served as a happy medium, supplemented with the occasional English or German word or phrase, with everyone serving as interpreter according to need. Cake, and coffee 'mit Schlag' arrived; and Frau Schütze graciously offered to serve, topping each cup with cumulous clouds of whipped cream.

Good company that they were, the Schützes respected our wish to be brought up to date with local news, which they were easily able to do. In fact, they had recently dined with Chancellor Schuschnigg and were pleased to report he was looking well at last.

'You see, our poor Chancellor lost his wife two years ago in a motor accident,' explained Frau Schütze, 'not long after Nazis assassinated Chancellor Dollfuss.'

'It is rumoured that Nazis drugged the driver,' added the Professor.

'You can understand that Herr Bundeskanzler was much shaken. We have known him for many years. He served with my brother Josef on the Italian Front and was taken prisoner.'

'And thanks to von Starhemberg, he has been their prisoner ever since.'

'Now, now Kurti, we are much in need of Mussolini's support. So long as Il Duce lends us his protection, our darling Austria can sing her lovely songs. You are planning to come to Salzburg for the festival, yes? Bruno Walter is conducting a new production of *The Marriage of Figaro*.'

'Bruno Walter?' Mr Sotheby grew excited, 'Why, he conducted Mahler's Ninth Symphony when I last visited Vienna.'

'The premiere? After Mahler's death? Kurti and I were at that very concert! And so was your father, Phoebe. We spent our youth under Mahler's auspices. Have you heard any of Mahler's works?'

'No, I'm afraid, although Dad much admired his music.'

'It is magnificent!'

'Indeed,' added Mr Sotheby.

'It came at a price. Mahler was a despot and the orchestra detested him,' remarked the Professor. 'Not to mention that he converted to gain the position.'

'With the result that we were blessed with a composer and conductor par excellence,' asserted his wife.

'They make a mockery of our faith.'

'It is difficult for the Jews, Kurti. And no one is spared the grace of God. Phoebe, your late father summed Mahler up very well. Roderick said (I hope you do not mind that I call him by his Christian name?) that Mahler was the quintessential Austrian. His melodies and harmonies encapsulated our empire: Catholic,

Jewish, Bohemian, German, traditional and modern, all under the autocratic rule of a maestro who was as much a part of that complex whole as he was an outsider, an exile. Given what became of Mahler himself, and of dear Kaiser Karl after the War, Roddy could not have spoken more truthfully. Now, about Salzburg, Phoebe. We would be delighted to have you as our guest. Our children are very eager to meet you.'

'How very kind!' gushed Mrs Sotheby.

'Thank you, but no,' I replied. 'I first wish to see Vienna for myself.'

Frau Schütze placated Mrs Sotheby with a half-smile and added an understanding nod in my direction. 'Our eldest daughter Zita is the same. Young ladies seem to know their own minds these days.' ('Too much,' muttered her husband.) 'Zita was supposed to join us here this afternoon; but no, she made plans to visit friends. Perhaps, then, you would allow us to show you Vienna before we return?'

The Sothebys' arrangement to meet the Schützes the following day for luncheon and a tour of central Vienna, promised me at last some time to myself.

Since my plans had nothing to do with any of the city's attractions, I left my chaperones at Stephansdom, Vienna's cathedral, walked through Stephansplatz, and headed down Kärntner Strasse.

The cobbled street was busy but unhurried. Cars maintained an ordered route, paying the horse traffic deep respect. Porters dozed outside buildings. Pedestrians, be they society ladies, businessmen, children, or tradesmen, strolled in a relaxed fashion. If there was any urgency in their purpose they concealed it behind calm politesse. 'Grüß Gott,' a gentleman nodded, touching his hat. 'Grüß Gott,' I answered, almost making a curtsey. 'Grüß Gott', 'Grüß Gott', and so it went, to the point that my journey felt like a high-class theatrical production in which the passers-by were costumed to reflect their station, and the timing and manner of their greetings had been thoroughly rehearsed.

The performance was enjoyed by edifices as glamorous as opera patrons. Ornate mouldings clung to façades like snug-fitting necklets on plump ladies; windows were as sharply tailored as gentlemen's breast pockets, their curtains tucked like handkerchiefs; smart brass knobs buttoned the doors.

I traversed the once-walled boundary of the Ringstrasse, rounded a park, and continued along another wide boulevard, Linke Wienzeile, which featured on one side a long succession of five-storey apartments, each rivalling the other for fashion and style: one was ornate as a wedding cake; another, steeply gabled, showed off its sunshine yellow front and terracotta brickwork; the Classical restraint of a third compensated for the excesses of the former two; and all gazed with solid condescension at the humble canvas umbrellas and canopies of the equally extensive market opposite.

Finally, I arrived at Dad's Vienna address.

With its mosaic façade, the building reminded me of his best brocade waistcoat. Featuring pink poppies with gold stems combined with summery sea blues and greens, it seemed oblivious to the fact that it was only Wednesday. 'Just like Dad,' I thought, 'Dressed to the nines for a morning jaunt to the barber.'

A happy tune clinked from the street organ outside one of the ground level shops, a bookstore. Given the contents tastefully displayed in the enormous plate glass window, I figured that Dad must have been a regular customer, and speculated whether the bookseller, one E. Kirschbaum, counted among his acquaintance. Furthermore, I wanted something else to read, and had a desperate need for writing paper.

But the man who sidled from a back room when I entered, seemed too young to be known to Dad. So much for the pleasantries of the street, I thought when he sneered at my greeting and, in response to my enquiry, grimaced at the shelf containing works in English; and when from that point I glanced at him for verification, he had resumed his backroom conversation which clearly was far more absorbing than any service he preferred not to render to me. From what I could overhear, the discussion seemed rather technical; while its tone, being punctuated with giggles and kisses, was romantic. Minutes later, a bohemian young woman holding a large cardboard cylinder left the shop. And when I turned back to the bookshelves, I came face to face with the bookseller whose jagged grin revealed chipped and crooked teeth, yellowed with tobacco.

I decided I would derive more entertainment from *The Complete Works of William Shakespeare* than Gibbon's *Decline and Fall of the Roman Empire*. Having initiated the transaction, I asked where I could purchase stationery. The bookseller kept a stock of bond. Despite his gruff manner, business progressed smoothly. Indeed, it became quite fascinating. My receipt he wrote in a manuscript rivalling that of a modern sign writer for quality and style: The 'O's' were perfect circles; the proportions of the 'P' acknowledged the golden mean; the verticals were beautifully upright; the angles of the 'A' were measured and even. SHAKESPEARE COMPLETE WORKS was a calligraphic masterpiece. 'Schreibpapier' was similarly configured. And as he counted my change, his calculations clip-clopped like hoofs down a thoroughfare, and the schillings jingled like harnesses. Curiously, his face was like a street: cobbled with pockmarks; ill-swept of its stubble; and in deplorable condition, the bridge of his nose being crushed, rendering its crooked remains a hazardous projection.

'Is Herr Kirschbaum here?' I enquired.

'Herr Kirschbaum is dead,' he answered while, with precision, he mitred the paper which he had cut with an acute sense of the perpendicular. He wrapped my purchases, and deftly fastened the string.

'I bet he strangled him,' I surmised; and having concluded that he was equally capable of twisting some string round my neck, I made a swift retreat.

'You were gone an awfully long time,' Mrs Sotheby scolded that evening. 'The Schützes were hoping to see you before they returned to Salzburg.'

'I stopped at a café for cake and spent the afternoon reading.'

'I don't know how you can be so mysogynic.'

'I think you mean misanthropic, my dear,' advised her husband.

'I'm nothing of the sort.'

'You've been brooding ever since you said good bye to that Turk. It's frightfully inconsiderate of you. Anyway, Klara Schütze told me she would send you news when she's back in Vienna. And I hope you're not going to be stand-offish when she does,' she added with a cross sigh. 'Heaven only knows what goes on in that pretty head of yours.'

Why, oh why did I not tell Kerem! Certainly, I had told him much, but I had never mentioned Maman's murder. I should have trusted him! But I did not wish to contaminate his goodness. Nor did I have any desire for him to think evil of me. A man of the world, with experience, means, and wisdom, he would have helped rather than hindered my quest. He would have known what to do, what to say, and what to do next.

As it was, I sat alone in the café and attempted letter after letter. How could I explain in writing the exact, horrible terms of my 'family business'; that I was foolish to encourage his affection; and that I had could never see him again? And where would I send the letter? I had no address. 'I will wait till he writes,' I sighed at the scrunched papers littering my table. 'And if he comes first, I will tell him everything in person. That is the best way.'

'We shouldn't prattle on our last night together,' Mrs Sotheby continued. 'I bought you a parting gift.' It was a prettily styled lilac suit with a shell-pink top in the softest cashmere. 'It's the latest fashion! Given your figure it should look splendid. I suppose we won't see you till Christmas. Do write. It's only four months, but

I'll be worried sick. What are you going to do with yourself?'

'This and that.'

'Well, be careful. I'm terrified Mr Solak is going to lure you to his harem, and we'll never hear from you again.'

24

Linke Wienzeile 40

WAVING HANDKERCHIEFS, and calling 'Auf wiedersehen!' the Sothebys departed the following afternoon. Free at last, I took a cab to my new home.

Dad's name was still in the apartment directory: Roderick Raye k.u.k. Hofmusiker Geiger – a fragment of a past world. Why I expected the interior to be drab and dark, I knew not; probably because the interiors of many Sydney apartments are dingy and staid. Not so Linke Wienzeile 40. Light frolicked about the foyer. Like the skirt of a flamenco dancer, the white marble stairway twirled in a captivating spiral and flaunted the wrought iron lace of its banister petticoat. Upwards it curled, hugging the erect body of the elevator shaft. I followed the passage of weights and cables and marvelled at the buoyant descent of the glass carriage. Lavishly ornamented gates parted, and a stylish elderly couple bid me good afternoon. All about were sounds of a summer fiesta: the plink-plonk of pianos picking out songs; broadcasts on wirelesses; children laughing in courtyards, and, as is not exceptional on such occasions, the disturbing tones of heated argument somewhere high in the building.

'Fräulein Raye?'

A grey-haired woman in widow's weeds introduced herself as Frau Geplapper.

'Why, you are the very image of your father, God rest his soul! Mein Beileid, mein Beileid! I never knew one as sweet-natured as Herr Hofmusiker Raye. Herzlich willkommen! I assure you, his rooms are just as he left them, save I had them cleaned when your trunks arrived. Such a rush to be off: a single valise and his violin, that was all, so excited was he to see his little family. How many years has it been? Twenty-three? Doesn't time fly? "I'll be back before the leaves turn gold," he called. But we never saw him again.'

'One wonders why some people marry,' a portly gentleman declared as he plodded down the stairs, indicating with his brows the distant argument.

'You can be certain the child is the only reason— if they are married at all, Herr Weissmüller,' returned Frau Geplapper, 'Which I doubt. He's already seeing another,' she added for my benefit once the gentleman had left the building. 'And right under her nose, too. No morals. They never do have any. Thirty-two years was I married to Herr Geplapper, may he rest in peace, and we never argued like that. Thank God it's stopped! Ever since she moved in they've fought from dawn to dusk. It's no way to raise a child, let me tell you.'

The elevator opened, and a young blonde fettered by high heels and a summer suit several sizes too small pushed out a baby carriage. 'Grüß Gott,' she greeted us. Her breasts were crammed into her brassiere, while her blouse struggled to fulfil a restraining order it was ill-equipped to execute. Her jacket had already given up, its large buttons unable to curtail her girth and hips. Given Frau Geplapper's silence, she was clearly guilty of the upstairs disturbance.

'You are not married, Fräulein Raye?' asked Frau Geplapper.

'No. I will go to my apartment, thank you.'

'It is on the top floor, Fräulein. Andreas!'

A heavy-set, middle-aged dullard wandered blearily into view. His mother ordered him to take my bag and lead the way.

What Aladdin's cave awaited me? I turned the key and flicked the light, and there before me was Dad! Dad in the full flower of youth; his handsome, clean-shaven face topped with a whimsical array of black curls. Dressed in a folkloric waistcoat embroidered with botanical motifs and a loose peasant shirt which hung over his breeches, he stood with one leg perched on a low stool. In his right hand he balanced a violin on his thigh, while his left hand rested confidently on his hip.

It was a portrait, a colourful oil sketch, the sinuous lines and louche splashes of colour of which challenged and complemented the assurance and energy of its subject: a young man certain of his future, whose future certainty lent much relish to his present delight. What would have been his expression had he known his true fate? Perhaps it was well he did not know, or I would have been denied that moment's pleasure.

But what an ego! Fancy hanging a picture of yourself for all to see the moment they walk in the door!

I circled the spacious interior, drew back the drapes, and opened the French doors. Fresh air and sunshine raced inside like two excited children running for ice cream – a delightful spread of vanilla cream walls and gold plasterwork. A large round rug featuring entwined blooms in lemon sorbet, strawberry pink, and mint softened the parquetry floor. The chairs and lounge were simple by comparison, being elegantly restrained rather than baroque in style, and, with their plush, plump seats, by no means uncomfortable. A grand piano with a walnut finish occupied an alcove which also featured portraits of Haydn, Mozart and Beethoven, the musician's holy trinity, arranged in a triangle on the wall behind. At the foot of the piano lay a lacquered violin case which contained the instrument Dad held in the painting, a very pretty violin decorated with two winged cupids in mother of pearl inlay.

Schubert's sweet A Major Piano Sonata rested on the piano stand. It was strange to think of Dad as a pianist as well as a violinist, and that that tender, meandering little tune was one of the last pieces he ever played. Unfortunately, the piano was terribly out of temper; but the melody had entered my head nonetheless. I could also hear Death's whispers in the bass, but Death could wait. Here, for now, was radiant hope, life, and joy.

'How curious,' I reflected as I wandered, 'It feels as if someone has been here. It smells as if someone has been here.' Frau Geplapper had aired the rooms thoroughly indeed, even the small servant's room at the far end. But I whiffed tobacco. Did Frau Geplapper smoke? No. She smelt of lavender.

Then I gasped when what I assumed would be a bedroom turned out to be a nursery. Initially, I feared that whatever I fondled would disintegrate like the treasures touched by Carter and Carnarvon when they opened King Tut's tomb; or that I would be cursed if I disturbed the contents. Silly superstition! This nursery was no charnel house filled with items for the Fields of Aaru. It was a room devoted to Life: my life.

Instead, I smoothed my hands over the cot quilt, cuddled the teddy bear and laid his head on the pillow, and studied the sampler which read 'Phoebe Joy Raye 17th January 1914': a gift, no doubt, but from whom? Opening the music box on the shelf, I listened to the dainty lullaby as I took out the little frocks folded away in the robe. It was easy to imagine Dad in the fullness of life and health, shopping for the various pieces, hanging pictures, moving furniture, bringing all his artistry into play and combining it with that fatherly touch I knew well and yet had often doubted, shadowed as it was by the circumstances of my conception. Here, however, I saw confirmation of his love; here was the affirmation that I was both wanted and eagerly awaited. This room was mine, intimately mine.

'Do you like it?' I heard him say.

'Very much. And I will keep it as it is.'

'Do you think Maman would have liked it?'

'Why don't you ask her?' I teased, only to be embarrassed by his silence.

'Yes, Dad,' I owned, 'Maman would have liked it very much.'

Pigeon-holed in the desk in his study were calling cards and letters, some of which bore the Imperial and Royal insignia. A calendar for 1914 stood next to the ink well. Filed alongside appointment books were notebooks – dozens of them – filled with practice notes. Ice skates lay at the bottom of a closet which also housed a fur-trimmed coat and winter hat, a knapsack and hiking staff, a pair of sturdy boots, and costumes from foreign parts. German and English classics filled the bookcase along with well-thumbed editions of *The Strad*, reference works, and a dictionary bereft of its spine. Two framed posters adorned the walls: one announcing Dad's performance of Mozart's 4th Violin Concerto at the Rudolfinium in Prague in November 1910; the other an advertisement for a series of Klimt Quartet concerts featuring Haydn's Opus 76 Quartets.

It turned out that Dad had left his cologne in the cabinet of the bathroom, a paradise of blue, green, and gold tiles, with a generous tub and even a shower; while his last beverage must have been a cup of tea, since a cup had been left above the kitchen sink to drain. Curiously, the tea in the nearby canister smelt fresh, which prompted me to brew some for myself.

The kettle still had water in it.

I tipped out the water.

It was clear.

And the tea towel hanging on the stove was damp and crumpled.

Perhaps it was Frau Geplapper; although Frau Geplapper did not strike me as one to take liberties.

But I discovered similar laxity in the bedroom. True, it was dusted, and the photographs on the side table were pleasingly arranged. I would have studied them, for they were pictures I thought lost – a wedding portrait, and a miniature of Maman – but the bedspread was creased; neither were the bedsheets pulled taut, nor were they pressed. Someone had tried to be neat, but they had not done a professional job.

I flung back the sheets and found them dirty.

Frau Geplapper assured me she had left the apartment spick and span. No one had been inside, save her. She never smoked, and the kitchen was bare when she left. How could the sheets be soiled? Clean sheets were fitted in anticipation of my coming. Only she had a key; and these were respectable apartments in a respectable part of town. As for Andreas, he was a good boy. I sensed it was unwise to lose her favour and apologised, even though I thought it more appropriate that she should apologise to me; but clearly, she was innocent.

That evening I refused to leave lest an intruder should come. I preferred to remain hungry than risk dining out. But I could not sleep. What if someone came? And how could I sleep in that filthy bed? It was too hot to sleep, anyway. I opened the balcony doors and paced the lounge room, determined to face whoever might enter.

Tiny scratches stirred me from the settee. A key turned in the lock. The handle twisted, the front door creaked, and...

In crept the bookseller.

25

Trespasses

'WHAT'S UP?' a fresh-faced youth bent over me. His smooth, light olive complexion was enhanced by a rosy glow as if he had just returned from a brisk walk. Had his dark eyes been small and shifty, their expression would have been harsh; but they were attractively almond shaped, and their long lashes screened a merry gleam. Everything about his face was in juxtaposition: angular cheekbones were countered by soft, black curly hair; a pointed nose and chin balanced a prettily shaped, rather sensuous mouth. He stretched and yawned: a slim, streamlined figure slightly below medium height. A tuft of dark hair peeked out from his billowy shirt. And his hands were beautiful – both hands were beautiful – with elegant fingers and manicured nails.

The portrait was come to life!

Upon closer study, I could see the reasoning behind Dad's more familiar moustache: it made him look older, more masculine; whereas in his present state one could easily think him effeminate and he knew it. He bristled with wit.

'The bookseller!' I cried. 'He came inside! He's been sleeping here!'

'Bit of hanky-panky going on, eh?'

'How can you make light of it? It's disgraceful!'

'You're right there, Possum. Love's a disgrace. Nothing but trouble. Take my advice: Don't trust your heart.'

'Useless!'

I jolted at the sound of my own voice and found myself alone.

'Oh, I could have sworn you were real!' I rubbed my eyes and stared at the painting. 'I must have been dreaming.'

But I had not been dreaming— At least, not in part. I stared at the porcelain fragments scattered over the parquetry. The table lamp still glowed, but the room was bright with sunlight. Shouts of children playing in the courtyard drifted through the open balcony doors. Still sleepy, I opened the front door, expecting to see again my intruder fleeing like Frankenstein's monster, but no one was there.

A clock struck ten. Had I been asleep all that time?

The sheets!

No, in that I was not mistaken. I gathered the unwashed linen and ran down the stairs.

'Good morning, Fräulein,' the bookseller grinned as I dumped the sheets on the counter before him. If he was guilty, he was unperturbed. 'I expected you might drop in.'

'How long have you been sleeping there? Don't deny it! You've been sleeping in my apartment! I can tell!'

'I don't deny it.'

'What right—'

'What right? Given the homelessness and poverty in this city, tell me this: What right has a former court musician to leave an apartment vacant for more than twenty years while thousands go without a decent place to live? Besides, how do I know you yourself are not squatting?'

'How dare you! I have the deeds. I am the daughter of Herr Hofmusiker Raye!'

'Are you now? Well then, you wouldn't have minded me sleeping there. He wouldn't have.'

'What do you mean?'

'You're his daughter: you should know,' he shrugged.

Was he homeless? If he hadn't slept in the apartment last night, where had he slept? Wherever it was, he had not slept well. His yellowed shirt was wrinkled, while locks of dark hair stuck out like tram wires. But why should I care where he slept? Only because what he said was true: In a way, Dad would not have minded.

'D—did you know my father? Did you know Herr Hofmusiker Raye?'

'Why do you want to know?'

'What business is that of yours?'

'What happened to him?'

'He left Vienna in 1914 and couldn't return. It was the War—'

'Enough said,' he interrupted. 'When I was a child, I once had to visit an uncle who lived in the apartment below. He didn't like hearing your father practise, so he sent me to ask him to stop, which pleased me because I did not like my uncle, and I was curious. Your father played his violin for me and let me try. It was the one opportunity I ever had to play a musical instrument. My

uncle ended up making his request in person. He was an ill-
tempered, miserly, and unreasonable man whom your father bore
very well. On parting, your father told me I was welcome any time.
I took up the offer,' he smirked.

'Well you've taken the offer too far. And you can wash the
sheets.'

'I'll see they are laundered. Are you hungry?'

'What does it matter if I'm hungry?'

'Have you eaten anything?'

I had not eaten anything. I had no idea where to eat, or what to
do, where to go, or who to ask. I wished I did not have to eat. But
oh, how my stomach rumbled!

'I have a table at the coffee house next door. I will take you.
Then I will show you where you can do some shopping.'

'There's no need.'

'Given your father's generosity in allowing me the use of your
apartment, I, in gratitude, should at least provide you with coffee.
We should also address each other by name. My name is Emil
Fährmann, and I will not object to you calling me Emil. What is
your name? I assume you have an identity other than Herrn
Hofmusiker's daughter?'

Herr Fährmann bundled the sheets and clumped into the back
room. He re-emerged sporting a grubby linen jacket which had
been pulped into shape. Taking a newsy cap and walking cane, he
lumbered toward the door which he held open to allow me
passage. Despite his courtesy, however, he was a thing most
brutish. He stood knock-kneed, his right foot skewed outwards,
his torso listing to the left. I hurried past him, embarrassed that
he took such trouble and fearful of what he might do or say next.

'You watch my shop for me, Albrecht,' he instructed the organ
grinder, giving him friendly pat on the back.

'How can he? He's blind.'

'You are mistaken. He sees in the dark.'

With its massive chandelier, vast mirrors, rose marble panels
and voluptuous gold figurines, the nearby Café Wienzeile seemed
too sumptuous a venue for breakfast. Herr Fährmann ordered
Kurze and croissants and inquired of the waiter whether he had
anything for a headache. The waiter nodded, studying me as a
doctor would a new patient. 'For me,' advised Herr Fährmann. 'The
young lady seems in good health.'

The waiter returned with a newspaper, the *Arbeiterzeitung*,[3]
which he recommended as a cure for most headaches these days.
Herr Fährmann eagerly took the paper, and with the waiter began
discussing the recent developments in Spain. Both were concerned

---

[3] *Arbeiterzeitung*: Left-wing newspaper banned by the State, printed and
circulated in secret.

for the whereabouts of a friend who had left Vienna to fight for the Republicans.

In my attempt to follow their conversation, I consulted a nearby edition of the *Wiener Zeitung*.[4] The Basques had surrendered to the Nationals, which was much lamented by Herr Fährmann and the waiter, both of whom thought Spain had become a Fascist playground. Even worse was that with the fall of Santander, in northern Spain, the Republic not only looked set to be crushed from without by Franco, Mussolini, and Hitler, but also destroyed from within by Stalin.

We left the café, and as we continued along Linke Wienzeile I realised that my misshapen guide was unhampered by his deformity. So quickly did his body arch and turn in time with his knock-kneed gait, that I felt I was walking alongside a broadsheet the wind had scooped from the pavement and was whipping down the street. Upon crossing the road, he halted as if he had been buffeted into a fence.

'That's Karlsplatz railway station,' he flicked his stick forward and angled it to the left. 'It was designed by Otto Wagner, who also designed our building – the Majolikahaus – and the adjacent apartments. Across the way,' he indicated a large baroque structure, 'is the Theatre an der Wien. The road follows the left bank of the Wien and forms the boundary of Mariahilf, the sixth district. The right bank is yonder and marks the district of Wieden.'

'Where is the river?'

'Underground.'

'Was it like this when my father was here?'

'Vienna used to be plagued by cholera in the summer. That is, those who couldn't afford a luxurious seaside holiday or mountain villa were plagued by cholera— cholera and floods. Since such inconveniences interfered with bourgeois pleasure, the authorities devised a system of vaults over the Wien and built up its banks. That way, the filth was contained and directed underground. Much like Vienna itself: garbage hidden behind ostentation. Musil didn't call it *Kakanien* for nothing. This is the Naschmarkt,' he led me into the market. 'Here you can buy all you need.'

We cut through the bustle of maids and housewives, Emil (he insisted I call him Emil) using his stick in equal measure as scythe and support. A basket overflowing with gold and red capsicums heavy, full, and fleshy, caught my attention. Nearby was a crate of tomatoes, some scarlet, others almost purple, perfect for goulash. This I mentioned to my guide who then helped me procure the freshest veal, speck cured in nutmeg and juniper, and the most pungent paprika I had ever smelt. He knew exactly which stalls to

---

[4] *Wiener Zeitung*: the official newspaper of the Austrian Republic.

visit, whereupon he introduced me in a dialect which, translated, approximated something like: 'This is Fräulein Raye. Look after her; she deserves nothing but the finest.'

'Then Fräulein Raye does well to come here. Ah, Misha,' winked the plump paprika lady, 'he buys my spices now. When he was a boy, he used to steal them.'

'Misha' turned out to be the pet name by which Emil was known to one and all. 'My father called me Misha,' was all he offered by way of explanation. Emil Fährmann may have disdained titles, but he had his own method of observing social distinctions. He permitted no further enquiry, nor did he invite me to address him thus.

But he did welcome my invitation to come to supper that evening. It was not the most prudent act on my part; but given his generous assistance, it seemed an appropriate gesture. After all, if he wished, he could have declined.

Emil arrived with a bottle of wine and the copy of Gibbon I had refrained from purchasing the other day.

'Your father?' he indicated the portrait. 'When I met him, he had a beard. In retrospect, he looked like a mini Trotsky without the glasses. Do you think it a good likeness?'

'Very much so.'

'It was painted by Egon Schiele. Schiele used to live in Vienna but died during the War. He and your father would have been about the same age.'

Emil knew every nook and cranny of the apartment, every ornament, picture and piece of furniture. The light fittings were designed by the architect, he informed me, the easy chair in the corner by Hoffmann, the dining table by Adolf Loos. The Madonna and child on the wall in the bedroom was a Romanian glass painting; the sideboard, a fine piece of Slovenian carving; the glassware, Bohemian.

'Might I add,' he continued, 'that was a very valuable vase you hurled at me last night.'

'You deserved it. You seem very knowledgeable. Are you an artist?'

'I am an architect.'

'But why—?'

'Do I work in a bookshop? Because there are no jobs for architects. The corporate state does not wish to house its citizens. It builds churches like the Vater-Unser-Garage— the new church in the Sandleitenhof. I design homes, not churches. Of what use are churches? We have churches on every street corner, and what do we find inside? Statues. Your father was killed in the War, yes?'

'No. He was badly injured. He passed away last year.'

'Ah, hence the *Trauerkleidung*,' he sneered, arching an eyebrow at my black dress. 'Well, you'll have no trouble feeling at home in Wien. We have a cemetery half the size of Zurich and twice as much fun. Death governs this city. The clericals persist in subjugating us with pious nonsense, assuring us that we will be rewarded in Heaven if we forego our rights and liberties and remain content with poverty. Meanwhile, the privileged classes indulge in debauchery and corruption, convinced that when they receive final absolution Heaven will welcome them. They pay a priest to say Mass for the repose of their souls. Church bells toll. They are entombed with ceremony, their graves marked with ornate headstones and tended by loved ones – Death's slaves – in heavy mourning. The rich have entire armoires devoted to death – full mourning, half-mourning, light mourning – while the poor must dye black their every garment and mourn till the end of their days.'

'And do you not think there might be some genuine feeling associated with the loss of someone dear? Clearly, you have never mourned.'

'You are right: I have never mourned. What's the point? I lost my entire family during the War. My sister died during the winter of 1916; my mother was blown apart in a factory explosion; my father drowned when his ship was torpedoed. I have seen comrades fall in battle. Kirschbaum, the former owner of the shop, whom I treasured as a friend and mentor, died at the hands of the fascist state. Anyway, what is death? Merely a trip on the Seventy-One.'

'A trip on the what?'

'Ah, the Seventy-One is the tram to the central cemetery,' Emil relished my ignorance. 'My family and friends have been the victims of a wasteful, imperialist war and a clerical regime. If I mourn them, I submit to that vile culture of death the imperialists and clericals so fondly promote. My life becomes death. No, I live for Life. Life is more important. And after Life? Nothing. Look at you: all in black, a showpiece of sorrow, riddled with guilt. You have a lump lodged in your throat. Why?'

'Guilt, schmilt. You are very forward.'

'And you are discreet?' he snickered. 'You take little trouble to hide the queries crossing your face, whereas I give my thoughts expression.'

'During which time you have given me little opportunity to express mine.'

'You are right. Come then, tell me a few things. I do not mind listening. Or ply me with questions. I am not afraid to answer. This is finger licking good, by the way,' he dangled his fork over the goulash.

Here I should note that our conversation proceeded in German, for Emil knew no English; the result being that Dad's dictionary became a third guest at our table. He was amused by my frequent consultations, many of which were unsuccessful because of his dialect. But he was patient with me, and gradually condescended to more standard parlance.

I learned that his father emigrated to Vienna where he worked on the barges, having been forced to leave his native Ukraine during a Czarist pogrom. His mother was a 'Herzogowiener'; that is, her family was originally from Herzegovina, although she was born in Vienna.

Orphaned during the War, Emil lived on the streets until he was befriended by Kirschbaum, the bookshop owner, who had no wife or family. He passed his remaining youth working in the shop, educating himself through extensive reading. Kirschbaum, on seeing his aptitude for draughtsmanship, arranged for him to study architecture. The banking collapse preventing him from exercising his profession, he returned to the bookshop and assisted his mentor until the latter's death, after which he took over the management of the store.

I asked him about his crooked leg, and he said it was caused by rickets, the consequence of starvation during the War and its aftermath. His nose was broken during Die Schreckentage, or 'Days of Terror'.

'In 1927,' he explained, 'there was a trial in which the offenders were acquitted of the murder of a war veteran and a child in Schattendorf, a village in the Burgenland. Burgenland is a region to the east, on the border with Hungary. The victims, who were associated with the Social Democrats, were marching in a demonstration when they were ambushed and shot from behind. The men arrested were Frontkämpfer.'

'Frontkämpfer?'

'A pro-German paramilitary group formed after the War. The "honourable gentlemen" pleaded self-defence. Self-defence? Shooting a one-eyed man and an eight-year-old boy is self-defence? They got off, thanks to their Hakenkreuzler lawyer. Do you know what that is?'

He pulled out a pencil and paper and drew a swastika. 'It is the symbol of the German National Socialist Worker's Party – the DNSAP. In principle, the party was abolished by the Ständestaat, our present government (for want of a better word); but it has always been affiliated with Hitler's mob, the National Socialist German Worker's Party, or NSDAP.[5]

'I was employed on a building site at the time,' he continued,

---

[5] *DNSAP*: Deutsche Nationalsozialistiche Arbeiterpartei.
    NSDAP: Nationalsozialistiche Deutsche Arbeiterpartei.

'and was shocked when I read the verdict in the morning paper. Everyone was— Clericals as well as Democrats. We all expected a conviction. Instead of going to work, I joined my comrades on the Ringstrasse and marched in protest to the Palace of Justice. Thousands had gathered – men, women, and children. Despite the numbers and the intensity of feeling, our demonstration was peaceful. We carried no arms; nor was our paramilitary, the Schützbund, involved.

'But the authorities called in mounted police. Many grew anxious. Then the police were ordered to charge. They came at us with sabres. I tried to get out of the way, but I tripped and fell under a horse. When I came to, I was in hospital with my face in bandages. I then learned that the Justizpalast had been set ablaze, and that Chancellor Seipel – Der Prälat ohne Milde – had instructed for the police to be issued with military weapons and to fire at the crowd. At least eighty died and hundreds were wounded. Of course, the Bloody Prelate blamed us for the fire – the Red Antichrist he called us. We didn't do it. We held a majority in the government. It was not in our interest to ruin our reputation through destruction. Besides, what would we gain by putting our own at risk? I am certain it was the Swastikas who set fire to the Justizpalast.

'That day marked the end of democracy in Austria. The Republic had made provision for trial by jury; but in the Schattendorf Verdict, either the jury was rigged, or the jurors allowed their politics to influence their conclusion. Where is the democracy in that? Furthermore, our leaders told us that we could not demonstrate against a verdict returned by a jury. Do we not have a right to express our views? We have always been able to protest an unjust decision. Again, where is the democracy in that? After Die Schreckentage, any protest or strike was suppressed by the Heimwehr, and the press was regulated. Now, there is no democracy. Mark my words, though, one day there will be no Ständestaat.'

'What do you mean?'

'My face may be broken; but that doesn't make me a broken man.'

I don't know whether you know it, Roddy, but there is a sculpture of a boxer fashioned at the end of the Greek Golden Age, following Philip of Macedon's conquest of the City States. He has been in a fight, for his hands are still strapped, and his muscular body is bruised and bloody. He sits with his legs apart, leaning forward slightly; his forearms rest on his thighs, his strong hands are softly folded. His head is turned slightly, his gaze directed upward to reveal a battered face with a broken nose and furrowed brow. His ears bulge; his beard is thick and ragged. Worn out, he has not been victorious. Nor is he defeated. He knows how to take the blows. There will come another day, another fight, and he will rise, retape his hands, and face his foe once more.

Looking at Emil Fährman, I was convinced that somehow the ancient boxer had come to life, donned a crumpled suit, and travelled to Vienna; for there he was, at my dining table, enjoying a plate of goulash. But unlike that Hellenic pugilist whose eyes were empty hollows, Emil's smouldering blue orbs were full of expression. His defiant glare reminded me of another figure: Michelangelo's David. Here was a man who knew his own mind, who could size up his enemy and fearlessly take him on. My guest was no fatalist; he was biding his time between bouts.

'And what happened to the men who were acquitted?' I asked.

'It would not surprise me if retribution was carried out some other way.'

'And would you have been satisfied with that?'

'Retaliation of that kind is no resolution; it perpetuates the conflict.'

'So, you would have preferred to see lawful justice run its course?'

'Lawful justice?' he sniggered. 'Laws are made for the exploitation of those who don't understand them, or who are prevented by naked misery from obeying them. That is all. Ten years have passed since the Schattendorf Verdict, and, I tell you, if it had happened today, the Frontkampfer would have been found guilty and hanged. And if, by some curious circumstance they were acquitted, we would have been hanged for demonstrating.'

'And what if they were never caught and tried in the first place?'

'You are very inquisitive. Why?'

'Because it interests me.'

'You are more discreet than I thought. Why does it interest you so much?' he lit a cigarette.

The lamplight glimmered in his eyes, and I thought once more of the ancient boxer. Tawdry as it might seem to modern taste, the Greeks of antiquity were fond of painting their statues, with the result that the cold, hard marble figures, which we deem the epitome of restrained beauty, would have exhibited vitality and passion confronting to the modern viewer. Sometimes, precious stones were used for eyes; and I wondered whether such was the case with the boxer – that his eyes were void because once upon a time they had been inlaid with jewels. How extraordinary, that one who was little more than a slave – whose sport had more in common with beasts than civilised men – could be so ennobled and testify to Art and Civilisation. But it was the spirit of the man that had been enshrined: his integrity which remained intact despite humiliation and debasement.

Likewise, Emil's battered face and rumpled hair, swarthy complexion and rough manner coloured him in a way that was confronting, improper. But, in the jewels that were his eyes lay conviction, determination, honesty, and kindness. Dark-rimmed, they sparkled like rare blue diamonds in a coal-lined cavern. Glittering through the sfumato of cigarette smoke, Emil's eyes tantalised me so much that I desired to snatch them, like a thief desecrating an idol, and risk being cursed forevermore. What I coveted, though, was not the jewels themselves, but what they represented: integrity, courage, and strength of purpose forged from hardship. So, to steal would have been counter to my deeper wishes. Instead, what was required of me was to tell the truth, and Emil's gaze compelled me to tell it ruthlessly.

'Because my mother was murdered, and the murderer got away,' I replied. 'There was no arrest, and a trial would have been pointless anyway because of inconclusive evidence. It is not right that people should commit crimes and not be punished. I don't see what's so funny!'

'Your naivety is touching,' he guffawed.

'You don't need to be patronising, either. I intend to find the murderer. I have evidence. It was my aunt and I will find her, and, and—'

'What? Bump her off?'

'Would you?'

'I wouldn't do anything. Not my goat—⁶'

'Don't mock me!'

'Well, I suppose you have your reasons, just as your aunt probably had reason to kill your mother.'

'Whose side are you on?'

'Must I take sides? It's a fact of life: every action is a reaction.'

'But it's wrong to kill.'

'Why do you say that?'

'You don't think so?'

He rolled another cigarette and scraped the match against the tinder. 'Personally,' he exhaled a swirling stream of smoke, 'I wouldn't kill, because for me to oppress another individual is counter to everything I uphold. Not because some deity has decreed that it is wrong to kill. God is a fiction. Nor because those in power deem it a crime and will punish me if I'm caught. In certain circumstances it is necessary to kill. Our beloved government, for instance, thinks it has every right and duty to

---

⁶ *Not my goat*: Part of a Yiddish expression, 'not my goat and not my Hanukkah candle', meaning 'none of my business'.

string up those who disagree; so petty thieves are hanged, and big ones pardoned.

'You know what you should do?' he leaned forward and puffed thoughtfully, 'Confront your aunt about the murder and make her pay with her own blood. Then, complete the cycle by killing yourself. I don't envy your position,' he revelled in the effect of his remark. 'So, you've come to Vienna to fulfil a vendetta?'

'No. My aunt lives in Paris. I intend to leave in November.'

'That's lucky! Dining with a potential murderess doesn't augur much for comfort.'

'And the same could be said of a guest who breaks into other peoples' apartments. How did you get in, anyway?'

He chuckled, stubbed his cigarette, and brandished a skeleton key. 'Now that you are here, I promise I will not break in again. You are not familiar with Vienna?'

'Not yet.'

'Then permit me to show you around. Business is slow in the summer and I could spare an afternoon or two.'

'I do not wish to be a tourist.'

'More reason to have a native for a guide.'

'There is no need to go to any trouble, especially with your sore leg—'

'My leg does not bother me. Besides, I have an excellent way to show you Vienna without walking far at all.'

26

The Giant Wheel

'I TOLD YOU, I didn't want to be a tourist,' I complained as Emil assisted me from the tram the following Sunday afternoon. We arrived at the Prater, Vienna's amusement park, amidst a mass display of Americans in floral chiffon and crisp suiting. Decked with cameras and shaded by spacious millinery, the various individuals bore the hallmarks of common ancestry and demonstrated an astonishing command of spoken English.

An enormous Ferris wheel, the Riesenrad, dominated the park. In the distance opposite, down a broad avenue lined with chestnut trees, I glimpsed a palatial building.

'That relic of Imperialist-Capitalist hegemony is the Rotunde,' Emil remarked. 'It was constructed for the 1873 World Trade Fair.'

While we walked, I could not help staring at the Orthodox Jews with dark curled sideburns, top hats, and long coats. Meanwhile, Emil pointed out (and greeted) the occasional artist or entertainer.

In the fairground proper, older men found youth in the company of fanciful blondes; couples romanced on the carousel; and dizzy youngsters flirted on the shifting boards of the Mysterious Hotel. Well-heeled parents succumbed to the whims of children demanding rides and treats. Americans captured memories in movies, while fashionable Brits attempted communication by shouting in English. And there were those for whom wealth was foreign, who counted the pennies they had saved for a ride on the roller coaster. Some lone figures perhaps had come to lose their sorrows in the surrounding merriment; while with a puritanical sneer, others scorned the transitory and vain. A few unfortunates brought their discord with them – these, the crazy jollity could not placate.

'Vienna's highest ideals are realised in the Prater,' Emil assumed a learned tone, 'Classlessness and pleasure.'

'I wonder you condescend to such entertainment.'

'And I wonder at your disdain. Visiting in mourning, what possessed you?'

'I didn't intend to come here!'

'You wished to see Vienna. Well, I guarantee you will see Vienna in its entirety here. Ah, this should brighten you up!' He purchased a posy of pansies from a flower seller and presented it. Then he fixed my hat with daisies.

'Emil, I must look a fool!'

'Then you will not be out of place. See for yourself.'

We entered a Hall of Mirrors whereupon I came face to face with a grotesquely fat young lady accompanied by a twisted man with a gargoyle face. Through this Versailles of sorcerers' eyes we passed, spectral thin, squat, distended, uneven; and by the time we re-entered the fairground I was none the wiser regarding my ludicrousness.

Emil suggested a gelato. 'And now,' he continued as he passed me my cone, 'I will introduce you to the most powerful man in Europe.'

The illustrustrissimo in question turned out to be Eduard, the Riesenrad operator.

'You see, although everyone is entitled to ride, Eduard determines who is on top, and who is on the bottom; who gets on, and who gets off. Is that not so, Eduard, mein Chaver?[7] Emil clapped the operator on the back

'A revolution for only a couple of Groschen,' Eduard smiled, 'And sometimes you can enjoy it for free,'

Slowly, gracefully, the wheel lifted us high above the city. Down we swept and up again in a steady, stately circle before we halted, our carriage topmost. 'We better take what we can get while we're on top of the horse,' Emil passed me a small pair of binoculars. 'See?' he chuckled, pointing at St Stephen's spire, 'We're higher than old Steffl. Not even the bishop can claim superiority when you're at the top of the Riesenrad.'

He pointed out the distant woods and hills, and described the districts radiating from the central ring: bustling Mariahilf with its many shops; Simmering, where the population was mostly deceased, being interred in Vienna's main cemetery, the Zentralfriedhof; Favoriten, a predominantly working-class area; Hietzing on the western outskirts, the domain of the aristocracy; and Döbling with its vineyards and taverns.

The wheel jolted, and I would have fallen had not Emil steadied me. 'You'll have to balance better than that,' he grinned, 'or you'll never succeed in bumping off your aunt.'

I wrenched myself away from him so hard that I fell properly with my ice cream upturned on the floor. He laughed and chivalrously extended his hand. Accepting his offer, I pulled him

---

[7]   Roddy, the only way to do justice to Emil's multi-pronged turn of phrase is to leave it be. So, I've footnoted the meanings of his Yiddish expressions for your ready reference. *Mein Chaver*: my friend (a Yiddish term of endearment); my comrade (in left-wing organisations).

down with me.

'See?' he laughed even harder as he wiped the ice cream off his clothes, 'Sprawling in the muck with the rest of us. Ah well, at least there's beer. Let's have a pint.'

'He's no Christian gentleman, I can tell you,' remarked Frau Geplapper when I met her in the vestibule next morning. She nodded in the direction of the upstairs argument. To escape the vituperation, I had left to do some errands, for the persons involved lived directly opposite me.

'Would you believe,' Frau Geplapper leant across, 'he refused to have the child baptised? I'll wager he's stained with Hebrew blood. I haven't lived the last sixty years without being able to spot a Jew when I meet one. Now he won't admit he's the father. Ha! She bears a child as dark as that, and he claims he had nothing to do with it?'

A door slammed, and the lift began its descent. I tried to excuse myself, but Frau Geplapper had some advice:

'He has a way with women, and it doesn't matter their rank, their shape, or their age. She has only to wear a skirt and you can be certain what he will do. I've seen him with all sorts, from a countess to a common servant girl— and I no longer have fingers and toes to keep track. Be careful, Fräulein Raye. He likes them young, and he particularly amuses himself with those who are unspoiled. The curly-headed good-for-nothing, I cannot think what they see in him. Hush! Here he comes!'

Emil limped out of the elevator. Frau Geplapper glared as he passed, while I reeled from a rush of heat, tasted again strawberry ice cream and grew heady with the scent of love-in-idleness.

But what had Frau Geplapper seen? Had she seen me charmed by Emil's coarse chivalry? Had she noticed that we returned late, having spent most of the evening drinking, dining and dancing in the courtyard of the Schweizerhaus, and that he had escorted me as far as my apartment?

As for Emil...

'This is a pleasant intrusion,' he looked up from his accounts with a gleam of amused affection. 'I suppose you've come for the sheets. I have them here.'

'Why did you take me to the Prater?'

'To show you round and to give you a good time. You had a good time, didn't you? Or did you want more than that?' he leered.

'How dare you!'

'Mind you, you need kissing, and lots of it; but if you want kissing, look elsewhere. My hands are full. It always starts with a kiss. And if I were you, I wouldn't believe all our worthy caretaker's shmues[8] about the curly-headed good-for-nothing.'

'Is it true that you're married?'

'Why should I be?'

'I should think it perfectly obvious why!'

'Ah! Do you mean Odalia? Oda? The blonde with the baby upstairs? Now why would I want to do that? If I married her, I'd have to divorce her. No, my chaste and pretty Phoebe, I am not married.'

'And are you Jewish?'

'Is this a Jewish nose?' he tapped his broken nose and winked.

'Never mind,' I shrugged, 'It's not really my business.'

'No, it isn't. And nor is it the State's. Still, the one, holy, catholic and apostolic Ständestaat requires me to have a religion and to stipulate it on my child's birth certificate. I am *konfessionslos*: without religion. So, I must instead give my parents' religion. But my parents were also *konfessionslos*. Feh! What do I put? If you went back far enough, you'd find a few tallits and kippahs; but what has that nonsense to do with me? And why does the State want to know? To further oppress us? Anyway, as luck would have it, I'm not the father; so, I will not put a mark on that kid's birth certificate, which is what the argument upstairs was about. Is that what you're getting at?'

I nodded.

'Listen, I had a fling with Oda about a year ago— I was drunk, it was cold, and Oda was willing. She certainly let me believe I was responsible. If that were the case, I would provide for the kid. The problem is, he has brown eyes. My eyes are blue. Oda also has blue eyes. How can I be the father? That blonde kurveh[9] took advantage of me. She even ousted me from my home; which was why I was sleeping in your apartment.'

'Among other things. So, you mean to say you live directly opposite me?'

'I am looking after the apartment for a comrade, Mendel, who these days is a journalist in Paris.'

'Well you're not doing a very good job of it. Where are you sleeping now?'

'Hotel Kirschbaum,' he glanced over his shoulder. 'There are rooms behind the shop. Albrecht also sleeps there. Unfortunately, it's not the Metropole, but so long as there's health... Anyway, Oda must leave. And if she can't look after the baby, she must put him up for adoption. Give the poor kid a decent start.'

'Who's the father?'

'Ask Oda,' he shrugged.

---

[8] *Shmues* (schmooze): small talk, gossip.
[9] *Kurveh*: (profane) whore, slut, bitch.

Despite his indifference, I could see in his eyes slubs of compassion and regret. Similarly, his nubbly body and nose, his stubbled chin and wryly curled lips twisted around a kind heart; and in his actions, choice and circumstance, purpose and passion, virtue and vice were knotted into an uneven homespun.

It could be said that character is the craft of fate, and that life's spindle does not always produce a smooth thread; and while one might show a preference for silk, it is good to remember that those fine and lustrous filaments are the work of a worm. As for quality muslin, it is the uniform product of mills and machinery. And what of rayon, silk's counterfeit? A scientific extrusion, limp and cheap. Homespun, drawn out by human hands, might not make fine fabric; but the cloth is strong and durable, and with time wears soft.

'Well, thank you for yesterday, Emil.'

'Nito farvos.[10] Now, since you don't wish to be trifled with, and I don't wish to trifle with you, we can be friends, yes? Do you need any more help?'

'As a matter of fact, I would like to know where I might find this bakery.'

'Ah, that's in Die Mazzesinsel,' he mumbled upon studying the address. 'Come with me.'

Die Mazzesinsel, Emil explained, was the local soubriquet for Vienna's Jewish Quarter. Situated across the canal, it derived its nickname from the unleavened Matzo bread baked at Passover. The district was officially named Leopoldstadt, in honour of the emperor who banished the Jews from Vienna. 'And then they came back,' my guide added in rebellious delight. Aside from the Riesenrad which dominated the skyline, there was nothing especially unusual about the district. The buildings – even the synagogues – were in keeping with the wide-eaved, solid neo-baroque style of the rest of the city; likewise, the combination of cafes and theatres, shops and apartments, churches and markets, wealthy and poor, was no different. But what a mix of races and languages! Men and women touting modern fashions walked alongside peasants from far-flung parts of Europe. Children in robes and rags romped in the street; bearded gentlemen in caftans argued and bartered.

We stopped at a chocolate shop where I purchased a selection to take to Mr Epstein's family. The shopkeeper could have been my sister, so closely did she resemble me; and in our exchange, I almost expected her to address me by name. Instead she smiled

---

[10] *Nito farvos*: Don't mention it.

knowingly. Clearly, she had formed the same impression.

And as we continued along Taborstrasse, the main street, I beheld my features in face after face. Usually I was the olive, dark-eyed exception to the blonde norm – the exotic misfit among my peers. Here, I blended in, and I relaxed in my newfound obscurity. Of course, my speech and manners gave me away as a foreigner; but if I kept quiet, I passed unnoticed.

'Judenschwein! Judenschwein!'

Shopkeepers hurried outside, and housewives leant out from open windows. Others retired indoors. The boldly inclined cussed back. A loutish rabble of youths, bored with summer and full of beer, barged down the thoroughfare. They pushed past a man, then tugged his beard to test if it was real. Snatching his hat, they tossed it onto a pile of manure and made him stamp on it. A policeman's whistle blew. The youths took flight, shoving their victim so hard that he, too, fell in the dung.

Emil rescued him and used his stick to retrieve the hat which he wiped as clean as he could, before passing it back with what I assumed was an apology.

'What language was that, Emil?'

'Yiddish. Yiddish was the language my parents had in common. He's from the Ukraine,' he indicated the gentleman, 'and, like a thousand others, has fled Stalin's purges. Ah, here is the bakery.'

The bakery was full of women, many of whom looked as if they wore wigs – cushions of hair in identical neat arrangements. 'It is customary for Jewish women to cover their heads when they marry. Some shave their hair, and then they cover their heads with more hair.' Emil explained, relishing the irony.

Fresh soap and lavender mingled with the baking smells I had known and loved since my childhood days with the Epsteins - rye, nutty and earthy; and peppery, fennelly caraway. Behind the counter, a boy of about thirteen years scurried like a ferret in a burrow, taking orders and fetching loaves, surfacing only to hand purchases and count change. I enquired after Herr David Epstein, Mr Epstein's youngest brother. The boy called into the kitchen, from which came a man in an apron, his forearms dusted with flour. Short and stocky, and lean from his labours, he had the same bespectacled Schubertian face as the man who was a second father to me.

'Fräulein Phoebe Raye?' he wiped his hands and mopped his forehead. 'Fräulein Phoebe? Herzlich willkommen! My dear ladies, this is Fräulein Raye, the daughter of my oldest brother's best friend all the way from Australia! May his memory be for a blessing! Jockel!' he called to the boy. 'Run upstairs and tell your grandfather!' The boy returned assisting an old man, a silver-haired version of his son. Introductions were repeated for the sake of Herr Epstein the Elder and the benefit of anyone else who had happened to enter either from necessity or curiosity.

'Misha!' Herr David Epstein spotted Emil at the back of the shop, 'What brings you here?'

'Davido,' he grinned, 'It's been a long time.'

'Do you know each other?' I asked.

'Know each other? I should be asking the same of you!' exclaimed David Epstein. 'We spent our childhood together down by the canal where the Rabbi would round us up and chase us off to school. Misha always escaped. You will share our *mittag* with us? Both of you, come upstairs, I insist. Jockel, fetch your mother and sisters. Vati and I will finish serving. And take care!'

In the simply furnished flat upstairs, we met David Epstein's new young wife, Pauline, and his mother, elderly Frau Epstein who immediately laid extra places at their table. Jockel or Jakob returned with his mother and sisters: Bela Austerlitz (Mr Epstein's sister), nine-year-old Mitzi, and Rosa who was but a toddler. Mani Austerlitz, Bela's husband, who ran the family stall in the Naschmarkt, followed soon after.

Old Mr Epstein explained that when Dad arrived in Vienna at the age of sixteen, he rented rooms in Leopoldstadt, a few doors further down the street. He then told me a story I knew well but did not mind hearing again, my recent experience having furnished me with context.

The Epsteins' son Reuben (Mr Epstein) had fallen victim to Jew-baiting. Dad, who had been bullied as a child, detested bullying of any sort and took on the thugs. The skirmish earned him a black eye, bruised knuckles, and a meal with the Epstein family, following which he pulled out a cigarette and lit it on the menorah.

'The look on his face when he realised what he had done!' old Mr Epstein imitated Dad's embarrassed expression, one hand over his mouth and his dark eyes wide open. 'He did not know about Hanukkah. We saw him every Sabbath after that.'

'And between times,' added his wife. 'Boys! Always hungry!'

'Always hungry eh, Jockel?' the old man winked at Jakob who was helping himself to seconds. 'He repaid us with his violin, and Reuben played piano for him. Beautiful! We knew he'd go far.'

'And give no end of trouble. We have the rascal to thank for introducing our son to a shiksa.'[11]

'Now, now, Friedl, they went with my blessing. It has been a happy marriage.'

---

[11] *Shiksa*: (derog.) non-Jewish girl.

'Feh! I give him four children, and he has the gall to say a childless marriage is a happy one! Why did I go to the trouble?'

'It was hard to let him go, but time has shown Reuben took the better path. We could have lost him as well as Josef in the War.'

'Instead, we lose Reuben in Australia. Australia? What is Australia?'

'It could have been worse. You left him well?'

I gave a positive account of life at home and passed the gifts Mrs Epstein had packed for her in-laws.

'See, Friedl, she is like a grand-daughter. You were not troubled on your way here, Phoebe?'

I told them of the street thugs.

'It is not the first time, and so long as the Ostjuden remain it won't be the last,' old Mr Epstein observed. 'Look, Misha, what your Stalin has done to us.'

'My Stalin?' Emil protested.

'You have mellowed in your middle age,' teased David Epstein.

'I was never a Stalinist. Why should I be?' Emil did not appreciate the jest. 'The Stalinists ought to take a lesson from our Riesenrad. A stately rotation is as much a revolution as the whirling blade of a circular saw. Here in Vienna we proved that Marx's dictatorship of the proletariat could be achieved democratically. Stalin's usurpation of power is counter to the communist spirit, and his purges are worse than the Czars'. Furthermore, you forget that the Ostjuden fought for democracy in Russia just as we did in 'eighteen. They should be welcomed as comrades, not alienated or persecuted.'

'They alienate themselves, and they will continue to be persecuted if they do not conform,' countered old Mr Epstein. 'When my father brought us to Vienna from Brünn I watched him trim his beard. As soon as he could, he bought a new suit. He insisted upon us speaking German and made sure we learned to read and write. We worked hard for the liberty to live as Austrians and worship as Jews. And we stand to lose everything if they do not do the same.'

'And if they refuse?'

'Then they should go, Misha. Maybe we need a Jewish state after all.'

'You share Herr Hitler's views?' Emil teased.

'Heaven forbid! I would sooner have Herr Bundeskanzler Schuschnigg.'

'And better Schuschnigg than Stalin eh, Misha?' winked David Epstein.

'Why are we going this way?' I asked Emil as he helped me into a tram going the opposite direction; but I received no reply until we arrived at a massive red and yellow brick fortress that was quite unlike the majestic white buildings of the rest of the city.

'This is Karl-Marx-Hof,' Emil proudly tapped his stick on the window. While the mighty arches, towers, and crenels recalled medieval castles, the colourful brickwork and numerous stark, square windows presented a striking, modern façade. The building continued for another half a mile.

'Did you design it, Emil?'

'I helped with the design, drafted the plans, and assisted on the construction. It was a dream come true. Before the War, my family lived in a single room tenement near where we visited today. It had no window, and I spent whole winters inside. We slept in one bed and washed when we could. The water we shared with three other families, and a single latrine had to suffice for twenty people. That was my home until my sister and my parents died, after which I had no home at all, for I could not pay the rent to the wealthy scumbag who owned the habitation.

'Thousands lived like that— and still do, while the rich have estates and palaces. When we established the Republic, we cleared some of the slums and built homes subsidised by soaking the bourgeois classes, where families could live in safety and comfort on rents a working man could afford. We provided playgrounds and courtyards, decent laundries, medical facilities, shops, and kindergartens. In Karl-Marx-Hof every apartment has a window and a balcony. I made sure of that.'

'But what are those dents in the walls, Emil?' One section of the building was riddled with cavities.

'You have not seen artillery damage before?'

'No, never.'

'And you think you have trouble!' he scoffed. 'During the Civil War, in February 1934, we barricaded ourselves here. The State's paramilitary, the Heimwehr, opened fire without heeding the families inside. Many of my best friends died in the conflict or were executed afterwards. Those who survived fled either to Spain or to the Soviets and I've heard nothing since.

'Here in Vienna we are like children playing Ringa, Ringa, Reia: we hold hands and circle, first to the left, then to the right; then down we fall crying shoo. "Husch, Husch, Husch!" Do you think husch will keep Hitler out? Or Stalin?' Then he leant into me and whispered, 'Who cares about your vendetta?'

Was he mocking me? Goading me? Belittling me? I could not tell.

'*I* do,' I glared.

27

Rats

EMIL AND I PARTED COMPANY at the bookshop; and upon reaching my apartment, I found a visitor.

Frau Geplapper was right about my new friend fancying younger women. Odalia was about twenty years old (Emil was in his early thirties). Her scarlet bolero and rhinestone necklace glamorised a plain, tight-fitting frock.

'Well, Emil, if you were drunk when you met her, she must have been equally inebriated,' I thought, for Oda was tanned and very blonde – almost white blonde – tall, and well endowed: a composite of the Venus of Willendorf and Mae West.

'Be careful of the rats,' she warned, her pale eyes as round and luminous as two rose windows. 'They are everywhere. I saw a large one this morning, in my apartment. They come in through the drains. You will need this.'

The box of rat bait she handed me was an unusual housewarming, to say the least.

'I have more if you need it,' she added, pleased to help. In fact, that was all she wished to do; for when I invited her in for coffee, she declined.

'I suppose she's concerned for her baby,' I surveyed my lounge for signs of infiltration. 'And I know what you're going to say,' I cautioned the Portrait. 'They're all part of God's creation. That may be so, but Mr Samuel Whiskers is not going to get the better of me.'

Other neighbours extended more conventional welcomes. Herr Weissmüller, who lived below and worked as a banker, introduced me to his wife and lively young boys, Hugo and Georg. Frau Weissmüller was happy to help me hire a maid, should I have need of one. Doktor and Frau Blumenthal, an elderly couple, had resided in the Majolikahaus since it was built. They remembered Dad, and were pleased to hear the violin again, as was Herr Frankl, the owner of the building. Opposite the Blumenthals lived Professor and Frau Professor Lehrer.

In a friendly gesture, Frau Weissmüller invited me to join her for coffee one morning.

We sat on the balcony, soaking in the sunshine and watching Georg and Hugo at play in the courtyard, when music began to blare. Frau Weissmüller urged her boys inside. Minutes later, Odalia marched into the courtyard, dressed in a playsuit – a short, buttoned garment reserved for the seaside or for sports – and assumed centre stage, legs spanned, arms on hips, her figure testifying to a childhood rich in cheese and butter. No doubt there were hundreds of Odalias scattered across the Austrian countryside herding goats, tending sheep, pressing against cows and squirting milk into pails; but to witness one enter the genteel confines of a Viennese courtyard was akin to watching a cow trot into a concert hall. She began to swing her arms up and down, right and left; she twisted her torso, reached for the sky, and plunged to her toes. Up, down, up and down, circling, skipping, kicking, squatting: every move a rhythmic and vigorous expression of the music.

'Always Von Suppé,' Frau Weissmüller rolled her eyes as we watched through the window.

And we were not her only secret audience.

'Andreas!' Frau Geplapper yelled, 'Come inside!'

I soon became familiar with Odalia's drill and the music which accompanied it – the sprightly, jubilant March from *Boccaccio*. The moment her gramophone sounded, drapes were closed and children called. Dr Blumenthal took his paper indoors. Andreas Geplapper loitered around the lower courtyard entrance. And once the session concluded, everyone resumed their morning activities as if nothing unusual had occurred. Aside from the Weissmüller boys who protested when called inside, and who staged a whimsical version of the routine upon release, no one complained. After all, Odalia was as much entitled to her *Lebensraum* as everyone else. Perhaps concern for her newly acquired motherhood permitted tolerance of her eccentricity. Or was it the universal dislike of her 'irresponsible communist rake of a "husband" the bookseller' (Frau Weissmüller's description) that prompted sympathy?

For Emil was the Quasimodo of the Majolikahaus – a deformed and shadowy presence who confined his activities to either very early in the morning, or very late at night. What visits he paid to his upstairs apartment, he timed to coincide with Odalia's calisthenics routine. Laden with provisions, he scuttled about, and re-emerged with a bag of dirty laundry. These tasks he undertook at considerable personal risk; for whenever he and Oda collided, hysterics ensued, which upset her baby son Waldemar, and everyone else.

Aside from Odalia, Emil looked after Albrecht the organ grinder. Conscripted into the army in middle age, and blinded during the War, the older man was without home or family. Emil kept him fed, sheltered, and clothed; he read to him and took him to the park, and, once a week, to the Turkish baths in Mariahilf. Albrecht, in turn, minded the shop. He could be relied upon to give an account of the various comings and goings in Emil's absence, describing visitors in detail – their height and build, their sex and occupation, from which part of the city they hailed, and how well-off they might be. Me, he knew by my footsteps and my perfume; and he always greeted me before I greeted him. Sometimes he called me Trudl, and when I asked him why, he replied:

'She was my little girl. She used to be my eyes. She died from influenza when she was sixteen. Ask Misha, and he will tell you she was very beautiful (he fancied her, you know). Like you, gnädiges Fräulein. You must be very beautiful.'

I saw Albrecht every day, for I often called into the bookshop to ask Emil's advice on everything from trams to piano tuners. Always he liked to know the latest news, which I soon realised had nothing to do with the headlines, but concerned instead the theatres, the book I was reading, or any forthcoming concerts. These topics he discussed at length and with great enthusiasm, drawing on a vast pre-war archive. Meanwhile, my many requests provided Emil with an excuse to liberate himself from the boredom of shopkeeping; and my gratitude earned him an evening meal in my apartment, to which Albrecht was also invited, and which was followed by a request for me to perform. Piano or violin it mattered not. They enjoyed both.

'You're not quite so fancy free as I thought,' the Portrait observed after Emil and I parted company one evening. 'Seems that Robin Goodfellow's rubbed potion in your eyes and you've fallen in love with the first creature to come your way.' His eyes twinkled, and his lips had curled into an amused little smile.

'At least he's not an ass. Anyway, I, for one, have other, more important priorities.'

'More important than love?'

I opened his lacquered violin case and made ready to practise.

'What do you think of her?'

'A very pretty instrument, with remarkable fire in the tone: a genuine gypsy violin.'

'Picked her up in Budapest. She plays well. Mind you, I can play anything.'

'Well, don't think you can play me. Now if you don't mind, I need to work. I am meeting Professor Rosé.'

'Ha, ha! He'll sort you out. And send him my fondest regards.'

28

Musical Royalty

PROFESSOR ARNOLD ROSÉ, fifty years the concertmaster of the Vienna Philharmonic; leader of the renowned Rosé Quartet; friend of Brahms, Wagner, and Mahler; known to every leading conductor and artist in the music world; and last, but not least, Dad's teacher...

What would he think of me?

Such were my thoughts which rumbled along with the Döbling tram, and which paused when I compared the stops with Emil's directions.

I soon arrived at the Professor's apartment on Pyrkergasse, a classic broad-eaved, symmetrical, white-bricked Viennese residence which had the added distinction of a front garden. A maid brought me inside, and while I waited, I viewed the print of Michelangelo's *Creation of Man* that hung in the hall.

'Well, if Professor Rosé thinks anything of me, I hope it won't be in a match-making capacity. What do I want with men?' I spied beautiful, wide-eyed Eve, lovingly wrapped in the muscular arm of God the Creator. 'And why are You so mindful of man when he is so unmindful of You?' I demanded of the stern, fatherly God in the picture.

There would be no limp-wristed Adam if Emil lay in his place. The hand would be turned upwards and the *digitus impudicus* raised. 'What do you think of that?' I asked the paternal Creator. 'And what is the point of loving someone who does not love you in return?'

A month had passed since I left Istanbul, and there had been no letter from Kerem; while Emil's friendship was merely an extension of his enlightened sense of social justice, as became clear earlier that morning when, in seeking his advice on travelling to Döbling, I found the bookshop closed.

'He is not here, Fräulein Raye,' Albrecht tipped his hat. 'Zusa's back in town.'

And who was Zusa? Well, whoever she was, she possessed the transformative power of the princess who kissed the frog; for when

Emil did appear, he had a spring in his step and a spark in his eye; and his mangy clothes were topped with a splendidly knitted Fairisle vest which he wore like a king.

'Fräulein Raye, good afternoon,' a stately young woman introduced herself. Tall, groomed to perfection, her polo shirt and pencil skirt smoothed over her curves, her wavy dark hair perfectly set, her cheeks like apples, her brown eyes soulful, Alma Rosé was stunning. Escorting her was an Alsatian named Arno. 'He's quite harmless,' she assured me as she hugged and stroked her pet. Arno growled and grinned. Alma, who spoke English well, gushed regret at Dad's passing, and apologised for not being able to meet sooner, 'but Mutti is not well these days. You should have come to Salzburg for the festival. Everyone was there. I would have introduced you.'

While Dad had only talked of Professor Rosé with the utmost respect, I had attuned to the affectionate tones of his voice and imagined a milder personality than the man who descended *alla breve*. He was tall and stout, with black-rimmed spectacles, thick white hair and a trim goatee.

'Herr Hofrat,' I greeted him in obeisance to Dad's guidelines and instinctively dropped to a curtsey as if I had been presented at Court. But the moment I bent my knees, I sensed I had been too formal and blushed and did not know whether to remain curtsied or stand again.

'And you must be "Possum",' he extended his hand, assisted my rise, and escorted me to his music room. A second maid served tea. There were further condolences, enquiries after my health and trip, and apologies for lack of prior contact. I passed him my gift – a small portrait of Rosé himself holding a violin.

'I wanted to know what you looked like, so Dad painted you for me.'

'He flatters me. I am not quite so young. Ha! The Kreutzer!' he laughed upon scrutinising the music on the stand in the picture. 'And Mein Beethoven,' he smilingly indicated the bust of the composer whom Dad had depicted scowling, with an eyebrow comically raised in approval. Little wonder the detail pleased him. A more solemn version atop a nearby cabinet presided over the room in which we sat. 'The outlining and vivid pigments remind me of Romanian folk painting. Have you seen Romanian icons?'

'There is a Madonna and Child in my apartment.' But I had not made the connection between that vignette and Dad's art, which I deemed quirky and modern.

'Now tell me, Fräulein, why does he call you Possum?'

'When Dad came home late from concerts he would call into my nursery and find me awake. I was never upset. It was as if I was waiting up for him. Apparently, I was nocturnal as a baby, and my eyes were so large they were like a possum's. Dad used to unwind during those midnight hours by lifting me from my cot and playing with me. Then he'd give me a bottle, change my nappy, and sing me to sleep. Sometimes we used to fall asleep together on the lounge, he was so tired.'

'I see. I remember when you were born.'

'Dad said he was performing the Mendelssohn.'

'Moments before we walked on stage, he burst into the dressing room, violin in one hand, a telegram in the other, shouting, "Es ist ein Mädchen! Ich bin ein Vater! Ich bin ein Vater!" But he was sad he was not at your mother's side, to see you and hold you. To compensate, he imagined you with him on the concert platform. His violin was his baby girl and he cradled you and sang to you. I have never heard that opening melody played so plaintively— a little too much portamento, but it was tasteful. The second movement was a heart-wrenching lullaby, and in the third movement we heard his joy. Your father received an ovation which lasted twenty minutes. Before playing his encore, he announced your birth and requested the audience's permission to indulge in *Schlafe mein Prinzchen, Schlaf ein*. Do you know it?'

'He used to sing it to me when I was small. Except he would sing "meine Prinzessin".'

'He performed it that night with delightful improvisation. The audience, even the Emperor himself, was moved to tears. It was a rapturous debut.'

Rosé's eyes misted. But when I looked at Alma, who had been attending to our tea, she was seething.

'Almschi,' Rosé, too, was aware of his daughter's mood, 'we mustn't leave Mutti alone.'

Alma left to check on her mother, and Professor Rose proceeded with even greater confidentiality. He expressed his sorrow for Dad's passing, and his remarks revealed his grasp of earlier events. 'I understand he purchased a plot when they moved your mother. He is buried with her, yes? I recall him telling me there were two angels on the headstone. And the epitaph?'

'*Be ye therefore merciful.*' Explicit though they were, it was clear his questions were motivated by a fatherly love which had spanned Dad's adult life.

'I thought you might like to see some photographs.'

Rosé lifted an album from a side table and found the image he wished to show me, a picture of Dad and Maman taken while on an alpine holiday: Dad in lederhosen, his skinny legs covered with long socks, and a Tyrolean hat with a feather cocked in its band. Maman, her hair braided, wore a dirndl with an apron and fitted bodice.

'He brought her to visit when we were in Bad Aussee one summer. He wanted my approval. They were young, but they were well suited.'

And he was right. While I had seen my parents' affection captured in later mementos, I tended to construe it as the consequence of a bad situation made good. Here, I beheld their love for one another years before they married.

'In sickness and in health, yes?' Rosé reflected. 'Ah!' he pulled out a photograph of himself and Dad in concert dress and looking proud. 'Now this was taken the night you were born.' But I could easily date it by Dad's goatee – his Mephisto phase as we called it. But the beard, being identical to Rosé's, was as much an expression of adulation as it was an attempt to look older; not to mention a defiant jibe at Grandfather, who thought the violin an instrument of the Devil. Typical Dad.

'My son and heir,' Rosé murmured.

'You will play for me?' He made that dreaded request in a more businesslike manner. 'I am not teaching much nowadays, but I promised your father I would help you.'

'I hope I won't disappoint.'

'We shall see, we shall see.'

29

A Pale Cast of Thought

SEPTEMBER PROGRESSED, and the Viennese fluttered to life like butterflies from aurous chrysalids. Holiday-makers, refreshed by mountain air, returned to work; students crammed the coffeehouses; the Opera and Concert Hall opened their doors; and Frau Schütze sent me an invitation to dine.

In a park opposite the Schönbrunn Palace, I sat beneath a spreading horse-chestnut. The leaves were wet from recent rain, and the moisture enhanced their lushness. Soon, however, they would join their golden companions in opulent display, then fall and curl into a brittle pile.

I pulled out a bunch of grapes. I was tempted to pull out the bottle of wine I had also brought; but that was a present for Frau Schütze and her family.

'Should have brought two bottles. And a corkscrew. I could drink it all— anything to stop Professor Rosé's shouts.'

My lesson that afternoon began well. I played the Cesar Franck Sonata, an old favourite. Rosé, however, stopped me half-way through the first movement. 'You have your father's left hand,' he observed, which I assumed was a compliment; but instead of encouraging me to proceed, he abruptly requested Joachim's cadenza to the Rondo of the Beethoven Violin Concerto.

If you have studied that cadenza, Roddy, you will know that it is extremely difficult. Professor Rosé neither praised nor criticised my rendition. He simply asked for a Wienawski étude, which happened to be the piece I was studying when Dad died. I tried to play. My memory lapsed. More discussion: the professor composed, analytical; me, fighting tears. Sight-reading followed. Rosé selected some light parlour music which he asked me to play a second time, using his fingering. And did I know the Bach Double Concerto?

Taking up his instrument, he insisted I follow his bowings and rhythmic emphases, and brought upon me the full force of his orchestral authority. Fifty years' experience voiced chill requests for precision which ill-supplied my cravings for warmth and praise. My bow shook, and my mistakes increased.

'Fräulein Raye!'

'I can't!' I sobbed. 'I'm sorry! I cannot do it! I've lost my talent!'

'You have lost your father,' Rose replied.

No amount of playing would ever bring Dad back. Try as I might to conjure him to life with my music, the experience was ephemeral; the ensuing silence unbearable. All my efforts to impress Rosé had turned to dust.

Sunlight streamed through the grey clouds, causing the amber leaves to glow against glistening ebony branches. A songbird warbled, bidding me lift my gaze from the leaf-strewn lawn.

'Your father used to play the Dvorak Humoresque without his violin,' Rosé resumed once I controlled my tears. 'He would put on a gramophone recording, and while the music played, he would roll his eyes and twitch his mouth in time, contorting his face according to the pitch and mood. He could even do portamento with his face. Did he ever perform it for you?'

'Many, many times,' I tried to smile, 'He used to do that when he watched me play. It was impossible to concentrate. He was even worse with the Paganini Caprices.'

'Would you play me the Humoresque?'

Exhausted, I made one final attempt to play well; and the piece was simple enough to restore my composure. I would not let Dad down with the Humoresque.

'Vàša?' Alma burst in, shocked and tearful. 'I'm sorry—' she backed away upon seeing me, my bow poised mid-phrase. 'I thought— the wireless—'

'I am finishing with Fräulein Raye,' her father replied. 'Is dinner ready, Almschi? Come, Fräulein Phoebe, I will show you out. And if, as you say, you have lost your talent, then you must find it again. You cannot lose something you did not once have.'

But Professor Rosé gave no indication there would be any further lessons. Besides, there was little time for more. Another month and I would have to leave. The surrounding woods, however, seemed impenetrable, while the blazing red and tangerine leaves of maples scattered through the park sent a fiery message that it would be unwise to stay. Indeed, only days ago, the Rotunde was engulfed in flames.

Initially, everyone – even the President – was rather jocund about the disaster. 'Roll up! Roll up! Pyrotechnics at the Prater!' was bantered up and down Linke Wienzeile as if the circus was in town; and the few whose curiosity had gotten the better of their midday meals, wandered outside to see.

'It was built for the International Exhibition, Fräulein,' Albrecht informed me when I joined him on the pavement in front of the bookshop, 'and inside was filled with machines and modern inventions and costumes and handcrafts. My father told me all about it. Father even met our good Emperor Franz Josef. The world came to Vienna that summer. You could ride a gondola and walk through a Japanese garden. Then my little sister died from cholera,' he sighed, 'and Vati's business collapsed— But, thank God, he recovered his fortune. He became a K. und K. printer and stationer, Fräulein Phoebe. I myself remember the automobiles, and the hunting exhibition. Then there was the lake created for a magnificent naval showcase— '

'Naval showcase?' Emil sneered.

'The *Adriaaustellung*, before the War— Ah, Misha, but that is luck, ja? A little birdie that flies in and warbles a pretty tune on the windowsill and flies away again.'

'Given it was built on a swamp, it's a wonder the building survived this long,' observed Emil.

'The largest dome in the world,' Albrecht clung to his pre-War visions.

'Not any more, Albrecht, the dome's collapsed.'

'Von Hasenauer was the architect, yes, Misha?'

'He couldn't have built it without foreign assistance: Austrian design and Italian inspiration combined with German construction and British engineering—'

'And Jewish gold,' Albrecht chuckled.

'Do you think the fire was deliberate?' I asked.

'The Rotunde's a tinder box. Toss a cigarette, and culture and education go up in flames. Well, bye, bye, Rotunde. Soon, all that will be left is a song for Albrecht to churn on his barrel organ. Isn't that right, Albrecht? You can play an Abschiedslied in the Rotunde's honour.'

'Farewell! No more will I return,' Albrecht began to sing.

'I will not leave a footprint on this dear land,' Emil joined in, 'My friends I must forget...'

Later, I asked Emil what he really thought.

'The Rotunde could have burned any time in the last sixty years, and the day after a major Nazi rally in Nuremberg it's razed. That fire has swastika written all over it. Hitler wants Austria: "One blood, one Reich," he says. One Reich, much blood, if you ask me.'

'Will there be a war?'

'War is like love. It always finds a way. Mark my words: if she resists, Austria will become another Spain.'

Wagonloads of corpses, and women wailing over dead children

flickered through my mind's dark cinema. Over the last weeks, El Mazuco had been bombed by German Junker planes. Thanks to Hitler, the Republican cause was all but lost, the newsreel commentary crowed.

'Well, if there's going to be a war, I ought to take up my dagger and scales and grope my way to Paris,' I studied the trail that twisted through gibbet-like trees. 'There's no harm in doing so. After all, I'm not bent on wanton destruction. I seek truth and justice. I have every right to confront Ailine. Then, I suppose, it's off to Oxford,' I sighed as I opened a letter from Lucy.

Oxford, 14th September, 1937.

Dearest Phoebe,

> *Hopefully this letter finds you in good health and happily settled into your new home. The Sothebys arrived safely, and from their description of the palaces and galleries, not to mention the hospitality of your father's friends, I can imagine your delight amidst such beauty and history.*

'Goodness, she can gabble! Five pages of Fred and Maggie monotony! What possessed her to think I should be interested in such house and garden tripe? And three paragraphs on cricket! ... *and we held a fine tea to celebrate the close of season ...* Thank heavens it's over! ... *Wally ...* bla, bla, bla ... *commencing doctoral work in Immunology.* Well, bully for him. *And I had the good fortune to attend a series of master classes in London with Guilhermina Suggia.* And bully for you. *Teaching two afternoons a week ...* bla, bla ... *performing Schubert's* <u>Arpeggione</u> *with Wally at the next Schubert Society meeting ...* how amateur ... *think of you and our many soirees ... looking forward to playing the Mendelssohn Trio again, and introducing you to our friends ...* I'm sure you are. And I bet the only reason you penned an epistle of this magnitude was to escape your mother-in-law.' I could easily imagine Lucy excusing herself with an 'I'll be writing a letter to Phoebe Raye now,' and devoting an afternoon to the project.

> *Now, will you be coming for Christmas? Letty mentioned you would; and it's a happy thought indeed that we should see each other again after so long— More than a year, is it not? Well, however long it's been, you'll find our door wide open and a pot of tea on the fire. And you needn't worry about a bed, we've plenty to spare.*
>
> *Sending you a warm embrace and many blessings,*

Your friend,
Lúighseach. [Lucy always used her Irish name.]

Christmas with Lucy: carols and Midnight Mass; a table laden with treats; a convivial gathering of family and friends; the Sothebys showering one and all with gifts and Brandy Alexanders. Wally and Lucy devoted as ever. 'I bet they'll have "news"'. Across the table, 'to make up the numbers', an eligible young man – Oxbridge no doubt – vetted by my well-meaning friend. Finally, me, in mourning, unwedded, with blood on my hands.

And they would know me for a murderess. I could never quite meet Lucy in the eye, she was so short-sighted. Only when she removed her glasses could I really look. Then her eyes were beautiful – clear and green and guileless – and I could look with confidence because I knew she could not make out my expression. But I would not want to look. Lucy's innocence would reinforce my guilt. Wally I could never look in the eye at the best of times. His principled, purposeful glare and wary manner made me quake.

'No doubt, Wally, you'll find a cure for tuberculosis— perhaps you'll receive a Nobel Prize for having destroyed a germ. Your task is easy compared to mine. A germ doesn't have a human face. It cannot outwit you and laugh at you. Nor can you commit a crime because you act in the name of Science; whereas I, in my effort to rid the world of a human pestilence, risk conviction. I become a criminal in a rightful cause.

'And you, Lucy, you'll make light of your troubles; but I know winter is not kind to you. You'll rest on Christmas afternoon, and on Boxing Day you'll hardly be able to move. But your paralysis is nothing compared to mine. If I kill Ailine, I will be a moral outcast. If I am caught, I will be condemned. Yet, if I do not act, I cannot move on. I have no support. There is no one I can trust, no one to protect me. How can you possibly love someone who wishes evil upon another?

'And why has Kerem not written? Surely, he would be back from China by now? Had he met with an accident? Might he be dead? Or maybe he was leading a life of crime. Could he really be a thief? He is a thief, even if he didn't take my cigarette case, for he stole my heart!'

I shied, and only narrowly avoided the missile that might have ended me and spared me any action whatsoever. A dog bounded towards me and skidded to a crouch, his eyes transfixed on the offending object: a stick. I flung it a short distance and he sprang off. Seconds later he dropped it at my feet and gazed dolefully. He wanted it thrown further afield. I obliged.

The dog fetched the stick, tossing and gnawing it as if boasting his skill. Then he pricked his ears and ran off, abandoning his toy with a bark, only to rethink his decision and dart back. Just as I threw the stick, there approached the largest pair of shoes I had ever seen. With the brown hartwist trousers above, they comprised the garb of a towering gentleman. A long, full-skirted overcoat, a scarf in vibrant autumn hues, and a trilby, replete with feather, completed his outer attire.

He bowed, and as he drew himself erect, he twitched his nose in an abrupt but well-practised manner, whereby it performed a function that his hands, at that moment, could not, for they were occupied with restraining his pet: *vis*, adjust his spectacles.

'Grüß Gott,' he said, with an embarrassing falter on the first 'G'. 'Verzeihen Sie mir. Ich hoffe, gnädige Frau,' again he stuttered terribly, 'mein Hund hat Ihnen keine Probleme verursacht.'

I replied that the dog had been a welcome distraction. As for the stick, well, suffice it to say I was lucky.

Bowing again, he tipped his hat and adjusted his glasses as before. He looked young, but his face was as solemn as an undertaker's.

'Mein Beileid,' he stammered. 'Grüß Gott.' And before I could converse any further, he turned and ambled away, his coat tails swaying behind him, his canine companion prancing at his side, nudging him to hurl the stick. This he did with prowess, sending it an enormous distance.

The dog ran full pelt and fetched it as before. The gentleman then pretended to throw the stick, cajoling his pet with far more confidence compared with his former stuttered address. A tug of war followed whereby the man overbalanced and rolled onto a bed of leaves, wrestling with his dog until he succeeded in prising the stick and throwing it again. The dog charged ahead while his owner traced a leisurely course through the trees. A church bell chimed the evening Angelus, which for me was a warning that I had neglected my social commitments. I stuffed away my thoughts, gathered my parcels, and hastened to the Schützes'.

30

The Case of the Open Window

HAD I SUCCUMBED to my mood that evening, I would have likened the Schützes' shabby Rococo villa to a jilted bride; but in doing so, I would have given a false impression. Her gown may have been yellowed and torn, for the cream coloured stucco crumbled on the façade; but she was instead a matriarch whose shapely portal offered a mother's comforting embrace when the double front door opened and Frau Schütze stepped out with open arms.

She thanked me for my gifts, helped me with my coat, and worried over my well-being. Did I have difficulty catching a cab? she probed the reason for my lateness. I had taken the tram. Did I get lost? Not at all. Emil had provided directions as always.

An elegant Imperial staircase took us to the belle étage; and as we approached the curved half-landing, I viewed the vestibule below. The parquetry floor, scuffed no doubt from children skidding over the surface, glowed beneath the chandelier. Two gilded chairs, like footmen in faded brocade, flanked a white and gold console, and guarded an enormous vase. The vase depicted a frilly pastoral scene in the style of Fragonard; but the romance of shepherd and shepherdess there featured was disturbed by a jagged crack. On the wall behind the vase hung an antique mirror, the silver backing of which had begun to flake; and despite its high polish, the glass no longer delivered a clear reflection.

'Who opened the window?' Professor Schütze broke onto the landing, red-faced and teeth clenched, for he had a reed in his mouth.

Frau Schütze denied knowledge and drew her husband's attention to me. He nodded an abrupt greeting, and was about to interrogate me about the window when he realised the impossibility of my being responsible and lectured me instead, the reed in his mouth wagging furiously:

'I welcome you as a guest in my house, but it is imperative that you leave a room exactly as you found it. Exactly!' He thumped his fist on the palm of his other hand and stormed away.

'He has a concert on Saturday,' his wife apologised, and guided me into the dining room. There, a willowy young girl, her long fair hair in plaits, was finishing the table preparations. The girl was about to pick up a glass filled with cane strips when she was stopped by her mother. 'No, no, Heidi! They're Vati's reeds. We must leave them be.' Frau Schütze's warning was opportune, for the Professor entered, still furious about the open window.

'Did you open the window in the salon?' he demanded of the second, slightly older girl who entered bearing a tureen. 'Nein, Vati,' she replied. Sisi, otherwise known as Elisabeta Schütze, was tall and slender like her sister, with hazel eyes and beautiful chestnut tresses. She wore a dark brown pinafore which became her well but was a sombre contrast to Heidi's pastel floral.

In came a third daughter. Again, the Professor raised the matter of the salon window. Another denial, and Zita Schütze joined the table. She was closer to me in age and height, with eyeglasses, and wavy dark hair bobbed in a modern style. Her cardigan was a neat-fitting mosaic of pattern; and while I suspected it was a make-do piece of handwork, its multifarious colours had been combined with consummate skill.

Zita was followed by a man of similar height and age, whose affable manner remained unperturbed despite the Professor's mounting choler. No, he had nothing to do with the window, and in the same breath smilingly introduced himself as Otto-Franz-Josef.

Thinking I would relax more by conversing in my native tongue, Frau Schütze spoke in English, articulating clearly and frequently pausing to allow her husband and children to follow while she told me about her home. The mansion had been in her family for several generations, she explained, and was but walking distance from the palace, which was convenient since the von Rechtschaffens had enjoyed a long association with the crown. Both her father and grandfather had served as judges; and there were other significant aristocratic connections which were lost on me. In 1800, Beethoven performed with the Austrian composer and pianist, Josef Wölfl. 'Your father mentioned in his letters that you play very well,' she continued, 'Our second son, Hubert, is also very fond of music. Ah! Here he is at last!'

In stalked the same tall young gentleman I had encountered in the park.

'Hast du das Fenster offen gelassen?' Professor Schütze demanded.

'Ja.'

Professor Schütze stood, and his rage rolled like the crescendo of a kettle drum: softly at first, then building in vigour and intensity. 'How many times do I have to say to members of my own family to keep the rooms exactly as you found them? Exactly!' he crashed his fist on the table. 'If a door is open, leave it open! If a window is closed, leave it closed! How can I make good reeds if the temperature is not kept constant? Constant, do you hear? Constant! Do not open the windows if they are not open! Leave everything exactly—! Exactly!' With every 'Exactly!' he thumped. Heidi cringed, while her adult siblings wearily raised their brows, mouthed 'Exactly!' and rapped their fingers on the table in perfect time.

'Exactly!' The Professor glared at his son. 'Well, Hubert?'

'My humblest apologies, Father. I was— s-s-s-moking a cig-cig-cig-arette and thought it wise to— ventilate—'

'Him! Of all people! *He* opens the window!'

'He has to smoke for his asthma,' Frau Schütze whispered to me. 'Huberle,' she coaxed the tall young man, 'This is Fräulein Raye. Phoebe,' she smiled and continued sweet as a flute, 'This is our second son, Franz-Hubert.'

Had his complexion been fairer, Franz-Hubert Schütze von Rechtschaffen would have blushed. Heidi giggled and was shooshed by Sisi, who looked to her mother for guidance. Otto-Franz-Josef nudged Zita and winked. The Professor glanced at me, then glared at Franz-Hubert who bowed and took his place. Artfully heeding their father's cautions regarding the reeds, his siblings passed salt and pepper, wine, water, and bread so rapidly that Franz-Hubert Schütze was spared from having to say anything other than 'Danke' or 'Bitte' as required. Even then, he stuttered.

Meanwhile, the conversation focussed on Dad's funeral, whereupon it became clear that monosyllabic answers were grossly insufficient. Herr and Frau Professor had taken the trouble to enquire, and they expected from me the courtesy of providing them with detailed information. Failure to do so was an affront, not only to my host and hostess, who had gone to great lengths to express their concern (which included, it seemed, a dinner invitation), but also to Dad's memory. Despite my misgivings, I proceeded:

'Dad's death prompted such a widespread and heartfelt response that his funeral was held in the Cathedral. Nearly a thousand people, from every walk of life, filled the church. There was a choir, too, which sang a setting of the Beatitudes, which Dad wrote years before, while he was sick. We found the music among his papers. I never knew he composed.'

'He studied composition with Schönberg,' remarked the Professor.

'It was haunting – the most unusual harmonies – quite beautiful. The first part of every beatitude ended strangely but was resolved very simply with each "For they shall". It was the most comforting piece of music. As if— As if—'

'As if he were convinced of the promise of Heaven?' Frau

Schütze smiled.

'Yes,' I whispered.

'We had Masses offered for the repose of your father's soul,' assured the more serious Sisi. 'Hubie made arrangements for a regular Mass to be said, didn't you, Hubie?'

No reply from the tall young gentleman.

'Was he buried with military honours?' inquired Professor Schütze.

'There was a flag, a procession, and a gun salute. Dad was buried with Maman in Waverley Cemetery, which overlooks the sea.'

'And what flowers did you place on his grave?' asked Frau Schütze.

'Roses. Red roses. Dad liked red roses.'

'In the wintertime, too?'

'Roses are quite readily available year-round in Australia.'

'How beautiful! Roderick so loved fresh flowers. The brighter the better.'

'Huberle is fond of gardening,' Zita prompted.

'Huberle' said nothing.

'Did you ever perform with my father?' I asked the Professor.

'I performed the Mozart Oboe Quartet with his little group. I managed to make him play in tune for once.'

Impossible! Judging from his recordings, Dad's intonation was perfect; and since an impeccable left-hand technique was the one aspect of the violin he could demonstrate, nothing annoyed him more than a student who dared display fault in that regard. 'F sharp!' he would call. 'F bloody sharp!' he called if he was really exasperated. Yet there was Professor Schütze, glib as could be, sipping his wine like a god, implying the very opposite. He couldn't be serious?

'Will you play for us sometime, Phoebe? We would love to hear you. And if you require an accompanist, Hubert or Franz I am certain will oblige,' Frau Schütze offered.

'I can play, too,' added Heidi. 'I am improving, am I not, Hubie? Hubie is teaching me.'

'I think, darling, it would be better if one of the boys played for Fräulein Raye,' advised her mother.

Heidi's 'But why?' Frau Schütze curtailed by enquiring after my homeward plans, and recommended I travel in company. It would be safer, and Hubert would be happy to take me. Happy? He didn't know the meaning of the word. Hubert turned to Otto-Franz-Joseph who smirked and raised an eyebrow at Zita, thereby forging an agreement that the three siblings would provide escort.

For the two men, the trip presented an opportunity for astronomy. Hubert, despite wearing glasses, possessed sharper sight than his brother. He pointed out a fading star and their mutual interest slowed their pace, leaving me in Zita's company. She had an unusual name, I remarked. It was her parents' doing, she sighed. They had named her after the exiled Empress of Austria, who in turn was named in honour of St Zita of Lucca. She helped her mother run the house and had done so for some years. 'As befits my name,' she added in a tone of ironic inevitability, 'St Zita: patron of maids and domestic servants.' Did she mind? Mind? It allowed her plenty of time for her own pursuits. She joked that she had completed three university degrees without the bother of having to sit examinations, for her brothers had passed their books her way; furthermore, she had the advantage of being free to think as she pleased.

'Not that it makes much difference. Anyway,' she concluded, 'be patient with Hubie. He only stutters when he's nervous. You get used to it. Besides, actions speak louder than words. Und es gibt nichts Gutes, außer man tut es.'

'There is nothing good, unless you do it,' I translated.

31

Sweet Union

'CURSE YOU, DAD!' I raged at the Portrait the moment I arrived home. 'An interesting young man? Scheming rascal! You arranged a courtship! Who do you think you are? Prospero? Bringing me to Vienna to contrive my meeting Franz-Hubert Schütze von Rechtschaffen! How did you think I would fall for that? And not only you. His mother's in on it: "Huberle," I imitated Frau Schütze's mellifluity. "Would you be so kind as to take Fräulein Raye home?"'

I heard Heidi giggle; saw Otto-Franz raise his brows and Sisi smile; and recalled Zita's trite adage:

'"Taten sagen mehr als Worte,"' I chanted. '"Taten sagen..." The man can't even string a sentence together! "M-m-mein Beileid", "G-g-g-gnädige Frau". I'd sooner be partnered with a horse! I'll never consent! Never, never, never!'

The next morning, three solemn knocks at my door announced the tall young gentleman himself.

'Herr Schütze,' I greeted him

He tipped his hat and bowed. 'Gnädiges Fräulein, bitte nennen Sie mich Herr D-d-d-doktor Schütze.'

A doctor? Ridiculous! Imagine his bedside manner. Must be a vet, I surmised as I watched him twitch his spectacles. His magnified eyes, brown like his mother's, bored into mine. I studied his oak brown, three-piece suit. Exceedingly well-cut in the streamlined pre-war style that Dad used to wear, it was as old as, if not older than, its owner, and thereby suggested the constraint of poverty. Herr Doktor Franz-Hubert Maria Schütze von Rechtschaffen may have been a 'von', and he may have been a doctor; but he was slumming it, the difference being that he was slumming in quality tweed, with a bow tie to boot.

He apologised for disturbing me. Then followed another pause. I waited and watched his lips, which were full but rather firm, form his next words.

'M-m-m-eine Mutter,' he faltered and paused again. 'M-m-m-eine—'

Ah yes, your m-m-mother... And you should be embarrassed, I glared.

'Bitte seien Sie so fr—,' he handed me an envelope and gestured that I open it.

Frau Schütze had sent another invitation to dine, this time on Saturday midday, and to spend the afternoon with the family. Should I accept, Hubert would come for me at noon.

The following Saturday, five minutes before the appointed hour, my chaperone arrived.

'Don't do anything I wouldn't do.' Such was the libertine advice of the Portrait, issued while I arranged my hat. 'By the way, Possum,' he winked, 'you look peachy.'

Hubert Schütze escorted me without a word. So long were his feet that he took the stairs at an angle. He was quite cautious about the descent, not only because of his feet, but also because of the case he carried, which was no physician's bag.

'You play French Horn,' I remarked in German once we had found a seat on the tram.

'Ja.' His legs were too long for the bench, which brought his knees closer to his chest. Between the two he wedged his case which he stroked with fingers like spatulas.

Two stops later, a more detailed answer stumbled out:

'But this is not a Fr-ench Horn.'

The tram slowed.

'This is a V-v-v-ienna— Horn.'

'So, you are a Doctor of Music and not of Medicine?'

'I-I-I play horn in the— Phil-harmoniker,' he pushed his glasses back onto his nose. 'We were in rehearsal this—'

But the word failed to manifest, as did my patience.

'Morning,' I finished his sentence.

'Ja.'

'Do you have a concert tonight?'

'Ja.'

We reached the Schütze home in the company of at least ten individuals, some quite dishevelled. A more decently clad gentleman asked directions. Dr Schütze matched his courtesy and advised that Herr Oberstabsarzt would be served a m-m-meal if he f-followed the others down the— side of the house to the (pause) rear entrance. Clearly, Herr Oberstabsarzt was not used to rear entrances; and Dr Schütze, sadly aware of the fact, apologised as he bowed, and stuttered his wishes for better prospects.

The dog barked an enthusiastic welcome as he skidded across the parquetry. Dr Schütze lavished him with affection and let him lick his cheek. He then instructed his pet, whose name was Sirius, to— (gesture) sit and to please shake hands with F-f-f-räulein Raye. Sirius seemed happy to renew the acquaintance. Perhaps he recalled the stick incident, for he wagged his tail and wriggled his rump as if anticipating another game.

Then followed a sweet greeting as Frau Schütze fussed over her son's hat and scarf, and worried whether their visitors had disturbed me. The economy may have improved, she explained, but many were still out of work and without homes; and the family did what it could to provide meals.

That afternoon, Karl-Alois Schütze, the eldest son, joined the family table along with his wife, Maria-Sofia (Fifi), who was heavily pregnant with their first child. It astonished me to see how like Karl-Alois was to Hubert. He had the same long face and solemn expression, the same tortoiseshell glasses and magnified brown eyes, the same tawny complexion. His hair, however, was cropped as befitted his soldierly occupation (he was a lieutenant engineer), whereas Hubert possessed a full head of wavy chestnut locks. If there was the same stutter, I was unaware of it because Karl-Alois seemed even more taciturn. Were they twins? I queried. Why yes, smiled Frau Schütze, proud of her achievement.

'And I am the oldest,' added Karl-Alois, 'Even if it is by only ten minutes.'

As for Otto-Franz, he was in every way the opposite. Short, fair, and rather tubby, he had a generous share in his mother's full-cream freshness, while his lively eyes were blue as cornflowers and undistorted by ill-fitting spectacles. He also sported what looked like his first moustache. In addition to his moustache, he sported a promising legal career, having secured employment in the office of the State Councillor immediately upon graduation, which details he conveyed to me with the ease and warmth of a favourite teddy bear come to life. His manner thus was quite distinct from his brothers. Karl-Alois Schütze was more concerned for his wife, a simple, decent girl, who in turn looked forward to the birth of her child. And Hubert Schütze? With his large, staring eyes, he reminded me of the wise old owl which sat in an oak:

> The more he saw the less he spoke
> The less he spoke the more he heard

'And how dull it would be if we were all like that bird,' I sighed to myself.

According to Frau Schütze, fifteen unemployed and homeless men had turned up for soup that day. There had just been enough to feed them. Sisi reported a similar situation at the hospital where she worked. And it was only going to worsen. With winter fast approaching who was to say how many more would come?

It would be solved, proffered Otto-Franz, by uniting with Germany.

Impossible, argued Professor Schütze. Unification was against the Treaties of Versailles and St Germain.

Failure to join Austria with Germany in 1919 was a violation of treaty, countered Otto-Franz. Did not Versailles make provision for the unification of peoples based on common language and self-determination? Then the separation of German Austria from Greater Germany failed to comply with the spirit of that very agreement. Austria should be permitted to re-join the German Reich from which she had been expelled after the conclusion of the German wars.

'Unification with Prussia?' queried his indignant mother. 'Pfui!'

'And you, of all people, oppose it,' Otto-Franz replied. 'Why, you entered into an anschluss! You married a German.'

'But I am not Prussian,' asserted the Professor. 'I am Bavarian.'

'You are German.'

'Yes, but more importantly I am Catholic, and I joined with your mother in holy matrimony, a union of faith and love, not of conquest and oppression. There was no kulturkampf when I married your mother.'

'But Hitler's—'

'Hitler's Germany? Are you mad? The Nazis are pagans obsessed with a myth of race and blood, who do all they can to undermine the authority of the Church. We depend on the Fatherland Front to preserve the integrity of our country as a Catholic German nation, while simultaneously observing every point of treaty which, Anschluss aside, forbids us to maintain an army of more than thirty thousand.'

'Hitler won't always be in power,' Otto-Franz protested. 'He's a puppet: a means to an end. Besides, any Anschluss would be a peaceful conjugation, a federation of German people, a synthesis of German culture: A *Zusammenschluss*,' he relished the word as he would fine cuisine.

'Then why has Germany violated the treaty and begun to rearm?'

'There would be no need for force for most are in favour.'

'Who is in favour? Who? I am not in favour! Nor is your mother!'

'My friends are. And my siblings. You're in favour, aren't you, Karl?'

'I am a Lieutenant in the Austrian army because I am in favour of Anschluss? Franzwurst, logic, please!'

'You are a Lieutenant in the Austrian army because you couldn't get a job as an engineer.'

'I am a Lieutenant in the Austrian army because I happen to believe in Austria's independence, and in her importance for

European affairs.'

'I doubt the lower ranks would share your views. What about you, Huberle?' Otto-Franz watched his brother struggle to answer and didn't bother to wait. 'Besides, most of those men you fed today, Mutti, are in favour. You wouldn't have to feed them if we united with Germany, for they would have jobs and homes.'

'But-but—' interrupted Hubert, 'at what expense, Franz?'

'Brown shirts,' scoffed Karl-Alois.

'The German government has co-ordinated public works operatives and relief programmes,' Franz argued. 'Of all people, Hubie, you should know that. You lived there.'

Hubert hesitated.

'And?' Franz feigned patience.

'And, rather than p-p-put up with what I have to say, I think it would be of greater— interest to learn the— view of a foreigner.' And slowly, shyly, he looked across at me.

'What would a woman know about politics?' scoffed Franz, his eyes agleam.

'Fie, Franzl!' Zita chimed in, 'We have the right to vote, and we are capable of forming political opinions, as you very well know.'

'None of which you have expressed.'

'Schwätzer! You haven't given us a chance!'

'And even if I did, which opinion would you espouse? You change them as frequently as you do boyfriends. And, mark my words, you will change them again when you marry. For regardless of whether they have the vote or not, women should take their husbands' view in such matters.'

'Nonsense! Anyhow, Fräulein Raye is unmarried, so she is free to express her mind.'

'Ja, because once she gets hitched, she'll have n-n-nothing to say,' Franz winked in Hubert's direction.

'Then it is— best she s-s-speaks while she can. And what is your view, F-f-räulein Raye?'

'Are you a communist like your father?' questioned the Professor. 'When I first met him, he was red from head to toe.'

'Red? Dad?'

'The War must have turned his head—'

'It turned everyone else's,' added Franz.

'The only time I ever heard Dad advocating Communism was when he was talking about Hitler,' I retorted, recalling Dad's teasing of Eric. 'Otherwise, he was obsessed with restoring the Austrian monarchy.'

'And do you share your father's Legitimist ideas?' probed Otto-Franz.

'He is my father, not my husband, so why should I?' I parried, much to his delight, and his reaction inspired in me the confidence to continue. 'Personally, I think most systems of government are testimonies to human failure. I mean, if we can barely govern ourselves, what hope have we for being governed, or of governing others?'

'Ah! We have a Cynic in our midst! Tell me, now that winter is approaching, will you walk outside barefoot?'

'Have you visited the Schönbrunn yet, Phoebe?' interrupted Frau Schütze.

'No, not yet.'

'Then perhaps you would like to see it this afternoon? Huberle would be pleased to show you.'

'Huberle' protested, insisting that he needed to walk his d-dog. Nonsense! scolded his mother, 'Vati' could take care of the dog. 'And Hubie can walk Fräulein Raye instead,' teased Franz, while Frau Schütze overruled her husband's objections regarding the dog. He had time to walk Sirius as well as attend to his reeds this afternoon, and still be rested for tonight's performance. Professor Schütze growled acquiescence. Hubert, as much under petticoat rule as his father, also capitulated on the condition that his younger brother and sisters join the excursion.

Now Franz complained. The Schönbrunn was only visited by tourists, and the thought of being a tourist in one's own country was demeaning, to say the least. 'Franzl' was scolded by his mother for a lack of patriotism. In response, he maintained that he did not lack patriotism. He was proudly a German Austrian, and in being a German Austrian, he refused to join company with a herd of Americans and receive instruction in royal 'obsoletism'.

'Now, now, Franzl, the Americans have all gone home,' replied Frau Schütze.

'And we have Berliners to contend with instead,' groaned Sisi.

'Then why don't we pretend we're Berliners, too?' Zita proposed. 'We will be the Piefkenesers.'

Franzl laughed and began goose-stepping around the dining room, inspecting its adornments as a stiff-lipped German general would his troops. His droll commentary on the martial attributes of the dining room portraits which, in featuring ladies with lapdogs and parasols, and gentlemen with beauty spots and powdered wigs, were most unmilitary, invited gleeful contributions in exaggerated Berlinerdeutsche from everyone. Everyone save Hubert, that is, whose speech impediment set him apart.

32

A Study in Statuary

WERE WE CHILDREN, we might have pretended our journey to the Schönbrunn was Hänsel and Gretel's adventure to the witch's house, for we wended through an enormous park. As it was, we were more akin to the Joneses calling upon the Smiths, strolling in through the back gate, given that an obscure side entrance provided access; and I expected at any minute to spy an out-house and clothesline. Heidi and Sisi ran ahead, Franz and Zita goose-stepped and giggled, while Hubert and I walked behind in silence. A chill I had never known – icy, arctic sharp – sliced my skin. 'If this is autumn, what would winter be like?' I wondered as I hurried to keep apace.

'I must commend you on your Viennese,' Hubert remarked in English with the admixture of lilt and drawl that characterised his native tongue. For once there was no trace of a stutter.

'Why didn't you tell me you spoke English? Given your brother's political claptrap over lunch, I would have appreciated having someone translate for me.'

'I fear much would have been lost had I done so.' Was he joking at his own expense? He was so poker faced it was impossible to tell. 'Franzl is exhausting. You managed well.'

'You can thank my father for that. He learnt to speak German when he came here to study.'

'Ah, but I did not say German. I said Viennese. Your *Viennese* is very good. And I am certain your father is to thank.'

'Your English is also very good,' I felt obliged to return the compliment.

'For that, too, you can thank your father. I had much trouble learning the English at school. My father recommended I practise by writing letters. He told me about your father, about the War...' he lingered, 'I confess I thought it a work of mercy at first – writing letters to comfort a crippled veteran – but it became an agreeable correspondence. His replies were most entertaining. Initially, he wrote in both English and German to help me understand. He asked many questions, yes?'

'And he expected good answers.'

His slow nod suggested that such responses had been in frequent demand. 'Your father took great care with my expression, and in my final year I topped my class in English. It is strange, yes, but I do not—' and for the first time he struggled. 'Forgive me, "S-s-s-stottern"?'

'Stutter.'

The irony seemed to amuse him. 'Same word, ja?'

'Jaaa, same verrd,' I could not resist imitating his drawl.

'I do not – stutter – so much when I speak in English. I miss your father's letters. He was an extraordinarily kind and generous man. I beg your pardon. I did not wish to upset you.'

Offering his breast pocket handkerchief, he broached another topic which he thought might be of mutual concern. He introduced it with a pause, his lips silently rehearsing his next words. 'I must also apologise for my mother. Since Karl's marriage she has been looking forward to similar fate befalling me. I am afraid she is of the opinion that because I am a single young man, I must be in want of a wife. Well, I may be single, but, unfortunately, I am not in possession of large fortune and so— That is right, yes? You have read *Pride and Prejudice*?'

'Yes, yes, of course. Only I'm surprised that you have.'

'Your father sent to me the Christmas before he passed away.'

'Did you enjoy it?'

'Very much.'

'Did he send you other books?'

'Every year since I was fifteen years old, ja. *The Scarlet Pimpernel* was the first.'

'Dad used to call it "The Scarlet Pumpernickel".'

'You have read?'

'I prefer the Pumpernickel stories to *Pride and Prejudice*. I don't quite share Miss Austen's – or your mother's – interest in marriage. I did not come to Vienna to find a husband.'

'Then why did you come?'

'Vienna was Dad's happy place and I want to know why.'

'I am truly sorry for your loss. I was looking forward to meeting him. He was my godfather.'

'He mentioned you were his godson. He was looking forward to meeting you, too.'

'I suppose that makes us cousins-of-sorts, yes? Then perhaps you might like to call me Hubie. That is what my cousins call me.'

'You have cousins?'

'In Holland, ja.'

'Very well, then. And you, Cousin Hubie, may call me Phoebe. Oh!' I gasped.

A verdant carpet rolled down a slope to a bedstead of trees, beyond which a patchwork coverlet parterre was spread. The palace, jaundiced and pale, slept beneath a canopy of soft grey sky. Like a family watching by a sickbed, the surrounding city kept vigil, as if awaiting the passing of a soul.

My new status of 'cousin' much pleased the younger Schützes who explained that they had little by way of extended family. Of course, the War was to blame (it invariably was), for they had lost two uncles on their mother's side to the Russians and the Italians. The Church provided the other reason (as it invariably did), having led their one surviving aunt to the Poor Clares. On their father's side, one uncle had been killed on the Somme, while another, who lived in Munich, did not have children. Given they had not seen their Dutch cousins for seven years, the visit of a cousin-of-sorts from such a remote part of the world as Australia was a novelty indeed, not to mention a welcome deflection from romantic speculation; and by the time we reached the fountain at the bottom of the hill, we were on first name terms.

'D-d-do you know the names of the fountain statues, Heidi?' Hubie asked in German.

'It's Neptune!'

'Why Neptune?' I inquired.

'At the time this garden was landscaped, the Habsburg lands extended to the Adriatic, and the Nederlands.'

'Versailles took away our ports. And our navy,' Franz lit a cigarette.

'Phoebe, you are familiar with the— Holy Roman Empire?' Hubie enquired.

'Dad taught me a little. Frankly, I thought it outmoded and arcane: a medieval cabal of Catholic feudal lords.'

'Is that so? The Holy Roman Empire is about— How do you say in English? It is Christendom, yes? The Christian world has been threatened since its inception by pagan tribes, Moors, and heretics. The defence of the Church and Her members, in war and— peace, has always been relevant. That was the role of the Holy Roman Empire. In some respects, it was not unlike today's so-called League of Nations, which the Americans think such a m-m-m-modern innovation. So, it can hardly be called outmoded, let alone clandestine. Perhaps it was ahead of its time?

'But there is an interesting symbolism in this fountain,' my very learned guide proceeded. 'Observe the statues on either side. Do you recognise them?'

'How's your ancient history?' Franz flicked some ash into the fountain.

'Trojan Wars?' hinted Zita.

'Is that Achilles?' asked Sisi.

'Ja,' replied Hubie. 'And the other?'

'Is it Helen?' asked Heidi.

'Helen you will see in the— main garden.'

'Thetis?' I ventured.

'You are right! She represents Empress Maria Theresia under whom the garden was designed. The figure of Achilles represents her son and successor, Josef II. It is interesting, is it not, that they portrayed themselves as lesser deities and demigods, yes?'

'But higher than mere mortals, nonetheless,' Franz interposed.

'But when you compare the fountain with that of— Versailles in which Louis XIV is explicitly linked with Apollo, it presents a different image of royal power, does it not, Franzl?'

'It is still about absolutism.'

'I disagree. The Habsburgs recognise a higher authority, God Himself, and acknowledge human imperfection. Achilles may have been a demigod, but he was weakened. Remember his heel. As for the S-s-sun King, he has been humanised. Come Phoebe, you will find France represented in the person of the cowardly P-p-p-paris over here. And next to him is Hannibal, whom I believe represents England.'

'How so?'

'As a Carthaginian, he was a Phoenician, and thus he belonged to a race of merchants. It is a fitting— symbol for a nation of shopkeepers, yes?

'There is a measure of wit in the design,' I smiled.

'The work of a woman who knew her own mind,' observed Zita.

'And you would do well to follow suit.' Franz escaped before Zita could retort, so she chased him instead.

The parterre was flanked on either side with statues. While we strolled from one to the next, a friendly competition ensued as Heidi, Sisi and I endeavoured to identify each figure. Hubie hinted and supplemented as required, which was frequent given the challenging array of subjects.

In doing so he presented an account of the efforts taken by Maria Theresia to consolidate her position as a female monarch, in which task she was remarkably successful. Through far-reaching family alliances and a policy of just warfare, her benevolent rule encouraged prosperity and peace for all, and enabled the flourishing of the arts and sciences. For Hubie the Holy Roman Empire proved the epitome of civilisation, and the Schönbrunn exemplified it. He had a point. The garden, ordered and symmetrical, headed toward a splendid Baroque palace, not a twisted castle in a Gothic horror.

Franz and Zita, meanwhile, positioned themselves between statues and imitated the various poses. Half-way down the concourse, Zita popped up as a vestal virgin. A few yards further, and Franz was poised as Apollo. While Hubie told of Aspasia, the Milesian courtesan, her patronage of intellectual life and her influence on Athenian politics, Zita assumed the role leaning contrapposta against her brother who was curled up to represent her shield; and during his explanation of the Order of the Golden Fleece, Franz mimicked Jason holding the prized token. But when they modelled Aenaeas carrying his father from the burning Troy, Franz with Zita draped over his shoulder, they toppled.

We next saw them as Lucius Junius Brutus supporting the dead Lucretia; Franz holding a cigarette instead of a dagger.

'What on earth is Brutus doing there?' To me, the principal actor in the creation of the Roman Republic seemed incongruous.

'Do you not remember that Brutus vowed to avenge the rape of Lucretia by Sextus Tarquinius, the son of the last king of Rome, who demanded Lucretia become his wife and future queen under pain of death?' Franz gave his cigarette a nonchalant puff.

'But what has that to do with the Habsburgs?'

'It is a warning to King Frederick the Great of Prussia, who was a C-c-calvinist, and who offered marriage to Empress Maria Theresia to increase Prussia's might at Austria's expense,' Hubie elaborated.

'Old Fritz should have known better than to mess with a woman,' Zita added from her very awkward semi-reclined position.

'Like Lucretia did Tarquinius, M-m-m-maria Theresia refused him; and like— Brutus, she was prepared to fight. In doing so she preserved the integrity of Holy Roman Empire,' Hubie continued. 'But Brutus himself has more to do with the ideals of the Empire than you might think.'

'Nonsense!' Zita protested. 'Brutus is the hero of Republicanism.'

'For the F-f-french perhaps. For us, no,' Hubie shrugged.

'Then pray, oh Learned One, why is Lucius Junius Brutus featured in the Habsburg iconography?'

'In the creation of the Roman Republic, the consuls swore an oath that they would take no entreaties or bribes from— kings,' Hubie remained unperturbed. 'And nor would the Habsburgs submit to bribes from the Hohenzollerns. Furthermore, the Roman Republic was governed by c-c-consuls; likewise, in the Holy Roman Empire power was delegated among several rulers who governed in co-operation. Also, like the Rex Sacrorum of the Republic, the— Church functioned in a similar manner, independent of the State in spiritual matters, yet intimately connected with it, with the Pope as P-p-pontifex Maximus, a title itself used in the Republic. Despite its difficulties, the Holy Roman Empire was the apotheosis of the greatness that was Rome. Brutus, therefore, is not quite so out of place.'

'I think it would be more appropriate to call you Professor Schütze like your father, rather than Cousin Hubie,' I remarked.

'It would be most— inappropriate, for I am no authority at all.'

33

Mid Pleasures and Palaces

'PITY DAD'S NOT HERE,' I thought as we entered the palace, Hubie and Franz debating the success of Josef II's Germanification policies. 'He would enjoy a tour like this, not to mention the company.'

'Phoebe, your father met Emperor Franz Josef, yes?' Hubie asked as he guided me up the stairs.

'On numerous occasions, I understand. I have correspondence, too.'

'Franz Josef was available to all his subjects. He worked from five in the morning till late at night. In his own words, he was the servant of the state.'

'The rooms are quite plain for a palace.' Although its rich golden-brown walls and ivory panels and solid furniture reflected both wealth and taste, the Emperor's study was modestly proportioned; and its photographs and paintings testified to a preference for family over worldly pomp by a monarch fond of smoking old pipes, judging by the collection on the desk stand. 'Was the Emperor a severe man?'

'No more severe than most fathers. I doubt you would describe your own father in such terms.'

'Dad was tough, though – tough on himself but generous with others, almost to a fault.'

'And yet you are sceptical of one's capacity for self-government. Why is that?'

'I have good reason to be.'

'My impression is that you yourself do not seem deficient in that regard— And you do well to give it importance. Indeed, I agree with you: self-mastery is essential for government. But I do not share your assumption that individual fallibility renders government fruitless. Nor do I consider such discipline an end in itself. These are the chambers of Franz Josef's wife, Empress Elisabeth, or Sisi as she was known.'

'And this is the Empress?' I indicated the portrait of a dark-haired woman wearing a white dress and a blue cape loosely fastened with a ribbon. I tried to look her in the eye. Unsmiling, she had a petite mouth which had the capacity to say much, if she so permitted. But she demanded respect. 'I understand you,' I wanted to tell her, 'You intend to lead your own life, have your own thoughts. You won't be dictated to.'

'I wish I had not been named after her,' the tall, chestnut-haired Sisi Schütze declared.

'You do not like her?'

'I will take another name when I enter the convent. I am going to be a nursing sister, Phoebe.'

'I suppose that's one good reason for becoming a nun,' laughed Zita. 'I'm stuck with Zita and scarred for life. Besides, it wasn't easy for Empress Elisabeth. Imagine being pushed into a marriage and a role for which you are unprepared. She even had to fight to mother her own children. And she was a prisoner here, her life only bearable because she demanded the freedom to pursue her own interests.'

'Which she did, extravagantly and capriciously,' argued Sisi. 'Building a villa in Greece only to abandon it upon completion; travelling hither and thither; meddling with the Hungarians; spending half a morning having her hair groomed; living on starvation rations and riding for hours on horseback for the sake of her figure. She wasn't a prisoner in Schönbrunn or anywhere else. She was a prisoner of her own shrivelled heart.'

'She was not always like that, Sisi. And you forget, Zita,' added Hubie, 'that from an early age the emperor was also— pushed into marriage and duties of state to which he devoted himself for sixty-eight years. And despite his wife's behaviour, there is no denying that he— loved her.'

'Not to mention the actress.'

'The friendship with Katharina Schratt was a— platonic one which the Empress encouraged for the sake of her blessed— independence. At least Franz Josef tried to love his wife. And I believe he was faithful to her. Furthermore, he had an empire to rule.'

'Which was falling to bits, physically and morally,' remarked Franz.

'Details of which we can spare the ladies,' warned Hubie.

'No need to spare us, Huberle,' teased Zita.

'She's not as innocent as she looks,' Franz winked insinuatingly.

'It is not necessary,' Hubie pontificated. 'Especially in front of the younger girls.'

'There you go again, avoiding the topic,' his brother complained.

'Franz,' Hubie paused, and I observed him struggle with his stutter, 'I— think it better to examine the m-merits of the empire which, by any standards, are— considerable, particularly given the circumstances. How, following the French Revolution, that most bitter and— misguided upheaval which has deprived you of your role as the secular guardian of C-c-c-christendom, do you rule a people, some of whom have placed nationalism and autonomy above any other higher concern, in an age in which p-p-power is increasingly defined by industrial— might, as was proven in the last war? When you are faced with P-p-prussian aggression to the west and Czarist— manipulation to the east, not to mention c-c-conspiracy within? Whatever his faults, I have deep— respect for Franz-Josef. And, as far as morals are concerned, rather than indulge in the— scandals of Archduke Otto, and the suicide of Crown Prince Rudolf, I prefer to look at the virtues of Karl—'

'Who failed dismally from the moment he assumed the throne.'

'He— strove to do what he knew to be right, despite the opposition. He will be canonised one day.'

'Amen, amen, and so we will have a saint. But we will never have an emperor.'

'Isn't she a bit young to become a nun?' I remarked to Hubie as we followed Sisi through the Empress' apartments.

'How old were you when you decided upon a musical career?'

'Fourteen.'

'Sisi is sixteen. I myself considered the religious life at a similar age. Your father helped me much. He advised me not to be hasty. If I studied hard and played well, and loved my family and friends, my vocation would reveal itself in time. Youth is better spent making discoveries, not decisions, he wrote. He recommended I seek the company of people I admire and trust, starting with my father.'

Odd instruction, I thought, from a man who in his youth was so impetuous, and whose relationship with his father was fraught with misunderstanding.

'Vati arranged for me to spend the summer in a monastery; which accorded with your father's recommendation that I be attentive to the innermost workings of my heart. His wisdom stood me in good stead.'

Would that I had benefitted from his wisdom when I was fourteen!

'Sisi has been discerning her vocation for some years. She is already working at the Hartmannspital, the hospital run by the Franciscan Sisters of Christian Charity, the order she has requested to join. But it will be a while before she enters, for she needs a mitgift— that is not the right word? What a woman takes with her when she marries?'

'A dowry?'

'Ah, danke. She will need a dowry. At present, all she has are the jewels left her by our grandmother. We are trying to save for her. It is easier now that Franz and I have jobs as well as Father. Sisi is happy, and it is important she knows that she goes with our blessing. If she were to marry, we would do the same. The choice is hers and hers alone, not like Archduchess Maria Elizabeth here.' And he directed me to the portrait of a beautiful young woman.

'Who is she?'

'She was the eldest daughter of Empress Maria Theresia. Unfortunately, she was afflicted with smallpox which badly scarred her face. Otherwise she would have married the King Louis XVI of France. The only path left open to her was a cloistered life. But it is not as bad as it sounds. She became abbess of a certain... Convent for Noble Ladies. Her sister Marie-Antoinette married King Louis instead— And you know what happened to poor Marie-Antoinette.'

I figured that Hubie was about my age, more likely a year or two older; which meant that while I had been shut in an orphanage, he and Dad had been corresponding. Why had Dad never written to me? Why had I never considered writing to him? I mustn't think ill of him! Perhaps it was his condition, I sighed. I had not featured in Vienna before the War, that safe and happy world into which he had retreated after Maman died; whereas Hubie, whom he knew as a baby, had. Still, how could he have remembered his godson and not his own daughter?

'I understand your father, like ours, was a c-c-court musician before the War.' If Hubie had been talking, I was unaware of it. I sensed we had covered some territory, for we entered a sparse white and gold antechamber that appeared more formal than the Empress' suite.

What had I missed?

'We are about to enter the Great Gallery where the orchestra sometimes played.'

'Did I ever tell you the story about the kangaroo and the king?' Dad asked his nieces and nephews one Christmas in Ballarat.

'Was it King George?' asked Jack.

'This king was much older than King George.'

'King Edward?' asked Beatie.

'Older even than King Edward.'

'King Arthur?' asked Billy.

'Not quite so old. But he was the oldest king of all the kings at the time. Franz Josef was his name, and he had white whiskers like Grandfather. He ruled over a beautiful country full of castles and palaces and churches, and rivers and mountains and forests.

There were reindeer, too, and wild boar. But, you know what? There weren't any kangaroos.

'Well, once upon a time, a kangaroo arrived in that faraway land; and being rather unusual, he attracted a fair bit of attention. Now, the old king had seen lions and tigers and giraffes and elephants, for he had his own special zoo; but never had he seen a kangaroo. So, he invited the kangaroo to court.

'Kangaroo, upon receiving the royal invitation, hopped to the palace and was shown into the grandest room he had ever seen. It was white and gold, with mirrors all the way down one wall and windows down the other. And on the ceiling was a beautiful painting of blue heavens and wispy white clouds, with a king and a queen in its centre, and folk from foreign lands all around. And there was an enormous chandelier with thousands of candles that flickered a thousand times, for the mirrors caught their reflection. Now the king, well he sat on a gold throne at the far end of the room, surrounded by courtiers and princes and princesses. And knights,' he added for Billy's entertainment.

'Kangaroo bowed to His Majesty who asked, "Tell me, Herr Kangaroo. What can you do?"

'"I can play the violin," Kangaroo replied.

'"Will you play for me, good Kangaroo?" asked the King.

'"With pleasure, Your Majesty," replied Kangaroo, and he pulled his violin from his pouch.

'Uncle Roderick?' Jack interrupted.

'What's up?'

'Boy kangaroos don't have pouches.'

Dad stared at the little boy in mock-surprise. 'I do believe you're right. Better watch that one,' he added in a whisper to Uncle Alec. 'Now, where was I? That's right. Kangaroo needed a violin, didn't he? So, he hopped up to the concert master and asked very politely if he could please borrow his Strad. Being a generous sort, the concert master obliged, and Kangaroo began to play.'

Fragrant honey from molten wax melded with sandalwood Eau de Cologne and rose parfum. Medals gleamed from gentlemen's chests, diamond necklets glittered, and pearls glowed in the golden candlelight. Lustrous pastel satins, laces, and skin like alabaster brushed against jackets and trousers regal red, royal blue, and ivory. Stout male figures, and ladies with waists pulled tight listened to the filigrees of Mozart, intimate and pure, played by the fine-boned fiddler.

Melancholy shadows stretched across the parquetry. I shivered at my reflection: a solitary, slender figure in a black princess coat and pert hat. How meagre I seemed in that immense gilded mirror.

Then I saw Dad laid out on white sheets.

'Phoebe!' Hubie and Sisi ran across the hall.

'We buried him in his concert clothes,' I murmured.

'You are very pale!' Sisi's brown eyes were filled with worry. 'I thought you were going to faint!'

'We have— neglected you, dear Cousin. Please, take my arm.'

'I'm quite all right, thank you. Oh, it's so empty! And to think it was once filled with music! Dad graduated from the Academy with highest honours, and his playing attracted the attention of the Emperor. He was only nineteen. He performed a Mozart concerto in this very room, which he followed with some Paganini. Dad told me the event became so much like a family gathering that he wondered why he had bothered being nervous. He even chatted with Archduke Franz Ferdinand, who had visited Australia, about shooting wildlife in Victoria. It's hard to believe that only a few years later the Archduke would be assassinated, the world plunged into war, and a way of life would vanish forever.'

'That is very true,' Hubie replied. 'Much of the fate of the Empire was decided in this wing of the palace.' He guided me into a beautiful salon bedecked with Chinese paper wall hangings. 'Here, our last emperor, Karl I, renounced involvement in state affairs. Unlike Kaiser Wilhelm – or your King Edward – he never abdicated, which means our present monarch, Crown Prince Otto, is in exile. Napoleon slept here,' he indicated another room in passing. 'He claimed an imperial title for himself, which was an abuse of the highest order, I might add. Are you feeling better? If so, would you permit me to show you my favourite room?'

We entered a narrow, highly ornamented blue and white salon. Fascinated, I studied the intimate blue ink sketches of rustic oriental scenes which adorned the walls from floor to ceiling. 'They are primarily the work of Maria Theresia's husband and children, who had much to do with the decoration of the palace,' Hubie commented. 'Even some of the furniture was made by an emperor or archduke.'

'It is very peaceful and homely.'

And, believe it or not, it was. Even though the first impression was of lavish wealth, if you bothered to look more carefully, that wealth comprised antiques lovingly preserved, personal details, discarded items put to new purpose, and quality purchases made to last a century.

'Yes. A family lived here. Unfortunately, the Schönbrunn, along with the all the common Habsburg property, was confiscated after the Republic of German Austria was declared. Two years ago, however, Chancellor Schuschnigg restored some private residences to the family, but not the palace.'

'Was it ever put to any other use after the emperor left?' I asked as we resumed our tour.

'For a short time, it was a hospital for returned soldiers. Also, it was an orphanage. But it is not easy to maintain – too expensive. So now we leave it for the Americans, the French and the British to enjoy when they deign to visit. They seem pleased that it is empty.'

There was the trace of a sneer in Hubie's voice. He was not angry, though, nor was he bitter. He was hurt, like a noble beast – a stag or an elk – that had been shot in the rump and had taken shelter to nurse its wound.

'This is Franz II,' he indicated the full-length portrait his siblings were studying. 'He was the last of the— Holy Roman Emperors. After the Napoleonic Wars, he became F-f-franz I of Austria.'

'Poor old Huberle,' Franz patted him on the back. 'He still wishes the world was subject to Austria. My dear brother, you will have to accept that the Holy Roman Empire is no more, its emperors entombed in the Capuchin Church. He was born in the wrong century,' he whispered, nudging me.

34

A Little Punschkrapferl

'**M**UST YOU STUDY every painting, every door knob, every chair and table?' Professor Schütze complained to Hubie the moment we returned, far later than expected.

'Kurti, you know how much Huberle loves the Schönbrunn,' remonstrated Frau Schütze.

'The sons I have! Hubert thinks too much, Franz talks too much, and Karl neither thinks nor talks unless the object in question has moving parts!'

'Huberle, your shirt and tie are pressed.' Frau Schütze herded him out of his father's way. 'Eat and dress for the concert and try not to keep Vati waiting.'

But Professor Schütze had more to grumble about. He could not tie his bow tie, and his wife could not tie it quickly enough. Where was Hubert? They would miss the tram if he didn't get a move on. And what was the world coming to that they had to take the tram anyway? Oh, for the days when transport to the Musikverein came courtesy of an Imperial and Royal carriage! All present refrained from comment. Apparently, such lamentations were a means of quelling nerves.

Frau Schütze helped him into his tailcoat and evening coat and tied his scarf. 'Do you have your best reed, Kurti?' He had left it on his music stand. Sisi dashed upstairs to retrieve it. 'Fraülein Rayel!' the Professor shouted, unaware that I was right behind him and much surprised when I appeared so quickly. 'Found it!' Sisi called from the landing. And where was Hubert? Zita was helping him with his tie. Why can't he tie his own tie? Hubie loped out in white tie and tails. As we left the house, father and son donned top hats and I found myself under the protection of giants.

Professor Schütze spent his travel time puckering and loosening his lips and making odd clicking rhythms with his tongue. Hubie relaxed with a pungent cigarette and a book; and took leave of his reading only when we reached my stop, whereby he assisted me from the tram all the while assuring his father that he would not be late.

'You have been to concert, Phoebe?' he asked.

'Not yet. I—I was wait— I haven't quite brought myself to do so.'

'But you intend to go to concert while you are here? My cousin,' he chastised, 'to visit the City of Music and hear no music is unforgivable.'

'You are putting me under grave obligation,' I smiled.

'Do you have favourite composer?'

'I don't mind what I listen to. It's always interesting. What is tonight's programme?'

'Let me see... Vivaldi, *Concerto Grosso*, Saint-Saens' *Organ Symphony*, Bizet's *L'Arlesienne*, and Mussorskgy's *Pictures at an Exhibition*. Toscanini is conducting. We have small problem, however. Half the orchestra is missing Furtwängler, who conducted us in Salzburg. Toscanini is very precise, very exacting. Furtwängler, on the other hand, is more intelligent. Vati prefers Toscanini—'

'And you prefer Furtwängler?'

'I know why I am musician when Furtwängler conducts. Under Toscanini we play music. Under Furtwängler, we create it.'

'Well, break a leg tonight.'

'Ah, Danke! In German we say, "Hals- und Beinbruch!" I am afraid we are a little more violent. We also break the neck.'

Thereafter, Hubie and I frequently coincided – in front of the Karlskirche, on the Linke Wienzeile tram, outside shops and coffee houses. Our encounters followed a pattern: a polite bow and handkuss on Hubie's part, an enquiry after my health, and an offer of escort. If I accepted, his only words were a good-bye closed with a handkuss upon reaching my destination, which left me wondering why he went to so much trouble, particularly since my journeys invariably took him out of his way.

Meanwhile, Zita made my acquaintance known to every leading shop, gallery, museum, and café in the city. She proved an informative, fun-loving, albeit garrulous guide who regarded me as a welcome escape from domesticity, and a confidante.

I learned that she had entertained a string of suitors, an account of which she provided over an afternoon tea of Punschkrapferl, a delectable rum-soaked apricotty-chocolatey *petit four* prettily coated in pink fondant. She received her first attentions from a committed Trotskyite whom her father promptly banished. The next contestant was more to her parents' taste, for he was devout and of good family; but he entered the priesthood instead.

Zita's third beau, again much to her parents' relief, was a good Catholic boy from the provinces who was tragically killed in the summer of 1934. Yes, it was a shock, but there had been no real affection between them, despite everyone's thoughts to the contrary. Her mother then tried to match her with a young man of aristocratic descent. 'What a bore!' she groaned. Meanwhile, there were overtures from another aristocrat living abroad; but he was penniless, and too far from home. Nor was she especially interested.

Finally, there was Rudi— Franz-Rudolf to be precise; but considering there were so many Franz-something-or-others, Rudi sufficed. Zita liked him well enough.

'Well enough for what?'

'Well enough to marry, of course. He's my fiancé.'

'You don't love him?'

'There's no point in being romantic,' she dusted some crumbs from her candy stripe blouse, which garment looked like something she had been made to wear, for it did not suit her; but Zita did enjoy experimenting with fashion as far as her figure permitted. 'Romance has little to do with it. I'll make it work.'

'How you can be so pragmatic?'

'I have to be. I don't possess your good fortune.'

'I have a room of my own and a private income,' I scoffed. 'That makes me independent. It doesn't necessarily make me happy.'

'You desire to share it?' she smiled coyly.

'I might. But what is the point if I am not loved in return?'

'A failed romance! What happened?'

Reluctantly, and then with much relief, I told her of Eric's deceit and Kerem's abandonment.

'A Turk? How fascinating! But you poor thing! You are just like Madame Butterfly.'

'Don't be silly!'

'Anyway, if you wish to keep it secret, you can trust me. My lips are sealed as a tomb. Did you know that my mother and your father—'

'What?'

'They had a brief infatuation! Mutti told me about his quartet. The Klimt Quartet, wasn't it? She said it was a fantastic novelty to see two gentlemen and two ladies playing together in public, which amused me no end because Mutti is so very conservative. The older generation disapproved, but that didn't stop any Klimt Quartet concert being attended by every person under thirty. Word would get out, and everyone would leave home, telling their parents they were performing works of charity or taking tea with maiden aunts. Mutti said the girls came to see the first violin, and the boys the cellist. But I later heard that some girls came to see the cellist, and some boys the first violin. Why did he call it the Klimt Quartet? Did your father know Klimt?'

'Apparently the name was my aunt's idea.'

'Then I suppose she knew Klimt. Perhaps she was one of his mistresses,' she added gleefully.

'That wouldn't surprise me. Who is Klimt, anyway?'

'Lord! Don't you know? He was one of the most renowned artists in Vienna!'

Then and there she arranged for us to visit Frau Lederer, who kept one of society's most opulent and influential salons. Zita had seen the Lederer's Klimt collection countless times. 'For inspiration,' she said.

'Ah, the dashing violinist in the Sternberg affair,' Frau Lederer nodded when she learned of my connection to Dad.

'One of the more notorious scandals of *la belle époque*,' Zita explained as our hostess brought us into her drawing room. 'Something between a Count and a young lady half his age. Mutti knows more about it than me,' she shrugged when I pressed her for more.

'Well, Dad was no count, and could never have been involved with a woman half his age,' I concluded with some relief as I joined Zita in viewing the paintings.

Imprisoned in a dazzling labyrinth of pattern, women stared; their expressions fixed and determined, intelligent and inquiring. With their delicate faces, they were victims as much as subjects. Naked bodies, slender and nymphal, stretched and curved in a shamelessly sensuous fashion across vast canvases. Other nude forms were wizened, grotesque contortions. One woman was even with child. Each voluptuous figure evinced the same remarkable draughtsmanship.

Entranced by the lavish and intricate geometry, the gold leaf and brilliant hues; and intrigued yet repelled by the forms, I studied the faces, hoping and dreading that Ailine might be featured. Not a one resembled her. Still, it seemed she was present in every painting. The orgy of nudity recalled for me her studio and I began to feel queasy.

'You're not the first person to feel like that,' remarked Zita who suggested I recover with coffee and cake (her solution to most problems). I suggested my apartment, which invitation she accepted with nervous excitement. 'The authorities refused to hang the frieze Klimt painted for the University. There was even a court case over it. If it wasn't for the Lederers his work might have been destroyed.' As for scandal, I had better get used to it.

'Egon Schiele!' she exclaimed when she saw Dad's portrait. 'He's a favourite of mine. Did you know he was infatuated with his own sister? Oh, that's nothing!' she laughed, seeing my shock. 'Klimt had at least a dozen mistresses and goodness knows how many illegitimate children. I'm surprised your father never told you any of this. After all, he performed in the finest salons in Vienna, including Alma Mahler's. Didn't you say Arnold Rosé was his teacher? Well, Rosé was Gustav Mahler's brother-in-law, you see. Mahler's wife Alma is a composer in her own right. Not that Mahler gave her any credit— which is shameful if you ask me, and probably the reason behind her affairs with Kokoschka and Walter Gropius. She married Franz Werfel the poet, but they'd been having an affair for years. I'm surprised you haven't been introduced. She is an extraordinary woman.'

'I don't see how having several affairs makes her extraordinary.' Zita's gossip made Dad and Maman's pre-marital affair look very tame indeed.

'Why are you so shocked? It happens all the time. Marriage is a means, not an end. And, if you ask me, women have as much right as men to develop their talents. Surely, you must agree with that?'

She noticed me eyeing the small portfolio she had brought with her.

'They're porcelain designs. It was a private commission, but the Augarten wants me to do more. Have a peek while I powder my nose.'

'Bathroom's the second door on the left,' I advised as I undid the portfolio strings. I needn't have bothered. Zita was quite capable of locating the bathroom on her own merits.

The designs were for a coffee set. With their streamlined, elegant silhouette they were strikingly modern; while my friend's flair for colour was exhibited in a brilliant circular motif finely outlined in gold and black. Klimt's influence was obvious, and in more ways than one I realised when I saw the signature.

No! It couldn't be!

There, in the corner, stylishly printed, was the name *Zusa*.

'What do you think?' she asked, proud of her skill. 'Mutti says it's a little stark, but, as you can see from our house, she's very old-fashioned. I keep telling her times are changing, and people nowadays aren't interested in fuddy-duddy Baroque ornament; but Mutti only laughs and says beauty, like truth and goodness, is as relevant now as it was three centuries ago. But why should we conform to past notions? Art is dynamic. I mean— you and I are living beings, and we are artists. Our ability to create beauty resides entirely with us, not with another's aesthetic mandate. Wouldn't you agree?'

All I could think of was that Zita's remarks were a variation on the mantra chanted from a certain shop on the ground floor. No! She couldn't be having an affair with Emil! Perhaps it was coincidental that the signature was the same; but another chance occurrence disproved that notion.

The following Thursday, while leaving the Epstein's bakery in Leopoldstadt, I spotted Zita exiting a nearby hotel – the kind that rents rooms for an hourly rate. Five minutes later, from the same building, Emil pulled up his collar and lumbered away in the opposite direction.

The bookshop had re-opened by the time I returned. Since there were no customers, Emil was drawing plans in the back room.

'I met Zusa the other day,' I began.

'Did you?' he measured an angle.

'She's a family friend.'

'Hobnobbing with the Hietzing toffs, are we?'

'I could say the same of you. I didn't think you would have such grandiose pretentions. You do realise she's getting married, don't you?'

'Feh! To that pisher?[12] He leans against his house,'[13] he sniggered. 'Now, my little Fräulein, kindly step into my shoes. What would you do if you were bored witless and an attractive young woman walked into your shop and propositioned you? Would you refuse?'

'You're disgusting! Anyway, I don't know what you find so attractive about her— dumpy, bespectacled little creature.'

'Take your eyes in your own hands. Besides, I have the right to love whomsoever I choose.'

'You speak of love in the same way you do public housing. Love is not a right!'

'But we hunger for it, don't we? Nothing is going to stop me – neither church, nor state, nor law, nor family, nor you. I love Zita Schütze. I always have. And I intend to people this corner of the world with our progeny. So, you leave me to my affair, and I will leave you to your charming vendetta. I needn't comment which is the more desirable.'

I glared at the unkempt stray of a man as he sat at his draughtsman's table – a man who was shorter than he ought to be – and saw the malnourished, rickety orphan within. He shifted and straightened his vest, showing off its intricate Fairisle work, and a triumphant little smirk stole across his lips. He was loved, and I was not. Someone had taken the trouble to knit for him; and I knew where I had seen Zita's cardigan before.

'How long have you known her?'

'We met some years ago at the Wiener Werkstätte, an artists' union which ran workshops. It's closed now. I assisted her with a project. She has the mind of a first-rate architect. Not that her family would know. No one appreciates her the way I do. Now if

---

[12] *Pisher*. (lit.) pisser, bed-wetter; (sl.) a young, inexperienced, presumptuous person; a nobody.

[13] *He leans against his house*: an insinuation about impotence, alluding figuratively to Job 8:15, 'He shall lean upon his house, but it shall not stand; he shall hold it fast, but it shall not endure.

you would excuse me, I have plans to finish.'

'What are you working on?'

'Our dream-home. Zusa and I have been collaborating.'

'I like the window.'

'Whenever I design a house, I include a round window. This one will have a view over the fields. On a summer's day when you look out and see the grass mown and dried, perhaps you will think of the adage, "The world is a haystack, from which each man plucks what he can". I have plucked my straw, and I intend to hold on to it.'

I left the shop, only to collide with Hubie. 'Not now!' I thought. I did not wish to endure his silent deliberations while Zita's amours filled my mind. He greeted me with his usual handkuss and enquiry after my health, but for once he did not offer to escort me. Instead, after much hesitation, he presented me with a ticket to next Saturday's concert.

While I was preparing for the evening's entertainment, Alma Rosé knocked at my door.

'Be a dear and take this for me,' she handed me the parcel she was carrying, and entered before I as much as invited her inside. 'I need some diversion. Vasa's been a beast, Heini's out of town, Mutti is ill, and Vati is in one of his dark brown moods. I thought to pop in to see how you're getting on. Have you been out much?'

'Quite a lot, thank you. Mainly museums and galleries. And the Schönbrunn.'

'All the dead places. I suppose you'll visit the cemetery next. Shall I arrange a plot for you?'

'I don't think that will be necessary,' I smiled. 'Not yet, anyway.'

'And you've had company?'

'As a matter of fact, I'm attending a concert tonight.'

'At the Musikwerein? I'll look out for you. Now, I have a favour to ask. One of my girls won't be able to do our New Year's Eve engagement. She's emigrating. Of course, I wish her well, but ... Anyway, I need a substitute. Are you available?'

'For what?'

Alma stared at me as if I were a little backward. 'I have an orchestra, the Wiener Walzermädeln, and I am offering you a position.'

'Oh, my goodness! I was planning to leave next month.'

'And miss Carnivale? Are you mad? You wouldn't consider postponing? I'm desperate! Besides, Vati recommended you.'

'Professor Rosé recommended me?'

'I don't know why you're so surprised. You're experienced, you have good tone and excellent technique, you can hold your own in an ensemble, and Vati says you have your father's aptitude for sight-reading and memorisation. Besides, I need someone who isn't going to let me down because they're running in the wedding stakes. You obviously have no romantic inclinations.'

'What makes you say that?'

'You are still in black.'

'I'm mourning my father.'

'How long has it been? Two years? Even by Viennese standards, that's a long time for a child to mourn a parent. If you were widowed, one might understand. Anyway, no decent man will make overtures while you're dressed like that. You're not averse to wearing a gown for professional engagements, are you? I mean, I cannot have you perform in black; it would spoil the ensemble.'

'I'll wear the gown.'

'Good. I have it here. Put it on. I want to see how you look.'

The gown was a gorgeous creation in sky blue chiffon. To better assess the fit and feel, I made a twirl and watched the frills and flounces froth and bubble.

'May I come in?' Alma called.

In my mirror I beheld her, imperious and impeccably groomed, a just-kissed Galatea scrutinising me from top to toe.

'My, you are a sylph! You haven't quite grown up yet, have you?'

'I beg your pardon?'

'I didn't mean to offend.'

'Well, I'm twenty-three. I simply choose not to spend my time in pointless flirtation.'

'Flirtation is never pointless. How is it that you're still single? I was married at twenty-four. Married at twenty-four, divorced at thirty,' she sighed. 'You know, there's no need to be afraid of being a woman. Or are you afraid of being loved?'

'It's betrayal I fear.'

'You are wiser than I thought. Careful,' she smiled wryly, 'else you grow old before your time.'

Come evening, a dank blanket of cold covered the Danube. I decided to catch the tram, and in doing so avoided not only the rain but also the rabble of youths outside. I knew their hallmark now. They were strong and healthy – 'the type that thrives on a trade' as Dad would say – and their cropped hair and white socks indicated their affiliation with the NSDAP, despite its being outlawed. But even though the economic situation had improved (so reported the papers), there were still few trades to be had. So, instead of working, these young men prowled the streets in packs, taunted Jews, and chalked up swastikas. When not on the streets, I imagined they lived with their mothers – hardworking women who took in laundry and scrubbed stairwells to supplement their meagre pensions and feed their sons. One could only wonder what these careworn matriarchs thought. And their fathers? Well, given that they were either buried on the Russian front, dredged out of the Danube, or drowning their sorrows in a Beisl, they thought of it not at all.

In contrast, the Musikwerein furnished living proof that what was missing from the Schönbrunn was still alive and well. Magnificently costumed, diamonds round every naked throat, Vienna's privileged and wealthy gave the illusion of being unaffected by the swastika jackals outside; but their hurried entrances and gushing welcomes – sighs of relief rather than salutations – betrayed them. Chancellor Schuschnigg arrived, shadowed by bodyguards unused to tailcoats. Now there was a worried man. Although only forty years of age, he was stooped, his face lined from long hours and endless negotiations, having just returned from Czechoslovakia. Apparently, music was his solace. 'Schuschnigg survives on music and the Sancta Missa. Amen,' Emil once intoned.

I would be worried, too, if I saw my face plastered with swastikas every morning, I thought.

Judging from the looks I received, I was an anomaly and I could not tell why. My beaded black dress was equal in style to the other gowns. Perhaps it was the colour. I held my head high and moved with seeming purpose through the crowd. 'Consign me to the netherworld if you wish; but my father was a Viennese citizen, and I have as much right to be here as you,' I glared at a young woman whose sneer would have slaughtered me had I been in a more furtive mood.

But I felt neither lonely nor out of place, for there was something very familiar about the goings on; and when I saw a gentleman in his evening regalia greet a party of close friends, I knew what it was: Dad. The courtly affability – polite even to the devil – the bows and handküsse; the easy formality, dripping with charm, was played out a hundredfold before me. What always seemed so delightfully eccentric at home was commonplace here. I could have laughed – not to mock – but out of sheer relief. Instead, I restricted myself to a smile. Thinking I was smiling at him, an elderly gentleman bowed. His wife noted my expression and nodded rather more sternly. She did not look directly at me, however. It seemed she had noticed my sleeve was torn. I followed her gaze and realised what was so unusual about my presence:

I was without a chaperone.

Alma hailed me over to her circle and introduced me to her brother Alfred, his wife Maria, and Lorelei (Lori) Kusch her concertmistress.

'This is fortuitous,' Lori smiled. She was an elegant and vivacious girl about my age. 'I've been looking forward to meeting you.'

'You're not on your own?' Alma scolded.

'I have a— a cousin playing in the orchestra. Do you know him?' I further inquired of Lori who was curious as to my musical connections.

'Hubie Schütze? Good Lord! We studied at the ac-c-c-ademy together,' she giggled.

You more than studied together, I thought.

Interlude

.

Musikverein, New Year's Day 1957

'And this is where Dad played the Mendelssohn?' Finally, as we entered between two great fluted golden columns, young Roddy indulged his curiosity and gazed around the Großer Musikvereinssaal, Vienna's jewel box of sound. So preoccupied had he been with manners – opening doors, offering his arm, walking curb-side, and not gawping – that his conversation had been even more sparse than usual.

Courtesy aside, he's going to have to learn to look people in the eye, I thought, or they'll think he's terribly rude.

'I can see him now, Roddy, violin in hand, dapper and spry in white tie and tails, tripping onto that concert platform, quite in love with the audience. The Emperor would have sat in gallery five, up to the left, amidst his people. He liked to sit with the common folk. It's magnificent, isn't it?'

Garlands of pink and white roses decked the stage, above which stood the great golden organ gallery, its majestic pipes flanked with caryatids and topped with a pediment. 'Take a look at the ceiling, and you'll find Apollo and his nine muses,' I encouraged him. Look up, boy. Feast on the splendour.

'Will Dr Schütze and his father be playing?'

'Sadly, no, Roddy. Boskowsky's conducting Strauss. Quite an inane concert, really. Everyone clapping along to music that ought to be danced to and getting all nostalgic about Austria's long-gone imperial past; all the while doing their best to uphold neutrality, observe class protocol, be good little socialists, attend church, and forget about the Soviets. Have you seen *Sissi*?'

'What's *Sissi*?'

'The film about Empress Elisabeth— Roddy, it's compulsory viewing; and it will give you a much better idea of Dad's world than I could even attempt. I've seen it four times already. It's still playing at the Bellaria, down near the museums. The sequel came out at Christmas. It'll do wonders for your German. When's your Academy audition?'

'March.' He didn't like being reminded and lapsed into silence.

'Do you still play?' he asked.

'Occasionally.'

'Would you consider accompanying me?'

'Roddy, I'd be delighted! What's the programme?'

'Well, the Franck, for one.'

'Might start a family tradition,' I smiled.

'I'd be glad of that. Are you worried?'

'About your audition?'

'No. About the Soviets. You always get ironic and change the subject when you're worried.'

'Do I?' I found myself wishing for a sharp-eyed glimmer – that look Dad gave whenever he probed my heart, but Roddy avoided my gaze; and whether it was out of fear of retaliation on my part, or because his attention was taken by the onstage preparations of the orchestra, I could not say. It seemed, however, that he genuinely wished to know. At least, that was what I construed from his single nod and quiet 'Mmm hmm', delivered as he took stock of the string section. He knew he was right. And he was.

'Well, yes, I am. The Soviets claim that Austria has violated her neutrality because she has accepted Hungarian refugees. Given the clamp-down in Hungary, anything could happen, Roddy. We're lucky to have the freedom we have after nearly twenty years of occupation. I hope we can hold onto it. No society's perfect, but I look at the Schönbrunn and the Musikverein, and recall all that has happened since I first visited, and I can't help but think that we once lived in Arcady. Truly, Roddy, those days marked the end of a golden age.'

Part Three

·

Et in Arcadia Ego

·

October 1937

Even in Arcady, there am I

Attributed to Cardinal Rospigliosi (later Pope Clement IX, 1667-69)

35

Arcady

'PROSIT!' Franz, Hubie, and Zita raised their glasses, and we toasted each other one by one. Having been to the pictures to see *La Grande Illusion*, we stopped for refreshment and further entertainment at the Theatre Ronacher where Alma and her orchestra played. The Wiener Walzermädeln comprised part of what Franz called a *Schrammel* – a variety show – and as we drank, a clarinet and oompah band accompanied a female impersonator dressed as an Austrian shepherdess who sang of her love for a boy in Berlin.

'*She* should be in love with the blonde chap next door,' Zita chuckled, 'But the dark Berliner has taken her fancy, and despite his being penniless, she's prepared to give him anything he wants.'

Hubie drew languidly on his cigarette and watched the smoke waft towards the dusty glass clusters of the centre chandelier. The chandelier was set in the middle of an enormous, elaborately moulded vault lined with three tiers of similarly ornamented stalls, the columns and tracery of which, like Miss Havisham's wedding cake, were draped with cobwebs; while the whitewash fondant of the walls was flaked and cracked, thereby exposing a marzipan layer of tobacco-grimed plaster. The Ronacher had given up being grand.

The happy groups gathered round mismatched tables cheered and applauded the shepherdess, tossed down drinks, and welcomed Alma's orchestra. Like nereids in a frilly chiffon river, the Walzermädeln swayed as they played Strauss' Beautiful Blue Danube, while Alma, their leader, seemed to stand on the waves of the Danube itself. Her shapely arms curved round her violin, and her large eyes dreamed into the distance. Couples waltzing in close embrace exuded sweat, stale brandy, and cheap scent.

'Congratulations on your job, Phoebe,' Franz continued. 'The Wiener Walzermädeln is much admired.'

'It's not the Philharmoniker, I'm afraid.'

'But there is far more to admire in the Walzermädeln than in the Philharmoniker. For instance, in the Philharmoniker, I don't think I will ever see a brunette as charming as that harpist, yes?

Of course, there's our Huberle, but—'

'Franzl!' Zita teased. 'What would Inge say if she heard you?'

'She would agree, I hope. And if she fancies any of the brunettes in the Philharmoniker, I would like to know about it. And as for Rudi—

'He fancies the blondes! Prosit!'

'Who does Alma Rosé think she is?' I complained to Hubie during one of our odd little promenades. While my week of rehearsal had been a welcome change from my usual routine, I had forgotten the rigours of orchestral work.

Alma reminded me soon enough. It was not going to be said that she, daughter of the concert master of the Vienna Philharmonic, and niece of the great Gustav Mahler, was any lesser musician. Nor was her orchestra a second-rate ensemble because it comprised only women. Oh, no! Not only had she made a choice selection of players, she was as demanding as her father.

She assigned me third violin, which part required intense concentration. I had to weave in and out of melody and harmony, and play the occasional solo, all as part of an ensemble that moved, and even laughed as one in time to the music. Furthermore, I had some thirty pieces to master by memory. Let me say now, Roddy, that the nymphal charm of the Walzermädeln, as with much of Vienna's lavishness and frivolity – be it architectural splendour, exquisite pastry, or feminine beauty – was the fruit of slavish dedication.

'And I tell you, Hubie, if anyone's riding on their father's merits, it's Alma Rosé. She's capable— I'll give her that. But she's not brilliant— not by a long shot. Yet how everyone lionises her! I was dining at the Hotel Bristol yesterday when Alma breezed in and flirted with every Tom, Dick, and Harry, while waiters kowtowed to her every request. Even policemen stop traffic to allow her passage. I saw it. A constable waved her through with a bow and she cruised along in that great white convertible of hers, with her horrid Alsatian sitting beside her. Then there's her boyfriend. Boyfriend? Hah! Toyfriend more like! Would you believe he's eight years her junior?'

'Do you always express yourself with such passion?' Hubie had listened in the utmost silence, ambling beside me, hands clasped behind his back, and pushing his spectacles onto his nose as required.

'Is that all you can say? If I feel passionately for my subject, well yes, I do.'

'Would you read to me one day, Phoebe? I am convinced you would read beautifully. When I read books in English, I comprehend the words, but my accent impedes my appreciation, for I do not capture well the expression. But you—'

'Hubie, did you pay any attention at all?'

'To every word.'

❖ ❖ ❖

Not only did Professor Rosé generously honour his promise to Dad by helping me find work, he also passed me tickets to the Rosé Quartet's Brahms cycle. The performance series commemorated the fortieth anniversary of the premiere of Brahms' G Minor Quartet, which the quartet originally performed from manuscript. During lessons I felt he was a teacher, a grandfather, and a friend combined. But there was a wistfulness in his manner that suggested he was reliving halcyon days. Was he also trying to conjure Dad to life?

'Dad said he heard Ysaÿe perform the Franck Sonata in Paris,' I loosened my bow after playing the sonata he had requested.

'It was written as a wedding present for Ysaÿe. The finale is like the exchange of vows, and the sonata ends in a joyous peal of bells. Your father told me he and your mother played it at their own wedding celebration.' No wonder the piece was so special to me – I had heard it rehearsed and performed almost since conception. 'Herr Roderick always liked to tell a story with his music. What story will you tell, Fräulein? You should perform the Franck.'

'Where will I find an accompanist?'

'Leave that with me. And now, I will play you a recording of your father.'

'Ah, Roddy! What a gypsy you were,' he sighed as we listened to a transcription of a Chopin Nocturne. 'Who was it first taught him?'

'A Mr Szabo. And the Countess Elizabeth Wolff-Metternich taught him piano. Dad said the Countess Wolff-Metternich was his first lady love. He was seven at the time.'

'That vibrato,' Rosé complained as if he were correcting Dad himself. 'Too much Zigeunermusik, I used to say. But Roddy was stubborn. We achieved a pleasing balance; but he made sure he had the last word. He used to assist me with recordings by going ahead to the studio and organising the microphone. He was fascinated by the process. On this occasion,' Rosé nodded at the gramophone, 'the studio engineers asked me to make a second recording. Apparently, there had been complications. After they pressed the discs, they invited me to select which recording I thought was better. I selected the one you just heard.'

'But—

'Your father had made his own recording earlier that morning and they played it instead of one of mine. I can see him sitting there now, the rascal, suppressing his smile. And I admit— his was the better interpretation. What a beautiful sound! Full and strong, but delicate, pure, elegant. Smooth as silk. I keep this record to remind myself that nothing is finite. We must change, renew, rejuvenate ourselves; otherwise, we harden and die. You have family close by?'

'I have a friend in Oxford whom I am planning to visit for Christmas. She's a cellist. We used to play a lot together. Alma suggested I travel by 'plane so I could be back for the New Year's festivities.' My Paris trip I had postponed till February.

'That sounds like Almschi. You young people, you move too fast. Now, you are able to come to dinner on Sunday after the midday concert?'

That Sunday afternoon, a familial group gathered around the Rosé table. Aside from the Professor and his wife Justine, the party included Alfred and Maria Rosé, Alma and her young beau Heini, Lori and her brother Eugene, and Hubert Schütze-Rechtschaffen.

Given everyone's common interests, not to mention the fact that Hubie had been acquainted with the Rosés through orchestral circles since he was a boy, I expected him to be more relaxed. The family welcomed him in a congenial manner, albeit tinged with the deference due to his aristocratic background; for despite the professed egalitarianism of the Republic, many customs of the Imperial *Ancien Régime* still prevailed. Hubie was courteous, but his solemn and aloof demeanour was at odds with the others' conviviality. If he had been included for my sake, he made no special effort apart from a shy acknowledgement of my presence. Instead, he sought the company of Heini and Eugene, both of whom he knew through university circles. Lori, he ignored.

Much of my attention was taken up by Rosé's wife Justine. A stout, solid woman, her serious heart condition coupled with diabetes rendered her housebound, and she seized upon any opportunity to engage with the outside world whenever her health permitted.

Aside from her family, whom she adored, she cherished anything even remotely connected with the glorious past world of her dear departed brother Gustav (the famous Mahler), and had arranged for apricot dumplings to conclude the bill of fare. Apparently, both 'Uncle Gustav' and Dad were particularly fond of them, and she hoped I would enjoy them as much (a given, I assure you).

All through lunch, she recounted Dad's many and varied courtships – 'a dark, dramatic young cellist' (Ailine); a petite redheaded baroness (Frau Schütze?); an ugly, ungainly violinist in service as an au pair (Mrs Epstein, no doubt); a ballet dancer; a Jewish lass 'not worth considering' – and laughed at the effect of her *skandal*. 'They all came to nothing, my dear, nothing at all— Roddy was in love with love itself. He quite transformed when he met your mother. Why, I could see them with a dozen children between them.'

Alfred Rosé's recollections had more to do with the Ned Kelly stories with which Dad had entertained him as a boy.

'Your father would have had us believe he was the only civilised person to have hailed from the Antipodes,' jested Professor Rosé.

'And now we have bushrangers of our own to contend with,' Alfred added drily. 'Hitler and his gang. It is a pity someone has not yet shot the German Führer in the back of the knee.'

'—Perhaps they have tried and not— succeeded,' Hubie took leave of his conversation with Heini to comment.

'Would it make any difference if they did?' Eugene contested.

'If you are referring to the— Jews, you are overgeneralising,' answered Hubie. 'True, there have been p-p-pogroms, some of which were a regrettable usurpation of— power. But there was also protection. And you forget Emperor Franz Joseph granted you civil rights.'

'But prohibited us from holding court positions.'

'What do you expect? Our Empire was a Christian one. In addition to the duties of State, participation in the sacramental life of the Church was a fundamental part of court life. To employ a Jew at court would have been equivalent to an orchestra recruiting someone who does not play an instrument; or holding a dinner party and inviting a guest who refuses to eat. Should the man who is not a musician claim he has a right to belong to the orchestra? And the man who refuses to eat? Should he complain that he receives no invitation to dine? You cannot have everything.'

'And it is attitudes such as yours which explain why we need our own nation. The Jewish People have as much right to self-determination as any German, Austrian, Czech, or Pole. My friends have established a kibbutz outside Jerusalem. I will join them after I graduate.'

'My brother is completing his doctorate in history so he can be a farmer,' Lori joked.

'And upon what will you base your "right" to your "grande illusion"? On belief or on blood? And will you exclude others on either account? And which form of your religion will you espouse in your— promised land?' countered Hubie.

'Every man has a right to basic civil liberties, which includes the freedom to worship as he pleases,' remarked Professor Rosé.

'Why should the Jews concern us anyway? We are Catholic,' added his wife.

'Baptised by the Cardinal himself,' Alma smirked.

'It would not matter if you were baptised by the poorest— priest from the most remote parish in the Tyrol, the Baptism is still the same,' Hubie retorted with a supercilious air. 'And as far as Hitler is concerned, it is not a question of Baptism, but of the blood in your veins. And he is as much opposed to the— Catholic Church as he is the Jews.'

'It is a wonder he has remained in power so long,' Rosé concluded. 'Surely he cannot last? That the man could captivate so many exceeds the credulity of any intelligent person.'

'Nationalism is a scourge!'

A week had passed, and Hubie's deprecation was his first attempt at conversation since we had dined at the Rosés'.

The glorious, crisp autumn afternoon was perfect for a Sunday excursion; and the Vienna Woods were filled with nymphs in dirndls and shepherds in lederhosen who had come away to pass the day in jollity. Not that my cousin-of-sorts and I joined the various displays of ease and happy love we glimpsed as we wandered. Hubie, for a start, wore plus fours, while I possessed no dirndl; and he invited me to commence our walk by praying the Angelus at a wayside shrine.

We diverged onto a path less trodden lined with black-trunked beech decked in a livery of golden leaves. 'I remember when Emperor Franz Josef died,' Hubie continued. 'His funeral was one of my earliest impressions. The first snow had fallen— It marked the start of a long winter. Everyone was in black, except the army. Vati lifted me up to see the procession, at the front of which I was astonished to spy a boy my own age: Crown Prince Otto von Österreich. Later, we became playmates— one of the benefits of living near a palace. After the monarchy was exiled, I did not see the Crown Prince until many years later. We became good friends. Your father knew Emperor Karl, yes?'

'Look, Hubie, some fawns hiding in a thicket!' I had never seen such animals in the wild. The little deer watched me with fearful eyes. A fox skulked past. Bushy tailed squirrels, chattering over winter preparations, scurried up tree trunks. In a nearby branch perched a goldfinch masked in scarlet. Then a pheasant strutted through the undergrowth, concealed save for his throat of regal blue.

'Your father knew Emperor Karl, yes?'

'They lunched together,' I conceded, my attempt to distract him from his political ramblings having failed. Well, at least he was talking. 'Dad said Archduke Karl, as he was known at the time, was interested in the federation of the Australian colonies. He had a notion the Archduke wanted the same for Austria-Hungary.'

'That is correct. Unfortunately, nationalist interests won out and received ample support at Versailles, while our Emperor was deprived of a voice. There has been trouble ever since: pogroms, the marginalisation of racial minorities formerly protected by the Empire; political turmoil; depletion of natural resources; trade disagreements. Furthermore, there are now too many separate, small states with insufficient means to resist the advances and overtures of either Germany or Russia. The Empire safeguarded against that.'

'Some people— people without means or privilege blame the Empire for their problems. Take the War, for instance—'

'And I suppose they say that the poverty experienced under their socialist regime was acceptable because the lower classes were no longer being exploited?' Hubie was scathing. 'Such persons are so repressed by their notions of class struggle that they cannot consider society in any other light. There will always be poverty; and we must all contribute to its alleviation. After all, what is the purpose of wealth if it is not used for the benefit of all? Certainly, it is true: nothing impoverishes a society like war. You do what you can to prevent it— and if you cannot prevent it, you try to minimise its effects. For centuries, that has been our policy; and we attempted repeatedly to resolve the last conflict.'

'We? You speak as if you were personally responsible.'

'I am a baron,' he answered with much hauteur, 'Of course I am personally responsible. It is my duty to preserve and protect civilisation; and I will argue that such goals are better achieved through marital union than war, and through principled dedication to the common good. My position is one of service, not power.

'To return to the Empire,' he overruled my query concerning the Republic's abolition of titles. 'Unfortunately, for the last century and a half, aggressive nationalist agitation has so drained our resources that we have had little to spare. But our Empire was bound by stronger ties than language, race, borders, or blood; for our faith transcended our differences. Like the birds and animals of the forest, in which there is such abundant beauty and variety: each a part of God's creation, each uniquely blessed, and each with its own role to play in subservience to its Creator. Hush!'

'Bushrangers,' Hubie whispered as he slowly crept from tree to tree.

'What a rousing song!' I remarked as I followed, for a cheery tune was being sung with great lust and feeling. The 'bushrangers' responsible were young men in hiking gear gathered in brotherly camaraderie.

'It is the "Horst-Wessel-Lied", a Nazi anthem. You have never heard it?' And quietly he sang so I could catch the words:

232 ♦ BY VIOLENCE UNAVENGED

Clear the streets for the brown battalions,
Clear the streets for the storm division!
Millions are looking upon the swastika full of hope,
The day of freedom and of bread dawns!
Millions are looking upon the swastika full of hope,
The day of freedom and of bread dawns!

Then one youth outstretched his arm in the manner of the German crowds I had seen in newsreels. His followers did likewise before dispersing into the woods.

'Well, Phoebe, with your own two eyes you have witnessed the dangers we face: Nationalism and Socialism. Combine them and add German to the mix, and the result is toxic.

'But what does it mean to be German? Is it to speak the language? You speak German and you are not German. Is it to be born on German soil? Well, that could be said for the newborn child of a Ukrainian refugee. Is it a question of blood? If so, how can it be measured? My father is from Germany, yet he will always say he is Bavarian.

'Of one thing, however, I am certain: to be German is not to be a crude militaristic, swastika wearing, prejudiced, immoral and irreligious thug who believes he can crush and usurp and claim the right to territory purely on the superiority of his race. The Germany of Hitler is not German. And the idea that so-called German Austria should be part of that Germany is a fallacy. We are not "German"! We are much more than "German"! We are Austrian! And to be Austrian is to be deeply Catholic! And to be deeply Catholic is to possess the fullness of Truth and to embrace all people in Faith and Hope and Love! That is what it means to be universal! And when we say *Austria Est Imperare Orbe Universo*, that is what we mean! Austria is nailed to the cross of Christ, with one arm extended to the east, the other to the west. She has nothing to do with German tyranny. We will never be German! *I* will never be German!'

And as he gloomily trudged ahead, gold leaves shimmered towards the black earth, leaving skeletal trees, with bony branches outstretched, fingering heaven's raiment, as if pleading restoration.

36

Allerheiligen

'MY, YOU DO LOOK GLAM,' Emil sneered when we coincided outside the elevator the following morning. 'Where are you going?'

'To Hietzing cemetery.'

'So eine schöne Leiche! One would think you were attending your own funeral.'

'Are you seeing Zusa today?'

'She's with her shaygetz[14] fiancé. When will you be back?'

'Really, Emil, you're like a stray dog scavenging meat from dustbins in an alley. I'm not a dustbin and I haven't any meat for you.'

'Saving your meat for her pious schmuck[15] of a brother, are you? If so, be careful your sanctimony doesn't get you into trouble,' he called down the stairwell, 'Does he know your murderous little secret?'

Church bells had been merrily clanging since sunrise. It was *Allerheiligen* – All Saints Day – and a holiday. Shaved and spruced, a rosebud in his buttonhole, Albrecht blithely churned his organ barrel and doffed his hat as schillings dropped in his cup. 'Thank God for the light in your eyes,' he called, then continued to sing how in this fair world there's little point in running around without hope or rest. Just trust. For the Good Lord always knows best.

Even those in deepest mourning were brightened by the posies they carried – joyful patches of colour amidst the city's pale and frosty monochrome. Kerem's splendid bunch of tulips bloomed in my memory. How I wished he would call, like Mr Rochester, and that I would hear him across mountains and valleys! Could there be such communion if he was no Christian, and I Christian in

---

[14] *Shaygetz*: disparaging term for a non-Jewish male; an impudent young man; a scoundrel (with the implication that the offending person is brutish or violent).

[15] *Schmuck*: (vulgar slang) jerk; an obnoxious, detestable, or contemptible person.

name only?

Instead, more Hubie. He was kind in his way, but I couldn't decide which was worse: his long silences or his political explications. Now he was waiting at the cemetery gates, dangling a bouquet of pinks.

'I thought you— might like these, Phoebe, to remember your father. I remember you saying he was fond of roses.'

Across the cemetery, where families had gathered as if celebrating a wedding, lanterns glowed from flower-laden graves. Like the patriarch of an enormous clan, the elderly parish priest feted with gusto, joked with children, and exchanged words in confidence. His young offsider chatted with a gang of older boys, and a brass band played hymns and songs.

Hubie, meanwhile, brought me to the von Rechtschaffen family vault. Had it not been destined for morbid purpose, the mausoleum could have passed for a house a child might desire as a cubby, for it was proportioned to suit a seven-year-old, although its columns and solid double-door were somewhat imposing. Three generations of forebears were there entombed.

'My mother's family is not an old chivalric family— unlike my father's, which can be traced to the Crusades,' he instructed, and I regretted my earlier questioning of his social position.

So that's why he was so insistent upon my coming today, I thought. Had his mother not joined forces (that I should spend Allerheiligen alone was unthinkable), I would have adamantly refused.

'Vati's family has long been without property; but, you see, it is service, not wealth, which determines status. A Count may be forced by penury to sweep the streets; however, if he has kept his honour, he remains a Count. My mother's great-great grandfather was ennobled by Joseph II, and successive generations have faithfully fulfilled court and civil appointments. My grandfather was Baron Alois Josef von Rechtschaffen.'

'So, had the monarchy remained, you would have inherited the title. Is that right?'

'I am a baron, regardless. Outside Austria, my title holds. It is not dependent upon the masses; I did not receive it via the ballot box. My authority and position, like that of my ancestors, come from God through His temporal and secular representative the Emperor, and I have a serious obligation to fulfil the duties of my state in accordance with His decrees, for at my death I will be called to account. It is the purpose of society, you see, to pave the way to Heaven – through the professions, through manual work, through culture, through all that is good and beautiful in God's world. You might consider my notions irrelevant and arcane,' he added defensively, rightly sensing that my attention had wavered,

'But that does not change the truth of the matter; nor does it alter my duty to remain beholden.'

'I marvel such attitudes survive. I gather, then, your family was much affected by the changes after the War.'

'The enlightened minds of Wilson, Clémenceau, and Lloyd George could hardly be described as supportive of the old Imperial order.'

'You sound like my father.'

'We frequently corresponded on the subject. Your father agreed that in dissolving the Austro-Hungarian Empire the allied forces upset the balance of power in Europe at a time when the balance of power required restoration rather than revision. With the establishment of the Republic, Grandfather lost his title and was forced into retirement. Whatever our circumstances, however, we have never lost our honour, nor our principles. Nor have we lost our traditions.'

'Well, you can wax all you like about position and tradition and suchlike, but what does it amount to? Really? Hubie, I am not my father, and I don't share his political views, nor am I that interested.'

'I thought— Please understand I was greatly looking forward— I'm sorry. I presumed—'

'Did you ever correspond on the subject of my mother?'

'I knew she died young and in tragic circumstances, but I never broached the subject. I did not think it my place. Your father most certainly never raised it.'

'Well you are right, Hubie, about my mother's death. The police thought she suicided, whereas in fact—'

'Hubie!' Heidi Schütze ran towards us. 'Karl's arrived! Fifi's had the baby! It's a boy!'

Hubie ran to congratulate his brother who was eagerly recounting his news to the crowd gathered around the family. Frau Schütze tearfully hugged her oldest son. Sisi and Heidi gabbled details to all and sundry. Franz fetched the priest who bestowed a blessing. The band joined in, and everyone began to sing.

I saw little point in remaining and crept away.

Long did I walk, following the canal until it reached a point. I turned into a cove, anticipating that it would lead me again to the river. Eventually I found a path and reached the Danube, heeding little the growing gloom as I listened to the lapping waves. One by one, I threw my wilted roses and watched them drift and swirl and disappear.

'Are you all right, Fräulein?' called a voice, and through the fog came a tall man holding a lantern.

'Where am I?'

'You're in Albern. Are you sure you're all right?'

'Everyone is so absorbed with politics and social mores! Am I of no importance? Do my troubles count for nothing?'

'Hold still, now. The Good Lord knows best. It's a hard time of year when the cold comes. Folk turn morbid. And when they get morbid, they do morbid things. You're not looking for someone?'

'Not exactly.'

'I only ask 'cause we had a woman wash up the other week, and no one could tell who she was. I buried her over here.'

He brought me through a small park to a grave marked with a black wrought iron cross and a silver crucifix. It was one of many such graves set amidst leafless trees. Each was dressed in the same way, with a lighted candle in a lantern, and fresh flowers at its head. I read the inscription on the cross:

Namenlos

'Folk wash up here all the time, an' who's to say how they been drowned— whether they throwed themselves in, or whether they was throwed in, or whether it was an accident. Little Seppel here, I found him in a box, just newborn, and gave him my own name. Yonder's a young lad, Wilhelm, was drowned by another. And there are many poor souls whom nobody knows. That's where I come in. I looks after their mortal remains. I gives them a final resting place and tends their graves; and seeing as I ain't got no idea how they landed here, I treats 'em all the same: same cross, same flowers, same lantern, same prayers.'

'My mother was murdered. I barely remember her; and when I do, it's not without recalling her tragic end. She was a quiet, private person, and there seems to be nothing left of her: Nothing, nothing at all!'

'Well, she had a name. That's a blessing. And she has a daughter. That's another blessing. Don't you worry; the Lord God knows where she's at. You know, when I takes the body of a life cut short, I can't help thinking there's got to be more than this here and now. It doesn't make sense any other way, does it? If they throwed themselves in, well, there's something not right upstairs made 'em do it. And if they was throwed in— well, mark my words, him who did the throwing will get his comeuppance.

'Meanwhile, I do the tending. It's their feast day tomorrow – All Souls' Day – that's why their lanterns are lit. They'll be lit all this month, it being the month of the Dead, you see. You take heart, miss. Life has a way of sorting itself out. Things can change fast, and they change overnight. When a body comes my way, I know it's my job to care for it. It's no accident they're washed up here. Just like you. A little voice told me I'd find someone. Didn't expect 'em to be alive. I don't know you, miss, and we might never see each other again, but you and I came together for a reason. It's like you've taken a bump on the riverbank, and I'm here to set you back on course. You come a long way?'

'From Mariahilf.'

'On foot? That's far. And you're chilled to the bone. Take my cape. My missus will make you a cup of coffee and we'll see you safely home again. And next Sunday, I'll light a candle for your mother and put it on a raft, and it'll float all the way down the Danube. We do that every year to remember the folk who've drowned here. Not that your mother drowned, but who's going to know that save you and me? May she rest in peace, and may you find comfort. We've a chapel if you wish to pray. The Chapel of the Resurrection it's called, 'cause there's always hope, isn't there?'

37

Café Nihilism

O N A DREAR, DRIZZLY November afternoon, a few days later, I cast my eye over the wet road and leaden sky, and yearned for sunshine and summer evenings. 'Guy Fawkes Night,' I mused while dodging a puddle. *Remember, remember the fifth of November.* 'Bet there'll be the usual bonfire up the road. And boys with bangers... Well, there's been all sorts of "gunpowder, treason and plot" since I arrived in Vienna.' A tram clanged mournfully, and I took advantage of its approach to hasten my journey.

Heeding my wish to widen my circle of acquaintance, Zita suggested we meet at one of her favourite cafes, Café Museum. 'Café Ni-hil-ism?' Emil drawled when I asked for directions. 'That's the one on Operngasse, just down from Karlsplatz.'

Through smoke haze and chatter she hailed me to a crescent shaped booth upholstered in red ersatz leather, where she sat with Franz and two of their friends: Inge Seyss, Franz's girlfriend, was the epitome of blonde elegance; while Zita's fiancé, Rudi Ströhmann, was an Adonis in a slide fastening sweater who looked as if he played too much tennis.

We huddled around a marble-topped table strewn with newspapers, half-eaten pastries, ashtrays, and coffee cups. Franz ordered more coffee and inquired as to my preference for cake.

'I wouldn't order the Orignal Sachertorte if I were you, Phoebe,' he chortled. 'They will serve you a very mouldy specimen. A century old cake! It will make you sick.'

'Kasperle!' Zita teased. 'We have been talking about you, Phoebe— Well, we have been talking about your former king, the Duke of Windsor. Hitler pulled out all the stops for him in Berlin, didn't he?'

'I was saying to Franzl it is a pity he could not remain on the English throne,' Rudi remarked.

'It was not permissible,' I replied.

'Could not Parliament have considered a morganatic marriage?' asked Franz.

'Neither the British Cabinet nor the British dominions would accept it. Mrs Simpson was twice divorced, with a husband still living. King Edward had his supporters, though.'

'Edward would have done much to improve relations between our countries had he remained on the throne,' Franz replied. 'He has deep affection for the German people. Certainly, while he is in Austria, he will be of great assistance to the Anschluss.'

One would think they still ruled the world! I silently moaned at the great chrome spheres that lit the café. Would they ever talk of anything other than politics? Thoroughly fed up, I decided to sport with them instead:

'But I have heard that measures are being taken to restore the monarchy.'

'Mistah Karl— he dead,' smirked Rudi, much to everyone's amusement. 'And the monarchy's prohibited by law.'

'But isn't an Anschluss prohibited by treaty?'

Franz cut his remaining cake into chunks, each of which he used to enumerate his points. 'I can guarantee, Phoebe, there will be no international opposition. After what's happened in Spain, nobody wants a war. The Duke of Windsor will ensure Britain's support, and Mussolini has now allied himself with Hitler. And Herr Bundeskanzler? Why, he'll capitulate to preserve Austro-German relations. All we have to do is make it legitimate.'

'Franzl,' giggled Inge, 'You sound like daddy.'

Smiling, Franz requested from Zita the loan of her glasses. 'Of course, dearest Inge, I mean no disrespect to your esteemed father.' He slowly folded his hands, leant across the table to Rudi, and assumed a tone of quiet deliberation: 'Meister, might I have a word?'

'My good Doctor Seyss,' Rudi assumed the role of the Austrian Chancellor. 'What is it you wish to discuss?'

'I think it is time to consider the welfare of the Better Germany.'

Much of what followed was a tongue-in-cheek exposé of legal possibilities and parameters taken to logical extremes and delivered in the most convoluted turn of phrase I had ever heard, and in such a fawning manner that Inge, Rudi and Zita were laughing so much they were in tears. 'Oh! Franzl, stop!' Zita cried. 'If only I could see properly! Oh, I wish I could see!'

'Servus, mein kleine Sängerknabe!' Rudi called and waved, and along came Hubie.

'You are well, yes, Gretel?' he inquired of Rudi, patting him on the back as he did; but he declined the invitation to pull up a chair, indicating with his characteristic mixture of stutter and gesture that he had his usual *Stammtisch*, or reserved table, in the far corner. Was he avoiding me? During his explanation he barely looked my way, and we had not coincided anywhere all week. To his table he retired, ordered a coffee, and pulled out a book. In fact, he ordered two coffees, for he directed the waiter to serve the second drink to the tramp reading a paper nearby.

Meanwhile, my conspiratorial companions pursued their discussion of Wilson's original Fourteen Points, and divulged plans for a Better and Greater German Federation based on shared language and common identity. Franz postulated that this should involve the reintegration of German speaking lands lost under the Treaty of Versailles. Of course, such grand-scale unification would be achieved peaceably through the exercise of the right to self-determination as advocated in said Treaty. The great German people should not be ruled by a foreign power. Already the Saar had voted its return. Similarly, those parts of Czechoslovakia, Denmark, and Poland, which had been lost, should be given the same opportunity. Then of course there was Alsace and Malmedy.

'But what of Holland and Switzerland?' I ventured, 'Aren't they Germanic in origin, like Austria?'

'You are right, Phoebe!' Thrilled by my suggestion, Franz proposed further union, which Rudi endorsed. By the time they finished their coffee, their map of Europe, drawn on a serviette, resembled the Europe of about five centuries prior. Given that only weeks ago the more progressive and enlightened Otto-Franz-Josef had criticised Hubie for being born in the wrong epoch, I found their conclusion ironic. And they seemed convinced that they could realise their vision without opposition. How could they be so certain?

'As our beloved Beethoven will tell you, dear Phoebe, it is all to do with beer and sausages. Beer and sausages,' Franz assured me. 'So long as we have them, we will not revolt.'

Preferring to walk off the coffee and cake, and not wishing to partake in further discussion, I declined to join them on the Hietzing tram. I had just passed Karlsplatz when I sensed someone closing in from behind.

It was Hubie.

'You seemed very engrossed in your book,' I was surprised he had left the café so soon, let alone followed me. 'What were you reading?'

'Friedrich Halm's *Das Auge Gottes*. You have read?'

'You over-estimate my German. What's it about?'

'It is about a medieval knight who is determined to restore his family's wealth and honour. He becomes more obsessive and bitter with every failure, to the point that he blames God for his misfortune and desecrates an icon. When he finally obtains the riches and power he desires, he is struck blind; and in his insanity he destroys himself.'

'It sounds rather grim.'

'It is a cautionary tale.'

'Why did you call him that? Rudi. Rudi Ströhmann. In the café back then.'

'Gretel? Ah, it is choir nickname. Believe it or not, Rudi once looked and sang like an angel. We were in the Vienna Boys' Choir together. No doubt you have heard?'

I fondly recounted to him Dad's involvement with the choristers when the choir visited Australia.

'Previously, it was the Imperial Chapel Choir, which was disbanded when Emperor Charles went into exile. Vati helped Father Schnitt, the choir director, re-establish it as the Vienna Boys' Choir. Karl and I sang for only a year before our voices broke, but Franz and Rudi belonged from the beginning. They performed *Hänsel und Gretel* together. Franzl played Hänsel; so, you can guess which role Rudi performed.'

'Then why didn't you join us in the café, Hubie?' I smiled. 'You would have balanced the discussion. Franz was talking nonsense.'

'If that was the case, my presence would have had little effect.'

'Do you think he's right about an Anschluss?'

'What is my opinion worth?' he grew testy. 'As Franzl says, and it is my impression you agree, I was born in the wrong century.'

'You didn't see his map. It was positively medieval.'

At that point we bumped into Emil. Hubie touched his hat and made an apologetic bow which Emil acknowledged with an obsequious leer. Like two dogs on neutral territory they warily eyed each other, cautiously circling before resuming opposite paths.

'How do you know Emil Fährmann?' I remarked.

'He tried to court Zita,' Hubie replied after some delay.

Well, I thought, he's doing a fair bit more than that now.

'My father refused his permission. Zita was but sixteen years old at the time and very impressionable. Herr Fährmann was giving her drawing lessons. Being an atheist and a Trotskyite, the sordid fellow was a dangerous influence. She became so infatuated that she was blind to the merits of any other suitors. He was trouble from the beginning, filling her head with rubbish and threatening her reputation. I do not believe for a minute that he had any intention of marrying her. As a Communist he scorned marriage. He had to be stopped. It was my duty as her brother to prohibit him from seeing her. He would have ferried her, as he has done others, to eternal darkness.'

'Do you really think so?'

'Do you know what damage they have done? Aside from destroying our empire and indulging their Marxist pipedreams after the War; when they finally fell from power, they undermined internal stability and discredited Austria in the eyes of other nations, particularly during Dollfuss' Chancellorship. Chancellor Dollfuss was the one leader who actively opposed Hitler.'

'Wasn't he assassinated? Dad was up in arms about it. He said the Nazis were responsible.'

'They were. But it would not have been beyond the realms of possibility for the Communists to have done the same. Chancellor Dollfuss, you see, had outlawed the Communists as well as the Nazis and Social Democrats.'

'So, do you think there will be an Anschluss?'

'Do you really wish to know?'

'I think you wish to tell me.'

'Danke, Phoebe,' he replied with much relief as we waited for the lift to my apartment; and I sensed I was among the few people in whom he chose to confide. 'Chancellor Schuschnigg, while a good and upright man, has to his detriment allowed his desire for German unity to override his Christian principles by signing a Treaty of Friendship with Germany and establishing a committee to promote Austro-German relations. Perhaps, ironically, his Christian principles prompted him to seek peaceful negotiations between our countries; but that means co-operating with German National Socialism, which does not have quite the same goals.

'Our chancellor has made too many concessions to Hitler and has weakened his position within Austria and in Europe. He is a lone voice now; which illustrates that it takes more than an individual to govern a society. It takes a dynasty. Meanwhile, Hitler has defied international regulation and aggressively rearmed. Mussolini, who supported us against Hitler after Dollfuss' assassination, will not support us now that he has allied himself with Germany; while our own army has been so drastically reduced under the Treaty of St Germain, that despite our efforts to rebuild it, it is no match for the Wehrmacht. Vat ist—?!'

Hubie stared in horror at the rat bait covering the landing outside my apartment.

'Oh, not again! It's Oda, my neighbour. She keeps putting it out. Not that I have ever seen a rat; but she's convinced the place is infested.'

'You have the concierge informed of the matter?'

'It's not worth it.' If I informed Frau Geplapper, Emil would incur the blame. 'I'll sweep it up. Don't worry, Hubie. Come and meet Dad.'

'Glücklich! Glücklich! Dich hab' ich gefunden,' he whispered as he studied first Dad's portrait, then me, then the portrait, amassing details and making what seemed a thousand connections. 'It is a good likeness, yes?'

'He had the most expressive face, which could be quite menacing at times; yet he was so tender, so charming. Always, though, there was that gleam in his eye: a bright, penetrating gleam that could see something deep inside which you couldn't see for yourself.'

'We have photographs of him at home that I will show you one day; but I find a painting captures more than a photograph. There is the same wit and vivacity in that face as I have read in many a letter. If at this moment I could have a wish granted, Phoebe, it would be that he stepped out from that picture for me to shake his hand. As it is, you have a beautiful *Andenken*. It must be of great consolation to have him here.'

'Will you stay for a little supper? I have some soup on the stove.'

'Nein, my good cousin. I have piano lessons to give. I teach the Weissmüller boys who live in the apartment below you. We will meet again at the Baptism on Sunday. You are coming, yes, to see little Karl baptised?'

'I— I haven't been to church since my father died.'

'You will come, please? I— My mother is expecting you.'

'Very well, Hubie. Yes, I will come.'

'Gutt,' he bowed, 'Then I bid you good evening.'

38

New Life

EARLY SUNDAY MORNING, a distant rumble rattled Emil's shop window. The drone intensified, rousing Vienna from beneath its foggy coverlet. Bleary, pallid house lamps blinked from old façades, curious as to the source of the noise. A low-flying biplane emerged, sputtering, and left in its trail a shower of dark flakes. A paper Swastika fluttered into my outstretched hand. Soon, thousands were scattered over Linke Wienzeile. An old street sweeper swung his broom into action, and with steady, well-practiced strokes pushed the twisted crosses into the gutter. A tram clanged and I hurried across the road to catch it.

The swastika cloud must have by-passed Hietzing, for not one black jot marred the district's Sunday tranquillity. My destination, Our Lady of Hietzing, the small, white parish church, its gothic spire enhanced by the dove grey sky and illumined by a pearly morning sun, wore a reverent shawl of mist; and a lace cloth of frost was spread across the square. There was something perennial about the families gathered outside in their evergreen coats and capes and Tyrolean hats. Certainly, I would have encountered minimal difficulty recognising ancestors had I the fortune to travel back in time.

Hubie insisted upon introducing me to the family members and fellow parishioners who cooed over baby Karl-Konrad in his antique christening gown. All the gentlemen were costumed in white knitted hose, their breeches fastened with leather thong; and those more impervious to the cold wore their jackets unfastened, whereby I noted the brass buttons of festive waistcoats; while the women's capes covered full skirts and close-fitting bodices.

A young priest – the same one I had seen in the cemetery the previous week – emerged from the church. It was an especial occasion, he announced. The baptism was his first since being ordained only months prior. Moreover, it was the baptism of the first son of a dear friend; for he, Herr Steffan,[16] had known Karl-Alois since choir days.

He summoned the godparents. Hubie stepped forward, erect and ardent, guiding the more relaxed Zita who was captivated by the tiny nephew she cradled in her arms.

'What are you asking of God's Church?' Herr Steffan asked.

'Faith,' Hubie and Zita replied.

'What does faith hold out to you?'

'Everlasting life.'

'If, then, you wish to inherit everlasting life, keep the commandments, "Love the Lord your God with all your heart, with all your soul, and with all your mind; and love your neighbour as yourself."'

'That was your father twenty-five years ago, Phoebe,' Professor Schütze whispered.

'In leather breeches?'

'And just as honoured and just as nervous,' beamed Frau Schütze. 'As Hubie has no doubt told you, your dear father was the best of godparents.'

But I was seized with intense sadness, for incarnated before me was the bond between Dad and Hubie, which comprised not only a mutual interest in politics and history, but Faith which I had conscientiously shunned, and which I knew had caused Dad much hurt. Hubie had been blessed with the full portion of my father's plate, while I had elected to eat the fallen crumbs. I crept to the back of the group to lick the mange that covered my soul, and from that distance watched the ceremony.

Herr Steffan breathed thrice upon the infant and marked him thrice with the sign of the cross. He laid his hands upon him and prayed that he might observe the commandments, and in so doing attain the glory of heaven. Then he bid Satan be gone. To think that such a rosy, placid babe had partaken of the fruit of the tree of knowledge! The priest was exorcising the wrong person. The foul and tainted inclinations were mine, not little Karl's. Yet over the child he continued to pray. He blessed salt and placed a grain in the infant's mouth. Baby Karl squirmed, while Herr Steffan prayed that he be preserved in grace and goodness and be ever hungry for heavenly nourishment. Indeed, may he be so! For what is worse: sin or the knowledge of it? The depraved act or the heart now hollowed of goodness? Would that I be likewise purged! Again, the little one was thrice blessed. Herr Steffan placed his stole upon

---

[16] *Herr Steffan*: Our Lady of Hietzing belongs to Klosterneuburg Abbey, a chapter of Augustinian canons. 'Herr' is the title used to address Augustinian canons. In English, Herr Steffan would be addressed as Reverend or Dom Steffan, rather than Father Steffan.

him and welcomed him into the church, a place I did not belong.

'You know that's what I wanted for you, don't you?' whispered Dad's voice.

Wretched creature that I was, I knew in my soul I was dead. My tears burning, I turned and faced the empty square, its lacy frost muddied by the tramp of feet.

'Phoebe?' Heidi tapped me and indicated her hymnal. 'We share. Come,' And she placed her arm in mine and drew me inside. Accompanied by the organ, Sisi's pure, youthful soprano floated from the choir loft:

> *My soul He doth restore again,*
> *And me to walk doth make*
> *Within the paths of righteousness,*
> *E'en for His own Namesake.*

Standing tall and straight by the baptismal font, Hubie renounced Satan on behalf of tiny Karl, and affirmed each point of faith. Every faculty he harnessed to pronounce 'I do believe' without a stutter, his measured responses reflecting a conviction sound as oak. He was devoted to his godson. Baby Karl did not appreciate being rid of Original Sin by a triple tipping of cold water and required much soothing. Hubie relieved Zita of the crying child, and gently rocked him. At that point our eyes met. Hubie twitched his glasses back in place, whereupon I could have sworn he nearly smiled.

He sat next to me for the Mass and received the Blessed Sacrament with deep reverence, while I remained in my pew. I could not receive, for I had many sins: sins which I ought to confess, not to mention desires I had no intention of renouncing. Was it wrong to desire justice? It was very right. But it was wrong to kill. Was it wrong to execute? I was not sure. But that was what I wanted to do. All that barred me from commission was circumstantial: my physical ability to carry out the task, and the opportunity to do so. I had to find Ailine. I required her confession before I could ever make my own. Meanwhile, I was condemned to a phantasmic existence, inert and starved of grace.

As for confiding in Hubie, how could I? He was so righteous, so principled! Such hideous ideas would never cross his mind. He would be shocked and disgusted. How he sang! A man at ease with himself and his Maker. He knew the final hymn by heart and his rich baritone engulfed my own pitiful mezzo:

> *O may this bounteous God*
> *Through all our life be near us,*
> *With ever joyful hearts*
> *And blessed peace to cheer us;*
> *And keep us in His grace,*

And guide us when perplexed;
And free us from all ills,
In this world and the next!

The organist also knew the hymn well – too well, I feared, for he took warped delight in counterpoint, experimenting with conflicting phrase lines and dissonant chords which offered little hope of resolution. Fortunately, by the final verse, he had progressed his harmonies so that they rendered proper thanks to the one eternal God Whom Earth and heaven adore; but not without a fight.

'Our organist had too much to drink last night?' observed a quiet, bespectacled man who also thought the improvisation macabre, and who had joined the Schützes outside. Franz, who was responsible for the cacophony, sheepishly deflected attention from the truth by introducing me. The bespectacled gentleman was his boss and Inge's father, Dr Arthur Seyss-Inquart, who broke into a knowing smile.

'Roderick? Roderick Raye? Das Kleine Känguru? Ah! Willkommen!' he exclaimed in delight and amazement; and explained that he was studying Law in Vienna while Dad was studying music. 'The Little Kangaroo' happened to be Dad's nickname among his coffee-house peers, partly because of his antipodean origins, and partly because he never sat still for more than a minute.

'He was always hopping about,' Dr Seyss remarked. An ardent music lover, he spoke knowledgeably of the chamber repertoire and was looking forward to the next Rosé concert. And Haydn's works counted among his favourites.

'The Klimt Quartet did Haydn great justice,' he continued. 'Their vivacious performances had much to do with the tension between the group. I remember the second violin and viola being an harmonious pair whose warmth of tone made your father's playing sparkle, while the cellist goaded his virtuosity to ecstatic heights. Do you also play, Fräulein?'

'Yes, she does,' Franz clapped and rubbed his hands in cheerful bonhomie. 'In fact, she will be playing today! Isn't that so, Phoebe?'

'I beg your pardon?' The idea of Ailine goading Dad's virtuosity to 'ecstatic heights' had prevented my answering promptly.

'I am spending the morning with Inge, and I need a pianist to fill in for me. You play piano, yes? Then it is settled! Phoebe can play the Mozart,' Franz informed his father as he left.

After breakfast, Frau Schütze showed me to the ballroom – Herr

Beethoven's Room – which was where most of the family's music-making took place.

It was a spacious, circular salon with long, slender windows and a Juliet balcony looking over the city. The original vista would have been more picturesque; for through the course of the last century or so, later generations had witnessed the diminution of forest and fields. Consequently, the thrill and charm of the round internal space seemed sadly at odds with the jagged geometry of the roads and buildings that comprised its modern aspect.

The room itself, with its light gold walls, was pleasingly airy, the winter sunlight being diffused throughout by clerestory windows positioned at the base of a central cupola. Directly beneath, a multi-pointed star was beautifully crafted in wood mosaic and enclosed in a circle of like tiles, from which emanated a rippling concentric pattern comprising alternate rings of birch and mahogany parquet. A grand piano stood to one side. Unfortunately, it was not the piano Beethoven had played; but it had its own significance, having been presented to Frau Schütze on her sixteenth birthday.

'And this was where my parents performed the Kreutzer?' I asked.

'Your mother played this very piano. As you know, the Kreutzer is not for the fainthearted, and so long as God gives me life, I will never forget that evening. They were so young! We all knew your father was brilliant; but that night his genius glistened. He unleashed the spirit of the music – tempestuous, strange, reverent, and hauntingly beautiful – in a way no other artist in my experience has been able to do— and I have heard many violinists. What was equally extraordinary was your mother. Who would have thought she could play with such purity, and yet so passionately? She provided a perfect accompaniment. Some joked afterwards that like Faustus, Herr Roderick had made a pact with the devil and had spirited Fräulein Juliette away, for it was quite plain she adored him.'

'Was it really like that?'

'I have upset you? Ah, Phoebe, I remember talking with your mother afterwards. She was only eighteen, and unused to society; nor did her temperament incline her to it. I tried to make her feel at home. We ended up talking about the history of this room and discussing the piano for which she had only compliments. Then her face lit up and she smiled. What prompted that beautiful reaction? I wondered. Well, across the room was your father. The flow of conversation may have carried him along another course, but in spirit he was at her side. Ah, the look he gave her! So gentle and happy – rare expressions in that mischievous face of his. He was in love; and so was she.'

Her affectionate description confirmed what Zita had earlier told me: Frau Schütze knew Dad very well— too well for my comfort.

'He once offered to pay me suit,' she fondly admitted. 'But my father refused permission because Roderick was a commoner. We remained good friends. In fact, Roddy introduced me to Kurti.'

'Frau Schütze, did you know my aunt? My mother's sister?'

'Why, yes; but not very well. I thought her the prettier of the two girls, and it puzzled me why your father did not pursue her. I don't believe they had been intimate, but the familiarity between them suggested a certain understanding. Now, if memory serves me well, your aunt was there that night. Yes! She was next to your father, talking with Count Bernhard von Sternberg. Their conversation was very animated, although your father wasn't paying as much attention as usual. Isn't it odd how details from long ago spring to mind?

'But that concert was quite an event. You see, within the week, the Klimt Quartet disbanded, the Devereaux family left Vienna, and the Countess von Sternberg filed for divorce. It was my first exposure to scandal, because I knew the parties concerned. Countess von Sternberg, you see, was my mother's cousin. The Count had been unfaithful and the Devereaux family were implicated. Roderick was questioned because of his friendship with Madame Devereaux and her daughters. Then suddenly the matter was hushed.'

'When did this happen?'

'Let me see... It was before the War, of course, and after Kurti and I were engaged. It must have been during the season, for Kurti and I were introduced the previous Summer and married the following Spring. That would make it the Winter of 1910, perhaps early 1911. Why do you ask, dear?'

Sternberg. Could Ailine's use of the name Stern have any connection with Sternberg, I wondered? 'I had a cousin, Sabine, who was born in 1911. She had congenital handicaps and was institutionalised. She died toward the end of the War.'

'Oh, I am sorry, dear,' Frau Schütze murmured.

'What's the matter?' It seemed unlikely that such a thoughtful person as Frau Schütze would be distracted by trivialities.

'You see, when Count von Sternberg died ten years ago, he left a generous bequest to a French orphanage. No one knew of any connection, and it begged the question as to whether he kept a mistress, which in turn reignited the earlier scandal. Goodness me.'

'But how was my father involved?'

'He wasn't, dear. He was dashing off to Paris at every opportunity, though, which led to rumours that he was having an affair. Everyone assumed it was your aunt. I thought it most out of character because he was always far too absorbed in his music;

and after what I had witnessed the night of the soiree, I did not
believe it. Unable to bear the gossip, I managed to speak to him
alone. Was it Juliette? I asked him, for he was being very coy. He
acknowledged it was; and only did so out of gratitude that
someone had noticed. They were betrothed. Being newly married
myself, I was very happy for them.'

'He always insisted he was faithful to Maman.'

'Then, if that is what he said, it is true. Try not to be too
perturbed by what you hear, dear. No doubt Zita's told you a tale
or two. When I hear such gossip, I wonder how would I have coped
if something like that happened to me? Would I have had the
strength of character to withstand such temptation? Furthermore,
remember that redemption is the consequence of a Fall, and that
some of God's greatest saints have also been His greatest sinners.
And if I know your father, I imagine he's enjoying Heaven as much
as he enjoyed life here on earth.'

'Sometimes I wonder, what is the point of it all?' I sighed as I
followed the parquetry pattern to the edge of the room. 'Dad never
had any regrets— Well, I suppose he learned not to. Now he's
gone.'

'And you are here. And while you are here, this is your home
and we are your family.'

Frau Schütze left to attend to her morning duties, and I began
a slow orbit round the centre star. Where was my place in time
and space? What was my purpose? Would I always be a moon, a
pale reflection of my parents' tragedy? A cold sphere, set in a dark
expanse, waxing and waning for the sake of revenge? Must destiny
exert such binding gravity? Would that some meteor shatter the
earth and set me on a happier course!

Instead, my ears were shattered by a blast. Instruments in
hand, Zita, Hubie, and Karl stood at the door.

'My, how you jumped!' Zita laughed. 'You were miles away! Are
you well? You look upset.'

'I am fine, but somewhat tired. It's been a long morning. I'm not
used to waking so early.'

'Then it is time to revive with some M-m-mozart,' Hubie replied.
'You will accept our apologies for our brother, dear cousin, in
placing you in this daunting position. Franzl is in pursuit of—
higher causes these days,' he added as he warmed his hands at
the Kachelofen.

'I hope your sight reading's good,' Zita tucked her clarinet
under her arm and organised her music stand. 'We haven't been
working on the Mozart long, but Vati is demanding nonetheless.'

'Rest assured, Phoebe, we are all under the same pressure,'
Karl-Alois sadly shook his head at his bassoon and drew up a

chair.

In came the Professor, oboe in hand. Amidst his children's blowing and spluttering, he attempted to advise me on interpretation, inserting what English he knew to emphasise his points. Within minutes he was shouting instructions, so loud were the clarinet scales, sustained horn tones, and honking of the bassoon; and it was all I could do to refrain from smiling. Being a violinist, I tended to view the woodwind as an inferior people who supplied harmonies for my melodies as they would a landowner with raw materials. And here I was, taking orders from the oboe! As for the brass, it was an unruly, exclusively male third estate which, if left unchecked, created untold upheaval, and celebrated its victories with beer. On this occasion, though, the brass player was a very genteel chap indeed. If he had a wild side, he concealed it well.

Hubie was right about Mozart. Wolfgang Amadeus' quintet for piano, woodwind and horn was most refreshing, despite my having to sight-read. The Schützes were pleasant and encouraging, not to mention highly-trained musicians.

Time compressed that morning. There I was, in the company of a family in costumes it had worn for generations, playing in a salon where Beethoven, too, had performed, and where Dad and Maman had played the music that changed their lives. Oh, to be born anew! If only everything was as perfect as Herr Beethoven's Room! I would never leave it, nor would I let the music end.

But end it did.

'Franzl's back!' Heidi burst in. 'And guess what? Rudi's driving a new motorcar!'

39

Man of Straw

COSTUMED DUKE OF WINDSOR style in cap and sweater, bow-tie, bags, and two-toned brogues, Rudi lifted the bonnet of his shiny red roadster and showed off the engine which Karl and the Professor examined with enthusiasm. Heidi bounced happily in the passenger seat, while Franz sat at the wheel and tooted the horn the moment his father bent under the hood. Frau-Schütze embraced Rudi, brought him inside, and invited him to share their Sunday meal.

He sat next to me and was keen to practise his English. Did he always live in Vienna? I asked. No, he replied. He originally hailed from Bozen.

'It is now Bolzano called,' he explained.

'In Italy? Are you Italian?'

'Do I look Italian? You look more Italian than I. No, I am German. Bozen was originally part of Austria, for it of the Tyrol was a part. It seceded to Italy at the end of the War.' But he preferred not to discuss the subject neither in German nor English, and with a stranger to boot; nor did I wish to be swamped with politics.

His account of his hobbies provided a satisfactory explanation for his healthy complexion and muscular physique. A member of the Austro-German Alpine Club, he enjoyed scaling rugged mountain passes; and his descriptions of 'Boy's Own' adventures, punctuated with numerous glances and smiles in Hubie and Karl's direction, were designed to impress the Schütze twins more than they were me. He had hoped to participate in a Himalayan climb and was quite peevish about having to turn down an invitation to join a forthcoming expedition to Tibet.

'Unfortunately, my bride-to-be does not fancy a mountain honeymoon,' he joked.

'Indeed, I do not,' Zita remarked with the air of a cat snubbing its food.

'There will be plenty more time for climbing, Rudi,' Professor Schütze sympathised. 'You have had good news of your doctorate, yes?'

'My thesis has been approved. Hence the car. I graduate next May.'

'Congratulations!' Frau Schütze raised her glass. 'Now we will have two doctors graduating. Huberle, too, has defended his thesis.'

'I thought you already had a doctorate in Music?' I queried.

'And soon he will also be Doctor of Law,' his mother beamed.

'And I have more good news,' Rudi reasserted himself. 'I have been appointed to the University.'

'Prosit, Rudi!' smiled the Professor. 'A toast to Herr Professor Doktor Ströhmann!'

'Herr Professor Doktor Krain,' corrected Rudi. 'I have decided to revert to my father's name. With my forthcoming marriage, I think it right to acknowledge my ancestry. Should my wife-to-be bear me a son, I should like to honour him.'

'Your father was a brave man,' Frau Schütze smiled in her kindly way, 'And you look just like he did when he was your age, right down to the duelling scar. Rudi's father was in the War, too, Phoebe,' she whispered.

'And you are happy with that?' Karl inquired of Zita.

'Should it make any difference to me?' she shrugged. 'After all, what's in a name?'

'"Was uns Rose heißt, Wie es auch heiße, würde lieblich duften,"' enjoined Franz with a knowing wink in my direction. 'And our Rudi will always smell sweet, yes? Is that *Pour un Homme* you are wearing, my friend?'

'Ja,' Rudi smiled.

'I knew it! I have a fine nose for scents!'

'And a fine brain for nonsense,' teased Zita.

'What will you be professor of, Rudi?' I inquired.

'Biochemistry,' he replied. Initially, he had enrolled in medicine to appease his mother and step-father, who were both doctors, but he didn't agree with the training. 'Too many physicians, particularly in Vienna, focus on cure, and not enough on prevention. Diet, hygiene, and exercise are far more important,' he claimed. 'So, I devoted myself to a higher science.'

His specialty was something called genetics: the study of inherited traits. Applied to agriculture it meant that plants could be selected and propagated for their superior nutritive properties. 'When cultivated on a large scale,' he continued, 'think what a single quality strain of wheat could do for the health of a nation.'

Frau Schütze's excellent culinary preparations he relished; and while luncheon continued, he extolled the merits of biodynamic food production and of a diet rich in legumes, grains, fruit and vegetables. He had even dabbled with vegetarianism; but since it gave too much offence, had decided it was not in his best interests. I, in turn, could not help pondering whether his best interests were driven by altruism or vanity; and it amused me much that such a strapping young man was once made to wear a dress and plaited wig and sing the role of Gretel.

'I humour you?' his baby-blue eyes grew suspicious. My smile during his expostulation of sex-linked white eye mutation in fruit flies had been ill-timed and I was forced to justify myself. Rudi did not appreciate being reminded of his years as a chorister.

'Well, some of us grow up, while others will always be choirboys,' he sneered in Hubie's direction.

Hubie's only exchange with Rudi had been an expression of disappointment that he did not attend the Baptism. 'Too early, Huberle,' Rudi smilingly complained.

'And I— gather you heard a later M-m-mass, Rudi?' he questioned in the manner of a school prefect.

'I caught the twelve at Stephansdom,' the other replied as though he had leapt onto the final carriage of a departing train. Still, whenever I looked across the table, my cousin-of-sorts was staring my way, following every word of conversation; but when, at the end of lunch, I sought him out, he had disappeared.

Frau Schütze thought Hubie had taken Sirius for his walk; and indeed, that appeared to be so, since the dog was nowhere to be found. Only later that afternoon, when I ventured onto the back terrace for some fresh air, did I see him.

Legs astride, Hubie stood at one edge of the lawn with his canine companion poised beside him. In a single steady motion, he raised and drew a longbow, and discharged an arrow which sped toward a target at the opposite end. The arrow struck hard, lodging itself in the centre. Sirius barked, bounded across the lawn, and pranced about the target. Hubie inspected the arrow, and from his pocket pulled out a pouch. Ears pricked, rump wagging, Sirius followed every movement and gobbled the titbit his master gave him.

'Good dog,' Hubie patted his pet. 'You are ready to hunt. Soon it will be Advent and the deer will come down from the mountain. I hope we see the stag this year. You would like to hunt the stag, Sirius, yes?'

Sirius, however, trotted to me and invited me to join the game.

'You have not seen archery before, my cousin?' Hubie pulled the arrows from the bullseye. 'Perhaps you would like to try?' He was cordial enough; but from the tone of his voice, I knew I had disturbed him.

'You're angry.'

'And if I am, what of it?'

He whistled to Sirius, strode back across the lawn, and fired another arrow which also hit the target's centre.

'It's Rudi, isn't it?'

'Rudi is neglecting his Faith.'

'Hubie, you really are a choirboy.'

'Being a choirboy, as you say, has nothing to do with it. In six months, he will marry Zita.'

'Don't tell me you're going to hold that against him. I haven't received the Sacraments in years. Are you going to hold that against me?'

'No, I am not, dear cousin. But you are not getting married. Phoebe, it is a grave matter. They will make vows before God and man. Rudi will be husband to my sister and father to her children. How will he fulfil his commitment to honour her and to educate his family if he does not take his faith seriously? He did not hear Mass at Steffl's this morning, I am certain of that. Or if he did, he left early.'

'Perhaps he drives fast.'

Hubie fired another arrow which hit the centre as before. Driving through Vienna at breakneck speed he considered an equally serious offence.

'Anyway, I have no idea what he sees in her,' I observed as we followed Sirius to the target, 'For she sees nothing in him. In fact, I find it hard to believe they were recently engaged. You would think they had tired of each other after twenty years of marriage! She intuits his every need, while he assumes his every need will be met. And he paid her no attention over lunch, he was so bent on impressing me; and she didn't care! What are they going to be like when they marry?'

'You are very astute, dear cousin. But Zita and Rudi have been friends since childhood, and our families are close. And yes, it puzzles me, too, that they wish to marry. I am sorry to say that much has to do with money. When the Empire collapsed, and the communists assumed control in Hungary, my mother's family estate was confiscated. All we have left now is this house and a hunting lodge. Zita has little in the way of a dowry. She is obliged to marry well if she wishes to live comfortably— and Zita is fond of the good life. But to marry Rudi—'

'Why does she have to marry at all? She's quite capable of making her own way. I've seen some of her porcelain designs. She's very talented.'

'But why should she take the job of a man who has a family to support, especially in such difficult times? Besides, her help is needed at home, the value of which outweighs any employment.'

'You're not serious? Kinder, Küche, Kirche?'

'A mother holds the past, the present, and the future in her heart and hands: she is the custodian of tradition; she nurtures her husband and family; while her children carry forward all she imparts to them. A woman's work is noble and beautiful. Why would she want the work of a man? But, to return to my sister. Given there are so few men in employment, Zita's prospects of marrying, let alone marrying well, are greatly reduced. She is clutching at wheat now.'

'Clutching at straws, you mean.'

'Danke. My sister's lack of judgement surprises and saddens me; and Vati is blind to Rudi's faults. Even if he were to refuse permission, Zita is of age and is quite capable of defiance. She is much in need of support and companionship. You are strong, my cousin. You can help her.'

'My friendship is of little benefit to her if she cannot be strong in herself. Besides, why do you say I am strong? You hardly know me.'

'You spent your adolescence looking after your father. He rarely mentioned you in letters, but when he did it was always with much affection. Whatever your faults, you have the devotion and loyalty of Ruth. I see it in your eyes. You have borne a heavy burden, and you have done so with love and courage.'

Sirius seemed to endorse his master's words, for he wagged his tail and sniffed my hand. Patting him was great comfort.

'Hubie, if only you knew what I felt!' No one had ever spoken so kindly.

'Take heart!' he passed me his handkerchief. 'You can be sure of your father's intercession. It is time now for him to take care of you. Come, try your hand at the bow. This smaller one will suit you well; and I have some gloves belonging to my sisters that should fit.'

'I doubt I will have much success,' I sniffed. 'I am a trifle short-sighted.'

'Eyesight has little to do with accuracy in this sport. An archer who relies too heavily on his ability to see will falter once he fails to place his shot. He must also consider the wind, the distance, the height of the target, and his own strength if he wishes to hit the bullseye. And when he hunts game, he must know intimately the animal he hunts. Judgement is paramount: sound judgement, and nerves of steel.'

Having demonstrated how to hold and draw, he bid me fire. My arm shook with the effort and the arrow fell short and wide of the mark. Sirius was most put out and hesitated whether he should pursue.

'You haven't the strength to strike from this distance, Phoebe. Come forward and you will have more success.'

'Dad was a terrible shot. In the War, he was so bad with a gun they assigned him to duty behind the lines. He couldn't bring it upon himself to kill anyone.'

'I can understand. Hunting a beast for food is one matter; killing a man, quite another.'

'I suppose it's a question of motive. You know my mother was murdered, don't you?'

'Murdered? That is terrible. Was it ever brought to justice?'

'No. One day, though, it will be. I will see to that.'

After several botched attempts I managed to stand firm. I lowered the bow and smiled at the arrow lodged in the outer circle.

'I thought you were Ruth,' Hubie twitched up his glasses. 'But it seems you are quite ruth-less. Instead, dear cousin, you are Judith.'

40

Krampus

YES, HUBIE, IT IS FLATTERING you should think me like Judith. I have shed my mourning garb, donned fine garments, and adorned myself with jewels. My hair I have prettily curled. You marvel at my resolve; but in attributing such righteousness to me, you deceive yourself. I have no share in Judith's virtue. I am not given to humble prayer and penance. I have not found favour with God; for beneath my fair features lurks most foul intent.

Nor do you realise that I further deceive you by allowing you to think highly of me. You stand close and guide my arm. Your quiet contentment fuels my confidence. My arrows hit the target and win me your praise and good opinion. Have you any idea what you have done? You have engendered in me the power to slay!

Would that I knew God favoured my cause! Providence stood by the prayerful Judith who protected her people from cruel Nebuchadnezzar. With feminine charm she seduced his general Holofernes, who succumbed to his vices while she remained unsullied. Then she beheaded him, and under the cover of darkness returned to her people with his head in a sack. Then, when at dawn the Babylonians saw their leader's head impaled on a stake in the Israelite camp, they fled. God was on Judith's side. Was God on mine? Perhaps the realisation of my capacity to kill was indicative of divine support.

Or was I deceiving myself? I relished the bloodless achievement of hitting a bullseye. How satisfying it was to harness every mental faculty, every muscle, every instinct toward lethal penetration! But a series of concentric circles positioned at the opposite end of a manicured lawn was a far cry from a human face pleading for mercy: the geometric neutrality of the target dulled any moral concerns. The arrows of Justice, drawn on Reason's bow, and carried by the winds of Vengeance could strike the centre with conviction. In killing Ailine could I be equally certain? Or would one swift and decisive shot to Ailine's heart lay bare the truth of my own transgression? Would I lament the blood of my victim, or would I rejoice?

My chicanery should have disposed me to the deception around me. But, as is often the case when we deceive, we are so bent on our own wicked pursuits that we fail to credit another's subterfuge. I had witnessed unawares a cunning heist: a seasonal embezzlement of emeralds, rubies, and gold as leaf after leaf fell from the trees. Its success lay in the fact that Autumn drew no attention to his skulduggery – after all, leaves are supposed to fall from trees during Autumn – and I had been duped by his beauty and charm.

But one night in early December, Autumn stole away with Raffles-like panache; and when I awoke and looked out the window, Linke Wienzeile was blanched with snow. White flakes drifted from cashmere clouds. Icicle fringes hung from sculptured eaves. Leafless trees donned elegant gloves of frost. Snow-sprinkled stalls huddled in the Naschmarkt. Trams swished along wet rails; horses with red flannel blankets tossed icy crumbs from their manes; and harness bells jingled.

In the snow-covered courtyard, Oda, still clad in her scanty playsuit, continued with her calisthenics. Nothing and no one, it seemed, could stop her until the Weissmüller boys played hookey one morning and launched a snowball attack.

Albrecht churned his barrel organ only on fine days, and otherwise occupied a cosy old chair by the Kachelofen in the bookshop. From there he kept up to date with the comings and goings, which were many; for Emil had plenty of business, although it involved little money, and more than books were exchanged. Indeed, the shop functioned more as a depot for parcels, messages, and letters, the most significant of which was a long-awaited piece of news delivered courtesy of a 'customer'.

'It's from Matti,' Emil announced. Albrecht's son, Matthias 'Matti' Drücker, had fled the country after the Februarkämpfe of 1934.

'Gott sei Dank he is safe! He is in Spain, yes, Misha?'

'Letter's from France.' Apparently, Matthias Drucker had worked his way westward, where he eventually took up arms in favour of the Republican cause. However, with Franco's Nationals aided by Hitler and Mussolini, the Republicans were heavily outnumbered. Following Nationalist attacks in Asturias, Matthias had narrowly escaped across the Pyrenees.

'I told him, I told him there'd be trouble,' Albrecht waggled a knobbly arthritic finger, 'You boys and your Marxist fantasies.'

'The Stalinists are the trouble,' Emil retaliated. 'They've taken control of the Republican forces. Cabellero has been arrested. Soviet imperialism has nothing to do with the spirit of Communism. Stalin has undermined the Revolution! What has become of the Proletariat?'

'What did you expect, Misha? The Garden of Eden?'

'Feh! We have the right to resist oppression!'

'Fräulein Phoebe, have you noticed how our Misha always talks about oppression? Be happy with your portion, my boy.'

'My portion? Thanks to Millimetternich and his Jesuitical successor I get bupkes![17] Now, across the border, that Nazi paskudnik[18] to whom everyone grovels – Mussolini, Jesuit Schuschnigg, and idiot British aristocrats lured by hunting trips and duped by anti-Red rhetoric – has his eye on the pickings.'

'Please, Phoebe,' Sisi Schütze begged. 'I need a second angel for the St Nicholas pageant. All you need to do is carry a basket and hand out treats to the children. Please.'

'Can't Heidi do it?'

'Herr Steffan's asked her to be an angel in the pageant at church. Besides, she's grown too tall to accompany Zita and Franz. It would look silly.'

If Franz was involved there was bound to be mischief.

'I am St Nicholas,' he twinkled.

'Are you going, Hubie?'

Hubie glanced from his book. 'I am Krampus.'

Bemused, I looked from Hubie to Zita, to Franz, to Heidi who giggled, and finally to Sisi.

'It is tradition,' Hubie explained, twitching a smile. 'Krampus is the devil who accompanies St Nicholas on his visit. He is the one who— punishes naughty children.'

'This year we have two Krampuses,' announced Sisi. 'Rudi also said he'd come.'

Sisi would accept no refusal, and on St Nicholas' Day, 6th December, she bid me dress in a white floor-length robe and fur-trimmed cape, and in that costume play the role of the Christmas Angel. Zita was similarly attired, only she carried an enormous leather-bound book and feather quill. Heidi handed me a basket filled with gingerbread St Nicholases which she and Frau Schütze had baked and decorated. Each was wrapped in cellophane and tied to a twig. 'Part of Krampus' switch,' she told me, 'to remind the children of what will happen to them if they are naughty.'

When Franz joined us in the vestibule, he was dressed in long robes topped with a cloak and a bishop's mitre; while his merry blue eyes were enhanced by a white moustache and a beard which flowed to his waist. 'Are you as angelic as you look, Phoebe?' he whispered. 'And you, Heidi? You have been a good girl, yes?'

'Some adults could do with a visit from Krampus,' Heidi pushed

---

[17] *Bupkes*: (lit.) beans; (fig.) nothing.
[18] *Paskudnik*: a revolting, horrible, evil person.

him away. 'Where are the Krampuses, anyway? You will be late if they don't hurry up.'

'Mind you don't pee in my Krampus trousers, Rudi!' Karl-Alois warned from the landing. 'Hubie can pee in his own trousers, but if you do that in mine, I'll kill you!'

A great horned figure with knee-high boots, furry breeches and a shaggy goat hair coat roared in reply. Cowbells, hung from a belt around his waist, clanged as he trudged along the *piano nobile*. He stood at the top of the staircase and brandished a bundle of sticks. In his other hand he swung a chain. Down the stairs he stomped. His mask with its aquiline nose and forehead scored with angry furrows, its gaping mouth full of fangs, and swaying forked tongue, was truly hideous.

A second, even taller horned and masked demon holding a black sack over his shoulder and rattling a chain, lumbered behind him. Clanging, swishing, and slashing, he drew close to me and pressed into my hand a small, hard case.

'Would you look after my glasses for me, Phoebe?' he whispered.

'Heaven only knows what you would do to me if I didn't, Hubie.'

Into the roadster we piled, with St Nicholas squashed between the Krampuses; the angels, book, and basket crammed into the dickie seat. Even though Rudi had to remove his headpiece to drive, we created quite a scene as we sped toward the Hartmannspital, with not a few snowballs being hurled at the car, one hitting Hubie square on the shoulder. Apparently, it was traditional to pelt the Krampus with snow.

Sisi escorted us to the children's ward and the Krampuses entered, cackling and clanking amidst shrieks of terror and delight. I peeped through the glass and glimpsed them swooping across the room and round the beds.

'When we were children, the more terrifying the Krampus the better,' laughed Zita.

'We enjoyed some good ones, too,' Franz agreed. 'Some of the world's most renowned conductors have made the best Krampuses. Little wonder, given they are so well-practiced in scaring the living daylights out of the orchestra.'

'St Nicholas, come quickly! St Nicholas, come quickly!' the children called.

'Come, my angels!' winked Franz.

A seven-foot Krampus held a small boy over his shoulder and was about to pile him into his sack when St Nicholas pointed his staff at him and cried, 'Be gone!' Krampus dropped the (very relieved) child and snivelled and scurried – his legs and arms like tentacles – into a corner. There he crouched, taunting St Nicholas who with his staff was prodding the second Krampus under a bed.

The children and their families, the doctors and nursing sisters all cheered; and to each we paid a call. Zita, the Guardian Angel, opened her book which purportedly contained the sins of every child. Pretending to read, she whispered to St Nicholas whose eyes widened with horror as he heard each account. In one case, she had the hide to turn the page as she related a particularly long list of misdemeanours.

'Krampus is out!' shrieked the children every time the cackling Krampuses crept forward, shaking their bells and chains.

'Away, Krampus! Peter promises he will be good, ja?' (Witness boy concerned clutching his mother for dear life and fervently nodding his head.) 'Eat your sauerkraut, Peter,' St Nicholas advised, and signalled for me, the Christmas Angel, to hand Peter his treat.

Each child received timely advice: 'Share your toys', 'Obey your parents', 'Be kind to your brothers and sisters', 'Say your prayers', and marvelled wide-eyed as to how on earth St Nicholas knew their sins.

'Thank you very much for coming,' the Sister in charge showed us out. 'The children have had a wonderful time.'

'So have we.' Franz had revelled in his role as a benevolent Deus-ex-machina.

'Father will be very busy when he hears their confessions tomorrow. The children will be well-prepared for Christmas.'

'If only evil were so easily recognisable and so easily crushed,' lamented Hubie.

'Indeed,' nodded Sister, 'but as with every one of Satan's tricks it always wears a mask.'

'You shouldn't play Krampus, Huberle,' Rudi patted him on the back.

'I don't think I have seen a more terrifying one,' Sister remarked. 'You made me want to be a child all over again. God bless you all!'

'We'll go for a beer, ja?' proposed Rudi.

'Ja,' Franz agreed. 'Only make sure you don't pee in Karl's pants.'

Beer and schnitzel were but the beginnings of our amusement. Since *Der Mann, der Sherlock Holmes war* was still screening, Franz proposed we see it (the film was an enormous favourite of his), particularly since its 'Englishness' was bound to appeal to me. 'It's a comedy,' he explained, 'featuring two British conmen who travel to the Continent dressed as Sherlock Holmes and Dr Watson. They insist they are travelling incognito, but they take advantage of the fact that everyone they meet assumes they are really the famous detective and his companion. In that capacity, they are hired to uncover a counterfeit operation, only to be arrested and tried for being impersonators, and acquitted when Conan Doyle himself attends the trial.'

The film was rollicking entertainment, and it created a hearty appetite. 'Schnapps or coffee?' asked Zita.
'Both,' replied Franz.
'And cake,' added Rudi.
Cafe Central was near enough, so there we adjourned, Franz and Rudi escorting us with a jaunty rendition of 'Jawohl, meine Herren', which Messrs 'Holmes' and 'Watson' had sung in the film.
Given the cold and dark and snow outside, the café was a sanctuary of light and warmth. Steam hissed from the coffee machine on the central counter – the altar for the Viennese sacrifice of beans to the glory of Civilised Thought. And through the airy expanse – an ambulatory of pale marble columns and elegant cross-vaulting – liqueur-laced tobacco wafted like incense from the thurible mouths of intellectual votaries who whispered in booths positioned like radiating chapels round an apse, each one dedicated to political principles. Through this hallowed space we wandered as pilgrims.
'Ah, the KPÖ[19] is playing chess,' Rudi nudged Franz and indicated the bristly, bohemian collective huddled around a table further down the café.
'That is about all they are good for nowadays.'
'Knight to E4 did you say? Ho, ho!' I heard Albrecht chuckle, 'You have him in your grasp, my boy! You have him!'
The game concluded amidst applause, argument, and ongoing analysis. Wagers were settled and the vanquished left his seat. The victor celebrated with a Fiaker which the waiter handed to him with great deference. Unshaven, shoddily clad in a herringbone carriage coat, a dirty red scarf coiled about his neck, Emil Fährmann picked off the maraschino cherry from its cushion of cream and consumed it with a dignified air. He took the glass in hands warmed by tattered fingerless gloves with woollen corkscrew strands protruding at odd angles.
'Welcome,' he grinned. 'You have come to chess school? Take a seat, please, gentlemen.'
'Master?' Franz winked at Rudi.
'Doctor?' Rudi winked at Franz.
Emil lit a cigarette and watched them like a fox savouring the prospect of catching two chickens for his dinner. Eventually Rudi took the chair.
'Zita, it is not— prudent,' cautioned Hubie.

---

[19] *KPÖ: Kommunistische Partei Österreichs*, Communist Party of Austria.

'Huberle, you're such a fuddy duddy. How could anything be imprudent with you around?' Zita pushed her way into the group, leaving Hubie little choice but to accompany her, which pleased me much for I was eager to see the match.

Emil easily foiled Rudi's attempt at a Queen's gambit, and soon captured the queen with a far-ranging move on the part of his bishop which he did not hesitate to sacrifice in the process. 'You're a scoundrel, Misha,' teased Albrecht, who followed the game through a blow by blow report from one of the spectators. 'Feh! The Lady was there for the taking; and to hell with the Bishop,' replied Emil, whose every move was deft and calculated. Rudi grew vexatious, and with Franz withdrew in hushed deliberation.

'Use your knight, silly.' Zita proposed. But Rudi paid no attention, which fatal error lost him the match.

'Perhaps you need to go to chess kindergarten,' Emil suggested.

'Chess is merely an ivory tower pastime,' Rudi sneered, 'Nowadays, wars are won by science and technology.'

'And what are science and technology without tactics?'

'And what are tactics, but coffeehouse speculation?'

'All wars are brewed in coffeehouses. Another match? Or maybe your genzel[20] will oblige?' Emil winked at Franz who promptly declined. 'Would one of the ladies deign to play?' And he deviously insinuated Zita while gleaming at me.

'I will play you.' Hubie stepped forward.

'Fräulein, you are most welcome,' Emil extended his hand.

During the previous game, Hubie had closely followed every move. Only his stutter had prevented him from criticising Rudi's blunders, which made him frustrated and tense. He shook Emil's hand and sat opposite.

'You are not going to fetch Cardinal Innitzer to say a blessing before you begin?' Emil taunted. 'After all, if the Ständestaat builds new public toilets, and invites his Eminence to bless the latrines, why not bless a game of chess?'

Lot fell to Hubie to play black, forcing him to mount a defence. This he did with skill; but he was unprepared for Emil's clever positioning and rapid attack. Yet Emil seemed impressed— either that or he was out for blood, for he offered Hubie a second game and invited him to play with white.

After much deliberation, Hubie opened play. A quick repartee from black. White answered with a second, carefully considered move. Black replied. Hubie pondered his third point of attack, hesitated, and then refrained. Emil grew impatient. Another cautious placement; another swift response.

Further hesitation.

'Hubie, you fool!' Zita protested. 'What did you do that for?'

---

[20] *Genzel:* (lit.) gosling; (sl.) an inexperienced youth; (sl.) a catamite.

Emil sniggered as he captured Hubie's queen. But he scowled when he saw the board. His quickness and confidence had been flattered. White's apparently negligent move was deliberate. Hubie had taken his opponent's measure and caught him off guard. Emil, too, lost his queen. And from that point, it was a contest of wit.

'You play like a monarch, sir,' Albrecht observed.

Indeed, my cousin-of-sort's command of chess reflected his appreciation of its origins. Medieval society was conjured to life on that amber and ebony board. Knights and pawns were employed in defence and attack, assisted by judicious intervention from the bishop. No piece was spared for the sake of the realm; while the king was an active combatant who directed the course of play, ably assisted by pawns and rooks, and eventually his queen whom he reclaimed.

Hubie assumed control of the board, and of the game— but not without a fight. Emil's creative strategy derived from the quick-witted pragmatism of the slums. His every move invited commentary, while Hubie's manoeuvres prompted hushed critique. Time ticked by. The air grew thick with smoke. More coffees were ordered. A distant clock chimed midnight. No end was in sight. The waiters and manager joined the intrigue. Coffee was served on the house.

Finally, at one in the morning:

'Checkmate.'

Exhausted, Hubie leant back and stared at his hard-won victory. Whatever titles, responsibilities, and position had been denied him by society, he made certain were still his within the realms of abstraction of Café Central. Surprisingly nonchalant about his defeat, Emil deferred by lighting Hubie's cigarette. But his wily glance at Zita, and that tiny smirk on his lips told that he knew he had won a victory all his own, in the material world, where it counted.

41

A-Hunting We Will Go

LATER THAT MORNING, while I was sipping a strong espresso, there arrived a note from Frau Schütze informing me that the deer had come down from the mountain, and that in two days' time the family would be travelling to their lodge in the Styrian Alps. I was most cordially invited to join them.

'We'll catch a giraffe and make him laugh!' the Portrait seemed to sing.

'Not likely,' I replied. 'I greatly fear we'll catch a deer.'

'And eat her up for tea? It's good game. You ought to try it. Caught myself a very pretty doe and married her too. Will you be the lucky hunter this time?'

'Me? Hunt? I am no hunter.'

'Then perhaps you'll be the hart?'

'I am no hart.'

'Better be careful, not every man will find you attractive. Your mirror might flatter you, but those inky brows and bugle eyes won't always hold their charm; while your dark tresses and creamy skin—'

'My skin is not pale.'

'If I were you, Possum, I'd count your blessings there's a man who thinks well enough to pursue you.'

'Nonsense! Who?'

'Young Hubie, of course.'

'You and your silly notions.'

'He doesn't praise you? Wait on you? Flatter you? Woo you with verse?'

'If he did, I would despise him.'

'Ha, ha! Ein wahrer Jägersmann! He'll catch his hind!'

'He pays me kind attention as befits a cousin-of-sorts. I am content with that. I wish him to go no further—'

'And sully your quaint honour with his affection?'

'I'm quite at a loss as to what to pack,' I sighed. 'What does one wear on such occasions?'

'Try my lederhosen. Dress as a youth and see what he does then.'

'Don a man's clothes? I think not. My hips are too wide, my waist too slender. I feel as if I should wear a dirndl.'

'You'd look a right shepherdess if you did. Oh Phoebe, Phoebe, Phoebe!' he smooched.

'Stop it! Tweed will have to do.'

Violin in one hand, suitcase in the other and hatbox under my arm, I ventured into the silver dawn. Sirius, his head sticking out of a cab, barked. What was I thinking of, —carting luggage on my own? Hubie chastised as he escorted me to the front seat, an unnecessary luxury given that he had to double over to fit in the back with Sirius and Zita.

At the Südbahnhof, Hubie made special arrangements for his dog, who had to travel in a separate box, while the rest of the family busily organised baggage and tickets. We settled in two compartments: Herr and Frau Professor with Karl-Alois, Fifi and baby Karl in one; myself, Hubie, and the younger Schützes in the other.

The train chugged past farms and fields and forested slopes, while we snacked on coffee and croissants and played cards. Then we began to sing. The Schützes were determined to teach me the Orchestra Song and did a wonderful job of impersonating all the instruments. In return, they insisted I teach them an Australian song; and after some thought, I decided on *The Road to Gundagai*. Only Hubie had any real command of English, but his accent was heavily influenced by his native tongue. As for his brother and sisters, the song was best explained with the help of actions. It was like teaching kindergarten. No one took offence – they enjoyed the music too much – and before long I was improvising on the violin, Zita and Heidi were providing a rhythm accompaniment, Hubie an oom-pah bass, and Franz and Sisi were harmonising.

Gundagai's etymology fascinated Hubie for he could discern no Latin, Greek, Germanic or Slavic roots (he spoke six languages). That was nothing compared with other Australian place names, I teased, and wrote down a few more for him to get his head (not to mention his tongue) around: Yarrawonga, Coonabarabran, Woolloomooloo, Gulargambone, Ulladulla, Oodnadatta... Soon I was explaining Murray's Undies, Dunedoo, Burping Gary and Coober Peed 'Ere (but he didn't pee over there).

We entered a wide snow-clad valley, where the town of Admont nestled beneath mist shrouded mountains. Church bells chimed the midday Angelus and the family paused to pray before alighting. Waiting at the station were the gamekeeper, who was Fifi's father Herr Merth, the local veterinarian (Fifi's Uncle Josef), and the parish priest (another relative) who helped us load our luggage onto the three sleighs that formed our transport. Sirius leaped up to join his master. Out of the town we journeyed, past an enormous monastery, and over the River Enns. A wayside shrine marked the entrance to Hall, a cache of cottages in a mountain casket. My high-spirited companions kept their minds off the cold by changing the words of our new song to fit the present setting:

> *There's a track winding back*
> *To an ancient mountain shack*
> *Along the road through Hall Bei*

'Hier sind wir!' Franz announced. 'Our "shack"!'

Shack? True, the Schützes' property was not one of the quasi-palatial villas owned by the former monarchy— but shack it was not. A steep-roofed lodge typical of the homes in the area, it was solid and centuries-old, with two tidy rows of windows. Inside, heavy wooden beams stretched across the ceiling. Thick walls punctuated by large timber doors with marquetry panels and carved architraves kept the cold at bay while log fires provided cosy comfort.

Still in the hall, Hubie respectfully tipped his hat. Wondering whom he was greeting, I turned in the direction of his gesture and screamed.

'You have not seen a stag before, my cousin?' I could have sworn I heard him chuckle.

'No, I haven't,' I gulped. 'Neither that close nor that dead.'

'He is handsome, yes?'

Such admiration and pride as that which shone in his eyes set me to wonder. I did not like the conclusion I reached.

'You didn't shoot him, did you?'

'Last season.' And if it were possible for Hubie to appear even taller, well, that possibility manifested there and then. He swelled his chest and squared his shoulders. 'We made this shrine. The crucifix between the antlers has been in Vati's family for many generations. Karl carved the wood for the banner below, and I painted the inscription.

'"Sancte Huberte ora pro nobis",' I read the gothic lettering. 'St Hubertus pray for us. Your namesake?'

'He is my patron saint, and the patron saint of hunters. St Hubertus was a nobleman who lost his wife in childbirth. Filled with sorrow, he withdrew from courtly life and became much addicted to the chase. One Good Friday, instead of honouring Our Lord's Passion, he went hunting. He was pursuing a magnificent stag when it suddenly turned and faced him, and between its antlers Hubertus beheld a cross: a warning from God urging him to mend his ways and lead a holy life. He renounced his birthright in favour of his infant son, gave his wealth to the poor, and was ordained priest. Later, he was consecrated bishop. St Hubertus was a most frugal and prayerful man of God who was responsible for the conversion of many pagans. I have much devotion to him.

'As for the stag, he and I have grown up together. He was a good trophy – a hart of ten – and fit for a shrine. But, Phoebe, you would prefer to see a live deer, yes? Sirius, I know, is very keen. Sollen wir gehen und Rehe jagen, mein treuer Hund?'

The mist lifted that afternoon to reveal a massive snow-covered mountain glowing gold in the late sunshine. Dark conifers with icicle epaulettes marched down the nearby slopes, and threatened to invade snowy fields, the borders of which were poorly manned by meagre birch with faded red leaves.

Upon kneeling to examine the scent his dog had so cleverly detected, Hubie noticed a trace of blood. There was a doe nearby, he told me, and she was on heat for the blood was from her urine. Fresh tracks led us to an ancient grove where gnarled apple trees formed a haggard cluster. Frost crowned fruit still hung from forked boughs, while dried leaves, grassy tufts, and earthy patches mingled with the snow. Forward crept Hubie, who positioned himself behind a tree and beckoned me to follow. Yonder, a deer was grazing on fallen apples. She dug a little with her front hoofs, nuzzled the fruit loose, and nibbled contentedly.

'Baoh! Baoh!' A buck emerged from the neighbouring copse. He lifted his head and let out a massive groan. The young doe continued to feast. 'Baoh! Baoh! Baoh!' He gambolled round her, and lustily tossed his antlers. She sniffed the air; while her large, pretty eyes averted their gaze from her suitor, and instead surveyed the orchard lest someone be privy to the flirtations, which were becoming increasingly frolicsome. Sirius barked, and the couple darted away.

'Please tell me you are not going to shoot her,' I whispered.

'Wie schön sie ist!' Hubie continued to watch. 'No, dear cousin, I will not shoot her. Perhaps she will fawn in the spring? Nor will I shoot her gentleman friend. He is young, but already he is too mature and lean for meat, and it is meat we are after. I wish them well. Come, let us walk some more. You are warm enough?'

He picked an apple from high on the branches, dusted off the snow and passed it to me. How crisp and cold it was! We trudged toward the mountains, munching our sweet and juicy fruit, our shadows lengthening over gilded fields.

Desirous to know more of what happened to Maman, Hubie broached the subject cautiously, hesitating to speak until he was assured, not only of my confidence, but of absolute privacy. I told him all that I remembered as a child and detailed the complications.

'The police said Maman suicided. She didn't. It was framed as a suicide for there was a note, but it was a forgery. Dad suspected murder, and no one believed him. The detective in charge thought him delusional due to shell shock from the War, and never bothered investigating further. Dad suffered a nervous breakdown as a result.'

'Vati told me your father had been very ill. I assumed it was the War. And what happened to you?'

'I spent my remaining childhood in an orphanage.'

'I am most genuinely sorry. I can hardly imagine how it would be to live with something like that.'

'Fortunately, many years later, we found evidence which proved my mother did not take her own life; and the police re-opened her case. We also know who committed the crime. It was my aunt, Maman's sister.'

'That is Ailine Devereaux, yes?' Hubie remarked after I recounted to him the evidence we uncovered.

'You sound as if you know her.'

'Well, about three years ago, while I was working in Munich, your father wrote me and asked me to try and find her.'

'He did what?'

'Shhh! He never mentioned why. All he said was that he understood she was living in Dresden and that he wished to renew contact with her.'

'Dresden? Are you sure? But I was going to go to Paris to look for her! Ailine used to live in Paris. She came from Paris to— And she returned— But— Dresden? How did he know that? Well, I suppose I'll have to go to Germany instead. I must find her!'

'Nein!' Hubie grabbed me by the elbow, 'Nein, my dear cousin, do not go to Germany!'

'But—'

'Hush, Phoebe! Please listen. I made enquiries and obtained an address. Unfortunately, it proved incorrect. I investigated further on your father's behalf— he seemed most anxious; but I am afraid it became increasingly difficult. You see, when Hitler assumed power it became unwise to ask too many questions. How do I explain this?' he sighed and paused. 'Your aunt was an artist, yes? Well, if she in any way opposed the NSDAP, she was in great danger.'

'Ailine couldn't care less about politics.'

'Ah, but Hitler does. Phoebe,' he wavered, 'I briefly met with your aunt. But when I went to visit a second time, she had disappeared.'

'What are you trying to tell me?'

'Apparently, there had been a police raid. You see, people disappear in Germany. And when you disappear, you cease to exist. There are no records. No one is going to tell what they know. They are too afraid. If you talk, you could get into trouble. Someone might be listening.'

'Are you certain of this?'

'I know what the situation is. It is possible your aunt is no longer alive.'

'How can I be sure?'

'I am afraid you may never find out.'

'But— I was going to look for her!'

'You— you do not plan to remain in Vienna?'

'No, that was never my intention! Oh, if only I knew!'

'You are trembling. Do not fear, my sweet cousin! Be calm! Would you permit me to offer you some advice?'

'What is it?'

'Perhaps it is better to think of your aunt as dead. She may not be brought to justice in this life, but she will face God. And you have your own life to lead. Would it not be better to try and forget?'

Forget! What a glorious temptation! Could it be possible? Could it be so simple? Could fate have acted in my favour, liberating me from a loathsome vendetta?

'And if she is dead,' Hubie continued, 'do you need to leave?'

'I was planning to leave next Spring,' I murmured.

'Must you?'

'Do you think I wish to?'

'Then let me try and find out more. The orchestra is travelling to Berlin early next year. I will see what I can do through people I can trust. Your father was of great help to me, and I promise I will assist you in any way I can.'

'You would do that for me?'

'Of course. But I must ask something of you in return. I ask that you be patient. In the meantime, we can be friends, yes?'

'Yes, of course, Hubie. Of course, we can be friends.'

And I beheld what appeared to be a smile. Well, at any rate, it was a slight upward turn of his lips.

'Look how the mountain glows red and gold!' he touched my elbow. The colours dulled and dimmed and disappeared with the setting sun. A crescent moon appeared in the purple twilight. 'That is Mercury,' he said, pointing to an early star. 'He is heaven's friendly messenger. Tomorrow will be a fine day, perfect for hunting. It is beautiful, yes?'

'And so wondrously calm.'

The mountain blackened, and darkness cloaked the conifer army. A barn owl swooped silently and pounced on a mouse. The gloom only enhanced the beauty of the stars which shyly peeped from the heavens. With Sirius trotting behind, we returned arm in arm to the lodge, a beacon of life and warmth with its promise of hot meals and fireside comfort.

'So, he decided to come after all,' Hubie mused.

Sure enough, parked out front was Rudi's red roadster.

42

Halli, Hallo!

THUDDING BOOTS, and a mellow baritone roused me from my slumber the following dawn. Dressed in an old mottled jumper and leather breeches, the faithful Sirius at his side, Hubie strode down the hall in joyous song:

> *Im Wald und auf der Heide,*
> *Da such ich meine Freude,*
> *Ich bin ein Jägersmann;*
> *Ich bin ein Jägersmann*
> *Die Forsten treu zu pflegen,*
> *Das Wildbret zu erlegen,*
> *Mein' Lust hab' ich daran;*
> *Mein' Lust hab' ich daran*

Rudi's even more robust tenor took up a chorus, and Hubie immediately sang in harmony:

> *Halli, hallo, halli, hallo,*
> *Mein' Lust hab' ich daran.*
> *Halli, hallo, halli, hallo,*
> *Mein' Lust hab' ich daran.*

The morning's chorale continued the previous night's festivities. Having discussed their plans, the men made merry, singing with gusto while they fine-tuned their weapons, organised their packs, and polished their boots. Father Merth called by and joined them for schnapps; then they knelt for a blessing around the St Hubertus shrine:

> *By the intercession of St. Hubert,*
> *patron saint of hunters,*
> *may you always honour God the Creator,*
> *who set man in dominion over all the animals.*
>
> *May the Lord God make you*
> *an honourable hunter*
> *who respects fellow hunters,*
> *the animals, and all creation;*

May He keep safe you
and all who share the field or the forest;
May He make all hunters
proud of their kill, generous with their meat,
and thankful in all circumstances.

May God bless you: Father, Son, and Holy Ghost.

All save Franz, who instead elected to spend the evening at the piano with me in a boisterous rendition of Dvorak's Slavonic Dances. 'Now run and we swap, Phoebe!' he called midway through the third dance. And while he shifted from Primo to Secondo, assuming my part with a syncopated single note, I rushed round the grand piano and took my seat at the treble in time for my entry. On we played, giggling and gasping whilst playing quavers against triplets, until Hubie appeared in the doorway. 'You are helping M-m-mutti bake the Linzertorte tomorrow, Franzwurst?' his taunt belying the more serious demand that his younger brother consider his hunting obligations.

Now Zita was knocking at his bedroom door and threatening culinary duties. Franz blundered out, tucking his shirt into his breeches.

'Horrido,' he mumbled in response to Rudi's slap on the back. It might have been a traditional hunting salutation, but my impression was that 'horrid' in English was more in keeping with his real sentiments. Poor Franzl had barely sipped his coffee when Hubie sounded his plesshorn. Out onto the snow he trooped, fumbling with his pack, and was swallowed by the vast white mist.

'They will not have to go far to find the deer,' Frau Schütze waved off her husband and sons. Cloud had covered last night's moon, she explained, so the deer would be out foraging in the morning. When the men returned, they would be cold and hungry; so, it was imperative the midday meal be ready. 'Can you cook, Phoebe?'

In the kitchen, heat glowed from the enormous wood stove. Great round pumpkins, striped like tabby cats, nestled in a corner. All the way down the long oak table stood baskets of onions, potatoes, parsnips and turnips. And there were carrots of molten colours – yellow, deep orange, purple, and nearly black. Zita cut open a pumpkin, scooped out the seeds, chopped the sumptuously golden flesh, and placed the pieces on an enormous platter – a great colourful wheel of vegetables.

I offered to make a strudel, having learnt how from Mr Epstein many years ago, and selected the best of the apples, soaked some raisins in last night's Schnapps obstwasser (brandy made from apples and pears), and fortified myself with a small glass of the same. I had the good fortune to work with the freshest, creamiest butter, and flour that seemed milled for the purpose; for, after resting the dough, I was able to stretch it smooth and sheer as silk. Onto the pastry I drizzled melted butter and scattered breadcrumbs toasted golden in (more) butter. I mounded cubes of apple, sugar and cinnamon, and raisins plump with brandy. Then, folding the pastry over the filling, I brushed it with still more butter and caressed it into a fat, fruit-filled log.

Sisi let me sample the Wurzelfleisch, the hearty pork stew which simmered in an enormous pot. A knock at the door announced Liesl, Fifi's sister, who had come to help with the potatoes. Peeling potatoes was Liesl's job and had been for years. In fact, it was one of the few jobs of which she was capable (she was intellectually deficient); and, with a company of grown men to feed, Frau Schütze needed a lot of potatoes. Heidi churned the butter and helped her mother with the Linzertorte.

Later that morning Fifi, who with Karl-Alois was spending the weekend with her parents, arrived with her mother and baby Karl. They brought between them a basket of fresh bread, Verhackert, sauerkraut, and several bottles of beer; and as we sat down for a well-earned snack, we savoured the buttery, spicy sweet aroma of the baking strudel.

'Ah! Sammeln der Jäger!' Frau Schütze announced, and I heard a trio of horns.

A spotted doe lay on the snow with a spray of oak on her belly. Similarly laid out beside her was a stag in whose mouth a second small branch had been placed. Hubie, Dr Merth, and the gamekeeper took up their horns and honoured each with a short anthem.

Professor Schütze gave thanks for the hunt and recounted the harvest. The hunters had followed a trail to a favourite glade where the deer were grazing on acorns. They closed in on the herd, at which point they made their kill. The horn trio sounded a mournful celebration: the hunters had been victorious, but noble beasts had been slain. Credit for the morning's achievements went to Rudi and Franz. In tribute, the Professor dipped the oak sprays in the animals' blood and placed them in the hats of the two men. Sirius, too, was rewarded with a branch in his collar, for he had tracked the doe. 'Halali!' sounded the horns. The hunt was over. 'To the meal!' the horns called.

'It is my first harvest!' Franz boasted.

'And m-m-may it be your last,' Hubie scorned. 'You would be better off with the girls in the k-k-kitchen.'

'Sour grapes,' Rudi teased.

'All her— good meat is wasted,' Hubie lamented.

Karl explained that while they had successfully tracked the herd, the deer took fright as they were about to strike. Instead of refraining, Franz fired his arrow and hit the doe on the run, penetrating her hind leg. A second arrow was needed to kill her.

'Instead, Franz, you will have your fill of the— sausage you so fancy. Her meat will be too tough for anything else.' I had never known Hubie to be so scathing. 'I hope your— beer is plentiful.'

'Always plentiful, Huberle,' Franz smiled.

'We came for food, and what do we have?' Hubie raised his arms in dismay.

'Huberle, you are upset over two deer?' Rudi soothed. 'There are thousands out there. We risk being overrun with deer. What does a trophy matter?'

'If you wanted to— prove yourself with a trophy, then you should have chosen an older— cunning animal, a stag worth the prize.'

'I knew I could hit him, and I did. He was weak— a Gobo. He did not deserve to live.'

'He was— tired from the rut.'

'He was too lean, Huberle. It is unlikely he would survive the winter,' Professor Schütze intervened.

'You do not know that!'

'It would have been far worse to die from starvation.'

'There is still plenty of good— fodder, Vati, and the deer know where to find it. He would regain his strength. You should not have allowed it.'

'Enough!' warned the Professor.

'At least it was a clean kill,' Rudi retaliated.

'It was a v-v-violation,' Hubie raised his fists.

'Enough!' the Professor pushed him back.

'And if you wanted an easy target, why did you not— choose a yearling?' Hubie struggled against his father. 'There was an older yearling in the herd whose antlers had— branched. Then we would have had the m-m-m-meat and you would have had your p-p-paltry trophy. As it is, we have to harvest another.'

'Hubert! I said, enough!' And had Hubie been ten years younger, his father would have boxed his ears.

Hubie remained silent all through lunch. Not that there was anything particularly unusual about that – meals and mealtime conversation tended to happen around him as a rule. On this occasion, however, he looked very glum indeed. 'Er schaut ins Narrenkastl wie üblich,' was the expression used in exasperation by the family. Not even his mother could lift his spirits, and she tried a dozen times to do so, her last resort being lavish praise for my strudel. 'Ja, ist es gut,' he shrugged, and excused himself the moment he finished.

'It is his favourite,' Frau Schütze whispered to me.

His sullen demeanour had only enhanced Franz and Rudi's jollity.

'Phoebe, it is well you are not Jewish, ja?' Rudi gestured, glass in hand. 'This pork is too good. Ah, poor Jews, they do not know what they are missing out on.'

'All the more for us,' Franz helped himself to seconds of the Werzelfleisch.

'Then you should thank the Jews for leaving you with more than your fill,' Sisi flashed her dark eyes, 'You both eat like pigs.'

Rudi and Franz laughed, then further amused themselves by imitating various university professors; and when they were no longer capable of mimicry, they lapsed into happy carousing.

'How odd it is that I miss him,' I looked at Hubie's empty chair. There would have been very little conversation if he had remained, regardless of his mood. But whenever I glanced in his direction, our eyes usually met. I missed his warm gaze. Nor did I like seeing him upset. Poor fellow! He tried so hard to control his stutter and it had returned with a vengeance right when he needed to make his point. Where was he? I had a good mind to look for him.

'Good heavens!' I gasped. Trudging across the snow were the unmistakable figures of Hubie, now dragging a sled, and Sirius.

'Don't worry. He won't go far, or for long,' Karl-Alois remarked with a puff of his cigarette.

'But it's freezing out there!'

'Hubie is sensible. He knows he must take care. Asthma.'

'Does he get it badly?'

'Ja. Cigarette?'

I accepted. 'And you tell me not to worry.'

'It's not as severe as it used to be,' he hid any concern with a flick of his lighter and offered me the flame. 'He'll be back soon.'

'He takes it all terribly seriously.'

'For Huberle, hunting is a divine right and sacred duty. Not so the others. For Rudi it's sport. For Franz, opportunity.'

'And for Karl?'

'Christmas dinner,' he grinned as I shook my head at him. Hunting one's own food was understandable, albeit disconcertingly primitive; while the idea of venison in lieu of turkey on the Christmas table was completely foreign to me.

'We are all different, yes?' he laughed. 'Rudi and Franz are immature. Their judgement is unsound; and unfortunately, they do not always wish to take advice. Huberle is far more astute and is a stickler for correctness; and his skill is outstanding. He does the hunt great honour. The trouble is that he expects others to share his view – which is usually right – and to have his ability – which is superlative – and he is angered when they do not. And when he is angry, he cannot express himself; then Franz and Rudi gain the advantage. Vati tries to moderate and ends up having to discipline. Somehow Franz and Rudi escape unscathed while

Hubie comes off the worst. Brothers!' he sighed.

'But Hubie was right, wasn't he?'

'And he knows it.'

'Then why did you not come to his defence?'

'Is it worth a fight? Besides, there were other issues at stake that were more important than making a correct kill. After all these years, Franzl finally managed to hit a deer, and that was praiseworthy, even if it was a botch up. And Vati had a point about the stag: he was weaker than the rest of the herd and may not have survived the winter. Compassion – for both the hunter and his quarry – influenced my father's judgement. In the grand scheme of life, is that so wrong?'

'Given you put it like that, perhaps not. But Rudi and Franz are positively crowing. Listen to them!' They were singing Lehár, rivalling each other on the high notes, and wallowing in the soaring melody:

> *Vilja, O Vilja, Du Waldmägdelein,*
> *Fass' mich und lass' mich*
> *Dein Trautliebster sein!*
> *Vilja, O Vilja, was tust Du mir an?*
> *Bang fleht ein liebkranker Mann!*

Karl tapped his cigarette. 'Perhaps there lies the error.'

'Or your father is too lenient.'

'You have a point. Vati has always had a soft spot for Rudi. Rudi's father was injured in the War and his family had fallen on hard times when Vati "discovered" him during one of his door-knock recruitments for the choir. He arranged for Rudi's board and education and brought him into our family circle so that he would have some semblance of childhood; while his mother, Frau Krain as she was at the time, could care for her husband. Otherwise, Rudi might have ended up on the streets. It was very generous of my father, and a situation you might well understand, yes? Where are you going?'

My hunch that Hubie had taken the path we followed yesterday proved right.

In the apple grove, a doe stood transfixed by the tall figure that stepped from behind a tree. Hubie drew his bow and fired. The deer sprang and staggered. Her legs crumpled beneath her and she collapsed on the snow. Sirius bounded ahead, sniffed her and barked in triumph. The doe struggled to lift her head, shuddered, and fell still. Kneeling, Hubie removed his hat and stroked her.

'Bring some branches, Phoebe,' he beckoned me over.

I hastily plucked all I could, and we arranged the foliage around the fallen creature. Hubie pulled out his plesshorn and a stately, solemn call sounded across the fields.

'Rehwild tot,' he sighed. 'A deer is dead.'

'How could you?'

'She is a maiden doe. She missed out on the rut. How plump she is! She has a belly full of apples and pears and acorns and chestnuts. Her meat will be very sweet. Fear not, Phoebe. The arrow pierced her lung. Our little deer did not suffer.'

'You killed her in cold blood! I saw you! You didn't flinch!'

'And now I must dress her. Perhaps, it is better you do not look.'

He pulled a knife from his belt, rolled the deer onto her back and cut her open. I covered my face and continued to watch by peeking through gaps in my gloves. Removing her entrails, Hubie cleaned her insides and drained her blood with the knowledge and experience of a man well-versed in the art. Little was wasted. The heart, lungs, kidneys and liver he returned to the carcass (for sausage); while Sirius, who with profuse slobber had followed his master's every move, he rewarded with the intestines.

'Had I hesitated, I would have missed and wounded her instead,' Hubie explained as he worked. 'That would have been far worse. It is the art of hunting: to know how to kill without harming. We hunters have our laws which we are bound to obey, and our traditions which teach us to respect the animals we hunt, for we have been entrusted by God to care for creation. We must carefully choose our quarry. It is forbidden to kill a deer with fawn, or a deer that is too young. If we shoot a trophy, it should be a stag that has reached his prime, and we must be certain there are younger stags ready to take his place. We must not shoot more deer than we require for our needs and for the health of the herd. And when we harvest, we use the meat well – to feed our families and those who have none to eat; the skins we use for clothes. That is our role as caretaker of the forest, and we take rightful pride in it. Come Phoebe, let us head home and celebrate, for we have caught our Christmas deer.'

And hoisting the doe onto the sled, he slung his bow across his shoulder, and whistled to Sirius who trotted along, dragging the entrails.

'Often, I have wondered what it would be like to kill,' I glanced at the pool of blood on the snow behind us. Hubie said nothing. The weight of the deer made his progress arduous. 'I mean, it is one thing to poison. There is a certain distance about the crime. It is quiet and calculated, anonymous. Shooting is altogether different. To look your victim or opponent in the eye and kill them the way you did with that doe, that requires conviction. Could you do that to someone?'

'Could I kill a person? Nein! Never. It is a sin to kill. Could you?'

'I would want to be able to, if I had to. My aunt, for instance.'

'Is that why you wanted to find her? For revenge?'

'For justice' sake. She killed my mother. I wanted to confront her; and yes, Hubie, I have often desired to kill her.'

'Phoebe, that is very wrong. Your aunt's fate is for the law to determine, not you.'

'But what if my mother's case cannot be proven?'

'It is still wrong. Nor is it justice. You, too, will have murdered, regardless of your intention. You would have put nothing right, only added your transgression to hers. Did your father share your view?'

'He never wanted the matter taken to court because of the inconclusiveness of the evidence. He couldn't bear the possibility of a miscarriage of justice. Even if my aunt confessed to the crime, Dad did not wish her to be tried because he disapproved of capital punishment.'

'I can understand his reservation, particularly regarding the death penalty. Chancellor Dollfuss reintroduced it because of the grave political and economic situation here in Austria. Unfortunately, the first to be executed were not the political enemies for whom the penalty was intended. It was a serious error of judgement on the part of an otherwise sound government; and it had unfortunate consequences, for it alienated groups who might have lent their support. Nor did it deter the Nazis and Communists. So, what did your father do?'

'The only way he could deal with it was to forgive her.'

'And you did not approve?'

'I despised him for it. He took the weakest position.'

'To forgive is weak? I have often thought it requires great strength. To discount one's own anguish of heart and choose instead to love one's enemy is perhaps the most difficult task of all. And do not think that in saying so I am condoning evil or excusing your aunt's crime. The crime, and the sin, remain. There must be atonement, preferably in this life, but also in the hereafter.'

'Then is it not right that I should call her to account for what she did?'

'Of course, it is right. But not to satisfy a vendetta.'

'I will never forgive my aunt. I will have her hang!'

'Phoebe, no! That is not good.'

'Hubie, she made my life a misery. As a child, I witnessed my father's mental and physical deterioration, and I was left at the mercy of others' charity. My aunt herself abused me and nearly drove me to despair.'

'But she didn't succeed. And now, through the mercy of God, if your aunt is dead, you have been spared from wrongful choice.'

'But He has also spared me from rightful satisfaction.'

'Try not to dwell on it, Phoebe. It is a temptation designed to rob you of your peace. While it is understandable that you should feel this way; if you are not careful, you will drive your passions to ill-purpose and suffer great bitterness. Then your aunt will indeed have made your life a misery. You have spoken of your troubles to a priest, yes?'

'Of what benefit would that be?'

'You would receive grace and guidance. I myself confess often, not because I have greatly sinned – thanks be to God, my trespasses are usually small – but because God, Who is infinitely merciful, is ready to forgive my wrongs. Brother Rosengarten, my spiritual director, is a good and holy man. You should talk to him. He would advise you well and would pray for you. I, too, will pray. How long has it been since you received the Sacraments?'

'About ten years.'

'Your father did not encourage you?'

'That was another matter we never agreed upon. I was a great disappointment to him in that regard. It seems he had more success with you. How often do you confess?'

'At least once a month.'

'Good heavens! Hast thou committed fornication?'

'Phoebe—'

'Or art thou a liar and a thief?'

'I am neither. But I have my faults, and I am as much in need of cleansing as the most hardened sinner. You bathe daily, yes? And not because you are dirty. Indeed, if you are anything like Zita, I'll wager that for you a hot bath every evening is a foretaste of Paradise. I myself am looking forward to a good soak after I have hung our quarry.'

Little wonder. Hubie was warm with the weight of the animal he pulled, and his sweat mixed with the smell of the deer – her earthy coat, her guts and drying blood. And there was another vile, pungent odour which became especially marked when we entered the lodge.

'Hubie, you stink! What is that smell?'

'It is deer urine.'

43

Sleep in Heavenly Peace

D RESDEN. What had lured Ailine to Dresden? I had a vague notion I had heard her mention Dresden in conversations; but given her use of name-dropping to lord it over her clique of enlightened and artistic minds, I had dismissed the reference as being of little relevance to philistines such as myself.

Dad had not been so foolish.

'How did you know?' I demanded of the Portrait; but I received no reply.

'And what, exactly, were you going to do about it?'

Again, silence.

'Dresden? Why, it's been an artistic centre for years!' exclaimed Zita. 'Look, you'll have a better idea if I show you the Kirchner.'

The painting in question was her favourite of the many artworks owned by Rudi's parents, and she immediately arranged a visit in company with her mother.

Since the Ströhmanns lived on the outskirts of Hietzing, I tried to reconcile the aesthetic contradiction of a modern artwork displayed in a Rococo mansion. I need not have bothered. An asymmetrical stack of stuccoed white cubes interspersed with terraces and windows of various shapes and sizes, the Ströhmann home looked as if it owed its construction to a team of ambitious Eskimos. Amidst the snow, it seemed to offer little respite from the cold; but the house turned out to be a refreshing blend of open spaces and cosy nooks, parquetry floors, and walls of books. From the inside, the irregular placement of windows made sense: they framed forest scenes and garden views, and so added a botanical component to an extensive art collection.

'It's magnificent, isn't it?' Zita shared my delight. 'A friend of mine designed it.' One look at the enormous round window circling the snow-capped woods told me exactly who that 'friend' was.

Given Rudi's smugness, I expected his mother to be weak and

over-indulgent. But if Frau Schütze was quality pastry, then Frau Elsa Ströhmann, or, I should say, Dr Elsa Ströhmann, was select dessert wine. Not a French sauterne, mind you; there was nothing syrupy or voluptuous about her. Instead, Dr Elsa had a cool and practical manner. Everything about her carriage and speech bespoke professional expertise and common sense. Her navy wrap dress and court shoes suited her svelte, athletic figure; and since she required reading glasses, she wore them on a chain around her neck. But she was neither aloof nor officious. Her sangfroid was simply the frost you taste in a late harvest Dürnsteiner; for her conversation was warm and intelligent, borne of education and experience and, as I learned from Zita and her mother, extreme personal hardship.

Her first marriage, to Captain Josef von Krain, had been difficult. Severely injured during the War, he was not the man she had vowed to love and cherish during those days of wine and roses that had defined the old Empire. But she had been faithful to him, had cared for him and supported him, and had nursed him through his final illness; which details Frau Schütze emphasised for her daughter's benefit. Those years of fermentation had developed in the fruit that was her soul a complex nectar. Physically, she had aged gracefully. Her face was lined, and her makeup confined to subtle tints for she was very fair; while her square jaw, prominent nose, and heavy-lidded eyes rendered her handsome rather than pretty. But the strength and harmony of her features, combined with her calm and unpretentious demeanour made her beautiful.

As for the Kirchner, its jagged lines and garish colours fully convinced me of Ailine's selection of Dresden as a suitable address. Dr Elsa, however, was very fond of the painting which had originally belonged to a Jewish colleague who had been obliged to sell his art collection to finance his emigration from Germany.

'I would not go to Germany if I were you,' she replied when I mentioned my travel plans; for I was determined to find out about Ailine in person. 'We travelled to Berlin for the Olympics. Having heard of Hitler's less than savoury activities from friends, we wanted to see for ourselves. All seemed in order during the Games; but afterwards, one only had to look Jewish to be barred from restaurants and hotels. You would not fare well.' She did not need to say more: a stroll down Taborstrasse sufficed.

Like Hubie, Dr Elsa's caution was imbued with the same wariness; but it carried greater authority, given her more recent experience and professional competence. As one of Vienna School of Medicine's first women graduates, whose career had included the treatment of war injuries, she was a resolute, forward thinking, and thoroughly modern woman who had no time for

Hitler's Germany. She and her husband, Dr Robert Ströhmann, had championed Chancellor Dollfuss, not only for his opposition to Hitler, but also because they admired his vision of Austria as a democratic republic, built on the principles of *Rerum Novarum*, which respected the common dignity of all regardless of race, rank, wealth, or class. Later, they were appalled by the Ständestaat's truncation of political rights; and were so disgusted by Dollfuss' outlawing of the Social Democrats that they allied themselves with the offended party.

The Ständestaat, Frau Schütze countered, had been necessary to combat Nazism and Communism during grave economic crisis. Now that Austria was recovering, political freedoms would soon be restored. Even the monarchy might return, which in that good lady's eyes constituted the best resolution. Could Austria hold out in the meantime? her hostess questioned. If Austria was Elsa Ströhmann, I thought, she probably would.

Little wonder she was fond of Zita, who possessed similar independence of mind and will. In that regard, Zita was perhaps as much inspired by her future mother-in-law as she was by Emil; although her ideas were put to rather different ends. To what extent, if any, was Dr Elsa aware that Zita was cheating on her son? None, it seemed. Zita was so blithe she appeared incapable of deceit; and while Dr Elsa was reserved, she was sincere; and she expected (and no doubt received) the same candour from others. Both women enjoyed art and architecture and thrived on intelligent conversation. Upon listening to their discussion of the layout of a small alcove and witnessing Dr Elsa's very favourable reception of Zita's coffee set (which she had commissioned), I concluded that she was looking forward to the latter's marriage to Rudi because she would acquire a daughter who shared her tastes and aspirations. That her son was taking a wife was incidental.

While I would have been more satisfied if I had seen her corpse, the likelihood that Ailine had died at the hands of the Swastikas also became increasingly plausible. Nazi thuggery was irrepressible. Before the hunting trip, the body of a young man was recovered from forests in Burgenland. The newspapers reported that he had been murdered by four youths, all NSDAP members, in retribution for leaving the outlawed party.

Then, after I returned, I visited the Epstein's bakery and found the windows smashed. The Swastikas were responsible, David Epstein informed me as he swept the glass. Apparently, a Jewish merchant, protesting the persecution of Jews in Germany, had hurled a brick though the window of Vienna's German tourist office, opposite the Opernhaus, in which hung a large portrait of Hitler. One thousand windows must be smashed to atone for the insult, the Nazis proclaimed, so hooligans armed with bricks and crow bars wreaked havoc in Leopoldstadt.

Meanwhile, floral tributes piled outside the tourist office, and the window remained unrepaired despite the cold. Frau Geplapper herself deposited a bunch of daisies in reparation for the 'disgraceful act of Jewish Bolshevism'.

'He ought to be ashamed of himself,' she remarked, implying Emil. Nazi sympathisers were many, it seemed, and if the government could not keep order, they argued, well, the sooner an Anschluss with Germany, the better.

Then, while I was Christmas shopping in Mariahilf, a stink bomb exploded in Herzmansky's store. Sickened by the stench of rotten egg, I hurried outside with hundreds of women in furs, kid gloves, and elegant millinery. What next? Nazi vengeance was limitless. And if that was what they did to innocent people, it was quite understandable that they could kill someone like Ailine.

My recent experiences gave me good reason to believe Hubie's testimony; and from the brevity of his explanations, which he communicated in fearful tones, I inferred that he had made his enquiries at considerable personal risk. Still, although I knew him to be incapable of fabrication, I sensed he was withholding critical details and pressed him for more during a long walk through the Schönbrunn grounds one mild winter's afternoon.

'Anyway, Hubie, why were you in Munich?'

'I told you, Phoebe. I was working in my uncle's law firm.'

'And you actually met with Ailine in Dresden?'

'Very briefly. But when I visited a couple of days later as arranged, her apartment was empty. The Gestapo—'

'Gestapo?'

'The Geheime Staatspolizei. It is the Nazi state police force.'

'Was she arrested?'

'I beg of you not to ask me anymore, Phoebe. If your aunt is imprisoned, think that she is serving a just sentence for murdering your mother. If she is dead, it is in God's hands. I promised I would try to find out for you when I am next in Berlin. Meanwhile, can you not leave the matter be?'

But I could not and wondered how else I was to find out.

Quite by accident, an opportunity came my way via Café Museum when the Socialists underwent one of Franz's cake-fork dissections. The only way Austria could maintain independence in the wake of the current disturbances was if Chancellor Schuschnigg sought Social Democrat support, Franzl observed as he pulled apart his cherry strudel. Even the Legitimists were in favour of making concessions to ensure Socialist collaboration against Hitler. Schuschnigg would never agree, argued Hubie, and rightly so.

'You would not enlist the support of the Socialists, Huberle?' queried Rudi.

'Never. Concede to the Socialists and we would rot from the inside. Chancellor Schuschnigg does well to oppose them. We have the Socialists to thank for the political turmoil we have suffered for nearly a century.'

'Not to mention the Jews,' Franz added. 'After all, most Socialists are Jews.'

'You mean, they are Jews by birth,' acknowledged Hubie, 'but remember, Franzl, not all Jews are Socialists.'

'Maybe so,' Rudi remarked, 'but there are further connections. After all, Stalin's pogroms have been responsible for our more recent Jewish problem, and the Jews in Russia supported the Bolsheviks.'

'The Ostjuden are entirely Stalin's fault,' agreed Franz.

'You forget Hitler,' Hubie added. 'If it wasn't for Germany's trading policies with Romania, there wouldn't be so many Jews coming to Austria from those parts.'

'Listen to you!' I scolded. 'I cannot believe you're all so prejudiced!'

'You have missed the p-p-point, Phoebe,' Hubie replied. 'The gist of our observations is that the recent immigration of Jews from the East has provoked a surge in anti-Semitism in Austria, which arises more from the unemployment crisis in the lower classes than from attitudes to religion or race.'

'Even the Jews are anti-Semitic,' Franz mused. 'Perhaps they need their Promised Land after all.'

'And where would that be?' Hubie prompted.

'Madagascar,' chortled Rudi.

'But why not the Land of Israel?'

'Pfui, Huberle! The British won't allow it. Nor will the Arabs.'

'Then where should they go, Franzl? You are always advocating self-determination. Do not the Jews have a right to establish their own n-n-nation like everyone else?'

'Perhaps. Meanwhile, if we united with Germany,' Franz prodded his strudel with his fork, 'we could handle the Semite and the Bolshevik simultaneously.'

'I suppose it is to Hitler's credit that he has put an end to Communism,' Hubie acknowledged.

Now, if anything united the three young men, it was their hatred of Bolshevism. For Hubie, it had caused the downfall of his beloved monarchy, and its loathsome atheism was a violation of nature, morality, tradition, righteousness, and the social order.

'True, true,' observed Rudi, who added that the Marxist nirvana of classlessness was counter to natural hierarchy. 'Always there will be predators and there will be prey, and within every species there is natural selection. Those who survive do so because they are best fitted. It is a fact of life.'

'I would not fare well in a Communist society,' Franz dabbed the cherries and cream from his lips. 'Consider this. For the Marxists, crime is justified by class exploitation, and the true criminals are the bureaucrats and capitalists. Those who make the laws are the ones responsible for the crimes. And the criminal? He is a victim of the system and should be shown clemency rather than be punished. Since I am a bureaucrat, they would regard me as a criminal. Me? A criminal? How can I be a criminal? All I do is implement legislation, so I am as much a victim of the law as those I prosecute. For I tell you, to be a lawyer is to suffer on two accounts: My clients exploit me, and so does the system. Perhaps I should stage a revolution.'

'And if you did, it would get no further than this c-c-coffeehouse,' Hubie jested in his dry way.

'You are right, Huberle. I will exploit another strudel instead. More coffee, anyone?'

Hubie excused himself, for he had a concert.

'I understand that Hitler's work camps have been particularly successful in dealing with the Reds,' Rudi continued after Hubie had left. 'I once saw a film about one near Dachau. The inmates experience life in an authentic commune, instead of frittering their time away on speculation. Class distinctions are eliminated. Everyone follows a strict regime of work according to ability, productivity, and skill. Of course, work is balanced by adequate recreation. After all, isn't that what they campaign for? Each camp is self-sufficient. And, to top it off, there's a healthy degree of repression to encourage revolution. It has a tremendous reforming effect. Nothing like being beaten with your own stick, yes?'

'Ah, Communism!' Franz tucked into his second strudel. 'What a panacea for communists!'

'Are women imprisoned in these camps?' I inquired.

'A camp for women has been established in Saxony. Why do you wish to know?'

'An aunt of mine was arrested in Dresden.' And I enriched my account with my own experience of Ailine's self-serving cant regarding common ownership and equality – maxims by which she had justified her destruction of my home.

'Marxist scum, ja? Listen, I have colleague from Dresden who is at present staying with me.' Rudi kept an apartment near the university. 'His father is *Kriminalkommissar*. He may be able to assist you. Would you like me to make inquiries?'

❖❖❖

I had further reason to discuss the Jewish Question with Hubie the following afternoon. We met, as arranged, after a Walzermädeln rehearsal at the Ronacher. My cousin-of-sorts was polite, but his frigid bow and stuttered greeting to Alma and Lori were tinged with acerbity. The only other occasion I had encountered a similar tone in Hubie's manners was with Emil, whom he regarded as the vilest representative of 'Atheist Bolshevism'. But neither Alma nor Lori were in any way connected with the Left. Lori's father was a wealthy industrialist; Alma was part of the cultural elite. Could his coldness be because the two women were Jewish? Not that being Jewish mattered in any way to them, for neither had genuine interest in anything beyond life's little luxuries, which they enjoyed aplenty. Alma, furthermore, had not forgotten the dressing down Hubie had given her during that Sunday lunch with her family, and she glared at him in her superior, slightly short-sighted way. Lori smiled glibly, tossed her curls, and hurried after her friend.

'Why you are all so hostile?' I complained as they drove away, Alma hugging her boyfriend, and Lori next to Arno the Alsatian in the back.

'You are upset?' Hubie was genuinely surprised. 'The two ladies are very fine musicians,' he added by way of appeasement.

'And so are you. You have much in common; which is why I don't understand your coldness.'

'I had chance to accompany Lori for recitals at the Academy...' Words refused to manifest, or else he denied them utterance, and he barricaded his adjutant emotions behind a single frustrated shake of his head.

'You fancied her?'

'Ja.'

And Lori had snubbed him.

'So, it's not because she's Jewish?'

'Is that what you think? Nothing could be further from the truth. Lori's brother Eugene is a good fellow. We have our differences, but he is sincere and thoughtful. His religion is as important to him as mine is to me. I hope his kibbutz is a success. I don't agree with it, but better a success than a failure, yes?

'Regarding Alma, what can I say, Phoebe?' he resumed after another lengthy silence. 'Her father is my concertmaster. He is a good man in his way, and I owe him and his family respect. All I will tell you is that I do not dislike Alma because she is Jewish. I have no reason to hate the Jews. I have Jewish ancestry, and I do not know a single person in Vienna who does not have Jewish blood. I work alongside Jews and have Jewish friends; most of my music teachers and university professors have been Jews; I owe my life to Jewish doctors. The Faith I profess is the perfection of

Jewish religion. The God I worship came to earth as a Jew. Everything I cherish has some connection with Jews. But do not ask me to approve scandalous or frivolous behaviour, or to allow anyone to ridicule in any way my beliefs. I see no reason to cultivate friendship with such people regardless of their race or creed. I apologise if I appeared hostile. I will rectify that.'

A few days before Christmas, Rudi knocked at my door.

'Forgive me if my visit is inopportune,' he began, 'I happened to be in the neighbourhood. Would another time be more convenient? It is only that I have news of considerable importance to tell you. What a beautiful apartment you live in,' he smiled.

'It was my father's.'

'He has very— how do you say, eclectic taste.'

'In that regard, I would say it is rather like your parents' home.' And while the coffee brewed, I told him what I knew of the various pieces.

'And that is your father, yes?' he indicated the portrait. 'It must be! I see a resemblance. Schöner, ja?'

He waited until I was seated before proceeding.

'I have information received concerning your aunt,' Rudi combined a soupçon of charm with an equal measure of deference and stirred it into his coffee. 'It seems Huberle was right. Your aunt was indeed person of interest. In June 1934, she was detained by the Gestapo in Dresden. Since then, she has ceased to be of concern.'

'Meaning what? Is she dead?'

'Ja, she is dead, Phoebe,' he spoke gently and handed me a letter. 'She suffered heart attack whilst in prison. No more will she trouble you.'

How could someone without a heart suffer a heart attack? Well, it was possible; for there, neatly typed on the official letterhead of the Geheime Staatspolizei, a mere paragraph to the effect, and a signature. Was her death as clean and efficient? I pictured Ailine in a dark cell, cold and motionless, her eyes staring. Had she suffered maltreatment, or had she perished from guilt or fear? Yet, what a gross injustice that I, the victim, was exonerated from the arbitration of her fate. Pity she had died of natural causes. But what did it matter? My hunt was over! Ailine was chaff in the wind, while I could flourish like the laurel.

'May I get you a drink, Phoebe?'

'More than that, Rudi. You can get me my fur, for we are going to celebrate!'

❖❖❖

I lay in a soft meadow surrounded by tulips, listening to the waves and the distant calls to prayers.

'Ah, Kerem,' I sighed and smiled at the figure seated nearby, 'How I have missed you!'

'Phoebe, it is I, Hubie.'

'Hubie? What are you doing here?'

'You are a case!' laughed a nymph.

'Shh, Zita!' A plump hand touched my own. 'Phoebe, this is Frau Schütze, and you are home in Hietzing.'

'Hietzing? How did I manage that?'

'Trottel! Don't you remember? Hubie found you singing in front of the German Tourist Office. How he managed to get you on the tram I don't know, for you were more than merry when you arrived here. "Dear and blessed friends!" you crowed, "Let us raise our glasses to the Good Spirit and drink the golden wine of joy!" Mutti tried to give you some coffee, but you refused. You said it was the Devil's drink. "Bring me the fruit of paradise! I wish to eat of the cherry tree!" you shouted. It was hopeless explaining to you that we didn't have any cherries; it only made you demand them more. And then you waltzed around the foyer singing, "She's up to her neck in a river of blood!" Hubie eventually caught you and you cried, "Take me to Cithera!" and vomited all over him.'

'I thought I was in the harem at the Sultan's palace.'

'No chance of that!'

'Zita! Stop giggling and help me make some coffee for Phoebe.'

'You are in the Ottoman room, dear cousin,' Hubie's explanation enabled me to make sense of the bed with its scrolled headboard and sumptuous canopy, the heavy swagged curtains, and the exotic Persian prints and golden arabesques. Hubie, in contrast, wore his tweed suit and bow tie. 'It is the room we reserve for guests,' he continued. 'Are you comfortable?'

'As if I were in Paradise. But oh, my head is pounding! Did you know, Hubie, that Ailine is dead?'

'And you, my dear cousin, have hangover. Who is Kerem?'

'A handsome prince who inspires my dreams. Hubie, I need to confess.'

'You may— confess later. For now, you must rest.'

Shadowed in the confessional, I admitted my drunkenness, for drunk I was. According to Hubie, who was so distressed by the incident that he blamed himself for not being with me, I was blind drunk when he brought me to his home at one o'clock in the morning.

'All I can remember is drinking kirsch and dancing in the snow; and I vaguely remember a zither playing. If I did anything else wrong, I have no recollection of it.'

'Was anyone with you, my child?' inquired the gentle, ghostly voice from the other side of the screen.

'A friend. He drove me to a tavern where we celebrated. It was only a couple of drinks.'

And Rudi had left me none the wiser when I asked him. 'Drunk?' he laughed, 'You? Dead drunk? You were sober when we parted company at the Opernhaus. You said you wanted to wait for Hubie. You were up to mischief, yes?'

But if you think I will present here a complete account of my misdemeanours, Roddy, think again. Suffice it to say that I gave my psychotic monologue full voice and told all my sins with guileless simplicity, succumbing to a practice I had known since childhood. And it was quite understandable that I did; for what is the Jesuit expression? Give me the child of seven?

But there was nothing Jesuitical about my confessor (for a start, Brother Rosengarten was a Capuchin).[21] Nor was he the snivelling, conniving, lustful scoundrel one finds in gothic fiction. He was a martyr: a priest pelted daily with the sins of countless penitents; and he heard me with patience and calm. He was more concerned that I had not received the Sacraments than he was about my murderous intentions. And his advice? Well, forget sophisticated psychoanalysis. It was positively saccharine:

'Pray for your aunt's soul,' he whispered, 'and I will remember her, and you, and your parents in my Mass tomorrow. Receive Holy Communion and use this time before Christmas to prepare your heart for the Christ Child. In penance say one Hail Holy Queen; and now make the Act of Contrition.'

Illumined by rows of votive candles, Hubie was praying in a side chapel when I floated from the confessional, my sins shriven; my heart light; my mind freed of its nightmare. I deposited a Groschen, lit a candle, and made my penance. Then I took another candle and prayed for Ailine. Had Brother Rosengarten required that I forgive Ailine, well that would have been a penance I could not fulfil. But I could pray for her now that she was dead. Forgiveness I would consign to God, the Father of Mercies. It was no longer my affair.

'You have ice skates, yes?' asked Hubie as we left the Kapuzinerkirche.

'I found some skates in my apartment. If they belonged to Dad, they'd probably fit me. We shared the same shoe size. Dad loved to joke about it.'

'Then join us at the Eislaufverein! You do not know how to

---

[21] *Brother Rosengarten:* In Austria, ordained Capuchins insist on being called 'Brother' rather than 'Father'.

skate? Don't worry! I will teach you.'

'Very well. But first, Hubie, I must send an urgent telegram. I'll meet you there.'

At the Post Office I penned the following:

Lucy. Apologies late notice. Not coming Christmas. Will write soon. Phoebe.

And then, upon returning home to fetch my skates, I picked up my scrapbook, took it to the tourist office, and tossed it onto the pile of floral tributes. I stood in the snow, wrapped in my white mink coat, and gazed at my reflection which in the wintery twilight spread a spectral haze across the broken glass. My eyes, with their large, liquid orbs, retained their spaniel sweetness; but behind them lurked the German Führer's cold, hard stare. How odd, that such a harsh expression could arise from a flaccid, commonplace face. I could easily imagine Hitler selling chestnuts on the street corner; whereas the nearby portly gentleman handing a cone to a hungry lad could never be a Chancellor. Had I fulfilled my vendetta, I suppose my eyes might also have turned mean and callous. Or maybe, by some strange magic, my beauty might be preserved but my soul befouled like Dorian Gray's portrait. Yes, like Dorian, I would prefer beauty at any cost.

'So, it is well that *you* have seen to the crime. The sins are yours, not mine,' I told Herr Hitler.

Certainly, I could not condone everything Hitler did, but I was grateful for what he had done for me.

Interlude

.

Café Bellaria, Vienna, 12 January 1957

'I would like to be a queen when I grow up,' Mellie declared as we took our seats and ordered coffee, chocolate, and cake. We had been to see *Sissi: The Young Empress*, and, as well as the film, which was screened to a full house, a café afternoon tea was an extra special treat for the children.

'Then you must be very wise, kind, and good,' I replied, fondly recalling the young Empress' graciousness towards the Magyars who opposed her being crowned Queen of Hungary.

'I will ride a horse across the plains like Count Andrassy,' Klem began rising to the trot, but resisted further temptation to use his chair as a saddle and whip himself into a canter.

'And may you be a good master, Klem.'

'Was it like that when you were little, Mumija?'[22]

'Oh no. That was a hundred years ago. I'm not quite that old.' Since the Soviets smothered Hungary's independence, however, a century felt like a millenium.

'Is Očka[23] looking after the Hungarians?' asked Mellie.

'Yes, Očka is looking after the Hungarians.'

'Will he be riding a horse?'

'I don't think so, Klemi.'

'How long will he be away this time?' asked Roddy.

'He'll be back and forth. Ah, here we are!' Klem and Mellie clapped as the waiter served their treats.

---

[22] *Mumija*: (Slovenian) Mummy.
[23] *Očka*: (Slovenian) Daddy.

Peter had left at dawn that morning, a work pattern that had been in place since October when the first refugees escaped over the Hungarian border.

The crisis itself had erupted after university students in Budapest protested the Hungarian Communist government's increasingly Soviet policies. They cut the hammer and sickle from the Hungarian Flag. Chanting 'Russia go home!' they removed Stalin's two storey bronze statue from its site (formerly that of a church). Their demands they voiced via a nationwide wireless broadcast, at which point the state police fired shots into the gathering crowds. In the early hours of the following morning, Soviet tanks rolled into Budapest. Fighting continued for five days, the rebels successful. The government collapsed, its leaders fled to Russia, and the Soviets withdrew. Hungary's new leaders formed an independent government. A week later, seventeen Soviet divisions entered the country, easily overcame the hastily organised resistance, and surrounded Budapest. Over breakfast we listened, stunned, as Kossuth Rádió, broadcasting from that city, fell silent. What began as a trickle, soon became a flood as students, families, orphans, prominent rebels, and members of the military fled over the border into Austria. The onset of winter brought its own complications, with many refugees suffering from hyperthermia and illness, not to mention wounds, in addition to their woes. Peter was co-ordinating medical treatment and relief.

I could easily imagine what Hubie would say of the situation.

'So, Dresden?' Roddy interrupted my thoughts, which had roamed freely, given the children were happily occupied.

'Dresden. To this day, Roddy, I have no idea how Dad knew about Ailine being in Dresden.'

'Mr Straughan told me.'

'I beg your pardon?'

'Lucy's dad. He's been like a father to me. Told me when we were working together on the bike. I ride a motorcycle,' he added, noting my surprise. 'Yeah, Mum wasn't too pleased about it, either. Sold it before I sailed. Mr Straughan said Dad asked him years ago. Told Dad that he heard Ailine enthusiastically mention Dresden in conversation.'

'You've been doing a bit of sleuthing yourself.'

'So?'

'Dad,' I sighed. 'To this day, Roddy, I regret how harsh I was with him. Then again, as he himself liked to say, nothing happens that is not intended for our salvation. He was a gentle man – and a gentleman – through and through. Despite his many and considerable talents, he never boasted. He was handsome without being vain; charming— passionate even, yet never licentious;

generous to a fault, and a friend to all. I only wish he was alive to tell.'

'You're lucky. I wish—'

I had seen it before, that angry flash, on the rare occasions Roddy dared look me in the face. Obscured by spectacles, his eyes were a softer brown than Dad's; but his glance was electric.

'Roddy, I don't know what is worse: the death of a parent you knew, or the death of a parent you never knew. The pain of loss; or the pain of ignorance. To be left with feeble, childish memories; or to be denied memory altogether. But, as a daughter, a wife, and a mother, what I can say is that Dad loved you.'

'He never knew me! He never even knew I existed!'

'He loved your mother; and in loving her, he was prepared to love any children she would bear. He *began* to love you. His love lay in his hope. Had he lived to see you, Roddy, from what I know of Dad, I cannot fathom the depth of his affection.'

Part Four

•

Germany Awaken!

•

December 1937

44

Joy to the World

'I ASSURE YOU, IT WILL NOT take you long to get your balance,' Hubie coaxed me onto Vienna's enormous open-air ice rink. I wobbled on the blades of my skates and wondered which foot to move first. Arms flailing, I shuffled along the ice, slipped, and stopped myself falling by clutching Hubie who drifted beside me, his tall form surprisingly graceful. 'That is good, Phoebe!' he held me steady. 'With practice, you will glide!'

Truly, I have all winter to practise, I mused as I blundered along. And the next. And a third, if I chose. I could stay in Vienna my whole life long if I wanted. I may have looked like a chicken trying to fly; but my heart was skating as smoothly as Franz and Rudi who zipped through the crowds in a lively game of tag.

'Hubie, Phoebe, come! We're taking photos!' Zita swished past. 'Karl wants to try out his new camera!'

Heidi, Inge, Fifi, Sisi, Zita and I huddled on a bench. Franz, Rudi, Hubie, and Karl clustered behind us. We called a fellow skater to take our picture: a gleeful portrait of family and friends.

'Until tonight!' I farewelled them and popped in to see Emil.

'I need to buy a Christmas tree.'

'And you come to a bookshop?'

'You know what I mean.'

'Come on, then,' he grumbled. Having abandoned shaving since the cold set in, he now sported a short bushy beard, and curls scrambled round his collar. 'Mind the shop for me, Albrecht,' he patted his elderly friend on the shoulder. 'We're getting a tree for Yoyzl Nacht.'[24]

Give Emil a project and you could rest assured that he would carry it out to the last detail. Having bartered for the tree and lugged it home, he then took charge of the decoration using the ornaments I had found in a cupboard. He placed the baubles and trinkets and slender white candles on the branches, and

---

[24] *Yoyzl Nacht*: Christmas Eve (Yoyzl: slang diminutive for Jesus).

periodically stepped back to ascertain the aesthetics of his arrangement.

'Now remember,' he advised from high on the ladder, having fixed the angel to the top, 'You can't light the candles until nightfall. That's the tradition here.'

'Tradition? Since when has tradition mattered to you?'

'I thought it mattered to you. Do you have a nativity?'

The nativity figures were another discovery. That they were wrapped in pieces of foreign newspaper much intrigued my scruffy friend, for the paper turned out to be an early edition of *Pravda*, a carryover from Dad's Red youth, and, given his fascination with language, probably constituted an attempt to learn Russian. Emil, who could read Cyrillic, was as much absorbed with the paper as he was with arranging Mary and Joseph, shepherds and animals.

'It's all about the man in the street, isn't it?' he repositioned St Joseph for at least the fifth time. 'Well, he was a carpenter, wasn't he?'

'What?'

'Christmas. Working people matter. Children matter. Families matter. That the poor and needy are important.'

'I always thought it was about redemption.'

'But through love, not power. Is that right?'

'I suppose so.'

'Do you believe in it? All this,' he indicated the decorations. Observing my hesitation, he asked again, quite emphatically, 'Well, do you or not?'

'Since you insist, then yes.'

'You should if you go to all this trouble.'

'You're the one who's gone to the trouble.'

'May I show Albrecht?'

'Of course. And you're both invited for a meal. It's only fish, I'm afraid. I couldn't get anything else.'

'That's traditional.'

He was delighted with his present: a fountain pen engraved with his name; while Albrecht fondled his new cashmere scarf. 'It's blue, Albrecht,' Emil explained, 'like the sky in summer. I only have chocolates and a bottle of Gumpolds for you, Phoebe.'

'Then we can celebrate like kings! Frohe Weihnachten, Emil! Frohe Weihnachten, Albrecht!'

At the Schützes' later that night, I waited with Hubie and his siblings outside Herr Beethoven's Room while Professor and Frau Schütze decorated the tree. Tinkling a tiny crystal handbell, Frau Schütze welcomed her 'kinder' inside. The Schütze Christmas tree glowed with candles and was decked with handcrafted ornaments amassed over two decades of children, not to mention heirlooms from past generations. Sweets wrapped in coloured tissue were also tied to the branches, and Frau Schütze invited us all to partake. Professor Schütze sat at the piano and bid us sing 'Silent Night'.

Our presents were abundant in thoughtfulness rather than quantity. I received my first *trachten* – a dirndl and petticoats, blouse, bodice, and jacket – handmade and embroidered by Frau Schütze, Zita, Sisi, and Heidi. Did I approve? Given the care that had been put into the manufacture, and the authenticity of the garments, not to mention the generosity of the gift itself, to wear those clothes was an honour, and I said as much.

'Put them on, Phoebe!' clapped an eager Heidi.

I withdrew to the Ottoman Room where Zita laced me in full Austrian dress.

'What do you think?' she asked.

I felt the constraint of centuries – my breasts and waist cinched by tradition. While the outfit reinforced my sense of belonging, it also imposed upon me the obligation to conform to a set of values which, although appealing in their solidity and in their promise of security and devotion, challenged my preference for independence and self-sufficiency. Quaint, yet attractive (for it was attractive in its own way), such old-fashioned costuming would take getting used to if I were to feel at ease.

'Zita, should I braid my hair?'

'You'd look a scream in plaits. Frankly, I cannot imagine you singing, "My garland, whom will it happiness bring?". You're much too exotic. You'd be more suited to playing Scheherezade.'

I put my hand to my bare neck and recalled my laughter in the bazaar when Kerem bought me the Turkish scarf and tried to arrange it. I gathered my hair, twisted it up, and imagined the scarf with its glorious blues, and the sapphire earrings dangling in place of my pearls.

'Heavens, you've gone all teary!' teased Zita. 'I wasn't serious, you know. I wouldn't like my life depending upon my ability to entertain a Sultan.'

'Well, *I* can't see *you* tending sheep, either.'

'That is the role I must play. Although, I might enjoy it more in your company. Come on, dry up! You look charming. Let's show the others!'

Surprised that I had a present for him, Hubie opened his gift and stared at the pair of gold cufflinks inside.

'They have the Imperial Coat of Arms,' he whispered.

'Dad left them to you. But consider them as much a present from me as they are from him. They were a from the Emperor. There's a note inside explaining everything.'

He opened the yellowed paper that had been folded to fit in the top of the case, and read:

Presented to me by Emperor Franz Josef I, on occasion of my becoming a Viennese citizen the day of my twenty-first birthday, 24th March, 1911.

'Now that I know you, Hubie, I know they're in good hands.'

'I will greatly treasure them. Thank you. The Christkind has also brought something special for you, Phoebe.'

He lifted the Child from the manger and passed me the gift that lay amidst the straw. I undid the string and carefully pulled away the paper. Inside was a box. And inside that was an enamelled locket embellished with silver daisies with seed pearl centres. I opened one compartment and found two painted miniatures: one featuring Maman; the other, Dad.

Hubie paused before he spoke. 'I hope you do not think me too bold in doing this. I had the pictures painted from a photograph. It represents the past, the present, and the future. In your parents you have the happy memory of the past— for I am sure you have happy memories of them, yes? My gift of the locket is the present.'

'And the future?'

'Open the reverse compartment and you will see.'

'It's empty.'

'The future is for you to discover. May it, too, be happy, Phoebe. I hope— I hope that I might also be part of it. I would like to be part of it.'

'I would like that, too. Would you help me put it on?'

Reverently, he took the locket, and wondered how he was to perform such a task. I turned away and lifted my hair to make it easier. He lowered the locket over my breast.

'The clasp,' he murmured, 'I—I cannot fasten it.'

'They're always fiddly.'

After much fumbling, he secured the chain, and I turned again to show him. With his bashful, stag-like eyes, he gazed, hesitating, as if he sensed he should not; yet he could not help himself. The bright stars, the warm and peaceful room, the glowing candles, the sweet, spicy, woodland scents, invited contemplation.

'Come,' he held out his hand and smiled, heeding now the church bells' midnight chimes. 'Let us worship together.'

45

A Christmas Carol

MERRY WITH CHRISTMAS CHEER, Franz, Hubie, and I returned to Linke Wienzeile and raced each other up the stairs. Christmas had been a true communion. After midnight's Mass of the Angels, we heard the Shepherd's Mass at dawn, during which I received the Sacrament for the first time in almost a decade. How I cherished the holy calm! Then we adored the Child and joyously sang *Adeste Fideles*. Mass of the Divine Word followed later that morning, after which we feasted on tender venison stuffed with chestnuts; cabbage and apple spiced with caraway and fennel; roast potatoes, and cumin laced pumpkin. Professor Schütze brought out his finest apricot liqueur. 'Your health, and a blessed year to come!' we toasted. Linzertorte completed our fare. We laughed through charades, sang carol after carol, snacked on gingerbread, played hide the thimble, and shared family stories. Meanwhile, snow fell as tranquil as manna, blessing the wintry world beyond. Nourishing hidden shoots, it prepared a glorious Spring: another Resurrection.

'I keep this up, and I could join Rudi in a Himalayan climb!' wheezed Franz.

'Do you suppose there are rats in the Himalayas?' I panted, 'for there are rats here in the Majolikahaus: enormous rats. Big ones: big as motor cars. And fat: fat as bankers.'

'Huberle will know. Are there rats in Tibet, my brother?'

'I am not sure. But I can see two little mice before me. And I am a big p-p-pussy cat in need of some dinner. I will p-p-pounce if you are not— careful. Meow!'

The great six-and-a-half-foot pussycat sprang. Screaming, I grabbed Franz's hand, and we ran helter-skelter up the stairs, tripped on the top landing, and fell under Hubie's clutches.

'Now, who will I eat f-f-first?' he meowed. 'This chubby little boy mouse? He will be good meat, yes? Hmm... I think I might prefer the— pretty little girl mouse with her soft brown fur... '

'Stop it, Hubie! Let me go!' I screamed, for Hubie had scooped me in his arms, and was licking his lips over me, smacking his chops and purring unctuously. 'Put me down! Odalia's door is open! We'll wake the baby!'

The door to my neighbour's apartment was swung wide, and the light was on. Yet there were no sounds or movement to indicate that anyone was home.

'Oda!' I called, 'Are you there?'

'Shhh!' Hubie whispered, 'I hear something.'

We tip-toed through to the bedroom where we found the baby in his cot, cold, weak, and panting. Franz offered to fetch a doctor.

'Herr Fährmann, is that you?' called a voice.

Frau Weissmüller, wrapped in her dressing gown, her hair in curlers, stood outside the elevator. 'She's gone mad, I tell you, Fräulein Raye! And thank God you're dressed! Fetch Herr Fährmann!'

In the dark courtyard, amidst prancing snowflakes and illumined by a small wood fire, Oda wore a long robe, and her blonde hair was plaited in a single braid. She sang loudly in a strong but curiously childlike voice:

> Gentle Mother,
> From your pure blood
> Springs forth new life.
> How your child
> Will change the world!
> And you, fair mother,
> Will shine like a star;
> While your heart, like fire,
> Warms the earth.

From the shadows crept rotund Herr Weissmüller in his pyjamas. Slowly, he approached the singing Odalia, and nearly reached her when she turned on him.

'Nasty rat!' she shouted.

I ran downstairs and banged on the bookshop door.

Emil swore and snarled; then he bristled into action like a badger on the attack and joined Herr Weissmüller and Hubie, who had also ventured into the courtyard. In their attempt to capture Odalia, who brandished a flaming log like a torch, they triangulated, co-ordinating their moves with signals as they surrounded and closed in upon her. Oda, however, was no deer. She ran at Hubie and pushed him over. While Hubie groped for his glasses, Emil lumbered out in front while Herr Weissmüller launched a bumbling charge from behind.

'Get her, Vati!' the Weissmüller boys cheered from the balconies, in company with other residents. 'Go, Herr Fährmann! Come on, Dr Schütze!'

But Oda, now wielding two fiery torches, broke through all three and ran straight into Andreas Geplapper. He extinguished her flares in the snow, wrapped her with his coat, and took her inside to hails of applause. Siren blaring, a fire truck screeched to a halt and firemen thundered into the building. Their alarm subsided when they saw the smouldering pile in the middle of the courtyard, and they strolled back through the foyer with a curious air of disappointment and relief just as Franz arrived with Dr Elsa.

Aside from troublesome nappy rash, baby Waldo was dehydrated and cold. 'Had he been left any longer, he would have needed hospitalisation,' Dr Elsa observed. 'Still, he will need to be watched. Can I rely on you, Phoebe?'

'I've never looked after a baby before.'

'There's always a first time. Keep him warm. Feed him little and often; and if he needs changing, consider it a good sign.'

As she handed him to me, I wondered how I would accommodate him. But he snuggled happily against my breast and I began to rock him and sing and felt strangely content as I watched him grow heavy with sleep, comfortable in my arms. Never had I considered being a mother. With Ailine gone, however, motherhood was possible. A new world opened before me.

'Dr Elsa, do you think he could sleep in my nursery?'

We warmed the room, arranged my cot, and laid the little one down. Dr Elsa demonstrated on my teddy bear how to change a nappy.

'Herr Fährmann, how good to see you again!' A probing professionally raised eyebrow and tilt of the head accompanied her otherwise cordial greeting when Emil entered with scratch marks on his face and a baby bottle in hand. Dr Elsa formally introduced him to the Schütze boys, which was an unnecessary measure; but her qualifying remark, 'Emil Fährmann is a very fine architect. He designed our home,' raised Emil a little further out of the gutter, at least in Franzl's eyes.

'Just as well it's you, Elsa,' Emil replied. 'Oda's meshuga.'[25]

'Her mental state is confused; but she is calm,' Dr Elsa reported when later she joined us for us for a bowl of soup. 'Keep an eye on her overnight, Emil. See that she stays warm and that she doesn't wander. If any of her symptoms worsen, contact me immediately. Here is my card. Are you able to telephone? I will look in tomorrow morning. Boys,' she added to Hubie and Franz, 'My car's outside. I'll give you a lift.'

'How are you?' Emil asked the following morning. But whereas I had been relatively untroubled by my tiny charge, he had spent the night in vigilant attendance. Haggard and bleary-eyed, he

---

[25] *Meshuga*: crazy.

inquired whether I needed any help. My early morning attempt at changing baby had been a blunder involving three nappies, pricked fingers, and a child that squirmed and kicked in a way no teddy bear ever could.

'I had to look after my little sister while my mother was working,' he mumbled through the pins in his mouth as he folded the cloth with impeccable precision. 'I'm going to check on Albrecht. Oda's asleep. Watch her for me, will you?'

A little later, Dr Elsa arrived in the company of a tall and very distinguished gentleman whose high forehead and silver-streaked hair enhanced the kindest, darkest eyes I had ever seen: her husband, Dr Robert Ströhmann, who had recently returned from Boston.

'You've had an interesting night?' he remarked upon greeting me. He had a very polished, fatherly manner. 'And how is your little patient?'

Baby Waldo had recovered well. Dr Robert then examined the sleeping Oda, and quietly exchanged professional opinions with his wife, which discussion he suspended at intervals to question me.

Oda stirred. Both doctors rallied to her side. She opened her eyes and stared vacantly at Dr Elsa who helped her sit. Then she spied Dr Robert.

'Filthy rat!' she snarled as she wrinkled her nose and spat in his face.

'Oda? Odalia Kleidel? She was one of our housemaids,' Rudi explained during an evening of cards. For the past week, my nursery duties had rendered me housebound; my only engagements, visits from my friends. Meanwhile, news of the strange event in the courtyard had circulated through the Majolikahaus, and expressions of sympathy, offers of help, and donations of clothes, food, and blankets were a daily occurrence. Emil had transformed from Bolshevik swine to Good Samaritan; while Andreas Geplapper was viewed with some curiosity as a liberator.

'My parents hired her whilst holidaying in Salzburg a couple of years ago,' Rudi continued. 'They took her back with them to Vienna. Her family needed the money, and Mutti thought to give her an "opportunity".'

'Did she act strangely?' I asked.

'How should I know?' he sorted his cards, 'Mind you, she started coming on a bit strong when we were in Berlin last year. Mutti dismissed her and sent her home. Don't look at me! How could I be responsible for a child that dark? Besides, I think—,' he chuckled at baby Waldo who was being dangled, secure and happy, on Hubie's knee.

'If you know who the father is, then you should inform him,' Hubie attempted to play his hand – a difficult feat; for baby, who had been trying to grab his cards all evening, took the initiative to play a club when hearts were trumps.

'My bet is it happened during that hike she attended – when the League of German Maidens teamed up with the Hitler Youth. Wouldn't be the first time.'

'Regardless of who, how, when or where, Rudi, it's not fair that Emil's shouldered most of the responsibility when it was none of his to begin with,' I retorted.

'A responsible Communist! How refreshing!' Franz observed.

'He's been the beast of burden he so admires,' enjoined Rudi.

'Better a beast of burden than a thoroughbred whose only function is to sire,' Zita cut in.

'True, true,' Rudi accorded, 'It is good we have rid ourselves of the aristocracy, yes?'

'He's such a darling little fellow!' The last thing I wanted was an argument between Hubie and Rudi over the abolition of the upper classes. Fortunately, no one else appeared to want that argument either – not even Hubie – for they all agreed. 'He can roll, you know. This morning, I wanted to do some practice so I put him on the rug. Before I knew it, he was clutching my ankles!'

'I hope he has not inherited his mother's condition,' Rudi resumed. 'My step-father is convinced she has a screw loose.'

'Well, if someone spat in your face and called you a dirty rat, you'd think the same. She was terrifying. Where did they take her?'

'The Steinhof. Her parents arrived yesterday. Mutti suspects they're hiding something. Rural families like that, there's bound to be an imbecile, a loopy aunt or unacknowledged suicide somewhere in the family.'

'What's the Steinhof?'

'The loony bin,' Zita explained.

'What will they do to her?'

'Hydrotherapy, electrotherapy, sedation...' Rudi had long-term familiarity with all things medical.

'You know, Rudi,' Hubie began in an unusually cordial tone, 'I am very— glad you made the decision not to continue with your m-m-medical training. You have such little— interest in restoring health.'

'That is because I believe that preventing illness is far more effective than treating it, as you well know, Huberle. You are not travelling to London with the orchestra?'

'I— prefer to keep close to home during winter, so I am rostered with the Opera. Lucky me, for Bruno Walter is conducting.'

'Lord! Hubie travelling in January!' Zita groaned. 'Stinking out

the train with his cigarettes; scarf wound up to his ears; carrying a
suitcase full of powders and potions, not to mention the
Pneumostat, horn, trunk, an extra coat...'

'I would not wish Asthma on anyone.'

'It's the family curse,' added Franz. 'All of us, save Mutti, have
suffered from it in one form or other. Hubie worst of all.'

'Ja,' Hubie sighed, 'But it has not stopped me from living a full
life.'

'It's probably genetic,' observed Rudi.

'My father said, that after he was wounded a nurse told him the
only thing that could hold him back was a lack of ingenuity,' I
rallied to Hubie's cause. 'Now, if Dad had an abundance of
anything, it was ingenuity. His life after the War became as full as
his life before it.'

'Then he was lucky,' Rudi remarked.

'You call losing both your legs and the use of an arm lucky? He
wasn't lucky. He was determined. He painted, conducted business,
taught violin and languages, gave wireless broadcasts; and he was
a wonderful father.'

'Ja, I call that lucky. But tell me, what about those who are
incapable of living such a full life? Or living a life of any value at
all?'

'They are capable of being cared for,' I smiled at Dad's portrait.
Dad would have replied the same. And I added one of his favourite
maxims, 'Everyone and everything has a place: in time and in
space.'

'Pfui! Clearly you have never encountered *Die Verstümmelten*—
How do you say it in English? It is mutilated, yes? The men
without faces. The ones who have sections of railway platforms
reserved for them, or who are shut away in homes because no one
can bear to look. My father lost an eye, half his nose, and the
lower part of his jaw to shrapnel. He wore a mask of tin to cover
the injury and spent the remaining decade of his life sorting mail
in the back room of the Hietzing post office. A Captain in the
Imperial Army sorting mail! That was his place in time and in
space. And I wouldn't say he was capable of being cared for,
either. That is, unless you wanted to be hit.'

A few days later, I received a letter from Dr Elsa, who wished to
bring Odalia's parents, Herr and Frau Kleidel, to see the baby. She
requested that Emil and I be present.

The Kleidels were sturdy, fresh-faced, apple cheeked folk who
had never been to Vienna, let alone ridden in an elevator. That
afternoon, they arrived on my doorstep, innocent as lambs, having
been shepherded through the city and coaxed into the
Majolikahaus by the Doctors Ströhmann. They were shocked at

what had transpired concerning their daughter. Apparently, not long after Odalia left the Ströhmanns' employ, a family argument provoked her to leave home. No one knew she was pregnant at the time.

'We believe the incident occurred in Berlin,' Dr Robert Ströhmann informed them. 'Our son is at present making enquiries.'

'That is not possible,' Oda's father declared, 'Herr Hitler would not allow such bestiality. It could only happen in Vienna.'

'I assure you, it did not,' inserted Dr Elsa.

'You must be the father,' Herr Kleidel turned on Emil.

'I had nothing to do with it,' Emil protested. 'It so happened, that your daughter prost—'

'She was already pregnant when Herr Fährmann found her,' cut in Dr Robert. 'He has cared for her this past year.'

'Then who was the Jewish son of a bitch who did this?' questioned Herr Kleidel.

'I think Herr Fährmann deserves some compensation, or at least some gratitude for all he has done,' Dr Elsa interrupted. 'Likewise, Fräulein Raye has looked after the child while your daughter has been ill.'

'I do not believe it!' shouted Herr Kleidel. 'It's Jewish trickery on the part of this harlot and her pimp!' he pointed at Emil and me.

'Sir, you have said quite enough!' warned Dr Robert.

'My husband is very upset,' apologised Frau Kleidel. 'It has been a terrible shock. Thank you for all you have done.'

'Perhaps I should make some tea?' I offered. Herr Kleidel blatantly refused and insisted upon returning to Hietzing. The Ströhmanns took their leave more graciously.

'You know you are going to have to give him up,' Hubie reminded me when next he visited, this time in company with his mother and Heidi who provided me with a morning's respite by offering to bath little Waldo.

'But if the Kleidels won't take him, who will look after him? We can't put him in an orphanage! Please don't make me give him up to an orphanage, Hubie! He needs a family!'

'Which is why you cannot keep him.'

'But who? I couldn't bear giving him to someone who would be cruel to him!'

'Then it might comfort you to know that we have found a family. Karl and Fifi have agreed. They can manage. They hope to have many children and they would be happy to count him as their own. He will have a brother close in age, which I know from experience to be a blessing; loving grandparents; and a host of doting uncles and aunts. You will be able to see him, too. We have approached the Kleidels, who are taking Odalia home, and they have given consent.'

'Hubie! That is wonderful news!'

'Your piano is very beautiful,' he bashfully looked away. 'Would you permit me to play?'

'I would love to hear you. You mentioned you play the piano, yet I have never heard you. Do, please.'

'The piano was my second instrument at the Academy.' He adjusted the seat and struck a series of luminous chords. I knew the music at once. It was the Franck violin sonata.

'I accompanied Lori, who performed it for her final recital,' he continued to play, 'Professor Rosé mentioned you wanted to perform it and were looking for accompanist. I have been practising in my spare time and yearning for opportunity to play with you. Would you play with me?'

46

Carnivale

HAD WE BEEN STRANGERS, I would have found Hubie's accompaniment disconcerting. His interpretation was intense; his technique exacting; his tone robust. To make music with him was like scaling mountains that were far more dramatic than the lowly hills of former experience. And rather than protest that such limits were too difficult, I instead plied all my skill to reach the summit. My violin and bow proved able assistants. It had always perturbed me that I could never bring forth the nuances of tone I sensed were hiding inside my instrument – the laughter and tears Dad liked to say – but, for the first time I heard them, and experienced a euphoria hitherto unknown: an ecstatic penetration into the ethereal world of an Everest amidst clouds.

Strange to say, though, as we performed the Franck one evening in early January, in Herr Beethoven's Room, for the Schützes and their acquaintance (which included a delighted Professor Rosé), from those lofty musical peaks my thoughts drifted to Istanbul, with its shimmering domes, and how, on the deck of the *Izmir*, I snuggled into Kerem's arms as he told me the story of Husrev and Shirin:

'So, what happened after King Husrev and Shirin met at the bathing pool?' I asked him.

'As fate would have it, their paths crossed many times, but they rarely met. Yet every meeting confirmed their love. But Shirin would not marry Husrev until he saved Persia, his kingdom; which he did, aided by the Emperor of Byzantium.

'Husrev's victory came at a price, for he had to marry the Emperor's daughter in payment. Grieved by such misfortune, Shirin, now Queen of Armenia, forfeited her realm and journeyed to Persia to see him. Husrev, of course, still loved Shirin, and asked that she become his mistress; but Shirin, who was as virtuous as she was beautiful, refused. She locked herself in an ivory tower and would drink only milk.

'Concerned for his beloved, Husrev engaged a sculptor named Farhad to carve a channel to convey milk to Shirin. As Shirin watched him hew the stone with strength and determination, she fell in love; while Farhad, captivated by her beauty and goodness, worked only for her. And when he finished, he made known his heart's desire.

'King Husrev was overcome with jealousy and contrived to separate them by giving Fahrad the impossible task of carving a mountain of stairs up which he was to carry Shirin's statue. Spurred by love, Farhad again applied his might; and when his task was near complete, Shirin, now even more in love, visited him on the mountaintop. On her return, she nearly fell. Farhad rescued her and carried her down on his shoulders before returning to finish his work.

'Farhad's success only enraged King Husrev more. Growing treacherous, Husrev ordered a messenger up the mountain to inform Farhad of Shirin's death, which of course was untrue. Overcome with grief, Farhad took one last look at Shirin's statue and cast himself over the cliff.'

'Oh dear, Kerem! And then what happened?'

'That, my darling, I will save for another evening.'

Then Hubie began the fourth movement, its theme a sweet exchange of holy promises, and coaxed me back to the golden beauty and familial warmth of Hietzing.

'I must work hard to keep up with her,' he acknowledged our many compliments and mopped his brow with his handkerchief. 'To play with Fräulein Raye is both a challenge and a delight.'

'You seem quite far away, dear,' smiled Frau Schütze.

'You look beautifully exotic with those pendant earrings,' beamed Zita. 'Sapphires suit you. And what a gorgeous gown! That heart-shaped neckline is very becoming. And the colour! Lapis lazuli.'

'I must put my violin away,' I muttered.

'Never have I heard you play as you did tonight,' Hubie followed me out. 'You were magnificent.'

'I have never been so well accompanied.'

'We shall do it again, yes?'

'If you like,' I wrapped my violin in Kerem's scarf and locked my case. Never would I hear the rest of his story.

'Come!' he held out his hand, 'And let me introduce you to my friends.'

'We wondered what had become of our Huberle,' Seppel Braun, a choir friend, remarked upon introduction. 'It has been months since he graced us with his presence.'

'I have been most— pleasantly distracted,' Hubie smiled.

'He is like the great stag that ventures into the mountains alone,' teased a law school companion Ziggy Kowalski, 'and when it suits him, he condescends to join the rest of the herd. This time,

I see he's returned in the company of a charming doe.'

'By which, I think my husband means to say that you are most welcome, Phoebe,' added his wife Maria-Anna, whom they nicknamed Marina.

Throughout dreary January, we enjoyed evenings of music and song, poetry and conversation, accompanied by a steady supply of food and drink. My piano was rarely silent; my larder emptied daily. All that was good and true and beautiful found a place at my fireside. Emil, who had reoccupied the neighbouring apartment, left the door ajar to listen, but declined my invitation to join us for supper. He had plans to work on, he said.

'It reminds me of old times,' Frau Geplapper reminisced when we coincided the morning after a lively soiree. 'I could never keep track of your father's guests. And the music! I'm certain it stopped only when he was asleep. Save for Herr Petrovic, the uncle of that Bolshevik scoundrel bookstore owner, no one ever complained,' she smiled. Fortunately, no one seemed to mind me, either.

Not that we were indifferent or unaware as to what was going on outside. No one could ignore the barrage of Nazi violence and propaganda to which Vienna was subjected, be it planeloads of Swastikas falling onto the snow, vandalism of homes and shops, and even explosions. Perhaps Hitler would soon be overthrown. Not everyone in Germany supported him. The Church did not (Bishop von Galen had been particularly outspoken); nor did many of the aristocracy; even the military had their reservations.

Besides, what could we do?

Play Beethoven instead.

The Septet was rollicking fun. Karl took up his bassoon, Zita her clarinet, and Hubie his horn. I supplied the violin, Herr Steffan was an able violist, Ziggy played the bass, and Marina the cello.

Our amusements were by no means exceptional. To paraphrase my cousin-of-sorts, the doors of the dance hall, hitherto closed by St Catherine, were again flung open by the Three Holy Kings. It was Carnivale, a valedictory festival of dancing and dining before Spring's Lenten fast. Truly, the Viennese waltzed their way through Winter, for every guild and society hosted its annual ball during January and February. Having debuted with Alma Rosé's Wiener Walzermädeln at the Ronacher on New Year's Eve, my orchestral engagements would keep me busy until March.

'Do you dance as well as you play, Phoebe?' Franz inquired after a family soirée. 'The Opera Ball is next week. It's the highlight of the season.'

'Huberle has not told you?' Frau Schütze glanced at Hubie who flushed as if his mother had caught him scribbling on the walls.

'Will you come?' he asked as he escorted me home. 'As a

member of the orchestra, the occasion is a special one for me. I would very much like you to— You have a gown, yes?'

'Yes, but—'

'Would you do me the honour of being my partner?'

'Well, what do you think?' I asked the Portrait as I twirled in my ball gown, a black, fitted creation with a bodice embroidered in gold; its hem edged with golden sequins. 'You chose it, so you better not tell me you don't approve.'

'I chose well, didn't I?'

'More to the point, do you think Hubie will like it?'

When he arrived, punctual as always, Hubie stared, smiled, and shyly pushed his glasses onto his nose.

'I am wearing the cufflinks,' he sniffed a little as he showed me.

'You have a cold.'

'It is fortunate I am not playing tonight. Come! Let me assist you with your fur. We have hired a coach and four especially.'

The ball commenced with the arrival of Chancellor Schuschnigg. Everyone stood for the National Anthem. Being the second movement of Haydn's Kaiser Quartet, I knew the tune well; but the words were more difficult to follow, for everyone sang their own version. References to German labour and German love, and praise of equal duties and equal rights mingled with 'Deutschland über alles in der Welt' and 'Gott erhalte, Gott beschütze Unsern Kaiser, unser Land'.

Come the third verse, however, everyone sang in unison:

> *Laßt, durch keinen Zwist geschieden,*
> *Uns nach einem Ziele schau'n.*
> *Laßt in Eintracht und in Frieden*
> *Uns am Heil der Zukunft bau'n!*
> *Uns'red Volkes starke Jugend*
> *Werde ihren Ahnen gleich.*
> *Sei gesegnet, Heimaterde,*
> *Gott mit dir, mein Österreich!*

Viewed from high in our third-tier box, the opening ballet, a kaleidoscopic interplay of patriotic red and white, was a spectacle worthy of the great Ziegfeld. The presentation of debutantes followed – courtly elegance *en masse* – as rows of young ladies in white gowns, their gentlemen partners in black evening dress, paraded onto the Opernhaus' vast dance floor (the seats of the auditorium having been removed for the occasion). Hubie and his siblings all had attended the Elmayer School which was responsible for training the debutantes in every point of deportment, from the dance steps to the handkuss, ensuring that each gesture was performed with the utmost correctness and refinement. In tantalising, albeit restrained display was played out before me the courtesy to which I had become so accustomed.

'Phoebe,' Hubie bowed, 'will you do me the honour of the next dance?'

He offered me his arm and escorted me down the many flights of stairs. The orchestra began *Wiener Blut*. We took our position on the floor, whereupon I quivered as Hubie placed his gloved hand on my back.

'What is the matter?' he asked. 'Do you have a headache?'

'No, I'm quite all right. A passing memory, that's all.' For I had recalled how Kerem exposed his naked wrist for me to hold.

'A sad memory?'

'Quite the contrary,' I whispered.

And oh, how we danced! Here was none of the gentle vulnerability of my shipboard romance; nor was there the artfulness of one of Eric's tangos. Delicacy tempered Hubie's strength; goodness regulated his feelings. We whirled round the floor: past Duke Max von Hohenberg and Countess Maria Elisabeth Bona von Waldburg; past Prince Ernst and his new wife Marie-Therese Wood; past Karl-Alois and Fifi, who were enjoying a special night out; past Franz and pretty Inge Seyss-Inquart; past Rudi and Zita: In sweet sympathy we circled, laughing, floating, flying: hearts, minds, bodies swirling, borne by the lilt of the waltz. But if I ended breathless and confused, elated and surprised, Hubie was more so. Panting apologies, he then beckoned Karl to escort me to back to our box while he retired to smoke.

Like gods, the Schützes and the Ströhmanns noted the comings and goings of various personalities. Frau Schütze shared her opera glasses with me and pointed out the dignitaries. Chancellor Schuschnigg I had greeted whilst in Hubie's company. Von Papen, the German ambassador, suavely escorted a beautiful young woman from the floor. Franz's boss, State Councillor Arthur Seyss-Inquart and his elegant wife stood conversing with elderly President Miklas and the Foreign Minister Guido Schmidt.

'Our Chancellor has made the mistake of co-operation instead of persevering with his predecessor's steadfast resistance,' Dr Elsa remarked as she watched Schuschnigg nodding with von Papen. 'And he is not helped by his cabinet. Guido Schmidt is a rogue, von Starhemberg a lazy good-for-nothing, and Seyss a conniving scoundrel. He steers a ship of fools.'

'Indeed, he does,' smiled Frau Schütze, 'for we are landlocked.'

'I admire Herr Bundeskanzler,' observed Professor Schütze. 'He is a most loyal German Austrian whose burdensome position is not to be envied. He has observed every point of treaty; honoured the principles of the League of Nations; and is doing everything he can to preserve friendship with Germany whilst maintaining Austria's independence as a Catholic nation.'

'The problem is that Herr Hitler does not have the same sense of the law,' replied Dr Elsa. 'Hitler is determined to have Austria.'

'Apparently Adolf's desk is littered with picture postcards from Vienna,' joked Dr Robert. 'He is planning to redesign the city. And if that monstrosity of a stadium at Nuremberg is anything to go by, God help us if he does. Adolf's taste is appalling.'

'Schuschnigg should actively seek support from France and England. Unfortunately, he has done little in that regard,' Dr Elsa continued.

'Support of the French? Pfui!' Professor Schütze interjected. 'The French won't play policeman in Europe's affairs.'

'Don't underestimate the French, Kurti,' advised Dr Robert. 'France is suspicious of Germany, despite the latter's unscrupulous efforts at appeasement; and she will be more so if there is further alliance between our two nations. What is it the French like to say? *L'anschluss c'est la guerre.*'

'But France is governed by Socialists!' deplored the Professor.

'France is on the verge of not being governed at all!' remarked Frau Schütze.

'Unlike the Conservatives, at least the Socialists are opposed to Hitler's policies,' Dr Robert continued. 'And I will add that Dr Schuschnigg has erred in isolating our own Social Democrats. If the Chancellor wishes to resist Hitler, he should enlist their support – or at the very least the support of the Christian Workers Association.'

'And Crown Prince Otto,' added Frau Schütze. 'The Prince is prepared to work with the Socialists.'

'Socialists? They're all Red at heart! And it is against the constitution to involve the monarchy, Klara,' warned the Professor, not for the first time.

'Then I can think of no better time to involve the monarchy than Carnivale, when it is permissible to bend a few rules,' Frau Schütze cheekily retorted.

'Whoever is not a fool during Carnivale is a fool the rest of the year,' winked Dr Robert. 'Klara, should we restore the monarchy and create a Danube Federation?'

'The Nazis have put a price on the Crown Prince's head,' warned Dr Elsa, 'And there will be no Danube federation if there's a Habsburg in charge. Yugoslavia, for one, will not lend support.'

'Yugoslavia? Pfui!' scoffed Frau Schütze. 'What were they thinking when they created Yugoslavia?'

'Dad called it Bitzerland,' I chuckled, and, confident my company would easily understand, I resorted to English. 'He called it Bitzerland because it comprises bits of this and bits of that.'

'Ah, Franzl!' Dr Robert greeted Franz who had at that moment entered our box. 'We are sorting out the world's troubles. You usually have something to say on these matters. How should our little Austria protect herself against big bully Germany?'

'He has too much to say on these matters,' grumbled the Professor.

'Had Austria and Germany united after the War,' Franzl launched his well-versed patter with a smile, 'we would not be beset with the problems of the past two decades; and we would have been more fairly done by in accordance with the principles of Versailles. It is in our best interest to unite with Germany, after which we can sort out the matter of National Socialism. There are too many divisions among the Nazis for Hitler to maintain power. Look at all the scandal over General Blomberg! With the help of the army, we should topple the regime and create a Better Germany: a proper German Federation.'

'With my son in charge,' Professor Schütze nudged Dr Robert.

'A word if you please, Herr Doktor.' Franz garbled a message to Dr Robert who immediately rose to his feet.

'Hubie's collapsed,' he announced.

47

Ruminations

'**G**OOD MORNING, little Cinderella!' Emil greeted me on the landing, 'What brings you here so late— or so early? Your coach was turned into a pumpkin, yes, and you had to walk home?'

'Stop it, Emil.'

'Hey, you've been crying. Vus machs da?[26] Has a wicked fairy turned your Prince Charming into a toad? I'm going to make you some coffee. And while the coffee's brewing you're going to sit down and tell me what the matter is.'

'Hubie had an asthma attack. He went to smoke a cigarette— he has special cigarettes, with powders in them, to help him breathe. But he collapsed. They took him to hospital and he—'

Scenes throbbed through my head: Karl in his shirt sleeves pumping Hubie's chest; Professor Schütze running to his assistance; Dr Robert gravely checking Hubie's pulse; Prince Ernst dashing up the stairs, guiding ambulance men through the finery; the darkness and blasting snow; the sterile brightness of the hospital; nuns adept at urgent calm gliding swiftly down the corridors; and waiting, waiting, waiting and wondering; feeling my pearls, my satin gown and high heels to be useless trappings.

'He's dead?'

'Dr Ströhmann revived him with adrenalin. One of his lungs has collapsed. He's on oxygen. His family is with him. We're taking turns to look after him. I'm going back tonight.'

'Oy yoy yoy!'[27] he hugged me, 'Now, don't you worry. With such prompt attention, he'll recover; and if he doesn't pull through it won't be due to lack of care. Dr Robert Ströhmann is one of the most respected physicians in Vienna.'

When I visited him that night, Hubie looked as if he had transmogrified into a creature from a painting by Hieronymus Bosch. Covering his face was a leather mask from which a long

---

[26] *Vus machs da?*: What's up?
[27] *Oy yoy yoy!*: An expression of sorrow or lamentation.

tube travelled to the machine that administered the oxygen that was keeping him alive. I stroked his hand. Days ago, his fingers had dangled over the keys of my piano, rippling arpeggios with precision and ease. Now they lay on the blanket, limp and bluish. Oh, dear God, make them move again! Come back to me, Hubie! Dear Hubie, please come back! I pressed his hand to my cheek, held it there and fondled it, hoping for some response.

'He is a big man. Reviving him was hard work,' Dr Robert remarked. 'We nearly lost him. But nearly lost is not the same as losing, is it? Fear not, Gnädiges Fräulein. We are doing everything possible. It is but a matter of time. Asthma can be like that: one moment all is fine; the next you're at death's door. Hubie is otherwise in excellent health; and if I were he, and awoke tonight, I could not think of a more pleasant experience than to find a beautiful princess at my bedside. I will retire to my rooms. Sisi, have Sister notify me of any developments.'

'He might not be able to respond, but he can hear you, I'm certain,' Sisi observed. 'And he can feel you. I have nursed people in this condition. Your being there is a great consolation. You are doing more than you realise. Let's pray the rosary together. He will hear our prayers and find comfort.'

'And how's Prince Myshkin today?' asked Emil when he called by the following morning.

'Hubie, you mean? Dr Ströhmann says he's in a stable condition. And he's no fool, Emil.'

'A game of chess proved that. Besides, my remark was not intended as a put down. The world would be a better place if there were more Prince Myshkins. I hope he pulls through, for your sake especially.'

'For my sake?'

'He's courting you.'

'Whatever gave you that idea?'

'Why else do you think a macher[28] like that would invite you to Vienna's most illustrious ball?'

'We're cousins. Well, cousins-of-sorts.'

'And cousins play music with a passion that leaves your hair standing on end?'

'It's music, Emil. It's supposed to be passionate.'

'Is it now?'

'So, we're friends, and what of it?'

'Do you think love is no different?' he smirked. 'Either way, Hubert Schütze's attentions towards you have given me further

---

[28] *Macher*: an important person who is very active in an organisation; a big shot; a person with connections; also, a person who thinks he is very important.

reason to admire him. It takes a man of wit and courage to court a shrew.'

'And it takes a woman of questionable judgement to put up with you. What I don't understand is how you can behave so contemptuously towards people you respect. Clearly, you have a good rapport with the Ströhmanns; yet you are cuckolding their son. Now you tell me you hold Hubie in high esteem, but you have no qualms in defiling his sister. Why?'

'It is perfectly understandable that I have a good rapport with Elsa and Robert Ströhmann: they are fine, intelligent people. Rudi Ströhmann is a putz.[29] And whatever my opinion of your cousin Huberle might be, *he* looks upon me as a second-class citizen.'

'Conducting a liaison with a woman who is about to marry another man *is* behaving like a second-class citizen.'

'I love her.'

'But, if you love her, how could you let her marry a man she doesn't love?'

'I don't want that.'

'Then why don't you marry her?'

'Why do you think?'

'I suppose it's for the same reason you didn't marry Odalia: you'd have to divorce her.'

'Go threaten the geese!'

'Then do something about it, for heaven's sake, or it will come to no good!'

'Tell her father that! Tell her brother that! Years ago, I courted her! I offered my hand in marriage and they slammed the door in my face! Why? Because I am not a khnyokish[30] Catholic aristocrat!'

'And you criticise me for having a vendetta? That sounds awfully like a vendetta to me – ruining a girl's reputation because her father refused your suit. Behave like that and you'll further demonise yourself in their eyes. For when they find out, they will scorn you. As they ought!'

'See? There it is! One rule for the toffs and another for everyone else! "Ruining a girl's reputation!" So, my actions toward her are morally reprehensible, while her behaviour is merely scandalous? She will exonerate herself with a confession, while I will be damned; when all along the fact is that we each have equal right to do as we please.'

'What trollop! In doing as you please, you're both in the wrong. And any children Zita has, either by you or by Rudi, will bear the retribution. I know, because I am a child who had to shoulder my parents' pre-marital folly.'

---

[29] *Putz*: (extremely vulgar) fool, jerk.

[30] *Khynokish*: (derogatory) holier-than-thou; bigoted; priggish; can also mean molly-coddled, clumsy, soft-hearted, and sloppily dressed due to religious preoccupations or convictions.

'I still have my rights.'

'You and your rights! In their eyes, your rights have virtually destroyed the society they are struggling to preserve: the society that was responsible for some of the greatest achievements the world has ever known. Can you blame them for their hostility and mistrust? And most ironic of all is that it is their society which has protected you and nurtured you, and which has permitted you the considerable liberty to exercise your so-called rights to the point that you overturned everything they value. What astounds me is that they have not put you in a hole somewhere and chained you up!'

'A century ago they would have!'

'More's the pity!'

'Well! Have I news for you,' I announced to Hubie when I visited him a week later. He continued to languish, and there was little else to do but sit with him and hold his hand, and keep an eye on the oxygen levels, which I did night after night following my gigs with the Waldermädeln. For I took the graveyard shift from midnight to dawn, thus enabling family and friends to take much needed rest. Before lapsing into silence, I made a practice of telling him various happenings, even the most trivial, and became quite used to ruminating aloud. News that night, however, was far from trivial:

'The government police uncovered a plot in which Nazis working undercover were planning a host of bombings and disturbances in Vienna and all over Austria. Apparently, the plans were all signed by Rudolf Hess, Hitler's deputy.

'And do you know where they found them? In the office of the Committee of Seven in Teinfaltstrasse, the committee the Chancellor himself established to promote working relations between Austria and Germany. It all came to light when Dr Tavs, the secretary, had the gall to declare to the newspapers of all things, that the Austrian police would never prosecute Austrian Nazis for fear of German retaliation.

'That's what prompted the raid on the Teinfaltstrasse offices. It turns out they're the headquarters of the Nazi underground! They even found weapons! Honestly! All right under Chancellor Schuschnigg's nose! What's more, they discovered another scheme to burn down the German Embassy and murder von Papen, which was to be executed by Nazis dressed in uniforms of the Fatherland Front. Can you believe it?

'Then, amidst civil disruption, they would push for the Chancellor to resign; and Hitler's troops would invade to re-establish law and order. How's that for provocation? Little wonder Schuschnigg's preparing to meet with Hitler. Oh, and Emil sends his regards. In truth, he's very grateful for what you did for Oda's baby. Do you know what he said when I told him? "An aristocrat with a sense of social justice, there is hope yet". Hubie?'

No, I was not mistaken. Hubie squeezed my hand again; and from behind the leather mask with its trunk-like tube and goggles, he gazed at me.

48

Red-White-Red!

H UBIE DID NOT RETURN HOME until February. Assisted by a Pneumostat, he slowly recuperated; and it consoled me much to see him brighten, both in body and spirit. Since even short walks he found exhausting, he remained housebound and spent his days in slippers and dressing gown reading in a comfortable chair with Sirius beside him. He derived great pleasure from having me read him in English; and in this manner we enjoyed *Persuasion*:

Anne was tenderness itself, I read, *and she had the full worth of Captain Wentworth's affection. His profession was all that could ever make her friends wish that tenderness less, the dread of a future war all that could dim her sunshine. She gloried in being a sailor's wife, but she must pay the tax of quick alarm for belonging to that profession which is, if possible, more distinguished in its domestic virtues than in its national importance.*

'Well, Hubie, I suppose they lived happily ever after,' I sighed as I closed the book.

'You would not want that?'

'Would you?'

'I would want your happiness above all else.'

'Well, I don't see why happiness must necessarily be bound with domesticity.'

'I gathered as much. You would not be content to occupy yourself entirely with homely duties; although you would perform them with ease and skill, as you do most things.'

'Which doesn't mean I would derive pleasure from them.'

'All tasks, even those we find enjoyable, become burdensome when there is no love. When love is present, even mundane chores become sublime.'

'One shouldn't rely on others or other things for one's own happiness.'

'You are right. We must be happy in ourselves. And for that, we must be at peace with God. And to be at peace with God, we must learn to judge rightly and act accordingly. Of that, I think Miss Austen was aware.'

'And she exercised such good judgement that she was condemned forever to spinsterhood, and to the writing of novels.'

'Well and good if she were happy. Better the writing of novels than an unhappy marriage.'

'If I married, I would prefer to live as the Crofts, and share responsibility both inside and outside the home.'

'You would marry a man who is a loving husband but a poor driver?'

'If I loved him well enough, perhaps I might.'

'You would risk the cart being overturned?'

'It is not a given the cart will topple.'

'And if it did?'

'Are you a bad driver?'

'I have never driven. If I had charge of the reins I would endeavour to steer well; and if my steering were faulty, I would welcome your guidance. What shall we read next?'

'Emil passed you this.'

'*Der Idiot,*' he grimaced approvingly as he studied the spine.

'He said it's been sitting in the bookshop for too long and that it was about time someone read it. Not enough people read such works nowadays.'

'Herr Fährmann never ceases to surprise. I would have expected *Das Schloss* or *Der Untertan*, or even *Das Kapital*. Please thank him on my behalf.'

'I will. Dad was fond of the Russians.'

'I read *Schuld und Sühne* and *Krieg und Frieden* on his recommendation. But I would prefer that you read me an English classic before I leave for France.'

'France?'

'As soon as I am sufficiently recovered, I will be spending the remaining winter on the Riviera. It is doctor's orders. Sisi is coming, too. You will walk Sirius for me while I am gone, yes? And I promise you, dear Phoebe, I will write.'

A fortnight later, a post-card announced his safe arrival.
A letter soon followed:

Montpellier,
10 February, 1938

Dearest Phoebe,

Be pleased to know that we are comfortably settled, and that the milder climate is already proving beneficial. We have a splendid view of the sea which has greatly impressed Sisi for she has never seen the sea before; and since a picture is worth a thousand words (as I believe you like to say in

English), I include a small sketch for your benefit [here followed a very passable ink and colour landscape]. My breathing grows daily stronger and I expect to resume playing my horn very soon.

While I write, I recall when we first met. I am ashamed to admit that, upon learning you were coming to dine those months ago, I dreaded being introduced. In my foolish shyness, I took Sirius for a walk to avoid the encounter, only to meet you by accident in the park. How forlorn and yet how beautiful you looked that afternoon, in mourning, reading alone in the twilight.

I think of you now, reading this letter. Perhaps you are out walking; only you are not in mourning, the leaves are not dying, and the light is not fading. New shoots are sprouting underfoot, the snow is melting, and the days are lengthening. Is the Danube still frozen? Have the primroses bloomed amidst the snow drops? When the lilac blossoms in the Volksgarten expect my return. Meanwhile, do not be sad or lonely; our letters will take the place of our many conversations. For me, they will be treasured testaments of friendship I will read and read again. And when I walk (I am making small excursions now), I will think of what I will write you. How I yearn to hear from you! My Lenten fast has begun early, I fear, deprived as I am of your company. Write me soon and tell me all!

I wait, filled with hope, and with this letter send you my fondest regards,

Hubie.

Well, Hubie, where do I start? Since you departed, Vienna has turned quite mad! And it's all to do with Chancellor Schuschnigg's visit to Germany.

You see, Roddy, early in February, Hitler invited the Austrian Chancellor to his residence in Berchtesgarten for an 'unofficial' meeting 'reflecting the mutual desire to discuss all matters affecting relations between the German Reich and Austria'.

Well, that was how it was reported in the papers verbatim from Der Führer. But, in truth, Herr Bundeskanzler seemed of similar mind. The meeting was a diplomatic one, he announced, to uphold the terms of the 1936 agreement, 'thus ensuring a friendly relationship between the two countries, corresponding with their common national traditions'.

The most singular outcome of the discussion lay in the appointment of Arthur Seyss-Inquart as Minister of the Interior and Chief of Security; a move which especially delighted Franz, who saw in his boss's new position an opportunity for advancement in the civil service, and a positive step toward his beloved *Zusammenschluss*; for Seyss-Inquart was of similar opinion in that regard.

Not everyone shared his delight. Rumours circulated that concessions had been made to Nazi affiliates which jeopardised the stability of the government and the country. Many began to doubt the authority and capability of the Austrian Chancellor. Would Schuschnigg resign? He did not, mainly because no one was willing to assume the role – a most unenviable and burdensome one given the divisions within the country, not to mention Hitler's demagogic ravings.

This information I communicated to my cousin-of-sorts in a letter amounting to several pages. And before I received a much-anticipated response, Schuschnigg retaliated. In a speech before parliament, which was broadcast far and wide, he asserted Austria's independence, citing in his favour a litany of historical figures from the steadfast Maria Theresia through to his predecessor, the assassinated Dollfuss. Austria had conceded much to Germany. Now that her very independence was under threat, having been forced to acknowledge German National Socialism as a political entity within her own boundaries, even within her own parliament, enough was enough:

'It is not Nationalism or Socialism which is the watchword in Austria, but Patriotism! Unto death!' he passionately concluded. 'Red-White-Red! Austria!'

'Gott mit dir, mein Österreich!' sang Parliament, which jubilation spread to the streets.

Furious, Hitler nullified all concessions made to Austria in the Berchtesgarten meeting; demanded freedom of circulation of hitherto banned German party newspapers; recommended the integration of the Schilling with the Reichsmark; and insisted upon the restoration of political freedom to National Socialists in Austria and abroad, which included the release of activists from prisons and work camps, such as the scoundrels behind the recently discovered plot; and threatened invasion if the above were not met.

But Herr Bundeskanzler did not give way. In keeping with the principle of self-determination he resolved to uphold, Schuschnigg countered Hitler by announcing, to great applause, on Wednesday 9th March, that a referendum would be held four days later. Let the Austrian people decide their fate. Let the people declare to the world their desire for a 'free, German, independent, social, Christian and united' Austria.

Red and white rosettes bloomed amidst the melting, muddied

snow; and red and white streamers lined the streets. Trucks blaring, 'Are you with Schuschnigg for a free Austria? Yes!' and 'Every Austrian vote Yes!' cruised up and down Linke Wienzeile, round the Ringstrasse, and through every district of the city.

Frau Geplapper extolled the virtues of Herr Bundeskanzler, 'the champion of German Austria, of freedom, of peace, and of food for all', and hummed 'Sei gesegnet ohne Ende, Heimaterde wunderhold' while she worked. In their busy little bakery in Leopoldstadt, the Epsteins tied red and white ribbons round fresh-baked loaves. Children chalked 'Vote for free and independent Austria' on the pavements. Red and white banners cascading from buildings transformed Vienna into an enormous candy shop.

But although the Chancellor insisted on the right to campaign without opposition, there was nothing he could do to prevent German planes showering the streets with Nazi pamphlets. Occasionally, I spotted an Anschluss sympathiser with a swastika pin stuck in the lapel of his or her coat; but most wore patriotic ribbons.

His treasured political rights restored, Emil jaunted in and out of his shop, his body twisting more markedly than usual, and whistled the *Internationale* while he decorated his shopfront with Austrian flags and volumes of Nestroy, Halm, Zweig, Kafka, and Kraus. Characters whom I recalled sitting around the chessboard at Café Central frequented the store. Nor could I pass without one such individual raising his fist and greeting me with a cheery '*Freiheit*', before handing me a leaflet outlining the need to vote 'Yes' to democracy and 'No' to domination by Nazi war-mongers in cahoots with industrial capitalists. Meanwhile, Albrecht resumed his position under the eaves, churned his barrel organ and sang:

> *So long as there's wine;*
> *And the violin plays*
> *A tune divine;*
> *While near us*
> *Some pretty girls sit;*
> *'We have all we need!'*
> *We Viennese say;*
> *And never will we quit!*

To their chagrin, Zita and Franz found themselves to be under voting age, which had been raised to twenty-four. Rudi was especially furious, missing out on the opportunity to flex his democratic muscles by only three months.

'And probably just as well,' observed Professor Schütze. 'They would all vote for an Anschluss.'

'Franzl might,' retorted Zita, 'But I like the idea of a free, independent, and democratic Austria.'

Then, to add insult to injury, Franz received a summons for military service. 'Pfui! I must defend German Austria against invasion from fellow Germans, for whom I would prefer to knock down all defences!'

'This is not about Germans, Franzwurst,' countered Karl-Alois, who had been recalled to barracks. 'This is about National Socialism. Surely you would defend Austria from the Nazi menace?'

'Hitler and his gang won't last!'

'They have the means. And Austria's operetta army is no match for German forces. Our only hope of resistance is if the French and the British lend us support.'

'You are right, Karl. Unfortunately, though, we have stood in Germany's shadow too long,' added Dr Robert. 'And France and Britain have had no interest in Austria since they carved her up at Versailles.'

'I hope it does not come to war,' frowned Dr Elsa.

The possibility of war repulsed everyone, particularly the older family members who retained vivid memories of the previous conflict. After his older brother was killed in action on the Somme in 1916, Professor Schütze left his wife and four little children to take up arms, endured the horrors of the Western Front, and spent the last months of the war as a prisoner. Upon release, starving and exhausted, he made his way home on foot.

Frau Schütze had lost her two brothers: Alois on the Russian front, and Josef on the Italian front; and she grew tearful at the recollection of those years of separation from her husband – the worry of months without news – and of the struggle to feed and clothe her little family on depleting resources.

Both Dr Elsa and Dr Robert had seen more than their fair share of human suffering treating trainloads of wounded. Dr Robert's first wife, Marta, had died from complications in childbirth, which might have been circumvented. But the best doctors were focussed on the war effort.

And then there was the grim memory of Captain Krain, Rudi's father, disfigured by shrapnel; a man who could be neither loving husband nor father; who after the War suffered a decade of torture shunned by society, compelled to perform menial backroom tasks, or else imprisoned in his home sipping soup through a straw.

The next day, Friday, a pile of letters arrived, at the top of which was one from Kerem.

'I don't believe it!' I ripped open the letter while in the elevator:

Istanbul,
7ᵗʰ March, 1938.

My darling Houri,

Will you ever forgive me for not writing sooner? Having left your address in Istanbul, I had no means of reaching you. I have only recently returned from the East, the typhoon in Hong Kong last September leaving me stranded for several months.

Are you still in Vienna? If so, are you quite safe? My reason for asking is that since my return I have been beset with demands, mainly from Austrian Jews, to sell jewellery for passage or asylum. What is happening? Should you receive my letter, please send me news.

Dear Phoebe, if only we could shape our life in accordance with the wishes of our heart! Unfortunately, I do not expect to travel to Vienna any time soon and so must forsake my heaven on earth. The memories of our happy days together – so brief and yet so joyous – I will embrace as if you were in my arms. Every thought of you is a kiss, my Paradise! And may you remember always

Your humble servant,
Kerem

My knees shook, and my heart throbbed as tears of sorrow and joy flowed without restraint. Kerem! As gentle and passionate as when first we met! To think I had thought ill of him! My thoughts whirling, I opened the next letter without heeding the address. It turned out to be from Mrs Sotheby:

Dear Phoebe,

Having been thoroughly spoiled by Australian sunshine, we could bear the dreary English winter no longer and so decided to spend a month on the Côte d'Azur.

Anyway, I am writing to tell you of the most marvellous coincidence. When we arrived at Montpellier, thoroughly worn out after a bothersome trip from Calais (I am sorry to say, Le Train Bleu is not what it used to be), we happened to be pleasantly entertained by some superb piano playing from another of the guests. It reminded me very much of you, dear, for the pianist played many pieces which you yourself play so very well. I told the young gentleman as much once he finished. Thankfully, he spoke exceedingly good English, for I was too weary to converse in French. As it turned out, he was from Vienna of all places; and after he and Desmond discussed the to-do over there, I asked him whether he had made your acquaintance. Well! Indeed, he spoke most admiringly of you and with such great affection that there was no mistaking his feelings.

What a dark horse you are! No wonder you declined to come for Christmas! And a baronet, too! Well, dear, short of marrying a prince or a count, you can't do much better than marry a baron, and Baron von Rechtschaffen is quite the most charming man, even if he is rather tall, and far more suitable than that Turk. We spent a day in his company and met his sister, a serious girl but very striking, although it did concern me that she was planning to enter a convent. Anyway, I am so very happy for you, dear! You must miss him terribly!

Do tell us how it all works out; and I'm certain Lucy would love to hear your news. She did so miss you at Christmas for she wanted you to meet someone – an ice-hockey player, would you believe, whom I don't think you would find even remotely interesting. I told Lucy as much, but she did not heed me. She never does. Well, there's no need to worry now, is there? I am altogether too excited for words, except that I wish you all the very best.

Yours truly,
Letty Sotheby.

P.S. If you need a trousseau, write me and I will recommend a couturière.

'Marriage! Does the woman think of nothing else? And to Hubie of all people! How utterly ridiculous!'

'She's right, you know,' the Portrait seemed to twinkle.

'*You* have too much vested interest in this matter,' I glared.

I imagined Hubie at the piano, conversing with the Sothebys in his quaint but erudite English. What had he said? And did his words truly reveal that he loved me? Perhaps Emil was right. Indeed, from the moment I first met him, he had shown me much tenderness and refined affection; and I recalled how, reclined in his armchair and fondling Sirius between the ears, he had probed my thoughts and ambitions, and had listened so very carefully to all I had to say. But marriage! Could he really be thinking of marrying me?

And could I marry him? Pledge myself to him? Bear him children? Care for him? Be his friend and helpmeet?

I opened the empty portion of my silver locket and tried to

picture his portrait, fitted alongside my own.

'I ought to love him. In one sense, I do love him,' I mused, 'I am very fond of him, certainly. He is very good and kind, very upright and sensible, and we have many common interests. But is that love? I think of him and I am happy. But how my heart yearns for Kerem! Should I trust my passions? Kerem loves me, so it seems; but he is by nature affectionate. And I have feelings for him I never thought I had for anyone. How could it be that, after such a brief encounter, I could feel this way? Or am I deceiving myself?

'Let's read what Hubie has to say.'

Hubie's letter was dated a few days after Mrs Sotheby's. It was full of charming detail concerning excursions, natural history, cultural experiences, and literary ventures written so that I could imagine myself part of the scene. There was also an update on his health, so thorough that it bordered on hypochondria, and spared from being judged accordingly by his inclination to obsess over minutiae, not to mention that he knew I appreciated being well-informed. As for political observations, they were absent from his epistle, whereby I concluded that our letters had crossed paths. There was no mention of love, sentiment, or romance of any description.

'As I thought, Letty Sotheby, complete supposition and total nonsense!' I tucked Hubie's letter into its envelope and consulted the last of my mail, sent from Paris by one Mr F. Horne, Esquire.

Written with a scratchy nib on hotel paper, the letter had all the appearance being dashed off at the eleventh hour using whatever was to hand, including the ink which had to be changed mid-paragraph. But such details were mere devices. I only had to envisage the handwriting in a broad-nibbed fountain pen to realise that the author was none other than Hubie himself, writing in English:

My Dearest Cuz,

I hope you are safe and well in beautiful Vienna. What with the confabulations one reads in the press, it is impossible to know what to make of the situation there.

Here in Paris, I am enjoying a pleasant change of pace and scene. I feel perfectly guilty calling it a business trip, what with opera and concerts every evening, let alone the 'haute cuisine' and multitudinous opportunities to renew old acquaintance. Just the other day I had the good fortune to bump into dear old Eudes. We had a royal night out and a few too many Bourbons which left me with an almighty hangover. Do pass on to Aunty Clara his delight upon hearing news of the family and tell her he hopes to visit as soon as possible.

Well, that is all I have time for at present. I will write when I am back in London. Meanwhile, keep well, and know that I remain

Your favourite cousin,
Frank

'Ah, he's a clever boy!' Frau Schütze beamed as she read the note, which I passed her with some perturbation when we met at the Opernhaus that evening. For I was certain that the 'Aunty Clara' mentioned in 'Mr Horne's' letter was none other than Hubie's mother. Concerning the rest of the subterfuge, I had no idea. Frau Schütze, however, proved skilled in decryption.

'He has been to see Crown Prince Otto!' she whispered, much excited.

'How do you know?'

'Why, Eudes is the French form of Otto; and they had a *royal* night out. You see, the Crown Prince is descended from the Bourbons on his mother's side,' she added, delighting in her son's linguistic tricks. 'Empress Zita is the daughter of Robert, Duke of Parma, who is descended from Philip V of Spain; and of Duchess Louise d'Artois, who as the granddaughter of Charles X was *une petite fille de France.* Perhaps we might also construe that dear, clever Huberle has been talking with the French? Ah, Phoebe, there is hope for us yet! Our beloved monarchy may be restored after all!'

49

Until Death!

DAZED BY TATYANA'S profession of love for Onegin, I drifted down the white marble steps into the Opernhaus foyer. Weaving through the music of my thoughts was the text of the letter I had posted that evening:

Oh, dearest, dearest Kerem!

How wrongly I have judged you! When you did not write, I thought you had deserted me, and yet could not believe it true of you; nor did I wish to, for not a day has passed in which I have not thought of you. I thought I was deceiving myself in loving you, and, now you have written, know my heart's yearnings belong instead to that communion of kindred spirits; for, all the while, you were thinking of me. It had never occurred to me that you had suffered any calamity. See how silly I am? And will you ever forgive me?

I am still in Vienna and am quite safe and happy – so much so, that I have postponed any further travel, particularly since the family matter to which I alluded while in Istanbul has been most fortuitously resolved, leaving me free to live as I please.

To think I might never see you again! Prince of my dreams, it is I who have forsaken you! I permitted the attentions of another. He is a good man, a very fine man, and I have reason to think him fond of me. I am very fond of him. And yet my heart pines for you. You are wiser than me! What am I to do? Write me, write me soon!

Your heaven on earth,
Phoebe

Had I been too forward? And how would he reply? May he not rebuke me! Perhaps he might come! And if he came, what would he find? Something was amiss, for a crowd had gathered near the entrance.

'See what you can find out, Phoebe,' whispered Frau Schütze.

Hundreds of young men, dressed in brown and carrying flares, paraded through the darkness. All wore the swastika armbands of the Third Reich; and as they marched, the crooked black crosses swung like pendulums.

'Ein Volk! Ein Reich! Ein Volk! Ein Reich!' they chanted.

'German troops have crossed the border!' a gentleman returned in haste from the Opernhaus square.

'Are you sure of that?' queried another.

'Has the army been deployed?' questioned a third.

'There will be no war!' declared a fourth, who had followed the first newsbearer. 'Not a drop of blood will be spilled! The Chancellor has resigned!'

A hush descended, as if the hearers had attuned to seismic tremors deep below. Some began to sob. Others stood stunned, wondering when the earth would open to swallow them.

'Gott schütze Österreich!' muttered the gentleman beside me, heeding not the tears in his eyes, and joined in the singing:

> *Land of liberty, land of light*
> *God with thee, my Austria!*

Couples gathered their furs and coats and hurried away; and when we re-entered the theatre for the second act, we found many of the boxes and stall seats vacant (and quickly reoccupied by students).

I came out of the opera much subdued by the frozen wasteland that epitomised the soul of the bitter Onegin:

> *This is the will of Heaven: you are mine!*
> *All your life has been a pledge of our union!*
> *And be assured, I was sent to you by God,*
> *I am your protector to the grave!*

'Three cheers for noble Tatyana,' Frau Schütze interrupted my melancholy, 'for resisting the advances of the selfish blackguard.'

'I hope I never make such a mistake as either one. I couldn't bear to commit myself to a loveless marriage, nor be undermined by passion— be it my own, or another's.'

'God willing, you will succumb to neither fate, Phoebe. But for now, we are going to have to leave romance aside and work out to get home! What a tumult! Ah, there is Professor Schütze! Quick! Down the stairs!'

Swastika banners and fiery torches bobbed like a thousand

bell-less Inchcape rocks on a treacherous sea as the swollen crowd thrashed past the theatre. 'Sieg Heil, Adolf Hitler! Sieg Heil!' it chanted in jubilation, its flame-flickered faces resembling the redeemed in Tintoretto's *Descent into Hell*.

'Kurti, take off your Fatherland rosette!' pleaded Frau Schütze.

'I will do no such thing!' answered the Professor as he clutched his oboe case to his chest and drew a protective arm around his wife. 'Come, Klara! Phoebe, stay close!'

Three trams passed before we were finally able to board. With fellow opera patrons wrapped in mink and astrakhan, we clutched hold of what poles and handles we could, crammed as we were against Swastika youths lustily singing, with harmonies supplied courtesy of Austrian reservists in feldgrau who looked as if they had been booted out of a beisl:

> *For the last time, the call to arms is sounded!*
> *For the fight, we all stand prepared!*
> *Already Hitler's banners fly over all streets.*
> *The time of bondage will last but a little while now!*
> *Already Hitler's banners fly over all streets.*

It so happened that no troops were deployed, for no invasion had occurred. Seyss-Inquart, the newly appointed Minister of Security, merely ordered the withdrawal of the Austrian forces for the sake of 'peace and order', so we were informed by a much-relieved Franz when he arrived home the next day. Instead of drawing arms, all Franzl had ended up drawing was the cigarette he smoked courtesy of a fellow soldier from Munich.

The truth was, that to prevent a full-scale German invasion, Dr Schuschnigg had indeed resigned, and, after considerable deliberation and with great reluctance, President Miklas had appointed Seyss-Inquart in his place.

'Well, isn't that a coincidence? An Austrian National Socialist Chancellor,' Emil observed as together with Albrecht as we listened to the wireless broadcast in his apartment that afternoon. Full political rights had been granted to National Socialists in Austria, and the exile of Austrian Nazis abroad had been revoked.

The other news was that Sunday's plebiscite had been cancelled.

And when I awoke that Sunday morn, it was as if the scenery had changed between acts. The red and white banners had been bundled somewhere backstage, and the flags of the Third Reich unfurled.

'We are German now, Fräulein Raye,' Frau Geplapper beamed as we walked to Mass, and I spotted a Swastika pin on the lapel of her Sunday coat. Andreas Geplapper wore a Swastika band on his arm and was dressed in mis-matched browns. Church bells pealed in celebration, and during the Mass the priest gave thanks for an unbloody resolution to the crisis.

Upon arriving home, Emil beckoned me into his apartment where he had his wireless tuned to Berlin. A mild and clinical voice made the following formal declaration on Hitler's behalf. It was the Reich Minister of Propaganda, Joseph Goebbels:

> *The German Reich will not tolerate persecution of Germans in this region because they belong to our country or because they hold certain opinions. There must be peace and order. I have therefore decided to help the millions of Germans in Austria with the resources of the Reich.*
>
> *Since this morning, soldiers of the German Wehrmacht have marched over the German-Austrian borders. The new National Socialist government in Vienna has itself summoned panzer troops, infantry divisions, and SS legions on the ground and the German Luftwaffe in the blue sky. Our soldiers guarantee that the Austrian Volk will shortly be given the opportunity to determine their future themselves and thereby their fate with a plebiscite.*
>
> *Behind the legions stand the will and decisiveness of the entire German nation. I myself, as Führer and Chancellor of the German people, will be pleased to enter Austria, my homeland, once again as a German and a free citizen. But the world must convince itself that the German people in Austria have been seized by a soulful joy and see that their rescuing brothers have come to their aid in their hour of great need. Long live the National Socialist German Reich! Long live National Socialist German Austria!*

'Zur Hölle, zur Hölle, zur Hölle,' sneered Emil as he switched off the wireless.

'It doesn't make sense!' I blurted. 'Germans being persecuted? What a load of rot! As for peace and order, well, without the Nazi-led rioting and vandalism, I cannot imagine a place more devoted to harmony, with all the order and discipline that harmony requires, than Austria. And if the army has been recalled, why is it necessary for German troops to be summoned? Besides, it's ridiculous to label the fiasco a rescue operation. If anything, Austria needs rescuing from Germany! Well, at least there will be an opportunity to vote.'

'An opportunity to vote? Ha!'

'It reminds me of the Balkan situation before the War,' Albrecht observed. 'But that Germany should treat us as if we were recalcitrant Serbs, what an insult! There'll be trouble from this, Fräulein Phoebe,' he nudged me.

❖❖❖

As you know by now, Roddy, Central Vienna is not large; and from customarily greeting Herr und Frau von Adabei[31] you come to know faces, even though you might not know names. Later that day, I found myself nodding at all manner of strangers, and my usual 'Grüß Gott' was invariably answered with 'Heil Hitler'. By Sunday evening, the hotels, inns, and guest-houses were full; the cafés were bursting with customers; while the Prater, the parks and the picture palaces were filled with rustic tourists. Organ grinders churned out 'Heute gehört uns Deutschland und morgen die ganze Welt'. And there were men in every conceivable combination of brown: plus fours, trousers, not quite matching brown shirts, and Sam Brown belts, armed with rifles and marching. What was going on?

'Herr Hitler is coming!' smiled a woman, her braided hair in scrolls, and dressed to the nines in trachten, 'And Herr Göring has already arrived!'

Come nightfall, a tiny knock sounded at my door. It was Hubie's friend Ziggy Kowalski and his wife. Would I mind if they stayed overnight? 'Of course not,' I replied, and in they came, carrying suitcases.

'I'm sorry to trouble you,' Ziggy apologised. 'We are catching a train early tomorrow morning and Marina is so tired these days—she is expecting! It would help if we spent the night closer to the station.' Never had I witnessed such concern for a pregnant woman and public transport. I proposed a game of cards to bide the time. Emil obliged by making a foursome. The Kowalskis departed at dawn, thanking me profusely but in great haste.

And when I later visited the Schützes, I found out why.

'Duke Max and Prince Ernst have been arrested!' Frau Schütze tearily exclaimed. 'And Herr Bundeskanzler is imprisoned in his own home!' Phone call after phone call brought further news of arrests, escape attempts, shootings, and suicides. Prominent jurists, doctors, journalists, artists, businessmen and entertainers had been singled out by the National Socialist incumbents.

Immediately, I thought of Professor Rosé and hurried to Döbling. A fearful Alma opened the door. The family was safe (for the moment), but they worried over the welfare of friends. Bruno Walter was in Holland. How would he return to his Vienna home? Alma Mahler-Werfel and her husband had fled, having smuggled their riches to Switzerland.

'What will you do?' I asked.

'What can we do?' Alma replied. 'Mutti is too ill to travel.'

---

[31] *Adabei*: an image-conscious person who dresses to be seen and admired.

Emil cleared away his flags; his favourite volumes he relegated to their former dusty haunts; and instead he stacked multiple copies of *Mein Kampf* which he topped with swastika pennants and portraits of Hitler.

'What on earth are you doing that for?' I asked.

'Have you read it?'

'No.'

'Feh! The more people read "Mein Krampf", the more they'll realise what a crackpot Hitler is, the more likely they'll revolt. And since you're mishpucha,[32] this one's on me.' He passed me a copy and staggered down the street in his odd crooked way. When I next saw him, he sported a haircut and shave that rivalled the spiffy grooming of the boys in brown. He even wore a Swastika pin on his jacket. 'To show I'm not a Jew,' he explained.

But Vienna had to wait till Monday for the German Führer. Late that afternoon, Linke Wienzeile was lined with crowds six deep. Fighter planes roared and church bells clanged. And in the distance, rumbling towards the city, I spotted armoured tanks.

My only prior experience of a military parade was accompanying Dad on Anzac Day. Year after year, in dwindling ranks, the solemn parade commemorated heart-wrenching loss as ageing men, like Dad, marched for their mates, living and dead. Since the Anzacs were for the most part easy-going volunteers, not professional soldiers, the parade was by no means an exercise in precision. And the pubs afterwards were full of stories, memories, and choked back emotions which hopefully found release over a pint.

'There's something terribly wrong in all this,' I remarked to the Portrait while from my balcony I watched the police restrain the folk who jostled to see the files of German soldiers. 'I almost wish there had been a war, a fight, some show of resistance, a Judas Maccabeus to rise and attack by surprise. Just as well Hubie isn't here. Imagine what he would say!'

In the past, Imperial Austria had always resisted: had held out against the Turks; had taken on the might of Frederick the Great despite the odds; had battled against Napoleon; had struggled to withstand Wilhelm I and Bismarck. Now, the tiny nation was no match for German might. Her identity had been stripped away over the course of a century and a half. With the disbandment of the Holy Roman Empire, she had been forced to take her place as an imperial domain in an increasingly secular world whose modern empires were built on military strength and trade; only to be destroyed once more by war and reconfigured as a democratic nation, a concept utterly foreign to her given her centuries-old

---

[32] *Mishpucha:* (lit.) family; often means extended family and ring-ins.

monarchy and diverse culture. The Anschluss with Germany was a union with ancient roots, certainly, and one much desired by post-war idealists. But there was something quite vulgar about the display of tanks and troops parading down Linke Wienzeile, and I expressed as much in a letter to Hubie:

> *You could hardly call it a victory march. I mean, no battle has been fought; and yet the Germans parade like conquering heroes. It's awfully ostentatious. Men, women, and children alike hold their arms in the National Socialist salute and cry 'Heil!' and I wonder if they really know what they are doing or saying; for only days ago the very same people were behind Chancellor Schuschnigg. Can they really be that fickle? It is as if Dr Schuschnigg's resignation was an invitation to acknowledge the Anschluss without even a protest. Certainly, that is what the new Chancellor, Seyss-Inquart, advised. Anyone not in favour, I guess, is hiding away at home. There's nowhere else to go, since most of the shops are closed either in celebration or commiseration. Hubie, I tell you it is a most peculiar affair.*

'Are you coming, Phoebe?' An excited Franzl, dressed in trachten and sporting a Tyrol hat, interrupted my epistle the following morning. 'Hitler is speaking at the Heldenplatz! It's an historic occasion! Quick! We're meeting Rudi at Prince Eugene's statue!'

Poor Prince Eugene, who had protected Austria during the Turkish Wars, was swamped by National Socialist enthusiasts. Rudi, also attired in traditional dress, helped Zita and me mountaineer our way up, where we enjoyed a most advantageous position beneath the prince's rampant horse whose rump was covered with a Nazi flag. Opposite stood the Hofburg, the former palace of the Habsburgs, its façade flanked with red bannered swastikas, its solid brick wings lending liberal protection to the thousands that filled the square.

'Lieber Führer sei so nett, zeige dich am Fensterbrett!' clamoured the madding crowd. But it seemed an eternity before the entourage finally appeared as dark specks on the palace balcony and Hitler came forward to speak:

> *Within a few short days, a radical change has taken place in the German Volksgemeinschaft, whose dimensions we might see today, yet whose significance can only be fully appreciated by coming generations*

'Volksgemeinschaft? What's that?' I shouted amidst the cheering.

'Being the community of people linked by common heritage,

irrespective of class or wealth, Volksgemeinschaft is the foundation of nationhood,' Rudi explained at the top of his voice. 'It is what identifies us as German, as opposed to Poles or Slavs, for instance.'

'It seems rather parochial, if you ask me,' I called back.

'Parochial? Is that how you would describe the union of a great people?'

'Pardon?' I shouted, for Rudi's remaining response had been drowned in the din.

'I said, "You have a lot to learn".'

Boos and catcalls resounded through the square when Hitler mentioned the hated treaty. I knew well that Versailles' punitive humiliation of Austria-Hungary; its devaluation of her transcendent identity; its reduction of Austria to a miniscule country in a fragmented Europe; and its rejection of her desire to join with Germany, was much resented. But Hitler turned the matter to quite a different purpose. Against the will of the people, he claimed, Versailles, in preventing Austria's post-war union with Germany, had thwarted the creation of 'a genuinely great German Reich', and had blocked the path of the German people to the future.

Adolf Hitler then proposed a new mission for Austria. As the eastern outpost of the German Volk, Austria (or Östmark as he called her) was now to protect German freedom from oriental influence – rather a different role from her age-old imperial function of providing military protection to diverse peoples, regardless of their language or culture.

And how the crowd cheered! Austria now fully belonged to the German Reich! The reunification of Greater Germany had begun! Martial shouts of 'Sieg Heil! Sieg Heil! Sieg Heil!' rang out as thousands stretched out their arms in fervent and unanimous support.

But Franz remained silent.

'Did Hitler say Reichsstatthalter Seyss-Inquart?' he asked of Zita.

'I think so,' she shouted back. 'I didn't catch it all. What a din! It's like a football match!'

'Does this mean what I think it does?' he called, looking at Rudi, who was hanging out from Prince Eugene's horse like a monkey from a tree trunk, his other arm extended in salute.

'What's that, Franzl?' Rudi managed to reply and shout a 'Sieg Heil' in the one breath.

'Austria! Austria! Is she really gone?'

'I think so! Hallo! Steady, my friend!'

And had Rudi not grabbed him as quickly as he did, Franzl would have fallen a long, long way.

50

Rejoice and be Glad

EASTER THAT YEAR acquired an especial significance: A miracle had been wrought; an unbloody sacrifice had taken place. The Austrian people, lying dead in a democratic wasteland, in three days had risen to new life without recourse to war. Providence had appointed Adolf Hitler to deliver his people and bring them to their true Home. Spring sunshine and nourishing rain caused every branch in park and wood to sprout throughout Vienna; and fruits of black, red, and white began to form as Austria was grafted to the German Reich.

'It's a disgrace!' Professor Schütze declared in implacable rage when he returned from his Monday rehearsal, having abruptly announced that Professor Rosé had been dismissed from his post as Concertmaster. 'Fifty-seven years he has held that position! Fifty-seven years! I admit we have not always seen eye to eye; but to inform an old man that his services henceforth are no longer required, is a crime. And one of your mob,' he pointed at Franz, 'One of your mob had the gall to say to him, "Your days are numbered, Herr Hofrat,". Nor is Rosé alone. Seven violinists have been sacked! And there will be more before the season's finished. All because they are Jews!'

And without further ado, he resigned from the Philharmoniker. That evening, his friend Seyss-Inquart dropped by for schnapps, whereupon the two men had a lengthy discussion behind closed doors. Days later, Furtwängler came to dinner, and further discussion took place. Richard Strauss also paid a call. The Professor capitulated and resumed his post as Principal Oboe.

'I am not obliged to become a party member,' he explained to his wife and children. 'I do not have to swear an oath to stay in the orchestra. It is important that music remain independent of politics. We must show that music, family, and culture are above the Third Reich by continuing to play and live as we have always done. If we do not, our beloved orchestra will be dissolved.'

But the decision cost him dearly. I had never seen the Professor look as grave and sad as on that day.

He erupted again when Karl-Alois came home. As part of the regular army, Karl had retreated to the barracks at Wiener Neustadt when the troops were ordered to withdraw. The army held fast for a week, surrounded by the German Wermacht, in a last demonstration of independence staged in the hope that other nations would rally to Austria's cause. All was in vain. Both Britain and France, while ostensibly outraged, were reluctant to employ force at short notice, and instead favoured prudent observation and diplomacy. Several officers committed suicide rather than take the oath of allegiance to the Führer Adolf Hitler.

'And you?' questioned his father, 'Did you take the oath?'

Karl was silent.

'Well did you?'

'The oath is not valid, for it was taken under force.'

'You took the oath?'

'Would you prefer I take my own life? Or face a Nazi firing squad? Or would you want to find me dead in my own home courtesy of the Schutzstaffel? For don't tell me that General Zehner committed suicide. Of what good is death, Vati? Instead, you have one lieutenant less whose loyalty lies with the Reich. The Chancellor should not have resigned! Come what may, we were prepared to hold ground! Why did Britain not come to our aid? Heaven knows Britannia needs us to guard her colonial interests, poor bastion though we are against German involvement in the East. Now Austria is no more!'

In the Naschmarkt, my favourite stalls closed. Traffic down Linke Wienzeile came to a standstill when a prominent lawyer threw himself in front of a tram. Herzmansky's store in Mariahilf was plundered. Herr Weissmüller lost his position at the bank. Police pressed Jockel and Mitzi Austerlitz into painting yellow stars and 'Jud' on the bakery window; and an ominous asterism formed as yellow stars appeared in the neighbouring Taborstrasse shopfronts. Hardly anyone was in the street. People were afraid of going out lest their homes be looted by Nazi supporters. And if they did go out, they might be pressed into scrubbing the pro-Schuschnigg slogans off the pavement. The sight of Swastika-sporting officials supervising the haut monde, bejewelled and well-dressed (as always), on hands and knees in the middle of Mariahilferstrasse, slopping suds with hard bristled brushes, made you stop and stare in shock, as you would when unarmed you might witness a lion attack a lamb.

In Leopoldstadt, Nazi storm troopers (the official title of the boys in brown) rounded up several Jews and pushed them to the ground. 'Hüpfen! Hüpfen! Hüpfen!' they chanted as they kicked the gentlemen into performing rigorous calisthenics. Onlookers shrugged helplessly. Others cheered. The weary phrase, 'What can you do?' fell from many a lip.

And indeed, what could you do? To resist or complain ran the risk of increased brutality. To turn a blind eye showed you did not care. But I could not refrain from voicing my distress when, on my way to the Ronacher, I saw Dr Robert cleaning the pavement with a toothbrush at the behest of brownshirt thugs and gawped at by a crowd.

'Dr Ströhmann!' I called.

He glared at me. Then his 'supervisors' brought him to task. Dr Robert winced with pain.

The boys in brown poured acid on his hands.

And when I arrived for my morning Walzermädeln rehearsal, I found the theatre closed and Alma, Lori, and the orchestra girls gossiping outside. In their smart coats, coquettish hats, and high-heels they looked like mannequins from *Harper's Bazaar*. A Mercedes pulled up in front. Out stepped a man in black military attire with a swastika armband. The theatre was being 'Aryanised', he announced; and our orchestra, being a 'Jewish' orchestra, by order of the Reich, was no longer permitted to perform. Then he returned to his car, leaving two brown shirt accomplices to stand guard.

I was out of a job.

Towards the end of March, a letter arrived from Kerem.

Istanbul,
19ᵗʰ March 1938

My Darling Houri,

What a joy it was to receive your letter; and yet what a sorrow to think you have suffered, and continue to suffer, on my account. How I should love to be with you in Vienna! Unfortunately, I am sailing to Cape Town and will not return till September.

I wish I possessed the wisdom with which you have credited me. Still, considering I am nearly old enough to be your father, at least I can speak from experience. Perhaps what I am going to write will scrape your heart like a file; and were we to talk face to face, heart to heart, I would soothe you with the chamois of my caresses.

Phoebe, sometimes love is rough-hewn; other times it glitters; either way, it requires cutting and polishing to reveal its splendour. Like a jewel, it has many facets of which feelings are merely a part. If your young man is as good and kind as you say, and if he has honourable intentions, give

him time. Should you develop feelings for him, be realistic:
Give yourself to him without regret. If not, or if trouble befalls
you meanwhile, do not hesitate to send word. I promise I will
do all I can to help.

I wish only for your happiness, and remain
Your humble servant,
Kerem

'I suppose he's right,' I sighed as I folded the letter. But already
the hard edge of Kerem's wisdom was grinding my heart. 'Perhaps
I might never see him again!' I sobbed.

A sudden knock forced me to curb my tears.

'I was passing by,' Rudi smiled, 'and thought I would call by to
see how you are. It cannot be easy these days, a foreigner living
alone. What's the matter?'

'How is your step-father?' The cruelty of the Nazi police, my
own powerlessness, the spineless complicity (or was it shock?) of
the bystanders, and the humiliation of a decent and distinguished
man – a doctor devoted to caring for others – continued to haunt
me. Furthermore, I had no wish to disclose anything regarding
Kerem, especially to Rudi who seemed a little too curious for my
liking.

'Ah, scrubbing slogans off the pavement with toothbrushes was
the punishment inflicted on National Socialists by the Fatherland
Front,' he shrugged.

'And tipping acid on a surgeon's hands? Was that also part of
the treatment?'

'My step-father was an outspoken Dollfuss supporter. It's
coming back to bite him now.'

'You're not concerned?'

'It's merely a demonstration; a change of the political tide. Tit
for tat.'

'And is this how you imagined your Anschluss?'

'It is early days yet. Things will settle. Lover's quarrel?' he noted
my tear-stained face.

'It's none of your business.'

'I thought— Hubie—'

'He's practising his horn again and the other guests are
complaining, which he says is a good sign.'

Indeed, not a day passed without my receiving a packet
postmarked Montpellier. Heeding Kerem's advice to give Hubie
time, I followed the line of his discussions be they literary,
historical, musical, or otherwise; and abandoned my hitherto
perceived duty of furnishing him with news, given that he never
mentioned any of my updates in his correspondence. This I

welcomed, for I was growing tired of providing increasingly distressing accounts of vandalism, bullying, and suicide.

Would he never come home? 'When the lilacs blossom', he had said. Well, that had been weeks ago. Now the parks were verdant, the woods afresh, the flowerbeds brimming with blooms; and there was no indication that Hubie was coming back. Every letter, such as the one I received early in April, I opened in the hope that it would contain news of his return:

Dearest Phoebe,

I hope this letter continues to find you well. Life goes on much the same here; although the recent troublesome weather has done me more harm than good, and the asthma has returned despite the health regime to which I have so faithfully adhered. Fortunately, this latest attack has proved less serious than the last, but it has left me weak and breathless.

Yesterday, Doctor K. was good enough to visit. To ensure that I recover as fully as possible, he advised me to postpone my return. Do not despair. I am well but must continue to monitor my breathing.

How I long to see you again! Too many weeks have passed since we danced and played together. How I miss the sound of your voice, and long for the touch of your hand! I yearn to gaze into your eyes once more and lose myself in all their dark loveliness and passion.

Memory and hope must be my medicine. Indeed, they soothe; but they also intensify the pain of absence. You are far away; while I, imprisoned by my mortal frame, languish in a foreign land. The sea, which I first found so refreshing, now holds less attraction for me. I wish to visit the mountains again, to see the hamlets of pretty Austria, to immerse myself in the life and beauty of my home. Most of all I long for you, and I count the days when we will be reunited.

Be calm, dearest Phoebe, and do not worry. While we may not be close in body, we are close in spirit, and you may be certain you are constantly in my thoughts and prayers.

Yours,
Hubie.

'Oh dear!' I shivered. 'What a turnabout! Perhaps he really does love me. Oh! What am I to do? Kerem, I hope you're right. Time must unravel this, not I. Hurry, Hubie, and come home!'

There was no escaping the political campaign for the coming

referendum. 'Vote *Ja* for Adolf Hitler, and *Ja* for the German Reich.' *Ja* on the wireless. *Ja* in the cinema. *Ja* in the papers. Everywhere you walked, *Ja, Ja, Ja,* to the point that you did not want to utter such a commonplace word, even if you did agree with what was being said or offered. Posters featuring muscular blonde males with handsome jawlines proclaimed *Großdeutschland Ja!* Plastered high and low in cafes, parks, and markets, a show of hands in salute underscored *Das ganze Volk sagt am 10 April Ja!* Even postage stamps advocated *Ein Volk, Ein Reich, Ein Führer, 10 April 1938 Ja.* And looming larger than life on billboards all over town was Hitler's moustachioed face and *Ja.*

'I cannot believe that Cardinal Innitzer has encouraged everyone to vote Ja. To think that the Church could be so complicit!' complained Dr Robert who joined us for Sunday dinner at the Schützes', his blistered hands bandaged.

'It contravenes *Mit Brennender Sorge,*' agreed the Professor. 'Perhaps the Cardinal thought to protect his flock by dispensing them from any duty of conscience. But he should be speaking out! He'll be recalled.'

'I should think so,' Dr Robert replied. 'And Jews have been forbidden from voting, which means that the bulk of the country's professional classes are unable to exercise their democratic rights.'

'What difference would it make? Within the overall population, the Jews are a minority,' countered Rudi, 'so their voice wouldn't amount to much.'

'I don't care how large a percentage of the population is Jewish,' argued his mother, 'It's a violation of rights.'

'Mind you, assimilated Jews would swell the numbers considerably,' Franz observed.

'But how do you tell?' questioned Heidi. 'At school, some girls won't play with Gretl Schumaker anymore because they say she's Jewish. She said she wasn't. No one ever told her she was Jewish before. How do you know?'

'In many cases, you don't know,' answered her mother. 'You are being kind to Gretl, yes?'

'Elsa and I will not vote,' declared Doctor Robert. 'It will not be a legitimate referendum.'

'Will you vote "Ja" now that Hitler has lowered the voting age to twenty, Franzl?' the Professor asked.

'I don't know what I'm going to do. It's all gone rather wrong,' lamented a bewildered Franz, who had entertained every hope of promotion while Seyss-Inquart had briefly taken the Chancellor's role; but with the incorporation of Austria into the Reich, Arthur Seyss-Inquart was relegated to Reichsstatthalter, and all the positions of influence were being handed to Berliners.

Addressing the throngs in front of the Rathaus the day before the referendum, Hitler restated his God-given mission to peacefully restore Austria to Germany – that miracle wrought by God upon His great German people. Fervently he implored Germans everywhere to make their mark on history, and with one accord, in full submission to Almighty decree, affirm the Reich. 'It was like a Mass,' remarked Frau Geplapper, who heard the Führer speak at the Nordwestbahnhof later that afternoon. 'May God bless Greater Germany!'

'Are you going to vote?' I asked Emil. 'The Social Democrats have declared they will support Hiter.'

'Me? I'm not obliged to.'

Furthermore, he refused to take Albrecht to the polls.

'But I am an Austrian citizen!' Albrecht insisted. 'Just because I cannot see does not mean I cannot exercise my rights.'

'You can't vote, Albrecht.'

'You could help me mark the ballot paper, Misha. That would be valid, yes?'

'You're not permitted to vote. Not because you're blind, but because you're Jewish.'

Nor did Zita bother with the plebiscite, despite her blue-stocking leanings. 'They're printing everyone's address on the back of the ballot papers. Imagine what that will lead to! Would you fancy a visit from the boys in brown?' Instead, she spent the afternoon with Emil; and left his apartment looking very coy as she straightened her skirt and smoothed the seams of her hose.

On Sunday the tenth of April, the 'Ja' vote for 'the reunification of Austria with the German Reich that was enacted on 13 March 1938', and for the election of 'our leader Adolf Hitler', amounted to 99% across the Reich. How could it be otherwise? No Jew was entitled to vote. Any prominent opposition had been imprisoned, while more lucky suspects had fled for their lives. Who would dare put his mark to 'Nein'? Professor Schütze and his wife did, as did many of their acquaintance. 'But I am certain our votes have counted for nothing,' he concluded, 'for it was reported that the vote in Hietzing was unanimously in favour.'

And thus, by democratic decree, was reinstated a union medieval in origin, but hardly medieval in its expression, for this was no Holy Roman Empire.

Finally, amidst lilacs and May roses, a telegram announced Hubie's return. With his parents, I waited for him at the station. Only Sisi appeared. Hastily, she traversed the concourse.

'Hubie's been detained!' she gasped, her usually calm demeanour much disturbed. 'A man in a black leather coat noticed he was reading *Der Zauberberg* and pulled him aside. I don't understand! What's wrong with that?'

An hour passed. Frau Schütze grew anxious; the Professor more so. Finally, Hubie strode into view, more solemn than ever. He embraced his mother and father. Upon seeing me, he stood rooted to the ground. I gazed at him and read in his large, soft eyes an abundant affection.

'Phoebe!' he sighed as he took off his hat. 'Mein liebling, Phoebe!' Long he caressed me and stroked my hair, and when I next looked up at him, he was crying. 'How wonderful it is to see you again!'

51

A Matter of Black and White

BEWILDERED, I studied the pamphlet included in my morning mail: a document designed to help the people of 'Ostmark' determine their eligibility for Reich citizenship. A comprehensive genetic taxonomy demonstrated who was an Aryan, and therefore welcomed into Hitler's Pax Germanica; and who was a Jew, and consequently *persona non grata*.

Four columns featured diagrammatic rows of spots. Some were pure white vis: ○; others were completely black like so: ●. And there was a host of in-betweens: quarter-filled, half-filled, three-quarter filled, in sundry combinations, with annotations in Gothic text explaining what was permitted and what was 'Verbotem'. For those whose German ancestry was clear-cut, it was easy: ○ + ○ = ○ (Pure Aryan). Likewise, for those who were Jews (● + ●) it was a fait accompli. But for the rest – quarter + quarter, quarter + half, half + half, three-quarter + quarter, and so forth – there seemed to be a nasty piece of logic at work, whereby a solution would manifest via the exertion of a special sector of my brain.

Since I was not particularly fond of exercising that sector of my brain – science was never my strong suit (more from want of inclination than ability, according to Dad who shared my indifference) – I took the matter to an expert.

'What does it all mean, Rudi?'

'It's quite simple. Everyone must provide evidence of ancestry to qualify for citizenship. For most, it involves supplying certificates of infant baptism for their four grandparents,' he explained during an *al fresco* celebration at the Ströhmanns' in honour of his graduation one glorious May afternoon.

'Easier said than done.'

'That is very true, Phoebe,' nodded Frau Schütze. 'For many, it means writing to every part of the old Empire. How will we obtain records? Besides, everyone has some Jewish blood. Why, the first Baron von Rechtschaffen was a Jew, and there have been marriages to Jews in every subsequent generation of my family. Where else do you think my sons get their brains and their good looks?'

'I might have thought I had something to do with it,' the Professor remarked in his droll way. 'And you are right, Klara, there would not be a single Viennese family without some Jewish connection. Even in my own family there are Jews. Uncle Wilhelm in Holland, for instance.'

'Uncle Wilhelm?' echoed Heidi.

'He converted to Catholicism when he married your Aunty Jannike. They moved to Amsterdam before Hitler came to power. Now I see the wisdom of their decision.'

'Do you have Jewish blood, Phoebe?' asked Rudi.

'Apparently, my grandmother was Jewish.'

'And that is your father's mother?'

'My mother's. But her family never really bothered with religion. The little I know is that Maman's childhood baptism had something to do with the Dreyfus Affair.'

'It was not a good time to be Jewish,' accorded Frau Schütze. 'In Vienna, it was the same. Do you remember, Kurti, that concert in which some of the audience booed Mahler onto the stage? Emperor Franz-Josef also attended, and he refused to allow the performance to proceed until the offenders were removed.'

'And what of your mother's father?' asked Dr Elsa.

'I have no idea. What does it matter? I'm proud of my Jewish heritage. Bobeshi was an extraordinarily beautiful and talented woman. To reduce her to a black spot on a chart is absurd. In fact, with a Scottish grandfather, a Chinese grandmother, a Polish-French grandmother, not to mention an Hungarian-Australian grandfather, I think my ancestry's fascinating. Dad used to say with a face like mine I could walk the world over and fit in anywhere.'

'The Wandering Jew,' Franz joked.

'Well, Jewish or not, I'm going to have to wander the globe to obtain baptismal certificates.'

'I think the natives will keep the authorities busy for quite a while,' remarked Dr Elsa.

'I don't think you'll have to worry, Phoebe,' Frau Schütze reassured me. 'You have a foreign passport. Surely, Kurti, the laws do not apply to Phoebe?'

'They might if she wishes to stay in Vienna.'

'And she will need proof if she wishes to marry,' Franz winked.

'Speak for yourself, Franzl.'

'Ah, but I do not wish to marry, dear Phoebe.'

'And did I say I did? Besides, what about Inge?'

'Yes, Franzl, what about Inge?' echoed Frau Schütze. 'You haven't seen her lately.'

'She has broken off our courtship and is going out with a fellow in the Schutzstaffel.'

'She wishes to safeguard her purity,' Dr Elsa raised an eyebrow.

'Rudi and I had to obtain certificates quick sticks,' chimed in Zita. 'Luckily, there's nothing to worry about on my side after all: Grandmother von Rechtschaffen was baptised as a baby, and Rudi's a pedigree. Lord, if this continues, in a few generations we'll all end up like the Habsburgs! Well, didn't they think that inbreeding was the best way of preserving the royal line? And look what happened,' she stuck out her lower jaw, rolled her eyes skyward in an imbecilic expression, hunched over, and attempted to speak. 'I am pure Aryan,' she joked.

'It's bad science, if you ask me,' Rudi observed. 'We know very little about our genetic makeup, let alone about the relationship between genetics and ethnicity. No one has discovered an identifying gene or genes for Aryan, or Slav, or Jew and so on, let alone whether such genes are dominant or recessive. Mind you, if they're convinced that the Aryans are the master race, it would follow that the Aryan gene pool is the dominant pool. So, why should they worry?'

'You base your objection purely on scientific grounds?' queried his step-father.

'It's a valid one, yes? Furthermore, there are cultural factors, as well as genetic distinctions, at work. One cannot say that an assimilated German Jew is the same as an Ostjud; so, to determine everything by genetics, particularly inaccurate or faulty genetics, is untenable. And what do baptisms have to do with genetics?'

'Once a Jew, always a Jew. Ask any Jew and they will tell you the same,' smiled Franz.

'I wouldn't go to the trouble,' Dr Elsa sneered. 'Anti-Semitism is the Socialism of fools.'

'It is the sport of the rabble,' added Dr Robert. 'It always has been.'

'Moreover, it— maligns our Christendom,' Hubie commented for the first time that afternoon.

'That is very true,' nodded his mother. 'You have been very quiet, Huberle. Is everything all right?'

'I received a letter yesterday. The university will not confer my— doctorate. Apparently, my thesis on phenomenology, jurisprudence, and the creation of the Grand Duchy of Krakow is not in— keeping with the p-p-principles of National Socialism.'

'You too, Hubie? Well, you're not the first. The varsity doors are also slammed in my face,' replied Dr Robert.

'Robert has been dismissed from his post at the School of Medicine,' Dr Elsa explained.

'Why, Dr Ströhmann?' queried Sisi.

'According to our new authorities, I am a Jew, Sisi.'

'I didn't know that.'

'Few do. What concerns me, though, is how did they find out?

My family was not observant. We never attended synagogue. In fact, we celebrated Christmas like everyone else— For us, it was holiday season. I was baptised when I married Marta my first wife. That was the law in those days. It is true, I did not always attend Church, especially after Marta passed away— I didn't see the point in it. I do not need a priest— or a rabbi, for that matter, to tell me that I should be a good person.

'Anyway, since I married Elsa ten years ago, I have accompanied her to Sunday Mass; which means that some Nazi has been searching through pre-War records. Where would they find such information? My birth certificate? My academic history? Or have they been looking in the parish registers? And if they've been looking in parish files they have violated the concordat they made to refrain from interfering in Church affairs. Or has the priest volunteered details? Even worse is the possibility that family or close friends have informed them. Other than the priest, they are the only ones who would know. It's abhorrent!'

'People one thought reasonable have lost all common sense,' continued Dr Elsa. 'When she heard what had happened to Robert, a friend dared to suggest I divorce him because it is now forbidden for a Jew to have intimate relations with a German woman. This advice, from someone who hitherto would never have tolerated the idea of divorce!'

'My desk is already piled with divorce cases,' Franz added. With Jewish lawyers being dismissed in their hundreds, he had quickly found another job. 'All that is required for divorce under National Socialist law is proof of ethnicity. I even have clients admitting to adultery to protect their spouse and children. They are prepared to testify in court what they would only have revealed in Confession and perjure themselves accordingly. I tell you, the Cake War is a pleasant relief. Tell me, Rudi my friend, will they use genetics to prove that "The Original Sachertorte" is in fact the original Sachertorte?'

'What will you do, Robert?' inquired a concerned Frau Schütze.

'I have been offered a position as a consultant physician in Boston. When Schuschnigg signed the agreement with Hitler in 'thirty-six, we knew it was only a matter of time. Our trip to Germany that year confirmed our suspicions, so we prepared to emigrate. It is well we acted when we did. We would hardly stand a chance now given the thousands who are trying to get out. We will leave after the wedding.'

'We are going to miss you,' lamented the Professor, 'Both of you.'

'What are you going to do about your graduation?' I asked Hubie as he walked me home via the Schönbrunn grounds that evening.

'There is not much I can do,' he sighed.

'You're not going to protest?'

'I have no means of appeal. The university has been purged of any professors who opposed the National Socialists; not to mention all the Jewish academics, regardless of their views. Judges also have been dismissed. Professor von Hildebrand, who helped me most with my thesis, only narrowly escaped arrest and is no longer in the country.'

'It's shameful!'

'Dr Ströhmann is right. I am not the only one. I had coffee the other day with Eugene Kusch, Lori's brother. He also has been denied permission to graduate, but that is because he is Jewish, of course. His situation is direr than mine. Do you plan to stay in Vienna, Phoebe?'

'I don't see why I should leave. Do you want me to stay?'

He smiled a little – the slight, shy turn of the lips typical of the awkward, withdrawn, very formal young man I had met in the park the previous Autumn.

'You visited Paris as well as Montpellier?' I broke another silence, thinking that reference to his recent trip would prompt further conversation, and curious as to his purpose in sending that mysterious letter from 'Cousin Frank'. Since he arrived home, he had been extremely reticent.

'I did no such thing.'

'While you were away, I received news from Paris, from a cousin of mine, Mr Frank Horne. Do you know him?'

'I have heard of him. But whatever might concern your cousin has nothing to do with me,' he surveyed the parkland and cast a glance at the winding path behind us. Then he continued sotto voce, 'There are many Austrians abroad who are grieved at our situation, particularly the Crown Prince who, I know for a fact, attempted to ease our plight by encouraging Schuschnigg to resist Hitler, by offering to assume the Chancellor's role following Schuschnigg's resignation, and by advocating with the French on the grave need to lend military support. All his considerable efforts, however, were in vain. Instead, our belated Chancellor sacrificed us at the altar of his Germanic idol. Believe me when I tell you, Phoebe, the oblation will be total. Hitler will see to that. This is but the beginning.'

Zita and Rudi were married on a beautiful June day. Being part of the wedding party, I arrived at the Schütze home early that morning.

Karl-Alois opened the door. Contrary to my expectation, he was wearing wedding mufti instead of military dress. As he explained, swinging Waldo into his arms and adopting that inimitably Viennese tone of resignation, his new Wehrmacht dress uniform unfortunately was still with the tailor.

Where's Hubie? I asked; and with a raise of his brows, Karl indicated the argument coming from the belle étage.

'Aside from your opinion, if you have nothing to substantiate your case then the matter is closed!' Professor Schütze thundered as Hubie stormed out of the salon. 'Anyone would think it was him the one being married!' the Professor shook his head at me in fury.

I did not see Hubie until we left for the church. Like Karl, he wore a morning suit of dove grey striped trousers and matching cravat, topped with a waistcoat and coat the colour of a foreboding cumulonimbus.

'There will be no— Mass, only a ceremony,' he sighed as he helped his mother into the open-air carriage. 'The Ströhmanns have stopped practising and my father does not wish to embarrass them by not having them partake of Holy Communion at their son's wedding; particularly Dr Robert, who feels betrayed by the Church. Vati is also worried there will be too many guests who are in sympathy with National Socialism, and who risk making communion in a state of mortal sin. But to pledge one's troth to one's beloved before Our Lord, and yet not receive Him, is a grave pity.'

'Now, now, Huberle,' Frau Schütze remonstrated, 'it is Zita and Rudi's wedding, not yours. We do what is best for everyone.'

Outside the church, Hubie stood beside his mother, as grim and sombre as a pall bearer at a funeral. The guests he acknowledged solemnly, his iconic eyes staring forcefully into the soul of each. Frau Schütze was gracious and charming as always, if a little anxious.

'How is Zita?' Dr Elsa enquired between welcomes.

'Quite ill, I'm afraid. Wedding nerves.'

Dr Elsa contained her thoughts.

Opposite, the Ströhmanns stood like Roman sentries on the banks of the Danube surveying Gothic hordes. Dr Elsa, more austere than ever, scrutinised each guest in turn as if to ascertain how heavily armed they were. Dr Robert looked on in dignified and silent disgust. For decades he had dined with these people, prescribed treatment, holidayed with them, celebrated with them. Now he regarded them as little more than barbarians.

'I wonder he has the hide to show up,' Dr Robert muttered as he watched Reichsstatthalter Seyss-Inquart and his wife escorted from their car by Gestapo bodyguards.

'Robert, he is a long-standing friend of the Schützes. At least he has the decency not to wear his uniform.'

'I was pleased to hear of your appointment in Boston, Robert,' Seyss-Inquart warmly shook the hand Dr Robert had been obliged to extend. 'Have you obtained your exit visas?'

'We will make the necessary arrangements after the wedding, Arthur,' Dr Elsa informed him.

'Then let me know, and I will ensure that you have them in good time.'

'We have climbed mountains together! Now he cannot wait to be rid of me!' Dr Robert seethed between guests.

'With all due respect, Robert, I think Arthur's was a genuine offer, motivated by sympathy and companionship,' Frau Schütze performed yet another smiling curtsey.

There was some measure of truth in her observation. The short-sighted Reichsstatthalter was under considerable pressure. While his handshake had been warm, he could meet the gaze of neither the Ströhmanns nor the Schützes; and however sincere his offer may have been, a host of watchful eyes barred him from further explanation or expression.

Franz, as best man, ushered us to our pew with his usual bonhomie. Rudi was all smugness and charm; and when he took his place at the sanctuary steps, he rubbed his hands together and gazed down the church aisle like a salesman on the verge of clinching a deal.

Attired in an artful adaptation of her mother's wedding dress, Zita leaned wearily on her father's arm. It was odd to see her not wearing her glasses. She was surprisingly attractive without them; but her quirky intellectual charisma had vanished from her expression. Like Queen Mary of Scotland walking to her execution, she maintained a steady, solemn pace, while her dim stare extended beyond Rudi, beyond the gilded sanctuary, beyond the marble altar, and traversed the city to a certain bookstore in Linke Wienzeile.

Professor Schütze, meanwhile, wore that purposeful glare which so characterised his stage entrances. Only Sisi and Heidi, as bridesmaid and flower girl, looked as if they belonged in the tableau. Willowy and graceful, with a blue satin sash round her slender waist, her golden hair garlanded with white rosebuds and curled around her angelic features, Heidi was the epitome of innocence; while elegant, dark-haired Sisi fulfilled her role as helpmeet with that calm intelligence everyone so valued in her.

Wedding vows echoed through the vault. The couple did not tremble but spoke their promises with the ease and confidence of a well-rehearsed ritual. Assured and polished, Rudi maintained a commanding presence. He knew he made a handsome groom. As for Zita, she had blocked out all emotion. Sealed with a kiss, her vows already were fractured.

❖ ❖ ❖

Back at the Schützes', the silver coffee service poured rumour after rumour into countless demitasses. Guests sweetened and stirred their Kurze; and let slip that Rudi had reassumed his father's name to distance himself from his Jewish step-father. It was a wise decision, some remarked while adding judicious dollops of cream to their dark beverage, even though Ströhmann was not a particularly Jewish name. Krain, however, was thoroughly German.

One gentleman waived all offers of coffee, having maintained that it was the height of ingratitude on young Rudi's part toward a man who had done so much for him.

'Josef Krain was a brute,' he remarked, to which his confidante replied that it came as no surprise to her when Elsa Krain married Robert Ströhmann.

'They had been friends for years— even before she married von Krain,' she added with a look of 'I told you so' and received her melange with a gush of thanks. 'Now look what has come of it.'

Overall, most agreed it was a pity such misfortune should befall so fine and generous a man as Robert Ströhmann. So, they smiled at him and tried to converse cheerfully in his presence. Having overcome his earlier indignation, Dr Robert adopted a professional approach, and circulated from group to group as if he were passing through a hospital ward; his every handkuss akin to taking the pulse, every exchange a silent assessment of his patients' condition. And from his weary expression, he seemed faced with a malady of epidemic proportion for which he had no cure.

'It is fitting they look upon him as a scapegoat,' Hubie bleakly observed as we witnessed the doctor withdraw to the terrace to smoke, and we both noted the guilty countenances of the company whom he had left, 'For it is our own sins that have marked him out. Such is democracy.'

'It's all very well to criticise, but I tell you there was no democracy in that referendum, Hubie. Luckily, you were still convalescing in Montpellier when it took place.'

'That is true. But I did not suffer a relapse of asthma. I was advised to remain permanently in France for my own safety. You see, Phoebe, Dr K. who visited me in Montpellier was not a Doctor of Medicine but a Doctor of Law. And I will admit that his advice was very tempting. But not to return to Austria was unthinkable. I could not in conscience do that to my homeland. Nor could I do it to you. I should also say that the aforementioned Dr K, was Dr Ziggy Kowalski, and that he and Marina thank you for your hospitality.'

'What?'

'Ziggy only narrowly avoided arrest. He topped our year in law school and held strident views about the Nazis; and, yes, as you know, he is Jewish. So is Marina. They escaped minutes before the Gestapo came to their home. Since Marina is French on her father's side, they sought asylum in that country. Meanwhile, you provided a very timely refuge for which they are eternally grateful.'

'I see. And had you returned before the referendum, how would you have voted?'

'I do not know.'

Herr Professor Doktor and Frau Professor Doktor Franz-Rudolph Krain bid their guests adieu. In the midday sun, Rudi's roadster gleamed like a ruby; its white hubs ivory pure; jet black tyres unsullied; chrome trim glinting.

'Where will they spend their honeymoon?' I asked Hubie as they drove away.

'The Bavarian Alps. They are beautiful. They will visit my grandparents while they are there. The difficult political situation has prevented us from seeing Opa and Oma Schütze for some years. I write them often, but it is not the same. You would like my grandparents. I hope one day soon you will meet them.'

52

News

ONE LOVELY JULY MORNING, while still in my dressing gown, I wandered into my lounge room. It was slathered in buttery sunshine. Outside, a tram clanged, and a motor lazily puttered past. Wienerlieder oozed from neighbouring wirelesses. Down in the courtyard, the Weissmüller boys chanted and clapped, delighting in their freedom from pencils and books; for holidays had begun. I savoured the earthy, chocolaty aroma of the percolating coffee – a perfect complement to warm, sweet brioche and Frau Schütze's apricot conserve. On the dining table, my egg nested in its silver cooker. My preparations complete, I commenced a leisurely breakfast, and opened a letter from Lucy.

Oxford,
25th June, 1938

Dear Phoebe,

It has been months since we heard anything from you, and I can only hope you are safe and well. We receive such mixed news from your part of the world that it is difficult to know what to make of the situation. On the one hand, the papers tell how Austria welcomed Hitler with open arms, and yet we hear daily stories of terror and persecution.

How are you faring? Letty mentioned she wrote you from France and said you might have some news. I suppose you'll write when you're ready; but I'm letting you know that a line or two, however brief, would mean a lot.

Everything here has gone quiet since term finished. Last week, the pubs were filled with celebrating students. Now, they've all left for holidays. Wally, too, is looking forward to a well-deserved break, although he will spend most of it fixing up the nursery. That's right, Phoebe, the nursery! At long last, we are expecting! I am well, but tired. God willing, baby will be born in November.

When they heard our news, the Sothebys postponed their

return. Letty insisted we hire a maid, so we procured the services of a lassie, Esther, who recently arrived from Germany. She is a teacher by profession, but she is only permitted to do domestic work here. Her English is very good, which is a blessing; but her situation made me recall my own experience of hard times, of leaving family and friends behind. She hopes her fiancé and her parents will soon join her, but the emigration process is both costly and complex. I have been reading the paper with her, for she is anxious to hear news of the conference in France and hopes the many restrictions upon immigration will be lifted.

I think I forgot to mention that Esther is Jewish. Tell me, is it true about what is happening? How is Mr Epstein's family? And please let us know if there is anything we can do to help. Know also that there is always a place for you here if ever you need one.

With warmest wishes, I remain,

Your friend,
Lúighseach.

'Yes, Lucy, it's all quite true. And finally, a baby after nearly five years of marriage! I suppose I ought to write. Goodness gracious! No paper, no envelopes, and no stamps!' Certain that Emil would have a supply of one or the other I threw on a frock and ran down to the bookshop.

'Where's Albrecht?' I asked as I entered; for while the barrel organ was parked outside as usual, its gentlemanly operator was nowhere to be seen.

'He's been geschnappt,' Emil at that moment was donning his jacket and hat.

'Geschnappt? What's that?'

'Arrested.'

'Why? What's he done?'

'Multiple crimes: Technically, he's unemployed and homeless. He's blind, he's elderly, and he's a Jew. What a schlimazel![33] You coming?'

'Where?'

'To the police station.'

The real issue, though, as Emil explained en route, turned out to be a matter of 'registration'. The National Socialist bureaucracy now required that all German nationals, young men approaching military age, and Jews, purchase an official identification card from the local police. In Albrecht's case, the authorities made the task a little easier by providing a personal escort. Then they held

---

[33] *Schlimazel*: a hapless fellow; one who is a constant victim of bad luck.

him under lock and key while they worked out what to do with
him.

Albrecht could not see his Nazi captors and their Viennese
police cohorts; he could not see where they had taken him; and he
could not see the cell in which they had shoved him. Nor could he
fathom why he was being punished.

For punish him they did. To ascertain whether he was truly
blind, they took the dark shades that covered his eyes and
stamped on them. It should have been obvious, because all that
remained of Albrecht's eyes was a skin-lined hollow on one side,
and an eyelid that drooped over a sunken white orb on the other.
For dinner they served him dog meat which made him sick. Then
they forced him to clean up his mess – an impossible task for a
man who could not even see shadows – and they jeered at him and
called him a dirty Jew the while. They ended up assisting by
dousing Albrecht and his cell with buckets of cold water.

'I told them all they needed to know.' Albrecht clung to Emil
like a scared child does his father. 'They have given me my cards. I
want to go home. Why won't they let me go?'

Emil silently examined the passbook Albrecht pulled from his
coat pocket. It contained all his particulars – even his fingerprints
– and a photograph; and it was stamped with a red 'J' for Jew.

'Where's Matti? Will you write and tell him, Misha, what has
happened? Perhaps he will come back.'

'Matti can't come back, Albrecht. Listen, I promised I would
look after you, and I will. I'll get you out as soon as I can.'

Unemployed, homeless, blind, elderly, and Jewish he may have
been, but Albrecht could not be classed as a worthless tramp. A
war veteran, he presented a quandary for the Gestapo who
otherwise would have had him imprisoned for good. One police
officer turned out to be more sympathetic (his own father had lost
an arm in the War) and arranged Albrecht's release with the
proviso that he be placed in appropriate 'Jewish' accommodation
within the fortnight. But Albrecht could not or would not
understand that he had to leave his humble lodgings behind
Emil's shop. That Vienna was being 'Aryanised' made no sense to
him whatsoever.

'I am Viennese!' he protested. 'I have lived here all my life, and
my father and grandfather before me. We were printers to the
Emperor. I fought for my homeland. It was my duty as a citizen. I
paid my taxes. I tried my best to be a good husband and father.
Always I have endeavoured to do right. I have lost my sight, my
occupation, my family, my home; and now they want to take what
little I have left! What have I done that they should treat me so?'

But all Jews, Roddy, had to sell their businesses and vacate their premises; and if they had not already arranged to leave the country, they had to find lodgings in designated areas in Vienna. The ruling applied to every Jew living in Östmark, with the result that people from the provinces were pouring into the city.

Since the Epsteins already lived in Leopoldstadt, which was deemed one of the official Jewish zones, they were exempt from moving. But elderly Mr and Mrs Epstein, David and Pauline, had to accommodate Bela Austerlitz and her three children, who had given up their flat to strangers. In their flat above the bakery, a bookcase now divided the living room, and a mattress was stored behind the piano which in turn shared the confined space with the dining table. Extra sleeping accommodation was tucked under the lounge on the other side of the case. As far as I could see, that allowed beds for two. Where the remaining two slept was a mystery.

David assured me that the arrangement was a temporary one. Just after the Anschluss, Bela's husband Mani, who was Czech, fled Vienna for his hometown, Karlsbad, where he was living with family and looking for work. Bela, Jakob, Mitzi, and Rosa were now organising their immigration papers.

'But if Hitler gets his way with the Sudetenland as he did with Austria, I don't think we'll fare any better,' she sighed.

'And what will you do?' I asked David.

'Stay here, of course. My parents are too old to move, and Vienna is their home. If Pauline and I leave too, who will take care of them?'

'But—'

'It cannot last, Phoebe. Surely, it cannot last.'

When I returned from the Epsteins', Frau Geplapper was posting an eviction notice in the foyer of the Majolikahaus.

'I knew it!' she checked the list against her own private catalogue. 'Frau Weissmüller may have had her nose done, but it was obvious anyway. Weissmüller, yes, yes, Lehrer, Blumenthal, Mendel—'

'Mendel?' I queried. Mendel was the owner of Emil's apartment.

'Herr Mendel is sure to remain in Paris. But they have missed Herr Fährmann,' she pencilled a note to that effect. 'And I always knew Herr Frankl, who owns the building, suffered persecution complex.'

'I beg your pardon?'

'You did not know? He has been declared mad and has lost his property.'

Within days, the Weissmüllers packed all they could into suitcases and moved to Leopoldstadt. Elderly Dr and Frau Blumenthal, who had lived in the Majolikahaus for thirty years, left to stay with relatives in Poland. The Lehrers announced they were going on vacation. A week later, however, I chanced to meet them in Taborstrasse. It turned out that their passage was halted at the Swiss border and they were sent back to Vienna. Now they were applying for Palestine. Mere caretaker though she may have been, Frau Geplapper oversaw the departures like the lady of the manor viewing the banishment of serfs.

The Rosés, meanwhile, pleaded with the authorities to remain in their Döbling home while they deliberated what to do, for Justine Rosé was too sick to move. To their surprise, the authorities proved quite accommodating (not all the Nazis were uncivilised louts). The other family members, however, had lost their sources of income; Professor Rosé's pension had been cut; and much money had been spent on medicine. They had no money for the visas, taxes, and transport required for emigration.

Fortunately, the family gained assistance from their many influential friends abroad. Professor Rosé's hopes lifted when he learned that sponsorship for his emigration was being organised by Carl Flesch (yes Roddy, same as the scale manual) in London. For, to travel to another country, you required a formal invitation from a friend or relative already there.

Alfred reported with considerable relief that an opportunity for him in America had come about through the conductor Stowkowski, whom he had met in Berlin several years ago. Maria his wife, who was not Jewish, then went about obtaining the necessary affidavits for emigration, for it was too dangerous for Alfred to appear in public. Always, there was the risk of arrest and deportation, and Alfred was a prominent Nazi target. Professor Rosé, too, rarely left his home for fear of be handed a toothbrush by an S.A. thug and made to clean a latrine.

The Ströhmanns transferred the ownership of their distinctive Hietzing home to Rudi and Zita by way of a generous wedding gift and moved into Rudi's flat while they finalised their departure. This arrangement the National Socialist administration also deemed satisfactory. Perhaps Seyss-Inquart had something to do with it, for they were otherwise left alone. And not only by the officials. Aside from the Schützes, no one visited them. Nor, it seemed, did they welcome anyone. That Austria had been so complicit in her own downfall merited only their contempt.

❖❖❖

Rudi and Zita returned from their Bavarian honeymoon and celebrated a housewarming one midsummer eve. At the meal's conclusion, Rudi opened a bottle of Marillenschnapps and bashfully announced the future arrival of the first junior member of the Krain family.

'You're a biologist and you're surprised, Rudi,' laughed Karl. 'How did you think it happened? The stork?'

'Indeed, I am surprised. Very surprised,' Rudi nearly blushed.

'Can you spare a minute, Phoebe?' Zita immediately engineered a pretext for bringing me inside. Not that organising the coffee required an extra pair of hands, especially with a cook and a kitchen maid. Zita quickly issued instructions and invited me to see her new studio.

'What happened to the Kirchner?' I asked as we passed the living area.

'It's in the basement along with other so-called degenerate masterpieces. I swear we have enough down there to hold our own exhibition, and I'm not going to let Dr Goebbels add to his collection if I can help it. Phoebe,' she began the moment we reached the studio high in a secluded part of the house, 'would you mind this for me?'

She handed me a small package and bid me keep it out of sight. I was to hide it somewhere safe and not tell anyone about it. 'I know I can trust you. I have it on good authority that you can keep a secret.'

'And whose authority would that be?'

'Misha Fährmann's.'

'The baby isn't Rudi's, is it?'

'No. But it suits his purpose well to think it is. Phoebe, whatever happens, Rudi must not find out. Misha told me you knew about us, and I must say you've been very decent to keep quiet.'

'I wouldn't say I've been decent. It's simply that what mischief you and Emil get up to is none of my business.'

I ought to have refrained, but that evening my curiosity got the better of me. In the solace of my apartment, I opened the packet. It contained letters of friendship and deep affection which upon close reading had something to do with a cycling tour through Burgenland the previous summer, 'when we delighted in carefree days sampling cherries at leisure and spent nights in each other's arms knowing that what we shared was special'. 'Our love is that of gods and heroes!' another later letter proclaimed. 'It is pure, sublime!' Never would it be tainted by progeny; never would it be sullied by the duties of the married state.

But from what I could construe, the recipient was somewhat uneasy about the romance's implications, because the letter immediately following berated 'Mein sehr lieber Franzl' for his vacillation. How could they be at fault for loving each other? The fault was with society at large:

> *Why should we be considered criminals when we enjoy a more perfect union? We harm no one by our mutual affection. Yet we are forced to conceal our feelings behind sham marriages which society honours without acknowledging her own crime of valuing matter over form, and without realising the suffering she inflicts upon us in the name of propriety.*

'Curiouser and curiouser,' I perused a fourth epistle, 'Now we want to live in a Shangri-La! Will you refuse that, too, Franzl?'

Apparently, Franzl did, despite the conflict between 'his heart's affection' and 'the dictates of conscience'. In the final epistle the writer resigned himself to friendship, assured of the truth of the love that informed it. He vowed he would be patient, certain that the day would come when the tears would be wiped from his eyes. Forever would he be loyal; and he would do all in his power to protect his most precious love from shame or harm.

Each letter was signed by Rudi.

'I found them in the wastepaper bin when I was cleaning his room,' Zita explained when we coincided in the bookshop a couple of days later. 'For someone in the legal profession, he's incredibly careless. Franz and Rudi have always been thick as thieves. Mind you, I never thought they were *that* friendly.'

'And you're prepared to incriminate your own brother in some form of blackmail?'

'Franzl needn't worry. I mean, it's clear from the letters he realised his predicament and ended the affair. He had to. He risked losing his degree, his job, and his civil rights. Now, if the Nazis caught him, he'd be imprisoned. Besides, you can't have a lawyer committing a criminal offence, can you?'

'Given that most lawyers are criminals, Zusa, I believe you can,' Emil wryly remarked. 'Rudi, meanwhile, still has his little rendezvous in the park near Karlsplatz.'

'How do you know?' I asked.

'A little birdie told me,' he sniggered. 'What intrigues me, though, is that our Nazi comrades haven't caught him.'

'Rudi has to behave himself, especially now Herr Hitler's in town,' added Zita. 'The Führer doesn't like naughty boys.'

'And his parents? Zita, they'd be horrified if they knew. And I don't only mean about Rudi, I mean about you. They're very fond of you.'

'I know. But in a way, I'm doing them a service.'

'I cannot believe you actually married him!'

'It suits us both,' Zita shrugged. 'Rudi has his apartment – that is, he'll have it back again when his parents leave – and I have the house. I don't ask him what goes on in his apartment, and he doesn't ask me what I do at home. Clearly, though, I play a significant role in his little scheme, otherwise why would he have persevered? Now I have provided him with a child – his own so he thinks – he can maintain his image as a respectable man. Little does he realise two can play at that game,' Zita nudged Emil who put his hand over her tummy. They gleamed at me. How they revelled in their subversion!

And how I wished that Hubie would show me the same reckless affection! But Hubie had retreated into the forest of his thoughts. Of course, he had good reason. Added to his disappointment over his doctorate was the perennial worry that his desk in the orchestra was no longer secure, for like his father he declined to join the NSDAP. Of his companions, only Herr Steffan remained in the country. Towards me, he was civil enough, but time and again I had to contend with his ponderous silence. 'I assure you, Phoebe, that whatever the Nazis do, I will always be your friend,' he replied when I asked him whether I was in any way responsible. But why should circumstances so condition his feelings? They had little bearing on Emil.

'Zita, Emil! Have you no regard? If the Nazis find out, you could both be imprisoned or worse! What would become of the baby?'

'Isn't love worth the risk?' challenged Emil.

'You won't blab, will you?' Zita grew anxious.

'I wouldn't dream of it.'

53

Abschiedslied

ALBRECHT SAT IN HIS ARMCHAIR in his winter corner near the woodstove and refused to go out. Engines and horns now filled him with fear, and he warned Emil whenever he heard a vehicle pull up outside. If a customer entered, he cowered. Only familiar voices and the touch of those he knew and trusted soothed him. So, we took it in turns to sit with him, to read to him and talk to him, and to sing with him his favourite songs. As for his barrel organ, he had no desire to play it. He could not play it anyway, for it had been confiscated by Nazi officials. And his was not the only instrument they carted from Vienna. Over the course of that summer, the barrel organs and their vagabond operators disappeared from the city, their music never more to be heard.

'It is not dark in here, Fräulein Raye,' he tapped his forehead. 'The darkness is outside. The world in my head is the Vienna I know on a golden autumn afternoon. I have a place there. It is modest, but comfortable, and I do not need to ask for anything. I go to the theatre and concerts. I read the papers in the coffeehouse, and I play chess; and I take walks with my wife and family.

'Perhaps I made too much of a home in that beautiful Vienna. I was a printer and stationer before the War, Fräulein Phoebe, and I had the honour of printing invitations for imperial functions. I suppose I put too much faith in my achievements,' he sighed, 'for everything went to ruin after the Treaty.

'I lost my sight in the War; but maybe I lost it before then. Was I blind to the world around me? But I knew what was happening! Misha and my boys, they started using the press to print their leaflets. They thought I was oblivious to their mischief. No! I could smell the ink; I could feel it on their hands. And young men have a way of airing their opinions. Besides, what could I do? I was helpless! Now look where your Marxist notions have taken us, Misha.'

'I like that! You blame me for your misfortune?'

'You rid us of our Emperor and called it self-determination. I

met him, you know, Fräulein Phoebe, during the War. Emperor
Karl visited the military hospital. He took my hand and asked me
to pray for peace; and told me he was doing everything in his
power to end the war, to end the suffering of his people. He cared
for us, Misha. Even though, like a father, he could not always
provide for us as well as he would have liked, we mattered to him.
And when you are a father, Misha, you will understand. I always
tried to do the best for my family. That is what fathers do. I did not
always succeed, but I loved them regardless. We had our
differences, but it never changed the fact that I was their father
and they were my sons. Poor Oskar was killed outside the
Justizpalast, and Matti ran away to Spain. Have you written him
yet, Misha?'

'You still want me to write to Matti?'

'Tell him what's happened, Misha. Tell him he must not come
home. He's a good boy, Matti. He took care of me after Sonya
passed away. She was my wife, Fräulein Phoebe, and no man
could have asked for a better woman. Oskar's death broke her
heart— first Trudl, poor girl, from Influenza; then Oskar. A mother
should not have to bury her children. Vey is mir![34] My beautiful
Sonya!

'I am to blame. My transgressions led me and my family astray.
I took time away from God. I pretended to be greater than I am. I
tried to cover up my mistakes, and through my wrongdoing I
prompted others to err. Yes, I have wilfully sinned...' His words
became a soft chant; and although what he said appeared
disturbing, it seemed to soothe him; for he began to sway as he
murmured, like a motherless child rocking himself to sleep.

'What are you going to do with him?' enquired a concerned
Hubie.

Hubie now knew that whenever he was in the vicinity, he was
more likely to find me sitting with Albrecht than at home, and,
given that he had more time on his hands these days, he often
stopped by. As is often the case when families encounter
hardships, private music lessons are among the first 'luxuries' to
be sacrificed. Over the past weeks, Hubie had lost more than half
his piano students since most of his pupils were either of Jewish
extraction, or else they were from aristocratic families, most of
whom were preparing to leave. Entering the bookshop, however,
he regarded as something akin to crossing the Acheron to a
Bolshevik Inferno; and he did so with disdain and trepidation, only
to discover that Emil's shop was home to some of his favourite
works. The purchase of a volume of Halm, which he was missing
from his own considerable library, had a curiously mollifying

---

[34] *Vey is mir!*: Woe is me!

effect.

'He's farmutshet,'[35] Emil cast Albrecht a worried look. 'Aside from the War, Albrecht spent his entire life on Linke Wienzeile. He knows this street. I thought of putting him in the Jewish Institute for the Blind. They'd know what to do with him; but they're closing.'

Hubie mulled over the situation in his customary thoughtful way. 'The Schamalzhoftempl is not far from here. I could speak to the Rabbi on my way home if you wish. He may know of somewhere safe. Otherwise, Albrecht could stay with my family. I will ask my parents. I am certain they would not mind. He would have a comfortable room, good meals, and a family to look after him. We could say he is an ageing servant of many years' standing. Surely, the authorities cannot object?'

'You would do that?'

'Yes. And you would be welcome to visit him, Herr Fährmann— even stay with him until he settles. He does not look well. Has he seen a doctor? Dr Ströhmann would not charge. Let me fetch him.'

'You are going to have to, Hubie,' I added, for Albrecht's hand had fallen limp and frail from my own. 'I think he's died.'

Few mourned Albrecht. Despite him being a well-known and much-loved part of Linke Wienzeile, and even though barely two weeks had passed since he was taken away, people had grown accustomed to his absence. They passed by the shop without as much as a glance, whereas in times past they would have acknowledged his cheery salutation, paused to exchange news, and tossed him a coin. A few celebrated. 'Now we have one Jew less!' Frau Geplapper remarked when she heard.

We buried him in secret – well, as much in secret as we could. Funerals are conspicuous affairs, and Jewish funerals were favourite targets for Nazi affiliates who delighted in pelting the mourners and coffins with eggs and rotting vegetables. Emil and I left at sunrise and travelled to Zentralfriedhof by separate trams. Hubie, too, came to pay his condolences, having taken a similar circuitous route from Hietzing. We met the Rabbi at the gravesite. With the pall-bearers, he was the only one to enter the cemetery via the Jewish gate. Fortunately, he was given little trouble by the Brownshirts who stood guard: Albrecht's war service ensured that he was laid peacefully to rest.

'May you be comforted among all the mourners of Zion and Jerusalem,' Hubie extended his hand to Emil after the burial.

---

[35] *Farmutshet*: worn out, exhausted.

'And may you lie in the ground and bake bagels,'[36] Emil did not bother returning Hubie's gesture.

'Hubie means well, Emil.'

'His sort always means well,' Emil snarled. 'They think a pious condolence suffices for a death that should never have happened. Albrecht's reached his terminus – a poor, blind old man whose life was ruined by war – a war caused by *Hubie's* class. He joins his wife who died of exhaustion, a son who was gunned down by a prelate's decree, and a daughter dead from Influenza after years of deprivation. Yes, we have your Hubie and his ilk to thank for our misery, and he dishes out platitudes.'

'You would have me believe that Princip was a— monarchist; that we had no right to defend land and people we solemnly pledged to protect; that revolution is superior to statesmanship; and that God is dead. You are a fool, and I have no more words for you.' Hubie pushed up his glasses with a supercilious twitch and strode away, leaving me to thank the Rabbi on my own; for somehow Emil had slipped from the gravesite.

I spotted him a little further along, leaning on his stick before a simple headstone – one of many identical pieces marked with a Star of David:

V. Furmanski d. 1916
A. Furmanski d. 1916

'My sister and mother,' he indicated the grave. 'I germanised my name when I entered university. What is the point of it all? Albrecht has gone, as they have, to nothing! And when I go it will be as if we never lived!'

And he began to shake with grief. 'My mother left me to look after little Velvela while she worked in the factory. I couldn't keep her warm! It was freezing, and we had no money for coal! She was only two! Maminke[37] died a week later. Charity provided the burial; for if we could not afford coal, let alone food, how could we afford a headstone?'

'They're at peace now, Emil. And Albrecht, too.'

'Feh! And you, too, succumb to the opiate!'

'Sometimes, Emil, an opiate is necessary, not to lull a person into oblivion, but to dull the pain, and thereby enable the body to rest and heal. Yes, I would willingly take an injection of faith, for the sake of the consolation it provides and the hope it offers. Quite frankly, I wish I could increase the dose.'

'Why?'

'Because I saw my father, whom I dearly love, endure extreme hardship. And yet he was happy. I am convinced he suffered no

---

[36] A translation of 'Lign in drerd un bakn beygl!', which can be paraphrased as 'May you go to hell and bake the bagels you will never eat'.

[37] *Maminke*: Mummy (very affectionate).

delusion, but cleaved to Faith, knowing it to be greater than his meagre self.'

We clung to each other in fond embrace, united in sorrow, doubt, and fear. But whatever our passions might be, whatever our desires, they were not for each other. That, we both knew.

'Best go,' he whispered.

Upon returning to the bookshop, I retired to the kitchenette to make some coffee. The shop bell jingled as the coffee brewed and I listened for the greeting. Since the voice was unfamiliar, I peeked round the door. The customer was a well-dressed, bespectacled young man who spoke with a polished Viennese accent. Emil bent over to record the purchase.

'It is not selling as well as I expected,' he remarked as he wrote. 'More's the pity. Everyone should read it.'

'I was surprised you had *Mein Kampf* at all,' the young man replied.

'I always make sure I have ample stock of the best literature.'

'And you have the necessary authorisation to sell the writings of the Führer?'

'I am a bookseller. I believe that authorises me to sell books.'

'That is true. After all, Herr Fährmann, we would not want to think you are a Jew.'

'I would not wish you to think that.'

'I have the impression, Herr Fährmann, that you are being disingenuous. Ah, Herr Untersturmführer,' the young man greeted a second customer. 'I suspect we have a case of a Jew making unauthorised sales.'

'A Jew?' another equally well-dressed man sauntered to the counter. 'Why, Herr Fährmann does not look like a Jew. He does not have a Jewish nose. Perhaps he has some identification that would help us out.'

'I don't think I have any identification that would assist you,' Emil replied.

The two men briefly disappeared from the counter.

'It seems to me,' the young bespectacled man maintained his erudite manner, 'that Herr Fährmann keeps his identity well concealed.'

Emil turned aside and drew back. For a split second our eyes met. How hunched and ramshackle he looked compared to the clean-cut figures of the gentlemen who closed in upon him.

'Then there is only one way to find out,' replied the older man. 'Come, Herr Fährmann,' he gestured, 'Identification is a simple process which we can conduct in the privacy of your own shop; or, if you prefer, we can be a little less discreet.'

Emil pulled down his trousers. But he did not do so without urinating on his 'customers'.

54

Emil and the Detectives

'HAVE A SEAT, Phoebe,' Zita passed me a brandy. 'Where have they taken him?'

'I don't know. I enquired at the police station, but he's not there.'

'This is terrible! Poor Misha!'

'What is terrible?' Rudi appeared in the doorway.

'A friend of Phoebe's has been arrested!'

'I am sorry to hear that. What has he done, Phoebe?'

'Apparently, he's Jewish and he was selling copies of *Mein Kampf*.'

'A Jew? Selling *Mein Kampf*? That is absurd! But why did you come here?'

'I—I thought you might be able to help.'

'Why not Hubie?'

'We had an argument and he's very out of temper. Anyway, Rudi, you were so helpful regarding my aunt that I thought you might be able to assist. You have contacts with the police, don't you?'

'Yes, but not in Vienna. Besides, if it's to do with Jews breaking the law, you'll need to speak to the Geheime Staatspolizei.'

'You could at least accompany Phoebe,' urged Zita. 'Rudi, she can't go to the Gestapo on her own.'

'That is true. I'll give you a ride. We will go at once.'

The Hotel Metropole, where waiters in penguin suits once fawned on the rich and famous, was now an ants' nest of officialdom. Tall men in jodhpurs and jack boots, their black jackets emblazoned with insignia, strode purposefully amidst the marble and potted palms. Each had a special role well known to the other members of the colony, as indicated by their many salutes and multisyllabic modes of address.

Brownshirts, equally tall, but lacking the spit and polish of their dark-suited superiors, stood guard, or else performed more mundane administrative tasks which to their credit they carried out with meritorious energy; for I had the impression these gentlemen preferred more vigorous physical work. Typewriter bells clanged, and keys click-clacked; telephones rang, and messages were delivered in clipped tones. And, spinning on its blood red background, crawling spider-like up walls and columns, and encircling the upper arms of every officer, was the all-pervasive swastika.

The Metropole was now Gestapo headquarters.

'Might I suggest,' Rudi whispered as we were ushered into a room, 'that you give them your fullest co-operation. Tell them everything they need to know. I have found matters proceed very smoothly when you do.'

'You have been here before?'

'Once or twice,' he drawled in a resigned, somewhat philosophical manner, like a dutiful son faced with bailing out an alcoholic father. 'My parents...'

'Don't you have any sympathy for them?'

'They are sensible people. In arranging their emigration well in advance of the Anschluss, they acted prudently. You can always rely on my parents to act prudently,' he jested; but I detected a tone almost of regret that in some way he wished they had been less prudent.

'You wouldn't think to join them?'

'Emigrate? Why? I am not in any trouble.'

'I thought that out of a sense of loyalty you might have considered it.'

'Then it is better I stay. Zita would not dream of living anywhere else, and the last thing my parents would want is that some Nazi seizes their property.'

I heard the quick step of a man with a purpose. A handsome individual, spick and span in his magnificently tailored uniform, entered and apologised for keeping us waiting.

Rudi, determined to establish amicable working relations, and adept at diplomacy, took the initiative regarding introductions and exploited my status as an ignorant and helpless foreign damsel in distress.

Our interview lasted an hour, during which the proceedings were recorded in triplicate. I explained in more precise detail exactly who I was and my connection with Emil.

'He is a Jew?' inquired the official. 'And you, Fräulein?'

'I am Australian,' I glared at him. But my interrogator detected a yearning I could not entirely suppress.

'Fräulein,' he suavely smiled, 'I should warn you that it is against Nuremberg regulations for an Aryan woman to have sexual relations with a Jew.'

I maintained that I had had no such relations; but I felt myself redden, for the poignant truth was that I wished I had. Oh, to be loved! But while the Swastika crawled through Vienna, binding everything in its web, there was no hope of love, no hope of being loved.

'I assure you, Herr Untersturmführer, that Fräulein Raye is a woman of impeccable character,' Rudi affirmed.

We eventually learned that Emil was being held for questioning. Given that the sale of *Mein Kampf* was prohibited to Jews, he would incur a severe penalty.

'And what might that be?' I asked.

'He will be fined; and if he fails to pay, he faces a year's imprisonment – perhaps more, given the way he insulted the lieutenant,' remarked the Untersturmführer.

'I'll pay the fine,' I resolved.

'Can you afford to do so?' queried a concerned Rudi.

'Emil cannot; I know that much.'

Back at the bookshop, a chain of SA youths swung piles of books from one to another and dumped them into a truck. 'Germans awaken! Rise up from your dreams! Traitors have lulled thee with vile and wicked schemes!' they joyously sang.

'We're going to need a good bath tonight!' laughed one as he brushed the dust from his hands, 'The tub will be ringed with Jewish filth!'

Then, amidst the papers scattered under the shop window, I noticed Emil's house plans. I picked them up and discovered his fountain pen.

'Fräulein! Achtung!' one young man strode towards me. He could not have been more than sixteen years old, given the soft fuzz above his lips.

'What are you doing?' I demanded as I hid the pen in my purse.

'We are Aryanising the shop.'

'Aryanising the shop?' I shouted, incredulous, and thoroughly annoyed by his insolence. 'Aryanising? Look at the mess you've made!' Trembling, I furiously scrunched Emil's plans. 'I suppose you're going to Aryanise the street, too?'

'Of course.'

'I have just come from Gestapo headquarters, and if this rubbish is not cleared up immediately, I—I will file a report! This is a most unacceptable state of affairs!'

Late that afternoon, as I was ironing Emil's plans smooth again, Dr Elsa knocked on my apartment door. She was equipped as if on a house call.

'Zita told me what happened,' she began once she was well inside. 'Are they going to release him?'

'As soon as I've paid the fine.'

'What a relief!'

She pulled an envelope from her medical bag. 'Take care of this. It is about as much money as we can spare at present, but it will help. I will pass you more as soon as I can. Emil's a scoundrel, but he doesn't deserve Dachau. He will need to leave the country.'

'Why are you doing this for him?'

'You don't think I should?'

What could I say?

'Listen, Phoebe,' Dr Elsa leant close to me, 'If I was Zita, and I was married to Rudi, I would also be having an affair. Emil must go. Is there anyone else you know who needs assistance?' I immediately mentioned the Epsteins. 'Good,' she nodded. 'The Gestapo watches our every move. Robert will only leave home for professional reasons, and then only in my company, or Rudi's. He is permitted to tend Jews. I will visit you again before we depart. We will be travelling first to Holland where Professor Schütze's sister has agreed to accommodate us until our ship sails. Our passage is booked for October, so I should manage a couple more instalments. Whatever you do, Phoebe, be careful.'

I did not see Emil again for at least a week. To be quite honest, I smelt him before I saw him, for it was the vile stench of excrement, dirt, sweat, and unwashed flesh intensified by heat and humidity that caused me to glance up as I came out of Café Central. He was scruffier than ever. His hair was matted and greyed, his chin rough with stubble; and he had been badly beaten, for one eye was swollen and had bruised a nasty shade of purple-green. His other eye glittered defiantly.

Emil was in a queue that extended all the way down Wallnerstrasse, past the café, and on down Herrngasse. He had been there since dawn, apparently; his destination, the British Consulate. In front, a woman in haute couture held a handkerchief to her nose. Immediately behind, a gawky youth not long out of school tried to mind his own business; but it was clear he was studying my friend with a mixture of disgust, caution, and respect.

'Where are you living, Emil?'

'Since the room service at the Metropole was appalling, I found alternative accommodation with several generations of retired civil servants.'

'Do you need anything? Food? Clothes? A book?'

'I need to get out of here.'

'Have you had much success?'

'Feh! It appears a mass exodus of Bolshevik Jews doesn't augur well for world capitalism. The big shots at the Evian Conference seem to think my arrival on a foreign shore would upset their economy and create social and international unrest. To emigrate, I need money and relatives, neither of which I have. But there is a possibility I might be granted temporary residency in Britain. You have friends there, yes?

'Yes, yes.'

'Would they help me? Would you help me? Also, I have a better chance if I apply on a Christian ticket. They're baptising in the Anglican chapel. What must I do to be baptised? I – also – need – to – learn – to – speakt – Englisch,' he added in a very careful, broken version of my native tongue.

'Of course, I'll help you. Use my address as a forwarding address if you need. I'll pass you some books and some clean clothes. Where will I find you?'

And upon arriving home, I dashed off a letter to Lucy.

'So, you mean to say you are not coming to Salzburg?' Hubie concluded during an afternoon walk through shady woods.

'I cannot, Hubie. Not at present. Not while Emil's in trouble.'

'I wonder you waste your time with him,' he sneered.

'You're not jealous, are you?'

'Is there any reason I should be jealous of a man like that?'

'You tell me. And regardless of your opinion of him, he's a very dear friend. He's kind and generous, and he was good to me when I first arrived. He has no family, and his closest friends left the country years ago. Now he's in grave danger. I must help him.' I wanted to add that Emil was also the father of Zita's child, but in Hubie's eyes that might have been enough to see Emil condemned.

'When do you leave?' I asked instead.

'Next week,' he sighed. 'I wonder why we bother having a festival this year. Do you know, Phoebe, they have Germanised the entire libretto of *The Marriage of Figaro* because da Ponte was a Jew? There will be no Bruno Walter, no Toscanini. All the best soloists have boycotted. Nobody wants to come; or they cannot come because they are Jews! What do you propose to do about Herr Fährmann?'

'He needs to be baptised. Apparently, foreign countries seem to be more receptive if "Jewish" doesn't feature on an application form.'

'And you are going to help him?'

'Of course. The Anglican minister is offering baptism. Hundreds are being christened every day.'

'A man who doesn't believe in God, and who has only scorn for the Church, is asking to be baptised, and you agree to it?'

'What else do you do? Thousands of people are trying to leave, and the doors are closed to them due to ridiculous prejudices. You're just as bad.'

'I will not have my faith made use of in that way!'

'Then *you* get him baptised if you're so fussy about it! *You* prepare him! You talk about offering friendship in the face of enmity? Then take him to your Church and have him dunked by your priest of choice!'

Hubie blinked and awkwardly twitched his glasses onto his nose as he paused at the shrine marking the path's division. Gazing at the cloudless blue heaven, he sighed; then he faced again the Christ which hung with arms outstretched, as if indicating either path a viable one.

But what had he seen? Was it a stag with a cross between its antlers? Or had he heard someone? Something had startled him, for he stiffened. And when he turned to me, he wore an expression of firm resolve.

'Where will I find him?' he asked.

'I made arrangements to meet him this afternoon, if you care to come.'

'And where might that be?'

'Follow me.'

Interlude

·

Vienna, 20 January 1957

'Would you like to try Dad's violin?' I asked Roddy as we settled down to practise now that the children were fast asleep.

'Which one?'

'Take your pick. The Vuillaume, or the Hungarian.'

'Villaume's yours, though.' He claimed the Hungarian.

'Unfortunately, there's no chin rest.'

'I don't play with a chin rest.'

'Nor did Dad. When did you start learning?

'When I was eight. Played piano first. Then Aunt Rachel came up one Christmas with one of Dad's recordings. I knew a bit about Dad from photos and so forth. And his paintings. They terrified me. I hated that room. Anyway, I played that record so many times that Mum gave in and let me take lessons. By the time I turned seventeen, I had my diplomas – violin, viola, and piano.'

'All three? Well done! How did you manage that with school?'

'Left when I was fourteen.' Another source of dispute, I concluded, judging from that defiant thrust of his chin. 'School was torture. Lucky me: a teacher for a mother, and a Nip for a father.'

'A what?'

'A Nip. Japanese. I'm chink-eyed. Or hadn't you noticed?'

Roddy stared hard at me. He had Dad's slightly slanted, oriental eyes.

'Were you teased?'

'Since I never knew my father, they reckoned Mum— Worst happened when I was twelve. Got beaten with sticks and locked in a storeroom. Pay-back for what the Japanese did to someone's father in Changi, apparently. Cleaner found me.'

'Little wonder you didn't matriculate. I know it's hard, Roddy, but don't let it define you.'

'Aunt Rachel told me Dad got called a dingbat for being part-Chinese; and if he wasn't teased for that, he was teased because he was small. From the time he set foot in the schoolyard, he made it his mission to outwit, outride, and outplay the bullies.'

'And is that what you plan to do?'

'So far. So good.'

Roddy swung the violin under his chin and his fingers climbed about the pegs as he tuned fifths, fourths, and octaves. 'Pretty spicy,' he remarked upon rapidly executing a scale which he boldly finished with a double-stopped cadence. Legs purposefully astride, attired in turned up jeans and sneakers, topped with Cilla's Christmas cardigan, my young half-brother was a rebel with a cause.

'What would you like to work on first?' I asked.

'Frank Sinatra, I suppose.'

'What?'

'The Franck Sonata, if you don't mind. By the way,' he ventured with some hesitation before giving his bow a swish, 'what happened to Herr Fährmann?'

'That was but the beginning, Roddy.'

Peter arrived home amidst musical pyrotechnics, with Roddy pushing the tempo, me trying to hold him back, and the two of us swapping instruments to prove our respective points. An exhausted husband proved a welcome relief from an exhausting brother.

'They keep coming, braving the snow and the Soviets' tightening of border patrols,' he sighed as poured himself a Scotch and sank into the lounge. 'Prosit!'

As well as treating refugees at the border, Peter had visited the camps established in Salzburg and Graz. Despite the limited resources, all efforts were being made to help move people as quickly as possible to permanent homes in Austria or any country willing to take them.

'How many so far?' asked Roddy who had listened attentively to his rumbling account.

Peter stroked his beard, 'Be nearly a hundred thousand by now, most of whom we've managed to settle. It's the least we can do considering the multitudes forced to leave back in 'thirty-eight.'

'How could we turn anyone away after 'thirty-eight?' I added.

Part Five

·

Ein Volk!
Ein Reich!
Ein Führer!

·

August 1938

13·MÄRZ 1938
EIN VOLK EIN REICH
EIN FÜHRER

55

The Eternal Jew

T O THEIR GREAT GOOD FORTUNE, God had blessed the German people with three gifts: intelligence, decency, and National Socialism. But He did so with a proviso: they could only possess two at a time.

Such was the joke being bandied about Vienna that summer; but as far as my new neighbours were concerned, nothing could have been closer to the truth. The Germans who moved into Emil's apartment were very decent National Socialists. Well-groomed and conscientious, Herr Gottfried Geschmiert and his wife Liesl were keen to do their bit for the Reich and had come from Sankt Pölten for that purpose. To be perfectly correct, I should have said Hauptsturmführer Geschmiert; for when I met that gentleman one August morning, he was decked out in his SS uniform – the epitome of the round-faced Austrian, reared on his mother's strudel, trying hard to be Prussian – and was heading off to work, accompanied by fond wishes for a lovely day by his wife and children.

The Geschmierts were very friendly. So impressed were they by my violin and pianoforte skills that they invited me to teach their two daughters. I accepted, for I was rather in need of ready money.

To our mutual disadvantage, however, there was a catch. In being responsible for Jewish emigration, it was essential that Herr Hauptsturmführer observe the new citizenship requirements. Of course, foreigners were welcome in the Reich, he explained, and it was in Germany's best interest to maintain good relations with her non-German guests. Still, foreign Jews were Jews all the same; and considering my grandmother was Jewish...

'Does it really matter?' protested his wife.

'We do not know about her grandfather, Mausi. Are you Jewish, Fräulein Raye?' No, I was baptised as a baby and reared a Catholic. Did I have the necessary papers?

'Knuddelmuddel, darling, do let her teach Lindl and Hildi.'

Geschmiert turned the pages of my passport as if he were engrossed in a Russian novel. Then he cast me a lingering eye. 'My wife is lonely, and unused to Vienna. Very well, Mausi. And I am sure Fräulein Raye will find out about her grandfather.'

Since Grandfather Devereaux was born on the Victorian goldfields, I wrote to Aunt Rachel and requested she send me his Baptismal certificate.

'Please Mr Eichmann, may I go to Palestine?' Lindl Geschmiert chanted in the courtyard with the children of the other recent 'Aryan' residents.

'Only if you have the colour red,' chanted Hildi.

'Girls!' their mother called from my balcony. 'Do not play at being Jews! Pappi doesn't like it!'

'But we are playing at getting them out, Mammi!'

'Let them be, Mausi,' Geschmiert patted the empty sofa cushion and his wife resumed her place. 'It's good exercise. We hope soon to get a Jew out in less than a fortnight, Fräulein Raye. At present, it takes months.'

'Really?' I offered him cake. 'Do please explain.'

'We are streamlining the procedure. Currently, there's too much red tape,' he gestured with his cake fork, 'Far too much. You see, Fräulein Raye, to be issued with your *Steuerunbedenklichkeitsbescheignigung*—'

'Good heavens! What is that?'

'Let me see, Steuer-un-be-den-klich-keits-be-scheig-ni-gung, in English, how would you say it? Ah! I believe it is a-um *tax certificate*. Do you know it involves four separate departments simply to process payments and give approval? Four separate departments! That is too many forms; and far too many snouts in the trough. Even worse, it takes weeks to complete a single application. And if the applicant makes a mistake, they must start all over again.

'And that is only the beginning. Once you have your Steuerunbedenklichkeitsbescheignigung, you must proceed to the Devisenstelle to release your assets, as well as to the Geheime Staatspolizei in Prinz-Eugen-Strasse to obtain a certificate of good conduct and have your photograph and fingerprints taken. For the certificate you must produce your Kleiner Anmeldenachweis, previously issued by the Bezirkshauptmannschaft (which was earlier responsible for tax payments), provided it has not expired. Otherwise, back you go...

'Now, to obtain your passport, well, first you must visit the local police to lodge a request. When your request is granted, you apply to the emigration office in Herrngasse, and then to the passport office in Wehrgasse, Margareten. The last stage is the exit visa, which is granted upon payment of emigration tax. Once again, another office, another set of forms. And this is where it gets sticky: all the wheeling and dealing by the rich prevents the poorer

Jews getting through. Worse still, if your passport has expired in the meantime, then...'

'Back to the beginning,' I concluded. Geschmiert wiped the cream from his lips and nodded. 'Now, correct me if I'm wrong, Herr Hauptsturmführer, but, as well as fulfil the Reich emigration requirements, I suppose you must also apply for immigration to the authorities of other countries?'

'And bingo! You have it! In fact, you have to do that first!'

'Why, given the situation, that could take years!'

'And that is what we are trying to overcome!' he clapped. 'We are centralising the entire process: taxes, visas, passports, and interviews, so that everything takes place under the one administration; and, to ensure that many emigrate as quickly as possible, and not only the wealthy, we have arranged with local Jewish organisations to identify and assist applicants and organise funds. That way, *everyone* can leave. No one is excluded! A truly collaborative enterprise! National Socialism at its best! We'll soon have it shipshape!'

'In Sankt Pölten, my husband supervised operations at the Voith factory,' Frau Geschmiert beamed.

'We made turbines for reel-fed printing papers. So far thirty-five thousand Jews have departed, but we still have over one hundred thousand to go.'

'You have a lot of work to do, Herr Hauptsturmführer.'

'I do indeed, Fräulein Raye.'

The following morning, when I opened the paper, I learned some sad news. A sizeable notice, edged in black and conspicuously marked atop with a cross, announced the death of Justine Rosé.

Attendance at the funeral was sparse, however, since most of the Rosés' family and friends had left the country. Others, such as Richard Strauss, did not come, probably from fear of associating with someone branded as a Jew despite the Rosés' avoidance of anything Semitic. And the orchestra was at the Salzburg Festival.

Poor Professor Rosé seemed as if he had aged twenty years in a week. No longer was he the erect, purposeful concertmaster I had met the previous September. Accompanied by Alma and Alfred, he shuffled broken-hearted behind his wife's coffin. At least the Gestapo had the decorum to stay away, and I suspected they were following instructions. Seyss-Inquart was a music lover, after all, and had been a long-term subscriber to Rosé Quartet performances.

'Any news about your emigration?' I asked the grief-stricken Alma.

'Not much, I'm afraid. Alfred's had some success. Friends in

The Hague and London have offered travel assistance; and a friend of a friend has guaranteed accommodation in Cincinnati of all places. The affidavit arrived the other day. It's only a tiny flat above an office, but it means he and Maria can leave.'

'And you?'

'I could get to Czechoslovakia any time. I still have my passport, and Lori would help me,' Lori had fled to Bratislava, and Alma had driven her across the border. 'But I'll stay put until Vati's settled. Given the fracas in Sudetenland, though, I don't much like the idea of Czechoslovakia.'

A few days after the burial, I took a cramped tram to Leopoldstadt. Most of the passengers bustled out at the Nordwestbahnhof Exhibition Hall; and from the tram window I stared up at the enormous figure leering from the building's towering façade: a grotesque, hook-nosed and bearded Jew dressed in a black caftan set against a bright yellow background, greedily brandishing money in one hand, and holding a communist hammer and sickle behind his back. He was the 'mascot' of The Eternal Jew Exhibition.

'I have nightmares about the Jew,' Lindl Geschmiert once confided during a piano lesson. 'I don't like the way he gleams (the poster was illumined at night and could be seen from far and wide). I'm scared he might come through my window and take me from Mammi and Pappi. I wish he would go away. I wish all the Jews would go away.'

Hildi, who attended the exhibition with her parents, had found the noses interesting. 'You are lucky you don't have a Jewish nose, Fräulein Raye,' she remarked, having scrutinised my own modest proboscis instead of heeding my demonstration of a C major scale. 'But Pappi can tell you're a Slav, which is nearly as bad.'

The queue for the exhibition extended to the Prater. Hundreds walked down Taborstrasse: schoolchildren, brownshirts, men and women from all walks of life. But they avoided the shops, many of which had closed; while those still open had their broken windows boarded, and shabbily displayed their meagre wares in the visible space. All around, the word 'Jud' glared in garish yellow. I idled in front of the Epsteins' bakery and watched Jockel wipe down an already clean countertop.

'Good afternoon, Fräulein Raye,' he smiled sheepishly. 'If you've come for bread, I'm afraid we haven't much left. And what we do have, I wouldn't buy,' he added with a shifty glance.

'We cannot get any decent flour, Phoebe,' lamented David as he crept from the kitchen. 'And since today the yeast was rancid, we baked matzo. Jockel, find out if the grocer has any eggs. No eggs, no challah for Sabbath. Poor Jockel,' he sighed as he watched his nephew slouch down the street. 'Now that he's fourteen, the Nazis won't let him return to school. The Rabbi's arranged to give him lessons, but it looks like university's out of the question.'

'It goes from bad to worse. Have you had any news from Mani in Karlsbad?'

'He's trapped, Phoebe. He cannot get back into Austria because the borders are closed to Jews, and Bela and the children cannot get out. And if Hitler has his way with Sudetenland, they will all have to emigrate.'

David's brow furrowed more deeply, flour dust lining the channels. Having had his beloved bakery tarred and feathered with the yellow star, he was deprived of income and denied the means to exercise his trade to its usual excellent standard. Somehow, he had to support and protect his extended family. Always he risked being taken by the Gestapo; and with the brownshirt barracks around the corner in the Augarten, he had little means of escape. Worse still, such raids usually occurred in the dead of night, when its victims were most vulnerable. Little wonder he was scrawny and drawn.

'Phoebe, this Versailles business has gone too far! Let's hope something will be done to stop Hitler before it's too late. It cannot continue, surely?'

'Will there be war do you think?'

'Think? I would welcome a war! If we packed the Nazis off to a front line somewhere, they would wreak less havoc here and destroy themselves through their own violence.'

'War or no war, you're in danger either way. What are you going to do? Have you thought about going to Australia?'

'Why should I, Phoebe? Why should they force me to leave my home? And how could I leave my parents? They are too frail to travel. Bela, however, has written to Reuben. It will cost a fortune.'

'How much?'

'For Mani, Bela, and the children? Reuben says they need two hundred pounds at least. And that is without paying taxes, or obtaining passports, visas, and passage! We cannot afford such a sum!'

That evening, I wrote to Mr Epstein, as well as to Scylla. I figured the sale of two properties would provide funds for the Austerlitz family to emigrate. The letters I sent via air mail the next morning on my way to Hietzing cemetery.

The cemetery visit comprised part of a daily ritual I had maintained for much of the summer. I purchased a small bouquet and a few simple provisions and waited on a bench in a nearby park. Hubie, now returned from Salzburg, soon strode into view with Sirius at his side. Together we wandered through the cemetery and stopped outside the von Rechtschaffen vault.

I placed my flowers on a nearby headstone and coughed three times. The von Rechtschaffen mausoleum door opened and Emil emerged like Lazarus from the tomb. I passed him my purchases and assumed my post at a graveside where I kept watch with Sirius. Hubie and Emil meanwhile argued metaphysics and theology, the means whereby my cousin-of-sorts tried to prepare his Jewish-Bolshevik candidate for Baptism.

Their meetings so far had not gone well. The first session, in fact, lasted barely five minutes. 'He had the— gall to say, "Why must you teach me? I believe everything already!"' Hubie complained as he stormed off in disgust, having left Emil to read the Catechism on his own. Then, while Hubie was in Salzburg, Emil read the Bible, and St Augustine's *Confessions* at his mentor's recommendation; and continued instruction with Herr Steffan, who also supplied him with papal encyclicals, having decided that *Quas Primas*, *Rerum Novarum*, and *Quadragesimo Anno* would appeal to his heightened notions of social justice.

Meanwhile, and unbeknown to Hubie, Zita visited. It had been Zita's idea to put Emil up in the family tomb using a copy of the key she had pilfered from her mother. All through August she provided him with clean clothes and food; and Emil would fondle tenderly her pregnant belly as they walked hand in hand.

They were a most odd couple. True, he had a heart of gold and in it all her quirks found welcome repose. And, it seemed, the same could be said for her. But given Zita's marriage, not to mention the political dangers, what would become of them? And the child! What would happen to the poor child?

'Would they never see eye to eye?' I pondered as I watched Hubie parry another of Emil's intellectual thrusts. 'In a curious way they have so much in common! Perhaps his baptism will help. At least Hubie can no longer object to his religion.'

'He knows nothing!' Hubie returned to my company and we walked back through the Schönbrunn park. 'We have grown up in the same city! We have attended the same university, and yet he is ignorant about our Faith, our traditions, our culture!'

'He seems to be enjoying the discussion. And he didn't miss a single meeting while you were in Salzburg.'

'He feasts on cruelty.'

'Stop being so contemptuous! I think he's genuinely interested.'

'He is being exorcised tomorrow. It will be a miracle if he turns up.'

Smuggled into the presbytery of Pfarre Maria, Emil pronounced the responses to psalms he recalled from childhood. He took salt and placed it on his tongue, was breathed upon and spat upon, and submitted with surprising docility.

'Possum, never, ever underestimate God's grace,' I heard Dad's voice when, two days later, we entered the church proper and Emil knelt and prayed the Our Father. 'Whatever wretchedness we are capable of, whatever tribulations we suffer, I guarantee you, they pale before God's love, to the point that our very weaknesses and misfortunes become the unlikely means of our redemption.' Two stumpy legs and a crippled arm were proof enough in his eyes, so convinced was he of this fact. He staked everything upon it. Perhaps he needed to.

According to the Angelic Doctor, grace perfects nature; by which I understand that God works with the stuff of each human soul. Given our individuality, I suppose the process of perfection is unique to every person. So, when I saw Emil prostrate his rickety, twisted body on the church floor and profess the Creed, I concluded that grace truly had whims of its own. I also learnt that its *modus operandi* was not confined to the person being converted.

Contemplative by nature, Hubie became even more prayerful. He set aside his hostility and pride and continued to instruct Emil with calm resolve, while the risks involved increased his cunning. He seemed to enjoy devising secret meetings. And Emil? Well, do not think that he suddenly stood and walked about, leaping and praising God. Rather, like a prized truffle, he remained on the forest floor, ready to be snaffled by pigs, his pungent earthiness intensifying as he drew flavour from the litter of a sturdy oak.

Then, at dawn on the Feast of the Holy Cross, Hubie and I became godparents when our errant friend was baptised. Herr Steffan placed a white robe on Emil's shoulders while Emil watched the candle in his hands with all the fascination of a Faraday. He even elected to stay for Mass, during which he received Communion.

'There. You have your ticket,' Hubie sneered after the ceremony concluded.

'I believe I do,' Emil swaggered. 'And if what you have taught me is true, it's been paid for in blood— And it isn't yours.'

'Indeed, it is true. And because it is, I can be certain you will show as little regard for it as you do everyone and everything else.'

They parted civilly all the same, cordially shaking hands while Emil muttered a few words of gratitude which Hubie acknowledged with a stiff nod; and I continued to muse upon the workings of grace, if grace could be said to have worked at all.

56

Degenerate

'I AM ENQUIRING after a Mikhail Yemelyan Furmanski,' announced the plainclothes man who arrived on my doorstep the following day. I was getting to know them now, these Gestapo fellows, and was developing an aversion to men in well-cut suits, particularly if their demeanour was officious. My current visitor was a full six feet of Aryan arrogance and privilege.

'I'm sorry, I know no one by that name.'

'I understand that he lives here.'

Again, I denied knowledge.

'Perhaps you might know him as Misha?'

Now, I could not look blank; and the plainclothes man was adept at reading faces.

'You will inform us if you see him, Fräulein,' he smiled. 'Unless, of course, you wished us to think you had ties with the Communist Party.'

But when I went to warn Emil, he was not in the cemetery. Even worse, I sensed I was being watched, for a man I had never seen before was paying his respects. I continued my ritual, praying a rosary and placing fresh flowers in jars before taking a lengthy walk through the Schönbrunn grounds. Once assured that no one was following me, I hurried to Zita's.

'Have you seen—?'

'Phoebe, darling, how lovely to see you!' she beamed. 'Just in time for afternoon tea!' And issuing orders to the maid, she turned to me and whispered, 'What's up? Is it Misha?'

'They know about him. Why is he called Misha anyway?'

'He'd tell you it's his ghetto name, but really it's his Jewish name. It's a diminutive for Mikhail. And don't worry about him. He was here last night. The maids were at the pictures and Rudi was working late, so I smuggled him in. How many lies would you like me to tell?' she playfully added when I questioned as to where he might have gone. 'Anyway, I'm glad you came by. Will you come with me to the exhibition?'

'Which one?'

'The Degenerate Art exhibition, silly! Misha reckons you won't see a show like it this century, and I promised I'd give him a full report. By the way, admission's free— not bad given that we'll be treated to some of the finest examples of modern art.'

'I don't care whether it's free or not. I'd sooner view the paintings at the Schönbrunn or the Hofburg. Modern art's grotesque.'

'You share Herr Hitler's taste? Or Hubie's. Fuddy duddy Huberle won't have anything to do with it either. Personally, I think he's relieved modern art's been banned.'

'What do you see in it? Honestly, Zita, have you any idea what it's like to be scrutinised by someone who has no intention of respecting your integrity, and to have a crudely distorted version of yourself publicly displayed to be gawped at and analysed by people who care nothing for cause or consequence? Do you know what it's like to be a victim of someone else's perverted world view?'

'Yes, I do. You think I haven't been the subject of surrealist exploration, let alone some Nazi phrenologist crony? Frankly, I find it quite fascinating in what it reveals of another's mind. Besides, aren't we all victims of each other's world views? Perhaps your aunt's work will be there!'

'Now that would be the one enticement to come,' I smiled. It would be confirmation of Ailine's decadence, her immorality, and her disdain for what is right and good, I thought; and it pleased me much to think that the aesthetic so praised by her ilk was being publicly shamed. 'Where's it showing?'

'Salzburg.'

'All that way just for an exhibition?'

'Listen, it's not coming to Vienna for months, by which time I'm going to be full to the brim with motherhood, so I'm not going to have another opportunity. I'm already feeling fat, and I'm bored beyond belief!'

'Very well,' I sighed. 'But I don't want to stay long. I'm worried for Emil.'

'You are a good sort. We'll make it a day trip!'

Hubie was predictably disgusted when he learned of Zita's plans, and admonished her for her taste and for —complying with Nazi dictums. He was equally disdainful of Rudi for allowing her to attend such an exhibition, let alone travel on her own whilst pregnant. That I had agreed to go appeased him somewhat; but the Nazis remained a problem, which prompted him to act as chaperone, at least for the journey which we then had to arrange around his rehearsal schedule. He refused to have anything to do with the exhibition.

We left him in a café brushing up his French on an edition of *La Croix*. He had given up lecturing us. 'Honestly, Huberle!' Zita complained, 'Would I lend my support to those who insult my taste?'

Like Vienna, Salzburg was emblazoned with flags of the Third Reich in honour of the recent and ongoing festivities (the Hitlerspiel, Zita called it), while the absence of yellow stars and weary queues ensured a rather pristine atmosphere which no doubt was helped by the crisp mountain air.

'You could say it's Hitler's revenge for being rejected by the Vienna Academy,' Zita remarked as we walked to the exhibition building, 'Forget about art as a means of self-expression; forget the idea of art for art's sake. "Art must be about the German Volk!"' she continued, thumping her fist in her hand and contorting her face like the Führer. '"Not deformed cripples and cretins, women who inspire only disgust, men who are more like wild beasts, and children who, if they were alive, would be regarded as God's curse!" Let's go in!'

The first chamber of the exhibition was devoted to religious art, and above the entrance hung a crucifix. Carved in wood, in a sparse, almost primitive manner, it depicted a suffering, emaciated Christ turning, despite his agony, to the good thief Dismas, to deliver His promise of paradise.

Labelled, *This horror hung as a war memorial in the cathedral of Lübeck*, the crucifix introduced a room full of images categorised as 'Insolent mocking of the Divine under Centrist rule'. Indeed, it was not the sort of crucifix I was accustomed to seeing above an altar – the humble submission of the God-man as the supreme sacrifice for the sins of mankind – an image which, through thousandfold replication, had become so familiar to me that my complacency almost warranted a second crucifixion. Here, grotesque and strained, his very identity obliterated by a mask, was Divine Mercy amidst human injustice. Nailed to the cross – that most cruel act of human punishment – this degenerate Divine King opened the doors of Heaven to undeserving supplicants while the doors of the World were closing all about. It was strangely apt, given that nations were presently shutting out thousands of helpless, pleading souls.

Most of the paintings were hung askew. Some had even been stripped of their frames and were crammed one against the other in a way most unconducive to study. Labels such as, 'Crazy at any price', and 'Even museum bigwigs called this art of the German people', abounded. One work, by Otto Dix, had been conceived like a triptych in the manner of Dürer. But the subject was far from religious, its treatment antithetical to Renaissance perfection. Entitled *The War*, it depicted a battlefield in which dead and dying bodies coexisted amidst hellish conflagration.

Further along, another painting by the same artist compelled me to halt. A returned soldier caressed his wife. He tried to place his arm tenderly round her waist, but his arm had a hook for a hand. Given the mechanics of the hideous prosthetic, their lovemaking seemed a hopeless cause, and acknowledged as such by the couple's pained expression.

'For someone who professes to have little taste for modern art, you have a queer way of expressing your dislike,' Zita wryly raised an eyebrow. 'Do you need a handkerchief?'

'Thank you,' I sniffed. 'I would remove the ugly hook, and fondle what remained of his limb, and kiss him a thousand times.'

'If you ask me, it's war that's degenerate, not the art produced. Let's see what "The Revelation of the Jewish Racial Soul" is all about.'

'How can you have a racial soul? A soul is individual.'

'I have no idea.'

The 'Jewish Racial Soul', or whatever it was, was a vibrant display of colour and imagination.

'Zita, if I had the opportunity, I would purchase that painting, and hang it in my living room.' I indicated a painting by Chagall, labelled 'JUD', in which a fiddler with a green face danced on the roof of a cottage. Aside from its musical subject, I found its originality and boyish vitality most appealing.

'Bumpkins that they are, the Nazis don't even realise that what they are doing is an imitation of what the Dadaists did twenty years ago,' Zita laughed. 'Lord! They've hung a Kandinsky! He's nothing to do with Dada! Misha is going to love this!'

But if Zita's laughter was the desired response, the organisers had no idea what motivated it. She mocked the regime's ignorance and perversion, and she knew she could get away with it. Whatever Hitler's reasons were for staging the exhibition, Zita had come to rebel – to assert herself against a power that was persecuting all that she loved.

'And if your aunt's work is here, you ought to be proud of it,' she whispered. 'Goodness me. *Which paintings are by the inmates of a lunatic asylum?* I'll ask the fellow in charge. He'll know the answer; for the lunatics are certainly in control here.'

A broad patch of vermillion caught my eye and I wandered over to a cluster of portraits. The vibrant red turned out to be a dress worn by a little girl with large eyes and dark curly hair; and it had a wide white collar edged with lace.

'My dress,' I murmured.

'What is it?' Zita joined me.

'That's my dress. She bought me a dress like that from Paris.'

'It's so tactile! The impasto! I want to touch it! Is that your aunt's work? It must be. It says Devereaux down the bottom. Your aunt a lunatic? Phoebe, why she's a genius! It's so humane! Look at the expression! I've never seen anything so poignant! Who is it? Is it you?'

I knew exactly who it was. With her body writhing and twisted like the crucified Christ, her innocent face pained and pleading, the poor child was severely handicapped.

'It's my cousin Sabine.'

Zita read the Nazi caption below:

A Curse and a Burden. Unfit for Life. Unfit for Art.

'Nineteen thirty-six! She's alive!' I gasped.

57

A Curse and A Burden

BREATHLESS, I FLUNG MYSELF into a seat in the train carriage. The locomotive hissed from Salzburg station. Was that Hubie running onto the platform? Stay away, Hubie! For where I am going, you cannot come!

Onwards, onwards, past hamlets and churches; past tidy fields and farms. Forms blurred, and the fading light gave gradual exposure to my reflection. My countenance melded with Sabine's. I beheld my eyes bulge in their sockets. My cheeks grew sunken. My teeth began to buckle like loose shingles on a roof. My neck, distended, writhed in opposition to the contortions of my jaw. But my hair remained prettily curled, fixed instead with a large silk ribbon. And I wore a dress of plush red velvet, over which was spread a collar of lace.

Poor, pallid, weak little girl! How you were loved! Or were you doted upon like a favourite doll? Was your portrait the outpouring of precious memory or the product of perversion? Are you a daughter or a fetish? Who gave you form? A mother who cannot help but express her affection, or an artist bent on sensation? After all, Ailine, you are quite capable of immolating your own child for the sake of your Art. And where are you now? Alive and well in Dresden? How could that be?

A man entered the compartment, sat opposite me, and opened a copy of *Der Völkische Beobachter.*[38] Hitler's meeting in Bad Godesberg with Chamberlin, Daladier, and Mussolini regarding Czechoslovakia was spread across the front page. I turned away, only to have my attention caught by an advertisement which featured a medical orderly standing behind a man who, from his twisted posture and palsied hand, was crippled like Sabine. 'This hereditary patient costs the community 60,000RM to live. Citizen, this is your money too,' I translated.

A Curse and a Burden. Unfit for life. Unfit for art.

---

[38] *Der Völkische Beobachter:* the newspaper of the NSDAP.

But Sabine was never a curse and a burden. Ailine loved Sabine, Dad insisted; and if that portrait was anything to go by, he was right.

Did Sabine love Ailine? Judging from the plaintive expression and yearning in those large brown eyes, she did. But Ailine could well have painted those beseeching eyes for self-gratification. Either way, Sabine's portrait testified to dignity and love, to the worthiness of life however weak, however insignificant. And she had a name, which Ailine had neatly painted in the top left corner. Furthermore, the painting's recent date, 1936, challenged a regime that regarded children like Sabine a burden on the system.

'Papers!' called a Gestapo official.

'You are from Sydney, Australia?' He paused from his examination of my passport and looked sceptically at my complexion. His English was very good.

'Yes.' I stared at his leather trench coat.

'I have relatives in Klemzig. That is in South Australia, yes?'

'I have not heard of it.'

'There is a German community there. Soon we will be all over the world.'

He returned my passport and scrutinised the stranger's identity card in much the same manner. Something, however, did not meet with his approval and he bid the man leave the compartment.

Jews were not permitted to read *Der Völkische Beobachter.*

'If Ailine is alive and in Dresden, then I wish I had her courage,' I thought as I watched them leave. Sabine's portrait boldly proclaimed humanity in the face of a brutal system. Then again, when it came to her opinion, Ailine revelled in non-conformity. Typical Ailine, using your own daughter for political commentary.

'Besides, she is still a murderess. And if she is capable of love and compassion, then it only makes Maman's murder worse. Whatever good she has done, nothing will make up for what she has done to me. It's a pity Sabine died. My life might have been easier had she lived.'

I will find you, Ailine! I will find you somehow! And—

The train pulled in at Sankt Pölten. The man who had shared my compartment darted into view and collapsed on the platform. The officer in the trench coat stood over him. The fallen man crawled to his knees in supplication. The officer raised a pistol and shot him in the temple.

58

All is Lost!

'PHOEBE!' RUDI OPENED his front door, 'Back so soon?'
'I need to speak to you, Rudi.'
'Of course, of course! Come in. Where's Zita?'
'She's still in Salzburg with Hubie. What's going on?'
'It's the Alpine Club,' he grinned. 'We are planning an expedition. Let me introduce you.'

Gathered round a zither, Rudi's confreres sang heartily as they banged their tankards twice on the table and banged them together in time to the music:

> *Und selbst das reiche Wien,*
> *Hin ist's wie Lev-i-tin;*
> *Weint mit mir im gleichen Sinn,*
> *Alles is hin!*

'Gentlemen, gentlemen, a modicum of decorum, please! We have a lady present!'
'Rudi, I need to—'

But, in true Austrian style Rudi insisted upon presenting me to all his friends, each of whom was determined to outdo the other in charm.

'The trouble with this house is that the living area affords little privacy,' he sighed as he led me away. 'I believe the architect responsible was rather too enthusiastic about communal space. This nook here will have to suffice. Take a seat.' He offered me a sofa near Emil's round window. 'You look exhausted. Let me get you a drink. Kirsch?'

And while I told Rudi what had happened at the exhibition, his friends continued to sing:

> *O, du lieber Wittgenstein, Wittgenstein, Wittgenstein*
> *O, du lieber Wittgenstein, alles ist hin.*
> *Geld is weg, Mäd'l ist weg,*
> *Alles hin, Wittgenstein.*
> *O, du lieber Wittgenstein,*
> *Alles is hin.*

'Let's try Bauer!' someone called amidst the laughter.

'Nein, Bauer will not scan,' answered another. 'You need three syllables. Like Blu-men-thal:

> *Rock ist weg, Stock ist weg*
> *Blu-men-thal liegt im Dreck*

'But Blumenthal will not rhyme with Wien. Back to Augustine, chaps.'

> *O, du lieber Augustin, Augustin, Augustin,*
> *O, du lieber Augustin,*
> *Alles is hin!*

'So, since Ailine had dated the painting 1936, Rudi,' I explained, 'she couldn't have died in 1934.'

'Then the Dresden police must have made a clerical error. I cannot think how else it might have happened.'

'But Rudi, they're so punctilious. How could they possibly have made such a mistake? I could understand if it were Schmidt or Braun. But Devereaux? How could they muddle their records?'

'Glitches can happen,' he shrugged as he topped my glass. 'It must have been a terrible shock for you. What are you going to do about it?'

'Go to Dresden myself, I suppose, but I haven't a clue where to start.'

'Then permit me to pave the way. I will make contact on your behalf.'

'Would you?'

'Of course!' he smiled. 'After such a botch up, it's the least I can do. Come, join our celebration. Then I'll drive you home.'

Down Linke Wienzeile we sped. Fresh as snow was the wind on my face; happy, twinkling stars filled the night. I lolled my head against Rudi's shoulder and stroked his strong jaw. How smooth-shaven and tanned he was! How athletic!

'Rudi, you're like Apollo driving his chariot, launching the sun into the heavens!'

'And if you're going to retch, I'd prefer you do it in the gutter.'

'Whee! We are in the bosom of the sun! Really, Rudi, you are the most generousest, handsomestest man in the whole, wide world!'

'Am I?'

'Yes. But I don't love you. No. Not one teensy little bit. Because, you see, I'm in love with a Turk with one hand. Imagine that!'

'You mentioned him last time we celebrated. I believe you were drunk then, too.'

'Am I really drunk?'

'Very. Have you your key?'

'Do I need a key? I don't feel very drunk. But then I don't love you, either. I don't love anyone. Not with nasty Nazi spiders crawling about. But I do have a key. Look, Rudi! That's my key! To *my* apartment! Drunk or sober, I am a very, very independent young woman. Remember that. And tomorrow, you know what?'

'What?'

'I'm going hunting. Heigh-ho the dairy-o, a-hunting we will go!'

'Good night, Phoebe.'

'We'll catch my aunt and put her in a box and never let her go. Never ever. Never, never, never!'

'Good night, Phoebe.'

'You know, Rudi, I think men are very, very magnicifent. Just magnici— ! Magnifi—'

'Good night, Phoebe.'

The zither played on and I sang in the snow. Amidst the tombstones I danced like Salome and requested Ailine's head on a platter. Then I pulled out a gun and shot her. A single bullet in the temple. I fell into a grave full of rubies and floated down Phlegethon. *Augustin, Augustin, Leg' nur ins Grab dich hin!* Who would have thought there would be so much blood? Swirling currents of blood. A putrid river, full of dead fish and excrement. Sewerage poured over my hair and face.

'Kerem! Kerem! Help me!'

'Shh!'

Unfit for life. Unfit for Art.

A hand covered my mouth: a strong and putrid hand; the hand of an unkempt, crooked figure. Unfit for life.

'Phoebe! Phoebe! Wake up!'

'Emil?'

My head thumping, I wandered into my living room and found Emil wrapped in my pink silk dressing gown, burning his clothes in the Kachelofen.

'Hangover?' he asked.

'Everything's spinning the wrong way. Even the trams are going backwards. They were going backwards last night, too.'

'They've changed the traffic around to conform to Berlin. And you're right: everything's spinning the wrong way.'

'What's the time?'

'About six.'

'What are you doing here?'

'They raided the cemetery and I escaped through the sewers.

Listen, Phoebe, I know I promised never to trespass into your apartment again; but believe me when I tell you I had nowhere else to go.'

'Someone from the Gestapo was here only the other day. They know all about you, Mikhail Yemelyan Furmanski. They say you're a Communist.'

'We'll they're a bit behind the times. I joined the KPÖ while I was still in short trousers and left after Trotsky fell from power. That was more than a decade ago. Why the hangover?'

'It's a long story, Emil.'

'Ah, but is it a good story?'

'I haven't time for such luxuries as vendettas,' he remarked as we prepared to eat the omelettes he had cooked. 'I'm finding it difficult enough to stay alive.'

'But I have to find her, Emil.'

'Well, before you run amok, listen. I've spent the summer in a charnel house. According to your darling Hubie, it's quite an illustrious crowd lying there: courtiers, judges, and military personnel. All that's left are their mortal remains and what lurks in their descendants' memories. How do you wish to be remembered? As the woman whose one goal in life was revenge?'

'Of course not.'

'And you would forfeit the love of a mensch[39] for the sake of your cause?'

'What?'

'Hubie.'

'Emil, Hubie doesn't love me!'

'A man like that doesn't set foot in a bookshop like mine unless there's a woman involved.'

'Nonsense.'

'So, why do you think Hubert Schütze-Rechtschaffen went to the trouble of instructing me in his beloved faith?'

'He believed it the right thing to do.'

'And he wouldn't have dreamed of doing so if it hadn't been for you. He loves you.'

'Pfui! With all your affairs, you're a fine one to talk of love! What sort of love is yours?'

'The sort of love you have when all the doors are shut in your face. You, on the other hand—'

'I cannot love anyone while my aunt is still alive!'

'You can, and you must! You must! Or do you choose to hate? You would prefer to have a share in the hate that is all around you?'

'I want nothing to do with that.'

---

[39] *Mensch*: (very favourable) an honourable, upright, good person.

'But you wish to persecute your aunt, whom you see as responsible for your sorrow, in the same way the Swastikas persecute me, the filthy Communist Jew whom they believe is at the root of German grievance. They are out to kill me, as you are out to kill her.'

'But you've done nothing wrong.'

'Kafka couldn't write better. But hate is still hate, whatever the justification. Phoebe, a year ago, I believe I said words to the effect that given the injustice you have suffered, you had a duty to resolve the crime your aunt committed, and that you should take her life and then your own. Do that, and all you would have achieved is annihilation. I cannot hold to that now. You certainly cannot hold to it for it directly contravenes the essence of your beliefs. You do believe, don't you?'

'Yes.'

'You won't make a sham of it?'

'No. What are you saying, Emil?'

'What I'm saying, Phoebe, is that Life is more important. When I was baptised, the priest impressed upon me that the ceremony would take away all my sins, and that this would happen independent of my disposition, as the gracious act of a God Whose generosity knows no bounds. I dismissed it as superstition until he put that white cloth upon my shoulders. Then I looked at your crucified Christ and I saw myself as the thief who said, "Remember me when Thou comest into Thy kingdom." And, I kid you not, I heard those words, "Verily I say unto thee, this day thou shalt be with Me in Paradise". Only then did I know it was true: My Redeemer liveth. Before such goodness, how could I not be sorry? I have sinned in every possible way and have been washed clean. Indeed, I am a thief. I have stolen Grace.'

'You have not killed.'

'I have been forgiven every misdeed. And there have been many of those. Your God is a God who forgives. You can do no less.'

'You're saying I must forgive? You, who blamed an empire for the misfortunes of your childhood, and staged a revolution to destroy it? All I am asking is for one person to pay for their crime! Wouldn't you if you were in my situation? Look at you now! Can you forgive your persecutors?'

'I am too busy outwitting them at present. Perhaps my forgiveness of them will be my reprisal,' he mused as he sweetened his coffee, relishing the irony as much as he did the sugar, which he clearly had not enjoyed for some time.

'Emil, you said it is imperative I confront my aunt.'

'Certainly, you must confront her if you can; but not for the reasons you think. Beware your wrath—'

'Who is it?' I called in response to the knock at my door, while Emil scrambled into the kitchen.

'Phoebe? It is I, Hubie.'

'Thanks be to God you are still here!' Hubie's eyes were filled with mournful ardour. His lips quivered; and through his manly caress I felt his deep need for consolation. 'I came last night, as soon as I arrived, but no one was home. I thought I had lost you forever! Then I took Zita home, and Rudi told me you had visited. When I saw you run past the café in Salzburg, I thought something had happened to Zita and that you were getting help, so I dashed to the exhibition. Zita mentioned something about a painting being alive. She said you turned quite mad and ran out screaming; but my sister is fond of exaggeration, particularly if it enhances the drama. I ran to the station, but there was no sign of you. What happened?'

'But why did you see Rudi?' he asked once I finished.

'Last December, I told him about Ailine and he offered to make enquiries through a friend of his whose father was in the police. I learned that Ailine had died while in prison in the summer of 1934. You yourself said she had disappeared and suspected she was dead. Now Rudi thinks it was a mistake.'

'They call it "The Night of the Long Knives",' he murmured, as if he had not heard my account. 'How did you say you learnt of her death?'

'I received a letter via Rudi from the Dresden police. He told me he had connections.'

'I suppose he would. Is there anything I can do to help you?'

'Rudi said he would follow it up.'

'But do you think Ailine would still be in Germany? That is, if she is still alive. Much can happen in two years. Was ist—?'

Hubie stiffened and gestured at Emil who was standing at the living room entrance, dressed in my gown, grinning crookedly.

'He's hiding.'

'There is a Gestapo official residing in the opposite apartment, and he is hiding here?'

'There was a raid.'

'Have you no— respect, no honour, no principles?' he towered over Emil. 'You are putting Phoebe in grave danger! Get out! I tell you, get out!'

'Where, Hubie? Talk all you like of respect, honour, and principle, but Emil has no shelter and now he has no clothes, and winter is approaching! Where can he go?'

59

Auf, Auf zum Fröhlichen Jagen!

HUBIE DECIDED it would be safer if Emil stayed at the family hunting lodge and devised a plan to smuggle him out. To this end, he requested I purchase a bottle of peroxide. When I returned from the apothecary, Franz had arrived, and Emil was trying on one of his suits. After bleaching his hair and equipping him with a rustic walking stick and a pair of spectacles, Emil looked closer to fifty than thirty. A few days later, the trio set off for the Südbahnhof, laden with hunting gear.

'From whom did you get Emil's passes?' I whispered to Hubie.

'Herr Steffan has contacts. Franzl and I will return on Wednesday.'

But when I met them at the station that Wednesday afternoon, they were two very pale young men.

'Bow hunting is now forbidden,' Hubie stuttered.

'They've changed the regulations,' Franz added.

'Hunting regulations! What about Emil? Is he safe? Hubie—Franz—?'

Franz explained that the trip to Admont had proceeded smoothly. The Gestapo, however, were at the station (they were at every railway station), searching luggage. Upon discovering the bows and arrows, they grilled the brothers about their activities and confiscated their weapons. When, finally, they were released, Emil, whom they last saw on the station platform, had disappeared. Apparently, the gamekeeper witnessed police escorting a man to a car. The man fitted Emil's description.

'We think he's at Graz police station,' Franz replied while Hubie remained speechless.

'Think? Did you ask?'

'How could we? We were not travelling in company. If we made enquiries, the Gestapo would rightly suspect we were aiding and abetting Jews. Moreover, whom could we trust? Truly, Phoebe, I am very sorry.'

'Sorry? Is that all?'

'What else can I say?'

'It's not a question of saying, Franz! It's a question of doing!'
'But what could I do?'

So shattered was Hubie that he came down with a migraine
and spent the remainder of the week in bed.

'I implore you, Phoebe, to believe me when I say that I would
never betray Emil.'

Bleary and listless, he had little taste for the coffee his mother
served us on the back terrace of their Hietzing home when later I
visited; and as he spoke, he prodded his Linzertorte, which weary
activity he soon abandoned, leaving the silver fork propped against
the side of the plate and the cake uneaten. Any motion from
Sirius, be it sudden interest in a bird in the shrubbery or a prick
of the ears at the sound of a motor, and he jolted.

'Have you heard any news?' he asked.

'Hopefully, Emil's papers will arrive soon. Then I can go to the
Gestapo with the means to secure his release— assuming he's in
Gestapo hands. I cannot sleep thinking what he might be
suffering.'

'The brutality of the Gestapo is without measure.'

'Then why didn't you do something, Hubie?'

Hubie ruffled Sirius round the collar and gazed absently at the
abandoned target at the far end of the lawn.

'Hubie! How could you have been so utterly vapid?'

'You are aware that I have a law degree, yes?'

'Don't change the topic!'

'I am not changing the topic. I am attempting to explain why I
did not pursue the matter.'

'Well, it better be good!'

'Phoebe! Quieten, please!' he put his hands to his head. 'I will
tell you that as much as I love music and my orchestral work, my
original ambition was to become a lawyer, not a musician. In
1934, after I had completed my law degree, my Uncle Joachim
invited me to work for him. Uncle Joachim is my father's youngest
brother and has a successful legal practice in Munich.'

'Your father has never mentioned him. But what—?'

'Please allow me to continue. At the time, I was grateful for his
invitation. The banking collapse had brought further hardship
upon my family, and a job meant that I would not be a burden to
them. Even more fortunate was that most of my living expenses
were covered. Uncle Joachim is married, but since he and my
Aunt Mathilde are without children, they were happy to
accommodate me.

'Initially, I was content with my work, and I had opportunity to
play music in my spare time and visit my grandparents. I also
admit that I was intrigued by Hitler, for I was impressed by the
stand he had taken against the Communists; but I was not fully

aware of the truth of his policies.

'My work for my uncle opened my eyes to the ghastly reality of National Socialism. New laws, you see, had been passed. Jewish businesses were being liquidated; Jewish properties were being sold; and companies owned by Jews were being transferred into non-Jewish hands. My uncle profited greatly from these negotiations – both in terms of his career and his finances – which is why he could employ me and pay me well.

'My concerns I expressed in letters to your father, who was insightful and encouraging. I also sought the company of others in Munich who were critical of Hitler's regime. Among the many involved were the von Guttenbergs whose estate my grandfather manages. We used to gather in the house of Crown Prince Otto's grandmother where we began to consider how Hitler could be overthrown.

'It soon became untenable to live with and work for my uncle. I left his firm, played in bands, and rented a room. Then, one night in July, I was arrested. For three weeks the Gestapo interrogated me. Phoebe, they knew everything about me, about your father, about your aunt. All my correspondence had been read.

'Then they sent me to Dachau. I was not there long, but a week was enough. My uncle, you see, is an active member of the NSDAP. In fact, he is a Gestapo informant. He obtained my release on condition that I did not speak of what had happened. If I did, there would be trouble for me and my family, and that there would be no mercy. I returned immediately to Vienna. I was, however, very ill, and spent the remaining summer in a clinic. Thanks to excellent care I recovered, save for the stutter. I had managed to control it by the time I left school; but it became very severe after they tortured me.

'My father cut off all relations with my uncle, who now serves on the Reich judiciary; and I focussed instead on my music. As my health improved, I also completed my legal studies. Now I have been denied my doctorate.

'Apart from my father, my confessor, and later your father, I have never spoken of my experience in Munich. And now my beautiful Austria is under Hitler's domination. Yes, Phoebe, I am sorry to admit that like Dante, my soul has been hurt by cowardice which oftentimes encumbers a man so that it turns him back from honourable enterprise, as false seeing does a beast when it shies. I have failed to act as I should. From my own experience, I fear the worst for Emil; and my lack of courage has led to his capture and caused grievous harm to countless others. I am sorry, Phoebe. Truly, I am very sorry.'

He removed his glasses and mopped his tears. When shyly he glanced my way, his eyes, magnified once more by his lenses, were brimful with dolour.

'No, no, Hubie, it is I who should be sorry. Had I known what had befallen you, I would not have spoken so harshly. You cannot blame yourself for what has happened. From what you have told me, you've every reason to fear. And you have spoken out. Never have I heard you condone Hitler and his regime. You secretly visited the Crown Prince to advocate on behalf of your country. You have been good and brave in all you have done for Emil, despite your dislike. By nature, you are cautious and prudent. You must not confuse careful judgement with cowardice. Indeed, your action is the more courageous given your character and your suffering.'

'Stay a moment.' He pressed my hands to his lips and hurried inside. Minutes later, he returned with a letter in hand.

Trembling, for despite the years I instantly recognised the handwriting, I read:

'Schönbrunn',
Stanmore, N.S.W.,
30th July, 1935.

My dear Godson,

I received your letter this morning and am writing to tell you how deeply sorry I am to learn you have been so unwell; and I regret that by placing you in jeopardy, albeit unknowingly, I was partly responsible for your sufferings. While they might do little to alleviate you physically, I hope my profound apologies and most sincere compassion will give you some peace of mind.

Having followed events from afar, I share your anxiety. I have read and re-read Mein Kampf (thank you for sending me the copy), as well as the editions of Der Christliche Ständestaat you so generously forwarded to me, and I fear the dark times ahead. From what you have written, it seems they have already arrived. They are the sad repercussion not only of an unjust and brutal war, but also of a bitter peace determined by an unfair treaty. What remains of the Austria I so dearly love is in peril.

Those with whom I have spoken here do not heed the gravity of the situation, and instead look upon Herr Hitler's rise to power with a mixture of bewilderment, envy, and admiration. What rumours they have heard concerning the more sinister aspects of his regime, they marginalise in favour of other more positive outcomes for which we are all inclined to hope when life is tough. National Socialism, however, needs to be viewed on its own terms, in all seriousness, with due regard for consequences. There is dire need for counter measures, and those who wish to champion the good cannot allow themselves to be defeated.

Regarding the darkness you yourself experience, I know it well. It is the Abyss. Be assured that it will pass. <u>Nil desperandum</u>, my boy. Within those black depths lies another Vitality, a certainty of eternal Truths, and the loving power of One greater than yourself. You will emerge the better for it, and I will pray for your fullest recovery. Meanwhile, continue to do all you can to regain your health and strength. Seek rest and comfort in the beauty of your native land; read and draw; enjoy the gift of music; welcome the support of the family who loves you; relax in the company of friends; take time to do good; nourish your soul through frequent contemplation and regular, even daily reception of the sacraments regardless of your despondency.

I look forward to the day when we will finally meet. Too many years have passed since we were first introduced. You have no recollection of that encounter, for you were only a week old. For me, however, it is one I recall with pride, with tenderness, and with gratitude for the honour your parents bestowed upon me. Little did I realise then how much it would mean to me in later years.

I fondly remain,
Your Godfather,
Roderick.

'Sadly, I have let him down,' Hubie took the letter I reverently folded and slid it into his breast pocket. 'Instead, you came. He sent you to me – beautiful, passionate Phoebe! Gird me for the battle I must face! Help me walk the path of righteousness! Yet I fear that to act would be to end a martyr. Now is not the time for martyrs! I must survive! Somehow Hitler must be stopped, and our beloved monarchy restored. What should I do?'

'Be the master of your fate. Be the hunter, Hubie, not the prey. You are exceptionally skilled in tracking and shooting. Camouflage yourself. Psyche them into trusting you and bring them down. You can do it to a deer. Why not to Hitler?'

'You would not hesitate to assassinate?'

'All that would stop me is a lack of opportunity, and the fear of failure. Regarding my aunt, for instance, had I the means, and the occasion—'

'Base revenge is quite a different matter, Phoebe. You still have recourse to legitimate authority.'

'And if that authority should fail me?'

'That is not guaranteed. It is still possible for you to seek your aunt and obtain a willing confession. This you must do for her sake as well as your own peace of mind. If she is still alive, her crime must be accounted for, and she must be lawfully punished, hopefully with clemency, so that she might make reparation. She has a right to repentance, Phoebe. Regarding Hitler, we are faced with a most unjust usurpation of power, to the point that the law itself has been corrupted, as has its channels of enforcement. If no other means exist to remove him from office, then I suppose tyrannicide is our only resort, with the sole purpose of restoring rightful order. It has nothing to do with vengeance. Of course, were such a decision to be taken, it would needs be executed with the utmost prudence.'

'You would actually consider that?'

'If there was nothing more to be done, it would be my duty. And may God have mercy on me.'

60

Shattered Glass

I SEIZED MY OPPORTUNITY to find out more of Emil's fate
when I bumped into Geschmiert one Friday evening. Greeting
me with his usual eager politesse, he opened the elevator
door; and as we descended, I informed him of my friend's
predicament.

'He is a Jud-Boat?' he laughed.

'I beg your pardon?'

'He's gone under. Like— How do you say in English?
Submarine.'

'Submarine or no, he's applied for immigration to Britain. Herr
Hauptsturmführer, I was doing my utmost to assist him. After all,
being a Jew, we can't have him here.'

'Of course, of course,' Geschmiert nodded approvingly. Emil's
exodus was being arranged with due respect for procedure.

'But since he's been arrested, I cannot contact him when his
approval comes through! I have no idea where he is! What am I
going to do?'

'Don't worry, Fräulein, I will find out for you. And for this
favour,' he opened the elevator grill and helped me out with a bow,
'what will you do for me?'

Fortunately, I was spared a reply, for at that moment Hubie
entered.

'Dinner for two, Fräulein?' Geschmiert smiled.

'Yes.' But we did not tell Herr Hauptsturmführer that we were
first going to Stephansdom for a rosary celebration. That was a
secret. Hubie and I had heard of the event courtesy of Herr
Steffan, who whispered us an invitation during a casual meeting
after Mass the previous Sunday. The event honoured the Feast of
the Holy Rosary, which in turn celebrated the Victory of Lepanto of
1571, the battle whereby John of Austria saved Europe from the
Ottoman Turks.

'You have your rosary, yes, Phoebe?' Hubie asked.

I showed him. 'It was a gift to Dad from Archduke Karl.'

'Then you have a relic!' He took my beads and kissed the
crucifix; which mark of affection I would have happily welcomed

on the cheek or even the lips, had he offered. 'How pleased our former Emperor would be to know this is happening! He is bound to be smiling from Heaven.'

We walked down Kärntner Strasse with other couples and small groups, mostly high school or university age, all of whom were quietly heading towards Stephansplatz. Heidi waved us from the cathedral porch.

'About time! We'll be lucky to get seats,' she gabbled, 'It's already full. Sisi's gone inside to mind some; but that was ages ago, and people haven't stopped coming!'

When we did find Sisi, we had to squeeze in. So full was the enormous nave that there was barely room to kneel. And it was nearly silent, despite the thousands.

'I thought Franzl was coming,' I whispered.

Hubie, who was deep in prayer, merely indicated the organ loft.

'He's playing?'

The mighty organ thundered, and we stood to welcome a solemn procession of banners. Heavily tasselled, with grounds of azure, rose, gold, black and vert; and decorated with crosses, pictures of the Holy Family, the Blessed Virgin, the Sacred Heart and Blessed Sacrament – the insignia of the many parish groups attending – they enhanced the cathedral's medieval magnificence. Vibrant song matched the pageantry when the youthful congregation burst into a hymn of praise. A house of glory stands, they sang, and would outlast the ravages of Hell.

Hubie's resonant voice filled the cathedral nave. What had come over him? Only days ago, he was fearful, wary, and guilt-ridden. He professed to have no desire for martyrdom, yet here he was, all six and a half feet of him, joyfully singing 'Many thousands with great fervour have already shed their blood'. The idea of doing away with Hitler had injected in him a new sense of purpose. Did he intend to go through with it? If he did, how had he reconciled it with his beliefs? Or had he dismissed it altogether in favour of reckless defiance?

The rosary commenced: solemn, devout, yet joyful, the Our Fathers, Hail Marys, and Glory Bes prayed with all the energy of youth accustomed to shouting across playgrounds and cheering at games. Yet these same souls were equally capable of hushed attention. For when Cardinal Innitzer spoke, they hung on his every word.

In contrast to his earlier naïve compliance when he ordered the Cathedral bells to be rung to welcome Hitler, His Eminence gave a homily in which he not only apologised for his former position, but encouraged his young flock to affirm Christ, their true Führer, and 'preserve faith and give outward testimony thereof, difficult though that may be'. He pronounced a solemn blessing. Then Franzl on the organ thundered.

'O praise the Lord, ye youthful choirs,' we sang in jubilation. But murmurs accompanied our hymn, along with furtive glances at the back of the church, shrugs, and anxious grimaces. The Hitler Youth were at the cathedral door:

> *Raise the flag! The ranks tightly closed!*
> *The SA marches with calm, steady step.*

'Please return home quickly and hopefully safely,' Herr Steffan announced as 'Clear the streets for the brown battalions' resounded outside. And, just as everyone was about to comply, the organ thundered a final hymn.

'Phoebe, it's the "Herz Jesu Lied"!' Sisi grinned, and with her brother and sister and all the congregation, she sang with gusto:

> *Firm and strong to God we stand*
> *Despite all shame and taunts*
> *We good people will uphold*
> *Our Faith forever more*
> *And so again, we pledge anew*
> *To Jesus' Heart our loyalty true*

'Sieg Heil, Adolf Hitler!' shouted the Hitler Youth.

'Christ is our Führer!' shouted the ten-thousand strong crowd that pushed past the brown-shirted gang.

'Lieber Bischof sei so nett, zeige dich am Fensterbrett!' we chanted as we swarmed outside the Bishop's palace opposite the cathedral.

Innitzer opened a top story window, waved his handkerchief, and gave a blessing.

'Thank you, dear young men and women, and good evening!' he called.

'Ein Volk! Ein Reich! Ein Führer!' shouted the Hitler Youth.

'One People! One Empire! One Bishop!' we shouted back.

At Mass in Hietzing the following Sunday, we learned that Herr Steffan had been arrested.

'For inciting the youth against Hitler and providing Jews with false documentation,' the parish priest whispered. 'And that is not all. Old Father Kravanik at the Cathedral has had both his legs broken. He was pushed from a second story window.'

'But what has happened?' asked Hubie.

'During the night, the Hitler Youth battered down the gates to the Bishop's Palace and forced their way inside shouting, "Kill all the priests!".'

And when with countless others Hubie and I visited

Stephansplatz to see for ourselves, we found every window smashed, and a smouldering bonfire in the courtyard. Crucifixes and furniture were among the charred debris; but prayer books had also been burned and precious artefacts destroyed, including paintings which had been slashed with Charlemagne's sword, itself one of the palace treasures. Many of the Archbishop's personal effects – his rings, his crozier, and even his clothes – had been stolen, and the Archbishop himself had only narrowly escaped. The palace was sealed, and the SS stood guard.

'It was but a matter of time before they attacked the Church,' Hubie reflected. 'In a sense, I hope it continues so that people realise the terror of Nazism and resist. Sadly, those who would gladly see the back of the Jews only finally take offence when their own faith becomes a target. Nothing, however, will destroy our faith.' He took my arm in his. 'Come. Let us to the Cathedral and light a candle for Steffan.'

'And Emil, Hubie.'

'Yes, and Emil. Pray with me, Phoebe, that they be courageous. And may God give us courage, too.'

The ransacking of the archbishop's palace was but the start of the kulturkampf. Church marriages could not be performed without a prior civil ceremony. Education now belonged exclusively to the State. Church schools were closed, as were religious houses. The monastery near the Schütze's hunting lodge at Admont was converted into an SS institute. Membership of the Hitler Youth became compulsory, and all other youth organisations were folded. Traditional holidays and feasts were also banned. There was to be no All Saints Day holiday, no All Souls Day, no St Nicholas, no Krampus. 'Nonsense,' Zita jested, 'Krampus has simply taken to wearing a toothbrush moustache!' And instead of Christmas, a 'German' winter solstice celebration would be celebrated on 21st December.

'Well, remember for future reference, that if you wish to stage a demonstration, it must be for the state, not against it,' advised Dr Elsa when she heard our account at dinner a few days later.

'The Church is doomed!' Dr Robert was in a particularly bleak mood, for he and Dr Elsa had been forced to postpone their departure when the Reich invalidated all passports and required any subsequent applications (of Jews, that is) to be made in keeping with the 'improvements' established by the Centre for Jewish Emigration. His new passport, emblazoned with a red 'J' and made out in the name of Robert Israel Ströhmann, infuriated and disgusted him.

'Never!' declared Sisi.

'Haven't you been prevented from joining the Sisters?'

'Whether or not I join the Sisters changes nothing, Dr Ströhmann. I have already made my vows in my heart. Hitler cannot touch that. And if the Nazis should kill me, I will storm Heaven with my pleas that Hitler be overthrown and Austria restored. Alive or dead, I am victorious.'

'Mother Superior suggested she enter a sister house in Italy,' continued Frau Schütze.

'To which I do not wish to go. Can't you see that's what they want: for good people to leave?' Sisi cast a regretful look at Dr Robert and Dr Elsa.

'I'm afraid we must go,' responded Dr Elsa.

'And you, Sisi, must practise Holy Obedience,' lectured her father.

Sisi chewed a morsel of pork like a young horse resisting a bit that had been pushed into its mouth.

'I do not wish to go, either,' protested Heidi, who was to travel with the Ströhmanns to Holland where she would attend school with her cousins, her own school having been closed.

'I will not have you singing death wishes on Pope and Rabbi, extolling paganism, or thinking you need not practise any Christian virtue. Adolf Hitler is not your saviour,' lectured her father.

'Don't worry, Heidi, you will be home for Christmas,' soothed her mother.

'Such as it will be,' Hubie sighed.

Karl-Alois, too, had received orders. He was being transferred to the Sudetenland.

'Tank maintenance,' he explained in his usual laconic manner.

'Well, what Hitler needs tanks for, I'd like to know,' scorned Dr Elsa, 'He's managed perfectly well without them so far.'

'Russia,' Rudi joked.

'If so, he wishes to use me as cannon fodder in the process,' added Franz.

'He won't get very far, if that's the case,' Zita teased.

But Franz was too subdued for repartee. His organ playing during the rosary celebration had been noted, and the following Monday the Gestapo had removed him from his job. Curiously, he was spared imprisonment, and instead 'advised' to enter military service.

'It will only be for a couple of years, Franzl,' soothed Frau Schütze, 'And perhaps, thanks to Mr Chamberlain, you won't have to face combat.'

'Pfui! Peace in our time! Chamberlain should have cried havoc and let slip the dogs of war!' scoffed Dr Robert.

'Will you also be conscripted, Hubie?' I asked.

'My asthma prevents it. I am, however, going to Germany. A colleague in the Berlin Philharmonic has fallen ill and Furtwängler has invited me to substitute. We will be on tour. Do not worry, Phoebe, I will return mid-November for the Philharmonic Concert. And I will write often, I promise you.'

Professor Schütze poured the schnapps. Instead of raising his glass, however, he took the empty Bohemian carafe and smashed it against the Kachelofen. The pieces he gathered and handed to everyone present. Holding his wife's hand, he began his toast:

'To my dear friends and family. However far you travel, may these fragments remind you that our thoughts and prayers are always with you. Bring them back when we meet again. To Robert and Elsa, bon voyage! To Phoebe, wherever you go, remember your family in Hietzing. To Sisi, may your virtue be an example to us all! To my darling Heidi, who is growing up so fast, prosit! To Karl and Fifi, my blessing! To Rudi and Zita, new life! To Franzl, a safe return! To Huberle, Hals- und Beinbruch!'

61

Faithful Love Cannot Be Marred

'HAVE YOU HEARD FROM EMIL?' Zita asked over coffee and cake at her home one October afternoon. She was now obviously pregnant. 'I hope I can hold on! I might get away with it if baby comes at the end of January.'

'Don't worry, Zita. You know how resourceful Emil is.'

'But it's not like him to be silent! He's always sent me a message or arranged a meeting. It's much harder now. I'm being watched. I don't trust the maids. Both are in the Party.'

'Why don't you dismiss them?'

'How can I be sure the new maids won't be the same?'

'And Rudi? Does he suspect anything?'

'You know, I almost wish he did, just to see if he cared. He has his laboratory and his mountaineering, his car and his friends, and he is content.' Zita gazed out the round window and sniffed. 'I never wanted his affection— Not that he has much affection to give— I thought I could handle it. Rudi and I have always been friends— He's like family, really. Besides, Emil was always there! Now he's gone! Phoebe, I feel as if I'm living in a forest full of wolves. What am I going to do? What if the baby resembles Emil?'

'You should have thought of that!'

'I didn't expect to fall pregnant!'

'Then what did you expect?'

Alighting the tram, I walked down Linke Wienzeile where brittle leaves and paper scraps performed a *danse macabre* in a mournful wind. Thunder rolled, and the grey sky grew tearful. A woman passed, and I hesitated before greeting her. After all, my eyes were suspiciously brown, and I could never be certain of the sympathies of the person in the street. If I said, 'Grüß Gott', my salutation was out of step with the more correct 'Heil Hitler'; but outside the realms of officialdom, I was none too comfortable with that mode of address.

'Phoebe?' Like Bucephalus, Alma Rosé's large eyes possessed a wild, high-strung look. Indeed, she had every reason to fear, not her own shadow, but the shadows all about her.

'We had visitors the other night,' she whispered, using her umbrella to shield us.

'The Gestapo?'

'They took my car. Anyway, I'm glad I caught you. Vati has been asking after you. Pop in if you can.' Then she drew her coat about her and hurried away.

I was about to cross the street when another familiar voice spoke my name.

Kerem!

He was standing outside Café Wienzeile, and his two-tone shoes, camel coat and fedora brought a touch of Hollywood to the scene.

'My beautiful, beautiful houri,' he sighed as he stroked my hair.

'I thought I would never see you again!' I snuggled into his soft lapels.

'You are more beautiful than ever, even than in my dreams! A little more pensive, perhaps. And how the wells of your eyes are watered! It has been too long, far too long!'

'When did you come?'

'This afternoon, from Paris.'

'Have you dined?'

'I was hoping—'

'Of course!' And we entered the café together.

'You have made a home for yourself here, Phoebe,' he resumed, having deferred graciously and frequently to my knowledge of German while ordering.

'I have had many happy times.'

'And the young man of whom you wrote? How is he?' he inquired in a fatherly tone.

'He's on tour in Germany.'

'And has left you alone? I was hoping to meet him. I expected to see a ring on your finger. I hope he has been good to you? He is a nice boy, and well brought up?'

'Yes, Kerem—' My tears began to flood, and again I found comfort in his quiet and genuine attentiveness. 'I do miss him. And then I wonder why, for he hardly talks, and only shows me affection when it pertains to his concerns.'

'And I imagine they are many. Do you remember how I promised that when I came to Vienna we would go to the Opera or a concert? Look, I have tickets to tomorrow night's performance of *Die Ver*— How do you say this?'

'*The Bartered Bride*,' I giggled. 'Oh Kerem! How very appropriate!'

'Is that what it is about?' he laughed once I explained the story of Mařenka and her love dilemmas. 'And true love triumphs in the end? Then let us hope it will be the same for you.'

'But what brings you here?'

'Apart from you? Business thanks to a client I met in Marseilles. I made some valuations of his wife's jewellery. Such fine emeralds! He invited me to Vienna. In fact, he was responsible for the opera tickets. His French is not bad, but I think he would prefer doing business in German. I was wondering, Phoebe, would you translate for me?'

'Of course. When are we meeting him?'

'Tomorrow morning at Hotel Metropole. Dear Phoebe, what is the matter?'

'Kerem, don't you know? It's Gestapo Headquarters!'

Surely, he was not in league with the Nazis! I worried as the next morning I silently stepped into the taxi. Kerem had encountered fleeing Jews in Istanbul, I knew that much. But to profit from their situation? He was disturbingly nonchalant about the appointment. Legs crossed, his left arm extended across the back seat, he viewed the Ringstrasse sights and smiled at the pleasure. Meanwhile, I sat upright, clenching my gloved hands and pressing my knees together.

'We will not be long, my houri,' he soothed, 'And afterwards, perhaps you will show me a little more of beautiful Vienna?'

The client in question wore his smart, black uniform. He welcomed Kerem in schoolboy French while his summery blue eyes scanned every inch of my person.

'Wir treffen uns wieder, Fräulein Raye,' he bowed. He was none other than the Untersturmführer who interviewed me after Emil's first arrest. Evidently, he had enjoyed some recent good fortune, for he was much complimented as he escorted us from the lobby to his office.

'A fine antique,' Kerem remarked in clearly articulated French as a subordinate placed a silver box on the Untersturmführer's desk.

'That is merely l'entrée,' Herr Untersturmführer grinned, pleased that his language skills extended to metaphor. 'Ouvrez, Monsieur Solak, s'il vous plait.'

The treasures crammed inside were so entwined that Kerem could not separate the pieces without assistance, despite his one-handed dexterity. He whispered for me to assist. I untied a pearl necklace from a gold prayer box pendant, lifted a diamond choker and matching bracelet, and set a sapphire brooch upon his black velvet jeweller's mat. Hanging on the wall opposite, Hitler's portrait had its head turned haughtily sideways, as if indifferent to the riches laid beneath him.

The Untersturmführer watched Kerem examine each item with

the eagerness of a pupil submitting a paper of which he was rightfully proud, but uncertain of his master's assessment.

'Magnificent!' Kerem scrutinised the sapphire through his jeweller's glass.

'And the diamonds?' Herr Untersturmführer prompted, insinuating that the schoolmaster-jeweller had overlooked his working-out, for Kerem had barely glanced at the necklet.

Kerem removed his glass and replied with the gleam and authority of the connoisseur, 'They are paste.'

'Judenscheiss!' Herr Untersturmführer hissed with a mixture of good humour and regret. He was a good sport, despite missing out on *summa cum laude*.

Several rings lay scattered in the bottom of the box, one displaying a large square cut emerald, dazzlingly clear. I passed them one by one. Last of all was a pair of earrings.

'Phoebe! Are you well?' Kerem laid aside the emerald. 'You are very pale.'

'I've seen these before,' I murmured. 'Rubies surrounded by diamonds.' Where? Had I dreamt about them? Or had I seen them on someone? Who?

'Perhaps Fraulein Raye needs a glass of water?' suggested the Untersturmführer.

Kerem offered a sum for the emerald ring and sapphire brooch in British pounds. Herr Untersturmführer had quite underestimated their value, and accepted on the spot, clapping and rubbing his hands as Kerem opened his valise. It was filled with banknotes.

They concluded their exchange with much aplomb, Herr Untersturmführer himself seeing us to the taxi.

'He was a very charming young man on his honeymoon when I met him,' Kerem quietly observed as he helped me inside. 'I had no idea of his employment.'

'No, Kerem, you have no idea. You could have been buying bread and milk at a market stall! Do you know from where those rings and jewels have come?'

'Do you, Phoebe?'

'I have my suspicions. Now, since you wish to sight see, let's go! Prinz-Eugen-Strasse 20, please,' I instructed the cabbie.

Formerly the Albert Rothschild Palace, Prinz-Eugen-Strasse 20 was now the recently established Central Office for Jewish Emigration. The building's stately approach was filled with careworn applicants, their coats wrapped about them, huddling in the cold.

'The Nazis raid Jewish homes and steal whatever they can get their hands on. And I'll wager that what I saw in that office was but a portion of what that man has amassed. How could you do business with him, Kerem? How could you? Do you know that Jews are banned from parks, baths, swimming pools, cinemas, and sporting associations? They are forbidden to own motor cars and are restricted in their use of public transport. Theatres and concerts are barred to them, as are the schools, universities, and professions. They must adopt Jewish names and carry special identification. Everywhere they go they risk the most brutal intimidation, and anyone who dares protest risks imprisonment or even death. People sell their valuables to get out, or simply to pay for medicines or basic expenses because they have lost their livelihoods. Those you see here have been camping in line for days; and it's freezing, not to mention perilous. A friend of mine, for instance, was taken by the Gestapo and I have no idea where he is, or even if he is still alive. To make matters worse, immigration is restricted. Aside from the quotas, the only way you can get out is with a barrowload of cash and a guarantee from persons abroad.'

'At least it is emigration and not deportation.'

'Is that all you can say? Why should they leave at all?'

'Phoebe, is there anywhere we might converse in private?'

In the safety of my lounge room, Kerem removed the banknote bundles from his briefcase and flicked open a bottom section. From this hidden compartment he handed me an envelope. Inside were affidavits, visas, and passes – a half-dozen documents in all – each worth far, far more than the paper on which they were printed.

'I have negotiated extensively in South Africa, Egypt, France, and Turkey on behalf of Austrian Jews,' he explained, 'selling precious objects in return for passage or asylum. The jewellery I purchased today will be used for similar purpose.'

'I don't believe it!' I scanned each document in turn.

'I have seen that sort of fear before, Phoebe, when White Russians took refuge in Turkey following the Bolshevik Revolution. So, when Viennese Jews called on my business in Istanbul last February, I knew something was amiss.'

'How could I have doubted you?' I hugged him.

'Now it remains for me to deliver these documents. I have a list in my address book here.'

'I'll take care of that,' I grabbed hold of the book and flicked through the contents. 'It will be easier for me since I know the city and the language.'

'You must be careful. You may be given valuables or money. If so, keep them safe for me. I intend to come again to Vienna, and for reasons other than business,' he smiled. 'And now, Phoebe, I have something for you.'

From his jacket pocket he produced my cigarette case.

'The Sothebys said you'd stolen it! I knew you hadn't! I knew it! But they insisted you were a thief!'

'And they were right, Phoebe. I was, once, a thief.'

Time and again, I had seen how beauty bewitched him; how, lured by lapis lazuli, he had espied the prettiest scarf amidst thousands in a stall; how entranced he had been by the gems he had recently valued. Moments ago, the walnut glow of my piano prompted a brief reverie. Now, his eyes danced across my face as he recounted a chapter from his youth. It was a solemn dance, however, more a Baroque sarabande than a polka, for Kerem's tale was a sombre one:

'When I was sixteen, Phoebe, I entered the service of a wealthy and respectable man. He had two wives; rings adorned his fingers, and beautiful ornaments filled his home. I used to wonder how he had amassed such riches, while I was so unfortunate. My father died when I was nine, you see; my darling mother, when I was fourteen. I should have been more accepting of my lot. I was not ill-treated, had a roof over my head and food to eat. Instead, resentful of my lowliness and poverty, I befriended wrongdoing.

'First, I pocketed a silver coffee spoon. Other valuables soon passed my way, and I delighted in my cunning. Elusion thrilled me and the opportunity for gain enticed me. So ambitious did I become that one day I stole a golden goblet. My master caught me; and in his rage he insisted the full force of the law be brought upon me.'

'He cut off your hand? But why did you persist? Did you not know what punishment awaited you?'

'I was a cocksure lad who thought consequences applied to those less clever than myself. Besides, such severe measures functioned more as deterrents and were usually reserved for violent offences. Many checks and balances prevented their application on a broader scale. But war had been declared. My master's influence aside, the court made an example of me to demonstrate what awaited criminals in times of hardship: They would be rigorously punished and denied the honour of military service.'

I imagined Kerem, a slender youth with a mass of dark brown hair, clad in the gathered trousers, tunic and jerkin I had seen in *The Arabian Nights*, being led into the courtyard of his master's home. Perhaps he was blindfolded for his own good – that he would not see his brutal punishment – but the binding of his mysterious green eyes also obscured from his punishers and fellow servants his exotic beauty, and the truth that he was a lover, not a criminal: a hapless aesthete. The young man who so ardently esteemed visual perfection was to be deprived of it. His maiming would ruin his symmetry; a crude stump would soon replace the marvel of his hand. They placed his hand on a block. He could feel the tourniquet grip his arm, damming the flow of blood, a prelude to partial death. Silence marked the raising of the axe. A brief swish and his wrist was cleaved. Cold air penetrated his raw flesh; his agony swaddled in cotton bandages.

'I passed out shortly afterwards. I never saw my severed hand. By the time I regained consciousness, my wound was closed and tightly bound, and I was left alone to lament my sin and my loss. But do not think my master abandoned me. I was well cared for, Phoebe.'

A woollen stocking now concealed his defect. He always covered it in cold weather, he said. Tenderly, I stroked it and he did not tense. Nor did he protest when I peeled away the covering and wrapped his stump with my hands, as delicate tissue might encase paper thin porcelain.

'Did it hurt?'

'The physical pain dulled with time. Another pain, however, still resides deep in my heart. My punishment was considered a means of repentance. But how can fear and savagery inspire sincere contrition? What genuine conversion can be expected of a man forever known and scorned as a brigand, regardless of his personal disposition? I am not a strict adherent, but I do believe it is the spirit of the law and not its letter that is at the heart of Islam. Like in your Bible, when your own Prophet teaches that if your right hand causes you to sin you should cut it off, he is emphasising the gravity of sin, not advising the punishment. How can I truly repent when I am permanently maimed?'

'And did you never think to take revenge? It seems most unjust. To be put to death for murder is one thing; but to be so gravely harmed for stealing—'

'Phoebe, my punishment was permitted by law. Besides, I was too shocked, too young, too incapacitated to consider, let alone even attempt revenge. Nor am I violent by nature. I abhor violence. I would not wish such injury on anyone – the pain, the memory, the handicap, the degradation – worse still, the loss of liberty, by which I don't mean the inability to use my hand. I am shackled to atonement through disability, disfiguration, and scorn. I am forever marred, body and soul.'

'You are a fine man, Kerem,' I fondled his stump and kissed it as though I were kissing his fingers.

'When you do that,' he smiled, 'I can feel my hand again.'

'Then I will keep doing it. You are not marred. You are kind, thoughtful, generous, caring: a truly noble person.'

'It is odd you should say I am noble, for that is what my name means.'

'Then it suits you. So, was it from fear when on the boat to Istanbul you said you had been mauled by a cur?'

'It was how my sister put it when she learned what happened. She thought my master a brute. Nowadays people assume my injury to be the result of war and say nothing; but your guardian's direct question that evening put me in an awkward position. I did not wish to lie; yet how could I tell the truth? Who wishes to do business with a thief? Anyway, I assumed I would never see you again. One makes many a casual acquaintance on board ship. Little did I know. You do not hold my crime against me?'

'As you yourself said, it was a misfortune of youth. I fell in love with you in Istanbul. And when my cigarette case went missing and suspicions concerning you arose, I refused to attribute to you any wrongdoing.'

'Words cannot describe my feelings when I entered the meyhane after my delayed return from China. I had written you to explain my absence, uncertain you would receive my letter, let alone respond. Then, when your letter arrived—'

'I am so ashamed of that letter!'

'It was a most sincere expression of feeling. How it pained me to let you go! I posted my reply. Filled with nostalgia for our time together, I walked through the old city to the meyhane where we had taken our last meal. I had not been there since that most delightful evening; and when the waiter gave me your cigarette case, all my fears resurfaced. If I kept the case, I could be accused of theft. To dispose of it would, of course, be unthinkable. Most importantly, your sincerity and deep affection demanded I risk all, return it in person, and tell you the ghastly truth. Darling, I could never deceive you.'

'Even if you had stolen it, Kerem, I forgave you. I forgave you in my dream because I loved you. And when you wrote, life for me had changed as I never imagined it would. Now, everything has changed again. Kerem, I only wish I was as pure and beautiful as the houri you think me. Instead, I am a vengeful creature.'

'Murder is indeed heinous,' he remarked after he heard my woeful account, 'And it will be my most fervent wish that your aunt is duly punished for what she has done. But must others be so grievously deprived of your affection because of it?'

'Just as you feel shackled to your crime, so do I feel shackled to my cause. Dearest Kerem, what am I to do?'

'Do you trust me so much you would ask my advice?'

'I no longer trust myself, and you are so kind, so good, and so experienced in the ways of the world.'

'That you seek a just outcome makes me love you the more.

But must one choice necessarily exclude the other? Of course, you must resolve your aunt's crime. That, however, does not mean revenge. Too many misdeeds are committed through wrath,' he gestured with his missing hand. 'You say you had proof. That is good. Now, I would try to find out as much as you can. The more you know of your aunt, the better will be your understanding. With true understanding will come true justice. But remember, Phoebe, the scales of justice have two arms. One pertains to your aunt; the other to you. To pursue the case against your aunt at the expense of your own happiness would tip the balance too far against yourself. You can love and still see justice done. In fact, I would go so far as to say, love and you are bound to find the justice you crave.'

'You make it sound so possible.'

'It is possible, my darling. We will make it so. And now we must dress for the opera. How I am looking forward to spending the evening with you!'

The atmosphere at the Staatsoper was convivial, to say the least. Vienna's rich and privileged, now a tribe of Aryan elite (Nazi personnel and their Austrian lionisers, wives, and girl-friends) thought *The Bartered Bride* a fitting celebration of the Reich's acquisition of the Sudetenland. At the sight of every necklace, brooch, and bracelet (and there were many), I wondered to whom they really belonged. Meanwhile, Kerem drummed up further business with an English-speaking contact courtesy of Herr Untersturmführer who sat next to me during the performance. And my hope that no one would recognise me was dashed at interval when Reichskommissar Seyss-Inquart approached.

'Are you enjoying the opera, Herr Reichskommissar?'

'Immensely, Fräulein. It is very close to my heart, for I am from those parts. I was born in Stannern, a German speaking village in what was at the time Moravia.'

He asked after the Schützes, and his eyes shifted behind their thick glasses when, respecting the concerned tone of his question, I told him a little of the family; but he otherwise betrayed no emotion. Instead, he seized upon my mention of Hubie's playing Brahms' First Symphony in Berlin to turn the conversation back to music. Brahms, too, was a favourite; and he was looking forward to hearing Bruckner's Fifth in the upcoming subscription series. Was I also performing? Not since the Walzermädeln was disbanded.

'No more Rosé Quartet concerts for me, either,' he commiserated, thereby closing that avenue of conversation; and we parted company with best wishes, give my regards, and so forth, all of which were quite hollow. After all, how could either of us pass on such sentiments?

Kerem's willingness for me to take charge of the documents he had procured was much in keeping with his self-effacing nature. Himself electing to be noticed only by the Gestapo, he allowed me to be showered with the gratitude that was his due.

My deliveries I concealed in the chocolate boxes I brought as 'gifts'. A work permit enabled a young woman to nurse in a Cape Town hospital; a wife could now join her husband in Istanbul; a son, interned in Dachau, was able to 'holiday' in France.

Only in one case did a child secure passage for both his parents, who in turn were not easy to locate. Their apartment had been 'Aryanised' and I decided not to concern the present occupants with the reason for my visit. Jockel and Mitzi Austerlitz proved invaluable, since they could scout around now exclusively Jewish neighbourhoods without arousing suspicion, neither on the part of fearful residents nor watchful authorities; and they soon found Mr and Mrs Kramer's more modest residence.

A fifth delivery proved difficult, because the family concerned was under house arrest. How was I to penetrate the Gestapo barrier? Believing honesty to be the best policy, I approached Geschmiert who liked to give the emigration process a personal touch. He willingly escorted me and took it upon himself to explain my visit. I communicated my success to Kerem by letter, thanking him on behalf of my 'family' for his generous 'presents'.

My final mission, a study visa for the son of a wealthy Döbling couple, took me to Professor Rosé's neighbourhood. I placed the visa in my violin case and visited him on my way home.

He was very much alone. His son Alfred had already left for America. Now Alma, too, was away. Her Czech passport, which she possessed courtesy of her former marriage, enabled her to travel abroad without interference. She was lucky to retain it, for, since the takeover of Sudentenland, any Czech Jew in Vienna risked being rounded up and pushed over the border with little more than the clothes on their back.

'Almschi's in Amsterdam with Mengelberg and Bruno Walter,' Rosé explained. 'Then, she will visit London and Paris. I wonder, Fräulein Phoebe, how much time has she left before her passport is useless?'

'You don't hold much hope for Czechoslovakia?'

'And who will be next? Better not answer. Let us play Mozart. Will you play the Sinfonia Concertante with me?'

'I wish I had more of a Mozart touch.'

'You are going to refuse an old man? The Rosé Quartet has been playing since 1882. Every year, for the past ten years, we have been saying, "This season will be the last". And still we do another. Not even Hitler can stop us. Carl Flesch has raised the money to sponsor the quartet in London. Almschi will be playing second violin. Mozart touch or not, Fräulein Phoebe, we *must* keep the music alive.' He tapped me gently on the wrist, whereby I understood that 'We' also included me.

62

Fire and Ice

'**J**EWISH ASSASSINATION IN PARIS!' shouted the newsboy at the tram stop near Professor Rosé's.

'Heil Hitler,' he thanked me, my purchase having curtailed momentarily his hullabaloo.

'Hitler,' I muttered, and scanned the front page.

A Nazi diplomat had been shot.

'Probably deserved it,' I shrugged.

Two days later, the papers were still harping on the incident, especially when the diplomat, one Vom Rath, died of his wounds. I turned from the headlines and resumed my breakfast, as a villager would the shepherd boy who cried Wolf. Far more interesting and relevant was Scylla's letter. Dated 27th September, it was a remarkably prompt response to my earlier request:

> *Regarding your real estate* [it continued after upbraiding me for writing only to communicate on matters of business], *all the necessary arrangements are being made. Meanwhile, please understand that selling property takes time. Nor can I promise that the funds procured will guarantee the outcome you desire. Money is one matter, but permission to immigrate is a separate affair. Nevertheless, be certain that we will do all we can, only please be patient. Any slowness on our part is not due to lack of concern, I assure you. What news we hear only increases our worries. Whatever else you might do, take care of yourself, Phoebe. With the prospect of war in Europe, don't you think it's high time you came home?*
>
> *Warmest wishes &c,*
> *Cilla*

'No, I don't think it's high time I came home.' I opened Hubie's letter from Leipzig; and was about to take up my coffee when my spoon rattled on its saucer.

'Not another firecracker!' I groaned. The previous night marked the fifteenth anniversary of the Beer Hall Putsch, a sacred day in the National Socialist calendar. Celebrations had been lively to say the least, with the Geschmierts hosting a raucous party which did not finish until their many guests bellowed the 'Horst-Wessel-Lied' all the way down to the ground floor at two in the morning.

A distant siren, however, prompted me to abandon Hubie's enthusiasms on Bruckner's Fifth in favour of a shopping trip. I crept past Andreas Geplapper in his SA uniform, quite hung over, snoozing in his chair in the foyer, and headed outside.

Others had also wandered onto the street, hurriedly wrapping their coats about them and muffling their faces with scarves to keep out the smoke as well as the cold, for in the icy breeze was mingled fire and ash. My feet crunched broken glass, whereupon I beheld Emil's shop window smashed to pieces. A clanging firetruck hurtled towards the Karlskirche. A second truck charged from the opposite direction and swept around the corner into Mariahilf.

'Is the Schönbrunn on fire?' I enquired of the greengrocer at the Naschmarkt, for much of the blue-grey haze drifted from that direction.

'If it is, there's not much you can do about it,' he shrugged as he weighed my potatoes. 'And as far as I know, it's not the palace, it's the synagogue. And not much you can do about that, either, Fräulein. That'll be the Schmalzhoftempel,' he nodded in the direction of the smoke billowing from behind Linke Wienzeile.

I set off in that direction, taking advantage of side streets to reach my destination, and came face to face with a file of young men. Most unusual for Viennese, they were hatless and coatless, some minus jacket and tie. They marched with their hands on their heads.

'We're driving pigs to market!' laughed the merry voice of a brownshirt youth. 'Hie there, Judenschwein! Judenschwein, move along!'

Boozed-up and brandishing sticks, a Nazi gang poked their 'produce' down the lane. I sheltered under the eaves of a building; and as I watched, my eyes caught those of a man in the file. It was one of those spontaneous connections arising purely from circumstance: we happened to look in the same direction at the same time; and our expression was one of mutual concern. At least that was my interpretation. The young man, however, lingered. Did he know me by sight? From a coffee shop or concert or previous passing in the street?

'Move along, move along, little piggy-wig!' a brownshirt prodded him, and grinned when the man jumped back in step.

The troop passed, leaving me face to face with the brownshirt.

'How now, my little Jewish sow,' he sidled up and pressed me against the wall, grasped hold of my chin and wrenched my head to one side.

'Let me go!'

Struggling, I tried to bite myself free, but he thrust his body upon me and squeezed my breasts. Moisture seeped through my dress.

'Halt!'

Geschmiert, his uniform not quite buttoned, stepped out from a car. 'He is giving you trouble, Fräulein Raye?' he asked in English after saluting the brownshirt who struggled to execute the 'Heil Hitler' and adjust his trousers simultaneously. 'Your name, Mann?' Geschmiert turned again to the stormtrooper. 'Move on, before I report you.'

'There'll be trouble for you now, Claus, you klutz!' a rear guard called as the stormtrooper joined the marching party.

'I will take you home, Fräulein,' Geschmiert escorted me to his car, 'But first we must hasten to Schmalzhofgasse. Mach Schnell!' he tapped his driver on the shoulder.

The car sped through the streets, swerving past broken furniture and narrowly missing what I thought was a body. A woman wandering all a daze in fur coat and slippers jolted to attention when the driver honked his horn. It took a second blast for her to move out of the way. In every building, windows had been shattered and front doors hacked. Bedding and wares were strewn over pavements. Ahead, firemen hosed blocks of apartments while flames leapt from the burning synagogue, the drama watched by anxious bystanders.

A Rabbi stood forlorn amidst scrolls and sacred artefacts. Geschmiert introduced himself with a few well-lubricated phrases. In the distance a woman screamed, glass smashed, and shots were fired. The driver leaned against his car, lit a cigarette, and welcomed the company of the brownshirt who had sauntered over, having fulfilled certain duties pertaining to the welfare of 'Aryan' residents, so I overheard.

'So, who's the lady in the back seat?' he asked.

'Geschmiert's floozy,' the driver replied.

'Geschmiert?' His companion laughed as much from incredulity as delight in potential scandal. 'Geschmiert? With a Jewess? Impossible! That is Rassenschande!'[40]

'She's the piano teacher,' nudged the driver. 'Ein Untermensch. Mischling 2nd Degree.'

'Mission accomplished!' Geschmiert interrupted the driver's recounting of the side-street incident and instructed him to take care of some books.

'We arrived in the nick of time! Thank God the Rabbi had the

---

[40] *Rassenschande*: (lit. race disgrace) violation of Nuremberg Laws pertaining to sexual relations between Aryans and non-Aryans.

presence of mind to save the community records! Terrible business! Imagine if they had gone up in flames! And now, Fräulein Raye,' he patted me on the lap, 'we will take you home.'

If I had to bathe seven times to rid me of that vile contamination, I would have done so. I turned on the taps full force and poured rosewater into the tub. An Untermensch? I am no underling! Mischling? Second degree? What do they mean? Fumbling with buttons and clasps, I ripped off my clothes. Did I not have hands, organs, dimensions, senses, passions? I cleansed my arms and face in earnest, hoping to restore both body and soul in a steamy bubble bath. Apparently, I possessed not a shred of humanity. True, the brownshirt did not rape me – I could be thankful for that. His forcing himself upon me was not to vent his lust. In a sense, it was far worse. He did it out of malice: to shame and sully me, and to disparage a man who happened to be a Jew.

'You would not even treat an animal that way!'

Yet I had behaved as a wild creature, had succumbed to primitive instinct, a fierce urge to bite and scratch. How else could I defend myself? A brandy failed to drown the taste of Nazi flesh. Would that he be plastered with his own secretion! In the mirror, I beheld my figure draped in a white bathrobe, my hair dishevelled, hanging long and loose over my shoulders, its curls thick and wet. I stared at my own dark eyes, worried over my black brows and olive skin.

'No, I am not mad! Nor am I a subspecies!'

So, I corseted and costumed myself in my most stylish day dress, silk stockings, and high heels; I brushed my tresses and rolled them into an elegant chignon; then I plucked and pencilled my brows and reddened my lips. Smoothing my skirt about my hips and straightening my seams, I viewed myself once more and wished I were fashioned from impenetrable marble.

All day Vienna burned. Gun-metal clouds, thick with ash and embers, hung upon the city like a heavy, military coat. Nearly every synagogue was razed, ninety in all, to say nothing of shops, schools, homes, and businesses. And Vienna was not the only city afflicted. The destruction raged across the Reich; for the German Volk had spoken out against the disgraceful act of Jewish treachery – the cowardly, bloody deed of the murder-boy in Paris.

And who was this 'murder-boy'? The buck who dared lower his horns and charge at the wolf ravaging his herd? Seventeen-year-old Herschel Grynszpan, a Jew of Polish extraction, who was living illegally in Paris with relatives, having fled persecution in Germany. Upon hearing that his parents had been deported without notice to Poland, the lad purchased a gun and took

himself to the German embassy where he demanded to see the
ambassador. The ambassador being absent, Grynszpan saw his
secretary Vom Rath instead and shot him in the stomach.

The following morning, I hurried to Leopoldstadt where I found
the Epsteins' bakery gutted, and the family nowhere to be found.
All down Taborstrasse, every single Jewish shop had been
vandalised. Cash registers lay broken on the sidewalk, their tills
agape like the unbound mouths of corpses, and the street rattled
with the sound of swept glass. A woman wearing a man's overcoat
and work boots tossed dead rats and rotting vegetables onto a
bonfire of furniture. Two boys in pyjamas shovelled rubble, their
labour their only means of keeping warm.

No one would tell me anything of the baker and his family.

Finally, I spotted Bela Austerlitz pushing a barrow of rubbish. I
took off my scarf and wrapped it round her bare head.

'My mother is dead!' she cried.

At dawn the previous morning, the SA looted their apartment
and set fire to the bakery. The family escaped in time, except
elderly Frau Epstein who suffered a heart attack on the stairs and
was consumed by flames.

'At least I have some good news for you, Bela. I have authorised
the sale of property. As soon as the transactions are complete,
there will be money for your family to come to Australia. Where is
everyone?'

Bela's whispered answer took me through streets and alleys
strewn with glass and piled with garbage, into a building, and up
several flights of narrowing stairs to a garret room. I knocked three
times as instructed.

'Mama!' came the tiny voice of three-year-old Rosa Austerlitz.

'Who is it?' called her sister Mitzi.

'It's Phoebe.'

Old Mr Epstein opened the door and I sidled inside, for the
entrance was obstructed by a chair, one of two crammed into a
tiny space which also housed a table and a bed, not to mention
seven people. The floors were bare, and a wan red sun edged with
ashen clouds glowed through the single dirty casement. The bed
was occupied by David Epstein and his wife, both of whom were
ill, David with a severe cold, and Pauline with morning sickness,
for she was newly pregnant. Mr Epstein Senior brought me a
chair. Once again, I explained my plans.

'I could sell another property if I need to,' I concluded. 'You all
must leave!'

'I am too old and sick to travel,' replied the sad old man. 'I will
stay here with Freidl, may she rest in peace.'

'And who will look after Vati if we go?' added David. 'Besides, they have no right to destroy our home! Now that this has happened foreign intervention is bound to occur.'

'But you have a child on the way and now you are without work. How will you support your family? I will bring food and clothes,' I passed him what money I had. 'Don't worry. I have the means. Where's Jockel?'

As the sole fit male member of the family, Jockel had been snatched by the SA and imprisoned.

'It's an outrage!' I complained to Geschmiert that evening. 'You have a fourteen-year-old boy in custody!'

'A fourteen-year-old boy in custody is not the only outrage, Fräulein! The whole affair is utterly illegal! It has taken us months to co-ordinate everything! And what happens? They shove Jews in Dachau and we must get them out of Dachau as well as Vienna! What a mess! Has he papers?'

'No.'

'Then there is nothing I can do about it. You need to speak to the SA.'

Jockel, however, was not in Dachau. After being imprisoned by the brownshirts in a gymnasium, deprived of food and warmth, he was released three days later and joined his family. But for young Jockel, without any opportunity for school or work, that garret was itself a cell.

Upon learning the plight of my Jewish friends, Frau Schütze immediately filled two suitcases with clothing which she thought might help. These she entrusted to Franz who accompanied me to Leopoldstadt the following day.

'Mutti's packed enough for a skiing trip,' he quipped as he puffed along beside me. 'And they're good clothes, too. There are even some Knize suits. Speaking of Knize, I don't know what I'm going to do about my shirts, let alone my aftershave, now they're closed.'

'Perhaps you should have thought about that before the Anschluss.'

'Please don't think ill of me, Phoebe! I couldn't bear that from you. Believe me when I tell you that I abhor what has happened.'

'What do you think they'll do to the boy who shot Vom Rath?'

'It's a tricky situation. Under French law, Grynszpan's crime is a political one and as such merits the death penalty. But the last thing the Nazis want is a Jewish martyr.'

'Then that is what they should have.'

'Don't you think there have been enough Jewish martyrs?'

'Do you think Grynszpan was right in seeking to redress the injustice inflicted upon his family?'

'By buying a revolver and shooting a Nazi diplomat? No, I don't. Of course, the situation must be rectified, but not by a seventeen-year-old waif. Look at the effect of it! What good has it done? Grynszpan's crime has led to the unjust and violent persecution of thousands of innocent people already suffering dire hardship and humiliation. Imagine the international backlash if the French give him the death penalty. His lawyers will do whatever it takes to avoid him being convicted.'

'Do you think that's fair?'

'It's a reasonable approach.'

'Would you bend the law to save him?'

'If I could establish the crime as one of passion, I would. Besides, the shooting was a desperate response to a situation that is itself criminal. Do you think the boy would have anticipated such a reprisal?'

'How could anyone anticipate such hatred, Franzl?'

'Indeed. But now Hitler's regime has been fully discredited. Had it not been for the pogrom, Grynszpan's crime would have passed unnoticed. I hope he will be spared. I am truly ashamed, Phoebe, to call myself German.'

63

Kindertransport

NEITHER HUBIE nor I heeded his impeccable white tie; nor did we consider the thoughts of any onlookers when we embraced at Café Museum that evening, Hubie having arrived post-haste from Berlin.

'I have been asked to perform Mozart horn concerto at the Salzburg festival,' he began as he escorted me to his table, his eyes aglow. 'I performed all Mozart's horn concertos for my music doctorate. Would you practise with me? I know orchestral reductions are a curse for a pianist, but it would be wonderful to play with you again. Would you consider?'

'Of course,' I smiled for the first time in days, and it did me the world of good. 'But I cannot believe you are playing Beethoven's Pastoral tonight.'

'What is so strange about it? It's been on the programme for months.'

'Given recent events, waxing lyrical about pastoral bliss is a bit ironic, don't you think?'

'What would you have us perform, the Königgrätzer Marsch?[41] Personally, I would prefer the Choral Symphony, and be reminded of our true purpose in life – to seek God above all things; to be united in Love, and, in being so, filled with Joy.'

'Oh, Hubie, how is Joy possible amidst such horror? And where is God?'

'He is in the Tabernacle of every Church; and in the tabernacle of the hearts of those who love Him and who seek to do His will.'

'Which is no Nazi. What will they do next? Now they've fined the Jews one billion marks for the murder of Vom Rath. Moreover, the Jews must pay for the damage which they themselves have to repair! It's tempting to think of the violence as an act of insanity; that way there would be a plausible explanation. The trouble is

---

[41] *Königgrätzer Marsch*: march composed in 1866 by Johann Gottlieb Piefke, celebrating the decisive Prussian victory against Austria in the Battle of Königgrätz which concluded the Austro-Prussian War. The music featured in the Nuremberg Rally Parade in Leni Riefenstahl's film, *Triumph of the Will*, (1935).

that it was all terribly, terribly sane. The Nazis knew what they were doing and did it shamelessly.'

'In Berlin it was the same,' Hubie resigned himself to comment.

'It's quite Malebolgian. Vienna is now home to panderers and seducers, grafters, hypocrites, thieves and deceivers, schismatics and falsifiers, all under the protection of khaki clad titans. The only difference is that none of them suffer punishment. Instead, they glory in their misdeeds. To see a Nazi carrying his head as if it were a lantern would give me immense satisfaction. Will it never end?'

'It will end, I assure you. Evil is never eternal. Somehow good will triumph. Given the scale of the disaster, do you still intend to look for your aunt? Whilst in Germany I made some enquiries on your behalf, but to no avail.'

'Hubie, with all that's been happening, I'd almost forgotten about Ailine. I'm not even as angry as I used to be.'

'You have every right to be angry. Righteous anger is the spur that goads the steed of Justice; Mercy the bridle which tempers and guides.'

'But in my case, Anger was spurred by Hatred's heel, and I clung to the mane of Vengeance. I now know what hate does. Having witnessed such violence and fury, I refuse to partake in it. My troubles I will resolve some other way, although I know not how. Meanwhile, there are more pressing matters to hand— Emil's papers, for instance. And Emil's whereabouts— Hubie, I've heard nothing! And you should see how the Epsteins are living! And they have no means of restoring their bakery or their home for the insurance company won't pay. The Nazis are confiscating property by way of reparation. And Jews are no longer to own businesses or work in shops!'

'I believe I have a partial solution to your Jewish friends' problem,' Hubie informed me a week later. 'I visited the Weissmüllers this morning. I have been giving the boys piano lessons without charge these past months. Herr Weissmüller was taken away during the pogrom. Apparently, there is talk in Britain of evacuating Jewish children. Frau Weissmüller wishes to send her sons. It is a temporary measure, but if it works out it means the boys will be spared further horror. Perhaps your friend's children could also go to England? That way, they would be safe while their emigration is being arranged.'

A letter from Oxford confirmed Hubie's news. It was odd that the envelope opened more easily than I expected. I scrutinised the seal. Surely it had not been tampered with! Why would anyone bother with my mail?

'Well, they would have no chance of reading this,' I shook my head as I attempted to decipher the hideous scrawl. 'Wally, for Heaven's sake, why don't you type? And what's this? Twins? Trust Lucy! From no children to two at once!'

Oxford,
Saturday, November 26th, 1938

Dear Phoebe,

I thought to begin this letter with some good news. Mary Arondelle and Letitia Maeve were born in the early hours of 22nd November, and I am happy to report that mother and babies are doing well. The girls are identical twins, and I'm having a deuce of a time telling them apart, although Lu assures me there are differences. She is convinced their personalities have already begun to show, which I attribute alternatively to wishful thinking or mother's insight; for as far as I am concerned all they do is pee, sleep, and suckle, and I am yet to see any individuality manifest in any of those occupations. Nevertheless, the fact remains that they are little marvels.

Would you consider being godmother to our Maeve? We have scheduled the Baptism for 18th December in the hope that you will come. Should circumstances prevent your attendance, we can arrange for someone to stand in by proxy. That is, if you are willing to assume the responsibility. And, of course, you are welcome to stay for Christmas.

We were all of us much alarmed by the recent violence in your part of the world, which has increased our concerns for you and your Austrian friends. Certainly, you will be relieved to know that concerted efforts are being made here to facilitate immigration. Last night, in fact, Viscount Samuel broadcasted a request for families to foster Jewish children in distress. My parents have offered their home and will contact you the moment they receive instructions from the relevant authorities. No doubt you will know of a family in need. If so, would you be so kind as to make whatever arrangements are required from your end? I have also submitted letters and documents related to your friend Mr Fährmann's passage and will keep you posted.

Lu sends her best wishes and trusts you remain well. I second her thoughts.

We both hope to see you soon.

All best for your health and safety,
Wally.

Wally's invitation in hand, I approached Geschmiert. 'When I sought your help for my friend Herr Fährmann, you asked me what I could do for you in return, Herr Hauptsturmführer. Well, you will be pleased to know that I can help you fill your emigration quota. I have three more Jews who have found a home in England, and I need you to organise their papers.'

'Three more?' he complained. 'Everything was going tickety-boo, and now they all want to leave at once!'

'But isn't that what you want?'

'We had made lists and kept files up to date! The Jews were co-ordinating themselves. Now they are panicking. It's chaos! Chaos, Fräulein Raye! At this rate I'll be working through Christmas. Liesl won't be pleased.'

'Well, all I can say, Herr Hauptsturmführer, is that I've done my share. You find Misha Fährmann. If you don't, I guarantee I'll have twenty more Jews for you to process!'

But Bela Austerlitz refused to part with her children. The poor woman was still without news of her husband and she had taken on char work to support her family.

'I've since heard that a Dutch woman has made arrangements with the Centre for Jewish Emigration,' I explained. 'They are giving preference to children whose fathers are absent, and to those who have already been offered a place. Jockel, Mitzi, and Rosa will have a home.'

'They already have a home: with their mother!'

'The Sothebys are good, generous people.'

'They are not Jewish.'

'The children will be well looked after, I assure you. And friends of mine, who live close by, have a maid who is Jewish. Jockel and Mitzi will be able to attend school.'

'My husband leaves for Czechoslovakia, and now you ask me to give up my children!'

'You can write to them. It will only be for a short while. They can't live like this, Bela. Perhaps you and Mani will be able to join them later.'

'Then Jockel and Mitzi may go. Not Rosa. At least leave me my little one. I will stay in Vienna and wait for news from Mani. You go to Australia,' she turned to David and Pauline. 'I will look after Vati.'

On a chill night, a week before Christmas, Hubie and I journeyed to the Westbahnhof. The platform was crowded with children, every one of them tagged with manila tickets, their only luggage a single suitcase.

'Who would have thought there would be so many?' I wondered

as I tried to pick out familiar faces.

'I was here a fortnight ago and it was the same, and there are hundreds more to follow,' Hubie replied as he guided me through throngs of children. 'I believe another train is being arranged for some time in the new year.'

'Dr Schütze!' The Weissmüller boys ran to Hubie, and as they pulled him towards their mother, they rattled off a description of the number of carriages and pistons, the class of engine, and the stops the train would make in its journey across the continent. Frau Weissmüller tried to share their enthusiasm and smiled wearily after them as they dodged the crowds in their quest for more information, novelties, and friends to meet or make.

'I keep telling myself it will only be for a time,' she sighed as she dabbed her tears with her handkerchief. 'It's for the best, yes, Dr Schütze? He has organised everything, Fräulein Raye. I don't think I could have done it on my own.'

'Has there been any news of your husband?' I asked.

'Not a word.'

Jockel Austerlitz was relieved to be freed from the confines of his garret prison. In the past few months he had grown several inches taller and was heavier in the brow. Before long, he would be shaving. He squinted a little and shifted uncomfortably in his borrowed clothes. Clearly, he had had enough of his mother's advice; but there was plenty more to come, which he bore with a sigh.

'Jockel, you are the man of the family,' Bela fussed over his coat which was too large for him, but guaranteed to keep him warm, and no doubt would fit before the winter's end. 'It is your duty to observe the Law and the Commandments; and look after your sister.'

'He doesn't need to worry about me, Mutti,' Mitzi remarked from the suitcase on which she was sitting studying a map. 'I can manage.'

'And don't forget to write.'

A whistle blew, and with hugs and kisses and a thousand promises the children boarded the train. Faces, many eager, others more apprehensive, a few downright miserable, and some quite bewildered, crammed the carriage windows. Sons and daughters called, cried, and waved farewell. Parents waved and called back, staving off tears as they watched the train chug their precious cargo to foreign parts.

64

Ring Out, Wild Bells

'FRÄULEIN RAYE! Will you give a penny for the Winterhilfswerk?' Hildi Geschmiert, dressed in her Jungmädelbund uniform, jangled a tin can. I dropped a pfennig for her and she jangled the can even louder. Had I been certain the money would go somewhere worthwhile, I might have donated more; but I knew that the Epsteins, shivering in their garret, would see none of it.

Nor would Emil, wherever he was. What would he think of his beloved bookshop now that it had changed hands? The new owner was equally houseproud. He had replaced the glass, obliterated 'Kirschbaum' from the front door, purged the store of its remaining dusty classics, and put up a special shopfront display just in time for Christmas. Posters of vigorous, fair-haired young men advertised the Hitler Youth as Germany's Future; and a fierce St Nicholas wearing a winged helmet and holding a spear kept Krampus at bay, the latter's leering face featuring the Jewish caricature so loved by the Nazis. The Christmas cards for sale showed a German family – mother, father, and child – peacefully gathered around the hearth.

But the Christmas tree was the highlight. Decorated with gold and silver baubles and topped with a Swastika, it took up much of the window. Another Swastika formed the base of a wreath from which a candle glowed. 'Bit of a fire hazard,' I thought, as I scanned the volumes of *Mein Kampf* stacked under the tree and recommended as the perfect gift for any adult. And amidst Hitler's bestseller were colourful books for the children. *Trust No Fox on his Green Heath and No Jew on his Oath,* I read on a cover.

'Mami said I could have that one for Christmas,' Lindl pointed to the book with a picture of a toadstool with a Jew's face for its stalk as she handed me a cellophane packet of gingerbread.

'Thank you, Lindl. What a lovely treat,' I smiled. Then I noticed the biscuits were Swastika shaped.

'It's nice we can celebrate Christmas,' smiled their mother. 'After all, it's about family, isn't it?'

'You shouldn't have given her those. Papi says she's part Jew.' I heard Hildi scold her sister.

'Don't bicker, girls. It's Christmas. Come, let's sing "Hohe Nacht"!'

Their clear, innocent little voices carried like bells through the chill evening air. But Frau Geschmiert and her daughters would not sing much longer. The weather was about to turn nasty; for the wind, which like a wolf had prowled through the city all day, began to howl.

A horn tooted cheekily, and Rudi's red roadster halted under a frosty street lamp.

'Phoebe! I'm glad I found you. Hop in!'

'What's happened, Rudi? Is it Zita?'

Rapidly shifting gears, he sped towards Hietzing, screeched around the corner and skidded in front of the Schütze's.

A black crepe wreath adorned the front door of the stately old house.

'Thank you for coming, Phoebe,' Sisi, red-eyed, welcomed us in, 'Hubie will be so relieved to see you!'

'What's happened, Sisi? Is he ill?'

Every step of Hubie's descent seemed to jar his membranes. He attempted his usual handkuss, faltered, then broke into sobs. We sat on a small chaise-lounge in a tiny waiting room off the foyer, where, my arm around him, I listened to his sad account.

'But Heidi seemed fine when she arrived from Holland.'

'It has been years since she had asthma,' he sniffed. 'We thought she had grown out of it. She caught a chill while shopping yesterday and retired early. When Mutti later checked on her, she was struggling to breathe. Immediately, we called the ambulance. The hospital, however, was understaffed. Due to the regulations, many doctors and specialists can no longer practise. Heidi was declining rapidly and the doctor in charge did not act with the urgency required. Dr Ströhmann would have known instantly that she needed adrenaline, but he is no longer with us, Phoebe, and now my beloved little sister is dead! Will you pray with me, please, for the repose of her soul?'

'Treatment would have been of little value,' Being well-acquainted with medical matters, Rudi discussed illness the way polite society discussed the weather. And he had no qualms about raising the subject as he drove me home late that night.

'I find it utterly negligent.'

'There was not much they could do if she didn't have the resilience.'

'And I suppose you're going to attribute that to her having Jewish blood?'

'Heidi Schütze?'

'Like me, she's at least a quarter Jew, and you know it, Rudi.'

'I'll pretend I didn't hear that. Anyway, resilience or no, whether her condition has anything to do with race is pure speculation, although it wouldn't do to have the Master Race suffering from asthma, would it? Which underlines why it's important that racial theory be tested scientifically to prove the Nazis wrong. Or prove them right.'

'And how do you propose to do that?'

'I don't propose to do anything. It's not my field.'

'But you're a biochemist.'

'An agricultural biochemist. I analyse wheat grains. I'm not a eugenicist.'

On Christmas Eve, Professor and Frau Schütze decorated the tree as was their custom. Tinkling the Christmas bell, they invited us into Herr Beethoven's room. Karl and Fifi's little ones were mesmerised by the candles glowing on the enormous conifer. Gifts were exchanged warmly but solemnly, as though they might be the last, and the family crept to Midnight Mass, fearful and dolorous. The following day the table was laden as always, with venison sent up from Admont. But grief numbed all, so much did we miss the willowy, graceful, angelic Heidi.

'Now look what your Anschluss had done,' Professor Schütze broke the silence and pointed at Franz.

'Kurti, you cannot blame Franzl. The Anschluss is the work of our generation, not his. If anyone is to blame, it is I. I should have checked on Heidi sooner. But she gave no indication of being so sick. If only I had known!'

'We had no way of telling how quickly she would decline, Mutti,' Sisi soothed, 'Now we have an ally in heaven.'

'You are right, Sisi,' her mother took her hand. 'And we must share the sufferings of so many who are also missing loved ones this Christmas. We will use the Holy Mass to unite ourselves with our beautiful daughter and sister, whom we hope has gone to Heaven, and adore the Christ Child Who has come to Earth in a special way for us this Christmas.'

'If it wasn't a grave sin, I would kill myself,' Hubie sat at the piano, pale and glum, when late that afternoon I found him and offered him the egg nog I had brought.

'Think, Hubie, you are much needed and much loved. Heidi looked up to you. You were her big brother. You must keep going for her sake.'

'If only—'

'Don't torture yourself with possibilities, it won't change what has happened. Come, drink.' But he refused the beverage.

'When Dad died it was the silence I couldn't stand,' I resumed, unable to bear his gloom. 'Dad and his quips and his songs disappeared overnight. I'd try and practise, and, as much as it annoyed me while he was alive, I'd find myself wishing he'd interrupt. I can see him now, coming into the room with a paint tube in his mouth saying, "I can't get the lid off the bloody cadmium. Bach sounds good, by the way." But I am at peace, knowing he's at peace – a peace I never experienced with Maman. And believe it or not, even though he's gone, I still find ways to keep him close. And he still speaks to me. Take heart, Hubie.'

'It is my consolation that my darling sister is in the merciful hands of God, and in the company of His angels.'

Fearing his remark heralded further melancholy, I fingered the tune on the stand. It did not help that it was Schubert's F Minor Fantasie, which I considered a poor antidote, even though the pathos befitted his mood.

'You taught her to play piano, didn't you?'

'She was making good progress. We played this duet only last summer.'

'Let's play it now. And perhaps, Hubie, she will hear it.'

Close we sat on the piano stool. Hubie's plaintive melody lilted over the exquisite harmony of my gently pulsing bass. Not wishing to stop, we let our tears fall on the keys; and when we could no longer see the music, we trusted to memory until our hands caved in to our feelings.

The family dressed Heidi in her bridesmaid's dress and blue sash and wrapped a pearl rosary round her hands. We knelt beside her white coffin, and in long silence mourned her passing before laying her to rest in the family vault in Hietzing cemetery. So innocent! So pure! Too joyous a one to be taken so young!

After the wake, Hubie and I walked through the Schönbrunn. Despite the SS barracks now being constructed in the grounds, and that Jews were forbidden entry, the palace itself remained untouched by the regime. Hubie wandered from one painting to the next, examined the furniture, and silently gazed out the windows. Mighty Neptune's pond was a mass of ice; and the statues flanking the parterre were cloaked with snow.

'You do not think I am foolish in desiring a return of the old world?' he finally spoke as we walked through the park, both dressed in black.

'Not at all. Now that I have seen for myself, I understand my father's love for it, and what has been lost through war, bitter treaty, and vile usurpation. It is truly a noble mode of life, a worthy ideal; and he who fights for it, champions a just cause.'

'You understand that I do not wish the monarchy restored for its own sake – as merely an alternate form of government. It is the restoration of Christendom I desire.'

'I understand.'

'And I will fight for it, Phoebe. Would you lend me your support, as a lady would hold the stirrup of her lord as he mounts and rides into battle?'

I nodded.

'Even if it meant his riding to his death?'

'Yes, Hubie.'

'May God bless you.'

He bent his head; and his lips fell moist upon my own like dewfall on a fresh shoot. I quivered; then, nourished by his caress, pulsed with life. My arms coiled round his strong body; my lips drank kiss after kiss. But, just as reverently had his lips descended, so they withdrew.

'It's growing dark,' he whispered.

65

Most Friendship is Feigning

UBIE LEFT ME OUTSIDE Linke Wienzeile with his usual polite bow; but the kisses he had showered upon me in the palace garden drenched my heart. There, a hundred seeds had germinated since our lips had touched, and my bosom blazed with vibrant desert blooms. Bleak midwinter it might have been outside; but in my soul it was the height of summer.

In the foyer, I glanced over my mail and found a letter from Aunt Rachel. Postmarked October, it had reached me later than usual, and, like Wally's recent note, the envelope opened too easily for comfort. Noxious suspicion sprang from my heart's garden. Who was reading my mail? Frau Geplapper? Geschmiert? The postman?

Assuming they had good knowledge of English, the culprit would have read Rachel's epistle with ease; for she wrote in a good, clear hand, which was very unfortunate indeed, given what she had to say:

> You must have been wondering, dear, why I have taken so long to write; but I had to do a fair bit of research. After obtaining details of his death from your step-mother, I applied for his death certificate which disclosed your grandfather's birth name as Dobro, not Devereaux.
>
> Since he received a Catholic burial, I enquired in various churches of that denomination around Ballarat, as per your request. Unsuccessful, I then enquired of the other denominations; but my search left me no better informed.
>
> Not to be discouraged, I travelled further afield to Bendigo where again I searched in vain; that is, until it occurred to me to ask at the synagogue, which proved a most interesting excursion. The Rabbi was exceedingly helpful. We consulted the register and found your grandfather's birth recorded for June 18th, 1862. Since his name, David Zelman Dobro, and birth date concord with the details on his death certificate, I am certain he's the same person. He was circumcised on June 26th of the same year.

'Oh, help!' I bit my lip and continued:

Phoebe, do get to safety before it is too late. These days, my thoughts go back to the years before the War. How oblivious we were of the tinder box that was Old Europe; and yet, as your father and I discussed on many subsequent occasions, all the matches were there, waiting to be lit. Now, if the newspapers provide any indication, I can only conclude, again like your father, that war in Europe is but a matter of time. Please, dear, take care, and let me know that you are all right. I will not sleep soundly until I receive such assurance from you.

Much love,
Aunt Rachel.

P.S. Grandmother and Uncle Alec and family are well, although Grandmother's arthritis is troubling her more than ever. She will be eighty-six next month and sends her love.

'You have received bad news, Fräulein Raye?' Geschmiert's voice close behind made me jump. 'My heartfelt apologies! I did not mean to scare you. And my commiserations for your recent loss. But I have some New Year's cheer to lighten your sorrow. I received news of your friend Herr Fährmann at last! He is Tauglich!'

'Tauglich? What do you mean, Herr Hauptsturmführer?'

'Ah, I am sorry, Fräulein! It is... how do you say? Fit! In good health! He is architect, yes? Then I am pleased to tell you he has found employment. He is working on a building project in Mauthausen.'

'Mauthausen? Where is that?'

'You have not been to Mauthausen, Fräulein Raye? Why, it is my home town, and near the Führer's home town of Linz. It is very charming, with beautiful views of the Danube. My father is the shoemaker.'

'How might I contact him?'

'My father?'

'Emil— Herr Fährmann. I need to notify him when his immigration is approved.'

'Ah, Fräulein! You continue to help me keep things ship-shape.'

'If so, then you realise how urgent it is that I know how to contact him, Herr Hauptsturmführer.'

'Why you can write to him! Do not worry, Fräulein Raye, we all know each other in Mauthausen. Your letter will reach your friend the same as if he lived in the next street.'

'Mauthausen? Mauthausen?' Zita screamed when the following day I visited. 'You idiot! Don't you know what that is? Phoebe, it's a prison! Like Dachau! He'll never survive! We must get his papers! Have you not heard anything? Oh, my God! The baby!' she grabbed me hard. And when I looked at the floor I realised why.

Wilhelmina Adelheid Krain managed to wait until her mother had been rushed to hospital before making her debut on the world stage. A robust, fair-headed child, the medics declared she was a credit to her parents. Such praise, which was abundant, particularly when everyone remarked that little Wilma had her father's blue eyes, greatly allayed Zita's fears; while Rudi basked in his heroic role, attributing his wife's timely delivery to his virtuosic gear shifting and zappy engine.

Fatherhood suited him well. He doted on the child, and, come the baptism a week later, showed her off to his friends at a celebratory party. And as the wine flowed, he further entertained himself by teasing Hubie whose mood that day matched his mourning:

'I can never understand why old Huberle is always so sombre.'

'Let him be, my friend. He has good reason to grieve, as we all do,' Franz chimed in.

'But surely, Franzl, he would find comfort in new life? Look at her! Who's my precious little darling baba girl? Huberle has no concerns of which I am aware.'

'Then perhaps he is in love?' Franz winked at me.

'Don't be silly, Franz,' I felt myself flush; but whether it was from anger or desire, I could not tell. As far as Hubie was concerned, I could have melted into the snow after he kissed me at the Schönbrunn. When I showed him Aunt Rachel's letter, he curtly advised me to burn it, and did not so much as think to accompany his words with even the smallest gesture of comfort. Always, it seemed that the more I craved his affection, the more he withheld it. Now he remained silent, as he had been all afternoon.

'Then perhaps,' Rudi grew all the merrier, 'He is in debt to a Jew. Or a Jewess,' he gestured my way, 'Either whole or in part.'

'I would not— stoop so low,' Hubie coolly replied, and walked away without as much as a glance, leaving me to wilt from embarrassment.

Chuckling, Rudi uncorked a bottle of champagne. 'Anyway, next month we are travelling to New York where I have the opportunity to visit the Rockefeller Institute. Zita and Wilma are coming with me and will be staying with my mother in Boston. We are lucky, yes, Zita? What a woman! To have given birth to a child so strong and healthy despite being premature. Good genes, yes? To Zita,' he raised his glass.

Zita smiled, but was so pale that Frau Schütze wondered whether she had taken ill. 'It's been a long day,' she sighed. 'I think I need to lie down.'

Rudi followed, apologising for his wife and encouraging everyone to make themselves at home. Seeing that he did not return, Frau Schütze questioned whether everything was all right.

'I'll find out,' I offered.

I glimpsed Zita in the alcove, framed by Emil's round window.

'You might have told me you were planning for us to travel to America,' she complained, and I ducked out of sight.

'You knew I was going,' argued Rudi, 'The trip's been planned for months. Besides, you're my wife, aren't you? Why should you not accompany me? Furthermore, my mother and step-father are keen to see their granddaughter, and they cannot return to Vienna for obvious reasons. Considering all they have been through, it is only fair we should make the effort to visit. Or have you something to hide?'

'What makes you think I might?'

'Zita, you've played your little game long enough. That child was not born premature; and you are a straw bride.'

'Indeed, I am, for I am married to a man of straw.'

'I am no Ströh-mann.'

'And you talk of playing games? You know very well what I mean, Rudi. I have evidence enough to denounce you. Much good you'll do the Master Race. As your wife, I could hardly describe you as virile.'

'Ah, but what you do not know, my dear, is that when I was sixteen, I suffered a severe case of mumps. At the time, there was some concern regarding the effect it might have on certain functions. So, when you fell pregnant, I was indeed surprised. I then had tests performed which confirmed the doctors' prognosis: I am incapable of fathering a child.'

Rudi pulled out a cigarette and flicked his lighter. 'So, you admit you have been unfaithful?' he continued. 'And I suppose you assume your family has escaped Dachau entirely on their own merits? My dear, they owe me their freedom. Why else do you think Huberle has not been arrested? How did Franzl so fortuitously end up in military service? And your father? We all know his views. Not to mention your mother's royalist fantasies... Delve deep enough into her ancestry and she would join the emigration queues. Denounce me, and I will make certain you never see them again.'

'And if I denounce you?' I stepped from my hiding place.

'You?' Rudi laughingly flicked the ash from his cigarette. 'What could you possibly know?'

'Why, your little romance with "sehr lieber Franzl", of course,' Frantically, I pieced what scraps I could recall. 'What did you write? Ah, yes! "Our love is that of gods and heroes!" You and Franz had a lovely holiday in Burgenland, didn't you? I have your letters and there is no telling what I might do with them. For I, too, have connections, Rudi. My neighbour and friend, for instance, Hauptsturmführer Gottfried Geschmiert— Goodness! If the Gestapo caught wind of your amours, then who'd be in Dachau?'

'You wouldn't dare!'

'See that Emil Fährmann is released from Mauthausen within the week and I keep quiet; and that when his papers come through, he is to have safe passage to Britain. If anything happens to him, I will speak. Come, Rudi, you have influential friends. You were so helpful regarding my aunt. Surely you could do me another favour?'

'And what interest do you have in that Bolshie Jewish swine?'

'Rudi, don't tell me you thought I was honest with the Gestapo about my relationship with Emil?'

'What about Hubie?'

'Hubie?' I laughed, relieved to find an outlet for my hurt, and to quell my pounding heart. 'Hubie? Are you that mistaken? Why, we're merely cousins of sorts!'

'Cousins? I don't think he sees it that way. Does he know about your romance? Don't worry, Phoebe, your secrets are safe with me. I will do as you request. And you, I hope, will keep your word.'

'Tell me that what you just said is not true,' Zita whispered the moment Rudi left, her eyes flashing.

'Have you any reason to doubt me?'

'Plenty. Misha would never—'

'Then you have no need to worry.'

66

Most Loving Mere Folly

FOUR DAYS LATER, Emil arrived at dawn on the mail train. His gait, more exaggerated than ever, gave him away; and his eyes retained their steely gleam. But his head had been shaved and his clothes hung about him; while his grimy, moth-eaten vest offered little protection from the cold.

He leant heavily on my arm as we walked home; and we barely made the distance, so weakened was he from lack of food, and nearly crying with pain.

'Did you have a safe trip?' I asked, at a loss as to what to say.

'Bit of a schlep,[42]' he panted. 'Believe it or not, though, people have been very kind.'

'Well, at least I have some good news. Your papers arrived yesterday.'

But how was I to get him out of the country? His clothes were lice-ridden. The only food he could keep down was chicken broth. Chilled by the freezing journey, he developed a fever. Yet in two weeks he had to leave, otherwise he would face permanent incarceration or even death; and here he was, bedridden. I had to find a doctor, but whom could I trust?

Hubie would know. But no longer was he so easy to find. Whenever I called at the Schützes', he was not at home; nor did he venture to call upon me; and I never saw him in the street whereas our previous casual meetings had been frequent. In all his usual haunts – the Karlskirche, Café Museum, the Schönbrunn – he was nowhere to be found. Something had set our friendship rocking like a precious vase shaken on its pedestal.

Finally, I spotted him early one morning in the portal at Stephansdom, in the company of an older man. He glanced in my direction, and, with a polite bow, finished his conversation; whereupon he pointedly turned his back and walked away, shattering our friendship into a thousand pieces.

---

[42] *Schlep*: an annoyingly long and burdensome journey.

I followed him across Stephansplatz, holding tightly the sliver of acknowledgement he had dashed at my feet, and wondering to which part of the vessel it belonged. Hastily I pushed past the early morning pedestrians and followed him down Kärntner Strasse.

'Hubie! Stop!'

He stiffened, then resumed his passage. I increased my pace. He slowed enough to bid me a chill good morning.

'Who were you speaking with just then?' I gasped.

'Lieutenant Colonel von Lahousen. He served with my Uncle Alois and is acquainted with my family, if you must know. What do you want of me?' he added tersely.

'I need a doctor.'

'You are not well?'

'It's not for me, Hubie. It's Emil. He's ill.'

Hubie strode ahead so briskly I had to run.

'Emil's been released. I am finalising his passage to my friends in England. He's sick. He needs medical help.'

'I will do no such thing.'

'Hubie, please!'

'Given your allure and your evident resourcefulness, you are more than capable of finding a doctor yourself.'

'Please stop! I cannot keep up! What's the matter with you?'

'Why should you care about me? Am I not merely a cousin-of-sorts to you?' he sneered.

'What?'

'That is how you described me, yes?'

'What are you talking about?'

'Are you so fickle that you have no recollection? You laughed, and dismissed me as merely a cousin, as if I meant nothing whatsoever to you. And to Rudi! Of all people, to—'

'Rudi?'

'Do not feign innocence with me! I heard you say it! After the baptism, I heard—'

'You heard? Oh, Hubie! You don't understand!'

'Does merely a cousin-of-sorts take you into his confidence and cultivate a deep and loving friendship? Does merely a cousin-of-sorts hold you in his arms and waltz with you? Does he write you letter after letter while he is abroad? Does merely a cousin-of-sorts go to the ends of the earth to help you? Phoebe, I would lay down my life for you! I kissed you! Yet you— you dally with another man – and an ill-bred, lascivious ne'er do well at that!'

'That's not true, Hubie! I swear it's not true! You know me better than anyone! I would never do such a thing!'

'Don't think I have been blind to your affection for Emil Fährmann! I have seen you with him. And always, always, there is that look about you, as if you have already made love.'

'How dare you! Yes, I am fond of Emil. I won't deny it. But I would never, ever— and nor would he. How could you even think that of me? To be blatantly honest, I was protecting Zita. Rudi was threatening her. Emil is the father of her child.'

'That is impossible!'

'No, Hubie. It's the truth.'

He pored over my face as though hastily scanning a page of fine print for an obscure fact that might clinch an argument in his favour; but, adept scholar through he may have been, and however well-versed he was in the text before him, he could not find the detail he so desired.

'Mein Gott! And you knew this? How long have you known?'

'Since I met Zita.'

'All that time? You aided and abetted their affair?'

'I did nothing of the sort! It was entirely their doing. Emil loves your sister, and she loves him.'

'Pfui! Love! You are one to talk of love! For you it seems that love is merely physical attraction. Do you care nothing for the intimacy of the mind and heart?'

'I do care, and you know it! And as far as your sister and "that man" are concerned, I *am* talking as much of the intimacy of mind and heart as the body! You're the one at fault.'

'How can I be? She has abused a sacrament and a law! And *you* are culpable. You knew and kept silent!'

'And *you* are complicit! Through your disapproval, you deprived your sister of happiness by pushing her into a so-called suitable marriage, and to conduct an affair on the side because that was all she felt was left for her to do.'

'You are wrong! I have always considered Rudi a most unsuitable choice of husband; and Zita's decision regarding an affair is entirely her own devising. Furthermore, I had every reason and duty to disapprove of Emil Fährmann. Does Rudi know?'

'You must not tell Rudi!'

'This is outrageous!'

'Hubie, please! Had my parents been given permission to marry, there would have been no need for them to commit fornication, and perhaps their lives would have worked out differently, for the better.'

'Your parents eventually married. And they were free to marry.'

'Do you not think that Zita and Emil wanted the same? He wanted to do the right thing by her, but your father – and you, in particular – turned him away.'

'He is an amoral communist. Of course, I turned him away! I will not have a man like that marry my sister!'

'He's not an amoral communist any more, Hubie. And just because everyone is not like you, it doesn't mean they are not good. For all his faults and whatever his opinions, Emil is a kind and loving man who is as free to love as you or me. Furthermore, he deserves neither imprisonment nor death, which is what he faces if the affair is exposed. Surely, you can understand that. For his own safety, he must leave the country, but he is too sick to travel. He needs a doctor. He also needs to see Zita. Who knows how long he will be gone, or if he will ever return?'

The next morning, a doctor arrived. During his visit, he passed me a note on Hubie's behalf informing me that my cousin-of-sorts himself, along with Zita and Franz, 'would be pleased to accept my invitation for cards the following afternoon'.

Sure enough, they arrived promptly at two o'clock; but Hubie had business other than cards in mind.

'Where is he?' he enquired. Hubie entered Emil's room alone, insisting on the utmost privacy. Some considerable time passed before he bid Zita come inside, which she did, carrying little Wilhelmena in her arms.

'Is this our bubeleh?'[43] Emil asked, still weak and confined to bed. 'Let's have a look. She's beautiful, isn't she? Ah, Velvela, you're a pretty little lady, just like your mama,' he crooned.

'We should let them alone,' Hubie whispered, wiping his eyes. 'Come Franzl, Phoebe, we have some important business. But before we begin, I am sorry to tell you that Herr Steffan has died. He was imprisoned with Herr Fährmann. They were working in a quarry. The work proved too arduous for Herr Fährmann. Steffan came to his aid and was shot for doing so. And now, we must prepare the annulment of Zita's marriage. Phoebe, you will need to swear an affidavit testifying to your knowledge of Zita's liaison.'

'Will it be enough to dissolve the union?' I asked.

'In an ecclesial court, yes, especially since we can prove that the child was conceived outside wedlock; and if Herr Fährmann acknowledges paternity, which he is prepared to do.'

'But we cannot file for civil divorce,' continued Franz. 'Under National Socialist law, the fact that Herr Fährmann is a Jew makes their affair a criminal act.'

'You were right, Phoebe,' Hubie remarked, 'Emil could be hanged, and Zita imprisoned. As for the child, I hate to think.'

'And then there's Rudi to consider—'

'What do you know, Phoebe?' Franzl asked warily.

'Never you mind, Franzl.'

'Phoebe, I advise you not to withhold any information that could help us in our case,' Hubie urged.

And at his further insistence I fetched the packet Zita had given me the previous summer.

'How did you end up with these?' Red-faced, Franz mopped his

---

[43] *Bubeleh*: (dim.) term of endearment, darling; dear child.

brow while Hubie scanned the correspondence.

'Ask Zita.'

'And you also were aware of this grave impediment to your sister's marriage, Franz?'

'Rudi and I, we both decided— I encouraged him to court Zita. I thought it would help him. I didn't expect Zita to receive his attentions. She didn't have to.'

'What possessed her?' Hubie murmured. 'Why—?'

'Hubie, all my life I've had to play second fiddle to you and Karl and Franzl, and lead a sensible, dutiful existence,' Zita interrupted, bottle in hand. 'But I tell you, I have just as much right to make my own decisions, which include whom I love and how I will go about it.'

'Is that what you think, Zita? That I have a right to lead my own life?' Hubie blurted. 'How mistaken you are! And you think it acceptable to— I cannot even call it marriage, and at the same time conduct an affair?'

'Don't you understand? I want to be loved for my own sake – not for the children I can bear, not out of religious obligation, not for the sake of propriety – I want to be loved for me!'

'Part of who you are is how you are in relation to others. It is not merely about *you*, just as it is not merely about obligation. The two go hand in glove. Certainly, you must be loved for your own sake. But for your own sake you must consider others and your obligations to them.'

'Pfui, Huberle! You and your obligations!' Zita stomped off to the kitchen.

'What are you going to do, Hubie?' Franzl queried.

'You have ended this— this sodomy?'

'Yes.'

'You have confessed your sin?'

'Immediately.'

'And you have not succumbed to further temptation in that regard?'

'I— I— endeavoured to curb it through courtship. I hoped I might— But Inge did not really care for me, nor I her. And then—' he glanced at me and blushed. 'So, I made a vow of celibacy. It is a temporary vow, and a private one, and it is better that way. What are you going to do? They could kill me if they find out. And Rudi.'

'You have done right, Franzl.'

'You are not angry, my brother?'

'I am shocked, I admit. But I admire your humility. Given your earnest desire for amendment, I will do everything in my power to support and protect you.'

'What about the letters?'

Hubie handed them to him.

'Keep them, Hubie,' Franz passed them back. They are

important evidence. You are also a lawyer, and can determine how they are to be used, if they are to be used at all. But please look after Rudi. He is my dearest friend. If you consider what he has suffered with his own father, it is little wonder he craves affection. He needs help, Hubie.'

'Always you have an excuse for him! If he needs help, as you say, which is true, then sometimes help lies in the acknowledgement of the wrong committed, and in accepting the consequences, however painful. He must be exposed!'

'They'll put him in prison. Or worse! Is that what you want? Rudi in Dachau?'

'I would not wish Dachau upon anyone.'

'Then leave it alone, Huberle! Please.'

'The annulment is more important,' Hubie tucked the letters into the inner pocket of his jacket. 'We already have sufficient grounds for a case without recourse to such correspondence. Herr Fährmann has promised that, once the legalities are concluded, he will marry Zita, and that he will raise Wilma, and any other children they might have, as Catholics. Phoebe, I believe I owe you an apology. Both Zita and Herr Fährmann tell me that you spoke your mind to each of them in the hope that Zita would circumvent the marriage of her own accord. While you had the duty to make your knowledge public, perhaps you were not fully aware of your obligations. It was an error of youth and innocence, born neither of malice nor of a delight in scandal, and I do not hold it against you. Please, let us be friends again.'

'Always friends, Hubie. Always.'

Finally, having organised Emil's papers, I waited with him outside the Centre for Jewish Emigration. Being a former concentration camp inmate, he was lucky to join a special queue for such persons, whose papers were processed with extraordinary speed, fully respecting the fortnight's notice which bound the applicants. As Geschmiert explained, 'We can't have them in the country longer than we need.' Finally, I saw him onto the Calais train late one night, still in pain, leaning on a crutch, and dressed in new clothes which included a sweater knitted especially by Zita.

'Give my regards to Lucy and Wally, won't you. And a special kiss for the little twins. And I packed your house plans, so you don't forget to dream.'

'I'll write,' he patted the fountain pen in his jacket pocket, the pen I had given him for Christmas more than a year ago, and which I had kept safe since retrieving it the day the Schutzstaffel closed his shop. 'And you, Tshatshkele:[44] Abi gezunt dos leben ken

---

[44] *Tshatshkele*: (lit.) a trinket; (fig.) a young girl who uses her charms to reach her goals; a favourite child; a desirable young woman.

men zikh ale mol nemen. In Englisch, how to say? No help. I have it! Stay healthy,' he nudged me and winked, 'You can always kill yourself later.'

67

Courtship

A YEAR HAD PASSED since the Anschluss. Spring sunshine melted the snow, and the frozen, silent Danube broke into a giddy ice floe waltz. Cherry blossoms blushed amidst the swastikas, as if Vienna herself was both embarrassed and flattered by her Nazi paramour; and yet, by her show of soft blooms, determined to preserve her innocence. Perhaps she also blushed in commiseration as she watched vulnerable Czechoslovakia, her former border defences in German hands, her British and French guardians unwilling to act in her interest, ravished by the Reich. Now Germany was eyeing Danzig.

I, too, felt a rush of colour when a telegram arrived from Kerem. The afternoon his train was due, I wrapped his yazma about me and hurried to the Westbahnhof. Joyously, we embraced and walked arm in arm down the concourse to a nearby café.

'Did you not see the sign, Fräulein?' asked the waiter. 'We do not serve Jews.'

It mattered little that I protested, asserting my foreign nationality, brandishing my passport, resorting to English to underscore my point, and demanding to speak to the manager. A list, published courtesy of the Gestapo, featured my name under 'Mischlinge, first degree'.

'You have two Jewish grandparents, Fräulein,' the manager declared.

'Has this happened much, Phoebe?' Kerem whispered as he escorted me out.

'I suppose it was only a matter of time,' I sighed. 'People look at me strangely now and are not as friendly as they used to be. What upsets me is how they came by the information.'

'I have rooms booked at the Grand. Let us take a cab directly. Is there another café you would recommend?'

'The Sacher, I suppose. The Gestapo tend not to patronise it, and you can sample some of Vienna's famous torte.'

'Would you believe there's been a court case over this cake?' I dangled my fork over the chocolate culprit. 'Honestly, Kerem, amidst all the persecution and destruction, Demel's and Sacher's squabble over the rights to the Sachertorte. The Sacher calls this the *Original Sachertorte*. Tomorrow, we'll visit Demel's and you can sample the *Eduard-Sacher-Torte* and work out the difference for yourself. Try some.' I cut him a morsel.

'And I will look forward to tomorrow's pleasure,' Kerem smiled. 'This is very good, too,' he indicated his Nusstorte, 'Allow me.'

And as he offered me a forkful, a dark figure, far taller than the waitress who had served us, overshadowed our table.

'Grüß Gott, Phoebe,' Hubie bowed.

Bowing, Kerem made his acquaintance. Hubie declined my invitation to sit. He was due to resume rehearsals at the Opera.

'I hope you will enjoy a concert during your stay, Herr Solak,' he gushed.

'I have tickets for Saturday afternoon's Philharmoniker performance,' Kerem smiled.

'Ah, I believe the programme offers much romantic interest,' chill caution undercut Hubie's intellectual affability. 'Being a hornist, I prefer Strauss' *Heldleben*; however, Tchaikovsky's Overture to *Romeo and Juliet* might be more to Phoebe's taste,' he raised a questioning brow at me. 'Opening the concert is Siegfried Wagner's *Der Bärenhäuter* in which true love triumphs at the expense of two souls lost to the devil. Speaking of which, I will find myself in the latter situation if I am late. Knappertsbusch is conducting.'

'It's *Fidelio*, isn't it?' I asked.

'Yes. And a great personal favourite. I bid you good afternoon.'

He tipped the doorman who had assisted him with his coat; wrapped his scarf, took his hat, and loped across the cobbles to the Opernhaus.

'He seems a very fine man, Phoebe,' Kerem remarked.

'I forgot he takes coffee at the Sacher when he's rostered with the Opera,' I murmured. Then I felt Kerem's hand on mine; and when I had the courage to look him in the face, I beheld a most kindly expression.

'You will come with me to the concert, won't you?' he broke our silence. 'Furthermore, I have no business engagements. Not even diamonds could buy visas. My time is at your disposal. Pray tell me, the worries you confided to me when last I visited— concerning your aunt. Have you managed to resolve them?'

'I've had little opportunity, Kerem. I've been thinking to go to Paris. My aunt used to live there. If she's had any trouble with the Nazis, she could well have returned. But how can I leave Vienna while my friends remain in danger?'

'What is the matter?'

'You see, Kerem, emigration is all very well for those who can afford it— And even then, it's difficult, as you know. But there is little hope for the poor. I have arranged for property to be sold to help some friends. Once their papers are sorted, I can leave. It's taking ages! Nobody wants to buy real estate! Meanwhile, you should see how they are living.'

'Will you show me?'

'Now? Are you serious?'

'My time, Phoebe, is yours.'

Emigration had a ripple effect in Leopoldstadt. Persons able to leave the country vacated premises which tended to be better appointed, and their empty apartments were quickly filled at reduced rates by those who remained, whose dwellings in turn were occupied by persons less well off, and so on down the ranks. One such opportunity had arisen for the Epsteins who moved from their attic into two rooms on the floor below. They were still without running water and sanitation, but at least they had space. Bela had not heard from her husband in months. Pauline, whose baby was due in July, worked for a pittance in a laundry. David, who had spent the winter hauling coal and shovelling snow, now fired the ovens in a 'German' bakery.

'We even have a piano,' wheezed old Mr Epstein who sat huddled in a battered armchair, a shawl over his shoulders.

Nestled on his lap, little Rosa, pale and thin, smiled wanly when I fingered a melody on the ivory-less keys, the hammers of which poorly struck the strings of a dusty upright bereft of its candelabrae.

'I'm afraid it's not a patch on your Bösendorfer, Phoebe,' sighed David, who had cracked a lens of his spectacles, 'But, we can't have everything, can we?'

'Please thank your friend for the cake,' said Pauline. It had been Kerem's idea to bring the family some Sachertorte in addition to the food and flowers we had purchased en route.

Seated on a rickety stool, Kerem quietly noted the grey flannel blanket that curtained the single window, the faded prints of old Vienna hanging on the grimy walls, and the yellowed sheets on the bed. He smiled at the daffodils I had placed in a chipped vase.

'Phoebe,' he whispered, 'could you please tell your friends that I will provide them asylum in Istanbul.'

'Do you mean it?'

'I insist.'

The Epsteins listened, stunned, as I informed them.

'I will not leave until I hear from Mani,' warned Bela.

'But what if you never hear from him?' urged Pauline. 'What if—?'

'Then, if I go anywhere, I will go to Jockel and Mitzi in England.'

'Tell your friend, thank you, but I will stay with my daughter,' concluded old Mr Epstein.

'Pauline and I will go after the baby is born,' David resolved.

Rapidly, I translated Kerem's response:

'Herr Solak says he will finance your passage. You will be his guests in Istanbul. From there, you can safely arrange your move to Australia. And if, for whatever reason, your plans fail, you have his unconditional protection.'

'Together, Phoebe, we will help your friends,' Kerem escorted me down the stairs. 'If I ensure their safety, you will be free to travel to Paris if needs be and circumstances permit. And should you require further assistance, you must tell me. I do this for you, my love. For you alone.'

Chess being one of the few pastimes which the grieving Hubie found even remotely pleasurable, I challenged him to a game at Café Central one evening after Kerem departed. Although we were well matched, Hubie's apparent blunders invariably overturned my plans. This time, however, his errors were without craft, being manifestations of his gloomy and distracted temper; and his preoccupations resulted in the loss of his queen. I hesitated to take her, but for once I had the advantage. Even so, I kept my fingers on my knight in case his bishop or rook lurked on some remote square. I was lucky. My knight was safe, and my move provoked him to reveal what was undoubtedly uppermost in his thoughts.

'You have never mentioned Herr Solak before,' he remarked tersely as his unfortunate queen joined captured pawns.

'I had no need to.'

'Have you known him long?'

'We met in Alexandria while I was on my way here, and we travelled to Istanbul together. Since we did not correspond for many months, I wrongly assumed his acquaintance to be merely a flirtation. As it turned out, he was stranded in Hong Kong after the typhoon. He renewed contact early last year and has twice visited. He has been helping Jews to leave.'

'Helping Jews? Helping Jews is but a partial solution to our grave problems. He seems very fond of you. And you seem extremely fond of him. I assume you enjoyed your concert? Check,' Hubie played his rook.

'I am fond of him; and yes, I did enjoy the concert,' I moved a pawn in defence.

'How old is he?' Hubie captured my pawn and foolishly checked me again.

'About forty,' I moved my king to safety.

'He was in the War, yes?' Hubie brought his rook close, which predictable move again threatened my king; just as his question, and the quiet but hostile tone of its utterance, contrived an explanation for Kerem's missing hand.

'His injury prevented him from fighting.' I swept my queen

across the board and seized the offending rook.

'And he is a Turk?' Hubie advanced a pawn in what I suspected was a slow-paced journey to reclaim his queen.

'Yes. Check.'

Did he anticipate the threat from my queen? He pondered whether to sacrifice his bishop or move his king. Several minutes lapsed before he dragged the bishop into play. Hubie would have fared better playing his king. Judging from his next pointed and solemn question, however, the bishop had an inquisitorial role which laid bare an ancient enmity.

'And I assume he is of the Islamic faith?'

'Nominally, yes; although he is favourably disposed to Christianity. And I wouldn't take my queen if I were you,' I nodded at my own bishop as I took Hubie's.

'And you are receiving his attentions?' Hubie moved his king.

'Yes.' I manoeuvred my bishop.

'Would you seriously consider marrying such a man?' Hubie again advanced his pawn.

'I love him. Check.'

'Have you no sense of obligation?' he threatened my bishop with his knight. 'And, I suppose, were you certain of your aunt's death you would accept him outright?'

'If he proposed. He is warm-hearted, sincere, thoughtful, and wise to the ways of the world. He has his faults; but he wishes only to do right. Whatever his concerns, he has never treated me with the aloofness that mostly has been my lot from you ever since the Anschluss.'

Hubie tipped his king.

'Hubie! You could have conceded me a victory for once!'

'I no longer wish to play.'

68

Visitors

HUBIE TOOK A PLANE to Rome. A curt note posted from the Vienna aerodrome informed me of his sudden decision to join his parents who, with Sisi, were making an Easter pilgrimage. He hoped the journey would be a means of consolation and spiritual renewal that would shower grace upon the entire family, all of whom deeply mourned Heidi.

'And he left you alone?' asked Professor Rosé when next I visited. His Döbling apartment having been 'Aryanised', he was now living with friends.

'Rudi and Zita will be home in a couple of days,' I replied. None of the Schützes remained in Vienna. Franz had commenced military service, while Karl-Alois and his family had been transferred to Pilsen where Karl was supervising military vehicle production. 'Have you heard from Alma?'

'She and Heini arrived in London the day before the Germans invaded Czechoslovakia. Had they delayed, Almschi's passport would have been useless. And Almschi's train was late. She had to fly from Hamburg to make the boat to England. The violins are safe, too, thank God. I will be departing soon, Fräulein. Since I do not know whether we will meet again, I would like to give you these.'

He handed me two gramophone recordings. One I already knew, for it was the recording he had played me during one of my first visits. The other was Elgar's *Salut d'Amour*.

'I found it while we were packing,' he nodded at the Elgar, 'And yes, it is your father playing. I believe your mother is accompanying him.'

❖ ❖ ❖

Strange to say, I had no gramophone to play the precious recording. So, on my way home, I purchased one and eagerly awaited its delivery the following afternoon.

Gingerly, I placed the record on the machine and lowered the needle. Amidst hissing and bumps sounded the gentle pulse of piano. Maman! And Dad's silky-smooth violin! Perhaps he used too much portamento; but his was a lush and loving interpretation. And Maman, so unassuming and attuned, how tenderly she responded to his phrases!

'Beautiful!' I gazed at the Portrait.

Still entranced, I answered the knock at my door.

'Rudi! Back so soon! Come in! How are your parents? How is Zita?'

'My mother is well, thank you. Zita and little Wilma are still in America.'

'Is everything all right?'

'We decided it would be in Zita's best interests if she and her child remained. This is not a social call,' he removed his driving gloves, but declined my offer of coffee. 'I am filing for divorce, Phoebe. And don't feign innocence. I know that you and Zita have enjoyed a lengthy conspiracy regarding her Jew-lover. Since Zita has violated the race laws, I gave her a choice: return to Vienna and face arrest; or remain safe and sound in Boston. Her in-laws are prepared to put her up. One would think my mother cared more for that slut and her bastard than her own son. And my step-father? Well, it didn't take much research to expose his ancestry.

'Now, as you know, I honoured my side of our little bargain and had the Bolshevik Jew Fährmann released from Mauthausen. Where are the letters?'

'I don't have them. I got rid of them. After all, you wouldn't want such letters to see the light of day.'

'Why am I not convinced?'

'It's the truth, Rudi! I assure you, the letters are not here.'

'We shall see about that.'

From a chain in his trench coat pocket, Rudi flashed a disc labelled 'Geheime Staatspolizei'. He opened the front door and in came the Untersturmführer I knew from the Metropole.

'First a Jew, and then a Turk. Who will be next, Fräulein Raye?' he smiled, winking at Rudi who nodded an instruction.

Brownshirts teemed into my apartment: the 'Alpine Club' in uniform. They stripped the beds and turned the mattresses; emptied chests and ransacked shelves, drawers, and cabinets. Books, music, violin strings, rosin, clothes, trinkets, photographs, and linen they dumped on the floor. 'Open the bureau!' the Untersturmführer ordered; and they searched its letters and notebooks.

'You lied to me, didn't you, Rudi?'

'That took you a while,' he smirked. 'I quite enjoyed composing that letter regarding your aunt. And yes, I made sure you were dead-drunk before I left you in front of the Opernhaus. You hold your liquor better than you used to. Sad to say, I didn't have quite the same success when you called in on your way home from Salzburg. Pity your aunt had to have a painting in that damn exhibition.'

'Why did you lie?'

'To win your trust, of course. What better way to keep tabs on our noble Huberle? But it seems darling Hubie plays his cards very close to his chest. Either that, or he's besotted with "your dark loveliness and your passion".'

'You've read my mail!'

'Herr Obersturmführer!' A brownshirt handed Rudi a package tied with a red velvet ribbon.

Rudi undid the ribbon, unfolded a letter, sneered, and tossed the package to the floor. The Untersturmführer reported the job complete and summoned his men. Rudi whispered one last command.

'What are you doing?' I cried. 'Leave it alone! That's my father! You can't take him!'

'It is a work of degenerate art,' Rudi replied as the brownshirt unhooked Dad's portrait.

'Rudi, please!'

'Consider it an eye for an eye. You "got rid" of my letters, so I will get rid of your painting. You little fool! To presume I might harm the Schützes, the family that is more a family to me than my own! And while I fulfilled my side of our bargain and did not harm your communist friend, I promised nothing about harming you, you little mongrel bitch. I would get out if I were you, Fräulein Phoebe.'

69

REGARD

DAD'S RECORD quietly circled on the gramophone. My hands shaking, I tried to reset the needle without harming the disc; and while the music played, I swept the smashed china, wrapped it in newspaper and placed it in the dustbin. The books I returned to their shelves, the music to its cabinet. I folded the clothes and remade the beds, piled the notebooks, and gathered and filed the correspondence, all the while avoiding the faded rectangle on my wall. Finally, back in the lounge room, I picked up the red velvet ribbon and one of the letters Rudi had tossed on the floor

'Maman!' I knew that loopy, upright French schoolgirl hand. Sure enough, the letter 'à mon très cher Roderick', was from 'ton petit bijou, Juliette.'

There were several dozen in all, mostly written from Paris before the War. They appeared to be more concerned with Ailine than Maman herself, for 'Lina' featured in many a line. Some letters had been sent from Chartres. The last, dated 1912, bore our Stanmore address.

Where were Dad's replies? I hunted through his bureau. Unfortunately, his habit of making copies of his correspondence dated from a later period; for I could find no copybooks. Maman's letters, however, mentioned numerous meetings.

Just as Frau Schütze said! Dashing off to Paris at every opportunity!

Did Dad keep a diary perchance? The only diaries Dad ever kept were the volumes he devoted to his music practice. There were, however, appointment books in which he jotted his daily doings with intelligent precision; but, unlike his meticulous and copious practice notes, the abbreviations he used regarding his daily doings rendered his documentation meaningless; at least at first sight.

I spread the letters across the table and, having located Dad's appointment books for 1911 and 1912, compiled a chronology. On a separate page, I made a list of Dad's abbreviations and tried to identify possible cross-references in Maman's correspondence. Over and again I examined the letters for facts concerning time, place, and circumstance, and made copious notes and observations. From the details communicated, it seemed that Maman confided exclusively in Dad. If only I had his replies! Perhaps Maman took his letters with her to Stanmore. So, I wrote to Scylla and asked her to search at home.

My excursion to post the letter was the first extended trip I had made in days.

But, upon my return, as I rounded the staircase's final spiral, I caught sight of a pair of jackboots and fled at once.

'Phoebe!'

Dressed in trachten, Hubie leant over the bannister.

'You must pack immediately!' he ran towards me. 'I have a cab waiting downstairs and there is a train leaving for Paris in an hour.'

'What do you mean?'

'I have your ticket and have booked rooms for you at Hotel Lutetia. Do not ask me how! It is imperative that you leave! The Gestapo—!'

'Hubie, I cannot go to Paris at the drop of a hat! What about the Epsteins?'

'Mutti is fully informed of their predicament and will look after them. Write her when you have settled. Should you wish to enquire after me, refer to me as Cousin Frank.'

'What—?'

'The less you know the better. We must hasten!'

I gathered my notes and grabbed Dad's diaries, packed all I could into a case and picked up my violin.

'But what about my apartment, Hubie?'

'Trust me, Phoebe. I will ensure that it is kept safe.'

In silence we drove to the Westbahnhof where a final call sounded for the Orient Express.

'When will I ever see you again?' I asked.

'I cannot say. But know that wherever you go, whatever happens, you are much loved here in Vienna. Last year, while I was in France, I bought you this ring. Please accept it as a token of my most fervent regard. The stones, in fact, form an acronym for that word. At least in French, they do. In German, it would be "Wertschätzung", which would be a little too complicated for such a tiny setting, yes?'

'Ruby, Emerald, Garnet, Amethyst, Ruby, Diamond,' I admired the setting and tried to restrain my tears. 'It's beautiful, Hubie. I wish I had something to give you in return.'

'You have given all you can. And now it is time to part. Auf Wiedersehen, liebe Phoebe!' he whispered, embracing me long. 'May God protect you!' And, upon helping me into the train, he handed me a letter. 'Please do me the favour of reading this. It will explain all that can be explained.'

A cloud of steam; a hand raised in farewell; Hubie's stately, solemn figure shrinking from sight; a suitcase and a violin my only possessions. Vienna, for me, was gone.

'Pardon me, ma'am, but if you want my advice, leave the Krauts to their own devices,' drawled a multi-chinned, tobacco stained American with whom, it appeared, I was to share my journey. 'Tell you what, I'm lucky to get a transfer. Guess I'll have to improve my Française. Skenazy's the name: Sam Skenazy. International News Service. Reckon you can't get more Jewish than Skenazy. Pair it with Samuel and I'm barred from every café and hotel in Wien. You look as if you've quite a story.'

'Which I am not going to tell you. Now if you'll excuse me, I have a letter requiring my utmost attention.'

Hietzing,
21ˢᵗ April, 1939

Dearest Phoebe,

With what words shall I express the comfort and consolation you have been to me these past months? Your understanding and patience in the face of my deepest melancholy have been heaven-sent; your beauty a haven of repose. In your tender company, I buried my sorrow; your gentle encouragement filled me with hope and purpose. For your generosity and courage in the face of tribulation, I have only the most profound admiration; and for you, my sincerest affection.

Yet I must let you go. Believe me when I tell you how much I have pondered what I should do; how this, my final decision, has arisen from months of prayer, of reflection, and of sleepless nights. Since the moment I first met you I have been captivated by your mysterious beauty and fine intelligence, your passion and your integrity; and my feelings have only increased with knowledge. Long have I desired to honour and treasure you, to have and to hold you; in short, to love you as my wife; but I cannot. Phoebe, I cannot marry you.

Do not suppose for a moment that my conclusion stems from the current regulations. Were that the case, I would have left the country long ago with you at my side. At the time of the Anschluss, I considered inviting you to France and marrying you abroad. Nor I did rule out the possibility of emigrating with you to England or Australia. To indulge my private desires, however, would be to betray my duty to my people at a time when my service is most urgently required.

Perhaps it was providential that I refrained from making my intentions known, for subsequent happenings caused me to question not only my situation but also your readiness and suitability. I refer particularly to the issue of my sister's marriage. Your reticence about her affair, which matter constituted a valid impediment to an essentially inappropriate union, exposed in you a lack of authentic respect for, and understanding of, the seriousness inherent to the taking of vows.

In your defence, your empathy for, and criticism of my sister's situation is justified; and to your credit you privately voiced your concern to the offending parties. With you, I concord that my sister is ultimately responsible for her actions; and as I explained on an earlier occasion, I attribute your complicity more to naivety than a desire to do wrong or to see wrong committed. In that, there is much to learn for us all. So, do not think I love you any less for your mistake – we all make mistakes; and I, too, am guilty regarding failure to act. Nor would I ever shun you on such an account.

The incident, however, did make me reconsider your suitability as my prospective wife. While feelings are important, the decision to marry must be grounded more on morality than emotion. Given your preparedness to favour feeling over duty in the choice of a spouse, I had no guarantee that you were ready for the responsibilities of such a commitment, particularly when your friendship with my sister's lover also drew my attention to the possibility that your feelings towards me might not be of the same degree as my feelings towards you. And however wrongly I construed the nature of that friendship, it alerted me to that possibility, which was later confirmed upon meeting your Turkish lover. While I believe your affection for me is genuine, your evident fondness for, and intimacy with the latter individual led me to conclude, with the deepest sorrow, that you do not love me.

Even if you were to convince me of the depth of your affection, the liberty of my fully returning it has been greatly constrained by the difficulties of the past year. Indeed, the circumstances in which we find ourselves must now dictate our course. Romance of any description has no place in this present crisis. It is imperative that you get to safety. As for me, I must make my own way. There is an old hunting expression: 'Who does not shoot also misses'. Whatever action I take, I doubt I will survive.

I hope that during your time in Paris you will find out more about your aunt. That situation you must resolve one way or another for the sake of your conscience. I know you will not find the peace you crave until you do. My most fervent prayer *is that you find a rightful solution. Once again, while I love you dearly and feel for your plight, I could not marry you while you are harbouring a grudge.*

Then go back to Australia, Phoebe. Get to safety. Should you meet and choose to marry someone in the meantime, you have my heartfelt blessing (May he be a kind and virtuous man, a good Catholic who loves you deeply!), and I wish you peace and joy and every blessing in this life and the next. I only ask that you remember me in your prayers. Be assured that I will always think of you with the greatest fondness and will ever cherish our moments together.

I remain your cousin-of-sorts,
Hubie.

P.S. I request that you make no copy of this letter, that you conceal it, that you make no mention of it neither in conversation nor in writing, and that you burn it at the first possible opportunity.

'All out of love, huh?' grinned Skenazy. 'A little lady like you shouldn't have that kinda trouble.'

Here ends
BY VIOLENCE UNAVENGED
First volume of
IN THE HEARTS OF KINGS.

Outside Heaven's Sway

Second volume of
In the Hearts of Kings

*If our choice determines our end ...
What determines our choice?*

Phoebe searches for Ailine in Paris despite the onset of war. When France falls, Phoebe must choose between her vendetta, Nazi occupation, and her love for Kerem Solak. And when Hubert Schütze reappears, her life takes another dramatic turn.

*Jazz ... Deception ... Sabotage
... Betrayal ...*

Glossary of

German Words and Phrases

Ch. 1   *Meine Prinzessin*: my princess

Ch. 12   *Schwammi*: little mushroom

           Maler: painter

Ch. 18   *Phoebe, mit wem sprichst du?*: Phoebe, to whom are you speaking?

           Er ist nur der Postbote, Vati: It's only the postman, Dad.

           Grüß Gott: (lit.) God's greeting (traditional Austrian greeting)

           Du hast für... Phoebe?: Have you signed for it, Phoebe?

           Ah, gut!... in letzter Sekunde!: Ah, good! The Austrian consul at the eleventh hour!

           Danke schön, mein guter Herr: Thank you, my good man

Ch. 20   *Prosit!*: Cheers!

           meine kleine Prinzessin: my little princess

Ch. 23   *Herr Bundeskanzler*: Chancellor

           Mein Beileid: my condolences

           Schreibpapier: writing paper

Ch. 24   *Auf Wiedersehen*: Good-bye

           k.u.k.: Kaiserliche und Königliche, meaning Imperial and Royal

           Hofmusiker: court musician

           Geiger: violinist

           Herzlich Willkommen: a hearty welcome

Ch. 25   *Trauerkleidung*: mourning clothes

           Der Prälat ohne Milde: the prelate without mercy

Ch. 26   *Groschen*: penny

           Judenschwein: Jew-pig (extremely derogatory)

           Mittag: lunch

Ch. 27   *Lebensraum*: living space

           gnädiges Fräulein: dear lady

Ch. 28   *Mutti*: mummy

           Mein Beethoven: my Beethoven

           Herr Hofrat: an official honorary title for persons in the highest echelons of federal, state, or academic service.

           Es ist ein Mädchen: It's a girl

           Ich bin ein Vater: I'm a father

           Lederhosen: short leather trousers worn as part of men's alpine costumes

CH. 29   *Abscheidslied*: song of farewell

          Verzeihen Sie mir... verursacht: Pardon me, dear lady, I hope my dog has not caused you trouble

CH. 30   *Hast du... gelassen*: did you leave the window open

          Danke: thank you

          Bitte: please

CH. 31   *Taten sagen mehr als Worte*: Actions speak louder than words

          bitte nennen Sie mich: please address me as

          Bitte seien Sie: please be

          Oberstabsarzt: staff surgeon in the Austro-Hungarian army with the rank of colonel.

          Zusammenschluss: sweet union

          Schwätzer: windbag, talker of nonsense

CH. 34   *Beisl*: public house

          Handküss: a traditional respectful bow, performed out of service and humility, in which the gentleman takes the lady's offered hand but does not kiss it (unless he wishes to declare his love).

CH. 35   *Zigeunermusik*: gypsy music

          Skandal: intrigue, affair

CH. 36   *So eine schöne Leiche!*: Such a beautiful corpse!

CH. 37   *Meister*: master

          Servus: hello

          mein kleine Sängerknabe: my little choirboy

          Glücklich! Glücklich! Dich hab ich gefunden: Happy! How happy I have found thee (from Schiller, 'On Friendship')

          Andenken: memento

CH. 38   *Das Kleine Känguru*: the little kangaroo

          Was uns Rose heißt, Wie es auch heiße, würde lieblich duften: A rose by any other name would smell as sweet (Shakespeare, *Romeo and Juliet*, I, ii, 43-44, transl. Goethe)

          Kinder, Küche, Kirche: children, kitchen, church

CH. 40   *Fiaker*: a double espresso, mixed with kirsch and sugar, topped with whipped cream and served in a glass. Named after the coachmen, or *fiakern*, renowned for drinking it while driving their horse and carriage.

CH. 41   *Ein wahrer Jägersmann*: a true hunter

          Hier sind wir!: We're here!

          Sollen wir gehen... truer Hund: Shall we hunt the deer, my good dog

          Wie schön sie ist: How beautiful she is

CH. 42   *Er schaut ins Narrenkastl wie üblich*: he's staring into space (lit. looking into the fool's box)

CH. 43   *Kriminalkommissar*: detective superintendent

          Trottel: fool

          Kirsch: cherry brandy

Frohe Weihnachten: Merry Christmas

CH. 48 *Gott mit dir*: God be with you

Freiheit: Freedom (traditional Communist greeting)

CH. 49 *Ein Volk! Ein Reich!*: One people! One realm!

Gott schütze Österreich: God protect Austria

Sieg Heil!: Hail victory!

Mein Krampf: my convulsion (a pun on Hitler's *Mein Kampf*, My Struggle)

Zur Hölle: To Hell!

Lieber Führer sei so nett, zeige dich am Fensterbrett!: Dearest leader if you will, do please come to the windowsill!

Reichsstatthalter: Reich Governor charged with implementing Hitler's policies.

CH. 50 *Jud*: Jew

Hüpfen!: Hop!

Großdeutschland Ja!: Greater Germany, yes!

Das ganze Volk sagt am 10 April Ja!: All the [German] people say yes on 10 April!

Mein liebling: my darling

CH. 51 *Mein sehr lieber Franzl*: My dear Franzl

CH. 52 *Untersturmführer*: second lieutenant

Obersturmführer: first lieutenant

CH. 53 *Achtung!*: Attention!

CH. 55 *Hauptsturmführer*: captain

Kleiner Anmeldenachweis: minor proof of registration

Bezirkshauptmannschaft: district commission

CH. 59 *Auf, Auf zum Fröhlichen Jägen!*: Off, off to the jolly hunt!

CH. 60 *Lieber Bischof sei so nett, zeige dich am Fensterbrett!*: Dearest Bishop if you will, do please come to the windowsill!

CH. 61 *Judenscheiss*: Jewshit (offensive)

CH. 62 *Mach Schnell!*: Hurry!

Untermensch: underling

Mischling: half-breed

CH. 64 *Winterhilfswerk*: National Socialist annual winter charity fund

Jungmädelbund: League of German Maidens

CH. 66 *Mein Gott!*: My God!

Songs and Hymns

By Violence Unavenged includes excerpts of lyrics in the public domain from the following songs and hymns, listed in order of appearance:

'An die Musik' (1817). Lyrics, Franz von Schober. Music, Franz Schubert.

'Horst-Wessel-Lied' (1929). Lyrics, Horst Wessel (attrib.).

'Im Wald und auf der Heide' (1816). Lyrics, Johann Wilhelm Bornemann. Music, Ferdinand Ludwig Gehricke.

'Vilja Lied' (1905). Lyrics, Viktor Léon & Leo Stein. Music, Franz Lehár.

'Kernstock-hymne' (1920). Lyrics, Ottokar Kernstock. Music, Franz Josef Haydn.

'O du Lieber Augustin' (c.1679). Traditional. Marx Augustin (attrib.).

'Herz Jesu Lied' (1896). Lyrics, Josef Seeber. Music, Ignaz Mitterr.

The song in Chapter 48 is my own rendition of lines from Franz Prager's, 'Erst wann's aus wird sein' (1931). Hopefully, it captures something of the spirit of the Wienerlied genre.

Speeches

Speeches of Adolf Hitler quoted in *By Violence Unavenged*:

The English translations of Hitler's speeches used in *By Violence Unavenged* can be found at www.der-fuehrer.org. The author rejects the views of the creators of that site.

Chapter 48: Proclamation for the Anschluss of Austria, broadcast read by Dr. Joseph Goebbels, Berlin, 12 March 1938.

Chapter 49: Speech at Heldenplatz, Vienna, around 11:00, 15 March 1938.

Chapter 56: Speech in Munich, 18 July 1937.

QUESTIONS FOR BOOK CLUB DISCUSSION

1. The arrival of young Roderick provides the catalyst for Phoebe to tell her story. What is the function of the interludes in *By Violence Unavenged*? Consider plot, character, setting, and theme.

2. Discuss the various part names in *By Violence Unavenged* in relation to the plot.

3. Describe the relationship between Phoebe and her father. Is it a healthy father-daughter relationship? Why? Why not? Describe and explain the shifts in Phoebe's attitude to her father.

4. The older Phoebe describes Roderick senior as 'a gentle man – and a gentleman – through and through'. Is this a fair assessment? What does the description reveal about the older Phoebe?

5. How do Phoebe's views of Ailine Devereaux change through *By Violence Unavenged*? To what extent is Ailine's characterisation imprisoned by Phoebe's narrative? Why might this be?

6. Roderick senior remarks, 'A noose around anyone's neck is not justice.' Explain. Is this a fair assessment of capital punishment? Why? Why not?

7. Compare Roderick's attitude to Ailine's crime with that of Phoebe and Mrs Epstein. Can you have forgiveness without contrition?

8. Regarding Ailine's unresolved crime, Roderick advises Phoebe, 'how you handle this will affect your relationship with every-*one* and every-*thing*. Be careful.' To what extent is this true? How does Phoebe's attitude to Ailine affect her relationships? How does the Anschluss affect her judgement?

9. In what ways is Kerem a key character?

10. What is justice? What is mercy? What attitudes to justice and mercy are held by the following characters: Roderick, Emil, Kerem, Phoebe, and Hubie?

11. Hubie says to his sister Zita, 'Part of who you are is how you are in relation to others. It is not merely about *you*, just as it is not merely about obligation. The two go hand in glove. Certainly, you must be loved for your own sake. But for your own sake you must consider others and your obligations to them.' Discuss. Does Hubie himself achieve a prudent balance?

12. The Jews are not an homogenous group in *By Violence Unavenged*. Identify the various Jewish characters and discuss their differences.

13. The Viennese characters reflect the complex and fragmented nature of politics in Austria in the inter-war years. Identify and discuss the various political viewpoints and the different attitudes to Anschluss. To what extent was the Anschluss affected by political divisions?

14. What is Christendom? Why is Hubie Schütze so anxious to restore Christendom?

15. What is tyrannicide? What is Hubie's justification for tyrannicide?

16. Why is Sabine important?

17. Choose three chapters and discuss how the chapter title reflects the themes and concerns of the chapter.

18. Discuss the use of music in *By Violence Unavenged*.

19. How has your reading of *By Violence Unavenged* affected your understanding of the Anschluss in Austria?

20. Discuss the portrayal of Nazism and the various Nazi characters. In what ways does *By Violence Unavenged* show the emergence of a totalitarian society?

Further Reading

Black, Edwin. *IBM and the Holocaust, The Strategic Alliance between Nazi Germany and America's Most Powerful Corporation.* New York: Three Rivers Press, 2002.

Bogle, Joanna, & Bogle, James. *A Heart for Europe, The Lives of Emperor Charles and Empress Zita of Austria-Hungary.* Leominster: Gracewing, 2004.

Brook-Shepherd, Gordon. *Uncrowned Emperor, The Life and Times of Otto von Habsburg.* London: Hambledon & London, 2003.

Burleigh, Michael. *The Third Reich: A New History.* London: Pan Macmillan, 2004.

Fuchs, Martin (trans. Lumley). *Showdown in Vienna, The Death of Austria.* New York: G. P. Putnam's Sons, 1939.

Gedye, G.E.R. *Fallen Bastions, The Central European Tragedy.* Publisher Unknown, 1939.

Guttenberg, Baroness Elisabeth von. *Holding the Stirrup.* New York: Duell, Sloan & Pearce, 1955.

Hildebrand, Dietrich von (trans. Crosby). *My Battle Against Hitler: Faith, Truth, and Defiance in the Shadow of the Third Reich.* New York: Image, 2014.

Kaisler, Fritz. *Degenerate Art: The Exhibition Catalogue Guide in German and English.* Berlin: 1937, reprinted by Ostara Publications.

MacDonogh, Giles. *1938 Hitler's Gamble.* London: Constable & Robinson, 2010.

Pauley, Bruce. *From Prejudice to Persecution, A History of Austrian Anti-Semitism.* Chapel Hill: University of North Carolina Press, 1992.

Riebling, Mark. *Church of Spies: The Pope's Secret War Against Hitler.* New York: Basic Books, 2015.

Schuschnigg, Kurt von. *When Hitler Took Austria: A Memoir of Heroic Faith by the Chancellor's Son.* San Francisco: Ignatius Press, 2008.

Singer, Peter. *Pushing Time Away, My Grandfather and the Tragedy of Jewish Vienna.* London: Granta Books, 2005.

Weyr, Thomas. *The Setting of the Pearl: Vienna Under Hitler.* New York: Oxford University Press, 2005.

Zweig, Stefan (trans. Starritt). *A Chess Story.* London: Pushkin Press, 2014.

Zweig, Stefan (trans. Bell). *The World of Yesterday.* London: Pushkin Press, 2011.

Suggested Movies and Documentary Films

Emil and the Detectives (1931). Screenplay Billy Wilder, from the novel by Erich Kästner.

La Grande Illusion (1937). Dir. Jean Renoir.

M (Eine Stadt sucht einen Mörder) (1931). Dir. Fritz Lang. Peter Lorre.

The Man who was Sherlock Holmes (Der Mann, der Sherlock Holmes war) (1937). Dir. Karl Hartl. Hans Albers, Heinz Rühmann.

Sissi (1955). Dir. Ernst Marischka, Romy Schneider.

Sissi - The Young Empress (Die junge Kaiserin) (1956).

Sissi - Fateful Years of an Empress (Schicksalsjahre einer Kaiserin) (1957).

The Cabinet of Doctor Caligari (1920 silent). Dir. Robert Wiene.

The Cardinal (1963). Dir. Otto Preminger.

The Dancing Years (1950). Dennis Price. Play by Ivor Novello.

Woman in Gold (2015). Dir. Simon Curtis.

Apocalypse Hitler (2011, 2x50min). National Geographic.

Black Fox. The Rise and Fall of Adolf Hitler (1962, 20min). Narr. Marlene Dietrich.

Chronicle of the Third Reich (2010). Spiegel TV.

Hitler – a Profile (Hitler – ein Bilanz) (1995,6x50min). ZDF.

Hitler's Circle of Evil (2018, 10x52min). ZDF/Netflix.

Hitler's Österreich (2008, 2x50min). ZDF.

Pope vs Hitler (2016, 88min). National Geographic.

The Dark Charisma of Adolf Hitler (2012,3x58min).

The World at War (1974). 26x45min. Ep. 1. A New Germany, 1933-1939. Narr. Laurence Olivier. Thames Television.

A Distant Prospect

ISBN 9780987435101 paperback - 494 pages - 8 December 2012

In 1928 Sydney, Australia, an Irish school girl finds new hope, after polio and personal tragedy, while playing cello in a string quartet.

"a splendid account, full of insight into the minds of young people on the brink of adulthood ... wisdom, pathos, humour and a keen understanding of the human mind and soul." Christine McCarthy

"A real story of grit, determination, and hope for a world that needs it now." Jim Poston

"feeds the heart and mind with friendship and family, music and fine arts, and lives afflicted by suffering made whole through understanding." Clare Cannon, GoodReadingGuide.com

"an inconvenient journey of friendship" Lori Wilson

Clashing personalities. Chamber music. Post-War trauma. Is harmony possible?

Sent unwillingly to school, and thrust into a string quartet, crippled Irish cellist Lucy Straughan must choose between isolation and friendship in a foreign land.

What can the morose, math-loving Lucy offer? And will dainty Della Sotheby, hot-headed Pim Connolly and precocious Phoebe Raye ever accept her?

But Lucy has more to give than she realises. Nor is she alone in her troubles.

Meticulously crafted and true to life, *A Distant Prospect* is a heartwarming coming-of-age story set in 1920s Sydney, Australia.

"On my list of all-time favorite novels" Laura Pearl

www.ingramcontent.com/pod-product-compliance
Lightning Source LLC
Chambersburg PA
CBHW030848030726
47495CB00005B/1424